"YOU WILL NEVER FORGET MY TOUCH."

Rhea felt his hands loosening the laces of her bodice, and soon the smooth, pale flesh of her breasts was revealed to his possessive gaze. His mouth left a trail of fire blazing along the taut arch of her throat, where diamonds, now reflecting the warmth of the woman wearing them, lay against an erratically beating pulse.

Dante pulled the pins from Rhea's hair, releasing the thick, golden strands to tumble down the length of her back, the curling ends swaying round her hips as if alive. His lips were against the tender curve of breast so temptingly revealed by the parted laces, but it was not enough. Dante wanted to feel her naked flesh against his; to taste again the sweet-scented softness of her woman's body; to know again that ultimate moment of ecstasy when they became one.

And suddenly it was as if they still stood upon the warm sands of a lonely cove in the wilds of a land across the sea.

Other Avon Books by
Laurie McBain

CHANCE THE WINDS OF FORTUNE
DEVIL'S DESIRE
MOONSTRUCK MADNESS
TEARS OF GOLD

Dark Before The Rising Sun

Laurie McBain

AVON
PUBLISHERS OF BARD, CAMELOT, DISCUS AND FLARE BOOKS

DARK BEFORE THE RISING SUN is an original publication of
Avon Books. This work has never before appeared in book form.

AVON BOOKS
A division of
The Hearst Corporation
959 Eighth Avenue
New York, New York 10019

Copyright © 1982 by Laurie McBain
Published by arrangement with the author
Library of Congress Catalog Card Number: 81-52381
ISBN: 0-380-79848-4

First Avon Printing, May, 1982

AVON TRADEMARK REG. U. S. PAT. OFF. AND IN
OTHER COUNTRIES, MARCA REGISTRADA, HECHO EN
U. S. A.

Printed in the U. S. A.

WFH 10 9 8 7 6 5 4 3 2 1

For my sweet Bunny,
a gentle and loving cat
who enriched my life.

> *No light, but rather darkness visible.*
> John Milton

Prelude

ON the north coast of Devon, in the West Country, lay Merdraco. There was a timelessness about the stone towers rising starkly against a misty morn, as if destiny had decreed they stand sentinel throughout eternity. Although the towers of the ancient castle had been raised by mortal hand stone by rough-hewn stone, now there was only the endless sounding of the sea echoing along the time-worn battlements, climbing the stone steps spiraling into the towers.

At night the lonely hooting of an owl in one of the abandoned towers was the only sound. There was no ringing of emblazoned metal shields or battle-honed swords, raised in answer to the call to arms, no defiant battle cry cutting through the silent Great Hall. The lord of the castle was no longer there. There was only the restless whispering of the sea.

1

No footfall would disturb the stillness of a moon-shadowed passage. No impatient hand would destroy the intricate patterning of a finely spun cobweb. No human trespass would displace the gossamer coating of dust that had fallen soundlessly throughout the long years. There was only the insistent murmuring of the sea.

The many passing days had borne silent witness to the sun and the moon rising in the east. As their circling paths carried them across the skies above the windswept stone walls, the castle waited broodingly on the cliffs above the wild shore.

Slowly, centuries had passed. Each generation had lived out its life at Merdraco in both joy and sorrow. The descending sun, like one fallen from grace, had continued to fall to the sea beyond the towers of Merdraco while the vesper bells heralded the coming of eventide. And the moon, serene and proud, had continued to rise. But it too was destined to fall in its turn, gliding into the somber waters of a dawn sea while the song of the lark heralded the coming of morn, and golden streakings in the eastern sky touched the towers of Merdraco once again.

There was the sun and moon, the sea and Merdraco. Ever changing, yet forever constant.

Merdraco.

Created from stone and mortar, Merdraco was all that remained of a once great and noble family. Empty, now forgotten, it was still guardian of all that had once gone on. So pervasive a feeling of melancholia was there about the deserted battlements and abandoned towers that it seemed as if life at Merdraco must surely only be in abeyance, and soon all would be as it once had been.

The tattered banner, faded by sun and spindrift, would once again flutter with majestic brilliance and the sepulchral descant from the sea would soon be drowned out by a trumpet's clarion call stirring the castle to life. Where there was only the harsh cry of the sea gull there would soon be the frenzied barking of hounds and the jingling of harness and clattering of hooves on the paving stones of the courtyard. Mellifluous strains of flute and mandolin would drift on the wind with woodsmoke rising to meet the sea mists swirling close to shore.

But the wind sighed, fading as if it had never been at all. An unnatural quiet settled against the cold stone of the castle while an enveloping gloom altered the shadows into more than dusky images until nothing was its true self, and the clarity of line was blurred until there were only indistinct shapes. The fleeting shadow of a bird became an advancing apparition from the past, and the heraldic dragons carved into the stone of Merdraco were no longer stilled as their soundless roar became that of the sea in tempest.

But the dragons of Merdraco remained imprisoned. Crouched in stone above the gates to Merdraco, their baleful eyes cast downward and their writhing, serrated tails poised above horned heads ready to strike, the stone dragons waited and watched.

There was danger in the stillness of this night of no moon, and yet there was none to raise the drawbridge or let the portcullis down. Nor could that have protected Merdraco from its unrelenting enemy, for time was the ravager of Merdraco.

Merdraco was defenseless against this enemy, vulnerable to the night that hides things, victim to days filled with yet another enemy's falsehoods, envy, and avarice.

And time abetted this implacable enemy of the family that was no more. It gave comfort to an enemy who knew no pity where Merdraco was concerned. And in the deepening abyss of time, that enemy began to savor victory, to exult in the downfall and ruination of the family and the ultimate destruction of Merdraco.

Who was there left to mourn the fading hour but the pale, fleeting shadows of ghosts from another time. And who was there left to sing the lament of past glory but the wailing winds of a dying day.

But in the dark before the rising sun, where there was only the quiet weeping of the sea, Merdraco awaited the coming of its master. . . .

Happy he who like Ulysses a glorious voyage made.
Joachim Du Bellay

Chapter 1

BLACK as a tinker's pot was the moonless night in early
September of the year of our Lord seventeen hundred and
seventy, but no blacker than the waters of the River Thames
as it wended through the heart of London. The fog, like a
confused and disembodied spirit, rose silently from the waters
where the *Sea Dragon,* a Boston-built brigantine out of Charles
Town, in the Carolinas, rode at anchor. Her square-rigged sails
were furled, and the tall, stark masts swayed eerily in the mists
engulfing the ship, but strangely visible was the figurehead of
the grinning red dragon with the gilded tail and fins, its lolling
tongue having mocked many an adversary unfortunate enough
to fall afoul of the *Sea Dragon* and her captain, Dante Leighton,
adventurer and privateer. To those whose ships had felt the

fury of the fighting brig's guns the captain was little better than a bedeviling smuggler and much-damned pirate.

Dante Leighton was also, for certain people interested in his whereabouts, more than a mere ship's captain. He was also the Marquis of Jacqobi, and the last surviving descendant of a time-honored family. He was sole heir to all his forefathers had envisioned, possessor of an ancient, once-revered title, one that had been held by men of honor and valor, and by men who had been daring and ruthless enough to achieve greatness and found a dynasty.

But that was long ago, and now that glory was as faded as the flowers in the autumn of the year when the *Sea Dragon* and her master had at long last come home from the sea. Dante Leighton had returned to claim all that his father's fathers had bequeathed him.

He was lord and master of Merdraco.

But much had changed about the man who had fled England and his home so long ago. Dante Leighton was no longer the destitute young lord who had squandered his inheritance and gambled away his heritage during endless nights of debauchery.

He once had been so exquisite and graceful a young man. But his classically beautiful face had begun to bear the mark of libertine excesses. With the arrogance of youth he had continued his hellbent course, contemptuously mocking those who counseled against the advice of false friends and pleaded discretion to the profligate young man.

Recklessly he had turned a deaf ear to the voices of those whom he could truly have called friends. And with a blind eye to his own image in the mirror, he had not seen the dissipation being wrought by a cunning hand. And with that elegant air of indifference that bordered on insolence and showed him to be a gentleman of breeding, he had abandoned himself to a rakehell's fate, still believing there would always be a tomorrow.

But the morrow had dawned cold and dark and a bewildered young man had faced the tragic realization that he had been cruelly deceived by the very one he had idolized, betrayed by that former friend's treachery, and brought to ruination and dishonor by that same enemy's hatred and depravity.

A strangely chastened and despondent Dante Leighton had

disappeared into the night while fleeing creditors and jeering friends alike, ashamed of his own name.

But before he had bid farewell to everything, he had gambled away his last guinea in one final and defiant, or perhaps desperate, attempt to reclaim one of the priceless family heirlooms which he had so foolishly let slip through his fingers. But he had lost. And what once had belonged to him, belonged to another.

It had been Dante Leighton's darkest hour. Death seemed a welcomed reprieve. And yet, unbeknownst to him, this was the beginning of his salvation. Dante Leighton certainly would not have believed that, for the man who had witnessed his final humiliation had been an ill-bred and scornful fellow, hardly sympathetic to a proudly disdainful aristocrat's misfortune. The man had been a common sea captain, churlishly bad-mannered enough to refuse a gentleman's word of honor to redeem his pledge. He had forced that indolent, silk-clad gallant to work off the debt by serving on board his ship, the *Perdita*.

And Captain Sedgewick Christopher's *Perdita* had been no lumbering, worm-eaten merchantman but a sixteen-gun privateer, her letter of marque authorizing her to harass with impunity any sworn enemy of the Crown. She pursued that course with unparalleled skill and zeal while the continuing disputes between the French and English escalated into the Seven Years' War.

An abashed young lord quickly found himself facing that eagerly sought-after death, and yet, once his ultimate destruction seemed imminent, he experienced a sudden determination to survive at all costs. With that vow pledged upon what honor he had left, Dante Leighton had accepted his fate, knowing that one day he would wreak his vengeance on his enemy and would give no quarter.

Those first, long years at sea had not been without hardship, but the man Dante Leighton was maturing into had borne them without complaint. Given no preferential treatment because of his exalted rank in society, he had cleaned the deck of blood and debris, working alongside the lowliest swabber. He had ridden the rigging, his fingers numb with cold while sky and sea blurred into one. He had been gunner, loading and priming the cannon while the crew cleared for action. And, when bone-weary and half dead with fatigue he had fallen into his hammock, he had fought off sleep while strengthening his will to survive with a carefully thought-out plan of revenge.

As the years passed and he proved himself worthy of sailing with the *Perdita* crew, Dante Leighton rose from efficient deckhand to foretopman, to helmsman, and, finally, to master. He had earned the respect of his fellow mariners.

But more than that, Dante Leighton had earned the respect and friendship of Sedgewick Christopher, a man not easily given to friendship. A dour man—even harsh, some might have charged—Sedgewick Christopher had been a commanding figure as he'd walked the deck of his ship, his narrowed, cobalt blue eyes raking sails, masts, and men while he'd roared his orders. He had been an uncompromising captain, but his crew would have sailed with none other than Captain Sedgewick Christopher for he was a fair man and, above all else, the finest captain any of them had ever served. Were they not still alive. That was more than many an unfortunate crew could boast.

And when the good captain had died in battle, his last words an order for the enemy to haul down her colors, the crew had buried him at sea with full honors. Even the most hardened sailor had grieved. But the first mate had grieved deepest. Captain Sedgewick Christopher had left to him, his friend and next in command, what few possessions he had valued. In a worn sea chest Dante Leighton had discovered the captain's much-prized sextant and compass and one other item, seemingly of little value. Only two people had treasured it. One had been the man who had kept it safe for so many years. The other was the man who now possessed what had once been his.

It was the portrait of a stunningly beautiful woman and a child. Flaxen-haired and gray-eyed, the woman was an ethereal vision in gold and alabaster rising from the virescent sea mists swirling around her. She seemed poised between sea and sky, a spirit caught by the wind and uncertain of its destiny. The child at her side, a boy of not more than ten years, was gazing into her face, his gray eyes filled with adoration. His small hand was lost in the silken folds of her gown, as if he sought to hold onto something that was elusive and perhaps fleeting.

It was the portrait of Lady Elayne Jacqobi and her son, Dante Leighton.

As Dante Leighton stared down at the portrait he had believed forever lost to him, he had known that his mother appearing before him in the flesh could not have surprised him more. For so many guilt-ridden years he had pondered the whereabouts of that portrait, only to have discovered that the captain had possessed it all these years.

But when Dante Leighton read the captain's last will and testament, he finally understood so many unanswered questions. He knew at last the truth behind the captain's actions that inglorious night so many years ago when he had rescued a dissolute young man from destroying himself. That young man had meant nothing to him, and Dante Leighton had always wondered why Sedgewick Christopher had cared.

It had been because of the portrait. Perhaps, as the days fled by, a lonely man who sailed the seas and had no family of his own, no loving wife awaiting his safe return to shore, had come secretly to cherish a woman who had existed only on canvas and in the memory of an anguished young man.

A gruff, sometimes caustic man had fallen in love with the painted image of a woman he could never possess. She had died before he had ever known of her. How often, when gazing longingly upon that pale likeness, had he wondered about the strange sadness in her gray eyes?

In silence Dante Leighton stared down at the hastily scrawled message addressed to him and the words blurred:

... and so I've waited too long to be tellin' ye this, for if ye be reading my words now, well, I've gone by the board and it doesn't matter anymore. Except, maybe, to ye, lad? And that is why I think ye deserve an explanation, not that I'm even understanding the wherefores and whys. Some might have said 'twas one of them chances of fate, what happened that day, and maybe 'twas. I've seen too many a strange thing to be questioning that which I do not understand.

All I'm knowin' about is what I felt that day so long ago. I'd been at sea a long while, and I had few acquaintances in London. I was alone until I happened past a shop window and saw the portrait of a woman and a boy. I couldn't seem to take a step beyond that portrait. I had taken root to the ground, lad, and when I stared into those soft gray eyes, I felt as if she were staring into my own soul. And she was beckoning to me, Sedgewick Christopher, and to no one else. Suddenly I felt as if I could do something to banish the sadness from those eyes.

Aye, I'm a foolish old man, and the shopkeeper thought little better of me when I inquired so vehemently about the lady of the portrait. Her name was Lady Elayne Jacqobi. She was a true-born lady. Then I discovered that she had died tragically just months before my return to England, and I felt like I had received a mortal blow. The shopkeeper thought me a man crazed, especially when I readily paid the exorbitant price he was askin' for the portrait. Little did he realize that I would have paid ten times that amount for the portrait of that lady.

And with my purse far lighter, he was more than pleased to regale me with the gossip concerning her, and especially about that angelic-faced boy in the portrait. He was the lady's only son, and a wilder, more rakish young lord there wasn't in all of London. The innocent-looking boy of that portrait had become a scoundrel who had gambled away his fortune and his good name. Such wickedness, I thought, for even the portrait of his mother had been auctioned off to pay for this miscreant's debts.

I knew then what I must do. I sought ye out, lad. I think I must have been half mad, and may God forgive me, but I hoped to find ye to be the cursed swine I thought ye to be. Then I would somehow have tricked ye into challenging me. I wanted to kill ye, boy, but when I sat across the gaming table from ye and stared into gray eyes so much like the lady of the portrait's, I could see only hers and I couldn't destroy her son.

Of course, ye weren't exactly what I had been expecting. Aye, ye were arrogant enough, but that was in your blood and the way ye'd been raised, so I couldn't fault ye that. But I could plainly see that your drinking and whoring were getting the better of ye. Ye looked like ye was staring death in the face. I would've left ye to your fate, lad, except that I saw something in your eyes.

I saw regret and sadness, and that same, strange expression of longing that had been in your mother's eyes. 'Tis a mystery still, the cause of that sadness, for she knew it well long before ye brought your share of heartache to her. But ye were her son, and she would have loved ye dearly, and for that reason alone, I took pity on ye that night.

I vowed that I would make a decent man of ye. Either that, or I'd see ye on the bottom of the sea. And truth be known, lad, I had my doubts those first months when your resentment and lack of spirit nearly cost ye your life.

But ye survived. She would have been proud of ye. I never had the honor of meeting the lady of the portrait, but I have loved her as I have loved no other. 'Twas madness, and I fear that it has been my downfall, for I have been content to live with but a dream these many years. Aye, I've played the mooncalf, but I'd not change one day of that devotion.

However, there is one thing I would have changed. It has made me little better than a blackguard, and most deserving of your scorn. I took advantage of my knowledge of ye and hid the portrait, never telling ye I owned it. I had convinced myself that I was doing it for your own good, that ye needed to suffer while wondering what had become of the portrait of your mother. I knew ye were desperate to recover the portrait, for I'd been back to that shop, thinking to purchase something else of the Lady Elayne's. The shopkeeper told me ye'd been in, and that ye'd threatened him, but that he could tell ye nothing about me, not even my name. I knew then that ye'd been gambling just to get enough money to buy the portrait.

And so I have unjustly deprived ye of her comforting presence these long years of struggle, and I do now humbly beg your forgiveness. 'Twas wrong of me, lad, but we all have our weaknesses. Your mother has been mine. How many times have I cursed the fates for their cruel mischief-making!

I only wish that ... well, that's not to be now. I wanted ye to know the truth. I also wanted ye to know that I have come to think of ye as the son I never had. I could not have been prouder of my own flesh and blood. That is why I have left to you, son, my share of the *Perdita*. She could have no finer a captain. I hope my partners in her will keep ye on as her master, but they're a sorry lot of greedy merchants and may not be willing to risk their investment with a young captain at the helm. If so, then sell out and get yourself a ship of your own. Ye've got the makings of a fine captain, lad, on that I'd stake my reputation. Ye've got your share of the many prizes we've captured. 'Tis a small fortune ye've amassed. I know ye've not spent much of it, but for what purpose ye've been saving it, I've no knowledge. That be your business and not mine. But if I were ye, then I'd be usin' it to buy that ship, and have it free and clear, with no meddling partners to interfere. Be your own master, lad.

But one last word of advice from a man who has seen too much misfortune caused by anger and pride. Ye've become a good man. Ye be a decent man, with the respect of this crew. I cannot be faulting ye for being ruthless, for only the pitiless survives to sail into home port. While on board ship, ye're duty bound to your crew to keep your ship afloat at all costs. But, lad, your inflexibility and determination, when not in battle, should be tempered with compassion.

I've come to fear that ye're too unforgiving. Ye've survived these many years solely to avenge a wrong done ye. I cannot, in all honesty, blame ye for seeking a day of reckoning. I do worry, however, that your desire for vengeance has become an all-consuming fire. Beware, boy. 'Tis too often a sad truth that the price exacted of the person seeking revenge is far greater than the punishment meted out.

I have found that revenge is not so sweet and, indeed, can leave a terrible bitterness. Ye may lose more than ye win, remember that. And one final word of advice from an old sea dog. Don't sail too close to the wind, or ye just might find yourself caught between the devil and the deep.

> Have a care, lad,
> Sedgewick Oliver Christopher

When the *Perdita* docked, and word of the captain's death reached the privateer's owners, the late captain had been proven correct about one of his worries. The *Perdita* found herself under command of another captain. Dante Leighton sold his share and, the money combined with most of his savings, purchased a sleek little two-masted brigantine just in from the colonies. He christened her *Sea Dragon*, and had the figurehead of a dragon fixed on the stem just beneath her bowsprit.

For her first voyage under her new master she had a well-seasoned crew, for many of the *Perdita* crew chose to sail with Dante. Cobbs, the bos'n, Norfolk bred, had figured it best to be sailing with a man trained by Captain Christopher. MacDonald, the Scots sailmaker, had helped make a sailor out of Dante Leighton and knew no one better to sail with. Trevelawny, the ship's dour-faced Cornish carpenter, reckoned that Cobbs and MacDonald knew what they were about, and he had signed on with them.

There was one other individual who knew the captain well and was to be found aboard the *Sea Dragon;* however, he had a hard time finding his sea legs. During his first few months at sea, it seemed as if he never would. Never had there been so green-visaged a man as Houston Kirby, onetime footman at Merdraco, then personal valet to the old Marquis himself, and finally house steward for Lord Dante Jacqobi, the old Marquis' grandson and heir. That his master was captain of a ship, especially one called the *Sea Dragon*, meant an uncertain future for them both as far as its newest crew member was concerned.

For many years a loyal Houston Kirby had bided his time, fervently hoping that his lordship would tire of playing sailor. Alas, he had not, and Houston Kirby had finally come to the unhappy realization that he would have to go to sea if he were to serve his young master again, a duty entrusted to him by the old Marquis.

Houston Kirby and his father and grandfather before him had not served the Leighton family through strife and turmoil to sit idly by while the last of the Leighton line did his damnedest to end up on the bottom of the sea. Remembering the hedonistic young lord that Dante Leighton once had been, trepidation had gripped Houston Kirby as he determinedly climbed aboard the *Sea Dragon* one stormy night.

He had seen nothing of his young master for over eight years, and so could be forgiven for not at first recognizing the captain of the *Sea Dragon*. The bronze-skinned, broad-shouldered man who had courteously greeted him bore little resemblance to the pale, effete young aristocrat. And the gray eyes Houston Kirby thought he remembered so well had become the impersonal, measuring gaze of a stranger. And as he had stood before the man he no longer knew, those gray eyes narrowed thoughtfully, and Houston Kirby had shivered. He'd never seen so cold and calculating a stare. And strangely enough, he had known for a certainty that had he not measured up to *Captain* Dante Leighton's unyielding standards, he would have been thrown overboard like so much bilge water being pumped into the sea.

There had been times during the following years, when cannon fire splintered the deck beside him, that Houston Kirby had seriously doubted the wisdom of following his master to sea. He had come close to death too many times not to have wondered whether he and the captain would ever again see the towers of Merdraco.

He had not been at all displeased, therefore, when the Treaty of Paris was signed in '63, and the hostilities between England and France came to an end. He had been looking forward eagerly to returning to dry land. But only too quickly he discovered that the captain had quite different ideas for their future, and returning to England and a life of leisure on land had not been part of them.

Instead, the billowing sails of the *Sea Dragon* had caught a freshening offshore breeze while the captain ordered the helmsman to steer a southwesterly course. Soon the verdant, familiar shores of England disappeared over the horizon. A fortnight passed, and the Canary Islands fell astern as the *Sea Dragon* ran free before the northeast trades, their first landfall, Barbados.

A young Alastair Marlowe, now supercargo aboard the *Sea Dragon*, sailed with them. He had joined the crew rather abruptly one rainy night in Portsmouth two years earlier, and had Houston Kirby been asked about that night, he would most likely have chuckled in remembrance of the fancy young gentleman being carried aboard by the captain. The unconscious beau's velvet coat had been muddied beyond repair, and his fine silk stockings torn, and he had been sporting a nasty bruise on his forehead, the painful result of a cudgel swung by one of a press gang. They had been attempting, and quite successfully until the captain interfered, to kidnap for service aboard one of His Majesty's ships anyone clad in breeches who had been unfortunate enough to be walking the streets of Portsmouth.

As the younger son of a comfortably well-to-do country gentleman, the estate now in the hands of the firstborn son, Alastair Marlowe's future had been anything but inspiring. If he had intended to keep his creditors at arm's length, he would soon have had to become either a clergyman or a soldier, both proper occupations for down-at-heels gentlemen, but neither of which appealed to a young man starved for a bit of adventure and a decent income.

Only the captain of the *Sea Dragon* knew exactly why he had taken pity on a young gentleman in distress that night in Portsmouth. Generous displays of compassion were uncommon for Dante Leighton. But had anyone been so unwise as to question the captain's offering a town seedling a berth aboard the *Sea Dragon*, Alastair Marlowe would soon have silenced his doubts. He had quickly proven himself no stranger to hard work, and indeed had shown such a willingness to learn that many an old hand had halfheartedly grumbled about being made to look bad by comparison.

As the *Sea Dragon* followed a leisurely course north, her ultimate destination Charles Town, the bewitching West Indian sunsets and balmy breezes cast their spell over the crew, who still remembered only too vividly the gale force winds and crashing seas of the inhospitable North Atlantic. By the time they had sailed past the dense tropical forests and conical-shaped mountain peaks of Dominica, the *Sea Dragon* was shorthanded.

Barnaby Clarke, the *Sea Dragon*'s new quartermaster and a self-styled dandy out of Antigua, joined the crew in Jamaica. Longacres, the new coxswain and an old pirate with no first name and two missing front teeth, came aboard in New Providence. And Seumus Fitzsimmons, the first mate, a glib-tongued Irish colonial with revolutionary rhetoric, introduced himself to the captain in Charles Town.

Once, while lying at anchor in St. Kitts, the captain went ashore, returning a short while later accompanied by Conny Brady, the *Sea Dragon*'s cabin boy. Rumor had it that the captain had won the lad in a card game, winning him from the captain of a slaver who had treated the boy brutally. Houston Kirby, had he so wished, could have confirmed the story about how the captain, after having witnessed the seven-year-old cabin boy's unsuccessful attempt to jump ship in the Dutch free port of St. Eustatius, had sworn to rescue the lad from any future beatings, by fair means or foul.

The fact that the slaver had sailed to St. Kitts with the *Sea Dragon*, almost yardarm to yardarm, did little to dispel the story, especially because the *Sea Dragon* ought to have been bound for Jamaica. The story, which had spread quickly, as all good gossip does, had enhanced the growing mystique about the captain of the *Sea Dragon*. Here was a man compassionate enough to rescue a child, but also quite capable of blowing a ship out of the water.

And, of course, there was Jamaica, the ship's cat, rescued from a weighted-down burlap sack thrown into a rain barrel in some back alley in Port Royal. Dante Leighton had been seen carrying the scruffy, flea-bitten tom aboard the *Sea Dragon*. Five years later, anyone catching sight of a big, sleek-coated tabby prowling the docks or sunning himself on the taffrail of the *Sea Dragon* would have had good reason to wonder about the chance of fortune that had allowed the smug-looking cat to lose one of his nine lives in order to live out the remaining eight as a cosseted ship's mascot, a superstitious crew seeing to his every need.

The following years had found the *Sea Dragon* sailing with the prevailing winds as she smuggled goods between the Indies and the Carolinas. Unloading contraband cargo in coves along the wild shores, she managed to stay just out of reach of His Majesty's well-armed frigates and sloops, which patrolled the coastline from Falmouth in the north to St. Augustine in the south.

One of her more passionate adversaries had been Captain

Sir Morgan Lloyd of H.M.S. *Portcullis,* an eighteen-gun sloop. But the *Sea Dragon* had sailed under a lucky star, or had the devil's own luck, and the *Portcullis* never had overtaken her or maneuvered close enough even to fire a shot across her bow, much less a raking broadside.

But those were tales of yesterday, and the *Sea Dragon* and her proud master had come home. The winds of good fortune had filled her sails on what was to be her last voyage. With a cargo of treasure retrieved from a sunken Spanish galleon off the coast of Florida filling her hold, the captain and his crew had returned to their home country, all wealthy men with dreams soon to be fulfilled. And so for now any challenging roars from the dragon were stilled, and in the ensuing lull, there was only the forlorn sound of creaking masts above a deserted deck while the tide lapped gently against the curving hull of a tranquil ship.

The fog, moving like a great jaundiced cloud, drifted away from the floating forest of masts and desolate wharves. It swirled along the narrow, twisting lanes of the City, where pickpockets, footpads, watchmen, and sixpenny harlots went about their business. In the muffled silence the chiming of bells in church spires lost high in the enveloping mists was like the echoing of a thousand bells, and the discordant notes of a hurdy-gurdy man cranking out a tune reverberated like a banshee's wail. An anonymous fiddler's song was carried on the seaborne breeze, and like the cajoling voices of street vendors hawking their wares, the source remained unseen.

A swiftly moving carriage appeared suddenly out of the fog, its wheels rattling across the slick cobblestones as it slid into one of the many iron posts guarding the paved footways. The angry curses from ghostly shapes went unheeded while the carriage continued on, the bundled-up coachman whipping his team to an even greater burst of speed despite the danger to life and limb.

"Ye thick-skulled, fat-headed landlubber!" roared a short, bandy-legged man, his raised fist threatening dire consequences should the offending coachman have been foolhardy enough to halt.

"'Ere, stir your stumps! 'Aven't got t'whole bloody night, I 'aven't, t'be standin' 'ere dawdlin' while ye twiddle your thumbs, square-toes. Some of us 'as important business t'be seein' to. Can't all be gent*eel* folk struttin' around with our noses in t'air, I'm sure."

Houston Kirby snorted rudely. "The only important business ye be to, spouter, is tryin' to decide whose pocket to be pickin' next," he warned, and since his next utterance was little better than a growl, the malcontent moved along smartly, sparing no backward glance for so rude a fellow.

"Damned impertinence! Dunno what's happened to the City. 'Course, never did like it overmuch. People in too damned a hurry, and too busy to give a fellow directions, except tellin' him where to go for darin' to bother them," Houston Kirby mumbled, pausing briefly to glance down at the nicely rounded toes of his boots. "Might not be the most fashionable pair in all of London Town, but they ain't square-toed," he muttered indignantly. He spat into the gutter that was quickly filling with dirty water.

Hunching his shoulders against the cold drizzle sneaking down the back of his collar, he marched along the slippery footway. The gleaming pewter and brass, crystal and silver handsomely displayed behind the plate glass of an illumined shop window went unnoticed, as did the warm richness of velvet and silk in a linen draper's, the seductive sparkle of precious gems and gold in a jeweler's, and the mystifying potions, salves, and cure-alls of an apothecary's.

The rain was coming down in sheets by the time Houston Kirby had neared the arched entrance to the yard of Hawke's Bell Inn. The brown cloth of his greatcoat was soaked through and felt twice as heavy as it had when he'd first struggled into it. Besides that, it was far too long and the wet hem flapped around his knees with every step. But despite the growing discomfort of his ill-fitting coat and the awkwardness in finding safe footing on the slippery cobblestones, Houston Kirby continued to hurry along the lane.

Suddenly he made a great leap through the air toward the other side, or at least as far as his short legs could propel him. And just in time too, for out of the darkness clattered a coach-and-six, which rolled through the arch with a splattering of muddy water in all directions.

Had there been anyone within hearing distance, he would

have been left in little doubt as to the small man's opinion of the driver of that coach. With a sigh he glanced down at his gutter-splashed breeches and very sad-looking round-toed boots. Shaking his grizzled head for what the world must surely be coming to, he scurried into the yard. But peace was not to be found there, for stableboys and ostlers were bustling about, harnessing and unharnessing teams of horses and loading and unloading luggage with little regard for the contents, sublimely ignoring anyone questioning the condition of his trunk.

Houston Kirby sighed as he reached the comparative safety and tranquillity of the taproom, which was crowded with shivering patrons newly arrived from Bath or Bristol, or perhaps even from as far north as Edinburgh, Newcastle, or York. The week-long journey by stage along the Great North Road was considerably easier and quicker than it had once been.

Houston Kirby tried to elbow his way closer to the warmth of the fire blazing in the big hearth, but there always seemed to be a broad back, a wide pair of shoulders, or a muscular forearm barring his way. With an almost comical expression of disgruntlement settling on his face, he started to commandeer a small three-legged stool, thinking that this current state of affairs pretty well summed up the way most of the day had gone thus far.

But as he prepared to remove the stool from beneath a large booted foot, a voice hailed him from across the room. Glancing around, he saw two men he knew well sitting at a table within the warming glow of the fire.

Alastair Marlowe raised his arm, beckoning to the little man whose head he had seen watching bob up and down in the sea of shoulders. At the same time, Alastair caught the eye of one of the busy serving girls and ordered another tray of tankards to replace the empty ones on their table.

Houston Kirby snorted when he saw the smiling girl hustle off, knowing that an older gent like himself would not have received such quick and friendly service. Leave it to a young and handsome lad with a twinkling eye and plenty of coin in his pocket to find a table near the fire and a more than willing serving girl.

His wet coat sending up a cloud of steam from its peg near the fire, Houston Kirby sank down onto the bench where a space had been cleared for him between the two men. The gentlemanly Alastair had helped him out of his coat and placed it on the peg, which had been just out of reach of Kirby's fingertips.

Seumus Fitzsimmons' nostrils twitched. "Damned if someone hasn't kicked over a chamber pot," he muttered. Then as his offended senses located the source of the incredible odor, he raised a black brow inquiringly. "I do beg your pardon, Mr. Kirby, but where the *divil* have ye been?"

Houston Kirby took a hefty swallow of his buttered ale. Heated and sweetened with sugar, cinnamon, and butter, it sent a warm sensation all the way down to his frozen toes.

"The way I figure it, Mr. Fitzsimmons, I'm lucky to be here, stench and all, considering I've been insulted and nearly run down twice by runaway coaches. Beginnin' to think I was far safer aboard the *Sea Dragon* durin' the war than I am now walkin' down the street," Houston Kirby scowled before he emptied the contents of his tankard.

"Sounds like we got up on the wrong side of the bed this mornin'," Seumus Fitzsimmons commented smoothly.

"And since when have I been sharin' a bed with ye and one of your many lady friends?" Houston Kirby demanded. The Irishman chuckled and Kirby nodded his thanks to a grinning Alastair, who had placed another tankard within easy reach.

Seumus Fitzsimmons shook his head, his expression of self-disgust giving way to laughter. "Ye'd think I'd have learned by now not to bandy words with the likes of him. But now that ye've brought it to mind," he continued, apparently not having yet learned that lesson at all, "'twould have been a sight to have beheld. However, I think I'm man enough for the ladies without needin' your kind assistance."

"Thought ye'd be talkin' revolution with some of them hotheaded Irish friends of yours in some back room of a tavern patronized by colonials," Houston Kirby responded curtly.

"Still plenty o' time for that talk. The night's still young," Seumus Fitzsimmons answered with an irrepressible wink at his two uneasy friends. Such talk was heard more frequently nowadays and was far more dangerous to be associated with.

"What's troubling you, Kirby?" Alastair asked, changing the subject as easily as he had his tankard of ale.

"Aye, thought a man as rich as yourself wouldn't have a worry in his head. Thought ye'd be fair to splittin' your seams with ideas on how to be spendin' your share of the treasure," Seumus Fitzsimmons asked curiously. His share of the treasure was already destined toward a ship of his own, to be bought when he returned to the colonies.

"Reckon most the mates might have a sovereign or two left once they finish celebratin' here in London," Kirby said as he eyed a couple of familiar figures at another table. He might not have recognized any of them. Their fancy clothes were new and out of character.

"'Tis especially interestin' when ye consider that none of us has even gotten his hands on any of that treasure yet," Seumus Fitzsimmons commented dryly, thinking of his own new finery into which the tailor had been only too happy to fit him with the expectation of his customer's forthcoming riches.

"We've only been in port a few days now," Alastair reminded him. "The captain's got to clear himself of that warrant for his arrest before we can all sit down and have a proper accounting of the treasure. Then we can divide it up."

Houston Kirby snorted loudly, nearly choking on his ale. "With the rumors goin' around about the cap'n, his reputation's blacker now than 'twas when he left London all them years ago. And no thanks to certain people I could name," Kirby said as he eyed a crew member who was holding court at a table close to the conviviality of the hearth.

Longacres' outrageously lurid tales of pirates and highly exaggerated stories about the captain of the *Sea Dragon* were spreading through London like wildfire. And the old coxswain, in his loose-fitting breeches, square-cut jacket, and scarlet bandana, a pistol stuck in his broad belt, certainly looked the part of the bloodthirsty pirates of legend. The costume did little to damage his credibility. And the fact that this colorful old character was also a very wealthy man only added to his popularity.

"Reckon some folk don't know when to keep their mouths shut."

"He's harmless enough, Kirby. Just enjoyin' bein' the center of attention. Though I do wish he'd be buyin' himself some new clothes, or at least a new pair of breeches. He looks like he's still sailin' a ship flyin' the skull and crossed bones," Seumus Fitzsimmons grimaced.

Alastair Marlowe had been silent while studying the play of emotions across the little steward's face. He thought how much more complex a man Houston Kirby was than most people knew. "You're still troubled about something, aren't you, Kirby?"

For one of the few times in his life, Houston Kirby didn't have anything to say.

"If you're worrying about the captain getting those charges against him dropped, I wouldn't. He is, after all, a marquis, and a very wealthy gentleman now. I doubt whether even Their Honors will question him overmuch. 'Tis strange how another man's title and wealth can influence someone. And yet we all know the finest title Dante Leighton possesses is the one he bears as master of the *Sea Dragon*. Besides, he is innocent of any wrongdoing where this warrant is concerned," he added loyally, putting all their previous smuggling activities out of his mind.

"And when did that ever save a man from the gallows?" Seumus Fitzsimmons was curious to know. "But ye be right about one thing, Mr. Marlowe. Them fine and most respectable bewigged old gents ain't goin' to hang no wealthy marquis. No matter what he's done."

"At least not this time," Houston Kirby muttered into his ale, his shoulders slumped as if he carried the weight of the world.

"I hope you're not forgetting that the captain also has two very respectable witnesses to testify in his behalf. I doubt very seriously whether a duke's daughter or one of His Majesty's own officers would be suspected of perjury."

Seumus Fitzsimmons laughed heartily. "Aye, the captain's got the divil's own luck for sure. To think that Captain Sir Morgan Lloyd himself would be the character witness for our captain! 'Tis strange enough to have me and all of London believin' everythin' ol' Longacres is spoutin' off about."

The sad little steward hung his head even lower.

"Here, look alive, mates," the Irishman declared as the serving girl arrived with a heavily laden tray of succulent dishes. "All ye need, Kirby, is some of this venison pie fillin' your innards. That'll get ye back in good spirits," he promised as he eyed first the many platters being positioned on their table, then the décolletage of the smiling young serving girl.

With Seumus Fitzsimmons' attention fully occupied in flirting with the comely maid, Alastair took the opportunity to inquire softly of the little steward.

"You're worried about what the cap'n might be up to now that he's back in England to stay, aren't you, Kirby? You're worried because the cap'n has become a powerful man and is now in a position to settle an old score."

Kirby stared into his ale as if he might be able to divine the future in its mirrored surface. "I've lived too long with the fear of this day."

"But Kirby, everything is different now," Alastair told him with an encouraging smile.

"Is it?" Kirby asked doubtfully. "Ah, lad, I wish I could believe that, but I know the people involved too well to be easy."

"The cap'n is wealthy now. Indeed, he is far richer than he probably thought he'd ever be. That can mellow a man's need for revenge. The cap'n can now forget all the unhappiness of the past. He has returned to England a successful man, even a hero in the eyes of some. He can start anew. After all, Kirby, the cap'n was just a young man of twenty when he fled England, and that was close to sixteen years ago. He has lived most of that time out of this country. Don't you think he might feel differently now? London is not the same town he left, and I'll wager that Merdraco isn't the same place either, nor the people living around there. Everybody changes. And anyway," he added quietly, "have you forgotten Lady Rhea Claire? Would the cap'n risk losing her?"

The Lady Rhea Claire. No, she was certainly not someone you would forget. Even the mere mention of her name conjured up a vision of breathtaking grace and beauty in the minds of both men. Houston Kirby sighed. Although he was not given to romantic or poetic ramblings, he couldn't help but compare Lady Rhea Claire to a dawn sky. Her hair was as pure a gold as the first streakings of light in a morning sky. Her lovely eyes were a violet blue. And in Houston Kirby's opinion, *she* was the true treasure that the captain had brought home to

England, a far more priceless treasure than the Spanish gold the captain had discovered.

Of the chance of fate that had sent Lady Rhea Claire seeking refuge aboard the *Sea Dragon* that rainy afternoon in Charles Town, or the one that had put that treasure map in the captain's hands, well, he didn't know which was stranger. Neither story needed any high coloring in the telling, even in Longacres' tales, which came as naturally to the old pirate as breathing, especially when he had a full tankard of rum at his elbow.

Of course, thought Houston Kirby, he might be wrong about the notoriety being created by Longacres' babblings. The stories might just benefit the captain, for, in Longacres' highflown telling of the tale, the captain and crew of the *Sea Dragon* had saved the beautiful Lady Rhea Claire from certain death at the hands of murderous villains. The beloved daughter of the Duke and Duchess of Camareigh, she had been brutally kidnaped from the family's country estate and shipped to the the colonies to be sold as an indentured servant.

Half dead from the deprivations she had endured during the long sea voyage to the colonies, Lady Rhea Claire had been fleeing her captors along the docks in Charles Town when she sought refuge aboard the *Sea Dragon*. Quite naturally enough, the good captain and crew of that fine ship had taken the poor wee thing to their hearts. Had they not taken pity upon her, taking her with them when they'd sailed for the Indies, she most likely would have died either at the hands of her former kidnapers or of the fever, for she had collapsed soon after boarding the *Sea Dragon*.

By the time they dropped anchor in St. John's Harbour, Antigua, Lady Rhea Claire had not only made a full recovery, she and the captain had fallen in love. In fact, according to Longacres, it had been love at first sight, so the charge of kidnaping the lass from Charles Town was as false as dicers' oaths, and by that Longacres would have sworn. And if justice was to be done, Longacres had been heard to declare, then the crew of the *Sea Dragon* ought to have been knighted for their uncommon act of kindness, and certainly not questioned like criminals.

Actually, Houston Kirby remembered the affair in a slightly different manner. For one thing, the first encounter between the captain and Lady Rhea Claire had been anything but love at first sight, and although the voyage to Antigua had been fraught with nothing more dangerous than sun-filled, balmy days, the atmosphere on board had been stormy.

Of course, he couldn't truly blame Longacres for his wrong assumptions, for the coxswain hadn't been privy to certain information. And now that Kirby thought about it, he would just as soon not have known the real story himself.

And if there was anyone to lay the blame on for the predicament they now found themselves in, thought Houston Kirby, then it would have to be the Spanish foretopman who'd long ago survived the sinking of his ship in a hurricane. All aboard had been lost except for the cursed foretopman, including the galleon's cargo, a hold laden with chests of gold and silver newly minted in Mexico City. Not satisfied with merely escaping with his life, the Spanish foretopman had decided to press his luck further, and throughout the following years he had looted the ship of some of its fabulous wealth. His conscience troubling him, however, he had confessed his misdeeds in his last will and testament. Years later that document ended up in a card game in St. Eustatius in which the captain of the *Sea Dragon* was holding the winning hand. Perhaps because the information revealed on the parchment had been a dying man's last confession, Dante Leighton had considered it worth the journey to Trinidad. And in the ruins of a plantation overgrown with jungle, he discovered a strongbox containing a map. The sunken galleon's location was clearly marked.

Because secrets like that are hard to keep, and because many a man had dreamed of finding a fortune in sunken treasure and would have stopped at nothing to get it, Dante Leighton and the crew of the *Sea Dragon* had not been alone in their search. Many were after the misbegotten gold from the conquistadors' El Dorado.

And that was why, when the captain of the *Sea Dragon* had discovered the trespasser in his cabin, the prized treasure map spread across a table, Dante Leighton thought Lady Rhea Claire Dominick just another conniver out to get her hands on the fortune. The captain had found it hard to believe her outrageous tale about being kidnaped, and even harder to believe that she was the daughter of an English duke. It seemed obvious that she was a street urchin who'd been sent on board by a rival treasure hunter to find that map.

Her feeble explanation that she had accidentally stumbled across the map that had been so cleverly hidden from all of Charles Town had been yet another farfetched tale meant to confuse the captain.

They'd had very little choice. The girl having seen the map, Dante Leighton couldn't risk turning her loose. So she had sailed to the Indies with them, and only Houston Kirby, Alastair Marlowe, and the captain had known the real reason why she went with them.

Soon, however, when Lady Rhea Claire had recovered her health, it became clear that she was indeed the person she claimed to be. Even the cleverest actress could not have played so refined and gracious a lady. Every word, every action bespoke her aristocratic upbringing.

The captain had continued to display an unusual degree of antagonism toward her. Of course, the captain had just been involved in an unhappy love affair with a woman in Charles Town, a woman whose lies and selfish scheming had destroyed his love for her. But Lady Rhea Claire was so different from that other woman. There could be no comparison. The captain's ill-tempered moodiness confused Houston Kirby.

And then, suddenly, he had understood. The captain's behavior had not been because he *disliked* her, but rather because he had found himself becoming enamored of her.

That startling turn of events had had the little steward more concerned than if he'd spied an unfamiliar sail looming to starboard. If Lady Rhea Claire was indeed the kidnaped daughter of the Duke and Duchess of Camareigh, then she had no business aboard a smugglers' brig or, worse, becoming involved with a man most people thought little better than a pirate.

Houston Kirby could still remember thinking that their one chance of salvation had been the gentle innocence of Lady Rhea Claire. The only thing she had cared about was returning to her family in England. Once the *Sea Dragon* had reached Antigua and their lovely passenger went ashore, Lady Rhea Claire would have forgotten all about the *Sea Dragon*, and her captain. And although he might have had a harder time of it, eventually Dante Leighton would have forgotten the golden-haired, violet-eyed girl he should never have even known existed.

That was what should have happened when they'd docked in Antigua. Instead, the captain of the *Sea Dragon* had forbidden the lady to leave her cabin. The captain's explanation for keeping her aboard ship seemed quite reasonable. The voyage of the *Sea Dragon* was a quest, the outcome of which could change the lives of every man aboard. They could not afford to be detained and questioned in Antigua.

But Houston Kirby was not deceived. He had seen that determined glint in the captain's eye too many times. The real reason was only too evident: Dressed in a skirt made from bits and pieces of buckskin and leather donated by each member of the crew, and a blouse cut from one of the captain's fine cambric shirts, her golden hair swinging in braids entwined with colorful ribbons, Lady Rhea Claire had become an endearingly familiar figure aboard the *Sea Dragon* as she sat on the companion ladder, Jamaica curled in her lap.

And watching her from the deck above, Dante Leighton, the *Sea Dragon*'s slightly disreputable captain, had come to want the gentle-born lady who seemed to represent all he might once have possessed, and had lost when he had fled England. She was a very real ghost from his past, but just as elusive as his memories.

And Houston Kirby was afraid that his fears were to be sadly realized as the captain tried to hold on to a dream that could never be fulfilled and just might turn into a nightmare for the captain and the lady he seemed determined to possess.

She had become a challenge to Dante Leighton, and that made her all the more desirable. Everything Dante Leighton had achieved in life had been fought hard for—his ship, the respect of his crew, and the successes he had known as a privateer. Nothing had come easily in life for the man who'd had to fight even for his own self-respect.

But Lady Rhea Claire had been determined too, and the *Sea Dragon* had hardly dropped anchor in St. John's Harbour when Lady Rhea Claire tried to escape. She might have succeeded too, if fate hadn't intervened in the person of Conny Brady, the *Sea Dragon*'s young cabin boy. Lady Rhea Claire had befriended the orphan, and the lonely little boy had come openly to idolize the beautiful and kind lady from London who always seemed to have a special smile for him. When a search party went ashore to find their missing passenger, Conny Brady had been among them.

And as the captain had expected, Lady Rhea Claire, having reached port, found herself in difficulties. Dressed as she was, and having arrived aboard a smuggling vessel, she had hardly looked the part of an aristocrat. Lost and dejected, with every respectable door closed in her face, Lady Rhea Claire had fallen afoul of a group of rowdy, drunken seamen, and it had only been because of the timely interruption of Conny Brady, and then an English naval officer, that she had escaped serious harm.

But that other member of the crew had not fared so well. Conny Brady had been wounded trying to protect Lady Rhea Claire from her attackers. The intervention of the naval officer had prevented any further bloodshed, and that was where fate had played yet another trick on the unsuspecting crew of the *Sea Dragon;* for that obliging naval officer had been none other than Captain Sir Morgan Lloyd of H.M.S. *Portcullis,* the *Sea Dragon*'s old nemesis.

At that time no one aboard the *Sea Dragon* would have believed that encounter to have been anything but unlucky, and Dante Leighton certainly thought it damned unfortunate. But he was more concerned about his unconscious cabin boy and about what Lady Rhea Claire would say and do now that freedom was within her grasp than to be worrying about what the hand of fate was about to do next.

Lady Rhea Claire's actions in that moment had sealed not only her own fate but also that of the *Sea Dragon*'s crew as well. She said nothing about being forced to sail with them, about trying to escape. She didn't even mention her kidnaping from England. Instead, she had given her name and professed her willingness to cooperate fully in any charges to be made against the man who had stabbed young Conny Brady. Then she had returned voluntarily to the *Sea Dragon,* her one concern, Conny Brady.

Sir Morgan Lloyd must have felt more than a little foolish

when, upon his return to Charles Town, he heard about the warrant for the arrest of Dante Leighton on the charge of kidnaping Lady Rhea Claire Dominick, the very same lady he had just left in Antigua with the captain and crew of the *Sea Dragon*. And his bewilderment must have been heightened by the contradictory statements made by two women, complete strangers, both of whom claimed to have special knowledge of Lady Rhea Claire.

One, an acclaimed Charles Town beauty and former love of Dante Leighton's, stated quite caustically that any claim of kidnaping as had been declared in the many handbills being circulated about the colonies was false, for she had seen, with her very own eyes, the *lady* in question on board the *Sea Dragon,* and hardly complaining. In fact, she had deceived the whole lot of them. In her opinion, Dante Leighton and the *lady* deserved one another. Most people agreed, but secretly talked among themselves. After all, hadn't Helene Jordane lost her own chance to wed Dante Leighton? When she broke off their engagement, she had no idea that he was the Marquis of Jacqobi, and not just the smuggler captain she thought him to be. And whether Dante Leighton had been speaking the truth or not, what better way to mortify a woman who had callously broken off an engagement, then changed her mind, than to introduce her to the woman he now intended to wed?

Houston Kirby, who had witnessed the scene, could have told anyone interested enough to have asked, that it had been a bit of inspired play-acting on the part of the captain, and that Lady Rhea Claire had been half-delirious with fever at the time and remembered little of what had happened. And shortly thereafter, the *Sea Dragon* had sailed for the Indies; the captain and crew never having learned of the handbills describing their passenger and offering a reward for information, or of the strange revelations that would soon follow.

It had been the other woman's story, and a deathbed statement by the captain of the *London Lady,* that made Helene Jordane look the fool. Thin and frightened half out of her wits, a girl called Alys had come forward and told a story of having sailed from London aboard the *London Lady* with Lady Rhea Claire. The two had formed a friendship. Alys' tale of the suffering aboard that ship left little doubt that Lady Rhea Claire had indeed been kidnaped. Alys, who had been destined for indentured service, had one very important piece of evidence to corroborate her story: a locket and chain of purest gold which belonged to Lady Rhea Claire. That and the information revealed by the late captain of the *London Lady* had convinced the authorities to issue a warrant for the arrest of the captain of the *Sea Dragon*.

And so it was left to Captain Sir Morgan Lloyd to return to the Indies to try to find the captain of the *Sea Dragon* and his unusual passenger. That was how the captain of H.M.S. *Portcullis* had come to lend personal escort to the *Sea Dragon* on its homeward journey and to unwittingly give safe conduct to the ship whose hold was by then full of priceless treasure.

And that was also how Sir Morgan Lloyd of His Majesty's Navy had come to testify that day in London on behalf of the captain and crew of the *Sea Dragon*. He had been honor-bound to tell the truth, and that meant swearing on oath that he had seen the lady return to the *Sea Dragon* of her own free will.

By that time, Dante Leighton had found not only the sunken treasure, but his heart's desire as well.

In a secluded cove, where the tide lapped gently against sun-warmed sands and the sky turned savage with scarlet and gold, a man and a woman had become as one. And as night fell, their destinies became forever interwoven.

And that destiny, once they were back in England, was precisely why Houston Kirby was so worried as he sat drinking ale in the taproom of Hawke's Bell Inn.

"Well, Kirby? You don't think the cap'n would risk losing Lady Rhea Claire, do you? He has everything he wants. He should just let the past stay buried. The captain's no fool, Kirby. Kirby?"

But Houston Kirby was staring down in amazement at the chops and boiled potatoes piled high on a platter that had been placed right beneath his nose. The aromatic steam rising from his dinner, and Alastair Marlowe's words, jolted him back to the present, and he shivered with the damp that clung to his clothes.

"The Lady Rhea Claire?" Kirby mumbled. "No, I haven't forgotten the lady, and that is precisely why I am worried, Mr.

Marlowe. Things may be different now that the captain and
Lady Rhea Claire have returned to England."

"No, Kirby, I don't believe that. Haven't you seen how
different the cap'n is when he's around her? She's changed
him, Kirby. He is gentle when he is with her. And the way he
touches her, as if he is afraid she might disappear." Alastair's
voice left little doubt that he was half in love with the lady
himself.

"Aye." Houston Kirby surprised Alastair by agreeing. "And
like I said, that's why I'm concerned. There just might be other
folk who feel the same way about her. Like her family, for
instance? And they might not care for the stories they'll be
hearin' about the captain of the *Sea Dragon*. The cap'n had
it all his own way when we were in the Indies, but now that
we're back in England, Lady Rhea Claire's family may have
their own ideas about what is best for her. The cap'n may not
be a part of her future as far as the duke is concerned. And
from what I've heard about the Duke of Camareigh in these
past few days, our cap'n may have met his match."

"Lady Rhea Claire is in love with the captain. She'd never
leave him, Kirby."

"It might just be better for everyone involved if she did,"
the little steward said, not meaning to speak his thoughts aloud.

"What do you mean?" Alastair asked sharply, but he looked
as if he did not really want to know the answer.

"What I'm thinkin', lad, is that once the cap'n sets his mind
to somethin', there's no stoppin' him. And I wouldn't like to
see the young lady get caught up in what is bound to happen
if the cap'n, nay"—Houston Kirby paused and corrected himself—"if Lord Dante Jacqobi returns to Merdraco. Which he
will. Ye see," he continued slowly and thoughtfully, "there
might be other folk as well who haven't forgotten the past.
And them folk may be hellbent on revenge, too. Dante Leighton, though he's been gone these many years, is still the Marquis of Jacqobi. That much hasn't changed. And for some
people that title will revive old and bitter memories. When his
lordship returns to Merdraco, certain people might feel like
'twas only yesterday. Then all the old hatreds will flare up.
Nothin' quite like festerin' resentments to start poisonin' some
people's minds over and over again."

"But Kirby, the captain doesn't have to become involved in all that. He can—"

"He may not have any choice in the matter," the little steward interrupted harshly. "Reckon it might already be too late to stop what's been set into motion. Maybe we never even had a chance. 'Twas meant to be all along," Kirby spoke sadly, remembering another time. "Only this time Lord Dante Jacqobi isn't the betrayed young man who knew only how to run away. He has become a man who is more than a match for his enemy this time. And when the two meet up there's goin' to be hell to pay."

"It does not have to be that way," Alastair repeated, but he knew their captain too well really to believe himself. "Has the captain's struggle been for naught? If only the past could be forgotten," he spoke wistfully.

"Ye can't forget, Mr. Marlowe, because the past is what ye be today. 'Tis a part of ye, lad. Besides, some things may not be as much in the past as ye might be thinkin'," he added.

"What do you mean?"

"I mean that maybe the cap'n hasn't been idle all these years. Maybe he's been up to somethin', and that somethin' might not sit too well with a certain somebody, not if he finds out. Which he will, once we get to Merdraco. Aye, then the fat will be in the fire."

"To be sure, I've never seen such glum faces," Seumus Fitzsimmons exclaimed. "I'm beginnin' to think ye're not God-fearin' men. Haven't ye read Ecclesiastes? 'A man hath no better thing under the sun than to eat, and to drink, and to be merry.' Well, then? We've got the food and the drink, so let us be merry, mates! Damned if I'm goin' to let them two woebegone faces spoil me appetite," he declared, helping himself to a large wedge of thick-crusted cheese.

"Aye," Houston Kirby muttered as he picked up his own knife and fork, thinking the Irishman ought to be quoting Isaiah instead. Even gallows-bound men deserved a last meal, he decided, washing down a stubborn piece of pork with a hefty swig of ale.

The little steward glanced upward, toward the location of the private room where the captain of the *Sea Dragon* and Lady

Rhea Claire were dining, and he wondered if they, too, were suffering a lack of appetite.

Or were they, as the young so often were, blithely unaware of what the morrow might bring while they celebrated the end of a journey, little realizing that the end was often but another beginning?

> They say best men are molded out of faults,
> And, for the most, become much more the better
> For being a little bad.
>
> Shakespeare

Chapter 2

"ANOTHER piece of gooseberry pie, Conny?" Lady Rhea Claire smiled.

"No thank you, m'lady. I'm fair to bustin' me new breeches already," Conny Brady said, muffling a belch behind his hand as he looked up sheepishly.

"Do not forget your milk, Conny," she reminded him a second time.

Conny Brady sniffed, sounding like Houston Kirby when the little steward wasn't pleased about something. "Beggin' your pardon, m'lady, but I don't really take to milk. Heard tell it ain't good for a person. Reckon a wee swallow of ale might taste good, though," he said.

"Indeed? Well, I shall have to tell my mother and uncle about your views."

"M'lady?"

"You see, my mother swears by milk, as does my Uncle Richard. And they are both in quite good health."

"That be the Duchess, then, m'lady? She drinks milk?" Conny asked doubtfully, then eyed the mug of milk with a less suspicious eye.

"To please me, won't you drink just a little?" she cajoled, a slight smile curving her lips while she watched him take a deep breath, then down the contents like any good drinking man would have done.

"Thank you," she murmured, thinking how much he reminded her of her younger brother Robin. The boys were of a similar age, and both had dark hair and blue eyes. Both possessed a certain mischievous quality that should have given fair warning to anyone who might have mistakenly thought either one was the angel he appeared to be.

"Cap'n. M'lady. D'ye mind if I'm excused now? I'd kinda like to join me mates. Thought I saw Mr. Kirby comin' up the lane not more than half an hour past. And I heard Longacres down there in the taproom when I was passin' through. I'd kinda like to be havin' a word with him."

"Very well, Conny. Off with you," Lady Rhea Claire told him with an understanding grin, knowing that the boy could never get his fill of Longacres' pirate lore.

"Cap'n, sir?"

"Run along, Mr. Brady," his captain consented. "But go easy on the ale, Mr. Brady," he advised.

"Ye won't be needin' me anymore this evenin', then? D'ye want I should give Mr. Kirby a message?" he asked as he stepped away from the table that was now cluttered with empty platters, a linen napkin still tied round his neck and stained with gooseberry pie.

"No, I'll not be needing either of you anymore this evening. And, Conny, remember that you are a wealthy young man. You need no longer ask consent of any man, nor serve him. What you do from now on is your own business," Dante Leighton reminded the lad who had spent half his life serving aboard the *Sea Dragon*.

Conny Brady frowned slightly, the thought seemed to trouble him. Then, with a shrug of his thin shoulders, he bid them good evening. But as he opened the door to leave and join his friends below, he glanced back. There was a strange expression on his face, almost one of longing, as he gazed at the captain and Lady Rhea Claire sitting companionably in the warmth of the firelight.

When the door had closed behind his small figure, Rhea Claire carefully folded her napkin and placed it on the table. "He seems so lonely sometimes. He enjoys being with his mates, and listening to that old pirate's stories of buccaneers, but underneath he is a very lonely little boy, Dante," Rhea Claire said, her face sad. Although she had been raised in a loving family, she had come to know loneliness since being kidnaped from her home, and she worried about Conny.

It seemed as though Dante Leighton had forgotten those long days of loneliness when he had had no family. "Do not mistake him for your own brother, Rhea. Conny Brady's been more places and seen more things than many a man old enough to be his grandfather. He has become strong, Rhea. And he now has a future most of London would envy. He'll not want for anything. He doesn't need your pity, my dear."

"But perhaps he does need love, Dante, and a family who cares about him, and not just what his money might buy," Rhea responded quietly but firmly.

"A family? What, pray tell, is a family? A group of loving people dedicated to one another's happiness? Or a group of selfish people related by blood, but who couldn't care less about one another?" His slight smile was little better than a sneer.

"I think that is an absolutely horrid thing to say."

Pressing a warm kiss against her forehead, his expression apologetic, he realized he had shocked her, "I did not come from a loving family. My father lived in his own little world, which excluded me. For some reason he took a dislike to his only son. No, perhaps that is rather harsh," Dante amended. "Let us just say that he was disinterested in my welfare. And my esteemed grandfather, the old Marquis, was more concerned with upholding family tradition than seeing to the wants and needs of individual family members. We were, none of us, overly devoted to one another."

"And your mother?" Rhea asked softly, her violet eyes shadowed.

"My mother?" Dante repeated strangely, as if the word were foreign to him. "She loved me so much that she preferred death to watching her son grow into manhood. Not that I had given her much hope of seeing that boy become an honorable man, or even a son that she could be proud of. Too late I discovered my true enemy, and that my mother had never been happy with . . ." Dante paused, then continued, his voice harsh, "Well, suffice to say that I did not make her life any the more bearable. I suppose I am partly to blame for what followed. If only I had been more a friend to her. If only she had turned to me for help," Dante murmured more to himself than to Rhea. His eyes closed against the memories, he did not see the instinctive movement she made toward him.

He moved the hand that Rhea would have touched comfortingly, and impatiently ran his fingers through the soft, dark chestnut curls that framed his forehead and temples. "The despair she must have known. How she must have suffered because of me. Sometimes I wonder what must have been going through her mind in that fleeting yet endless moment of darkness just before the rising of the sun. If only she had waited, given me a chance to make things up to her. But she did not.

"We'd had an argument, just one of many in those last days. I had thought her wrong, and I had stormed out of the library, not sparing her even another glance. I heard her call my name, but I never stopped. And I never saw her again. I went off to London, and it was just a few days later that I received the news. They said it was an accident, that the path had been slippery after the rain, and she had lost her footing. Everyone knew she loved to walk the cliffs. Even with a storm coming she could be seen standing on the cliffs, gazing out to sea for hours at a time. I realize now that that was her way of escaping the torment of her life. Eventually it must have come to her that there could be another, more final escape. She must have thought it her salvation when she stared down at the tide breaking against the rocks so far below. And so, at dawn, she took that last step that ended it all. She no longer had to face the morrow and what it might bring."

"No, Dante, you cannot know that. She may truly have slipped," Rhea whispered, shaken by Dante's tormented memories.

"The last words she spoke to me, except for calling my name, were, 'Perhaps death will be my only escape from this hell I have created for those I have loved.' Then she asked for my forgiveness."

Dante opened gray eyes shadowed by the past, and Rhea felt as if she were staring into a stranger's eyes. "She wanted *my* forgiveness. Dear God, the irony of that! Her words still haunt me. The villagers of Merleigh say that her windswept figure can still be seen on stormy days silhouetted against the dawn above the cliffs near Merdraco. Some have even said that she haunts the Great Hall, and that her voice can be heard calling to someone, but of course there is no one to answer. Even the vicar of Westlea Abbot, a neighboring village, has claimed to have seen a specter that appears atop one of the towers of Merdraco on a moonless night. Of course," Dante added with the cynical look that Rhea knew only too well, "he preaches more from the bottle than from the Good Book, so you can't take his word as gospel."

"How do you know all this? I thought you'd not returned to Merdraco in over fifteen years." Rhea wanted to learn all she possibly could about this man she had come to love, yet knew so little about.

Dante seemed momentarily startled by her question, then he shrugged. "It is not important how I know," he said, unwilling to explain. "Most good people think it a sin for someone to take his own life. They believe that the soul will never find peace and is destined to wander for eternity, or perhaps be damned. My mother did not make a very good bargain when she traded one hell for another."

"Dante, I am so sorry," Rhea said awkwardly. "I never knew. You do not speak of the days before you left England. I wish you would tell me," Rhea urged, her slim hand touching the hardness of his tanned cheek.

But she was unprepared for the violence of his reaction when his fingers wrapped painfully round her hand and he pulled her from her chair and onto his lap. Staring deeply into her startled eyes, he spoke coldly. "You are not a part of that life. Never do I want you to be touched by it, or even learn of the man I once was. I wonder if you will continue to be faithful to me, no matter what may happen, or what you might learn. Or will you, my most beloved, find life with me so unbearable that you would turn away from me? Will I hurt you as I have everyone else in my life? Or will you remain true, little daffadilly?" he demanded, his gaze lingering on the golden glory of her hair.

"Dante, you know you have my love forevermore. I have pledged that to you."

Dante loosened his punishing grip when he saw the hurt expression in her eyes. Turning her palm upward, he pressed a gentle kiss against its softness.

"Forevermore? If only I could believe that. But I fear that nothing is forever. You will only be hurt all the more if you are deceived into believing that what happiness we have found today will be there tomorrow," Dante told her.

Perhaps he was unaware of the cruelty of his words. Rhea turned her face away. His casually spoken words frightened her. There was such a hopelessness about them.

Dante's touch was gentle this time as he turned her face to his. "I've hurt you, haven't I? I did not mean to, but now you can see how easily an ill-spoken word can cast doubt on or even destroy the feelings we thought inviolate," he warned her. "Never let anyone turn you against me, Rhea. Promise me that."

Rhea stared at him in silent confusion.

"Promise me?"

"I promise you," Rhea finally spoke the vow.

"You may have doubts about me one day, but never doubt that I love you. You may hear of scandal associated with my name, but however genuine it may sound, come to me and let me explain. Give me the chance to deny it. Or perhaps to confirm it. But give me that chance, Rhea. Never run away without letting me explain," he asked her, almost pleadingly, she was later to remember.

"I'll never leave you, Dante," she told him again, trying to reassure him, for she had just seen a side of Dante that few people knew about, and it had been anything but arrogant.

"How easy it is for you to promise that now, but what of later?" he murmured as his mouth closed over her lips and he parted them, savoring the familiar feel and taste of her.

Rhea's hands moved caressingly as she cradled his head and responded to his kisses with a growing passion of her own. It was always this way, she thought drowsily as she felt his fingers moving with purpose against the laces of her bodice. She could deny him nothing. She could think of none but him when he looked at her, touched her, made love to her. The rest of the world ceased to exist when they were together.

Unfortunately, however, the rest of the world still had business to take care of, and a persistent, not-to-be ignored knocking finally intruded into Rhea's consciousness. Reluctantly, she freed her lips from Dante's possessive kiss.

"There is someone at the door," she tried to tell him, but the words were little better than a breathless whisper.

"The damned fool can bide his time," Dante replied, unwilling to stir himself for some misadvised oaf demanding entrance, not when he could bury his face in the fragrant, golden tresses he had loosened to fall free about Rhea's pale shoulders.

"Dante, please," Rhea pleaded. She felt his mouth moving along the curve of breast revealed by her parted bodice. The knocking was becoming impatient.

"Either the bastard's crazed, or he has an army at his back, for few men would dare disturb my privacy. One of the few advantages of being thought the devil incarnate, my sweet," Dante muttered as the knocking continued and a noisy shuffling could be heard beyond the solid oak of the door.

"I do believe 'tis an army. I suppose there's nothing for it but to face the enemy," Dante sighed as he allowed Rhea to slide off his lap. He was far from being in good humor as he watched her cross the room and, her back to the door, straighten her bodice.

"Enter at your own risk! Pistols primed!" he called out, sounding more like the captain of the *Sea Dragon* than a gentleman of leisure.

Rhea spun round in surprise, expecting to see Dante standing with a pistol in each hand. But he was still sitting where she had left him. A wicked grin was widening his mouth as he stared at the door.

"I daresay the worst of your reputation has now been confirmed, and by your very own lips," Rhea commented dryly while adjusting the delicate fall of lace adorning the sleeves of her muslin gown. "Half of the maids in the inn are scared witless whenever they happen to cross your path. I truly believe that you enjoy causing an uproar," she accused him, but the smile curving her lips took the sting from her words.

"Do I really?" Dante asked, sounding genuinely surprised to hear such an accusation, but he was even more surprised by the sudden silence beyond the door.

"Well? Enter, or be damned!" he called out, ignoring Rhea's expression of feigned exasperation.

"Lord, 'elp us!" whispered one of the chambermaids cowering just outside the door.

"What'd Oi tell ye? A bloodthirsty pirate 'e is. Sailed from the Indies on the devil's own ship, 'e did. 'Eard tell, even, that one of them treasure chests full o' gold was filled with the bleached bones of pirates. Devil's treasure, 'tis," her companion declared.

"No tellin' what a gent like 'im might do, then?" the first maid questioned timidly, feeling a weakness in her knees at the thought uppermost in her mind.

"Aye, and 'tis somethin' a supposedly decent miss like yerself shouldn't even be knowin' about, much less thinkin' about," the elder of the two girls responded knowingly.

"Ooooh, but 'e is an 'andsome devil, though," the younger girl stated, unmindful of her more experienced friend's advice while she momentarily forgot, or perhaps dreamed, about Dante Leighton and his adventurer's less-than-respectable reputation.

"Well, ye don't 'ave t'be worryin' none."

"Ye think not? Don't reckon 'e'll be castin' them bonny eyes at either one o' us, not with her ladyship at his side," the young maid predicted wisely, even while tidying the mobcap perched atop her russet curls.

"Such a beauty she is, too. And sweet as can be, with not a mean word to anyone. Not at all snooty, either, if ye knows what Oi means. Why, just t'other day she says to me—"

"Damn the two of ye! I knew it, damned if I didn't!" roared the innkeeper as he stomped along the corridor, the two guilty maids fixed in his stare. "Knew ye'd be standin' here gossipin' while I've got customers to be fed and seen to. Don't know how a man can run a decent business nowadays, what with the wages bein' demanded and the poor service bein' given in return," he complained as he grimly eyed the nervous girls.

"We knocked! Again and again, we did! Even pounded on the door with our fists! 'Tis the truth!" they chorused.

"But we was frightened 'cause a voice, soundin' for all the world like the devil 'imself, says to enter or be damned!" one of the girls said on a rising note of hysteria.

"Good! Then we'll be wastin' no more time standin' here," the innkeeper declared, his appreciative laugh rumbling down the corridor and somewhat relieving the tension of the two young men standing at a safe distance, their arms full of carefully wrapped bundles.

Without further ado, the innkeeper opened the door and, with a hand clasped firmly on each girl's shrinking shoulder, escorted the two into the dragon's den.

"Ah, at last. I had begun to think my hearing was playing tricks on me," the captain of the *Sea Dragon* commented conversationally.

Without his coat and waistcoat, his ruffled shirtfront parted nearly to the waist and revealing a bronzed, muscular chest, the close-fitting buckskin breeches leaving no doubt of his virility, Dante Leighton looked every inch the piratical captain half of London suspected him of being.

Sitting with a booted foot resting casually against a tapestried stool while he idly toyed with the rapier lying across his lap, his languid pose was quite deceptive, for the narrowed gray eyes raked the newcomers and missed nothing.

"Beggin' yer pardon, m'lord, m'lady, but if ye're finished dinin', then the girls here will clear the table," the innkeeper explained at his most genial. His bonebreaker's grip was coming close to shattering each girl's shoulder as he pushed them toward the table.

"'Tis quite all right," Dante murmured, his gaze moving to the two uneasy young gentlemen hesitating in the opened doorway.

"It was a delicious meal, Mr. Parkham." Rhea Claire complimented him with a smile that took hostage of the gruff innkeeper's heart. "Our young friend, Mr. Brady, found the gooseberry pie especially delectable."

"Did he, now?" Mr. Parkham said with a beaming smile. "Well, I'll sure be tellin' Mrs. Parkham about yer kind words, m'lady. Be glad t'hear it, too. Ol' Nell Farquhar, proprietress of the King's Messenger, off St. Martin's Lane, claims she bakes the best gooseberry pies hereabouts, though I don't know how her customers have ever gotten a mouthful. I figure she eats most of 'em herself. A waist as round as a hogshead of molasses she has, and as mean as a—"

"If you will pardon me for interrupting, Mr. Parkham," Dante spoke softly, yet effectively halted the garrulous innkeeper. "What business do these gentlemen have here?"

"Says they be makin' a delivery, m'lord," Mr. Parkham replied while leveling a questioning stare of his own at the two men. "And they had better be tellin' me the truth, for if I finds out that they've bamboozled me, and be here to try to sell their wares on the sly, well . . ." he warned, the ugly glint in his eye promising swift retribution. There was little doubt that he meant it, for Mr. Parkham was a burly man who was well used to keeping order on his premises.

"Oh, 'tis true enough, m'lord," one of the young men quickly spoke up, preferring to address the gentleman who most likely would be tipping him. "We're from Madame Lambere. She sent us along with the clothes she finished for Lady Rhea Claire. She said to be quick about it, that her ladyship needed them, and Madame isn't one to disappoint a customer. The Dominicks always pay their bills, she said. Otherwise, m'lord, we wouldn't have intruded so late in the evening," the young man explained, although his eyes, once having located the lady in question, had never moved beyond that stunning vision in white.

"'Tis true, then, m'lord?" Mr. Parkham demanded, thinking privately that this glib young gent in his finery probably did more than just deliver packages for Madame Lambere. But at his lordship's nod, he had to acquiesce and, relaxing his defensive stance, he grudgingly allowed the two young gentlemen access to the room.

"Be about yer business, then, and don't be botherin' his lordship any longer than need be. And ye two, get clearin' the table," he ordered the two maids, who'd been standing in awed silence while ignoring their less than interesting duties. "Ye've work to see to, so quit yer gabbin' and gawkin' and get crackin'. I'll be expectin' to see them silly faces back in the kitchens by the time I've gotten there meself," he warned them, little realizing how quickly the two would follow in his very footsteps.

The two young gentlemen wasted little time unwrapping their bundles. Spreading the contents across the wide four-poster in the far corner, they revealed a dazzling sight.

A primrose yellow damask gown embroidered across the voluminous skirt with a scattering of delicate wildflowers and butterflies, and a blue quilted satin petticoat spilled forth like a breath of spring on a winter's eve. A rose brocade with a white silk stomacher, richly embroidered in a pale green leaf pattern with small satin rosebuds, and elbow-length sleeves trimmed with a cascade of three point-lace ruffles burst into glory, next followed by a watered silk turquoise taffeta, flounced and furbelowed with Valenciennes lace and violet bows on the sleeves. A lavender petticoat tumbled out next.

But it was the last gown revealed that drew gasps from the two mesmerized maids who were now staring quite openly at the finery piled high on the bed. The gown was an exquisite, ethereal creation of gold tissue which shimmered in the firelight like dancing fairy lights in the woodlands. The sleeves and ruffled skirt were trimmed in soft, silken blond lace that resembled gold-spun cobwebs.

The pelisse of sapphire blue velvet, trimmed with ermine, went almost unnoticed, as did the assortment of handkerchiefs, some edged in lace, some embroidered, some colored. And the silk stockings in every shade imaginable, with kid gloves to match, remained carefully folded and set aside. The rose-colored satin slippers and the purple velvet ones soon became lost under the mountain of velvet and satin and lace, along with the pair made of yellow kid. The lavender silk hat with violet plumes might have captured a quick glance, but the straw hat with jonquil ribbons and the Bergère with lovely sarcenet roses went unappreciated by the two bemused serving girls, their rounded eyes glued to the gown of shimmering golden threads.

"With m'lady's permission, I'll leave this package wrapped, for 'tis m'lady's chemises, stays, and under petticoats," the more talkative of the two men suggested courteously, but the look in his eye was anything but respectful.

"How considerate," Rhea said, ignoring the man's leering wink. "My mother and I have always been most pleased with our purchases from Madame Lambere's. We have never had reason to complain," Rhea said, the remark sounding quite innocent, especially so accompanied as it was by a sweet smile. "Madame Lambere has truly surpassed herself where this gown is concerned. 'Tis truly magnificent."

"Madame will be most pleased to hear your praise. Of course, m'lady has excellent taste. And, if I may be so indiscreet to say so, I knew the moment m'lady walked into Madame's that this gown could be for none other than her. In fact, Madame had quite often confided in me that the Duchess of Camareigh is her very favorite client. And, if I may be so bold, one of the most beautiful ladies in all the realm, as indeed is her daughter. How very fortunate a man His Grace is to have two such beautiful women gracing his home. Ah, and could there possibly be a more perfect setting for such unequaled beauty than the lovely perfection of Camareigh? To quote Madame, *C'est magnifique!*" the young man exclaimed, and kissed his fingers to his lips. His accent was atrocious, despite the eloquence of the gesture.

"Madame has told me how *extraordinaire* an estate Camareigh is. I believe Madame traveled to Camareigh just last year to sew many new creations for Her Grace and m'lady? Yes, indeed, His Grace is a most fortunate man," he added, his eyes lingering on Rhea's décolletage as if his fingers itched to take in a tuck or two along that entrancing curve of seam.

"Very perceptive of you to have noticed, *m'sieu,* but as I am the gentleman being billed for these garments, and not His Grace, you will in future kindly address any such remarks to me," Dante Leighton's cold voice interrupted the tête-à-tête and left the young gentleman from Madame Lambere's with little hope that his lordship would be generous about a tip. Indeed, as he risked a glance at the notorious captain of the *Sea Dragon,* he wondered if he might consider himself lucky to be leaving the room in one piece.

He was in fact edging toward the door with that very goal in mind when one of the serving girls let out an ear-piercing scream that must surely have raised several of the dead. Then, her tray of china scattered across the floor in shards, she fled the room, her cries of terror echoing along the corridor. Her squealing companion was not far behind.

The two young men were frozen in their tracks, denials of their guilt, whatever the offense may have been, quivering on their lips when Dante Leighton began to laugh. And since there was no apparent reason, his laughter did little to set either young man's mind at rest. Neither had any trouble envisioning Dante Leighton standing on the bloodied deck of his pirate ship, his demonic laughter ringing out while he urged some poor soul to walk the plank.

The lady, oddly, did not seem concerned. She glanced around the room, and then suddenly her gaze halted and she stared in fascination at the mound of blue velvet on the bed. It was moving like some beast awakened from slumber, its pale green eyes blinking open and glowing wickedly with firelight.

Each young man, although neither would admit to it later, felt the hair on the back of his neck rising.

"Jamaica," Rhea Claire murmured softly, her expression one of indulgence as a streak of orange bolted from hiding and landed in her outstretched arms. "Here you are, silly billy," she chuckled, scratching the cat on the back of his head until his purrs could be heard clearly across the room.

"Thank your mistress for delivering these gowns so quickly. And here is something to compensate you gentlemen for the fright you've had," Dante said, counting out a more than generous tip for both bemused young men. Their gushing thanks barely said, they disappeared from the room.

"Well, I daresay you now have as bad a reputation as I have, my dear," Dante commented with a grin of satisfaction. "Of course, I shall have a devil of a time keeping you from being burned as a witch, and ol' Jamaica from being thrown into the Thames as your familiar."

"He is not black," Rhea replied, unconcerned.

"Ah, but some might claim that you have cast a spell over him and over the captain and crew of the *Sea Dragon*. The men already think you are an enchantress, and I would have to swear that you bewitched me," Dante said provocatively, the look in his eye causing a blush to spread across Rhea's pale cheeks.

"Little daffadilly," he murmured softly, thinking of the exotically bright, at times discordant colors of the Indies, and how like an English garden Rhea had seemed by comparison. Even her scent was reminiscent of spring flowers for it was a delicate fragrance with a tantalizingly elusive hint of piquancy.

"I do not need to be my Aunt Mary to know what your thoughts are," Rhea said enigmatically as she pressed her cheek against Jamaica's head.

"Indeed? And what would this Aunt Mary of yours be able to tell you of my thoughts?" he asked. "She is not a soothsayer, is she?"

"Indeed she is," Rhea responded, her smile widening at his expression of surprise. "However, she is also very much a lady, and I doubt whether she would feel it quite proper to put your thoughts into words."

"My feelings exactly. Why waste breath talking about something when you can be doing it instead?" Dante queried softly, and started across the room toward her. There came another demanding knock.

"Most likely the good innkeeper come to assess the damage," Dante predicted, beginning to think he would never again have a moment's privacy with Rhea. "Sorry, my love."

A slight smile curved the corners of Rhea's mouth. "I am not going anywhere," Rhea promised. "Besides, there is always tomorrow," she told him, making herself comfortable before the fire while Jamaica yawned and curled contentedly in her lap. "And I am a very patient person."

"Damned if I am," Dante cursed as he went to the door.

Rhea held out her hands to the fire while the conversation of the innkeeper and the serving girls droned on, but soon their voices faded and Rhea's thoughts drifted far from London. She stared hypnotically at the flames dancing in the hearth, and suddenly she saw a peaceful valley where the wild iris and daffodil blossomed in the woodland, and the meadows were covered with bluebells. The crystalline reflection of swans floating across a sylvan lake was disturbed only by a soft breeze rippling the surface.

And in the distance, on a gently rising knoll, was Camareigh, its golden-hued walls basking in the warm glow of a somnolent late-summer afternoon.

That was the Camareigh she remembered, though it had been autumn the last time she saw her home. Almost a year had passed since the dawning of that fateful day when she had been kidnaped. The innocence of her life had vanished that autumn day redolent of rain and woodsmoke. Her destiny had been changed forever.

The girl who had ridden her mare, Skylark, along that narrow country lane with carefree abandon was no more. Rhea wondered how different it would be when she saw her family again. During those long months at sea aboard the *London Lady*, when she had known such a desperation of mind and spirit, she had despaired of ever seeing them again. How they must have suffered on her account. How many hours into days into months had they agonized over her fate, wondering perhaps if she were even still alive?

She was home, but had yet to see her family. She was so close, yet still so far. She had wanted to let her family know of her safe return immediately upon her arrival in London. But out of concern for Dante and the awkward position he was in because of her, she had waited, acquiescing to his wish to clear himself of the kidnaping charge before he faced her family.

Besides which, he had added with that mocking smile of his, she was his most important witness, and the only one who could completely prove his innocence. She didn't want to see him gallows-bound, did she? he had asked.

Dante Leighton could be most persuasive when he wanted something, and he presented his last argument quite convincingly. Would it not be better to travel to Camareigh and be reunited with her family there, rather than send an impersonal letter informing them of her arrival? Why make them travel to London, where the long-awaited reunion would have to take place among strangers? Surely they would come as soon as they heard the news. And, of course, the rest of her family would still be at Camareigh, and what kind of celebration would that be?

Rhea, never one to suspect ulterior motives, had believed in his sincerity, and had been touched by Dante's consideration for her family. It would not be until later that she would fully understand the deeper emotions conflicting within Dante. Houston Kirby would not have been so easily gulled, for he knew the captain too well not to question his actions, especially when they seemed wholly innocent. That was when it was best for a person to be on guard.

But Rhea was unsuspecting. And uppermost in her mind was the reunion with her family. She was anxious to return to them, and to Camareigh. She was homesick for the familiar sight of their faces and the sound of their voices. There was so much to say, so much to explain.

Rhea frowned slightly as she anticipated that reunion. Suddenly she was afraid of not being the same Rhea Claire they had once loved. So many things had happened to her. Would they think her too changed? Would they be able to accept what had happened? Could they accept the fact that she . . . ?

"Rhea?"

She turned her head, her mind still miles away.

"Rhea? Are you ill? You're so pale," Dante asked sharply.

Rhea gave a guilty start. She had momentarily forgotten her whereabouts, and with a look of surprise she noticed that the room was empty except for the two of them.

Dante was sitting at the table, cleared of cutlery and china. Spread out before him were several sheets of foolscap. A quill pen was held poised above one of the sheets already partly filled with neat lines of script.

"I am feeling quite well, thank you," Rhea replied politely. "I was just thinking about something." And still caught up in her private memories of Camareigh and her family, she didn't realize that the vagueness of her reply seemed to exclude Dante.

The scratching of the quill pen continued for a moment longer, then Dante carefully replaced the pen in the inkstand before methodically sprinkling fine sand from the pounce box over the slanting black letters.

"What are you thinking about?" he inquired casually while folding the parchment into a neat packet. Melting the sealing wax, Dante pressed his signet ring into the soft resin spreading across the two folds and firmly affixed his seal to the document.

Rhea sighed, shrugging. "About my family. About going home," she admitted, and to the man watching her, the soft smile of remembrance curving her lips bespoke a secret she was sharing with herself.

When Rhea became aware of Dante's fixed gaze, her smile widened to include him, but he didn't return her smile. In the flickering shadows of the firelight his expression seemed brooding, and for an uncomfortable instant Rhea felt as if she were staring into a stranger's face again.

Suddenly Dante smiled, and Rhea found herself letting out her breath, unaware that she had been holding it. To break the strange tension she felt growing between them, she glanced over to the letter.

"To whom have you been writing?" she asked curiously, thinking that Dante had few friends in England. "To someone in the colonies?"

"No," Dante answered, momentarily startled as he, too, stared at the letter. "It is to a business acquaintance. There are certain business transactions which I must conclude before 'tis too late."

His reticent response did not surprise Rhea, for there was much about Dante she did not know. If she had known everything she would probably not have understood, for they were as different as night and day.

"But let us not concern ourselves with business. I have a gift for you," he said as he got up and walked over to where a brown cloth greatcoat lay across the chest at the foot of the four-poster.

"I was going to present this to you tomorrow, but what better time could there be than now?" he asked as his hand disappeared into one of the deep pockets, reappearing seconds later with a small, flat leather case.

"You have already spent far too much on me," Rhea protested, genuinely concerned by his extravagance. It was so unnecessary. "I wish you hadn't ordered so many new gowns from Madame Lambere's. She is the most expensive dressmaker in London, and since her popularity has increased, so have her prices."

"Of course she is the best. Do you think I would buy anything but the best for you?" Dante asked. "You do not care for the gowns? Are they not up to her usual standard? If not, then I'll certainly have a word or two to say to her when—"

Rhea shook her head in amused exasperation, for Dante suddenly reminded her of a small boy whose surprise had been spoiled. "No, it is not that at all. Indeed, I think they are the most beautiful gowns I have ever seen, but—"

"My only concern is that you be pleased. Price is of no consequence," Dante interrupted, thinking he had put an end to her objections.

"It is just that I do have several wardrobes full of gowns at home, gowns I have scarcely worn. I just do not want you to waste your money, Dante," Rhea told him, trying to catch his eye in order to convince him of her sincerity. "My parents have seen to my every need. I have never wanted for anything, and I am certain that all of my possessions are still in my bedchamber at Camareigh. So, truly, you do not need to buy me anything, Dante."

The expression in Dante's eyes was unreadable, but his body suddenly tensed. He stood staring down at Rhea, his narrowed gaze lingering on the pure gold of her hair and the way the firelight seemed to be a living part of it.

"Your parents need no longer bear the responsibility for you, Rhea. Whatever you need, I will buy. Those possessions of yours are from another life. I want you to wear only what *I* have purchased for you. From the satin slippers on your feet to the velvet ribbons in your hair, I want everything you wear to have been bought by me and by no one else." His voice was implacable.

Rhea stared at him in amazed incomprehension. "I do not understand. You wish me to forget about my family and the life I lived before I was kidnaped from Camareigh?" Rhea spoke quietly, but there was a look of unease in her eyes when she met Dante's.

"My dear, you misunderstand me," Dante said quickly, realizing too late that he had gone too far. "What I meant was that I had no intention of returning you to Camareigh dressed as you were when aboard the *Sea Dragon*, despite the charming picture you made. Perhaps if you seem little changed, then your parents will be less suspicious of me," Dante speculated. "Perhaps your father will even allow me the opportunity of explaining before he tries to blow my head off. Not that I could truly blame him. If I were in his place and a gentleman of so disreputable a character came calling with my daughter on his arm, I would certainly waste little time in dispatching him to the devil," Dante added with a humorless smile.

"Oh, Dante," Rhea whispered, a smile of relief banishing the shadows from her eyes. She knew then why Dante had been so difficult of late, and why he'd been so determined to lavish her with gifts. He felt that he needed to buy her loyalty. And if she did not love him so much, she would have been offended. "For a man who is very clever, you can also be very foolish," she said softly. "Have I not convinced you yet that I shall always love you? And you needn't worry about my family, for they will welcome you into their hearts as soon as they meet you," Rhea predicted without hesitancy, forgetting her own doubts of only moments before.

"'Tis true, then, that love is indeed blind," Dante murmured with a smile of bitterness as he wondered how long it would be before Rhea was influenced by others and began to see him in a less than kindly light.

But until then...

Dante held out the slim case, just out of her reach. He grinned. "Perhaps you are correct, my dear, and I have been spending too much money on gilding a lily. Well, I am in a quandary, for I doubt that I can return this, or even trade it in on some good horseflesh. I suppose I shall be forced to find someone more appreciative. You wouldn't be able to suggest anybody, would you, my dear?" Dante asked, looking thoughtfully expectant. "I don't suppose you have a sister who is blond and blue-eyed, and avaricious enough not to mind trading her favors for a pretty bauble or two?"

Rhea lifted the sleeping Jamaica from her lap and, without causing a break in his purring, resettled him on the vacated seat. "As a matter of fact, I do have a sister. I believe I have mentioned her. Of course, the type of bauble she would be interested in would make your hand sticky. She is only two. No," Rhea corrected herself with a disbelieving shake of her head, "she is now three years old, and loves codlin tarts dripping with cream. No, I do not believe she will do at all, my dear. However," Rhea continued, looking quite serious even as she smothered her chuckle with a cough, "there is always Caroline. Yes, I can see that she will do quite splendidly for you, Dante. She is blond and blue-eyed and, unfortunately, quite avaricious. Shall I arrange introductions? She is from a most respectable family, and the daughter of my father's dear friend, Sir Jeremy Winters."

"She is the girl who was with you the day you were kidnaped?"

"Yes, and until yesterday I hadn't known if she was even still alive. As far as I knew, she could have died, as I thought Wesley Lawton had."

"Ah, yes, Wesley Lawton, the good and proper Earl of Dindale. If I remember correctly, you were quite concerned about him and quite relieved to hear of his miraculous recovery. You were going to wed the distinguished gentleman, were you not?" Dante asked, his voice too casual to be anything but sarcastically intended.

"He is the Earl of *Ren*dale," Rhea corrected him, knowing full well that Dante remembered the earl's proper name. "And he was nothing more than a family friend. Of course," Rhea added, not above a bit of teasing herself, "the thought had crossed my mind that he could become much more than that. In fact, had I not been kidnaped, I probably would have seriously considered marriage to Wesley Lawton."

"Indeed? Odd, isn't it, how one man's misfortune can turn into another man's good fortune," Dante commented, not overly concerned about the unfortunate trick fate had played on the pious Earl of Rendale. "However, this Caroline sounds promising," Dante continued with a glint in his eye, unwilling to let Rhea get away with her last remark. "Is she your size?" he inquired while his gaze raked Rhea's figure. "I should really hate to have to spend any more money on gowns, ribbons, or satin slippers."

Rhea's laughter was beginning to get the best of her. "I would not wish Caroline on even you, m'lord," Rhea conceded, thinking of that very determined young woman in hot pursuit of Dante, his marquis' title warming the cockles of Caroline's heart. "I do think it wise not to introduce her to Alastair. Now that he is a gentleman of fortune, he would never have a chance."

"'Tis a pity, but I do not think this Caroline, despite the charming picture you paint of her, is the person I am in search of. Do you have anyone else in mind?" Dante asked softly, holding out his gift enticingly.

"Only myself," Rhea replied, the gift forgotten as she stared up into his eyes, her gaze captured and held by his.

"Little daffadilly, will you be mine?" Dante's request was huskily spoken—barely audible, in fact—as he reached out to entwine around his forefinger one of the golden curls cascading over Rhea's shoulder.

Slowly Rhea moved closer, until she felt the heat of his body warming hers. She reached up to him, running her fingertips lightly along the hard line of his jaw before letting her palm come to rest against the curve of his chin.

"Always and forever," she promised, feeling that indefinable shiver spreading through her as she felt his mouth pressing a kiss into the softness of her opened palm.

Dante's arms slid around Rhea's waist, melding their bodies closer together; then his lips found hers, parting them, tasting them, as his tongue touched hers.

Rhea felt Dante's fingers at the nape of her neck, then gasped when she felt something cold touch her flesh. Reaching up, she was startled to feel the cold hardness of metal against her skin.

She glanced down, affording Dante an unrestricted view of the top of her head as she strained to see the necklace adorning her neck. "Oh, Dante, 'tis beautiful," Rhea breathed as she caught sight of the multicolored sparkle reflected by the brilliant-cut diamonds nestling against her breast. "You really shouldn't have, Dante," she protested even as a pleased smile tugged at the corners of her mouth.

"I thought we settled that argument once and for all. You had better get used to accepting gifts, for I shall never tire of trying to please you, my love," Dante reprimanded her gently as he stood back to admire the effect of his generosity. "Diamonds become you, my sweet. Although," Dante paused, his gaze critically assessing, "I think next we must have sapphires and rubies. They will reflect more perfectly your natural warmth, for you are not a cold woman, Rhea," Dante said, smiling when Rhea glanced up at him, the tears filling her eyes making him think of wild violets after a spring shower.

"I do not know why I deserve to have found such happiness,

especially when I have been so cruel as to jest about Caroline. Truly she is not as horrid as I have portrayed her. It was wrong of me when I know that she will never find the happiness I possess," Rhea said with a sense of shame, for in that quiet moment, with the fire emanating a benevolent, rosy glow, she believed that nothing could ever destroy the love she and Dante shared.

Dante kissed Rhea lingeringly. "That is why I love you, Rhea. You are so gentle and understanding, loyal and forgiving. When I am lost in my darkest thoughts, I think of you and I no longer feel hatred. Perhaps you were sent to be my salvation. I just pray never to lose the unselfish love you have given me, or fall from that high esteem you seem to hold me in."

"Never shall I change my love or my respect for you, Dante," Rhea vowed. "It has been given freely and will not be taken away, no matter what may happen. But you are so difficult to convince. What must I do, give my life for you?" Rhea bantered with a smile that quickly faded when Dante grasped her painfully by the arms, anger glinting in his gray eyes.

"Never, ever say that again," he commanded, the grimness of his expression frightening Rhea. "Never again, do you hear me? Promise me. I will never have your death on my conscience. I will not be held responsible for another's actions, not again, by God!"

Rhea swallowed hard. "I promise, Dante. I am sorry that you misunderstood me. Don't you realize that you could never do anything to cause me to take my own life? If that is what you are worried about, then, please, let your mind rest easy," Rhea reassured him, but the strange coldness in his eyes remained unchanged.

"You have not seen all of your jewelry," Dante said abruptly and, to Rhea's oversensitive ears, coldly.

Releasing Rhea from his embrace, as if her touch disturbed him, he turned his back on her and picked up his greatcoat. Digging deep into one of the pockets, he recovered several cases. Placing them on the table, he opened one, revealing a pair of diamond earrings gleaming against a blue velvet background. In another was a diamond aigrette shaped like a feather, and in yet another case lined with the same blue velvet was a bow-shaped diamond stomacher brooch accompanied by three smaller, identical brooches.

Rhea remained silent as she stared down at the glittering diamonds, her heart heavy. Never, since they had declared their love for one another, had Dante stared at her with that cold-blooded gaze that made his pale gray eyes seem so cruel and pitiless.

"They are exquisite," Rhea finally said, her voice tremulous as she stared down at the dazzling stones that seemed so lifeless. "Thank you," she said simply, biting her trembling lip as the diamonds blurred before her gaze and a hot tear escaped to drop down onto the back of Dante's hand.

He jerked as if the single teardrop had scalded him. "Rhea?" he questioned hesitantly, remorse overcoming him.

She was weeping silently and she tried to pull away from him, but she felt his arms pulling her around to face him, and he would not release her. She kept her face turned away from him. What pride she had left refused to let him see that he had hurt her as surely as if he had struck her.

But Dante was determined to look into her eyes. Cupping her chin, he forced her tear-stained face up to his searching gaze. "You frighten me, Rhea, in a way no other person has ever been able to frighten me," he surprised her by admitting. "You are still so young, so innocent of the many evils in the world. And you are so damned easy to hurt. Perhaps I have hurt you most by loving you. I wonder if it is good to be so vulnerable. One day you may not thank me for having loved you.

"Kirby warned me, but I would not listen. I had to have you, Rhea. I could not allow you to walk out of my life. But since then, I have been conscience-stricken by my selfishness, for I have come to fear that you may be too fragile and decent for a man like me. Too young, perhaps, not to be consumed and ultimately destroyed by emotions and passions which even I sometimes do not fully comprehend in myself."

Dante's arms tightened as he held her close against his heart. "How can you love a man decent people have scorned and who now seems only to bring you heartache?"

Rhea raised her face from his chest and, gazing up into his

eyes, she answered him with almost childlike ingenuousness. "Because without your love my heart would break."

Gently, Dante wiped the tears from her face, his eyes never leaving hers. "Then love me tonight, Rhea. Let us forget the tears and the angry words and misunderstandings between us," he whispered, his lips caressing the corner of her mouth. "Let us just think of this moment, then, and let there be no tomorrow to concern us."

Rhea parted her lips under the growing pressure of his, allowing his tongue an intimate touching with hers. Her body yielded to the caress of hands that had become as familiar, as natural to her as breathing and seemed just as necessary.

"Make me forget." Rhea's entreaty was an impassioned whisper.

"You are mine, Rhea. Never forget that. Whatever may happen, remember that no one else will ever be able to hold you as I do, or love you as completely as I shall tonight. You will never be able to forget my touch, nor I yours." Dante spoke almost defiantly, as if daring the fates to separate them.

Rhea felt his hands loosening the laces of her bodice, and soon the smooth, pale flesh of her breasts was revealed to his possessive gaze. His mouth left a trail of fire blazing along the taut arch of her throat where diamonds, now reflecting the warmth of the woman wearing them, lay against an erratically beating pulse.

Dante pulled the pins from Rhea's hair, releasing the thick, golden strands to tumble down the length of her back, the curling ends swaying around her hips as if alive. His lips were against the tender curve of breast so temptingly revealed by the parted laces, but it was not enough. Dante wanted to feel her naked flesh against his, to taste again the sweet-scented softness of her woman's body, to know again that ultimate moment of ecstasy when they became one.

And suddenly it was as if they were still standing on the warm sands of a lonely cove far across the sea, where the only sounds to disturb them were the melancholy cry of birds as night began to fall, and the indolent lapping of the tide against the shore. Rhea had come to him out of the water, like a sea nymph. Her pale body had been painted golden as the savagery of a dying sun set the wilderness sky ablaze in sheets of flaming copper.

Just then there was the patter of windblown rain against the windowpanes, and the crackling hiss of the fire. But it did not matter that there was no balmy breeze to warm them, nor pungent scent of sea and earth to arouse their senses, for the intensity of their passion was not diminished from that first coupling on the sun-kissed sands of a primitive shore.

For Rhea, indeed the sensations may have been heightened as she anticipated that more satisfying and intimate joining between them. Before that moment of sexual awakening upon the sands, she had been a child, with no knowledge of her own sensuality. Passion had not existed until then. Now she was a woman, and experiencing all the aching desire that Dante had helped her feel while initiating her in the ways of love. And now only Dante could assuage the fire which burned in her blood.

And his words of just moments before had been no idle threat, but rather a foreshadowing of the future; for whatever might happen, there could never be anyone else for her. Dante was a part of her, and now she would never be free of the need for his touch.

Dante's hand slid into the silken tangle of gold veiling the alabaster smoothness of her shoulders, his fingers gently grasping her nape and holding her head firmly tilted upward. With his other hand, he touched her flushed cheek, and then his thumb caressed her lips, teasing their trembling softness. For a long moment he stared down into the depths of her eyes, the thickly lashed lids half closed, heavy with passion. Then, slowly, Dante lowered his mouth to hers.

As Rhea responded to his kisses, she felt his fingers continuing their attack on the laces of her bodice, as well as those of her petticoats. When he slid the gown from her, the petticoats fell into a rumpled pile round her slippered feet, leaving her clad only in her corset, chemise, and stockings.

In the golden fire glow Rhea's pale flesh seemed gilded, reminding Dante of that night on the sands. The firelight dancing through the unbound silver gilt of her hair shimmered like a reflection of the sun and moon together. The twinkling of diamonds round her throat drew Dante's eyes to the gentle curve of breast quivering beneath the lacy edge of her corset. Then his gaze traveled lower, to linger on the seductive length of ivory-tinted thigh above her gartered stockings.

Dante's hands tightened around Rhea's waist as he lifted her clear of the discarded mound of muslin and lace. Her arms wrapped round his neck, he buried his face in the scented silkiness of her hair while holding her close against the muscular hardness of his body.

"You are becoming more voluptuous with each passing day. I can scarcely clasp my hands around your waist any longer," he said, his voice muffled by her hair. Then Rhea felt his warm breath against her ear as she nibbled the soft lobe, his tongue tickling the delicate inner flesh.

"You truly bewitch me, Rhea," he murmured thickly, setting her back on the floor, then turning her around quickly to deal efficiently with the remaining laces of her corset.

The corset landed atop the pile of discarded clothing. Then Dante swung Rhea up into his arms and dropped her onto the bed with ungentlemanly disregard for any ladylike modesty she might have tried to maintain. She landed indecorously against the quilted coverlet and soft pile of pillows. Her indrawn breath of surprise turned into low laughter that mingled with Dante's as she stared up at his grinning face. She did not realize that her chemise had ridden up above her hips, leaving her modesty completely compromised.

Dante knelt before her and began to unroll her silken stockings with studiously prolonged care, his fingers straying often from their task.

His work completed, Dante reluctantly allowed her small, arched feet to dangle over the edge of the bed as he rose and stepped back, a gentle expression softening the chiseled quality of his face.

Lazily crossing her arms behind her head, the chemise straining taut across the firm roundness of her breasts, Rhea settled herself comfortably against the pile of pillows. She sighed contentedly as she played with a long strand of hair and watched Dante pull off his shirt, baring a broad expanse of smoothly muscled chest and shoulder.

"Would you like to know a secret?" Rhea spoke hesitantly, a shy smile putting a slight dimple in her cheek.

"I intend to know all your secrets," Dante responded. He sounded quite serious, especially so when he added softly, "Never let there be any secrets between us. They can lead only to misunderstanding."

"Never," Rhea promised without hesitation, thinking that was a promise which could easily be kept.

Dante shook his head. He was amazed that she still steadfastly believed in truth and human goodness, despite the tragedy that had disrupted her life. She continued to be unsuspecting of the darker emotions which often drove people to acts of desperation and violence.

"Now tell me, what is this dark secret of yours?" Dante inquired.

"I fear 'tis not so much dark as foolish," Rhea admitted sheepishly. "You asked how it was that I came to love you. What if I told you that you reminded me of one of my family?"

"Good God! Not your father?" Dante demanded in mock horror.

"Silly," Rhea admonished him with a laugh, unaware that few people could have gotten away with a comment like that where Dante Leighton was concerned. "Of course, now that I do think about it, I do believe there is a certain similarity of character between the two of you," she speculated aloud, while privately and accurately suspecting that neither one would have readily admitted to such a thing. "'Twas an ancestor I had in mind. There is a portrait of him in the Long Gallery at Camareigh, and I used to be quite fascinated by it. In fact, it was my favorite painting, next to our family portrait, that is," she corrected.

"And who was this ancestor? An exemplary fellow, no doubt?" His attention centered on unfastening the buttons of his breeches, he did not catch the devilish glint in Rhea's eyes.

"Actually, he was a bit of a scoundrel."

Dante glanced up in surprise. "Indeed?"

"Hmmmm, 'fraid so," Rhea answered, her lips quivering as she tried to keep a straight face. "He was a privateer, but I suspect he sailed with the silent good wishes of Elizabeth I."

Dante's buckskin breeches landed with a soft thud atop Rhea's gown and petticoats. His turned-inside-out stockings and upended boots were scattered across the room.

"A privateer?" he repeated thoughtfully, not at all displeased. "Then it goes without saying that he was a scoundrel."

"From the look of him in the painting, I always thought he could have charmed the devil himself," Rhea continued, not quite so relaxed as she gazed at the masculine beauty of Dante's naked body. He came toward the bed and stood before her. "I wondered why you seemed so familiar to me when I first saw you aboard the *Sea Dragon,*" she continued. "Physically you do not resemble him at all, except perhaps in the leanness of build, but, well..." Rhea's voice trailed away as her confusion increased. She looked down at the golden strand she'd been twirling around her hand.

"Please, continue. You have piqued my curiosity," Dante murmured softly. Then the bed sagged as he sat down.

"'Twas just a certain arrogance about him, and perhaps that look of challenge in his eyes. I always used to feel a bit of a shiver when I walked past him, as if he might reach out of the painting and grab hold of me. And whenever I looked up into his dark eyes, I felt as if he somehow knew exactly what I was thinking and feeling. I suppose I was intrigued by the fearless daring of the man who had led an adventurer's life sailing the seas. When I came to know you," Rhea continued slowly, her voice growing husky, "you seemed the embodiment, at least in spirit, of my buccaneer ancestor."

Dante's arms encircled her as he enfolded her against his chest. A moment later her chemise floated to the floor, and then there was the comforting warmth of his body next to hers and his mouth pressing against her mouth.

"Forget about your man of the portrait. Feel me. I am flesh and blood. He cannot reach out for you, Rhea. He cannot hold you, and caress you, and kiss you until you ache with desire. Kiss me, Rhea," he whispered against her rosy lips, his tongue tasting freely of hers. "No painted image can love you as I do."

Rhea's fingers slid through the tangle of curling hair covering his wide chest. She reveled in the hardness of his body and in the way his hands moved over her, molding her to him in such a manner that she felt she no longer had an existence separate from his. She shivered when his tongue licked against a hardening nipple and his hands gently cupped her breasts as he buried his face against their softness. Rhea entwined her fingers through his thick chestnut hair, its smooth vibrancy curling beneath her touch.

His hands caressed her waist, then slid along the slight curving of hip and across the tautness of her stomach. They moved slowly along her slender thighs, exploring the delicate inner areas that were so sensitive to his touch.

Her hair spilled across the pillows like golden honey as she lay beneath him and stared up into the pale grayness of his eyes, the thick fringe of dark lashes masking their burning brightness. Then her own lids closed as his thighs pressed against hers, parting them. And then he was a part of her. His hips moved against her, and her response joined his. The pressure building gradually within her increased with the pulsating rhythm of his body until, arching against his hardness, she cried out with the exquisite pleasure which always came with his lovemaking. It left her breathlessly weak and trembling, yet with a fulfillment that no other pleasure could bring.

"Never, never, will I lose you," Dante vowed softly, but his words were inaudible to Rhea. She lay with her cheek pressed against the warm dampness of his chest, and the strong, steady beat of his heart was the only sound she heard. Resting contentedly within the circle of his arms, she took comfort from the gentle strength surrounding her.

Lingeringly, Dante pressed his lips against the pale transparency of her temple while carefully smoothing back a softly waving curl. Her golden head fell backward to fit snugly in the curve of his neck and shoulder. He closed his eyes, the sound of her quiet breathing filling him. And at last he was content to sleep, knowing that she would still be lying beside him when he awoke.

And when Dante did awaken several hours later, the pale sunlight of dawn was filtering through the small, dust-stained panes of the mullioned windows. The fire, which had burned so brightly the night before, lay in ashes.

Dante stared down at Rhea, who slept so peacefully beside him, the warmth of her body like a burning brand against his flesh. The golden sheen of her hair spreading across the pillows reminded Dante of the late-afternoon sunlight of autumn. Her delicate profile was etched against the deep bronze of his shoulder, and instinctively Dante started to reach out and touch the gentle curve of her mouth. Her dreams were sweet, he thought, and rather wistfully hoped that they were of him.

Dante resisted the temptation to awaken her, and carefully climbed from the bed. He could not resist gazing for a moment at the unadorned beauty of her body as she lay naked against the silk coverlet. She looked so ethereal, so pure and enchanting a vision, that he could scarcely believe she was the same warm-blooded woman he had held in his arms the night before. Where was the temptress who had responded to his lovemaking with such wild abandon?

She was so entrancingly lovely. And, strangely enough, she was his. But suddenly, on a dark feeling of despair and jealousy, Dante began to wonder how he could possibly hold on to her. She said she loved him, but what of those words she had so innocently spoken last night, when she said he reminded her of a man in a portrait which had fascinated her for years?

Fascination? Perhaps that was all that she really felt for him. What did she know of love? He knew he had taken unfair advantage of a young girl's first tentative steps into womanhood. He had tantalized and finally seduced her, making her vibrantly aware of emotions she had never suspected she possessed. Perhaps any other man could have elicited a similar response. So why should he think himself special, indispensable to her happiness?

What they had shared, that all-consuming passion, had been theirs for so short a duration that he found himself questioning its chances of surviving. Had those feelings even had a chance to become love? Once back with her family and friends, would her desire for him fade? Would she wish she'd never met him once a younger and more socially acceptable man entered her life?

And what of her family? Until he had come into her life, they had been her whole existence. He would be a stranger to them, an outsider, an intruder. Would they resent him? Would they try to turn Rhea against him? How could the brief interlude they had shared possibly withstand the influence of those deep family relationships?

Dante resettled the coverlet across Rhea's shoulders. "Little daffadilly," he spoke softly. "Have I already lost you?" Jamaica, who lay curled on the foot of the bed, cocked an ear and opened an eye at the sound of his master's voice. But when no other words followed, he stretched with lazy contentment and resumed his feline dreaming.

Suddenly the chill of early morning touched Dante's bare flesh. He slipped on his morning gown, tying the silk sash around his waist as he walked over to the table and the correspondence he had left there.

Dante glanced back at the bed, at the sleeping figure snuggled deep beneath the warmth of the quilts. With a newfound purpose, he took quill in hand and addressed the envelope he had sealed the night before.

For a long moment Dante stared down at the address he had written, the address which had become so familiar to him over the years:

> Sir Jacob Weare
> Sevenoaks House
> Westlea Abbot
> Devonshire

Then, abruptly, Dante placed the letter upright against the silver inkstand, knowing that the letter would be posted by Houston Kirby later in the day. But even Dante Leighton, who had thoughtfully planned out every move he was making, did not fully realize how far-reaching the repercussions of that letter would be once it was in the possession of a certain gentleman in Westlea Abbot.

> *A thousand ages in Thy sight*
> *Are like an evening gone;*
> *Short as the watch that ends the night*
> *Before the rising sun.*
>
> Isaac Watts

Chapter 3

EIGHT bells would have chimed the hour and the changing of the watch aboard H.M.S. *Hindrance,* a revenue cutter stationed in Bristol Channel. Patrolling a wild stretch of Devonshire coastline, it had been her duty to prevent smugglers from landing their contraband cargoes; untaxed spirits, tea, tobacco, silks, and scents deprived the Crown of much-needed revenue. But the secret coves, where during dark nights gangs of well-armed men waited with nervous impatience, were far too many. The Crown had not been able to halt the inland journey of the contraband. And because the riding officers were far too few, the tubs and bales and cases ended up stashed in neighboring farmhouses, barns, and inns. Or, perhaps, even sequestered in the sacred confines of a church cellar, along with the vicar's complimentary cask of brandy.

But on this day, the pale light of dawn showed the King's colors which had been hoisted before the warning shot had been fired at the smuggling lugger, now hanging in tatters. The roar of cannon fire which had followed was now silenced by the sea crashing across the splintered decks of a once proud ship, now foundering on the rocks. Most of her crew, those who had not been washed overboard and drowned, had abandoned ship.

She had been a good ship, served by a good captain and crew. Perhaps too good, she had been betrayed. Her course had been marked out in advance by an unfriendly hand and, her fate sealed, she had valiantly faced doom on the rocks of an inhospitable shore.

Cold and angry, the sea heaved and rolled and lifted H.M.S. *Hindrance* on the foaming crest of a wave rising toward shore, only to toss her down against the rocks yet again and again. Her canvas was in shreds and her mainmast had split and disappeared into the sea.

Against the gray, dawning light, the dark outline of the sheer cliffs could be seen climbing ever upward toward the heavens. And rising even higher atop the summit were the dark, solitary towers. From those towers the shining beacon of light had lured H.M.S. *Hindrance* toward the razor-edged reefs lurking just beneath the surface of a sullen sea.

At the base of the steep cliffs was a narrow crescent of sandy beach, a haven against the hungry grasp of the sea. And for those few desperate men who had managed to survive the sinking of their ship, it was their one hope of escaping the fierce undertow of the breakers crashing against the rocks. But the weakened and battered seamen who staggered ashore found no safe haven upon that isolated stretch of beach. Instead, they were met by the smuggling gang, armed with bludgeons and knives. The gang accomplished what the sea had not.

And as the sun rose high above the dark towers silhouetted against the morning sky, the infamy which had left bodies half buried in the sea-swept sands or floating out on the current toward a watery grave, was exposed to the damning light of day.

Dead men tell no tales. But if the captain of H.M.S. *Hindrance* could have moved his salt-encrusted, swollen lips, or raised a bloodied finger, he would have identified his murderer. In naming the traitor, he would have told a sad tale of how a ship and crew had come to be no more.

He would have told of the treachery and betrayal by a fellow officer of the Crown and how, suspecting there was an informant among the troop of dragoons stationed in Westlea Abbot, he had attempted to identify the traitor who had been warning the smugglers. But the fatal mistake the good captain made had been in confiding his suspicions to the wrong man. Too late, he had come to suspect the true villain.

The captain and the man he had so mistakenly trusted, a respected gentleman and a man in a high position of authority, had confronted the officer under suspicion. That officer had broken down and confessed his treachery, then had begged for mercy. With that plea for leniency had come the promise of valuable information concerning the activities of the smugglers. That very eve they were planning to land contraband in Bishop's Creek, he had informed them. Two flashes of light, then three, that was the signal for the all-clear. After the tubs had been unloaded, they would most likely have ended up at Bishop's Grave Inn, for Sam Lascombe and the smugglers were as thick as thieves.

Although it was against his better judgment, the captain had been persuaded against informing his superiors of the officer's confession, at least for the time being. The gentleman with him was, after all, the local magistrate. He had advised the utmost discretion. Tomorrow, he said, would be a far better time to send a dispatch. By dawn they would surely have arrested the leaders of the smuggling gang and have clapped the rest in irons. They would be able to report that they had put an end to this looting of the King's coffers.

Unsuspecting, the young captain of H.M.S. *Hindrance* agreed. With the magistrate's assurances that he would personally see the dishonored officer locked up in Westlea Abbot gaol with none the wiser, and then see that his men were at Bishop's Creek at the appointed hour to lend the captain all of the assistance he would need, the captain returned to his ship.

Perhaps he should have been more suspicious of the smuggling lugger when she sailed out of the dark, almost as if she had been waiting for a rendezvous. She had cut across the *Hindrance*'s bow, the smugglers calling out abuses and damning his majesty King George and all who served him, as if daring the other ship to give chase.

Thinking the game his, the captain of H.M.S. *Hindrance* ordered his helmsman to steer toward the smuggling lugger. Soon she was close to overtaking the lugger.

The captain had smelled victory in the air, along with the smell of gunpowder which still lingered from the last round of cannon fire which the *Hindrance* had shot across the smuggler's bow. In the distance he had seen the flashing of lights from Bishop's Creek; and instead of the two, followed by three, there had been four flashes of light to end the sequence. That had been his signal that the smugglers had been apprehended, and were now safely in the hands of the authorities.

He had the smuggler at the disadvantage. He had successfully cut off her escape to windward, trapping her between the mouth of the cove and the dragoons on shore. And because of her position, the smuggler was unable to fire her guns, except for small arms, and H.M.S. *Hindrance* was out of range.

Suddenly, however, the smuggling lugger sheered off, her bow turning into the wind. The sudden change in direction caught the captain of the *Hindrance* off guard, for the other captain surely knew that he would fall foul of the *Hindrance*, but before he could give the order to change course and bring the helm a-lee there was a horrible splintering noise that ripped through the *Hindrance*'s hull, bringing her to a shuddering stillness as she struck the reefs.

Like a prophetic sign, the sun brought out of shadow the dark towers on the bluff. Too late, the captain realized that they had not sailed into Bishop's Creek, but had been tricked into the treacherous waters of Dragon's Cove, a place no ship dared venture unless her captain was familiar with the one navigable channel through the reefs.

The narrow channel cut diagonally across the reefs which began to form just within the mouth of the cove; beyond that point there was no deep water for a ship to safely sail, only razor-backed reefs and shallows, and breakers, which rolled toward the bold shore wreathed in white water and mists of sea spray.

With his ship now at the mercy of the pitiless sea, the captain and those few seamen who could swim, or who had managed to grasp hold of a broken piece of mast, struggled ashore. And there, on the wet sands, the captain was met by the very traitor he'd thought locked up in the gaol in Westlea Abbot.

As the captain's glazed eyes stared heavenward, the last sight he caught was one of the dark towers of Merdraco. And out of the shadow of the tower moved a gentleman astride a horse. And in the first light of dawn, the dying captain of H.M.S. *Hindrance* cursed for all eternity the face of the man he had trusted with his life.

A fortnight later, in a small Welsh village on the far side of the channel, a solitary figure would stand in the burial ground of a simple church of gray stone. Braving the cold west winds blowing in off the channel, he would stare down at the newly turned earth of a grave while the silvery light of a bleak morning filtered through the branches of a cedar grove planted to shield the mourners.

He glanced up and gazed across the turbulent waters, knowing that beyond the swirling clouds hanging low against the horizon was the coast of England. He bowed his head and stared down at his brother's grave, his eyes watering from the winds blustering around his caped figure. Then, with a last farewell, and a promise to keep, he walked away slowly.

He would never forget the words chiseled on that cold, silent headstone:

Sacred
to the memory of
Benjamin Lloyd
Captain of H.M.S. *Hindrance*
Loved—Honored—Lamented

*Forever, Fortune, wilt thou prove
An unrelenting foe to love,
And, when we meet a mutual
    heart,
Come in and bid us part?*

James Thomson

Chapter 4

HOUSTON KIRBY cleared his throat, hesitating before he knocked. Even though the countless bells of the City had been chiming in a cacophony of sound since first light, he hated to disturb Lady Rhea Claire. She might have slept through the din, Kirby thought with a grimace, for he was no lover of bells since his own slumber had been so rudely interrupted. But he did have to post that letter for the captain, who had left Hawke's Bell Inn several hours earlier.

Readjusting his plain tye wig and straightening his neatly folded stock, the little steward started to raise his hand to knock

73

again but the door swung open and he found himself staring at the lady herself.

"M'lady!" Kirby said, flustered by her sudden appearance and by the manner in which she was dressed. "Oh, m'lady, ye shouldn't be lettin' people see ye dressed that way. What will people be sayin'?" he demanded, glancing over his shoulder worriedly while trying to stretch himself a few inches taller in order to shield Lady Rhea from any prying eyes in the corridor.

Rhea grinned, unconcerned. "They would surely comment on the fine fit, and perhaps even ask my dressmaker's name," she said as she smoothed her hands over the soft buckskin of her skirt.

"Oh, m'lady, please," Kirby said nervously, although secretly pleased, for they both knew it had been his nimble fingers that had neatly sewn together the many patches. "Ye shouldn't be makin' jest here in the corridor. 'Twouldn't be good for your reputation, m'lady, for anyone to be seein' ye. 'Twas all right aboard the *Sea Dragon*, but I shouldn't care to have anybody else seein' ye dressed in so—so," he paused awkwardly, staring up at her as he sought the proper word.

"In so improper a manner," Rhea kindly supplied.

"Beggin' your pardon, m'lady, but indeed so." He stiffened as they heard footsteps approaching along the corridor.

Relenting, Rhea allowed him to enter the room, then smiled when she heard the door shutting almost on his heels.

"Perhaps then, since you do not approve of my attire, you would be so kind as to select the gown you think I should be wearing," she invited while pointing to the two gowns she'd spread out across the bed.

"M'lady, I could never be disapprovin' of ye," Kirby quickly disabused her of that idea. "Indeed, I rather fancy ye in that, but that was when we was in the Indies," he said, a wistful expression lightening his customary frown.

Rhea understood. She herself had felt something akin to longing when she remembered those vivid blue skies and waters, and the balmy breezes warming her. Perhaps that was why she had suddenly felt like wearing the clothes she had worn while on board the *Sea Dragon*, for she knew she would never have need of them again.

"'Twas nice, wasn't it, Kirby?" she said softly.

"Aye, m'lady. Reckon I wish we was still sailin' in them waters. Strange how safe and untroubled they seem now that we're back in England." He sighed, then shook his head to free himself of those thoughts. Forgetting about his wig, it inched backward to perch at a precarious angle.

"Well," he said briskly, "'twill be a hard choice, m'lady, but I'm thinkin' the primrose would be lookin' mighty nice on ye. Reminds me of that Indies sunshine, something we sure don't see much of here, what with all of the soot and fog.

"Then the primrose it will be, Kirby," Rhea decided, thinking that she had forgotten how cold and gloomy England could be in autumn.

"Ah, here 'tis," Kirby muttered as he picked up the letter which was still propped against the inkstand. "Reckon I oughta be gettin' this posted," he said, his frown returning as he eyed the address. "Well, then, is there anythin' I can be doin' for ye, m'lady? If not, I'll be off. Got to meet the cap'n," he told her, the letter tucked safely away in his coat pocket.

"Will you be meeting Dante on board the *Sea Dragon?* He said when he left this morning that he had some banking to see to, and he also wanted to inspect the ship."

"Aye, m'lady. We was seein' to that earlier. The cap'n thinks she'll be needin' the weeds and barnacles burned off, then have to be retarred. He's seein' to the bankin' now. Reckon he'll be back shortly. 'Bout time for luncheon," he guessed.

"I see. And Conny? Have you seen him this morning?"

"Aye, m'lady," Kirby responded with a wide grin. "Had breakfast with me, he did. I'm wonderin' how someone so small can be puttin' away so much. Left me feelin' as queasy as I did the first time I stepped aboard the *Sea Dragon.* And from what I was hearin' from that puffed-up landlord, young Master Brady was puttin' away quite a bit of gooseberry pie the night before. 'Twas all that Parkham bloke could talk about, that and puttin' some female's nose out of joint because of it. Reckon I'm not understandin' these city folk much anymore," Kirby grumbled, shaking his wig back even farther.

"I suspect that you and Canfield, my mother's maid, would get along famously. She dislikes city folk," Rhea told him, thinking that the ever-proper Canfield would certainly not ap-

prove of the clothes Houston Kirby had gone to so much trouble
to make for her.

"Would ye be wantin' me to send up one of them servin'
girls to help ye dress, m'lady?" he inquired solicitously, his
former valet's training never far away.

"No, I'll be able to manage. And I can always wait and
have Dante assist me," Rhea said, thinking Dante would be far
more efficient than the giggling and gawking serving girls if
they could even get one to enter the room after their scare of
the night before.

"Very well, m'lady. But if ye be needin' anythin' at all,
just send one of them servin' girls to fetch me. After I post
this letter, I'll be downstairs in the taproom. The cap'n wanted
the crew to meet there and begin discussions on the dividin'
of our riches. Good thing the cap'n's an honest man, for with
the groggy heads from the night before, he could swindle us
out of our breeches. Beggin' your pardon, m'lady," Houston
Kirby said gruffly, mortified at his slip. "Well, guess I really
had better get goin'," he added, sounding as if he'd rather be
dangling by two fingers from a yardarm than meeting downstairs with his mates. He even looked as if he were walking
the plank as he made his way to the door.

"Thank you, Kirby," Rhea called after his departing figure.

"I don't s'pose that no-good, flea-bitten tom is around here
anywhere? Maybe masqueradin' as m'lady's slipper or her fur
muff?" he asked casually as he lingered in the doorway, his
glance suspicious as he peered beneath the bed.

Rhea laughed. "So you heard about that?"

"Aye, m'lady, talk of the taproom, 'tis," he said with a grin
of appreciation.

"Jamaica disappeared earlier, but I suspect he'll return in
time for luncheon," Rhea told the little steward, who didn't
seem a bit surprised at the news.

"Aye, reckon so, m'lady. A blind man would know we was
havin' fish for luncheon, so figure ol' Jamaica will be hot-
footin' it this way before long," Kirby agreed with a sniff that
attempted to discount any appearance of concern for the cat.

Then bowing elegantly, he left the room.

Rhea continued to stare at the closed door for a moment
longer, her thoughts concerned with something which had hap-

pened earlier that morning, soon after Dante had left. She had already begun to suspect as much, and now she was almost certain that she was with child. Rhea wrapped her arms around herself protectively. She prayed that she was right, for she wanted Dante's child. But as suddenly as a cloud drifting across the sun, her mood darkened as she wondered if Dante would be pleased. There were still too many things they did not know about one another. Their time together had been so brief.

A few more minutes passed while Rhea stood there deep in thought, but since nothing could come of speculation, she turned away and put her mind to more practical things. The thought that Madame Lambere might have to let out the seams in the newly purchased gowns was uppermost in Rhea's mind as she held the primrose gown against her waist and speculated a little sadly on how rotund she soon would be. But then came an even more disturbing thought. What would be Dante's re-action to that? Soon he would not be able to hold her, Rhea realized, her spirits plummeting.

An imperative, staccato knocking intruded on Rhea's thoughts and she hurried to answer the door.

With a welcoming smile, she swung the door wide. Only Jamaica, who sailed through the opening, heard her cry out.

Downstairs, in the crowded taproom of Hawke's Bell Inn, the sound of voices raised in song was drawing a deepening frown from the innkeeper, who was afraid that the exuberance of his guests would lead to trouble. And he certainly did not want any confrontations between the boisterous colonials and any Redcoats who might happen by and take exception to what they overheard. It did not lessen Mr. Parkham's worry any when he heard the out-of-tune voices chorusing yet another stanza of that unfortunate song:

> Yankee Doodle came to town
> Upon a little pony,
> He stuck a feather in his hat
> And called it macaroni.

> Yankee Doodle, keep it up,
> Yankee Doodle dandy,

Mind the music and the step,
And with the girls be handy.

Mr. Parkham shook his head. Pity it had such a catchy tune.
He had caught himself humming it, even after severely scolding
the serving girls for singing it. He could have sworn he caught
that damned Irishman's tenor drowning out the other voices.
It was bad enough that the man was a handsome and glib
Irishman, but to be a colonial, and a rich bastard as well. It
was a damned shame to waste good English sterling on one of
them misfits talking revolution.

With another shake of his head lest anyone mistakenly think
he approved of such tomfoolery, Mr. Parkham returned to the
kitchen, determined to advance luncheon before this bunch
drank him out of all his ale. Of course, thought Mr. Parkham
while slowing his pace considerably, at least the rowdies did
have plenty of money to pay for it, and a hardworking fellow
like himself couldn't always be too choosy about where his
profits came from.

For the past few days, the profits for Hawke's Bell Inn had
been coming out of the deep pockets of the thirsty crew of the
Sea Dragon. Gathered together in the taproom, where an almost
visible air of expectancy hung over the noisy group, the exulting
sailors were celebrating what had turned out to be a most
providential end to their association.

"And here's to sailin' before the wind!"

"And to fair weather!"

"And to havin' yer sails rappin' full!"

"Aye, and here's to every wee bonny lass who ever bid a
sad farewell to her laddie buck! And here's fair warnin' to any
landlubber who's been holdin' her hand—I be back in town!"

"Aye, and here's to every hell-raisin' Jack-tar here, may
your course always run smooth, at least till ye've got three
sheets in the wind like meself," Seumus Fitzsimmons toasted
his mates before sitting abruptly back down as his legs crumpled
beneath him.

"And here's a toast to that fine, upstandin' gent, Bertie
Mackay, and his scurvy crew of loose fish aboard the *Annie
Jeanne*, may they all end up in—" But the rest of the toast

was drowned in laughter as several interesting destinations for the rival smugglers were voiced.

Houston Kirby, sitting a little apart so he could keep an eye out for the captain's arrival, pushed his wig off his brow, where it had slipped while he'd tried to see his way clear of the milling crowd.

Aye, they were all here, he thought glumly, wondering if any of them would be able to come to their senses once they got their hands on their fortunes. How many would find happiness, the little steward worried, still feeling responsible for their well-being.

Some of them would do all right, Kirby decided as he glanced over the room, spotting familiar faces. Longacres was once again holding court near the fire, where he was surrounded by the usual spellbound listeners. Kirby figured that the old sea dog had been around so long that not much more could happen to him that hadn't already. He was planning to sail back to the Indies where, on St. Thomas, he would open a tavern. It would be the perfect setting for the wizened buccaneer and his hair-raising tales of piracy. Cobbs, the bos'n, had been dreaming of returning to Norfolk ever since he had left as a boy. Now he could return as a wealthy man and become the country gentleman of his dreams. Most of the mates were already referring to him as Squire Nabobs.

Kirby spied Alec MacDonald, the Scotsman, by the bluish haze hanging over his head from the pipe that was never far from his lips. He planned to open a shipyard along the banks of the Chesapeake. His future was in the colonies. And with war always on the horizon, he would probably become even wealthier. Certainly a far cry from his fellow clansmen who continued to live a hand-to-mouth existence in the Highlands of Scotland.

Kirby reckoned the jack-a-dandy, Barnaby Clarke, would play the London gentleman for a while and then return to Jamaica where, no doubt, he would live out his life as an indolent planter. Trevelawny, the ship's carpenter, who never said much and smiled even less, was going to invest in mining in his native Cornwall. And if he kept as tight a rein on his purse strings as he did his tongue, he would most likely own half of the West Country by the turn of the century.

And, of course, there was Seumus Fitzsimmons. Houston Kirby eyed the flushed face of the dark Irishman whose jokes and ready wit kept his mates laughing. Kirby suspected that the facetious Irishman was looking forward to war between the colonials and the Crown, for he intended to purchase a schooner and carry on the fine tradition of the *Sea Dragon*. Aye, Seumus Fitzsimmons might be the one to set the table roaring, but once he had a crew and a ship of his own, he would make a fine captain. And, just maybe, he would turn into a fairly decent gentleman.

On the other hand, thought Kirby, Alastair Marlowe was already a gentleman. But now he had a gentleman's means. What he would do, where he would ultimately settle, even Alastair Marlowe was not yet certain. He planned to pay a visit to his brother and the family home before making any decisions.

Houston Kirby narrowed his gaze, fixing it on a dark head bobbing up and down in the crowd around Longacres. The little steward was still pondering the orphaned cabin boy's future when he caught sight of the captain standing in the doorway.

Aye, now the captain was a fine-looking man indeed, Houston Kirby nodded approvingly as he noted the fine cut of the captain's frock coat and the snug fit of his pale buckskin breeches. And his riding boots still had a nice shine to them, while his stock was still neatly folded, yet Kirby knew the captain had been on the docks and in the streets of London where it was only too easy to befoul one's shoes.

The man who had accompanied Dante Leighton into the taproom soon held Houston Kirby's rapt gaze. It was none other than Sir Morgan Lloyd himself, captain of H.M.S. *Portcullis*.

The little steward had begun to push his way through the patrons when another toast brought an ear-shattering cheer from the group. It was probably the first and last time the health of an officer of the Crown had been toasted by smugglers.

"Never did I think to see the day," Sir Morgan Lloyd commented with a good-natured smile as he accepted an overflowing tankard from the outstretched hand of one of the crew of the *Sea Dragon*. He could not help but remember another time, in Charles Town, when he would have worried about moving through a group of smugglers, thinking his back too easy a target.

"To your health, Captain," Dante Leighton repeated the toast, raising his own tankard toward his former adversary.

"And to yours, Captain," Sir Morgan Lloyd responded politely, but as their eyes met above the gleaming pewter their glances were measuring ones.

"You will be staying in London for a while longer, or will you be returning to your station in the Carolinas?" Dante asked casually while adjusting the lace of his cuff.

"I shall remain in London for only a few days longer. One never quite seems to finish making reports to the Admiralty. Then I shall travel to Portsmouth on official business. But, perhaps, after my duty is done, I shall be able to take leave and return home to Wales." Sir Morgan spoke matter-of-factly, yet there was a note of longing in his voice which he could not conceal, nor may even have been aware of.

"You have a family there?" Dante asked curiously, for although he had played a dangerous game of cat-and-mouse with Sir Morgan for many years, he knew virtually nothing about the man's personal life.

Sir Morgan smiled. It was rather a sad smile. "No wife or children, but I do have a home, and a young brother I would like to see again. It has been far too long. It seems a lifetime ago that we wrestled in the gardens, much to my mother's despair. I fear we were too quick to get ourselves in trouble, and my widowed mother endured quite a lot before we received our commissions."

"Your brother is a fellow naval officer?" Dante inquired.

"Yes, he followed in my footsteps, much to my mother's disappointment. She would have preferred keeping at least one of her sons by her side, and I cannot blame her."

"My peace of mind would have been greatly disturbed, Sir Morgan, had I realized that I might well have had two of you crossing my bow," Dante told him with a disarming grin, privately thinking it would have been no circumstance for jest.

Sir Morgan laughed in appreciation. "You need not have worried, Captain. My brother captains a revenue cutter on patrol in Bristol Channel. That was, at least, one small comfort for my mother. She managed to see him once in a while. He was here to handle the funeral arrangements last year. I was, as you know, otherwise occupied."

"How fortunate, then, that I have forsaken smuggling," Dante remarked easily. "For I suspect this brother of yours is making quite a nuisance of himself to the local smugglers, if, of course, he is anything like his elder brother."

Sir Morgan's gaze narrowed thoughtfully as if a sudden thought had struck him. "I had forgotten. You are from the West Country, are you not, Captain?"

Dante Leighton smiled. "Yes, from Devonshire. On the north coast," Dante informed him further, saving him having to ask.

"Ah, yes," Sir Morgan murmured, but Dante had the distinct impression that the man had always known. "I do believe that particular stretch of wild coast is part of my brother's station. Are you familiar, perhaps, with a village known as Westlea Abbot?" the captain of H.M.S. *Portcullis* asked as he glanced casually about the room. He did not miss the slight start of surprise Dante Leighton was unable to suppress.

"Yes, 'tis a small village which lies on the coast, southwest of Merdraco, my home."

"Ah, I see."

"Indeed? And may I inquire as to your interest in an insignificant fishing village?" Dante asked, suddenly on guard, although the expression in his eyes would have led one to have believed him to be quite bored with the conversation.

"The village was mentioned in a letter I received from my brother not more than six months past. He also mentioned a village called Merleigh. It seems the locals, who are not overly friendly to the King's men, do a bit more than fish nowadays," Sir Morgan commented wryly. "You wouldn't happen to know about that?"

Dante's smile widened, and to Houston Kirby, who had finally managed to edge his way close, the smile boded ill.

"It is a quaint coastal village lying northeast of Merdraco. It was named for the castle, and in honor of my family name, Leighton. Of course, that was long ago."

Sir Morgan was silent for a moment. "How very interesting, for it would seem that Merdraco lies in a direct path between two villages under suspicion of harboring a notorious smuggling gang. Had I any doubts of your future intentions, *my lord*, I would certainly feel it necessary to inform my brother of your former unlawful activities. You are far too dangerous a gentleman to be ignored," Sir Morgan said, lifting his tankard in a silent toast to the well-known smuggling skills of the captain of the *Sea Dragon*.

Dante Leighton's laughter drew the attention of several grinning seamen, who thought it yet another remarkable trait of their captain's that he would stand drinking and laughing with an enemy.

"I shall indeed rest easier knowing you are safely back in the colonies, Sir Morgan," Dante replied. "I am already considered infamous enough to the villagers of Merleigh and Westlea Abbot without having my more recent past brought to light," Dante protested, his gaze meeting Kirby's for a single meaningful moment.

"What was it the villagers so fondly called me, Kirby?" he demanded of the little steward, who had been avidly listening while pretending not to hear.

"Now, now, Kirby," Dante cajoled. "You needn't spare my feelings. We both remember the endearment. I was known as the 'dragon's spawn.' And do not be mistaken, Sir Morgan," Dante warned him, "it was, for the most part, well deserved."

"Cap'n, sir!" Houston Kirby finally found his tongue. "The both of us knows ye didn't do half of what ye was accused of doin' by them villagers," he corrected him, unwilling to allow the captain to blacken the Leighton name in front of Sir Morgan. "Even to this day, I'm still believin' 'twas a bit of carefully planted malicious gossip which stirred up them villagers."

"Always the true and loyal friend," Dante murmured, thinking he truly did not deserve such devotion. "So you see, Captain," he continued, "when I return to Merdraco, I shall have only enemies to welcome me home, not a circle of fellow conspirators."

"Time, of course, will tell," Sir Morgan spoke quietly, telling himself that he should never be surprised by anything Dante Leighton might do. The man remained a puzzle.

"I can see that I have not completely allayed your suspicions. Once a smuggler, always a smuggler?" Dante asked with a low laugh. "I fear that the villagers around Merdraco feel much the same, only for them 'tis, 'Once a murderer, always a murderer,'" Dante said, a cynical smile curving his lips as he noted the look of stunned surprise crossing Sir Morgan's face. Had he glanced at Houston Kirby, he would have seen the little steward's forehead disappearing in a deep set of disapproving wrinkles. "I am surprised you had not already guessed my dark secret, or heard rumors concerning my past."

"'Twas suspicion, never proof!" Kirby spoke angrily, but whether the anger was directed at those responsible for such an accusation, or at the captain for repeating it, only Kirby knew.

"If I may be so impolite as to inquire?" Sir Morgan asked, his gaze drifting between the worried-looking steward and the indolent-seeming captain of the *Sea Dragon*. "Whom were you accused of murdering?"

"A young woman." Dante's voice shattered the awkward silence that had followed Sir Morgan's blunt question. "They say I took her out on the moors, seduced her, then strangled her."

For perhaps the first time in Sir Morgan Lloyd's life, he was ill at ease meeting another man's stare. With a sigh of relief he felt the pale gray eyes shift from him when Alec MacDonald drew Dante Leighton's attention.

Sir Morgan continued to gaze at the haughtily aristocratic and classical profile of Dante Leighton. The man was more the devil's spawn than any dragon's. He was charismatic and intelligent; and cunning had kept him alive these many years. The captain of the *Sea Dragon* was a dangerous man. As Marquis of Jacqobi, he was also a very powerful one. And Sir Morgan Lloyd found himself wondering how many more men the enigmatic Dante Leighton might be.

"Beggin' your pardon, Cap'n," Alec MacDonald began, his thumb and forefinger nervously smoothing the curling ends of his moustache. "We—that is, the crew and me—was wonderin', now that we be disbandin', if we could pay our respects tae Lady Rhea Claire. We figure we will never again see her ladyship, and we all wanted her tae know how honored we have been tae have had her aboard the *Sea Dragon* on her most important voyage," the Scotsman concluded, his face ruddy with embarrassment.

"Aye, her ladyship brought us luck, she did!" a voice piped in from somewhere behind the broad shoulders of the Scotsman.

"Here's to Lady Rhea Claire! May she be forever fair of face!" someone called out, and Kirby would have bet he caught a tinge of an Irish brogue in the slightly slurred words.

"And forever happy!"

"Aye, and may her bonny eyes be forever smilin' and—" another voice cried, but was cut off by loudly approving ayes, and cheers, and tankard banging, followed by further toasts to the lady's beauty, goodness, and grace.

Houston Kirby puffed out his chest and placed his hands on his hips while he glared around the room at the familiar faces, leaving them in little doubt of his disapproval. He didn't care to have the lady's name bandied about a common taproom by common sailors, or by any other riffraff or rabble off the streets who had joined the celebration.

But Dante Leighton was not offended. He grinningly accepted their good-natured tribute, for chants of his name had joined the toasts. He glanced upward, wondering if Rhea could hear the tumult, and he knew that she would be honored rather than offended by the crew's genuine affection for her.

"I believe, Captain, that you also expressed a desire to pay your respects to the lady? Perhaps this would be an opportune moment?" he suggested as he noticed for the first time the heavily laden trays being carried in by several serving girls. Under the watchful eye of Mr. Parkham, the girls moved between the tables, the aromatic dishes piled high on the trays effectively quieting the group which had seemed, just moments before, an unruly mob bent on destruction of the taproom of Hawke's Bell Inn.

"Mr. MacDonald," Dante turned to the *Sea Dragon*'s former sailmaker. "I shall carry your request to the lady, and I am certain she will be honored to meet with the crew."

"Thank you, Cap'n," MacDonald said simply. Nodding briefly, he turned away. His moustache was quivering, however, as he grinned widely at his mates, giving them the thumbs-up signal as he settled down to enjoy his luncheon.

Dante turned back to Sir Morgan, who had been waiting patiently while finishing off his tankard of ale. "Captain?" he inquired courteously of the King's officer while he set his own empty tankard down on a nearby table. "Shall we go? Now that you are aware of my unsavory past, you will, no doubt, be reassured to find Rhea is still alive," Dante told him, his pale gray eyes coldly impersonal, for he was well aware of Sir Morgan's unease at encountering his gaze. "She will, of course, be pleased to see you, since you are partly responsible for saving me from rotting away in Newgate."

"You are certain that I shall not be disturbing the lady? I would not wish to intrude," Sir Morgan said with frigid politeness, although he would have been greatly disappointed not to have the opportunity to greet Lady Rhea Claire.

"Kirby?"

"Lady Rhea Claire was concluding her toilette when I knocked not more than a quarter of an hour past," Kirby told him, hoping her ladyship had indeed completed dressing, for he'd not care to have Sir Morgan catch her *en déshabillé*. Kirby suspected Sir Morgan of having more than a friendly interest in her ladyship.

Kirby stood for a moment longer watching the two men climb the stairs. Then, with a shrug, he returned to the taproom and his own place at the table, but he heard little of the gossip circulating.

There was a strained silence between the two men as they made their way along the corridor, and it intensified when one of the serving girls who had been so terrified the night before scurried past like a frightened hare, her eyes round with fearful apprehension when she recognized the lean figure of the captain of the *Sea Dragon*. It seemed he was stalking her.

"You seem to have a rather strange effect on women," Sir Morgan commented, wishing as the words left his mouth that he had not.

But apparently Dante Leighton had not taken offense at the offhand remark and, in fact, replied conversationally. "'Tis a pity, but many a damaging rumor has started because of some innocent incident. For instance, our little friend there was in my room last evening. She and another highly imaginative creature were clearing the table of dinner when a pile of clothing on the bed began to move, and, because I am a man of questionable character, they immediately assumed the worst. They ran out of the room screaming. 'Twas a shame they did not stay to see the cat crawl out from under the clothing. They believed it to be some sorcery of mine," Dante said with a suddenly weary smile. "I have always thought it wise to remember that not everything is as it may seem," he added in a quiet voice, and there was an unmistakable warning to his words.

"A salutary lesson I shall indeed bear in mind, Captain," Sir Morgan responded, and the tension lessened somewhat as their eyes met candidly.

Lost in thought, they did not become aware until they stood before it that the door to Lady Rhea Claire's room stood open.

Neither could have been prepared for the scene inside. Lady Rhea Claire was standing in the center of the room, dressed in the outlandish buckskin outfit. But that was not what startled the two men. It was the fact that Rhea Claire was being held in the arms of a strange man. His broad back to the door, he held Rhea against his chest, his hand smoothing one of the long golden strands of her unbound hair. Then, to the utter amazement of both men, the man pressed his lips against her cheek in a gentle, loving kiss. Even more shocking was that the lady was not protesting. Indeed, she was snuggling closer to the gentleman.

The two people were unaware that their privacy had been intruded upon, but Jamaica, lying on the bed, sensed trouble brewing and, with feline dispatch, disappeared beneath the bed.

Perhaps it was the sound of Rhea's weeping which severed the invisible bonds holding Dante immobile, or perhaps the proprietorial way in which the man rested his cheek upon Rhea's bowed head. Whatever the reason, Dante Leighton was upon the man before Sir Morgan even thought to interfere.

Dante grabbed hold of the man's shoulder and spun him around, his hand going to his sword, but Rhea stepped between the two men.

"Dante, no! Please! You do not understand. This is my father!" Rhea cried.

Staring up at Dante, her face tear-stained, her lips quivering, she said quietly this time, "This is my father."

Something flickered momentarily in Dante Leighton's pale eyes, but whether it was fear or uncertainty, neither showed clearly on his face as he held the older man's hostile gaze.

Even had it not been for Rhea's declaration, Dante would have recognized the face of the Duke of Camareigh.

It was a face one remembered: It was scarred. Across his left cheek, a thin scar etched its way from just beneath his eye to the corner of his mouth, adding a sinister cast to his aquiline features. The years had not changed him much, Dante thought, remembering all those years ago when he had sat across from him over a gaming table. He was still tall, no stooping of shoulders; he was still lean, no bulging of his waistcoat. But there were more lines on his face to mark the passing of the years, and the expression in his sherry-colored eyes was more world-weary and cynical, except when his eyes rested on his daughter's face. Then they mirrored all the warmth of their coloring.

Yes, Dante remembered those eyes well, and their contempt for a reckless young man, contempt the Duke had not bothered to hide when he won a fortune from the dissolute Marquis of Jacqobi. Dante Leighton had felt a fool the last time he faced the man, and now, as he stepped back and released Lucien Dominick's shoulder, he realized that the years hadn't changed that either. He still felt a fool. Only this time there was enmity in the Duke's eyes, which he also did not bother to hide.

No, the Duke of Camareigh was not easily forgotten.

Sir Morgan received a similar impression. At Lady Rhea Claire's impassioned plea, Sir Morgan had come to an abrupt standstill, thinking discretion the better part of valor in this instance. But his hand continued to rest lightly on his sword hilt as he felt the Duke of Camareigh's penetrating gaze come to rest on him. Sir Morgan knew the Duke had not missed a single detail of his appearance while sizing him up and deciding whether he would be friend or foe. And Sir Morgan suddenly found himself wondering how so arrogant and harsh a man as the Duke of Camareigh could have sired so gentle and agreeable a daughter as Lady Rhea Claire. She took after her mother, he speculated idly, beginning to grow increasingly uncomfortable under the Duke's coldly imperious scrutiny. He had come up against interfering civilians in positions of authority too many times not to know that they could cause no end of trouble for a mere officer of the Crown, especially when that complaining civilian was a member of the House of Lords and mixed socially with high-ranking ministers, perhaps even with Sir Morgan's superiors at the Admiralty. If the Duke of Camareigh took a dislike to him, Sir Morgan knew, then the wrong word in the right ear would have his career in ruins.

"Father, this is Sir Morgan Lloyd, of H.M.S. *Portcullis*. He escorted us safely back to England. We owe him a great deal, for he came to my rescue while we were in Antigua."

With relief, Sir Morgan Lloyd heard Lady Rhea Claire introducing him.

"Captain," the Duke said, inclining his regal head slightly, "if what my daughter says is indeed true, and I have no reason to doubt her, then I owe you a debt of gratitude which can never be fully repaid. It is an honor to make your acquaintance," the Duke told him in all sincerity, and Sir Morgan suddenly found himself the recipient of a rare smile from the Duke of Camareigh.

"The honor is mine, Your Grace. Lady Rhea Claire is being too kind, for I did little more than my duty required. I am just thankful that I could be of some small service to her ladyship," Sir Morgan responded. Another man might have been suspected of unbecoming false modesty, but not Sir Morgan, whose deep sense of duty was evident in the straightforwardness with which he spoke and met the other man's eyes.

"Actually, the man who carries the onus of hero is Captain Leighton, who rescued Lady Rhea Claire from the Charles Town docks. His actions kept her out of the hands of her former kidnapers, who had been pursuing her with murderous intent."

In Sir Morgan's mind, he had just been speaking the plain truth, or at least what he knew of the truth, and so he was unprepared for the look of gratitude in Lady Rhea Claire's eyes as she heard his praise for Dante Leighton.

However, the Duke of Camareigh did not see the captain of the *Sea Dragon* in the same light.

"That was well over six months ago. I would hazard a guess that your route was rather leisurely circuitous? Or am I mistaken in thinking that England lies in a direction opposite Charles Town than do the West Indies?" the Duke asked in that overly polite soft tone that Rhea knew only too well masked displeasure.

"Father, I can explain. Please, I must tell you so many things about—"

"Rhea, allow the *gentleman* to explain why he has kept you aboard his ship for so long."

Dante Leighton had been standing quietly through the last few minutes of conversation, a thousand different memories spinning through his mind while he stared at Lucien Dominick, the embodiment of all he had left behind so many years before. For a brief moment, as the memories threatened to overtake the present, he felt the old confusion and sense of betrayal. But he was no longer the frightened, beaten young lord who had fled London. He would no longer be intimidated by anyone. And what was his, he vowed silently, he had the power to hold.

Something of Dante Leighton's antagonism and immovability must have transmitted itself to the Duke, for his gaze narrowed as he stared at the younger man, noting for the first time the aristocratic features stamped on the bronzed face. There was a certain arrogance in the way he stood, holding himself proudly tall, as if daring anyone to condescend to him. Suddenly something seemed familiar.

"Leighton?" the Duke murmured thoughtfully, a slight frown marring his brow. "The name is not unfamiliar. You *are* English, are you not?"

"Indeed, Your Grace. Although I have held the title of captain for these many years, I am also the Marquis of Jacqobi," Dante Leighton said curtly.

It was the Duke's turn to hide his surprise at the revelation of Dante Leighton's full identity, and it must have come as a shock to discover that the captain of the *Sea Dragon*, a notorious smuggling vessel, was also a peer of the realm.

The Duke remained silent for a moment, as if finding it difficult to digest this unexpected piece of information. The fact of Dante Leighton's being a titled lord changed many of the Duke's assumptions. But there was one thing it did not alter, and Lucien Dominick would have demanded an answer to that question from even His Majesty.

"I still do not have an explanation for your having kept my daughter aboard your ship. Nor do I understand why I was not contacted immediately upon your arrival in London. You have been here for several days, but had I not a man watching the docks in London I still would not know of your arrival. Is that correct?" the Duke inquired, just barely containing his anger.

"You seem to have forgotten that my daughter was brutally kidnaped from our home and that our family has suffered the agony of not knowing whether she was alive or dead. And now to discover that she has been here in London, while we have continued to wonder whether we would ever again see her alive." The Duke searched his daughter's flushed face for an explanation. Noting the sadly guilty look in her eyes, he shook his head in disbelief. That she could have been party to such a cruel deception. "Rhea?"

"Oh, Father, please try to understand," Rhea whispered brokenly, her tear-filled eyes beseeching his forgiveness for her unintentional cruelty. "A single day has never passed without my longing for you and Mother and the rest of the family. If you only knew how I have longed to see you, how I have missed you! I wanted to inform you of my safe return to England, but Dante and I did not wish to have him meet my family while he was under suspicion of kidnaping me from Charles Town. He knew he would not be allowed to leave London until he has answered those false charges, and I was one of the few people who could give evidence refuting the charge.

"Father, Dante has been cleared of any complicity in my kidnaping from Camareigh, or of having kept me aboard the *Sea Dragon* against my will. Sir Morgan was correct when he said that I would most likely have died in Charles Town if Dante hadn't taken me aboard the *Sea Dragon*. Houston Kirby, the ship's steward, nursed me back to health, and all on board could not have been kinder to me. We owe them our gratitude, Father, not our condemnation. How could I abandon them now, when they were in need of my support?" Rhea pleaded. "I had no other choice but to remain and testify on their behalf. Dante and his crew have been cleared of all charges. The crew has disbanded. And as soon as the treasure was divided among the crew members, we were leaving for Camareigh," Rhea said quietly, her glance moving between the two men who meant more to her than life itself. When her eyes met Dante's, there was a subtle change in her expression.

The Duke did not miss that tender exchange of glances, and it did not soothe him. It was becoming disturbingly clear that this Dante Leighton exerted a great deal of influence over Rhea.

"I think you should know that Rhea had every intention of letting you know that she was in London, but I persuaded her otherwise. For purely selfish reasons, I played upon her deep affection and love for her family," Dante admitted with brutal frankness. It would have been difficult to know whether Lucien Dominick or his daughter was more surprised by the admission.

"Dante?" Rhea asked, confused.

"'Tis true, my dear," Dante responded, purposely using the endearment. "You see, I had no intention of returning you to the bosom of your family while I was locked up in a cell in Newgate. I feared that, once behind bars, I might never again see the light of day. Knowing something of Lucien Dominick and of the power a duke can wield, I suspected he might react as I would have if my daughter had become involved with a man such as myself. Am I not correct, Your Grace?" Dante inquired. Meeting the Duke's unblinking stare, he knew he was right.

The Duke did not deny the accusation, and suddenly Rhea knew that Dante had been right. "Father? Say it is not true. You would never do something so horrible as to keep an innocent man in prison."

"There is nothing I would not do to ensure your happiness, or to avenge a wrong done to one of my family," the Duke said softly. In that moment he showed Rhea the ruthless side of his nature which she, his beloved daughter, had never been fully aware of.

"I think you should also be aware of the fact," Dante continued, "that Rhea had very little choice about staying aboard the *Sea Dragon* when she sailed from Charles Town."

"Dante, please," Rhea interrupted, her pale cheeks flushing. "It is not necess—"

"No, Rhea, I think it very necessary that your father know the truth. I want him to hear it from me, now, and not through rumors later on," Dante said evenly. "Upon arriving in Charles Town aboard the *London Lady*, Rhea escaped her kidnapers and fled along the docks. It was my ship, the *Sea Dragon*, that she chanced to climb aboard while seeking safety. She was half delirious when I found her in my cabin, and, because of certain circumstances, I disbelieved her story of having been kidnaped and of being the daughter of the Duke of Camareigh. I thought her a spy sent aboard my ship to cause mischief. I could not risk her giving some information she had accidentally stumbled across to my enemies, so I kept her aboard. When we sailed, Rhea sailed with us."

Lucien Dominick's scar whitened. "It must have been obvious, from what you yourself have admitted, and from what I have heard from other sources, that my daughter was a very sick young woman when she arrived in Charles Town. And whether you believed her story or not, I find it reprehensible that you would have so little pity for a frightened girl who must have pleaded with you to take her to the authorities and who was in dire need of a doctor's care. Are you so cold-blooded that you would turn a deaf ear to the desperate cries for help from a girl stricken with terror?" the Duke demanded in a voice so harsh that even Rhea became frightened of him.

Dante Leighton's bronzed face paled under the censure of the Duke of Camareigh's words. "Your anger and contempt are justified. Hindsight, of course, often changes one's opinion about one's actions and whether he would repeat them, but at the time I felt I had little choice. Considering the outcome, I have very few regrets," Dante said in a quiet, unapologetic voice, but it must have cost him quite an effort, for every so often a muscle in his cheek twitched slightly.

"As you may know, my past is not one to be proud of. Because of it, I left England and pursued a life totally different from what I had been accustomed to. I lost, through foolishness and misfortune, my family's heritage and my wealth. Through the years, however, I have managed to amass a considerable sum of money, but until now never enough to achieve certain goals I set many years ago," Dante explained, his eyes lingering on Rhea before meeting the Duke's accusing stare.

"When Rhea stumbled aboard the *Sea Dragon* in Charles Town, we were about to set sail on a voyage that would change the lives of every one of us. We were going after sunken Spanish treasure, gold enough to make every man aboard rich beyond his wildest dreams.

"With that treasure I could give up privateering and smuggling, and return to Merdraco and claim all that is rightfully mine. That goal was out of my reach until we discovered the treasure. I would not have let anything or anyone stand in my way of achieving that goal," Dante told the Duke of Camareigh, his words ringing with that same sense of purpose and determination which had led the *Sea Dragon* to that cove along the Florida coast.

"So to hell with my daughter and the rest of the world, was that it?" the Duke asked, his words sounding like a death knell as he stared contemptuously at the man who faced him so boldly while explaining his treachery.

"No, Your Grace," Dante replied, refusing to be baited, for he knew Lucien Dominick's fingers itched for the hilt of his sword. "As the voyage lengthened, I came to have another purpose in life," Dante added, his eyes returning to Rhea, and their crystalline quality softened as he met her trusting gaze. "I fell in love with your daughter, and I had no intention of allowing her to leave the *Sea Dragon*. I am guilty of trying to keep her aboard, against her will, in Antigua," Dante confessed, though not contritely. "But Rhea is most resourceful and managed to get ashore. Rhea is also completely unselfish and puts the welfare of others before her own. That was why, when an injured boy needed her, she returned to the *Sea Dragon* to care for him."

Lucien Dominick looked down at his daughter, unsurprised by this revelation. Unconsciously, he reached out to touch the long golden braid of hair. Sensing his tender regard, Rhea turned to meet his gaze, her eyes loving as she reached out to him. Her small hand was enveloped by his, just as it always had been. He had guided her with a steady hand when she took her first tentative steps and when she rode her pony for the first time. He had always been there.

But he had not been there this time, he thought sadly. His sweet Rhea Claire, his firstborn, had brought only happiness to their family. She was so incredibly lovely, so deeply beloved by all who knew her. That she, of all people, should have known the terrors of this past year hurt him more than any physical wound could have done.

Unaware of doing it, the Duke's fingers traced the line of his scar while he gazed at his daughter's exquisite face, and for an instant it was as if he were thinking of another face and another time. Whatever he was thinking, it tormented him.

"Father? Are you ill?" Rhea asked. She touched his arm tentatively, not wishing to startle him, then squeezed his hand in the reassuring way a parent would have a child's. It was a strange sensation to be comforting her father, for it had always been the other way around.

Lucien Dominick shook his head, clearing it of the haunting memories of the past year and of a face so similar to Rhea's. But that other face had masked an evil which had nearly destroyed his family.

"I am fine, now that you are safely returned to us, my dearest child," he said.

As the Duke gazed at his daughter, he gradually became aware of a difference in her appearance, a change which went beyond the physical.

He had to admit that he had been startled by her incredible beauty when she opened the door and he saw her for the first time in nearly a year. He was not certain exactly how he had expected her to look, but after so harrowing a time, he would not have been surprised to find her a pale shadow of her former self. Instead, she was breathtakingly beautiful. Rhea Claire had always been a lovely girl, but she now possessed a warmth and vibrancy which had only been hinted at before.

And although she was thinner, he couldn't help but notice how womanly her figure had become beneath the thin material of her bodice. Her femininity was emphasized. She was blossoming. The gold of her hair was richer, the violet of her eyes deeper, the blush in her cheeks rosier.

And suddenly it became all too clear to the Duke. Until the kidnaping she had possessed the innocence of a young girl. Now she was a woman. There was a new maturity about her. The Duke had sensed some indefinable difference in the way she held herself; proudly, but with a new, intimate knowledge. There was a natural seductiveness in her smile and her glance; it was not coy or flirtatious, but unconsciously alluring, especially when her eyes lingered on Dante Leighton, their look altered subtly to the tender, knowing glance of a lover's.

The Duke's face was ashen, his scar standing out angrily, as he came to his startling conclusion. Smoldering wrath flared inside him and communicated itself to Dante, who, meeting Lucien Dominick's blazing eyes, reached out a hand to Rhea.

Rhea reacted unthinkingly, stretching out her hand to his, locking her fingers with his, while her other hand was still clasped in her father's grasp.

"I think you should know, before you come to any more dangerous conclusions, the most important reason why Rhea stayed with me in London," Dante said quietly.

"Dante, please. I do not think this is the time. I wanted to explain everything to my mother and father. They need to understand—" Rhea began, only to fall silent as she glanced between the two men.

"I think now is the time," Dante said. "Your father has already assumed the worst. He believes I seduced you, perhaps even raped you. He believes we are lovers. I imagine he would gladly give half his fortune to see me hanging from the gibbets," Dante speculated grimly.

"No, Father, it is not true!"

Lucien Dominick glanced down at his daughter's beautiful, tear-stained face, an uncommon gentleness in his eyes as he reached out and cupped her chin. "My sweet child," he murmured sadly. "What you must have suffered. If only I could change the past. I do not blame you for what has happened. You are so young and innocent. You have been badly used by so many people. I only wish to protect you from further sorrow. I am going to take you home, Rhea."

"Father," Rhea said softly, placing her hand over his, "I love Dante. He has never made love to me without my consent," she admitted. Embarrassment stained her cheeks, but she met her father's gaze directly and the truth of her confession could not be mistaken.

It was not what Lucien Dominick wanted to hear. "Always so loyal. But I fear your loyalty is misplaced this time. It is painfully obvious to me that this man has seduced you. He took advantage of your innocence, my dear. He played on the confusion and loneliness you must have felt on finding yourself in a distant land, among strangers. You are merely the latest of his mistresses, and when he tires of you, he will discard you," the Duke said, meaning to destroy any illusions Rhea might have entertained about Dante Leighton. It was best for her to learn the bitter truth now no matter how cruel and un-feeling he might appear in her eyes.

"I love Rhea," Dante said simply. "I will not deny that I may have taken unfair advantage of her. Some might even be correct in accusing me of having seduced Rhea."

"Dante, no," Rhea pleaded, feeling the sudden tightening of her father's fingers against her chin. "I came to you will-ingly."

"You never really had any choice, Rhea. Once I decided I wanted you, I set about to make you desire me. Had I honored your virtue, then you would still be innocent in the ways of love. But it did not happen that way."

"You bastard." Lucien Dominick spoke the words so quietly that Rhea was not aware that he had spoken until she saw him reach for his sword.

"Father, please! You do not understand. Dante is my hus-band!" Rhea cried. Freeing her hand from Dante's possessive grip, she placed both her hands restrainingly against her father's sword arm.

If the Duke had been stabbed in the back, he could not have been more unpleasantly surprised. But Rhea's declaration, rather than mollifying him, seemed to snap what restraint he had left. "I shall have the marriage annulled. Have you for-gotten there is a Marriage Act? Rhea is underage, and she did not have parental consent. You would not have been able to obtain a license without it. Nor have you been in England long enough to have posted the banns."

"We were not wed in England," Dante said, deriving a certain pleasure from the expression on the Duke's face. "We were wed on New Providence Island, in the Bahamas. We made our promises to a clergyman, in a church, and before witnesses. Our marriage was entered in the parish register and signed by both of us. It is, in the eyes of God and man, indissoluble. And," Dante added, his eyes meeting the Duke's squarely, "it has been consummated."

Lucien Dominick was most dangerous when he seemed in-different. For a moment, it seemed he had not heard Dante Leighton's words.

"Then I shall see Rhea a widow before night falls," he said finally. There was no doubt that Dante Leighton understood the words spoken so softly and with such deadly intent, for his hand dropped to his sword as the Duke drew his.

And for Sir Morgan Lloyd, who had been standing in silence, his presence forgotten, there was no mistaking the smooth scraping sound of a sword being drawn from its scabbard. He had not wished to intrude and had been about to take his leave, but he felt he must interfere or there would be bloodshed. Could Lady Rhea Claire accept the death of either man at the hands of the other?

Sir Morgan had taken a step forward before he realized that Dante Leighton had not drawn his sword.

"I shall not raise a weapon against you. No matter what insult or provocation you give me, I shall not fight you," Dante told the Duke. "You are Rhea's father, and for that reason alone I spare your life.

"I am not a fool. I know I cannot really win a duel with you. If I allowed you the advantage, you most likely would kill me. If I fought you and won, then Rhea would turn against me for killing her father and I would lose her. So, should you still be intent upon letting my blood, think very carefully before doing so," Dante advised the silent Duke. "It would certainly be murder, for I would have been defenseless against your attack, and Sir Morgan would stand witness to the deed. Would you risk having Rhea turn against you? For you will have murdered her husband."

Sir Morgan breathed easier. The Duke was no fool either and must certainly heed Dante Leighton's words of undeniable wisdom, albeit cunningly inspired. Indeed, Sir Morgan was quite impressed by Dante Leighton's cool logic, and couldn't help but remember how elusive and challenging an adversary the captain of the *Sea Dragon* had been. The man possessed an instinct for survival which allowed him, in that first sensation of danger, to escape and profit at the same time.

But whether Dante Leighton's brilliant ploy would have succeeded on its own or not, no one would ever be sure, for Rhea Claire spoke then with quiet dignity.

"I am with child."

And whether the future father or the grandfather-to-be was the more startled was anyone's guess, for both men simultaneously lost whatever fight had been in them and stared in disbelief at the slim figure of the young woman standing between them.

Sir Morgan coughed softly, then loudly cleared his throat, successfully gaining the attention of the three people standing in unnatural silence. "I think it best if I take my leave. This is a family matter," Sir Morgan said with special emphasis on the relationship, which he sincerely hoped would eventually become less strained. "I fear I have already overstayed my welcome. Please do not concern yourselves that anything I have heard will go beyond this room. Your privacy will be respected," he reassured them.

"Thank you, Sir Morgan. I never feared that it would not," Rhea responded and walked toward him, feeling it safe now to leave her father and husband alone. She held out her hand. "I do not know how to thank you for your many kindnesses."

"Lady Rhea Claire, it truly has been my privilege," Sir Morgan said with a gallantry not usually associated with him. He took her hand and bent low. "I fear I shall not have the pleasure of your company again, and that is why I came to bid you *adieu*. May you find continued happiness, Lady Rhea Claire."

"Thank you, Sir Morgan. But I hope you are mistaken and that we shall be able to welcome you to our home. I am sure that I speak for my mother and father when I extend an invitation to visit Camareigh."

"Thank you. It would be an honor." Sir Morgan glanced beyond Rhea, to where the Duke of Camareigh and Dante Leighton were still standing in silence. "Your Grace, by your leave?" Sir Morgan bowed slightly, before turning to Dante Leighton. "Captain, this is not quite the manner in which I thought we should be ending our association, but certainly preferable to one of us ending on the bottom of the sea. I cannot say it has always been a pleasure knowing you, but it has always been a challenge," Sir Morgan admitted. "I fear that I shall be the only one to miss the figurehead of the grinning red dragon. Certainly not Bertie Mackay. You gave him too much competition, not to mention stealing much of his glory."

"Captain." Dante Leighton held out his hand in friendship and farewell, reflecting that he respected and liked the captain of H.M.S. *Portcullis*, and was relieved that they would no longer find themselves in conflict. "I wish you well."

"Thank you. Let us hope that Bertie Mackay is of a similar mind when I return to the Carolinas. And, from what I've heard downstairs in the taproom, I may have a hotheaded Irishman to be worrying about as well," Sir Morgan said with a wry grin. Then with another courteous bow he started for the door.

The Duke of Camareigh's voice halted his progress. "You will be in London awhile longer, will you not?"

Sir Morgan halted abruptly, for the question sounded like a command. Turning around, he faced the Duke with a look of surprised inquiry. "No, as a matter of fact I shall be leaving within a day or so. I shall travel to Portsmouth and, perhaps, time permitting, to my home in Wales."

Lucien Dominick seemed to be having a difficult time gathering his thoughts. His gaze kept returning to his daughter, as if still disbelieving of the incredible turn of events, and unwilling still to accept that there might not be anything he could do about the situation, or the circumstances surrounding it.

"I should like to have a few words with you, Sir Morgan, since you have firsthand knowledge of my daughter's experiences in the colonies. Perhaps, if you would not mind waiting for me in the taproom, we could discuss that, as well as certain other matters I am curious about," the Duke requested, his tone less peremptory this time. "I fear that we will not have the opportunity to talk later, for my daughter and I shall be leaving for Camareigh within the hour."

Sir Morgan nodded, his glance straying to Dante Leighton, who seemed startled by the news of his wife's impending departure. "I shall await your pleasure, Your Grace."

"Thank you, Sir Morgan. I shall be but a few more minutes."

As the door closed on Sir Morgan, Lucien Dominick held out his hands to his daughter, his expression no longer forbidding. "It is true?" he asked simply.

"Yes, Father. I had not wished to tell you in this manner. Not about the baby, or about the marriage. I wanted to tell you and Mother together, at Camareigh. I wished you both to share in my happiness. Even Dante did not know until this moment," she explained, her gaze uncertain as she glanced at her husband, for she had yet to discover how he felt about the child.

It was Dante Leighton's turn then to feel that events were moving beyond his control. "It would seem there is quite a lot happening here without my knowledge," he said quietly, his glance questioning. "Is it true? Have you decided to leave with your father?" he demanded, but his expression was doubting of any such thing.

Rhea nodded, confirming his worst suspicions. "Dante, my mother is ill. I must go to her now. When you and Sir Morgan entered, my father was just beginning to tell me about her illness. Please try to understand. I must go to her. She must know that I am safe." Although her eyes were beseeching, her voice made it only too clear that she had made up her mind to leave with her father, and nothing he could do or say could change that decision.

There was a glint of satisfaction in the Duke's eyes as he said, "I shall have a maid sent up to pack your clothes. You will, of course, wish to change," he added, distaste settling over his harsh features as he noted the buckskin skirt and the strange sandals with their rawhide straps entwined round Rhea's calves. "It will be drafty in the carriage," he commented, saying nothing further. "My carriage is below. We can be on the outskirts of London within the hour if we do not delay," he added, his meaning clear as his eyes rested on the indolent figure of his son-in-law.

"Fresh teams of horses await our arrival at several inns along the route, so we shall waste no time in seeing your mother. And, of course, Francis and Robin and the twins will be thrilled to see you, my dear," the Duke added, and Dante Leighton, who was a man not above suspecting another's motives, received the distinct impression they were being cleverly manipulated by the Duke.

"Do they know that I have returned?" Rhea asked eagerly.

"I am the only one who knows. I did not wish to raise their hopes unnecessarily. Until I arrived in London, and, indeed, actually saw you with my own eyes, I was not certain you had even returned to England aboard that ship. I was, however, quite prepared to question its captain concerning your whereabouts should you not have been aboard," the Duke explained, and he sounded almost sorry that he had not had that pleasure.

"I shall inform the coachman of our plans and have him

send up a couple of footmen to carry down your trunks," he said, changing the subject and apparently having thought out every detail except, perhaps, for one.

And that detail was making himself comfortable at the table, his plans very much his own as he contemplated the Duke, wondering if next the Duke would try and order him from the room, which wouldn't come as a surprise, for it was more than obvious that the Duke would enjoy nothing better than to send the captain of the *Sea Dragon* packing; and right out of his daughter's life.

"I trust it shall not disturb your schedule, Your Grace, if I have a word in private with my wife?" Dante asked quietly, his sarcasm like the cutting edge of a knife.

Lucien Dominick would have liked to deny him, or so it seemed as he stared at the former privateer as if he had outrageously requested a piece of the moon.

"I am certain those footmen you'll have sent up will be quite the strapping fellows, and more than happy to stand guard at the door should I be so foolish and try and leave, accompanied by my wife," Dante said with bitter mockery. "You need have no fear on that score, Your Grace, for I shall always know where to find Rhea."

"Father, please," Rhea asked. "Dante *is* my husband and the father of my child. I would like to have a few minutes alone with him," Rhea requested. "I have to change my clothes regardless, and you did wish to have a word with Sir Morgan, Father," Rhea reminded him, exerting a certain subtle persuasion of her own.

"Very well, but I shall not be long in conversation," the Duke said, finally conceding temporary defeat. But he was obviously reluctant to leave the two of them alone together, which was only too insultingly clear to Dante Leighton. He knew the battles were not over yet and was not surprised to hear the Duke add a parting shot. "Remember, my dear, the footmen will be right outside the door should you need assistance."

Rhea's eyes followed her father's progress across the room, and not until the door closed on his tall, commanding figure did she glance away. And it was only when Dante saw her shoulders shaking that he realized that she was crying.

"Rhea?" he inquired, and there was a new note of tender concern in his voice. "Are you ill? Shall I call for a doctor? Or your father?" He was worried enough to offer even that.

"No," Rhea answered huskily. "I am just happy. Until now, being back in England has felt like a dream. There was no reality to it until I saw my father standing at the door and heard his dear voice. Suddenly the horrible nightmare seemed truly over. I felt all my fears vanish and I knew that I had really come home," Rhea explained, feeling an overwhelming contentment as she rested her head against Dante's shoulder.

Her eyes were closed and she did not see the strange expression on Dante's face. "You have felt safe and happy with me, haven't you, Rhea?"

She glanced up in surprise. "Of course I have."

"And you are still pleased to be my wife?"

"Of course I am."

"And to be carrying my child?"

"More happy than I could ever tell you," Rhea answered, her eyes holding his for a long moment while she searched that pale grayness for some hint of his feelings about the baby.

"Good. Although it would have changed little had you felt any regrets. You are Lady Rhea Claire Jacqobi, and the child you will give birth to will be a Leighton. And that is the name of the family you have become part of, whether you like it or not. To call yourself a Dominick is no longer your right. Nor will your home ever again be Camareigh. Remember that, Rhea Claire," Dante warned her, and the intensity of his gaze frightened her.

Yet she replied calmly. "I accepted that when I wed you, Dante. I love you and always shall, please remember that," Rhea told him, and she began to feel some of the angry tension leave his body.

"I shall hold you to your word," Dante promised her.

"Dante, you are pleased about the baby?" Rhea asked shyly.

But no words could have surpassed the look of tender passion which spread across Dante Leighton's face, erasing the harshness that sometimes made him seem so remote.

"You will never escape me now," he murmured, his mouth lowering to hers, and they both found comfort in that intimate touching.

"I wouldn't be able to even if I so desired, for soon I shall be so big 'twill be difficult for me to get to my feet, much less run away," Rhea jested, yet the thought did give her cause for concern when she remembered how large her Uncle Richard's wife, Sarah, had become when she was expecting her first child. And with that thought, Rhea found herself wondering if Sarah had had a girl or a boy. And what other events had occurred at Camareigh while she had been absent this past year. There would be so much for her father and her to discuss on the journey.

"I cannot persuade you to stay?" Dante asked softly, his teeth nibbling along her parted lips. "I promise I shall not be long about this business of the treasure, for the crew grows impatient to be about their new lives of leisure."

"Please, Dante, do not make this any more difficult than it already is," Rhea begged as she fought off the aching longing she always felt when in his arms. "I must go," she said adamantly.

"I shall miss you," Dante whispered against the fragrant softness of her hair. "I haven't slept alone in many months. How shall I keep warm?"

"I shall instruct one of the serving girls to put an extra comforter on your bed, but that is all," Rhea offered, a warning glint in her eyes, but she was quickly succumbing to the sensual pleasure of his touch, her resolve fading as she felt his hand caressing the tender curve of her breast.

There was silence in the room until the sound of approaching feet along the corridor beyond the closed door penetrated Rhea's awareness and she freed her lips from Dante's. "Dante, I think there is someone at—"

Dante sighed, thinking they'd had a damned sight too many interruptions at this inn. He reluctantly released Rhea from his embrace as the knocking continued. "No doubt one of your father's eager watchdogs," Dante commented with an unpleasant glance toward the door.

Dante stood in front of the fire, staring broodingly into the flames while the two serving girls bustled about, packing the colorful gowns they'd admired the night before. Dante kept his back to the room, unwilling to participate in Rhea's departure, but when he heard the exclamations of pleasure from the girls as they helped Rhea dress, he couldn't resist the temptation of a glance.

Dressed in the pale primrose gown with the wildflowers and butterflies dancing across the voluminous skirt, she brought all the warmth of springtime into the chilly room. The gold hair had been confined in a simple twist on the back of her head, and it was with a certain sadness that Dante watched the ivory smoothness of her shoulders disappear beneath a blue velvet cloak.

Dante returned his gaze to the flames. He felt none of the warmth of the hearth, for at the back of his mind was the worrisome thought that once the Duke had Rhea back at Camareigh, he would do everything within his power to destroy their marriage.

Dante felt a gentle touch on his arm and, glancing down, stared hard at the small hand with his ring on the third finger.

"You *will* come soon?" Rhea asked, understanding his fears.

"Very soon. I trust you will be on the lookout for me. I doubt whether your father will allow me through the gates of Camareigh," Dante predicted. Lucien Dominick would not give up without a fight.

"I am sorry that your first meeting with my father was so unpleasant, but you must admit that the circumstances of our marriage are a bit unusual. And you must allow him a certain dismay at having discovered that I am wed to a man he thought may have kidnaped me." Rhea was hoping desperately that Dante and her father would be more understanding of one another. "Just give my father time to accept you, Dante. When he comes to see how much in love we are, he will raise no further objections to our marriage. The rest of my family will be anxious to meet you, especially my mother. You will adore her, Dante. She is just as wonderful as my father, only less severe. In fact, she is the only one who can tease him, and she never fails to steal a smile from him," Rhea told him. As she spoke of her family she became more anxious to see them again.

"Indeed?" Dante said with a smile. "Your mother must be a remarkable woman. I shall indeed look forward to making her acquaintance."

"I think you and she will get along quite well together.

Unless, of course, you anger her. She does have a temper. But she does not stay mad for long. Why, even Robin—" Rhea was saying when she suddenly remembered something. "Conny!"

"You needn't worry. He is downstairs listening to Longacres, so you will have a chance to say good-bye to him," Dante reassured her, understandingly.

"Whatever shall I say to him? I did not expect to leave London without taking him with me to Camareigh. He so wanted to visit, and I did promise him. I hope he will understand," Rhea fretted, worried both about his reaction to her sudden departure and leaving him alone in London.

"You worry about him too much, Rhea. He may still be a boy, but he is tough. However," Dante continued, "you may rest assured that I shall be keeping an eye on him. And when I arrive at Camareigh, Conny will be with me. I give you my word that he will not be abandoned. I have been giving a great deal of thought to his future, so you need not worry. And, furthermore," Dante added with a devilish grin reminiscent of their days aboard the *Sea Dragon,* "there is a room full of men downstairs who are waiting to pay their respects to you. Do you mind stopping and saying good-bye to them?"

Rhea's smile was sad. "Of course not. They are my friends," Rhea answered, suddenly recalling those languorous days aboard the *Sea Dragon* when the sun rode the yardarms and the sails billowed with the warm trades. And at night, under a black sky full of stars, the rising of a full moon turned the sea to shimmering silver. "I cannot believe it is over, Dante. It seems but a dream now, and soon those friends will be but names and barely remembered faces, but even then I shall always hold dear those days we shared aboard the *Sea Dragon.*"

"I know," Dante said, and gently taking Rhea into his arms, he held her close, wishing that they were once again standing on the warm sands of their cove. Their love for one another had been found there. That love had found its beginnings in a savage wilderness, yet it would meet its greatest challenge in another wild shore, where it would either endure or be destroyed.

Houston Kirby had continued to watch the door while nursing his third tankard of ale. He was merely curious when Sir

Morgan descended the stairs, looking uneasy. Sir Morgan entered the taproom and, finding himself a table near the door, ordered a brandy, which he quickly emptied. Kirby wondered what Sir Morgan was waiting for with so little patience. He was not to wonder for long, for shortly thereafter a very distinguished-looking gentleman dressed in a flowered silk suit of the finest quality descended the stairs. But it was the scar on the man's cheek that interested the little steward most. It reminded him of something, but the memory was elusive.

To Houston Kirby's surprise, only because the man seemed out of place in the taproom of Hawke's Bell Inn, the scar-faced gentleman sat down at Sir Morgan's table. The way Sir Morgan had bowed, one would have supposed the man to be King George himself.

Scowling, Houston Kirby looked down at his ale. There was something going on that had the hairs on the back of his neck rising. It didn't ease his mind any when the lordly gentleman, who was asking questions of Sir Morgan, continually glanced up and around the room, his narrowed gaze singling out individuals who had sailed aboard the *Sea Dragon*, including Houston Kirby. It was a gaze which did not invite introductions. In fact, it was insultingly assessing, even unfriendly.

"Arrogant bastard," Houston Kirby mumbled into his ale, beginning to feel as ill at ease as he had when just a young footman standing under the scrutiny of the old Marquis. And he was speculating about just what the old Marquis would have thought about the strange circumstances of his grandson and heir's return to England, when his curiosity became even more aroused by the sight of Lady Rhea Claire's trunks being carried down the stairs and out the door by two hulking footmen wearing livery he was not familiar with. And since he knew neither man, he was alarmed by their handling of Lady Rhea Claire's possessions. Besides, no one had told him she was leaving, and he had yet to see the captain's sea chest following the same route.

Houston Kirby had reached the door of the taproom by the time the captain and Lady Rhea Claire had reached the bottom of the stairs, and to the little steward's surprise, Lady Rhea Claire was wearing her cloak as if in preparation for a journey.

"Captain? M'lady?" Kirby questioned in growing concern, for her ladyship had been crying. And the captain, well, he didn't look at all pleased.

"Rhea," a voice caressed her ladyship's name from somewhere behind Houston Kirby's shoulders and, glancing around, he looked up until his eyes came to rest on the scarred cheek of the gentleman dressed in the flowered silk.

"Father, I am almost ready to leave."

Houston Kirby felt his knees giving way. Oh, Lord, he thought, *this* was the Duke of Camareigh? He understood only too well the reason for the captain's grim expression.

"I wish to say good-bye to my friends, Father. I will be but a few minutes," Rhea explained with that sweet smile that always managed to warm his heart.

"Oh, Kirby! This is my father, Lucien Dominick, Duke of Camareigh. Father, this is Houston Kirby, steward aboard the *Sea Dragon* and one of the gentlest, kindest men I have ever known. He saved my life when I was so ill. He has a broth that rivals anything Rawley could come up with, even Mrs. Taylor's Special Treat," Rhea said, laughing at the private joke between them.

"Your Grace," Kirby responded, bowing deeply, his face a bright red with the guilty embarrassment he was feeling as he remembered his uncomplimentary words of only moments before.

"Mr. Kirby." The Duke spoke to him graciously because Rhea would not have lied about the man's character. "It seems I owe you my deepest gratitude for your conscientious treatment of my daughter," the Duke said, amazed still that he should be thanking one of the men he had expected to have arrested as common outlaws deserving of his condemnation.

Houston Kirby mumbled some inane remark and suddenly remembered where he had seen the Duke before. Nervous, he spoke without thinking. "If I may say so, Your Grace, you don't look much different than when I saw you close to twenty-five years ago."

At Lucien Dominick's politely raised eyebrow, he elaborated quickly, lest the Duke think him impertinent. "I was valet to Lord Merton Jacqobi, the tenth Marquis. Remember well, I do, him sayin' that ye be a young buck to watch out for, 'cause ye had a temper, and 'cause the Dowager had too tight a rein on ye. 'Twould lead to certain trouble one day for the person who dared get in your way."

In the awkward silence that followed Houston Kirby's outrageous remark, the little steward wished the earth would open up and swallow him. Lord help him, he'd been living in the colonies too long. It came, therefore, as an astonishing surprise when the Duke's laughter filled his ears. Even Dante and Rhea looked startled.

"Yes, I remember Lord Merton Jacqobi only too well. He had much in common with my grandmother, the Dowager. They were both tyrants."

Lucien Dominick's glance rested briefly on Dante Leighton, as if seeing him through different eyes. Little did Houston Kirby realize that his innocently spoken remarks had revived old memories for the Duke, memories of the headstrong young man he once had been and of the slightly disreputable reputation he himself once had possessed.

But rather than lessening his concern where Dante Leighton was concerned, the realization of his own past caused him greater worry. To think that his daughter was now wed to a man who had equaled, if not surpassed, his own youthful follies. Remembering now how ruthless and unprincipled he had been as an ambitious young man, he couldn't help but wonder further about Dante Leighton. He would not have let anything or anyone stand in his way of achieving his goals, Leighton had stated. It was that single-minded determination which had Lucien Dominick worried, because Rhea was now caught up in Dante Leighton's destiny.

"Lady Rhea Claire!"

Someone in the crowded taproom had spotted the small group standing in conversation just beyond the door and, recognizing Rhea, had called out to her.

Much to the Duke of Camareigh's surprised disapproval, his daughter not only acknowledged the hail, but also intended to greet personally the uncouth fellow. Obviously he was a member of the crew of that cursed ship, for the man swaggered across the room as if still walking a slanting deck. And if that had not identified the man as a sailor, then his costume certainly would have, for the man looked like a pirate, the Duke thought in growing dismay.

But before the man with the almost toothless grin and cackling laugh could reach Rhea, Alec MacDonald, on the strength of having fought beside her Scots great-grandfather at the Battle of Culloden, stepped forward toward Rhea. He at least looked civilized, thought the Duke. But he continued to keep a watchful eye on the wizened gent with the knife protruding from his belt.

"Lady Rhea Claire, we thank ye for takin' the time tae see us," Alec MacDonald began nervously, for his gaze had not missed either man standing on each side of the lady, and neither man seemed overly pleased by the situation. The captain, he knew, but the other gentleman was a stranger, and the Scotsman, on noting the scar cutting across that austere face, decided he'd just as soon it stayed that way.

But Rhea was having none of that, and with a smile said, "Mr. MacDonald, this is my father."

Alec MacDonald's moustache twitched. "Your Grace," he said, but the Scotsman did not bow or nod in deference.

"Father, Mr. MacDonald fought beside my great-grandfather at Culloden. He remembers Mother and Aunt Mary. I told him Uncle Richard had rebuilt the castle and lives there during most of the year."

"Out of respect tae the memory of MacDanavel of MacDanavel, I would have fought tae protect any of his kin coming tae harm," Alec MacDonald said with simple pride and dignity. "MacDanavel of MacDanavel, a fine man he was, came tae my assistance and offered me the hospitality of his home in Timeredaloch. 'Tis been a rare privilege for me tae know his great-granddaughter."

Lucien Dominick sighed. Once again he had been cheated out of the pleasure of disliking one of the smugglers. Out of loyalty and decency, they had all befriended and protected his daughter.

"Thank you, Mr. MacDonald," the Duke replied, a smile lifting some of the harshness from his features and which must have been as rare as the sun shining on a winter's day in the Highlands. "My wife, who has always been proud of her Scottish heritage, will be quite touched to learn of your kindness to our daughter."

Alec MacDonald's moustache twitched again, and this time there was the beginning of a wide grin. "Aye, remember her well, I do. Dark as night and just as wild, she was. 'Twas the other sister, the one with the red hair, who had the gift. Heard stories about her, I did, but—"

Alec MacDonald glanced down at the elbow nudging him none too gently. Clearing his throat, he continued, "Well, as I was about tae say, on behalf of the crew of the *Sea Dragon*, we wanted tae thank you for bringing us good fortune."

"I fear I did little more than get in your way most of the time, but I shall cherish my memories of our voyage. And I wish all of you godspeed and keep you safe," Rhea said, her softly spoken words carrying to the men who had gathered close around her cloaked figure.

One man stepped out beyond the rest, his dark eyes sparkling as he bowed deeply. "To be sure, 'tis a sad occasion havin' to say farewell to so lovely a lady, but so she might not forget the bonny crew of the good ship *Sea Dragon*, we hope she will be acceptin' this small token of our esteem." Seumus Fitzsimmons recited his carefully memorized speech perfectly, then flourished a small leather case.

Under the expectant gaze of all the crew of the *Sea Dragon*, Rhea opened the surprise gift. Her expression did not disappoint them. Tears filled her eyes as she looked up at the rough men who had become her good friends.

"You should not have done this," she murmured, her fingertip lightly touching the exquisitely detailed jeweled brooch. It was a golden ship with diamond sails. A wave of emeralds and sapphires curled past her bow and there was even a rubied figurehead of a grinning red dragon.

Rhea was speechless. Their generosity was astounding. But her expression was satisfaction enough for them.

"We all own a piece of that wee ship," Alastair Marlowe commented, having moved up closer through the crowd.

"Thank you," Rhea whispered huskily. "I shall always treasure it," she promised. And before Alastair could realize her intentions, she had pressed a soft kiss against his cheek.

Bemused, he glanced around and encountered the gaze of

Dante Leighton and then the stranger's sherry-colored eyes. They seemed no more understanding than the captain's did.

His face turning a bright red, Alastair Marlowe stepped aside, allowing the others to crowd close in the hope of being treated in a similar fashion, which they all were. Even Longacres' grizzled old face was not ignored. After kissing them all Rhea glanced around worriedly, for there was one member of the crew whom she had not said good-bye to yet. But she could not find the small dark head. "I do not see him. I cannot leave without saying good-bye to him, Dante," Rhea said, her gaze searching the room anxiously now, for she felt her father's hand on her elbow.

"I will tell him what has happened, Rhea," Dante reassured her, smoothing a stray curl back from her cheek, his hand purposely lingering against its softness as he met Lucien Dominick's gaze above her head.

"I just hate to leave without explaining to Conny."

"Who is this Conny?" the Duke asked, still disturbed by the sight of his daughter mixing so freely with this rowdy group.

"He is the cabin boy aboard the *Sea Dragon,*" Dante explained. "Rhea became quite fond of him while she was aboard."

"We should be leaving, my dear," the Duke reminded her.

With a sigh of disappointment, Rhea nodded. She heard several voices toasting her name and she waved a last farewell to her friends. Clasping the jeweled replica of the *Sea Dragon* in her hands, she allowed her father to escort her from the room.

In the corridor she paused, her eyes meeting Dante's for a long, silent moment. But that was all; for they'd already said their good-byes in their room.

Suddenly Rhea felt a tug on her cloak and, turning back, she stared down at a small dark head. "Conny!" she cried out in relief, and before he could step away, she had wrapped him in her arms. "I did not think I would have the chance to say good-bye."

"Ye be leavin' then, truly?" he asked, looking up at her, his wide eyes swimming.

"Yes, Conny, I have to. This is my father," Rhea said, indicating the tall man at her side, his shadow seeming to cast a darkness across the hall. "He has told me that my mother is very ill. She needs me, Conny. I must go to her today, but when Dante comes, in a few days, will you come with him? I want you to come to Camareigh and meet my family."

"Ye really mean that, Lady Rhea?" Conny asked diffidently as he eyed the unfriendly face of the strange man. "He won't mind, then?" he asked, his gaze straying yet again to that scarred cheek.

"Father?"

Lucien Dominick felt he had lost all control of this re- markable situation. Now his daughter was inviting what was little better than a street urchin to Camareigh. But he could not deny her. "Certainly. We shall expect to see you there, ah, now what was the name?"

"Brady, Your Grace. Constantine Magnus Tyrone Brady. Conny to me mates," the cabin boy stated audaciously.

Lucien Dominick's lips quivered even as he replied quite seriously. "I see. I shall certainly remember the next time." And as he stared down into the little boy's proud, expectant face, he realized why Rhea had become so attached to the boy. He bore a certain resemblance to their Robin.

Lucien Dominick held out his hand to Rhea, helping her to her feet. With a last glance between Conny and Dante, Rhea turned away so they would not see her tears. She had almost reached the door when she suddenly thought of something and turned around.

"Oh, Kirby, Jamaica is under the bed," she called out to him, for he had been hovering near the door, curious, but wishing not to intrude.

"Aye, m'lady, I'll see to him," Kirby promised her, his voice sounding strangely muffled.

"He is welcome at Camareigh. My mother loves cats," Rhea reminded him. Then, with a last look at the three forlorn fig- ures, the steward, the cabin boy, and the captain of the *Sea Dragon* standing together in the hallway of Hawke's Bell Inn, Rhea moved through the opened doorway and disappeared into the waiting carriage that would take her home to Camareigh.

> *When night*
> *Darkens the streets, then wander forth*
> *the sons*
> *Of Belial, flown with insolence and wine.*
>   John Milton

Chapter 5

IN the darkness of a new moon rising there came two flashes of light, then three; the signal for the all-clear. Riding at anchor just within the mouth of Bishop's Creek, the smuggling sloop, with her fore- and aft-rigged sails, responded with a lantern's flash, and soon the tubs of brandy hidden beneath the false bottom of the ship were being unloaded by tackle and sling into many smaller boats, which had been rowed out for the illicit rendezvous.

The shallow-hulled boats, their contraband cargo safely aboard, began the return journey to shore while the sloop got under way and, settling the land, disappeared into the darkness. The boats, fully laden, rode low in the water, but they still scudded easily across the shoals, scraping bottom only when they were beached against the pebble-strewn sands.

The porters and tubmen, some thirty to forty who had been selected for their brawn, made quick work of the unloading. With two four-gallon casks slung over their shoulders, one hanging down in front and the other behind, they began the silent, arduous climb up the steep path winding to the cliff above. The only sound was the rushing of a wild moorland stream toward the beach far below.

Reaching the summit, the procession tramped along a well-used path until the men reached Merwest Cross, where the only light for miles shone forth from Bishop's Grave Inn. There, at the crossroads, the group divided, one to head north toward the sleepy village of Merleigh, the other south, toward Westlea Abbot.

Sam Lascombe, proprietor of Bishop's Grave Inn, was watching from an upstairs window as the clock on the stair landing struck the hour, chiming once. Sam Lascombe couldn't spy any movement below, but he knew they were there, led by Jack Shelby and ably guarded by batmen armed with cudgels, knives, and firearms. He pitied the poor soul who happened across the smugglers' path on a moonless night such as this.

"They be comin', then?" a voice demanded none too softly.

Sam Lascombe, who'd been craning his neck out of the window, reared up in surprise and banged the back of his head hard against the window frame. "Damn ye, woman!" he whispered, jerking himself back inside. "What are ye tryin' to do? Send me to an early grave? What d'ye mean sneakin' up on a man like that? Can't ye see I'm listenin' fer them?"

"If a man wasn't up to no good, then he wouldn't be worryin' about his wife comin' up behind him," the woman replied with simple logic as she peered past him into the darkness outside. "Don't see nor hear nothin'," she said, not bothering to lower her voice.

Sam Lascombe rolled his eyes heavenward. "That be the point, Dora. Ye ain't supposed to see or hear anythin' on a moonless night. And I figure I've got enough to be worryin' about these days just tryin' to stay alive, to be worryin' any about whether something is right or wrong," Sam Lascombe grumbled, for it was late and he was tired, and there would be a lot of work to do. Dawn was still a long way off.

"Reckon they'll be takin' our horses again?" the woman asked.

Sam Lascombe glanced over and tried to see his wife's face in the shadows. Was she making sport of him? "Aye, it's either that or have the Bishop burned down around our heads. Don't need to be remindin' ye, do I, about what happened to the Webbers when ol' Daniel got tired of lettin' them run his horses into the ground and refused to let them use them t'other evenin'?"

There was silence, for both remembered only too vividly the sight of the Webber farmhouse smoldering in ashes the following morning. Mary Webber was widowed, as well as homeless, when her husband was found at the bottom of a cliff. His neck had been broken, but before he had been thrown to his death he was brutally whipped.

And as the silence between them lengthened, they both heard the faint tramping of feet growing closer, louder. Suddenly it stopped. There was quiet. They waited, knowing that soon they would hear the muffled thud of horses' hooves and the creaking of harnesses as the smugglers resumed their midnight march through the darkness.

When there was only silence again, Sam Lascombe would go out to his empty stables and find perhaps twenty casks of fine French brandy, which were to stay hidden until they were collected sometime later. Of course, several of the casks were for Sam's private use and, untaxed, meant a handsome profit when the brandy was served to his customers.

Dora Lascombe sat down wearily. "When's it all goin' to end, Sam?" she asked for the thousandth time, though she knew there was no answer.

Sam Lascombe sighed, but not out of irritation. It was just that he was weary too as he sank down beside her on the edge of the bed they had slept in together for the past thirty years.

"Wasn't like this in the beginnin'," she said.

"I know," he said tiredly, rubbing his forehead.

"Ted says it all changed when Jack Shelby took over."

"Aye, your brother's right about that. Jack Shelby brought in them outsiders. Mostly deserters and criminals. All scum if ye ask me. Heard a couple of them was wanted for murder up Bristol way."

"Well, reckon we all be wanted for murder now," Dora reminded him.

"Aye. I didn't like what happened down there t'other night in Dragon's Cove. In the old days we might have cracked a preventive officer's head, or tied him up good and tight to keep him out of trouble, but never cold-blooded murder. It ain't the same," Sam Lascombe said.

"Murderin' them innocent men like that, even if they were the King's men," Dora said, voicing his worst thoughts. "'Twas bad enough, that, but to be killin' one of our *own*. Burnin' down a man's home and leavin' his wife a widow, his children fatherless and bound to starve. 'Tis a sin, Sam Lascombe, and ashamed I am to be associated with the likes o' them."

Sam Lascombe slapped his thigh in frustrated anger. "D'ye think I'm likin' it any better? That Jack Shelby and them cut-throats of his have terrified the whole countryside. Nobody dares say nay to them, especially now they've murdered them King's men. I'm 'fraid there's no stoppin' them now. What do they care for the poor, defenseless villagers and countryfolk? Come in here, they do, drink and eat their fill and don't pay for nothin'. Take whatever they wants from everybody. Heard it said they raped Mary Webber and her eldest daughter the night they burned them out of their home and killed Tom."

"Oh, dear Lord, I hadn't heard that," Dora gasped, thanking her lucky stars she was a grandmother as she thought of that rabble sitting downstairs in the taproom after a successful running of the goods.

"Call themselves the Sons of Belial," Sam Lascombe snorted derisively. "More likely sons of bitc—"

"Hush, Sam! Don't be speakin' that way," Dora cautioned him, for one never knew anymore who might be listening when they shouldn't be. A wrong word could get a person killed.

"I just hope Ted isn't speakin' so bluntly, or loudly," she added, worrying about her brother and his family over in Merleigh. "He's not one to be mincin' words when he's riled up about somethin'."

"Reckon he's got the right idea, though," Sam Lascombe

agreed. "Don't see why we can't form our own smugglin' gang hereabouts. Nothin' wrong with good, old-fashioned smugglin'," he continued almost wistfully. "Only way for a man to make a decent livin' nowadays, what with taxes bein' what they are. How can I expect to keep the Bishop open when I can't break even on a bottle of brandy I serve my customers, or on a cup of tea, or a mug of coffee? How can ye make your puddin's and jams when sugar costs an arm and a leg? Can't even dress ye as I would wish to, for even a yard of the cheapest woolen would bankrupt me, and unless I sneak a bit of cambric from one of the cargoes, I can't even afford to buy ye a decent petticoat for church."

"That's kind of ye, Sam, but my woolens keep me warmer," Dora said, not wanting him to worry about the sorry state of her underclothes.

"I tell ye, Dora, next they'll be wantin' to tax manure. I don't know what a man is s'posed to do in order to survive," he said, wondering how he was going to pay for hay to feed his horses.

"Ted said he could probably get half of the gang, mostly those from hereabouts, to join with him," Dora spoke softly, glancing over her shoulder worriedly even though there were only the two of them in the room.

"Aye, reckon most would like to join with him and get back to plain and simple smugglin' again. Don't know who picked Jack Shelby as our leader, anyways. Nobody asked me. He always seems to have plenty of spending money, though, and always knows where the dragoons are goin' to be. Don't s'pose anybody has any fondness for Jack Shelby, that's for sure. Ted knows I'll stand beside him."

"When's he goin' to talk to Jack Shelby?"

"Tomorrow I think, and 'tisn't somethin' I'd be lookin' forward to doin'. Your brother's got more courage than I do."

"Ye sound worried 'bout it," Dora said nervously.

"Aye, I am. That Jack Shelby has gotten meaner with every passin' year. Won't sit easy with him havin' Ted crossin' him like this."

"Or t'other gent."

"What d'ye mean?"

"Ted was sayin' that he thinks Jack Shelby ain't smart

enough to be the brains behind this smugglin' business. Says he has just about figured out who it really is," Dora said.

"Who?"

"Wouldn't tell me. Says he knows when to keep his mouth shut and when not to."

"Well, I just hope he doesn't bait Jack Shelby about not bein' smart enough. The man's got a streak of meanness that doesn't improve none when he gets mad."

"He always was the sullen one, weren't he? But it has gotten worse recently. Never been the same, he hasn't, since they found his daughter murdered out there on the moors. Been half crazed ever since. The man ought've been locked up long ago."

"Reckon so, Dora, only who's to do it now? Nobody in his right mind would say a word against Jack Shelby. Never be heard of again, they wouldn't. Even roughed up the vicar over at Westlea Abbot for darin' to criticize them. 'Course, the old gent must have been in his cups at the time, or he'd never have said what he did standin' there at the pulpit, especially with the vestry full of tea and brandy," Sam Lascombe said with a chuckle, then grew serious. "Of course, I s'pose we can be thankful for one thing."

"Eh?"

"That Merdraco still stands empty. Most likely the young master be on the bottom o' the sea with that ship o' his. Wasn't surprised to hear he'd turned privateer. Always was a wild one, him. And if he ain't on the bottom, then he's probably been hanged from the gallows. At least we don't have to be worryin' about that. Even the dragon's spawn wouldn't have the nerve to show his face around here anymore. Don't know what Jack Shelby might do if that was to happen. Go mad, most likely."

"Always thought 'twas a pity about the young master," Dora said now, although at the time she had believed the worst about him, just like the rest of the villagers. "Always thought him such a handsome young gentleman. Oh, he was wild enough, but 'twas just bein' young. Always thought that Lettie Shelby was no good, though. Knew she'd be comin' to grief one day. Wicked creature, she was, and probably got what she deserved. The way her father carries on about her, ye'd have thought she was a saint or somethin'."

"Well," Sam Lascombe said, muffling a tired yawn, "'tis

in the past now, and not likely to cause us any trouble. Got enough worries without thinkin' about the trouble there would be if his lordship returned to Merdraco. Lord help us, Dora, if that was to happen."

"Aye, 'twould be bad that. But I'll not be losin' any sleep over that," Dora allowed, privately wishing Jack Shelby ten feet under where he couldn't cause any more grief.

Two days later, Ted Samples disappeared while on his way home from having dinner with his sister, Dora Lascombe, and her husband, Sam, at Bishop's Grave Inn. Ted Samples was never seen or heard from again.

Full many a glorious morning have I seen.
                                        Shakespeare

Chapter 6

THE first light of dawn was just breaking beyond the gentle rise of hill toward the east when the coach carrying Lucien Dominick and his daughter rolled along the stately avenue lined with chestnut trees leading to Camareigh, for centuries the home of the Dominick family.

The great house stood silent and dark, shrouded by the morning mists. Its occupants, still lost in their dreams, remained unawakened from peaceful slumber. It was that strange hour of light between day and night, when reality could seem as elusive as dreams.

There was, however, one hearty soul who seemed to have escaped from the arms of Morpheus. As the coach creaked to a stop before the wide steps of the porticoed entrance, a large figure bustled over from the group of low, stone buildings which comprised the stables.

His breath was ragged, but still he managed effectively to bark out orders to the coachman and footmen and send the grooms scurrying to the lathered team of horses.

"Your Grace! Your Grace!" he cried, forgetting himself as he rushed forward and, pushing one of the footmen out of his way, swung open the door of the coach himself. "Is it true? Is it really true?" he asked again while peering into the shadowy confines of the coach. He stepped aside only when the tall shape of the Duke of Camareigh appeared.

The Duke remained silent as he turned and assisted his caped companion to descend the steps. As the rising sun's golden light illuminated the skies, the woman's hood fell back and she lifted her face to the warm sun.

"Oh, Lord," the big man breathed as he stared at the face. "Oh, dear Lord," he blubbered when he saw the smile. "It can't be true."

"Butterick," Rhea said, reaching out and touching the big man. He had been in charge of the stables at Camareigh since before she was born. "I am real, Butterick. And I've come home."

Butterick sniffed loudly, unashamedly brushing away the tears rolling down his ruddy cheeks. "Oh, Lady Rhea Claire, if ye only knew what this means. Her Grace will be so happy. We've all missed ye so. It just hasn't been the same around here since ye disappeared. I—I just can't be believin' these old eyes of mine," he said gruffly.

"Thank you, Butterick," Rhea said, touched. "'Tis good to be seeing you, too. I trust you've not let Skylark become too fat and lazy since I've been away?" she asked him.

"Oh, m'lady, certainly not," he replied seriously. "If I do say so, though, the little mare has sorely missed ye, despite the fact that Her Grace has been exercisin' her for ye," Butterick explained, sounding more like himself once he was back on the subject dearest to his heart. He warmed to his subject. "Of course, I knew I should've insisted that Her Grace take one of the grooms with her the last time she went ridin', but, and beggin' your pardon, Your Grace," he said apologetically as he glanced at the silent Duke, "ye know how stubborn Her

Grace can be at times. Took a tumble, Her Grace did, and got caught out in the rain. Soaked clean through to the bone, she was, when Her Grace and Skylark both came limpin' home. Oh, but we got her all fixed up right and proper, only took a poultice on her fetlock. Skylark, that is," he reassured Rhea. "Aye, if only I could be doin' as much for Her Grace," Butterick mumbled with a disgruntled sigh.

"Her Grace's condition has not worsened since I've been away, has it?" the Duke asked sharply, taking a step toward the entrance before Butterick could answer.

"'Bout the same, Your Grace."

"She doesn't know we've returned?" the Duke questioned as he glanced up toward the south wing of the house, where the family had their private rooms and where the Duchess of Camareigh's bedchamber overlooked the gardens.

"No, Your Grace. Just like ye ordered when ye sent the outrider on ahead to say that none of the family, especially Her Grace, was to hear about Lady Rhea Claire's return from anyone but yourself."

"Good. Come along, Rhea," the Duke said now as he glanced again toward the row of darkened windows in the south wing. "I think there is someone who would very much like to see you, my dear."

Butterick remained where he was for a moment longer while he watched the Duke and Lady Rhea Claire climb the steps. He was so happy to have the young lady back home with her family. But he was worried because the Duke didn't seem as happy as he should be. Worried, most likely, about Her Grace's health, he speculated as he roared further orders to the stable boys, who seemed to think they could just stand around, like gentry, enjoying the sunrise.

The joyous news of Rhea Claire's arrival spread fast through the halls of Camareigh, especially through the servants' quarters, where the housekeeper and underbutler were rousing sleepy maids and footmen. Soon the whole house would be in an uproar with celebrations.

The grand staircase was lighted by newly lit candles along its muraled length as Lucien Dominick and Rhea Claire Leighton ascended the steps, while along the silent corridors to the south wing, the light in the many wall sconces was flickering as the candles reached the end of their nighttime existence.

They passed through the Long Gallery, where the painted faces of Dominick ancestors stared down in mute curiosity at the early-morning trespassers. Rhea couldn't help but spare a quick glance at the portrait of her Elizabethan ancestor, the privateer. In the half light, she could have sworn that he was smiling. But when Rhea and her father passed beneath another portrait, Rhea kept staring straight ahead. Another day, perhaps, she would look at that particular portrait, but not today.

Standing before the double doors to the Duchess' private chambers, Lucien Dominick hesitated, then opened the doors and quietly escorted Rhea into the darkened room.

"Wait here for me, my dear," Lucien whispered. "I think I should go to warn her first. She has been very ill, and I do not wish to shock her. Once she knows you have returned safely, no doctor's cures could possibly benefit her more. She has despaired so that she has lost much of her spirit."

"I'll wait," Rhea said softly. "But if she is sleeping, then do not disturb her. I am not going anywhere."

"Lucien? Is that you?" a voice called from the shadows near the tall windows.

Lucien and Rhea spun around, both startled by the sound, and as they stared across the room, they realized that the long velvet hangings had been pulled open. Sitting curled up on the low window seat was a robed figure.

"Rina? What are you doing out of bed? You shouldn't be sitting here without a fire in the hearth. And I'd wager you don't have your slippers on, either. You mustn't become chilled, my dear," Lucien told her, his concern only too obvious as he hurried to her side.

"You sound like Rawley, always fussing about something," the Duchess responded huskily, still sounding as if she were suffering from a chest cold. "I was just sitting here watching the dawn. I do think the skies are finally clearing. Did you have a good journey to Bath? I do think Butterick should have accompanied you. He does have the best eye for horseflesh. I am glad you have returned. I missed you," the Duchess confided, holding out her hand to the Duke.

"You are feeling better?" Lucien asked as he took her cold

hand between his and, moving forward, partly blocked the Duchess' view of the door behind.

"Yes, I am. As you can hear, I've gotten my voice back," she said with a slight laugh that quickly became a cough. "Who is that with you? I thought I heard whispering. If that is you, Rawley, then you can take that dose of Mrs. Taylor's Special Treat yourself," the Duchess warned, but when no impertinent threat followed from Rawley, she frowned and strained to see into the darkness. "Rawley?"

Lucien Dominick stepped aside, allowing the pale shaft of sunlight to spread across the room and reveal the caped figure moving slowly closer.

"Mama?"

The Duchess of Camareigh looked as if she had been turned to stone.

"Rhea." The Duchess spoke her daughter's name, but no sound issued from her lips.

Then Rhea Claire was kneeling before her mother, her face pressed against her mother's breast as she felt those comforting arms holding her close. Sabrina Dominick's hands, shaking almost uncontrollably, caressed the golden curls. Then, cupping her daughter's face, she turned it upward so she could look into the violet eyes that were reflections of her own.

"My dearest child, my sweet Rhea Claire," she whispered, her voice choked with tears as she stared down at Rhea's upturned face in disbelief.

Lucien Dominick stood back, allowing them this moment together. His eyes blurred as he stared down at the two heads bent close together, one so dark, the other so fair, both so dear to him. Weary though he ought to have been, he felt no tiredness, for he knew an uplifting of spirit he had not felt since the nightmare had begun almost a year earlier. And as the early light streaked through the windows, he felt as if the darkness and gloom which had been so much a part of life at Camareigh since Rhea Claire's kidnaping were now banished forever.

Sabrina Dominick glanced across her daughter's head, her eyes meeting Lucien's. No words were needed. Rhea Claire had returned and, for the moment, that was all that mattered. The countless questions and answers would come later, but for now it was enough to have Rhea Claire there with them.

This repose did not last long, however, for an imperious knocking sounded at the door and, with the Duke's command to enter, a robust-looking woman with a sour-looking face charged into the room. She came to a halt when she caught sight of the two women silhouetted against the window.

"Well, I had to be seein' it with me own eyes. Lady Rhea Claire. I told them we'd have ye back here one of these days soon," the woman stated, apparently not overly surprised to find Rhea sitting with her mother. "Reckon I'll be needin' to bring Mrs. Taylor's Special Treat," she declared, and for the first time since Rhea had known her, which had been all of her young life, the grizzle-haired maid allowed herself a wide smile. As she stood there beaming, she looked almost pretty.

"Seein' your face, m'lady, will put the roses back in Her Grace's cheeks. And I must say, m'lady," she added in growing puzzlement, her eyes raking Rhea Claire's figure, for the cloak had fallen from Rhea's shoulders to reveal the décolletage of her gown, "that I've never seen ye lookin' so well. Here I was thinkin' I was goin' to have to put ye to bed and give ye an extra dose of Mrs.—"

"Taylor's Special Treat," Rhea finished for her. "Hello, Rawley," she greeted the maid.

"M'lady," Rawley said, her smile widening. "Well, the whole household is in an uproar, Your Grace," she said, addressing the Duke as if he had personally caused the upset. "Ye'd think, the way them silly maids are actin', 'twas Michaelmas. Poor Mrs. Peacham isn't goin' get any help from them today in cookin' the meals. Which reminds me, Your Grace. Ye'll be wantin' some breakfast first, or d'ye want to take a wee nap? Ye must be tired from the journey. Why, ye've made wonderful time, ye have," Rawley continued. Once started, Rawley was hard to stop.

"I couldn't sleep now, Father," Rhea said, her hand still held in her mother's. "I want to see the others."

"And I feel quite hungry for the first time in many, many months," the Duchess admitted.

Rhea Claire glanced up at her mother, noticing for the first time how very thin she had become. With her dark hair hanging down to her waist, she suddenly seemed so vulnerable, and

Rhea realized that the past year of worry had taken its toll on both of her parents' health.

"Ah, now that does me old heart good to hear ye talkin' like that, Your Grace," Rawley said, and Rhea could picture her rubbing her hands together.

"Tell Mrs. Peacham and Mason that we shall breakfast in here. I shall go and inform Francis and Robin of their sister's return. I would like you to see that we are not disturbed, Rawley, for at least the next half hour."

"Very well, Your Grace," Rawley said, promising herself that no one would get through that door. "Don't think Mason will ever be the same, though, Your Grace, seein' how ye got through the entrance without him bein' on duty to greet ye. The man's brokenhearted about it. Thinks he's let the family tradition down. He's gettin' hard of hearin', if ye asked me," Rawley muttered as she left the room.

"Now, sit down beside me, Rhea, and let me look at you," the Duchess said, thinking she would never get tired of staring at her daughter's face and wondering how many times during the past year had she dreamed of this very moment. "Rawley is right, my dear. I have never seen you looking more beautiful. Have you, Lucien? From what I heard from Alys, I expected you to be little more than skin and bones," the Duchess said with a sad smile, for it hurt her even to think of what had happened to her daughter on the ship.

"Father told me that you let Alys stay here at Camareigh. Thank you for that, Mother," Rhea said, remembering how she and Alys had become friends while sharing the misery of that voyage to the colonies.

"I could have done nothing less for the poor child. If it had not been for her, we would not have known you were still alive, or heard about that horrible voyage to the colonies. Even hearing the bad was some comfort, for at least you were alive. She told me how you became friends and how you told her so many stories about Camareigh and about your family. She was so frightened when she was brought here, but she seems to love Camareigh and the family so much that I hadn't the heart to send her back to London. She does not have a family of her own, and we have so much room here," the Duchess tried to explain away her tender heart.

"I remember I used to become almost irritated with her because she asked so many questions about Camareigh, but I realized that those reminiscences and stories were what kept me alive. They comforted me when I was cold and hungry and frightened of never seeing my family again," Rhea said, still haunted by memories.

"Alys has settled in quite nicely. In fact, she seems to have a gift for healing and has been taken under Rawley's wing. She knows she has a home here for life."

"I promised her that I would buy her indenture papers once I managed to return to Camareigh and told you about her," Rhea said, thankful that her parents had been kind enough to take the orphaned girl into their home.

"Now," the Duchess said, her eyes taking in every detail of Rhea's appearance, "you must tell me about everything. I want to know how—" she had started to ask, when a sudden thought struck her. Sabrina Dominick's violet eyes looked accusingly at her husband standing so negligently against the back of the sofa. "Lucien? How was it that you knew Rhea had returned? You did not go to Bath, did you? You lied to me."

Lucien Dominick sighed. He had known that this subject would come up eventually. "No, my dear, I did not go to Bath. I've been in London. Now, before you accuse me further," he interrupted his wife's first impassioned words, "I did not know if Rhea had even returned when I received word that a ship, which seemed to be the one Rhea was supposed to be aboard, had docked in London. You will remember that I have had men watching for any sign of that ship's arrival. Since you were ill, and because I did not know if Rhea Claire was aboard, I did not wish to get your hopes up only to have them dashed," Lucien explained in a most reasonable tone, though he expected an argument. Sabrina never liked to be coddled.

But Sabrina surprised Lucien by smiling and saying, "I cannot be angry with you. You did have my best interests at heart. And besides, I would have slowed you up. You promised me that you'd bring Rhea home, and now you have. Thank you, my love. You could not have given me anything more precious."

Lucien Dominick was deeply moved, and also slightly uneasy, for Sabrina had yet to learn all there was to Rhea's story.

"Now tell me, how is it that you returned to England aboard this same ship you left Charles Town on? And why has it taken so long? Why did he take you aboard his ship in the first place? We had word from our man in Charles Town of some outrageous rumor being spread by a woman about your having gone aboard voluntarily. A lie, of course. And what of the captain? What was his name, Lucien?" the Duchess demanded, her questions coming fast and to the point.

"Dante Leighton, Mama," Rhea told her.

"Yes, that is it. A pirate, isn't he? I trust he is locked up in Newgate?"

"He did not have anything to do with my kidnaping from Camareigh," Rhea said quickly, beginning to become worried lest her mother have Dante hanged before she could even make his acquaintance.

"No, I realize that. I suppose your father has explained to you about that?" she asked hesitantly, her eyes meeting Lucien's for confirmation.

Rhea nodded, but still she found it incredible that her kidnaping had been part of an insane plot for revenge devised by her father's cousin. Lady Katherine Anders, who, along with her twin brother, Percy, had fled England nearly twenty years before, had returned to exact a horrible punishment against her most hated enemy—Lucien Dominick. She had blamed the Duke for all the misfortune which had befallen her, including the untimely death of Percy in Venice.

Rhea remembered with a shudder the woman who had so kindly given her a ride in her carriage that rainy afternoon when she and Francis and their cousins had discovered the abandoned puppies. That woman, whose face she had never seen, had been planning her revenge even then. The kidnaping had been just a part of her scheme to torment Lucien Dominick before claiming her final revenge, his death.

Ultimately, she had failed, but not before she brought tragedy to Camareigh, and had murdered a harmless old man whose only crime had been remembering Lady Kate from the time when she and Percy had lived at Camareigh.

"It must have been horrible for you when she sent those poems, baiting you about my whereabouts. And then to send you that piece of my hair and the ring from my finger, to prove that she had indeed kidnaped me. And that night, when she tried to kill you, Father," Rhea said, for her father had told her of the terrible night when Kate walked the halls of Camareigh.

"But it *is* over now," the Duchess said firmly, "and Kate will never be able to hurt us again. And now that you are safely returned to us, she has failed completely in her attempt to destroy our family. Let us forget about it now, for it is in the past. Now that your father has told you about the reason behind the kidnaping, we will not speak of it again." It was all still too painful, and for too many long, endless hours she had thought about Kate and how very close that madwoman had come to destroying everything.

"You have not answered me about this man, this Dante Leighton," the Duchess said as she glanced between her husband and her daughter. Both the Duke and Rhea remained silent, neither quite knowing how to begin. "Nor do I understand why the authorities have not come to see us about this. Surely the man will have to answer the charge of kidnaping Rhea from Charles Town?"

"I am afraid, my dear, that it is not as simple a matter as we once thought. There are some other...factors which we must now take into consideration," the Duke said uncomfortably, for he sounded as if he were defending this Dante Leighton.

"What do you mean, Lucien? Exactly what more do I need to know about this man Dante Leighton?" the Duchess asked bluntly.

"All the charges against him have been dropped."

"What!"

"Yes, I felt a similar surprise myself upon hearing the news," Lucien told her, unable to conceal a certain bitterness.

"Mother," Rhea said, meeting her father's gaze only briefly, "it was due partly to my testimony that Dante is a free man. I was very ill when I went aboard the *Sea Dragon* in Charles Town, and although I would have liked to leave the ship there, I had no choice but to sail with them when they left Charles Town."

"Then I do not understand why the man is walking around free when he forced you to sail with him," the Duchess demanded.

"But when we reached Antigua, I stayed aboard voluntarily," Rhea explained, blushing slightly when she added softly, "I am in love with Dante Leighton, Mother."

It was only too painfully apparent that *that* was the last thing the Duchess was expecting to hear. Still, though startled, she was not terribly concerned until she glanced up at Lucien, who seemed rather too interested in the creases in his coat sleeve. "What exactly are you trying to tell me?" she asked slowly, sensing there was more to come, and that she might not like what she was about to hear.

"Mother, please, you must understand. I love Dante, and you will too when you meet him."

"He is here?" the Duchess asked in amazement, glancing toward the door as if he might be lurking in the corner of her bedchamber.

"No, he remained in London to settle his affairs. The crew of the *Sea Dragon* has disbanded, and they must divide the treasure," Rhea explained as if it were all very simple. "Then Dante will come."

The Duchess of Camareigh closed her eyes for a moment. "I think there is much here that I do not understand," she said finally, opening her eyes to stare at her husband. "There is more, isn't there? For I cannot see your accepting this man without good reason, Lucien. What is the reason?"

"Believe me, Rina, I have not accepted him," the Duke said emphatically. "I have merely temporarily bowed to our daughter's wishes."

"Mama, Dante Leighton is my husband," Rhea told her with simple directness.

The Duchess remained silent for several moments. "Lucien?"

"I am afraid it is the truth, my dear," he answered abruptly, unable to mask his disapproval.

"B-but it cannot be legal?"

"They were wed in the Indies. In a church. Apparently everything is quite legal. Your son-in-law, Dante Leighton, saw to that," Lucien added with a renewed feeling of frustration.

"You are accepting this. Why?" the Duchess demanded, unwilling to believe that her daughter could possibly be married, or that Lucien would accept such a mesalliance. Rhea Claire, married to a coarse, ill-bred sea captain? And despite what Rhea had said about being in love with the man, she couldn't believe she actually meant it. "Rhea? Why? I do not understand."

"Mama, I am sorry. I did not wish to upset you, but you must try to understand. Once you meet Dante, I think you will see why I love him. Father thinks he seduced me, but he didn't. Truly, he did not. I loved him almost from the beginning. He never harmed me in any way. In fact, if he had not insisted I stay aboard the *Sea Dragon*, then I most likely would have died. The ship's steward nursed me back to health."

"The fact that you are wed to this miscreant is harm enough, my child. The man must be a fortune hunter. Well, he is mistaken if he thinks to get a tuppence from us," the Duchess vowed.

"He was very hesitant to believe that I was the daughter of the Duke and Duchess of Camareigh, Mama. And he is no fortune hunter. Dante is very wealthy. He does not need any money from my family, nor indeed would he accept any," Rhea said proudly.

"It is obvious to me that this man has taken advantage of our daughter in some invidious manner. Have you met the man, Lucien? And he is still alive?" she asked, incredulous when Lucien nodded, for if there was one thing Sabrina Dominick was, it was quick-tempered, and she would have wasted little time with amenities had she come face to face with this Dante Leighton.

"Yes, I met him, along with most of the crew of the *Sea Dragon*. And if you are worried about Dante Leighton's being snubbed by proper folk, then do so no longer, for he happens to be the Marquis of Jacqobi. No doubt that was what impressed the authorities. Strangely, I knew his grandfather."

"Indeed? Well, I knew your grandmother, and that doesn't mean I liked your cousin Kate any the more, or that she was any the more sterling of character because of that connection," the Duchess reminded him, her cheeks flushing with anger.

"Oh, I almost forgot," the Duke remembered with timely purpose. "There was a Scot aboard the *Sea Dragon* who sent his personal respects to you."

The Duchess of Camareigh looked startled. "To me?"

"Yes, it seems this Scotsman fought beside your grandfather at the Battle of Culloden and remembers you and Mary quite well. He particularly asked to be remembered to you," the Duke informed her, unable to resist teasing her with so strange a coincidence. "He very proudly told me it was his honor to protect any of MacDanavel's kin."

The Duchess was momentarily speechless, which gave Lucien Dominick the chance to say, "In fact, I met quite a few interesting characters from the *Sea Dragon*. It would seem as if our daughter made quite an impression on them."

"Well, she seems to have made quite an impression on this Dante Leighton, too. Am I to believe that this man will be arriving here at Camareigh one of these fine days? And am I supposed to welcome him with open arms?" she demanded as she glanced between the two oddly silent people. "I still cannot believe that you would stand for this, Lucien. There is something else I do not know, isn't there?"

"My dear, I still have not accepted this marriage of Rhea's, but for the moment there is nothing I can do. Rhea claims that she is in love with the man, and he made it quite clear that she would hate me if I harmed him—not that he seemed to think I could," Lucien added, still offended by the man's effrontery. "He very kindly explained that the only reason he spared my life instead of dueling with me was because I was Rhea's father. A rather high opinion of himself is one of the finer points of his personality."

Sabrina Dominick closed her eyes. "My God, the arrogance. I am truly amazed at your restraint, Lucien. I would not have been so controlled in the face of the man's insolence."

"I very nearly was not. I had every intention of seeing that our daughter was a widow by evening," Lucien Dominick admitted. "And it was only because of her feelings that I did not kill him. Rhea has suffered too much already."

Glancing between them, the Duchess knew she had been correct, and that there was something else. She waited for the last revelation.

"Mama," Rhea said softly, "I am with child."

The Duchess of Camareigh stared helplessly at her daughter, her face growing pale. Tears welled in her eyes.

"Mama, are you ill?" Rhea asked, concerned that all the excitement had been too much.

Sabrina Dominick shook her head. Meeting her daughter's troubled gaze, she held out her arms. "Oh, my dearest child, I am so thankful to have you home, and yet I feel I have been blessed and cursed at the same time. You must give me the time to try to understand all that has happened to you," she pleaded.

"I know, Mama," Rhea said, her voice muffled as she buried her face against the Duchess' unbound hair. "I was almost afraid to come home to Camareigh. I thought you might find me too changed. That you might find it hard to accept what has happened. That you wouldn't love me as much and that—"

"Oh, my dear, never fear that we will ever turn away from you. We shall always love you, no matter what has happened. We shall always be here," the Duchess reassured her, remembering all the times during Rhea's childhood when she had held her in her arms and comforted her.

Lucien and Sabrina exchanged glances across Rhea's head. There would be much for all of them to accept if they were to resume their lives as a family again. And if that meant accepting Dante Leighton, then so it must be.

The more the merrier.
John Heywood

Chapter 7

FOR the first time since that tragic day a year earlier, the joyous sounds of unrestrained laughter drifted out of the private drawing room in the south wing of Camareigh. In the hearth, logs of maple and oak, scented with applewood, were burning brightly, for darkness came early in fall and brought with it cold winds blowing out of the West Country.

A spattering of rain blew against the tall, mullioned windows that framed the view of distant hills purpled by descending dusk. Soon the heavy, velvet hangings would be drawn, closing out the darkness, and countless candles would be lit, adding their brightness to the room.

The flickering light from the fire was reflected in the silver of the tea service, which had been set up before the two women who sat together on the rose-colored silk sofa near the hearth.

Rhea Claire glanced up from the cup she had just filled with the steaming dark brew and, under her mother's smiling regard, handed her the brimming cup in its delicate china saucer.

"This is certainly a welcome relief from Mrs. Taylor's Special Treat," the Duchess remarked with a wry smile. "Although, now that I ponder the thought, I suspect that Rawley has doctored my daily dose more than once with a drop or two of rum. I have truly come to regret the day she accompanied us to Verrick House and acquainted herself with Mrs. Taylor."

"You really are feeling better, Mama?" Rhea asked, her eyes searching her mother's pale face carefully. There was no sign of fever, and her mother hadn't coughed in more than an hour.

"I have not felt so well in nearly a year," the Duchess reassured her, and taking a sip of tea, she glanced around the room at the family. She knew she would find no contentment greater than this.

Rhea followed her mother's gaze, her own eyes resting for a moment on two golden heads. Her youngest brother and sister played together on the flowered carpet just beyond the tea table. Andrew seemed to have grown the more since she had been away, and his steps were less shaky as he toddled across the carpet toward her, his childish prattle alerting her to his intended destination: the tray with the buns, scones, and cakes.

Arden, whose mouth bore the traces of the chocolate sponge cake her sticky fingers had just held, wouldn't allow her twin to have anything she did not. Squealing, she crawled onto wobbly legs and teetered after him. But, unable to slow herself down when she lost her balance, she tumbled into him, knocking his short, chubby legs out from under him. His cry of surprise turned into a bellow of outrage when he realized what had happened and that the tray of sweets had been moved out of his reach.

But his older brother, Robin, was there to soothe him. Taking a codlin tart, he broke it in two and handed each twin a half piece of the apple pastry. "That should keep them quiet for at least a few minutes," he said with a pleased grin as silence descended on the pair.

"I am afraid they are becoming cross. They missed their nap today, but there has been so much excitement, and I hated to exclude them," the Duchess said while eyeing the two, her hand hesitating near the bell pull. They might have to send for O'Casey, the twins' nanny, very soon.

"Robin seems to have silenced them," Rhea said, thinking her brother had grown a foot taller since she had last seen him. He was thinner too, but his dark hair was just as curly and unruly, and the expression in his violet eyes just as mischievous. She wondered what pranks he'd been up to recently.

"He hasn't been himself since you were kidnaped, Rhea," the Duchess said, reading Rhea's mind. "He has been so subdued, almost sullen. I think you have always been closer to him than anybody else. He's been brokenhearted, and I really despaired of ever seeing the old Robin again."

"He does seem quieter, even troubled, but every so often I see that same look in his eyes, which means he has been up to something," Rhea said. She'd been on the receiving end of too many of his pranks to rest easy now.

"I think, however, that Francis has changed the most this past year," Rhea remarked of her other brother, who, as firstborn son, was heir to Camareigh and the ancient dukedom. "I had never before realized that he bore such a startling resemblance to Father. The eyes are different, but there is a remarkable similarity in bone structure and in the way he carries himself."

"Yes," the Duchess agreed, thinking that Francis had matured into a handsome and dignified young man that past year. "Your father and I are very proud of both Francis and Robin. If it had not been for their timely interruption that day, well . . ." The Duchess hesitated, trying not to relive the terror of seeing Lucien brought back to Camareigh, blood dripping from his coat sleeve.

"Do not think of it, Mama," Rhea urged. "Have you sent word to Uncle Richard and Sarah?"

The Duchess nodded, grateful for the change of subject. "Your father sent word immediately. Butterick picked one of the best riders in the stables. Thomas may be no bigger than a boy, but he has years of riding experience. If anyone can reach the Highlands within a week, then he can."

"I was so pleased to hear about Uncle Richard's and Sarah's daughter. Lady Dawn Ena Verrick. 'Tis a lovely name," Rhea said, thinking of her own child, whether it would be a boy or a girl, and what name she and Dante would choose.

Sabrina Dominick had not missed her uncertain yet wistful expression. She still found it difficult to believe that her daughter would soon be giving birth to their first grandchild. Sabrina glanced over to where Lucien was sitting talking with Francis. It seemed only yesterday that they had met, then wed, then named their firstborn child Rhea Claire. The Duchess of Camareigh shook her head in dismay. The years were passing so quickly, yet Lucien seemed not to have changed. In her eyes he was still as handsome as he had been the first time she had seen him. Although he still possessed a haughty arrogance which some people mistook for coldness, he was a far more compassionate man today than he had been that first time she had crossed his path. Their life together at Camareigh had been blessed, and although the past year had brought its share of tragedy, all that was over now. The Dominick family had survived, and they would continue to do so for generations to come. The Duchess of Camareigh did not need her sister Mary's gift to know that for a certainty.

The Duchess glanced again at her daughter, wishing for her the same deep happiness that she had had in her marriage to Lucien. She could only hope that Dante Leighton was half the man Lucien was.

"Word has also been sent to Mary and Terence," the Duchess remarked, then added with a shrug, "not that it was necessary, for unless I am mistaken, Mary will have sensed your return to Camareigh. Most likely she has already been on the road for hours and will pass our messenger on the way. I have had rooms prepared for them in the north wing. I suspect young Betsie must think me quite mad, having her lay the fires in unoccupied rooms, but she will learn soon enough that one cannot be unprepared where Mary is concerned."

As if on cue, there came a sudden commotion beyond the closed double doors, and then they opened to admit a group of noisy people who surged forward into the room, apparently unconcerned about their welcome. It was Lady Mary, her husband, General Sir Terence Fletcher, and their seven children, Ewan, George, James, Anna, Stuart, Margaret, and John.

Heartfelt cries of "Rhea Claire! Rhea Claire!" resounded

throughout the room as the family, just arrived from Green Willows, their estate in the southern uplands of Wiltshire, spotted the familiar figure of Rhea sitting with her mother on the sofa positioned close to the hearth.

"I always do try to time my arrivals," Lady Mary Fletcher announced with a shy, gentle smile as she saw the tea service set up before her sister and niece and tried to make light of her sudden arrival.

"By now I should know better than to ask how you knew Rhea had returned," the Duchess said with a welcoming smile for her sister and her family, but she was always too curious not to inquire.

"We met your messenger halfway between here and Green Willows, and he accompanied us back to Camareigh," Lady Mary explained, hugging Rhea. "Oh, my dear, it is so very good to see you again. I always knew we would, but, well, there were days when I knew you were close to death. I felt so helpless, for I could do nothing for you," Lady Mary explained apologetically. Even after having the second sight for all of her life, she still had not decided whether it was a blessing or a curse. "'Twas strange, but I saw a ship docking in London, and then I saw a cat, although why I don't know," she said with a self-conscious laugh, "for Sabrina has always loved cats, not me. But there the creature was, and, then"—she paused for effect—"I saw a very familiar figure dressed in the palest of yellows, and then I saw Camareigh, and I just knew that you had come home," Lady Mary explained. Making herself comfortable on the sofa, she gratefully accepted her sister's invitation to warm her frozen hands and feet before the fire. "The trip between here and Green Willows does seem longer, and the roads worse, and the weather even stormier with each journey. Or perhaps my aching bones only make it seem so."

"A cup of tea, Mary?" the Duchess asked, taking up her duties as hostess. Rhea was engulfed by her cousins and would certainly be occupied for quite some time trying to answer all their questions.

"Now you are the mind reader," Mary said with a grin and, breathing deeply of the fragrant steam, sipped the warming tea while she eyed her niece. "Rhea is looking exceptionally well, Rina. I can scarcely believe she has returned to us, even though

I see her standing there. My prayers have been answered. And perhaps now I can get a good night's sleep without visions haunting me."

"I know you do not believe it possible, but your visions have always been a comfort to me and, indeed, most helpful," Sabrina told her sister, thinking of all the times through the years when a warning from Mary had saved not only her own life, but also the lives of many of the members of the Dominick and Fletcher families.

"Sabrina," Sir Terence Fletcher greeted his sister-in-law affectionately as he approached, Lucien at his side. Taking her hands in his, he kissed her cheek, then eyed her as he would have a member of his troop who had caused him displeasure. "I thought I left orders for you to take care of yourself? You know I am not accustomed to having my orders disobeyed."

"And as you well know, Terence, I have never been very good about following orders," the Duchess smiled, pleased to see her brother-in-law looking so well. Tall and distinguished, even with hair that had grayed considerably over the years, he still had about him that certain look of military authority. She could still remember the first time she had met him. It had been on the battlefield, and she had just witnessed the death of her Scots grandfather at English hands. She had been but a child of little more than eleven, and Colonel Sir Terence Fletcher had been the English officer she tried to kill that day. The Battle of Culloden seemed so long ago now, but the memory of the scarlet-coated battalions of the King's army, its blue, yellow, and green standards flying so high in Scottish skies, was still vivid. Little had she realized that one day the English officer would marry her sister and become a much loved member of their family.

"Indeed, and I shall never understand how or why Lucien has put up with it for all these years," Terence responded with a grin, for Sabrina always managed to rob him of any pretensions of being in control.

"Who says I have?" Lucien demanded. He was always more at ease with Terence and Mary than with any other people, except for Sabrina.

"I cannot tell you how very pleased I was to see Rhea Claire sitting here beside you. Long ago I gave up doubting Mary's gift, but when she said that she knew Rhea was at Camareigh, I was afraid to believe it. We have all hoped for this day for so long. However," Terence Fletcher added, sounding more like a general addressing his troops, "Lucien has informed me of an unexpected difficulty. Is there nothing we can do about this Dante Leighton? The man's conduct is outrageous, and he certainly should not be allowed to go unpunished. I think you have suffered enough without having to bear the disgrace of this man's effrontery."

Lady Mary paused in her selection of a small iced cake. "And who is this Dante Leighton?" she asked.

"I was just about to tell Mary about him when you joined us," Sabrina said, wondering just how to explain.

"It has to do with dragons, does it not?" Mary surprised them with her abrupt statement.

"How on earth did you know that?" Sabrina demanded, startled.

"If you will remember, I have been seeing the strangest red and green dragons since this whole affair began. I eventually understood about the green dragons, for The Merry Green Dragon was the name of the inn where Kate and her murderous associates stayed while planning the abduction," Lady Mary reminded her attentive audience. "But I never could understand this red dragon I kept seeing in my dreams until several months ago when you mentioned the name of the ship Rhea Claire was supposed to be aboard. But"—Lady Mary paused, her gray eyes bright with knowledge no one else could possess—"I had forgotten about it, for I had not had the vision in a couple of months. Then, four or five days ago, I started to see this grinning red dragon again. By then I was seeing Camareigh, and a ship docking, and that strange cat, so I forgot about the red dragon." She faced her sister and asked, "Why should this man have anything more to do with you? Except, perhaps, for answering your questions about his part in this whole affair?" Lady Mary puzzled. "Terence sounded quite upset. Has the man demanded the reward for Rhea's return? That truly would be quite outrageous, considering his part in this business."

"I shouldn't put it past the man at all," Lucien remarked, his eyes meeting Sabrina's as if warning her to expect the worst when she met Dante Leighton.

"Lucien is the only one, except for Rhea, who has met this man, but I fear that soon we shall all have the pleasure of his company," Sabrina predicted worriedly.

"The man would actually come to Camareigh?" Lady Mary asked in disbelief, for few people of her acquaintance were so uncouth to force themselves on unwilling hosts, and she certainly knew that the man had not been invited to Camareigh. "The man must be little better than a savage. Poor Rhea Claire, to have had to suffer the man's presence for so long. And am I to understand that the man is now actually trying to further that acquaintance by coming to Camareigh? I can certainly see why you must feel quite outraged by the impertinence of the man. Cannot he be arrested? Surely he must be out of favor with the authorities? I shouldn't let him get past the front gates, Lucien," Lady Mary advised her brother-in-law, and coming from the gentle Mary Fletcher, that sounded quite extraordinary.

"Mary, Dante Leighton is Rhea's husband," Sabrina announced bluntly, then added hesitantly, for it was a difficult announcement to make considering the circumstances, "and is the father of the child she is carrying."

Lady Mary Fletcher choked on her tea, her cough drawing Rhea's attention. She realized that they must have just told her Aunt Mary about Dante, and for the first time since Dante had put his ring on her finger, Rhea glanced down at it self-consciously. She had been feeling awkward as she recounted again, this time for her cousins' apparently insatiable curiosity, her adventures since being abducted from Camareigh. Rather than becoming easier, the telling was far more difficult now, for she had come to expect amazement, horror, outrage, and embarrassment from her listeners. As a result, she found herself constrained to defend Dante's honor and integrity at every turn. And glancing over to where her aunt and uncle were in earnest conversation with her mother and father, she knew that they too were discussing Dante Leighton, and from the expressions on their faces, it was only too obvious that he had not made any friends among that group.

If only Dante were here. Then there would not be this tense waiting, and any suspicions they were entertaining could, once and for all, be laid to rest.

Rhea glanced over at Francis, meeting his understanding gaze while she tried to respond to her young cousins' questions. Francis' reaction to her marriage and the news of her pregnancy had surprised her, for it had been one of thoughtful deliberation, as if he were reconstructing in his mind every detail of her experience. Apparently he was not happy with his conclusion. He left her in little doubt that he thought Dante Leighton had taken ungentlemanly advantage of her.

"And were they actually pirates, Rhea?" young Stuart Fletcher was demanding, his eyes round with excitement. His cousin had always been, after all, just a girl, but now she had risen considerably in his estimation.

"There was this one man, wasn't there, Rhea, who actually knew Blackbeard and saw his chopped-off head swinging from the bowsprit of one of His Majesty's ships," Robin chimed in, thinking he would like to have been aboard the *Sea Dragon* and met some of these pirates.

"'Tisn't true," Stuart said with a disbelieving shake of his rusty curls.

"My father met the man in London," Robin informed him knowingly. "His name was Longacres, and Father said he'd never seen a more bloodthirsty-looking pirate."

Stuart Fletcher's mouth dropped open in awe as he stared over toward his uncle's tall figure, for he'd always had the highest opinion of the Duke, even though he was Robin's father.

"You look prettier than ever, Rhea," ten-year-old Anna said shyly. "Are you really married?" she asked hesitantly, her freckled face mirroring admiration.

"Yes, Anna, I am truly wed," Rhea told her, holding onto that thought as she realized she was the only adult in the room who was the least bit pleased about the fact.

"What is your name now?" eight-year-old Maggie wanted to know.

"Lady Rhea Claire Jacqobi." Rhea said the name then silently repeated it to herself over and over again as her thoughts drifted to Dante. What was he doing? Was he thinking of her?

"I don't like the sound of this man, this Dante Leighton," James Fletcher was saying as he glanced at Rhea Claire out of the corner of his eye. "He doesn't sound acceptable," he added jealously, for he had long been in love with his cousin.

"It doesn't matter what you think, James," his elder brother Ewan told him with his usual practicality. "The deed is done."

"A villainous deed," James maintained stoutly, thinking he would certainly give the man the cold shoulder should he dare to show his face at Camareigh. Francis had filled them in on the man's unsavory reputation. "Isn't there *anything* that can be done?" he demanded, his youthful jealousy riding high.

"You could always call him out, Francis," George commented, still impressed by his cousin's showing that day when the Duke had been attacked. "There's only one of him. You should be able to deal easily enough with the blackguard," he said eagerly.

"From what I've heard about the man from my father, the man's a former privateer and smuggler, and he wouldn't be alive today to be troubling us if he weren't a cunning devil. No, he is safe, for Rhea Claire would never forgive any of us if we did him an injury," Francis informed them, disappointment only too evident in his flat tone.

"We could arrange an accident," James suggested hopefully as he met his brother George's appreciative grin.

"James, go and get yourself a creamed bun," Ewan told his younger brother in exasperation.

"Well, I think 'tis a good idea," James grumbled. But he decided to get the bun when he saw Rhea, his youngest brother John's hand clasped firmly in hers, head toward the tray.

The three cousins continued to stand in silence, and when Francis Dominick's speculatively narrowed blue-gray eyes met the thoughtful gaze of Ewan Fletcher, whose eyes shifted to meet the shrewd stare of his brother George, no words were necessary among the three. The cousins knew that if they had their way, they would see that Dante Leighton never set foot on the hallowed grounds of Camareigh, or ever again saw Rhea Claire.

"We could always waylay him on the road. Give him something to think about."

"Send him off, with a flea in his ear, eh?" George agreed.

"How about buying him off? I've quite a bit of my allowance still."

"Won't do, that. He's filthy rich," Francis regrettably informed them.

"Didn't marry Rhea for her fortune, then?"

"You could always put on one of your father's old wigs and, pretending to be the Duke, scare the man off. Threaten him with dire consequences."

"He's a marquis. 'Twouldn't impress him."

"Damn it all, anyway. Isn't there anything we can do?"

"S'pose we'll just have to be rude to the man. Nothing else for it."

"I could wing him. Hide in the bushes. That'd scare him," George suggested.

But, alas, calmer thoughts prevailed and the three dissatisfied cousins accepted the fact that there was little they could do. Only no one made certain that James understood there was nothing to be done about Dante Leighton.

That afternoon seemed to set the pattern for the days that followed, and soon a week had passed. Dante Leighton had yet to arrive at Camareigh. The days seemed unnaturally long for Rhea, even though each hour was filled with the happiness of being with her family.

But every so often her eyes would stray to the tall windows and the vista beyond, in search of that figure approaching the great house. Or she would suddenly still, listening for the distinctive sound of coach wheels rolling up the drive. But day after day she was disappointed. Finally, however, visitors arrived at Camareigh. But Rhea Claire was not standing at one of the tall windows overlooking the stately drive, and so she did not witness the arrival of the coach as it pulled up before the wide steps.

Rhea was in the Long Gallery, standing before the portrait of her great-grandmother, her father, and his twin cousins. Her thoughts were troubled as she stared at the two fair-haired children sitting beside a very young Lucien Dominick. To think that such evil had existed behind those two angelic faces, that so much grief had resulted from Kate and Percy's insane hatred and enviousness. Rhea's glance lingered for a second on the late Dowager Duchess, Claire Lorraine Dominick, whose purpose in living had been to see that the Dominick family continued to survive and that Camareigh remained forever great. In her desire to see her wishes come true, she had become obsessive. Because of her single-mindedness, she was partly to blame for Kate and Percy's own obsessions. She had neglected the cousins on the distaff side of the family, for they could not perpetuate the name of Dominick, and so those cousins had come to hate Lucien Dominick for being heir to the Dominick name, title, and fortune.

As Rhea Claire, victim of their madness, stood before that portrait, she couldn't help but think of Dante's obsession to return to Merdraco and, apparently, to wreak revenge on somebody he held responsible for all of the misfortunes that had come his way.

Rhea turned away from the portrait with a shiver of premonition that Mary Fletcher would have understood and hurried along the gallery, away from all that unhappiness.

She slowed her pace as she saw a gangling figure approaching. Unconsciously she felt for her golden chain and locket with the miniature portraits of her mother and father inside. The remembrance of the day she had lost it was only too hauntingly vivid, but thanks to the girl standing before her, a wide smile of contentment on her plain face, she once again possessed one of her treasures.

"Good morning, Alys," Rhea greeted her friend, remembering.

"Ah, 'tis a lovely mornin', m'lady," Alys declared, oblivious to the rain cascading against the windowpanes. "Now that ye've returned home, why, no day can be bad."

"You do like living here at Camareigh, Alys?" Rhea asked, though the look in the girl's bright blue eyes was answer enough.

"Oh, m'lady," Alys said, her grin widening, "'tis all ye said it was. I never expected to be seein' it, though."

"I hear you've been learning a great deal from Rawley."

"Oh, aye, a fine woman that Rawley is, but," Alys said, lowering her voice confidentially, "Her Grace says I'm to start helpin' O'Casey soon with the twins. Look forward to bein' with the little ones. Always have liked babies. But I don't believe in coddlin' them too much."

"I have a feeling that Andrew and Arden are in for a surprise," Rhea predicted, thinking that Robin had had it far too easy with O'Casey and that the twins were beginning to get out of hand as well, but with Alys Meredith as their nanny, they would find not only love and affection but a firm hand as well.

"M'lady?" Alys began awkwardly. "I never got the chance to thank ye proper like for keepin' your promise about not forgettin' me."

"It was my mother who asked you to stay here," Rhea protested. "I only wish I could have helped you that day we were torn apart in Charles Town."

"Oh, ye did ye best. I guess ye faced even worse later on, and here I was comin' to your home with ye still missin'. Didn't seem fair. But Their Graces were so kind, and when they asked me what I wanted to do with me life, well," Alys said with a shy smile, "I said 'twould suit me just fine to stay here at Camareigh, if they didn't mind, that is. Told them I'd be happy scrubbin' the scullery, but Her Grace, well, she wouldn't have anythin' to do with that. Says I'm a friend of her daughter's, and I could live here as a guest forever, but, well, I'm not one for bein' idle. Like to think I'm payin' me way. So Her Grace says I'm to work at whatever I want."

"I told you they were wonderful."

"Aye, m'lady," Alys agreed, her tone reverent.

"When I was in the Indies, everything was so perfect, except that I didn't know what had happened to you. Then Sir Morgan Lloyd informed us that you had returned to England and were most likely at Camareigh. I knew then that everything would turn out for the best. I was not surprised to find you still here, and happy, and now that I am with my family, I have no more worries about anything," Rhea stated, convincing herself that everything *would* work out; it had to.

But Alys Meredith, for all her unworldliness, was not convinced. She had overheard too many hushed conversations, seen too many worried faces, to believe that events would evolve exactly in the manner Lady Rhea Claire seemed to think they would.

"A pity 'tis raining, for I would like a walk in the gardens," Rhea said wistfully, and looking beyond the rivulets of water glistening on the windows, she imagined the yew-hedged walks that led to the sunken gardens where her passage would be reflected in the shimmering surface of the lily pond. She would not have lingered long, however, and soon would have left behind the neatly trimmed topiary gardens, for her destination was the natural beauty of the parkland, where a gently sloping meadow descended to a lake where swans drifted peacefully in the quiet.

"Oh, m'lady," Alys gasped. "I nearly forgot! There be visitors newly arrived. They be down in the—"

But Rhea waited to hear no more. With a rustling of her skirts and a discreet flash of silken ankles, she was through the gallery and quickly to the Chinese Room, the first-floor salon where visitors were usually greeted.

Past the liveried footmen she sped, stopping only once, to glance quickly into one of the tall pier glasses before she entered through the double doors of the Chinese Room.

A man was standing with his back to the doors, talking with her father. Her eyes on that tall figure, Rhea did not notice the other occupants of the room. "Dante!" she cried, stopping in her tracks when the man turned around.

"Lady Rhea Claire!" cried Wesley Lawton, Earl of Rendale, forgetting his gentlemanly dignity as he rushed toward her, his hands held out. "Good Lord! I've never seen you looking so beautiful," he exclaimed, momentarily forgetting himself. His eyes missed nothing of her appearance. Dressed in a taffeta gown of turquoise trimmed in lace and violet bows, her golden hair entwined with turquoise and violet ribbons, she was stunning. This was hardly what Wesley Lawton had been expecting to find upon seeing Rhea for the first time since she was kidnaped and he was struck down by those murderous ruffians.

Rhea went numb. She had been expecting to see Dante's face, not the florid face of Wesley Lawton. Although undeniably handsome, he suddenly seemed less refined when compared to Dante's classical features, and, indeed, the Earl seemed less masculine to Rhea's critical eye when she remembered Dante's lean build and bronzed skin. Dressed in a strawberry-colored satin coat and breeches, the height of fashion, the Earl seemed all pink and white and soft.

And suddenly Rhea could barely stand to have him touch her flesh. But she held on to her manners. "How very kind of you to say so, Wesley. And I must say it is gratifying to see you looking so well. I had, until arriving back in England, thought you dead."

"Good Lord, not really. My dear Rhea Claire, I am only sorry that I was unsuccessful in saving you from attack. Didn't even have the pleasure of putting a hole in that one blackguard's head," the Earl fumed, his manly dignity still smarting.

"Rhea Claire! 'Tis just wonderful to be seeing you again, and I swear 'tisn't fair that you should be looking so well after all you've been through," the strident voice Rhea remembered only too well sounded behind her. Turning around, she found herself staring into the sweetly smiling face of Caroline Winters. "And whatever have you done to your skin? Why, lud, but you're as brown as a stable hand," Caroline crowed.

"Caroline. Sir Jeremy," Rhea greeted them, but there was genuine warmth in her voice only for the latter.

"My dear, it is good to see you. I have been so concerned about your welfare, not to mention being concerned about your mother and father. They have suffered so much." Sir Jeremy gave Rhea a fond hug and kissed her cheek.

"How is your gout? No more bad bouts?" Rhea asked as she hooked her arm through his, thankful to be able to disengage herself politely from conversation with Wesley Lawton and Caroline.

"How kind of you to ask, my dear," Sir Jeremy beamed, touched. His own daughter seldom mentioned his fitness except to complain about his infirmities keeping her from traveling to London as often as she wished.

Caroline Winters sighed. She'd been privy to those tiresome details for most of the journey to Camareigh. Not one to let an opportunity go by, she quickly linked her arm with Wesley Lawton's, a smug smile setting on her plump face as she guided him to the sofa. But despite her attempts to capture his attention, the Earl's eyes never strayed from Rhea.

"I was telling your father that we would have arrived even sooner, but Caroline insisted on waiting for Wesley to arrive at Winterhall, for we knew that Lucien had sent word to him as well. We thought we should all travel together—so much safer nowadays. If something like what happened to you, my dear, can happen once, then it can happen again. Can't be too safe." Sir Jeremy coughed in embarrassment as he realized he'd brought up a subject best left forgotten. "Well, I s'pose, m'dear, you'd rather not speak of that. Tch, tch. 'Twas a tragedy."

But his daughter, whose avid curiosity often bordered on rude impertinence, wanted to hear everything about the rumors they had been hearing.

"Now, Father," Caroline complained, a pout forming on her lips, "since I nearly lost my life in the affair, I think I have a right to hear all about what happened to Rhea after she left England. 'Tis the least she can do. Why, I've never been the same since. I still have nightmares about that dreadful affair and those horrible men," Caroline said dramatically while fanning herself, lest she become too unnerved and possibly faint right into the arms of the Earl of Rendale.

"My dear, really," Sir Jeremy reprimanded his daughter for her insensitive curiosity. "Rhea need say nothing more about the unfortunate affair. We should be quite satisfied just to know that she is safely back at Camareigh. And, as I said before, Lucien," Sir Jeremy said to his longtime friend, "we are honored that you invited us here. After all, Rhea has been back only a little over a week."

"We consider you part of the family, Jeremy," Lucien said, refraining from emphasizing the *you* as he would have liked. He supposed that Jeremy Winters had done the best he could in raising his motherless daughter. She was, after all, his only child.

"Oh, Papa, do not be foolish. Why, I am Rhea's best friend, and I am only interested because I feel it is my duty to set right the scandalous gossip spreading through London about Rhea Claire. Oh, my dear," Caroline Winters said with a sly glance from beneath coyly lowered lashes, "you do realize that your reputation is, well, not quite..." She paused, as if too embarrassed to continue, but she was certain that Wesley Lawton caught her drift. And if there was one thing Wesley Lawton, Earl of Rendale, was concerned about, it was his good name. It just would not do for a man in his position to align with a woman whose reputation had been damaged, even if she were the daughter of the powerful Duke of Camareigh.

"Caroline!" Sir Jeremy interjected, his face turning a bright pink with embarrassed exasperation.

"Well, 'tis the truth," Caroline protested, glancing around as though she were being unjustly accused. "Why, I daresay that Rhea Claire is no longer considered quite as eligible a catch as she once may have been. Oh, I think it just too awful, but what can one do?" she asked with a fine show of concern for the friend she had always heartily disliked. Her envy of Rhea Claire Dominick's title and fortune, not to mention incredible beauty, had helped sour her disposition into one of perpetual discontent.

Having sought to put the other young woman out of countenance with her cleverly aimed barbs, she was therefore startled to hear Rhea's gentle laughter. Caroline's words of commiseration died on her lips.

"You are very kind to be so concerned about my welfare, Caroline," Rhea said, thinking Caroline Winters had not changed much in the past year, "but you needn't worry. You see, I am *indeed* no longer eligible, but only because I am already wed."

Caroline's squeal of shock was nearly drowned out by the Earl's exclamation of disbelief. But Caroline's shocked dismay turned to exultation as she realized that she need no longer compete with Rhea Claire for the attentions of Wesley Lawton.

"My dear, how absolutely wonderful!" she cried, speaking the truth for the first time in her life when complimenting her former rival.

"This is true?" the Earl said, his voice an undignified squeak.

"Yes," Rhea answered simply, her eyes searching out her father's. But the Duke was sipping a brandy, his thoughts apparently lost in the swirling movement of the liquid.

"B-but I do not understand. Whom did you marry? You've just returned from the colonies. There hasn't been time," the Earl protested. He had always believed that Lady Rhea Claire Dominick would someday become his wife. He had intended it since he'd seen her first, a little girl held in her mother's arms. It was only right that their families, both revered for centuries, be united by the marriage of himself and Rhea Claire.

Poor Wesley, Rhea thought, feeling a certain amount of pity for the poor, pompous Earl of Rendale. He looked devastated, and she was about to suggest her father offer him a brandy to bring back some of his color when he asked with a beseeching look, "It was not a colonial you wed? Or, heaven forbid, a sailor?" he demanded, thinking he would never again be able to show his face in London if he had lost out to some low-born lout with neither family name nor fortune. The humiliation of it was almost too much even to consider.

Rhea shook her head, a smile tugging at her lips. She knew that the saving grace for the Earl of Rendale would be that, although she had married a man of questionable reputation, her husband was a titled gentleman of both fortune and family. "My husband's name is Dante Leighton. He was the captain of the *Sea Dragon*, the ship I found myself aboard after leaving Charles Town, and the ship which returned me safely to England."

If the Earl of Rendale had been a dog he would have been put out of his misery, for never had there been such a suffering look on a man than on the Earl's pale face in that instant. "A sea captain?" he said weakly. The man was probably not even English, he thought, not with that Italian-sounding first name.

"Yes," Rhea admitted, enjoying prolonging his misery. For, really, what business was it of his? She even allowed Caroline a few more moments of basking in scandalous pleasure before she said, "Oh, did I not mention that Dante is the Marquis of Jacqobi?" Even the Duke had to smile at the abrupt change of expressions on the two faces.

"A marquis?" Caroline whispered in despair. Rhea Claire, despite her misfortune, had managed to marry a marquis. She was a marchioness now, with a title more exalted even than that of countess, which was what Caroline would possess if she ever managed to get the Earl's ring on her plump finger. It was just too much, thought Caroline, fanning herself in earnest this time, for she was definitely feeling faint.

"Jacqobi?" the Earl repeated the name. He prided himself on being familiar with the titled families of the realm. "A West Country family? Devonshire, that's it. They had a castle. Dates from about the eleventh century, I believe. The title is quite old, yes, indeed. A most revered title," he said with a sigh of relief, for although he had lost Rhea Claire, at least he had lost out to a marquis. But then he remembered something. "I believe I am familiar with this Dante Leighton, the current holder of the title. He was a gambler. He lost most of the family fortune, am I not correct?" he asked patronizingly as he thought of his own bank account and the considerable holdings he possessed all over the country.

"Yes. Dante has supported himself as a privateer these past years, since he left England."

"I seem to remember a bit of scandal associated with his name," the Earl added. "Nothing I heard firsthand, of course. I believe I am quite a few years younger than he is."

"Really?" Caroline breathed, her depression lifting as she realized that Rhea had married a fortune hunter. "Oh, my dear, I am sorry. I suppose you will be living on your own fortune. Or has His Grace cut you off without a farthing?" she asked hopefully.

"Dante is a very wealthy man," Rhea informed the crest-fallen Caroline. Rhea did not feel in the least guilty about enjoying the other young woman's obvious unhappiness. Her mother had told her about Caroline's reprehensible behavior when questioned about the kidnaping. She had been found lying unconscious on the side of the road the day of the kidnaping, but rather than admit she had no important information to give them about the kidnapers, she had lied outrageously in order to play up her own role in the drama. Her lies had misled the searchers for several days, as they tried to track down the Gypsies of the girl's story. The Duchess never had believed Caroline's hare-brained tale of evil Gypsies and a dancing bear and had never forgiven Caroline for her lies.

"I must say I am relieved to hear that, for I have never cared to learn of a fellow member of the House of Lords squandering a fortune, let alone an irreplaceable inheritance. If I thought someone other than a Lawton might one day be living in Rendale House, well, I should burn the place to the ground this very instant. Must preserve family tradition at all costs," he said fervently.

"How rich *is* your husband?" Caroline asked fearfully.

"While I was aboard the *Sea Dragon* we discovered a sunken Spanish galleon, and in its hold was a fortune in gold and silver ingots. The crew members are all quite wealthy men now. In fact, one of the men is intending to return home and buy the manor house of the family his father used to foot for. If it is not for sale, then he says he will build the most elegant, palatial estate this side of Yarmouth," Rhea said, thinking the *Sea Dragon*'s ex-bos'n would most likely succeed.

The punctilious Earl of Rendale winced. A member of the lower classes being in possession of a fortune could lead only to disaster. The upstarts would try to buy themselves respectability, and because many of the best families, through misfortune and mismanagement, now found themselves in dire straits, untitled and boorish vermin would someday be dining in some of England's best homes.

With a great heaviness in his heart, the Earl glanced around at the tasteful furnishings of the Chinese Room, thinking what a pity it was that there would be no union between their two great families. He gratefully accepted the brandy which the footman, dressed in blue and gold livery, was serving with a quiet dignity one found in all the servants at Camareigh.

Caroline Winters selected a plateful of delicate cakes from a platter, but for once her heart wasn't in it and she only pecked at the delectable pastry. Although Rhea Claire was no longer a threat to her becoming the next Countess of Rendale, Caroline felt no great satisfaction. It just wasn't fair! *Lady* Rhea Claire Dom—no, Jacqobi, had always had everything—grace, beauty, intelligence, wealth, and now she was married to a marquis. It just wasn't fair! Caroline sulked, eyeing Rhea's turquoise gown with envy.

Wiping a dab of cream from the corner of her mouth, a sudden thought struck Caroline as she realized that she had yet to meet this insufferable Dante Leighton, this irritating Marquis of Jacqobi. "Where *is* your husband?" she asked, her voice cutting across the room and into the conversation Rhea was having with her father.

"He is still in London, seeing to his ship and crew," Rhea explained. "But we expect him soon, do we not, Father?"

The Duke of Camareigh smiled. Sir Jeremy knew from experience that Lucien Dominick's smile was not a reflection of pleasant thoughts. "Undoubtedly the gentleman in question will come. A gambling man could not resist the challenge," he predicted wisely. "Or the odds." And whether they were in Dante Leighton's favor or against, only the Duke of Camareigh seemed to know.

> *Necessity brings him here, not pleasure.*
>
> Dante

Chapter 8

IT was one of those rare autumn days, summerlike in warmth, when Dante Leighton saw Camareigh for the first time. Golden sunlight slanted down on the honey-hued walls of the great house, which sat like a shining crown atop a gentle knoll. Its position afforded it a commanding view of the peaceful Somerset countryside.

The stately gardens and carefully maintained parklands of the magnificent estate were surrounded by woodlands of ancient oak and evergreen, interspersed with sunlit glades where brambles of wild berries glistened with ripening fruit. A fallow deer bolted from the tangles beside the narrow road that meandered into the vale, sending a flock of white-throated warblers into the sky.

Dante Leighton's pale gray eyes narrowed as he gazed into

the sun and followed the birds as they flew above the verdant fields and hedgerowed lanes that twisted past the whitewashed, thatch-roofed cottages of the village nestling along the banks of a stream. Cascading down from the gentle slope of hillside in the distance, the waters flowed beside the old stone mill and kept the big mill wheel turning, grinding the farmers' grain into flour and meal.

"Ooooh, *'tis* Camareigh, isn't it?" Conny Brady asked for what seemed the hundredth time, for every time their coach had passed by an estate where the residence could be viewed through wrought-iron gates, closed against the curious, he had voiced the same hopeful question.

Dante Leighton, sitting astride a sorrel-maned chestnut, surveyed the pastoral scene below, musing that this private domain of the Dukes of Camareigh must have changed little through the centuries.

Glancing back at the young boy, hanging half out of the opened coach window, Dante Leighton answered. "Yes, this is Camareigh."

Even had he not inquired directions of the smith in the last hamlet they had passed through, Dante Leighton would have known from Rhea's loving description that the great house of time-mellowed stone, its mullioned windows reflecting the last warmth of the day, was Camareigh. From his vantage point on the hillside, he had a clear view of the Dominick estate. The great house was H-shaped with two wings, running east and west, and intersected by towers. Clustered about the great house were the low-roofed outbuildings, the largest being the stables. The central portico was reached by a long, chestnut-lined drive surrounded by copper beech, maple, and birch, all aflame with crimson and gold.

But before reaching the tree-lined avenue to Camareigh, one would have to gain access through the double, wrought-iron gates standing guard at the entrance. Reinforcing those barriers was a gatekeeper's cottage where, no doubt, several bloodthirsty mastiffs kept the gatekeeper and his well-primed blunderbuss company. Dante Leighton wondered what orders the gatekeeper and groundsmen had been issued concerning the arrival of an unwanted son-in-law.

"Aren't we going any farther?" Conny Brady asked in growing concern as Dante Leighton continued to sit astride the big stallion he rode with such ease. The young cabin boy, who'd never ridden anything except the rigging, wondered if there was anything his captain couldn't do.

Houston Kirby risked a glance out of the coach window, finding Camareigh just as impressive as he'd anticipated. He had a feeling similar to when he had faced cannon fire: There was no turning back. They were in the enemy camp and, except for Lady Rhea Claire, they had no allies. As Dante Leighton urged his mount down the curving road, the coach rumbling along in a cloud of dust behind him, the little steward realized that there would be no slipping quietly into Camareigh. Half the valley, especially someone in one of those golden towers, was probably watching their slow, noisy progress right then.

They traveled along the same lane that Lucien Dominick's cousin Kate and her cohorts had come down a year earlier, only this time it was Conny Brady who was craning his head out of the window time and time again, just to make certain that the great house, which was still just visible through the trees, had not vanished. After a few moments, Dante slowed his pace, allowing the coach to close the gap between them. They were entering the parklands of Camareigh, but still had quite a way to travel before the columned Dominick home. As Dante Leighton glanced back to inform an impatient Conny Brady and Houston Kirby of that fact, two riders appeared out of nowhere, their mounts blocking the road. One of them fired a shot into the ground in front of Dante's horse.

All hell broke loose. And then, just as suddenly, James Fletcher's and Lord Robin Dominick's plans went awry.

Their intended warning, "Halt and go no farther, or face death!" was never voiced, for the sudden, loud pistol report frightened the team of horses drawing the coach, and as the leaders reared, neighing with fear while their hooves raked the air and the startled coachman's whip cracked above their heads, Dante Leighton's mount bolted. Despite the coachman's curses, the panic-stricken team followed suit.

Dante just barely managed to keep his seat while holding the reins firmly in one hand, and, gently patting the stallion's sweating neck, he spoke quietly. He had just about calmed the horse, bringing those galloping hooves back to an even trot, and was straightening in the saddle when an overhanging bough caught him across the head and shoulders, knocking him off the horse.

The team, also under control, had been halted just around the curve, allowing Conny Brady and Houston Kirby, who had quickly jumped from the dangerously rocking vehicle, a clear view of Dante Leighton being unseated from his mount.

Conny Brady let out a yell and began to run toward the fallen rider, a look of horror on his face as he stared down at the crumpled form. Houston Kirby, a little bit slower to reach his master's side and breathless from the effort, squatted beside the unconscious Dante Leighton, deeply concerned. Blood was seeping from a wound on the captain's ashen brow.

"He's dead, isn't he?" Conny cried, his voice carrying to the two boys, who, having quickly brought their own mounts under control, had hurried to the fallen rider.

"*Is* he dead?" Robin Dominick asked hesitantly as he stood beside a brokenhearted Conny Brady. And from the look of the gentleman lying there so strangely still, young Lord Robin Dominick had the awful feeling that the gentleman was indeed dead.

"Lord, we've done it now," James Fletcher mumbled through stiff lips, wishing he'd never overheard Francis and his brothers talking about waylaying Dante Leighton on the road.

Houston Kirby, having ascertained that the captain was indeed still alive, spared the strangers a glance, noticing for the first time the oddness of their dress. Although they were but young fellows, they were dressed in old-fashioned wigs. And from the peculiar bumps and mounds underneath their coats and vests, it seemed they had stuffed their clothing to give the impression of being much older. "Ye meant to kill him?" he asked them harshly, his eyes not missing the pistol held by the larger of the two boys. From the embarrassed, guilty looks on their faces, Kirby knew they had intended mischief and guessed it had gotten out of control.

James Fletcher suddenly seemed to have become deaf and dumb, for he continued to stare down in horrified fascination at the stream of blood trickling from the bruised flesh of the gentleman's forehead. He felt sick as he remembered the pistol he was still carrying. Too late, he realized that the man kneeling beside the injured Dante Leighton had seen it.

"We only meant to scare him off," Robin Dominick finally said, a little spurt of blood appearing where he'd been chewing on his lower lip. "No one wanted him to come to Camareigh!" Robin added defiantly, thinking that none of this would have happened if Rhea had not been kidnaped from Camareigh. Then everything would still be the way it had always been.

"And who are ye to be sayin' such a thing?" Kirby demanded of the little boy, but when he met the violet eyes so identical to Lady Rhea Claire's, he needed no introduction.

"I am Lord Robin Dominick. I live at Camareigh, and I know that nobody wants this Dante Leighton to come and take Rhea away!"

"So ye thought ye'd be takin' matters into your own hands, eh?" Kirby asked softly, pitying the young boy. Obviously he had acted on his own, without the consent of his family. "Nobody knows what ye've gone and done, do they, lad?" Kirby asked.

"O-of course they do! I told you the family doesn't like this Dante Leighton. We want him to go back to the colonies. Rhea doesn't love him. She said she never wanted to see the blackguard's face again as long as she lived. She doesn't want anything to do with any of you people she met while away from Camareigh. Why can't you just take him and leave?" Robin tried to bluff his way out of the predicament.

"It isn't true!" Conny Brady said, his mouth dropping open with incredulity. "She loves the cap'n. And she said I could come to Camareigh to see her. She wouldn't change her mind, would she, Mr. Kirby?" Conny Brady asked, his voice wobbly as he wondered if it might indeed be the truth.

"Of course not, lad," Kirby reassured him absently, his attention on the captain. There was nothing to do now but try to get him into the coach and then to Camareigh. Not exactly the way the captain had planned to arrive, Kirby thought, shaking his head. He sighed, wondering why there always had to be complications. At least this way they would get past the wrought-iron gates. Even the Duke of Camareigh wouldn't turn away an injured man.

Misinterpreting the little steward's mood, Conny Brady

reached out a hand and grabbed Robin Dominick by the lacy
stock folded so neatly around his neck.

"You killed him!" Conny Brady yelled as he eyed the small,
dark-haired boy. This was Lady Rhea Claire's young brother,
the boy she had always spoken of so lovingly, and who would
always come first in her heart. This pampered, rich little lord
had murdered the only person who had ever really cared about
him. He would avenge the captain's death. "I'll make ye pay
for this, ye cowardly, sly-faced cur! And Lady Rhea Claire
does love the captain. She'll *hate* ye for murderin' him!"

"I didn't murder him! And she won't hate me! She won't!"
Robin yelled back, realizing that this unmannered, scrawny-
looking boy was none other than that Conny Brady Rhea had
spoken about so much and seemed so fond of.

Robin tried to pull his neckcloth free of the upstart's grubby
hands, but the boy had too good a hold on it and didn't seem
to want to let loose, in fact, he was twisting it tighter by the
second. Robin gritted his teeth. Glaring at Conny Brady's grim
face, he kicked him in the shin. The other boy's yelp of pain
was satisfying to Robin, but only for a second, for before he
knew it, his feet had been knocked out from under him and
Conny Brady, an orphan boy wearing his first really fine pair
of breeches and matching coat, had landed on top of him.

Houston Kirby stared in amazement as the two boys rolled
and wrestled and traded punches in the middle of the lane. The
other young man tried to separate them but quickly found his
own feet knocked out from under him as he sat down abruptly
in a mud puddle.

The coachman climbed down from the box and approached
the scene of chaos, with a wide grin on his face. The two
fighting boys were spirited enough and, being of a similar age
and size, it looked to be a good fight.

"If ye can be sparin' me a moment, I could use a hand
helpin' his lordship into the coach," Houston Kirby suggested
none too politely. "We'll have to move him carefully," Kirby
told the man now that he'd finally managed to catch his attention.

They were half lifting, half dragging Dante Leighton when
a rider approached from the direction of the great house.
Houston Kirby glanced up, thinking to demand assistance, but

the words died on his lips as he stared into the scarred face of
the Duke of Camareigh himself.

Oh, Lord, Houston Kirby thought, wondering how he could
possibly defend the captain against whatever the Duke might
have in mind, now that His Grace had the captain of the *Sea
Dragon* at his mercy. But Houston Kirby was to be pleasantly
surprised, for Lucien Dominick quickly dismounted and hurried
to their side, lending a hand as if he were lifting a dear friend.

"What has happened?" he demanded as he helped the little
steward place Dante Leighton on the coach seat.

Houston Kirby opened his mouth to speak but didn't know
quite what to say. How could he tell the Duke of Camareigh
what his own son had done? But explanations were unnecessary, for at that moment the Duke's gaze found the two com-
batants slugging away at each other, James standing helplessly
to one side.

"James!" the Duke of Camareigh's voice pierced through
the daze James Fletcher had been lost in. With an even greater
feeling of disaster, that young man turned to see his uncle
approaching.

James Fletcher was the only one of the three young men
whom Lucien Dominick recognized, for the other two were
coated in clinging mud. However, when the two boys felt a
viselike hand gripping them and glanced up to encounter the
unsympathetic, displeased gaze, the mystery was solved. The
Duke knew the violet eyes of his son only too well, and, since
Dante Leighton was lying unconscious in the coach, the other
boy could be none other than Constantine Magnus Tyrone
Brady.

"I shall have an explanation of this affair, and from both
of you young gentlemen, although I do use the word with some
reservations," he said in that cold tone that Robin had heard
too often. There would be no peace of mind for Robin. "You,"
the Duke ordered Conny, "will climb into the coach and accompany your captain and Mr. Kirby to Camareigh. And you,
Robin, will climb back on your horse, which I see has wandered
down the lane a fair distance, and return to Camareigh. Once
you have made yourself decent, I shall expect to see you in
my study," he told his son, whose bent head was almost proof
enough of guilt.

"And, you, James," the Duke commanded of the young man who, having thought himself overlooked, was beginning to walk away. At the sound of his name, he halted. "I shall have an explanation from you while we ride back to Camareigh together," the Duke pronounced the death sentence on the hapless young man who had yet to face his own father, the general.

Dante Leighton awoke to a steady pounding in his temple. Groaning softly, he raised a hand to the aching spot and was surprised to encounter a soft bandage wrapped around his forehead. Opening a wary eye, he glanced around at his surroundings and was surprised yet again. He was not lying in the road but in a very comfortable four-poster bed with embroidered hangings and a matching quilted comforter which someone had carefully placed around his bare shoulders. The tall, mullioned windows were draped in sea green Italian silk damask hangings, drawn against the cool evening air. A cheerful fire was burning in the hearth, and while firelight danced on a woman he had never seen before, a clock on the pilastered mantel chimed the hour. The woman sleeping was in a high-backed wing chair upholstered in rose silk brocatelle, and even though she was sleeping, she had a watchdog look about her.

Keeping a watchful eye on her, Dante looked for the door, but it was on the far side of the room, and he would have to pass right in front of the woman in order to reach it, though why he should feel threatened in so lovely a room, he wasn't certain. He was being treated well: A bouquet of fragrant flowers was scenting the room from its china vase on a mahogany dressing table, while a silver tea tray sat on a small table just out of reach of his bed. As Dante glanced curiously around the room, he noticed for the first time the crystal goblet of brandy sitting on the bedside table within easy reach of his outstretched arm. With an appreciative sigh, he reached out and captured it, drinking all of it without hesitation.

Caught unawares, he choked, then coughed, a comical look of disbelief forming on his face as he eyed the evil-tasting brew that looked so much like brandy. "What the devil?" he exclaimed.

"I see ye've come to your senses at last," the woman commented from her place by the hearth, apparently unimpressed by the angry glint in Dante Leighton's pale gray eyes. "Best thing for clearin' your head of fog."

"Good Lord, woman. You could have killed me with this poison," Dante accused her. Sniffing the dregs, he questioned, "It *isn't* poison, is it?"

"Well, some think 'tis as bad as that when they're swallowing it, but later, when the roses come back to their cheeks, they aren't complainin'." The woman crinkled her wrinkled face with amusement.

"Madam, I have never desired to have roses in my cheeks," Dante informed the complacent busybody.

"Might d'ye some good, m'lord, if ye did. Never seen such a pale face, especially seein' how dark-skinned ye be from the sun. Mrs. Taylor's Special Treat will have ye back on your feet in no time," she said with the full irritating knowing air of someone who never had to take the medicine herself. "Ain't seein' double, are ye? Nor feelin' woozy?"

"Well, if I wasn't woozy before, then I certainly am now," Dante said, thinking how well she and his at times infuriating steward would get along. "And if I may be so bold as to inquire," Dante asked silkily, glaring at the unsympathetic woman, "just who the devil are you? And where is Kirby? And Conny Brady? And where the devil am I?"

"Ooooh, feelin' better, we are. Told ye, didn't I?" the woman said with a sniff, reminding Dante Leighton even more of his irritating little steward. "Well, now, *I* am Rawley. And *your* Mr. Kirby has gone down to the kitchens to prepare ye a meal. A more insufferable and bossy little man I've not had the pleasure of meeting. *Your* young Master Brady has finally been settled in another chamber, and a more ill-mannered and noisy young lad I've not had the pleasure of meeting either," Rawley informed him, leaving him in no doubt that she disapproved of all three of them. "Ye be a guest at Camareigh."

Dante Leighton was surprised, for although he had thought the room too elegantly furnished to be an inn, he could not believe that he had actually made it through the gates of Camareigh. His sudden chuckle startled Rawley. As she came closer with the tea table, she watched the gentleman carefully out of the corner of her eye and wondered if the stories were true. Had Lady Rhea Claire married herself a pirate? He certainly looked and acted the devil despite being a marquis.

"I am curious, Rawley," Dante asked politely, his sudden smile halting Rawley in her tracks and warming her heart as no other smile had ever done. "Why do you consider Conny Brady ill-mannered? I can well understand your feelings about Kirby, for he is set in his ways, but Conny?"

Rawley sniffed, placing her hands on her hips. As she eyed the relaxed man in the bed, she realized that all the tension had left him as soon as he'd learned he was at Camareigh. He seemed to feel in control of the situation, which was strange for a man lying on his back in bed.

"Well, seein' how ye was unconscious at the time," Rawley began, and as she faced the pale eyes of the captain of the *Sea Dragon* she suddenly felt uneasy. The man had a way of staring at you, as if daring you to lie to him. "Ye missed what happened after ye fell from yer horse."

"If I remember correctly, I was knocked from my mount after he bolted because of a shot fired directly in front of him." Dante's gaze narrowed as he saw her fidget nervously. "I take it you are familiar with my two would-be assassins?" he inquired smoothly.

"Oh, m'lord," Rawley said quickly, lest more damage be done, "they didn't mean any harm. Certainly not what happened. They only meant to frighten ye away from Camareigh. That was all," Rawley reassured him, hoping he was a reasonable gentleman. "'Twas just a childish prank."

"They?"

Rawley swallowed, wondering how it was she was having to explain all of the misunderstandings to this Dante Leighton? "'Twas young Lord Robin and his cousin, James Fletcher. They only thought to help," she explained, thinking it wisest to clear the air right then. Besides, it would save His Grace the embarrassment of having to explain and apologize to the man.

"Help me into a grave, that is," Dante said coldly. "Lord Robin? Ah, I do remember. Rhea's young brother. She warned me that he was usually up to mischief of some kind or another," Dante said reflectively, "but I had no idea how dangerous a youngster he was. I shall have to be on my guard in the future."

Rawley bit her lip. "Ye needn't worry, m'lord. Lord Robin was soundly disciplined by His Grace. I fear he'll not be sittin' down for a week of Sundays, nor will Master James. The general threatened to send him to his old sergeant major for some proper disciplining. Scared the poor lad half out of his mind, it did. Never heard such pleadin' that he'd never do anythin' bad again. Of course, we all knew that young James has been in love with Lady Rhea Claire since he's been out of swaddlin', so he couldn't help himself, really he couldn't."

"I s'pose Conny Brady was quite vocal in his defense of me?" Dante guessed.

"A bit more than vocal, m'lord," Rawley admitted. "He and Lord Robin came to fisticuffs on the road, and that was when His Grace came along and broke them apart. Don't know which one fared worse. Both have blackened eyes and swollen lips, not to mention teeth marks that'll most likely become infected. His Grace, well, never seen him so angry as when he stormed into the house and saw ye settled in here."

Dante Leighton seemed genuinely startled. "Lucien Dominick *personally* saw that I was brought to Camareigh?" he asked in disbelief.

"Aye, says I'm to see t'yer every need, and that nothin' was to happen t'ye while ye was a guest under his roof. He says that there has already been enough bloodshed and unhappiness caused by people tryin' to take matters into their own hands, and just because a person isn't likin' the way things are, that doesn't give them the right to try to change them—especially by foul means. Heard him sayin' this to Her Grace and to the rest of the family, which included the Fletchers and Lord Robin. Madder'n some hornet, he was," Rawley said with a shake of her grizzled head as she remembered all she had overheard.

Dante Leighton was astonished. Never had he thought to find an ally in the Duke of Camareigh. As he thought about it, he saw that he just might have to thank young Lord Robin for inadvertently assisting him in gaining access to Camareigh. And to his wife.

As though reading his thoughts, Rawley said, "Her ladyship's been in here all night long. She's been sittin' by yer side since ye was brought in here, but His Grace ordered her to get some rest, to think of her child. He says not to worry, that ye would be safe here. He promised her."

Dante smiled slightly. "That was one thing I always respected about Lucien Dominick. He was a gentleman, no matter what. Maybe I am not so unlucky in my choice of father-in-law?" he speculated, thinking that if he'd managed to gain some small support from the Duke, then the Duchess would be no problem at all.

"Aye, ye could do worse, m'lord. Of course, there is the Duchess still," Rawley said, once again reading his mind. That was a meeting she would like to witness!

"How is Rhea Claire? The journey from London was not too tiring for her?" Dante asked, wishing morning would come and he could hold her in his arms again.

"Oh, fine. Especially now that she is back home again. Reckon ye'll both be stayin' here awhile, now," Rawley predicted slyly.

Dante raised a questioning brow. "Indeed? That is something we shall have to decide."

"Well, unless I'm mistaken, m'lord, ye ain't goin' nowhere fast on that broken ankle of yours."

For the first time since he had recovered consciousness, Dante became aware of the throbbing in his ankle. Frowning with disbelief, he started to throw off the comforter and swing his feet to the floor.

"I wouldn't be doin' that if I was ye, m'lord," Rawley warned, thinking this Dante Leighton was a headstrong one for sure. "Seein' how ye ain't got no breeches on. Oh, don't be mindin' me, for I've seen just about everythin' a man has to offer. Worked in a London brothel for a while, till I got bored, that is. But I was thinkin' about your modesty, m'lord," she warned him in that insultingly offhand fashion that left him feeling about as masculine as a lad still in the nursery. Dante Leighton, who over the years had come to heed good advice, hesitated long enough to feel the cool draft sneaking beneath the bedcovers and over his bare skin. Resettling himself against the pillows, he eyed the smug-looking Rawley with suspicion.

"You *are* certain it is broken?" he asked doubtfully, thinking the woman had yet to prove her worth to him.

"Aye. Seen enough broken bones in my day to know what

I'm talkin' about. Even that short, sour-faced man of yours, who hasn't enough meat on his bones to feed a bird, agrees with me. Reckon he's seen enough swollen and bruised flesh to know what he's talkin' about, too," Rawley grudgingly admitted, as if holding Dante Leighton personally responsible for the actions of Houston Kirby.

And at that precise moment, as if he'd been standing just outside listening for his cue, Houston Kirby bustled into the room. Looking for all the world like a bird with ruffled feathers, the little steward cast an uneasy glance at the gaunt-faced woman who seemed to know so much and wasn't in the least bit shy about letting a person know that she did.

Houston Kirby sniffed in annoyance as he noted the empty goblet beside the captain's bed, but he was too pleased to see the captain awake to question him about the noxious brew that this Rawley woman had prepared with such vigor, and had succeeded in getting the captain to down.

"How ye feelin', m'lord?" he asked, thinking it best to be using the captain's proper title now that they were among decent folk. His master would get better service that way, for one thing.

"Like hell," Dante answered while he rubbed the back of his head.

"Not surprised, for ye took a fair crack to your head from that bough," the little steward agreed.

"And apparently to my ankle as well."

"Oh, already tried to get out of bed, did ye?" Kirby said, not at all surprised by his captain's reckless actions, and having personally removed his captain's breeches, he now eyed the stiff-backed Rawley with renewed interest.

"He didn't get far," Rawley felt obliged to declare, and despite her claims to the contrary, a pale pink was staining her thin cheeks.

"Well, glad to know that all of the sense wasn't knocked out of ye, m'lord," Kirby said with a chuckle as he placed his tray on the table beside the bed. "Brought ye some broth, me *own* special recipe," Kirby informed him, feeling much better now that he was back in charge of the captain's convalescence. "We'll have ye back on your feet in no time at all."

"Aye, that *we* will, m'lord. Now, if ye gentlemen will be

excusin' me, I'll be about my usual duties," Rawley said with a sniff that bettered any Houston Kirby could have summoned. "Got to be tellin' Lady Rhea Claire that ye've awakened."

"Don't disturb her," Dante said sharply, halting the woman in her tracks as easily as if she'd been a member of his crew.

Rawley hesitated. She worked for the Dominicks, but this gentleman sounded so authoritative. And he was, after all, Lady Rhea Claire's husband. His wishes would have to be followed. Besides which, he was right. Seeing how concerned he was about her ladyship, her opinion of Dante Leighton rose considerably. Just maybe he wasn't as bad as she'd first thought.

"Very well, m'lord. Was thinkin', myself, that it'd be better to let the young lady rest," Rawley agreed.

"Interferin', know-it-all woman," Kirby grumbled as he watched Rawley leave the room.

"Have you seen Rhea Claire?" Dante asked.

"Aye, lookin' as pretty as ever, even though worried half out of her mind about ye," Kirby informed Dante as he handed the captain the steaming bowl of broth.

"Am I correct in understanding that His Grace saw that I arrived at Camareigh safely?" Dante asked, still doubting his good fortune.

"Aye, helped lift ye into the coach himself, he did," Kirby said. "Thought at first he'd come to finish ye off, but surprised me by lendin' a hand. A real fine gentleman, he is."

"Have you met the Duchess yet?" Dante asked as he took a spoonful of broth. When the little steward remained silent, he glanced up curiously and had his third surprise of the night. Houston Kirby was actually blushing with embarrassment. Never before had Dante Leighton seen the little man looking so uncomfortable, even distressed. "What is wrong?"

"Nothin'."

"Come now, Kirby," Dante invited the other man's confidence, "you can tell me, can't you? You didn't get in an argument with the woman, did you? Lord, that would do it. I had hoped to greet Rhea's mother on a cordial note."

"Oh, no, 'twasn't anythin' like that," Kirby sighed. "Her Grace is the loveliest, most beautiful and kind lady I've ever laid eyes on. An angel, she is, m'lord. I can see that Lady Rhea takes after her, yes indeed."

Dante Leighton stared, incredulous. Never had Houston Kirby seemed so impressed by a woman. The only two women Dante ever had known the steward to accept had been Rhea Claire and Dante's mother, Lady Elayne.

"Why, you old sea dog," Dante murmured affectionately, and Houston Kirby glanced up gratefully, knowing the captain would say naught of this to a living soul. "I am sorry I did not have the pleasure of meeting this paragon."

"Ye did, only ye was unconscious at the time," Kirby told a startled Dante Leighton. "Oh, don't worry. Ye was decent. They'd just brought ye in and laid ye on the bed when she and Lady Rhea Claire came in. Her Grace was tryin' to calm the young lady down, for ye was lookin' pretty poorly. Thought ye was dead, she did. Never seen such an upset young lady. Reckon she still loves ye," Kirby said, sounding as if he had yet to approve of the relationship.

Dante Leighton relaxed against the pillows, feeling far better than he had since crossing bows with young Lord Robin Dominick and the other far from friendly young fellow.

"Wouldn't be lookin' so smug if I was ye. We've still a long way to go before we're accepted by this family," Kirby advised.

"Did Her Grace say anything?"

Houston Kirby sniffed. "Stood here beside your bed for a while, eyein' ye good. Don't reckon them bonny eyes missed a thing about ye, m'lord. Can't say, though, they was exactly friendly, or admirin'," Kirby said, taking the empty bowl.

"If she was of a mind similar to her young son's, then I am surprised she didn't whack me on the head while I lay unconscious," Dante said, yawning sleepily. "Are you certain she did not have a pistol tucked away in her shawl?"

"Ye wouldn't be sayin' that if ye could have seen that sweet face. Why, I don't s'pose there could be a less bloodthirsty person alive. Her Grace, bein' so small and dainty, struck me as a gentle and kindhearted lady who'd probably faint dead away at the sight of a pistol, much less know how to use one," Kirby defended her fiercely.

"Rhea looked sweet and innocent enough at first, yet she

nearly set afire our treasure map," the captain of the *Sea Dragon* reminded the little steward. Dante Leighton yawned again, his eyelids feeling heavy as he made himself more comfortable against the pillows Kirby had just plumped beneath his shoulders.

"Ye're feelin' pretty smart about gettin' into Camareigh, ain't ye, m'lord?" the little steward demanded with a suspicious glint in his eye, for the captain wasn't above pulling a trick or two if he thought it would help him achieve his aims. "If I hadn't seen ye knocked from that horse with my own eyes and seen that bump on your head and an ankle twice its size, I would be suspectin' ye of bein' up to one of your deceptions."

The Marquis of Jacqobi opened a lazy eye. "'Tis a pity I didn't think of it before that fire-eating brother of Rhea's did, for I would not have been quite so excessive. A sprained ankle at the most," Dante declared, thinking he would have to have a word with Robin Dominick. Either that or develop eyes in the back of his head.

Drowsily, Dante stared into the flames, fascinated by their flickering lights. When next he woke, Rhea Claire was sitting in the rose silk chair, and the fire was but a few glowing cinders.

"Little daffadilly," he murmured.

"Dante!" she cried in relief as she jumped to her feet.

"I've not been forgotten?" he asked as she sat down gently on the edge of the bed, her violet eyes searching his face for any sign of fever.

"Did you really think I could?" Her sweet smile changed to a different kind when she felt his arms sliding around her waist. He pulled her against his bare chest.

"I've missed you, Rhea," Dante whispered against the softness of her golden hair. "I haven't been truly warm since you left my bed."

"'Tis just as well then that we are reunited, for winter is coming quickly," Rhea said, sounding so practical that Dante winced, but before he could complain of the cold welcome, she had wrapped her arms around his neck and pressed her lips against his, taking the initiative away from him.

"I may be invalided because of this damned accident, but I've not lost my male instinct, no matter how unimpressed this

Rawley woman is," Dante said, his breath warm against her mouth.

Rhea laughed softly. "So you have met our Rawley?"

"Not only Rawley, but also some foul concoction called a 'special treat,'" Dante informed her with an injured look. "I still believe the woman meant to do me in. Now, *that* is carrying loyalty too far," Dante grinned.

"My poor sweetheart," Rhea said. After all, she had been brought up on Mrs. Taylor's Special Treat.

"I shall expect very loving care from you if I am to recover," he warned her.

Rhea's smile faded and her eyes clouded. "Dante, I—I do not know what to say. How can I explain my brother? He was acting out of love for me. Can you find it in your heart to forgive him? I could not bear it if you and Robin did not like one another," Rhea told him, pleading. To her vast relief, Dante smiled. How could he condemn in another the same passion he himself felt for Rhea? He knew that he, too, could not be held accountable for his actions should anything threaten his beloved.

"You are not angry?"

"I was, but perhaps not anymore. If he would allow me, I could commiserate with this Robin about the pains and joys of loving you," Dante admitted.

Rhea rested her head against Dante's shoulder, beginning to hope that all would be well now that Dante had arrived at Camareigh.

> *For Satan finds some mischief still*
> *For idle hands to do.*
>
> Isaac Watts

Chapter 9

"NOW, where did that mishief-maker get to?" Houston Kirby demanded of no one in particular as he stomped along the corridor. Glancing up, he encountered the haughty, cold stares of countless, nameless Dominick ancestors gracing the walls of the Long Gallery, and he slowed his pace and proceeded more circumspectly, for it never was wise to disturb the dead.

"Warned him, I did. Won't put up with none of his usual nonsense, I said. But does that flea-bitten, rascally tom listen?" the little steward demanded of himself, a grievous look settling on his face as he glanced around the quiet room, imagining what mischief the cat was up to at that very instant. But there was no trace of Jamaica. All was quiet. He should be grateful for small favors, Kirby thanked his lucky stars, for the room wasn't in a shambles. That was more than he could say for the kitchens.

Not over an hour past he had seen the orange and white tabby being chased from the kitchen by a broom-wielding scullery maid. And upon investigating further, being prepared even to come to the miserable feline's defense should it come to that, he had found, instead, the kitchen in an uproar with the staff threatening to mutiny.

The cook, despite being tiny, was raising hell while swinging a frying pan like so much gossamer. Mrs. Peacham was in charge of an incredible domain of copper pots and pans, newly washed china, and fats dripping from savory-smelling meats roasted on spits in the giant stone hearth which occupied the whole south end of the kitchen. Steam rose from countless kettles and black iron pots, and drying herbs, hanging in bunches from the rafters, added their spicy scents to the room.

Much to Houston Kirby's chagrin, though not his surprise, a thieving tomcat known by the name of Jamaica had sneaked into the room and, undetected until too late, licked clean a plate of freshly baked salmon, followed by a selection of kidneys and bacon. He had even managed to take a bite from a slice of beef. All of his meal had been destined for the family's breakfast.

Houston Kirby was muttering under his breath as he left the Long Gallery and turned toward the south wing and the rooms belonging to the Dominick family and their guests. Dante Leighton was in one of those rooms, and Houston Kirby decided that was where Jamaica had ended up. No one would dare skin an inch of fur from that feline's back while he enjoyed the protection of the captain.

Kirby had just about reached the corridor leading back into the wing when he noticed that the double doors of one of the rooms were ajar. Lying just outside the opened doors was a small piece of half-chewed meat. Kirby smiled. He had the thief cornered.

"Ah-hah! Got ye now, ye scurvy, hell-born piece of ballast!" he cried out as he jumped into the room, slamming the doors shut behind him. As he glared around, his knees nearly gave out. He was staring at the stunned face of the Duchess of

Camareigh. In her lap was none other than the conniving tom himself.

"Oh . . . nooo! Your Grace!" Kirby wailed in mortification, his bright red face the picture of abject misery. "Oh," he repeated, unable to find his wits.

Sabrina, Duchess of Camareigh, smiled. It was either that or start laughing, and that would never have done. "This *is* your cat, is it not?" she asked.

Houston Kirby nodded miserably.

"I take it he has been up to mischief? He stole the salmon intended for breakfast?" she guessed.

Houston Kirby's mouth dropped open. "How did ye know, Your Grace?"

The Duchess laughed aloud. "I can smell it on his breath," she told the embarrassed steward, and to his amazement, she rubbed the smugly purring tom under his chin while speaking softly to him.

"I'll take him back to the stables, Your Grace," Houston Kirby offered, promising himself he'd see that the old tomcat was soundly disciplined for causing such a disruption. "The captain'll be mighty upset to think Jamaica was botherin' ye."

"Oh, 'tis the captain's cat, too?"

"Well, more his than mine. Actually, Jamaica was the mascot aboard the *Sea Dragon,* but 'twas the captain who rescued him when he found him tied up in a sack in Port Royal."

"I can see that my son-in-law and I have at least two things in common," the Duchess remarked.

"Beggin' your pardon, Your Grace, but I don't see how ye could have much in common with the captain," Houston Kirby risked contradicting the Duchess, his eyes shining with admiration as he stared at her. Dressed in a gown of emerald green velvet and lace, her black hair waved into delicate curls and draped with pearls, the Duchess of Camareigh looked like a queen.

"We both love Rhea, and we both have a fondness for cats," she said with a grin that altered her appearance and made the little steward think of a mischievous child. Like her own son, Robin, in fact.

"And he does love Rhea, doesn't he, Mr. Kirby?" the Duchess asked softly, completely disarming Houston Kirby with her smile and the questioning look in those incredible violet eyes.

"Aye, Your Grace," he said simply. "The cap'n's not been the same since he first saw her. Loves her like he does Merdraco, and like he did his mum, the Lady Elayne, before she died. He still reveres her memory. There be only a few things Dante Leighton treasures in this world, and once he's given his heart to them, they're always a part of him. Reckon he'd go crazy if he lost either Rhea or Merdraco," Houston Kirby said firmly. He was uneasy thinking about what would happen when they got to Merdraco.

"A love like that can become obsessive," the Duchess said, thinking of Kate.

"Aye, that it can, Your Grace," Kirby agreed. "But, if I might say so, Lady Rhea Claire, being the gentle and understandin' lady she is, might make all the difference in the world to the cap'n's future. She has already influenced the cap'n in her own quiet way, I figure she'll always be doin' it. Reckon he's not even aware of it, though."

"How very astute of you, Mr. Kirby," the Duchess said, her smile warmer as she met the grizzled little man's wise eyes. "I have a feeling that you know both the captain and Rhea far better than either one may realize. You are not to be underestimated, Mr. Kirby."

"Please, Your Grace, just Kirby," he suggested in embarrassment. He was, after all, still the captain's steward, even though wealthy in his own right.

"Very well, Kirby, but I shall tell you now that I shall not look upon you as a servant. From what I have heard from my daughter, you may well have saved her life, and I shall always be grateful for your many kindnesses to her," she told the flustered man. "Besides, are you not a rich man now? Will you be leaving the captain?" she inquired in what sounded deceptively like mere polite conversation.

"Oh, no, Your Grace. My place will always be by his lordship's side and with his family, at least, as long as I am wanted. I was born at Merdraco, and I'll most likely die there. I'll continue to serve the captain and Lady Rhea Claire and their heirs," he said stoutly.

"Loyal and noble, yet not above a wee bit of larceny, I

suspect. You remind me of two friends I once knew far better than I do today, which is a pity. They live near Verrick House, my old home in Sussex. They stood by me when I was in need of their very broad shoulders for support and assistance," the Duchess said with a soft chuckle, as if remembering a private joke. "Will and John Taylor. How I do miss them and the days when we . . . well, that is not for today," the Duchess halted. The curled form of Jamaica seemed to be reminding her of another time, and of both sad and joyful memories best left forgotten. She shook her head to clear her thoughts.

"I am honored, Your Grace," Kirby said, bowing deeply, endearing himself to the Duchess without realizing it.

"And how is your master today, Kirby? Do you think he is up to a visitor? No," the Duchess answered her own question. "I shall wait until he is not at the disadvantage. He would feel obliged to stand in my presence, would he not?" she asked innocently, but Kirby had the distinct feeling that Rawley had been telling tales about the captain and his breeches and that the Duchess of Camareigh had found the stories amusing.

"Aye, Your Grace. The captain still knows how to be a gentleman when he wants to," Kirby said, not realizing how revealing a remark that was.

The Duchess was thoughtful. "I see. Rhea has told me that he has made his living quite successfully as a privateer and smuggler these many years," she said. "We have had several very interesting conversations about your Dante Leighton. He would seem to be a most enterprising gentleman."

"Oh?" Kirby said, not quite knowing whether the captain was being complimented or criticized. "Aye, he is that, but he's considered quite respectable, too. In the trade, that is." Kirby came quickly to his captain's defense. "He really *was* brought up a gentleman, Your Grace."

"You needn't defend his honor to me, Kirby. As a matter of fact, just between you and me, I have the utmost respect for a man who can make the most of adversity. Raised a gentleman, with few practical skills, Dante Leighton might have lived off others after he lost his fortune. But instead he went out and worked for the wealth he now possesses. There can be no disgrace in trying to survive as best one knows how. He can be proud of his years as a ship's captain.

"My family, before I wed His Grace, was not wealthy. Indeed, we had to struggle sometimes to keep food on the table. I was forced to help in any way I could, but I was determined to survive, Kirby, and I cannot condemn another for attempting to do the same."

Houston Kirby was speechless. He had hardly expected to hear admiration of the captain from the Duchess of Camareigh! Something of his surprise and pleasure must have shown on his face, for the Duchess felt compelled to say something further, but this time she spoke warningly.

"However, I do not condone his actions where my daughter was concerned. He took advantage of her innocence, and I shall not forgive him for that. At least I shall not until I am certain that he will make my daughter as happy as she would have been in a marriage to another man, and in less suspicious circumstances. Your Dante Leighton, Kirby, is a very handsome devil, and I suspect that he is used to having his way," the Duchess accurately accused. "My sweet Rhea Claire never had a chance, did she? No, please do not answer, for I would not ask disloyalty of you."

"No, Your Grace," Kirby said without guilt, "the cap'n can act like the devil. He isn't perfect, Your Grace, but underneath his arrogance and seemin' contempt for what some people would call bein' proper, he's a good man. I'd not have stayed with him all these years otherwise, Your Grace. I would've left him to his fate, whatever it might have been," Kirby said honestly.

"Yes, I believe you would," she said, her hands rubbing the soft fur of the pampered ship's mascot.

The Duchess of Camareigh continued to fondle Jamaica, but her thoughts were on something else, for when she glanced up at Houston Kirby, her expression was slightly troubled. "What *is* to be the fate of Dante Leighton, Kirby?"

Houston Kirby ran a finger beneath his stock while he cleared his throat, unprepared to answer. Not only was he uncertain of the captain's fate, but also his speculations would cause only worry for the Duchess.

"He returns to Merdraco with a purpose, does he not? He is determined, now that he is a wealthy man, to reclaim his heritage? Perhaps regain his honor?"

"Aye, Your Grace," Kirby admitted.

"Dreaming of success is far easier than achieving it, Kirby."

"Aye, Your Grace," Kirby agreed. "But the cap'n—his lordship, that is—is not the same young man who ran away fifteen years ago. He's become a man who knows no fear when it comes to achievin' his goals. But . . ." Kirby hesitated, not willing to put his most troubled thoughts into words.

"Kirby?"

"Well, even though the cap'n's been involved in breakin' the law, he's never been guilty of betrayin' another, nor of cheatin' at cards, if ye understand what I'm sayin'? The captain will fight to the death to win, Your Grace, but he'll not lose his honor doin' it. But . . . other folks may not play so fair," Kirby finished.

"So what you are telling me then, Kirby, is that my daughter could well find herself a widow before giving birth to her child?"

Houston Kirby swallowed, shifting his weight from foot to foot as he faced her searching gaze. "No, Your Grace," the little steward finally replied. "The cap'n and me, well, we've come a long way. 'Twas a struggle at times, but we made it. No, Your Grace, I have to believe now that he will succeed in becomin' master of Merdraco once again. I cannot believe that all of it will end in a cold grave on a hillside. No, Your Grace, I have to believe that the cap'n will overcome anything. His enemies may do as they like, but he will succeed. He will," Houston Kirby pronounced.

"I trust you are right, Kirby," the Duchess of Camareigh said slowly.

"The captain has to succeed," Houston Kirby repeated to himself later as he walked back along the shadowy gallery, Jamaica held firmly in his arms.

"Don't think ye could be sparin' the cap'n at least one of them nine lives of yours, d'ye, Jamaica, 'cause I got this achin' feelin' in me bones that he's goin' to be needin' all the luck he can find if we're to come out of this with a whole skin," the little steward muttered. The well-fed, contented tom eyed the newel post as they passed, as if he hadn't anything more to worry about than sharpening his claws.

* * *

"I'm beginning to wonder if there isn't something horribly wrong with this husband of yours, Rhea Claire. Why, 'tis nearly two weeks now since he was brought to Camareigh," Caroline Winters complained, her displeasure increasing as she noted the lovely primrose gown Rhea was wearing. Her friend was more beautiful than ever despite the fact that she was *enceinte.* Even that was hard to believe, for Rhea's waist was still smaller than her own, Caroline thought in dismay while selecting another dish of rice and apple pudding.

"Why, I can't believe he is as handsome as all the maids declare him to be," Caroline continued. Casting a sly glance at the Earl, who was absorbed in handling one of his host's pistols, she simpered, "Certainly not as handsome as Wesley. Wesley! You did hear what I said, didn't you?" she teased, but her voice was sharp. "Isn't it just like a man not to acknowledge a compliment," she said with a tight smile, for despite all of her wiles over the past fortnight, Wesley Lawton still had yet to appreciate her.

"The man's been ill with a fever since last week. Besides, it is difficult for someone with a broken ankle to get about. 'Twould be next to impossible for the gentleman to climb the stairs," Sir Jeremy explained patiently. "You know how much difficulty I have getting around when I'm suffering one of my attacks. Why, just the other day I—"

"Papa, what was it you heard in London about Rhea's husband? I've been trying to remember all day long." Caroline sighed, wishing she could recall that tantalizing snippet of gossip.

"It had something to do with his past. Of course," she added with a knowing look at Rhea, "I s'pose he's told you everything about why he left England so suddenly? I don't s'pose you have any secrets between you." She tried to bait her friend.

Lord Richard Wrainton, only brother of Mary and Sabrina, glanced up from his book and, peering over the tops of his spectacles at Caroline Winters, quoted, "'The secret of being a bore is to tell everything.' You might remember that, for it could serve you well someday," he advised, but her scowling attention was centered on the three Fletcher brothers and their cohort, Francis Dominick, who had rudely guffawed at the remark, their game of cards temporarily forgotten as they eavesdropped on the conversation. Their Uncle Richard always seemed to find something witty to say.

"Well, I think 'tis a bore to be too smart, and always quoting strange, nonsensical things from dusty ol' books," Caroline said, still smarting from having apparently been the butt of the joke, even if she hadn't quite understood it. "Anyway, as I was saying . . ." she tried to continue despite the renewed laughter—even from her own father, she realized in outraged indignation.

"Uncle Richard," Rhea said softly, "you're being a bully, picking on someone who could never understand you in a thousand years."

"I know," he said, "but she does irritate me so. Besides, you will not defend yourself against her remarks. 'Tis the privilege of your uncle to do that," he said with a boyish grin as he eyed his niece fondly. Rhea was holding his firstborn child, Dawn, in her lap, playing with her. "Now tell me again about this man aboard the *Sea Dragon* who actually knew my grandfather. 'Tis amazing the way life evolves. I have often wanted to chart the migrations of certain races, peoples, and families, and through the study of events, come to conclusive evidence supporting cause and effect. The one determining the other," Richard Verrick explained, his bluish-gray eyes glowing. "Do you not think it would be interesting?"

Rhea smiled. Her Uncle Richard was such a dear person. He had been only about Robin's age when her mother and father married, and, being an orphan, he had come to Camareigh to live. He had always been bookish, her mother said, as well as nearsighted. At times he seemed to live in his own world. He wasn't stuffy, though, and had always been happy to amuse his nieces and nephews, and had seemed more like an older brother than an uncle. Because he had always been close to their whole family, he had remained a contented bachelor until meeting Sarah Pargeter, the orphaned ward of his sister Mary's husband, General Sir Terence Fletcher. Richard Verrick, his myopic vision sharpening rapidly, fell in love with the quiet young woman who made no effort to attract the eligible young gentleman. He was a very wealthy marquis who could not only claim a rich duke as a brother-in-law, but who also possessed several estates of his own as well as a castle in the Scottish Highlands.

Rhea stared down at the child cradled in her arms. She liked the feel of the baby snuggling against her breast. Soon, soon she would know the warm feel of her own child's body.

"Oh, of course! I remember now!" Caroline exclaimed, glancing around for a proper show of appreciation of her mental prowess, but no one seemed to be paying her any attention. "Rhea Claire's husband was accused of murder!" Caroline cried. Satisfaction was hers, for she had succeeded at last in gaining the shocked attention of everyone in the room. "Why, Rhea Claire, I do believe you are surprised. You mean to say your husband never told you he was suspected of the brutal murder of a young girl?" Caroline asked.

"Good Lord," murmured the Earl of Rendale. He'd not known. "Is it true?" he asked.

Rhea's cheeks were turning a pale pink as she felt the embarrassing disquiet spreading through all the people in the room. She was thankful at least that her mother and father and her Aunt Mary and Uncle Terence were not present, for she had no answer.

"Can it be that you are actually wed to a murderer? Oh, my dear, it's just too awful. I should think you would be scared to death to be in the same room with him. I mean, if he does have an uncontrollable temper, why, he could do it again, couldn't he?" Caroline asked. Her feigned pity was almost unbearable, Rhea thought as she met the girl's gloating expression. "Or," Caroline went on, "it could have been a calculated murder. Why, he might already be planning your death in order to get your inheritance."

"Caroline! This time you have gone too far. I am ashamed of you," Sir Jeremy spoke harshly, his face turning beet red with shame. "Please, Rhea Claire, accept my deep apology on behalf of my daughter. She forgets herself."

"Oh, Papa, really!" Caroline pouted. "After all, you are the one who told me the story," she went on, hardly endearing herself to her father.

The Fletcher brothers and Francis Dominick had left their card game and were gathered behind the settee, on which Rhea and Richard Verrick were sitting quietly. Even the gentle chuckles of the baby had stopped.

When Caroline Winters saw the unfriendly faces staring at

her, she said huffily, "Well, I don't know why you should all be staring at me like that. *I'm* not the one accused of murder!"

"No, but you've repeated a piece of gossip you know little about, and with the express purpose of causing offense," Richard Verrick said, his voice unexpectedly harsh. His family glanced at him in surprise, for Richard Verrick was the soul of discretion and courtesy. "'Gossip is mischievous, light and easy to raise, but grievous to bear and hard to get rid of. No gossip ever dies away entirely if many people voice it. . . .'"

"Oh, you and your damned quotes and your damned red hair!" Caroline rudely interrupted. His unruly red curls had always bothered her. If not for them, she would gladly have determined to become the next Marchioness of Wrainton, but she just couldn't see being married to someone with red hair, or living in a moldy old castle in Scotland.

"Caroline! Apologize this very instant. Your behavior is outrageous," Sir Jeremy ordered.

"Well, how dare he speak to *me* in that manner?" she demanded, her cheeks puffing out with anger.

"I only wish I'd had the intelligence to take a switch to your derrière years ago, young woman!" Sir Jeremy roared. Struggling to his feet from the comfortable armchair he'd been resting in, he looked as if he intended to set the record straight right then and there, company or not.

"Oh!" Caroline wailed. Setting her half-uneaten dish of rice and apple pudding down on the table with a small bang, she jumped to her feet and stormed from the room, her skirts swishing as she threw open the doors.

Sir Jeremy was too embarrassed to stay. Politely excusing himself, he limped to the door. The Earl of Rendale, despite his curiosity to learn more of this scandalous incident concerning the Marquis of Jacqobi, decided it would be better to make his excuses as well, and with his usual gentlemanly show of manners he bowed and left the room. Francis Dominick watched his stiff-backed, retreating figure, surprised that for once the man realized he would have been *de trop* had he remained.

Walking around to the front of the settee, Francis squatted in front of his sister's still figure. "That was an unpleasant surprise for you, was it not?" he asked softly, his blue-gray eyes understanding. "I am sorry. I could strangle Caroline sometimes."

With a smile for the outraged-looking James Fletcher, he added, "But I shall refrain from doing so, and I trust you have not taken my words seriously, James," he warned, little realizing how much like the Duke he sounded. He wanted no repeat of the episode which had very nearly cost Dante Leighton his life.

"We're keeping an eye on him," Ewan Fletcher reassured his cousin while dodging a carefully aimed elbow from his hotheaded younger brother. For although James had been disciplined by both the Duke and the general, he had a dangerously short memory.

"I wouldn't do anything to her. Or to him," James denied. "Honestly I wouldn't, Rhea. You do believe me, don't you, Rhea?" James asked in growing concern lest his cousin become displeased with him again. He had agonized more over her disapproval of his act of recklessness than even his father's, which had been only too predictably severe.

"James, please do not trouble yourself any further, for I know you were only trying to help me. Dante will recover, and he forgives you. I know you would never do anything so reprehensible again," Rhea told her young cousin for the hundredth time. Turning to Francis, she said, "I was shocked, but only because I was unprepared to hear such a thing about Dante. Of course I do not believe it, and hope that no one else at Camareigh will either," Rhea said, her voice tremulous, for she was badly shaken.

"I think you should ask Dante about it," Richard advised, thinking that Francis had certainly matured in the past year, far more so than his younger cousins, he thought with a frowning glance at the two younger ones, who were about to come to fisticuffs as they argued about whether or not James could be trusted. "You should hear his side of the story, Rhea."

"I know, and I shall. 'Tis strange, but Dante warned me that I might hear unpleasant gossip about his past, and he made me promise that I would come to him for his explanation," Rhea said, remembering also how nervous he had seemed about it.

"He was expecting this?" Francis murmured, for he had

heard nothing bad about the man, and had secretly begun to respect Dante Leighton, who had left his home and family and led so adventurous a life. And from what he had come to learn, her husband was genuinely in love with Rhea and treated her well.

Rhea placed a gentle kiss on the top of Dawn Verrick's red curls. Carefully, she handed the child back to Richard Verrick's waiting arms.

"You're going up to him?" Francis wanted to know.

"Yes, but if you are concerned, I shall have one of the footmen follow me just in case Dante decides to attack me," Rhea said with uncharacteristic sharpness.

"Rhea, I didn't mean that, really I did not," Francis denied. Rhea closed her eyes, then smiled apologetically.

"I am sorry, too. I do not know what has come over me of late. I feel so snappish sometimes. Please forgive me, Francis."

"Always, you know that," her brother said, but he looked worried as he watched her leave the room, and he wondered why loving someone always seemed to make you less happy than you were when *not* in love.

Beyond the tall windows of the Long Gallery, lightning illumined the blackening skies. The sudden, blinding flash highlighted the lone figure standing so still before one of the portraits. In the golden glow from one of the wall sconces, its flame flickering, the painted figure looked almost medieval. The reds were Venetian; the yellows aged like antique gold; the greens as dark as a huntsman's cloak; and the blues of wild woad.

Dante Leighton stood staring up at the Elizabethan, wondering what manner of man he had been. His eyes were black as a raven's wing, as was his hair, the curls framing a boldly staring face. The lips curled in a slight smile, while the eyes remained coldly assessing, wary.

This was the Dominick who had so fascinated Rhea Claire. Dressed so finely, in embroidered doublet and lacy ruff, his bejeweled hand holding a pair of gauntlet gloves while the other rested on a decorative sword belt, he did not look much like an adventurer.

A deafening clap of thunder sounded overhead, followed

by another flash, and then a rumbling shook the room. The crystal chandeliers tinkled melodically. A thunderbolt hit with an earthshaking reverberation, and then rain hit the windows in cascading silver sheets.

Dante Leighton glanced at the painted image one last time, then hobbled toward a high-backed, tapestried chair set against the wall, the crutch Kirby had managed to produce for him keeping the weight off his ankle.

Resting the crutch against the paneled wall, he relaxed against the chair back, his eyes roving the darkened gallery as he wondered how many times Rhea Claire had walked along it, perhaps dreaming of her swashbuckling ancestor, little realizing that one day her own life would become entwined with an adventurer's.

Dante Leighton, former captain of the *Sea Dragon*, smiled as he sat there in the darkness. He had made it past those forbidding wrought-iron gates into Camareigh. He remembered the first and only time he had spoken to the Duke while under his roof. The arrogant Lucien Dominick had actually apologized to him, reassuring him that no similar incident would occur. Then, much to Dante's surprise, the Duke escorted two subdued, uncomfortable-looking boys into the room. Dante's gaze had gone first to the taller of the two. A red-headed lad, his face had turned nearly as red as his curls while he made a muffled, though sincere, apology. But when Dante's eyes encountered the violet eyes of Robin Dominick he had been mystified. There had been something so tantalizingly familiar about the lad with the curly black hair and strangely tinted eyes. Of course, the eyes were like Rhea's eyes, but still . . . there was something else about the small boy who made his apology with such stiff-backed pride and defiance.

The apologies included Houston Kirby and Conny Brady, whose presence the Duke had requested. But Dante could see, as he took note of the glaring glances exchanged between Conny Brady and Robin Dominick, that all was not settled between those two.

Dante stretched his leg with a sigh, cursing the injury which had kept him isolated from the rest of the household, making him feel like a pariah. But since he could get around on his crutch, that would change.

Just then he heard the staccato beat of heels approaching along the gallery. Remaining hidden in the shadows, he waited in silence to identify the trespasser. His hand tightened on the broad end of the crutch, for he felt naked without his sword. Indeed, he was quite defenseless, he suddenly realized, should anyone take it upon themselves to rid the Dominick family of its newest member. But as he waited patiently for the figure to approach, he understood that it was a woman. The swishing of skirts was unmistakable, and then, to his surprise, because she seemed in such a hurry, the woman stopped before the portrait of the Elizabethan.

"Does he continue to fascinate you, little daffadilly?" Dante asked quietly.

Startled, Rhea cried out, glancing upward, as if the man in the portrait had spoken those soft, seductive words.

"Rhea!" Dante struggled awkwardly to his feet, just managing to reach her in time to steady her. "I'm sorry, my dear. I didn't mean to frighten you," he apologized, his arms holding her close. Her body remained strangely stiff.

Rhea stared up into the shadowed face of her husband. Lightning flashed, and in the unnatural brightness, Dante saw that her eyes were wide with terror. It was an expression Dante had not seen in them since that first night he had come face to face with her aboard the *Sea Dragon* and she had looked upon him as someone to be feared.

"Rhea? What is wrong? Don't you recognize me?" The fearful expression remained.

Dante's pale gray eyes narrowed speculatively as he continued to search Rhea's ashen face. "Rhea! Look at me!" he commanded sharply, gently shaking her.

"Dante," Rhea whispered, her darkened eyes sliding away from his gaze. "You frightened me. I wasn't expecting to see you in the gallery. I thought you were still bedridden. How did you get in here?" she asked, and Dante could feel her body continuing to shake. "For a horrible moment I thought . . ." she began to say, then, shaking her head, she closed her eyes.

"You thought your Elizabethan had spoken to you?" Dante guessed. "Is that what frightened you? Oh, Rhea, you are such a child at times," he said, pressing his lips against her forehead affectionately. Placing a caressing hand against the soft roundness of her breast, he said, "Your heart is pounding so, you'll make yourself ill. Here, come and sit for a moment."

But Rhea jerked back, and whether she or Dante was the more surprised by her rejection, neither knew.

Another flash of lightning revealed their faces, and Rhea swallowed against the fear rising inside her as she met Dante's blazing eyes. "It was not your imagining that a ghost spoke to you that frightened you half out of your wits. I frightened you," Dante accused her, his hands tightening painfully on her shoulders. "Look at me! My God, you're scared to death of me, aren't you?" he demanded, his voice harsh with anger and, perhaps, with his own fear.

"No, please, Dante, that isn't it," Rhea told him breathlessly, trying to still the wild beating of her heart. "My mind was on something else, and when I stopped here by the portrait, trying to gather my thoughts, I was not expecting to hear your voice. I had expected to find you in your bed," she explained, her hands touching him now, caressing him.

"I think that may be our problem," Dante murmured more to himself than to her, for it had been almost a month since they had made love. "What were you thinking of? Not me, surely, or you would not have been so frightened. Or *were* you thinking of me, little daffadilly?" His voice was smooth, but smooth with sarcasm.

Rhea's awkward silence condemned her. "Has someone said something against me? Was I too rude to Rawley when she tried to force more of that concoction down my throat?" he demanded.

"No, Dante, it was..." Rhea began, but her words faded away, and she had to glance away from that penetrating gaze.

"What is it? You may as well tell me now."

Rhea glanced around the shadowy room. It was so quiet, except for the distant sound of thunder as the storm gathered against the hills. When the faint rumbling died, it was suddenly too quiet.

"Rhea, I will not let you leave me until I know the worst," Dante told her.

"Thunderstorms have always made me nervous," Rhea tried to lie, but she knew he could see right through her.

"I remember how you used to snuggle close against me

when the *Sea Dragon* rode out the storms. But I haven't been able to calm you this time, Rhea. Why?"

"Because no one accused you of murder before," Rhea said bluntly. Dante took a long, deep breath.

"And did you believe this person?"

Rhea placed her hand on his thigh, feeling the tensing of his muscles beneath the soft buckskin. "No."

Dante stared at her in the growing darkness, for twilight was falling, and he realized that it could only become darker before the dawn once again painted the eastern sky in rosy hues. "I had hoped you would be spared hearing the ugly story, but that was foolish. I ought to have told you myself. What exactly did you hear?"

"That you were accused of murdering a young girl."

"Suspected, not accused. There was never any evidence to try me. There was, however, some circumstantial evidence. Had they convicted me on that, they would have sent an innocent man to the gallows. I was innocent. I was *not* innocent of having a bad reputation, however, inviting trouble and scandal. I am not proud of that. But believe me, Rhea, I did not murder Lettie Shelby," Dante told her, and in the light, Rhea could see him staring at her with a pleading look. What had become of the arrogant captain of the *Sea Dragon?*

"Who was she?"

"A local girl, from Merleigh. Her father had been the bailiff at Merdraco until I discovered he was cheating me. I fired him. He had been buying and selling the cattle, taking care of the purchase of feed for the animals, as well as seeing to the tenants. Unfortunately, he was reporting a far lower amount in the books and pocketing the remainder. But what I objected to the most was his brutality where the tenants were concerned. Jack Shelby had a vicious streak and he misused his authority. However, I dismissed him too late, for his daughter had been hired to work at Merdraco by that time. The first time I saw her she was cleaning soot and ashes from the hearth in the salon. Even with her face smudged with ash, Lettie was beautiful. Not in a classical sense, but in a very earthy way. She was the type of woman who possessed a natural seductiveness. She knew how to catch a man's eye with the movement of her hips, how to make a man aware of the softness of her lips when she licked the dryness from them. Seduction came as easily to Lettie Shelby as breathing, and she knew how to use her talent to get whatever she wanted. I was very young and foolish, but I wasn't the only man she was free with. But I was the one she stole a watch from, and that watch was clutched in her hand when the body was found.

"What happened?"

"She apparently went to meet someone on the moors. Perhaps she had met the man there before. It was a secluded spot, very lonely and wild, certainly a place where lovers could enjoy complete privacy. But this time her rendezvous ended in her death. She was beaten, then strangled."

"And she had your watch?" Rhea questioned. "But that surely wasn't enough to cast suspicion on you, especially if what you said about her was true. Why didn't they suspect other men as well?"

"Because, the day before she died, she spoke in public of her 'gentleman lover' and how he was going to give her everything she wanted. She said he had promised her a big house in London and all the clothes and jewels she could ever ask for. Never before had she been so indiscreet, for although the villagers knew she wasn't above a roll in the hay with one of the local lads, she had never mentioned a gentleman before. I suppose she couldn't resist bragging. She said she was one of the few smart girls in Merleigh and knew how to get what she wanted out of life, that she would be the fine lady one day and make their lives hell for doubting her. She also had mentioned the gentleman to her father, and since he had seen Lettie and me together once, he assumed she meant me. He had a grudge against me anyway, and was only too quick to think me the murderer. I had a bad reputation and was one of the few gentlemen of wealth in the area, so suspicion fell heavily on me."

"You had no alibi?" Rhea asked curiously, but Dante remained silent. "Where were you when she was murdered?"

"I was with a woman."

"I don't understand, then. Why didn't you tell the authorities you were with someone?"

"Because she was a respectable woman, and I could not

destroy her reputation just to save mine. After all, mine had been blackened long before," Dante explained.

It was Rhea's turn to remain silent as she thought about what Dante had just told her. Finally she said, "You were involved with both Lettie and this other woman?"

Dante's laugh was harsh. "As well as others. I told you my reputation was hardly sterling. But after I became involved with this other woman, I had neither the time nor the inclination to be with Lettie. Strangely enough, Lettie seemed not to mind. Her gentleman lover must have kept her very busy."

"You loved this other woman?"

Dante smiled bitterly. "I thought I did at the time."

"And she loved you?"

"I thought she did."

"And she said nothing of that night? She let you be suspected of murdering that girl when she knew you were innocent?" Rhea demanded, feeling all the bitter anger Dante must have felt then.

"I could ask nothing of her. Besides, since nothing was proven against me, there was no harm done," Dante excused the woman's heartless actions. "We were young, Rhea. In fact, she was your age at that time, and because we thought we were in love, we risked everything to be together. If we'd been discovered, many people would have been hurt. But you do her an injustice, for she was willing to come forward, but certain events preceded the testimony she would have given, and then it did not matter anymore."

"Were you intending to wed her?" Rhea wanted to know.

"Yes. I asked her, and she accepted."

"Then it would not have ruined her reputation to say she had been with you."

"Rhea," Dante said gently, "I spent that night with her. We were lovers."

Rhea couldn't seem to find anything to say, for although she knew that Dante must have had mistresses, it was different to hear about one from his own lips.

"About that same time, my world fell apart. My mother died shortly thereafter, and it was, I am certain, because we discovered that the lands of Merdraco were beyond my reach— those not under titular ownership, I mean, the ones I had mortgaged because of a promise from a gentleman I trusted. He promised that there would be no time limit on repaying the money I had borrowed from him in order to pay off my debts. That man betrayed me. This man, who had been my guardian, made some very bad investments with my inheritance. That, combined with my own extravagances, left me penniless except for the castle. I was, of course, responsible for trusting another man so completely. The blame is mine for having been so blind—and for losing my land. The castle could not support itself without the revenues coming in from the rest of the estate. Everything was lost."

"You surely cannot take all the blame, Dante. You were young, and you trusted your guardian. That's understandable. You cannot be blamed for another man's treachery," Rhea protested.

"And even had my love defended me, I could not have married her. I was a penniless gentleman by then. I could not ask her to live the life I thought I was destined for. Not that I would have blamed her had she turned me down should I have had the effrontery to have asked her to elope with me," Dante added.

"I think you are being too kind to her. Because of her, you unfairly bore the suspicion of being a murderer. When you needed her love, she turned her back on you. She abandoned you," Rhea said, indignant and hurt over the betrayal.

"And you are being too hard on her, my sweet," Dante said, touched by her show of outrage on his behalf. "She was young. She had been raised to expect a life of luxury. I could not ask her to give that up."

"I would have given up everything for your love," Rhea told him, her hand touching his tentatively.

"Not for the man I was then," Dante said, his spirit returning as he felt the comforting warmth of her beside him. "I am not certain, had you been my lover, that I would have even bothered to ask you to join me, for I would have kidnaped you and fled into the night. The rest of the world be damned," he said softly, and this time when his arms pulled her close, and his lips tasted hers, Rhea responded with all of her love.

"Thank you for your belief in me," Dante murmured against the softness of her lips.

"I have told you before that you need never worry about that," Rhea reminded him. Her breathing was ragged again, but from the excitement of his touch, not from fear.

"The more precious something is, the more protective one is of it and fearful of losing it," Dante said.

Rhea rested her head against his shoulder contentedly. Watching the play of light in the storm clouds, she asked in puzzlement. "I still do not understand one thing."

"What is that?" Dante asked, but his mind was on other things as his lips left a trail of fire along Rhea's cheek and throat. It had been far too long since he had held his wife in his arms, and he was tired of conversation.

"It could not have been common knowledge that you were penniless, for you had just made the discovery yourself. It does seem strange that this woman learned of it just when she might have come forward to clear your name," Rhea demanded.

Dante grinned in appreciation. "You are beginning to become too worldly, my love. Her grandfather, who had raised her since her parents' deaths, was a friend of my family and just happened to be informed of the truth by my guardian."

"This guardian of yours certainly exerted a great influence on your life," said Rhea. "You trusted him. You even gave your lands to him for safekeeping. And because you trusted him, you also told him of your love for this woman. And when suspicion was cast against you, you confided in him, did you not? Having you accused of murder must have fitted into his plans most conveniently. Learning of your alibi, he had to make certain it never came to light. He let it be known that you were destitute in order to suppress your alibi."

"You amaze me, Rhea. I had thought you so innocent. But yes, I trusted my guardian, and would have with my life as well as my lands."

"Why did he wish to destroy you, Dante?"

Dante sighed. "Because he hated the name Leighton. He hated Merdraco and all it has always stood for. He was jealous and envious, and because of something which happened many years earlier, that dislike turned into hatred. He plotted the downfall of Merdraco, and he played both my mother and me for fools. She had tried to warn me against him, but..."

Dante's voice was full of all the regrets and bitterness of un-
satisfied revenge, all he had felt over the years.

"Then how could you have trusted him in the first place?"
Rhea asked, trying to read his expression.

"He was very clever. He pretended to be a friend. He maintained his air of kindly benevolence, always pretending to be
so concerned about me, and then playing the betrayed friend
when I was accused of murder. Quite the respected gentleman
of the community he is. But that was yesterday, my love, and
I am more concerned about today and having you to myself
for the first time in much too long," Dante said.

Rhea moved back a little, her eyes searching his face.
"Dante, this guardian of yours. He is still alive?"

Dante was quiet. Too quiet, Rhea thought.

"Where is he, Dante?"

"Soon he will be in hell, but for now he lives at Wolfingwold
Abbey. Whenever he approaches his lands, he must travel the
only road across the moors, and once he has reached Merwest
Cross, where the roads leading north and south cross, he cannot
help but see the towers of Merdraco standing proud against the
skies. He thinks of me then, Rhea, and he knows I am out
there somewhere, that I am waiting for the day I can send him
to his grave."

> *More exquisite than any other autumn rose.*
> Theodore Agrippa D'Aubigne

Chapter 10

IT came as no great surprise to Dante Leighton when, the following day, he received an imperious summons from the Duchess of Camareigh. The meeting was already long overdue, and Dante had a feeling that Her Grace's patience had run thin where he was concerned, especially in light of the latest disturbing piece of information she must have heard concerning her son-in-law.

"Now try to be pleasant, m'lord," Houston Kirby reminded his captain, a worried frown wrinkling his brow while he brushed a few stray cat hairs from the shoulder of Dante's dark blue frock coat.

"Why, Kirby, I am always pleasant and diplomatic."

"Aye, when ye're wantin' somethin'. But your honey-tongued words won't be makin' any impression whatsoever on

199

Her Grace," Kirby warned. "She's keen-eyed, that lady is. If ye're smart, ye'll be seein' that for yourself when ye meet her," the little steward warned the captain as he eyed him up and down with critical thoroughness. "Aye, ye'll do, then," he finally decided. The captain's dark chestnut curls were brushed neatly back and tied with a plain ribbon, and the clean white carefully folded stock was a startling contrast against the bronzed skin of his face, which was smoothly shaven and lightly scented. The captain's fawn-colored breeches still fit nicely, and although only one of his silk stockings was visible, it looked proper, as did his lordship's fashionable Spanish-leather pumps. "Aye, reckon ye *look* decent enough," allowed Kirby in a backhanded compliment.

"Thank you. Now I have no fear of facing what I am certain will be the even more critical eye of the Duchess of Camareigh," Dante said with a mocking grin. But underlying his apparent ease was a deep concern that all might not go well, and that could be disastrous for his relationship with Rhea. She was already disturbed by her father's continued coolness toward him, and should her mother show a similar tendency, it could only add strain. He promised himself to make the Duchess of Camareigh accept him, for he'd be damned if he was going to lose Rhea now.

"Here, don't be forgettin' your gift for Her Grace," Kirby reminded him as Dante started to hobble to the door. "Seems a strange thing to be givin' Her Grace if ye was askin' me," Kirby said, handing him the package. A bouquet of flowers, or even a jewelry box would have been more appropriate, but try to tell a person somethin' when they've got their minds set, thought Kirby.

"But I am not asking you, Kirby," the captain said with that devilish grin. The little steward held open the door and watched as the captain slowly made his way along the corridor on his crutch, his peculiar present tucked carefully beneath his arm.

A footman clad in blue and gold livery, his hair hidden beneath a neatly powdered wig, stepped aside deferentially as he opened the double doors to the Duchess of Camareigh's private salon.

"Lord Dante Jacqobi, Your Grace," he intoned in so serious

a voice that Dante stopped, expecting to see the man don his headsman's hood and lower an ax against the intruder's neck.

Dante Leighton paused in the center of a flowered carpet, surprise overtaking him. He could have sworn he heard a bird's song, yet the trees beyond the tall windows were bare. On the other hand, one would never suspect that winter could intrude in this room. There was a feeling of perpetual sunshine there. The white plasterwork ceiling and gilded scrollwork and carvings festooning the walls created a light, airy effect, reflected in the crystal chandelier with its sunbursts and beads. A couple of wing chairs upholstered in a delicate lilac floral motif were arranged along one side of the hearth, and a settee of pale yellow Chinese silk was opposite.

It appeared that the room was empty except for that strange chirping, and Dante Leighton was about to leave when he caught sight of a movement in one of the window seats.

As he stared at the woman sitting there, Dante Leighton was stunned. She was a ghost from his past, dressed in the palest of sea-green satin, with elegant lace adorning her décolletage and trailing from her sleeves. Her midnight black hair was simply coiffed, and several soft curls caressed the ivory smoothness of her shoulder.

Dante Leighton blinked, thinking the vision must surely disappear and he would find himself in bed, awaking from some bizarre dream. But when he looked again, she was still sitting there. This time he noticed that on either side of her were two fair-haired children, listening with enraptured expressions to the melodic notes the woman was creating by cranking the handle of a miniature barrel organ.

Every so often one of the two children would glance up into her face and say something, and she would laugh softly and turn the handle of the serinette again. After a moment she stopped. Glancing up, her violet eyes met Dante's mesmerized gaze. She smiled.

"Forgive me, Lord Jacqobi, for not having greeted you properly when you entered," she said in a soft, husky voice. Had Dante his wits about him, he would have realized that she'd had the opportunity to study him for several minutes while he stood in the center of the room.

"Lord Jacqobi? Are you quite all right? You look as if you

have seen a ghost," she said, little realizing how accurate her guess was; for Sabrina Dominick, Duchess of Camareigh and mother to Rhea Claire, was the very same woman Dante Leighton had seen in London and been enchanted by nearly twenty years earlier.

"Please, sit down," the Duchess said in growing concern as her son-in-law continued to stand there staring at her with the strangest expression on his face. But he didn't move, and she grew increasingly uneasy.

And then, quite suddenly, Dante Leighton began to laugh. At first he laughed softly, but then the sound grew into a deep, rich laugh which seemed to capture the untamed spirit of the man who, in risking the odds rather than meekly accepting his fate, had set out to make his fortune and create a future more to his liking. The Duchess, startled, clasped an arm around each of her children. But her children were not frightened, and, in fact, seemed to find the tall man leaning on the crutch and laughing rather funny. Their giggling laughter joined his.

The Duchess of Camareigh raised a rather haughty, inquiring brow as she stared at him, wondering if the man was losing his mind, and she had just about decided to call for assistance from one of the footmen standing outside of the double doors, when Dante Leighton's laughter faded. Having sensed her disquiet, he now managed, despite the crutch he was leaning on, to bow quite decently.

"My apologies, Your Grace," Dante said at last, "but your appearance startled me."

"Indeed?" the Duchess said frigidly. "I have come to expect varying reactions upon first acquaintances with strangers, but never has anyone laughed in my face," she said, her small chin raised regally, and Houston Kirby, had he been able to witness this first confrontation between the captain and the Duchess, would have felt like stringing the captain up from a yardarm of the *Sea Dragon,* for he'd gone and done just what the little steward had warned him not to do.

"Please accept my deepest and sincerest apologies, for I meant no offense," Dante said with one of his most engaging smiles, and it would indeed have been hard for even the Duchess of Camareigh not to have been mollified by that devilish charm that seemed to come so naturally to that very same captain of the *Sea Dragon*.

"Then you would not mind enlightening me?" the Duchess inquired silkily, her violet eyes still regarding him with cold wariness.

"I was thinking, Your Grace," Dante said, taking a step closer, "that you had not changed much in nearly twenty years. If it is possible, you are even more beautiful than you were then," was Dante's audacious reply, and it left Sabrina Dominick feeling no small amount of confusion, for his obviously heartfelt compliment was the last thing she had been expecting to hear.

"You will forgive me, Lord Jacqobi, but I am afraid I have no memory of such a meeting. I am certain I would have remembered you," she responded, but there was a new, searching look in her eyes as she tried to remember where she might have met her son-in-law before.

"I was a lad of sixteen when I saw you. You were in conversation with several older gentlemen and I was standing across the room, watching you. I remember thinking I had never seen so beautiful a young woman, although you were hardly older than I was at the time. You seemed to have caught every gentleman's eye, yet I could see that you were not happy. You held yourself so proudly, so defiantly, as if daring anyone to touch you, which was what most of those fine gentlemen about you would have given their fortunes to do."

"How extraordinary," Sabrina Dominick murmured. There was a strange expression on her face as she remembered back to her first season. It had not been a happy time for her.

"I returned to Devonshire shortly after seeing you that evening, and I never discovered your name or that you eventually wed Lucien Dominick. When I returned to London the following year, no one seemed to know anything about you. I never saw you again. Of course, my life during those years was confined mainly to gaming tables and other gentlemanly pursuits, and most likely I did not frequent the establishments a lady would. It was just a few years after that when I left England. To see you again and to discover that you are Rhea's mother," Dante spoke with a disbelieving shake of his head. "I never forgot your face, or those incredible violet eyes. *Now*

I realize why Rhea has always seemed so strangely familiar to me. It has had me puzzled." His pale gray eyes narrowed as he compared mother and daughter.

"That was long ago, and yet you have re-created vividly what I was feeling that evening," the Duchess said softly, staring up at the man who had captured her daughter's heart. She smiled, and for the first time since Dante Leighton had entered the room, it was a welcoming smile. "I am sorry that you did not find the nerve to approach and speak a few words with me. I think we would have had much to talk about, for I fear we are kindred spirits. I would have welcomed a friend, for I had only one wish then, and that was to return to the safe anonymity of Verrick House, my home in Sussex, which I managed to do shortly after that evening. I wed Lucien not long after that, and we stayed at Camareigh. With the birth of Rhea Claire, we preferred to spend our time in the country, establishing our family life without the constant interruptions of London and all the social functions that entails."

Dante Leighton was silent awhile. "Yes, I regret that I did not come forward," he said finally, feeling as if this woman had been his friend for years.

"Who is he?" one of the children snuggled close to the Duchess wanted to know.

"This is Dante Leighton, Lord Jacqobi, and he is your sister Rhea's husband. Say hello to him, Andrew. Arden," the Duchess said, her hand caressing and smoothing their golden curls.

"You're funny," Andrew said instead, and began giggling as he caught his twin's eye. And as Dante hopped forward, the two youngsters laughed more.

"You walk like a bunny rabbit," Arden squealed in delight.

"And I bet you like codlin tarts," Dante responded, his grin widening as he stared at Rhea's young brother and sister. Perhaps his own child would have the golden hair of the Dominick line.

"How did you know that?" she demanded, her eyes round with wonder.

"I always know what little girls like," Dante answered quite seriously.

"And do you know what Rhea Claire wants, Lord Jacqobi?" the Duchess asked smoothly.

"She has my love, Your Grace," Dante answered simply, sensing that a recital of his assets would not impress this woman.

"Then she will want for nothing else," the Duchess declared, her smile warm. "Please, sit down. We have many things to discuss, for there is much I wish to learn about you, Dante Leighton." Helping the twins to hop down from the window seat, she sent them to play on the carpet. She placed the serinette safely out of reach of small, eager hands, then made herself comfortable on the sofa, carefully spreading out her skirts. Dante Leighton closed his eyes, feeling almost incapable of carrying on as usual. It was still difficult for him to comprehend that *this* was Rhea's mother. Had he harbored doubts about taking Rhea for his wife, they vanished. The wheel of fortune had come full circle. His meeting with Rhea had been pre-ordained. Nothing would ever change his mind about that.

"Please, Lord Jacqobi, sit down. Your ankle must be paining you," the Duchess invited him. "I shall have a brandy sent in for you, and perhaps a sherry for myself, although I expect you to do most of the talking," she warned him, and Dante knew that although the Duchess was an incredibly beautiful woman, Houston Kirby was right. She was no fool.

"I have a small gift for you," Dante said as he handed her the package.

A look of surprise crossed Sabrina Dominick's face, but she graciously accepted his gift. "Thank you, although 'tis quite unnecessary. But I must admit that I do love surprises," she said with a dimpled smile which reminded him of Rhea's.

"'Tis nothing of great value compared with Your Grace's jewels, but I did not know what else to give a woman who seemed to have everything. As I pondered what Rhea had said about her mother, I thought you might appreciate this plunder from the sea," Dante Leighton explained, feeling some of the nervousness his little steward had felt now that he awaited the Duchess' reaction. She had every right to laugh in his face.

But Sabrina Dominick was no ordinary woman, and as she removed the layer of wrapping around the hardwood box, then opened the hinged lid, she gave a small cry of pleasure. Revealed to her admiring gaze were several exquisite shells, the likes of which she had never seen.

"Oh, beautiful," she breathed in awe, and her voice attracted the attention of the twins, who came tottering over.

"They are quite common in the Indies," Dante said modestly, although he was pleased by her reaction.

"Oh, they could never be common, Lord Jacqobi," the Duchess contradicted. "This one looks like a sunrise, for the swirling colors are golden pink. And this one would get the tangles out of my hair," she laughed as she held a cream-tinted shell with spiny teeth along its curved edge.

"Can we eat this one, Mama?" Andrew asked as his small finger tentatively touched a shell that resembled a flattened Banbury cake.

"'Twould be a bit dry, I am afraid," Dante advised. He noticed the Duchess picking up the shell that curved to a point in a winding fashion and had deep ridges with spines, and he said, "Hold it to your ear, Your Grace, and you will hear the song of the sea."

Sabrina Dominick listened, but there was a doubting expression in her eyes until suddenly they grew as round and full of wonder as her children's did when she held the shell cupped to each of their ears in turn, their squeals of delight nearly drowning out the sound.

"Thank you, 'tis a wonderful gift, and one I shall always cherish," she told him. Tilting her head sideways as she stared up at him, she asked, "And what manner of man are you, Dante Leighton?" Here was a man who had gambled away his inheritance, ruined his reputation, and even been accused of murder. Yet here also was a man who had found the strength to begin again, possessed the tenderness to save a stray cat, and to make an orphan boy his legal ward.

Dante Leighton met her curious gaze steadily. "I am the man who wed your daughter and who will make her happy. I admit that in the past I have done many things I am not proud of, but never will I betray the love which Rhea, for some reason, has decided to give me."

"I do not think it strange that Rhea loves you, now that I have finally met you," the Duchess commented, for the man could charm the devil himself. "Now, please sit down, or I shall be forced to think you are feverish. Then I shall have to call Rawley, and instead of a snifter of brandy, you will find yourself sipping some of Mrs. Taylor's Special Treat," the Duchess threatened, laughing as the man who had struck fear into the hearts of many a seaman sat down hastily.

And it was upon this casual and friendly scene that Lucien Dominick and Rhea Claire entered, each with a slightly different reaction.

"Mama? Dante?" Rhea said, glancing in wonderment between the two smiling people.

"My dear, please join us. I was about to offer Dante another brandy," the Duchess responded, realizing that the Duke had not missed her use of their son-in-law's given name. "Lucien? You will join us, too?" she questioned, her eyes almost challenging him to decline the invitation.

With a shrug, Lucien Dominick sat down beside his wife. Rhea sat down in one of the wing chairs next to Dante.

"You have had a pleasant talk?" Rhea asked, still feeling some nervous apprehension. If her mother and Dante had taken a dislike to one another, as had her father and her husband, then she would not have known what to do. Her place was by her husband's side now, and her loyalty was his.

"Indeed we have, my dear," the Duchess responded, and Rhea sighed softly. "In fact, I have been hearing about some of your husband's more daring exploits. It has been quite fascinating, for you know I have always enjoyed a bit of adventure and derring-do," she added with a smile as she met the Duke's startled gaze. "But, of course, being a respectable lady, I have never partaken of disreputable activities."

"'Tis a pity, Rina, that you did not give in to those tendencies," Lucien Dominick commented while he filled his son-in-law's glass, then poured himself a brandy, thinking he would have need of another one himself as he sat down, preparing to engage in polite conversation with a man he once wanted to kill. "I imagine you would have been quite skillful at breaking the law, my dear."

"Lucien, really," the Duchess laughed nervously, thinking she would have to bridle her tongue lest she bait him too far. He was not in a teasing mood as he sat there staring broodingly into his brandy.

"My mother and father are always jesting in this manner,

and none of us has ever understood the reason why," Rhea explained.

"What has them so conveniently occupied?" the Duke demanded as he caught sight of his youngest offspring at play in the center of the carpet.

"Plunder from the sea," the Duchess said, laughing at his mystified expression.

"Conny and I collected quite a few shells on the beach while we were waiting for the treasure to be found," Rhea confided impulsively as she remembered those warm, somnolent days under the palms. "These were a gift from Dante, were they not?" Rhea asked. "You must have him show you the contents of the sea chest he has aboard the *Sea Dragon,* for it is full of amazing artifacts he has retrieved from sunken ships. He even has a crystal decanter that some Spanish governor used—before his ship went down in a storm, that is," Rhea declared.

"I would not have thought you would have time or inclination for collecting, Lord Jacqobi," Lucien Dominick murmured.

"It all depends on *what* I am collecting, Your Grace," Dante responded, unwilling to allow the Duke to rile him. He realized that he had a long way to go before Lucien Dominick would accept him as a son-in-law.

Lucien Dominick's sherry-colored eyes lingered on his daughter's figure. Soon she would be showing her pregnancy, and he wanted nothing to disturb her while she was in such a delicate condition. His gaze moved to Dante Leighton, and he said, "I have often found that it is far more pleasurable to possess one item of great value than several of lesser quality. Have you not found that to be so?" he asked so softly that Dante almost didn't catch the underlying warning.

Dante Leighton held the Duke's narrowed gaze. "I am pleased, Your Grace, that we have finally agreed upon something."

"I have a request to make of you both," the Duchess began, sounding a little shy. She ignored Lucien's darkening expression. "It would mean so much to me if you would agree to repeat your marriage vows in the small chapel here at Camareigh," the Duchess requested. "Lucien does not seem to think it necessary, but I truly believe it would be a very wise move, not only because I could be present this time, but because... well..." She did not continue, as though she found the words too painful.

"Because some people less charitable than yourself might question the legitimacy of our child?" Dante helpfully supplied the reason.

"That is horrible!" Rhea cried, her hand going automatically to her gently rounding stomach. "We were wed in church. It was all quite legal."

"Although Lucien will not say as much," the Duchess said, "he knows I am right. I know how vicious gossip can become, and because there has already been so much gossip associated with your name, my dear, the fact that you were wed in the Indies will only fuel raging tongues."

Sabrina Dominick glanced at her husband. She knew that he still held hopes of seeing the marriage annulled, and she knew he wanted no part of making it even more binding. But she also knew there was nothing they could do about it.

"I will not stand idly by while our daughter's name is sneered at. I will not see her happiness destroyed by scandalmongering fools," the Duchess declared, her cheeks brightening with anger.

Rhea met Dante's questioning glance and nodded agreement as he said, "We would be honored to *repeat* our vows here at Camareigh. I know that Rhea has always been saddened because you and His Grace were not present at our wedding." Dante was feeling quite pleased. The second wedding would make virtually impossible any attempt the Duke might make to annul their marriage.

"I am so pleased. And I know that the Reverend Smalley will be, too, for he was quite disappointed to hear of your marriage. After all, the man christened you, my dear, and I think he always assumed that he would preside over your wedding. He was heartbroken over the whole affair." The Duchess always spoke affectionately of the clergyman who had ministered to the spiritual needs of the Dominick family since the time of the late Dowager Duchess, who, much to Reverend Smalley's despair, had declared herself in no need of his advice.

"I also intend to throw the grandest ball of the season in order to introduce our son-in-law to society properly and proudly," the Duchess declared. "I shall have no one thinking that we are not pleased with Rhea's husband, or that we are ashamed of her being with child."

"My dear," Lucien said with a slight smile curving his hard mouth, "if you think having Rhea and Lord Jacqobi repeat their marriage vows before us and the good reverend will help, then by all means it shall be done. Though I think that a grand ball, with our guests full of food and drink and their senses dulled, will go much further toward silencing gossip." He realized that he'd never had any choice once Sabrina made up her mind.

The Duke of Camareigh got to his feet and poured himself that second brandy. He was thinking exactly what Dante had been thinking. Once Rhea and Dante repeated their vows in the small medieval chapel that had stood witness for countless other Dominick marriages, including his own, there would no longer be any course for the Duke except to welcome the captain of the *Sea Dragon* into his family.

Let us forget and forgive injuries.
Cervantes

Chapter 11

THE first snowfall had long since melted, and only a small piece of the Yule log remained in the great hearth. As it was every Christmas, it had been burned with ceremonial reverence, the lighting followed by the gaiety of carols and feasting. The holly and mistletoe which had decorated the great hall were gone, removed by maids and footmen while they dusted and cleaned and polished, the servants' energy rivaling the March winds blustering and howling across the hills and rattling the windowpanes.

It was a genesis, a time of new life, new beginnings.

The untarnished gold of daffodils and the bright green buds unfurling on the bough were a harbinger of spring, and soon the hills and meadows would be covered in a profusion of wildflowers, daisies and cow parsley, spots of white among

211

the blues, lilacs, and pinks of speedwell, columbine and lords-and-ladies.

Dante Leighton, standing in solitude before one of the mullioned windows, caught the flash of a blackbird's wing. The wind carried it toward a copse of greenwood on the far side of the small lake where the medieval chapel stood in seclusion, surrounded by ancient cedar. Under that barrel-vaulted roof, with a pale, winter sunlight shining down through the small stained-glass windows, he and Rhea Claire had repeated their marriage vows. Crowded together in the ornately carved Jacobean stalls had been the strangely silent members of the Dominick and Fletcher families, their faces only a blur to Dante as he claimed Rhea as his wife once more. He repeated without hesitation the words spoken so solemnly by Reverend Smalley. Standing beneath the hooded pulpit in his black cassock and bands, the Reverend had looked like an ancient mystic, the shadowy light of the altar candles flickering eerily across his wizened features.

The former captain of the *Sea Dragon*, whose daring had never faltered when he faced cannon fire, was running a shaking hand through his already disorderly curls. Dante was frightened, frightened in a way he had never been frightened before, and there was nothing he could do about it.

For the thousandth time, he glanced up in the direction of the bedchamber decorated in delicate shades of blue, yellow, and silver, where the tall windows, draped in pale blue damask, overlooked the gardens below. Rhea Claire lay in the canopied bed giving birth to the fruit of their passion. Dante swallowed something lodged painfully in his throat as he remembered her agonized cries of that morning, when the pains had first wracked her. Despite her brave smiles, her eyes were shadowed to a dark purple and a cold sweat beaded her pale brow.

He had been sent from the room, his worried questions going unanswered as Rawley and the Duchess hurried to Rhea's bedside, closing the door firmly in his face. Dante took a hefty swig of brandy from the glass he had already emptied far too often. Feeling its warmth spread through his chilled body, he cursed himself for ever having laid a hand on one inch of that sweet-scented flesh.

Dante looked away from the distant hills, where the sun was falling like molten gold, and eyed the other occupants of the room in curious reflection. They no longer seemed strangers to him. Indeed, he had come to consider them his family. And now they were sharing with him the burden of waiting, and feeling all the fear he was feeling.

And as Dante stared at this newfound family of his, he thought back over the past few months and how, despite himself, he had come to like these people, even to cherish their friendship. It had been a strange experience for Dante to share his feelings. He had never had the companionship of brothers and sisters, or ever known that special relationship which usually existed between most fathers and sons.

But the situation had not changed overnight, for their suspicion of him had been deeply rooted and, even he admitted, well-founded. But with the Duchess' help, and her warmth toward him, their antagonism had gradually changed to a genuine effort at making him feel welcomed at Camareigh. He had suddenly found himself included in conversations, sometimes even the center of attention, especially among the younger members of the family, as he recounted many of his dangerous adventures as a privateer captain.

Dante's gaze lingered for a moment on the Fletcher family, who had arrived the night before, Lady Mary having had another one of her visions. He supposed Sir Terence had become used to it over the years, but it still gave Dante an uneasy feeling to think that this woman could actually see the future. As he stared at her sitting so calmly by the fire, her slim fingers busy with her needle and thread, he found himself feeling almost irritated with her, for Lady Mary looked as if all she had to worry about was dropping a stitch. He hadn't enough faith yet in her gift to relax and understand why she was unconcerned.

Dante had come to respect and like her husband, the retired general, even though Dante knew the man had been prepared to dislike him at first. Now they found much to talk about, and he knew that Sir Terence held no grudge against him. Even James, the lad who had very nearly killed him, had forgotten his embarrassment and joined his brothers and sisters in questioning Dante about his life aboard ship.

Francis Dominick, Rhea's brother and only a year younger than she, had been more difficult to win over. He had presented Dante with a haughtily lifted cold shoulder for several months. But he had been no match for Dante Leighton's charm, and was usually found elbow to elbow with his cousins Ewan and George as they tried to beat Dante at cards.

Dante also found himself liking Richard and Sarah Verrick, whom he knew MacDonald would have approved—and not only because of the red hair Richard had inherited from that clan chieftain MacDonald thought so highly of. Richard was an intelligent young man, with a deep sensitivity for the Highlands, where he made his home.

Thus far, Robin Dominick was Dante's only failure. He never had expected to receive a hand in friendship from Lucien Dominick, who still maintained a frigid politeness where his son-in-law was concerned, but he had hoped to persuade Robin Dominick that he was not quite the ogre he had been purported to be. He supposed that part of the difficulty was the strained relationship between Robin Dominick and Conny Brady, neither lad believing in forgiving and forgetting an injury. It hadn't helped matters that both were constantly demanding attention from Rhea, each feeling that the other might usurp his place in Rhea's heart. The rivalry became more bitter as the days went by.

Dante had had no small amount of trouble with Conny Brady, either, for the lad found it difficult to assume his new role as the ward of the Marquis of Jacqobi. He resisted joining in the Dominick family's activities, preferring to eat in the kitchen, or with Houston Kirby, who, although a wealthy man, said he was certainly too old to change his ways, and would take his meals in his room, where he could remain aloof from both master and servant. Dante had told the little steward that he no longer expected Kirby to serve him, but Houston Kirby, standing as tall as he could, declared with wounded dignity that, despite his wealth, it was his honor and duty to serve the Marquis of Jacqobi. One day soon, when his arthritic joints and rheumatic eyes failed him, perhaps he would consider training a young man for the privilege of serving the Leighton family. Then, with his lordship's permission, and God willing, he would live out his days in a small cottage on the estate.

Conny Brady was young enough to learn the ways of a well-bred gentleman, and since the lad had become his ward, Dante Leighton intended to see that Conny Brady never had reason to be ashamed of himself or to bring disgrace on his name through ignorance. When the Duke and Duchess invited the former cabin boy to dine with their family, Dante Leighton insisted Conny accept, telling him that, as his ward, Dante would expect the same obedience he had maintained while serving aboard ship.

"Is she goin' to die, Cap'n?" Conny Brady demanded just then, startling Dante. Standing beside his captain, his small shoulders slumped dejectedly, he eyed the man who had always been able to give him a straight answer. "Is she?"

Dante Leighton gazed helplessly down at that dark head and wondered what he could possibly say.

"Of course she isn't," Lady Mary said softly, her dove-gray eyes full of compassionate understanding. "First pregnancies always seem the most difficult, but Rhea Claire is young and healthy and wants this child very much. You must be patient," Lady Mary said in her always soothing voice.

"She *will* be all right, won't she?" Dante asked her, but he was asking for more than mere reassurance, and Lady Mary knew it.

She smiled slightly, and Dante was reminded again of the woman's serene beauty. Although her face was madonnalike in its purity of line, it was the gentle spirit of the woman more than anything else that made her so beautiful.

"I do not always understand what I have seen in a vision," Lady Mary began, her smile widening as Conny Brady's mouth dropped open, "therefore I prefer to keep them to myself, unless telling about a vision is necessary in order to help someone."

"You *have* seen something, then?" Dante demanded, his lips whitening.

Lady Mary's smile faded and she reached out and touched Dante's clenched fist. "You must learn to have more faith, Dante Leighton," she said, and her eyes suddenly seemed silvered with mystery. Dante felt a slight shiver going through him as he speculated on what she might be seeing.

"Now is not the time," she said strangely, her head tilted slightly, as though she were listening to something. "But someday I shall tell you of my vision of wild thyme and blackthorn, and of clouds edged in sungold. And I will tell you about the sun and the moon and the sea."

Dante Leighton frowned. Although sincerely fond of the woman, he was beginning to think her crazed. But just then the double doors of the private drawing room opened, and the Duchess of Camareigh came rushing in, her face pale and drawn. Lucien Dominick reached her first, taking her in his arms as she swayed. She leaned against his body, drawing strength from his touch.

"Rhea?"

Sabrina Dominick looked up from her husband's shoulder and managed a tired smile. "Rhea is fine. And you, Dante Leighton, are the proud father of a very noisy son."

Reverend Smalley found himself back behind the pulpit, sooner than propriety dictated, for the christening of Christopher Dominick Leighton, Earl of Sandrake and first grandchild of the Duke and Duchess of Camareigh. Lord Kit, as he had already been nicknamed, was a beautiful baby, with thick chestnut curls covering his small head, and a lusty cry that reverberated throughout the small chapel, causing the good reverend to wince. He couldn't even hear himself speaking.

His duty done, the reverend was pleased to return to the great house, Lord Kit's outraged cries not nearly so piercing in the high-ceilinged entrance hall or the charming Chinese Room. The reverend was not displeased when the young lord's mother excused herself and took the demanding Lord Kit for his feeding. The reverend was then able to sip his sherry in peace while considering the prospect of an early retirement.

Disengaging himself from conversation, Dante followed Rhea and caught up with her by the stairs. He took their son from her arms. Holding the now quiet baby easily with one arm, he held out his other for Rhea. Together they climbed the grand staircase.

"Did I thank you for our son?" he asked, his eyes lingering on the tiny profile just visible inside the lamb's-wool blanket.

"Many times, my lord," Rhea responded.

"And did I tell you how breathtakingly beautiful you are?"

"Many times, my lord," Rhea said, and smiled.

"And did I tell you how happy you have made me?" he asked.

"With much frequency, m'lord," she answered, her smile widening.

"And did I tell you how much I love you?" he queried further.

Rhea's eyes lowered. "Many, many times, m'lord, although 'twould be far more believable if you showed me," she said, startling him with the provocative statement. It had indeed been quite a few months since they had made love.

Dante glanced over at her, noting her fiery cheeks. "Aye, m'lady. 'Twould seem as if I do too much talking."

"Aye, m'lord," she agreed, coming to a stop, out of habit, as they passed beneath the portrait of the Elizabethan.

"He must be jealous," Dante said as he eyed the adventurer of old, then glanced down at their son.

"No, I think he would be pleased," Rhea said softly. Silently she bid farewell to her young girl's fantasy, her eyes lingering on her husband's beloved profile as they walked on down the gallery. They paused before another painting, this time because Dante wanted to.

"You seem fascinated by that portrait," Rhea commented, thinking how many things in her life had changed since the day her family stood for the portrait.

Dante smiled, his eyes on the painted violet eyes of the Duchess of Camareigh, before moving to stare lovingly at Rhea's image. "Someday I shall tell you about a young man's dream, and how all that he had wished for has come true and then some. I have no regrets about anything I have done, Rhea," he said with tantalizing obliqueness. Smiling down at her puzzled expression, he continued along the gallery.

Rhea laughed, nodding toward their son. "'Twould be a little late now to have any regrets, m'lord. Now you have a wife and son to support."

Standing before the windows of their room, Dante gazed out on the terraced gardens, past the clipped yew hedges and the roses and the lily pond, toward the open parkland in the distance. He sighed. Seldom had he known such peace. He understood why Rhea loved Camareigh so. Hearing her soft voice behind him, he turned around, staring at her while she talked softly to their son. Her golden head was bent low over the chestnut head of the baby suckling at her breast. His small hands were kneading against her while he received the nourishment from her body. Perhaps he was even unaware of the loving strength surrounding him.

"And did I thank you for naming him Christopher?" Dante asked. "I was surprised."

"I never forget anything you tell me," Rhea confessed, her fingers caressing the soft, fine curls covering her son's small head. "Captain Christopher was very important to you, more so, I think, than your own father was. I thought you would like to honor him by naming your firstborn son after him." Rhea pressed a kiss against Kit's forehead. "And I thank you for letting him bear the name Dominick, too. It means a great deal to my parents. Why did you choose my family name?"

Dante shrugged, a little uncomfortable admitting to the act of generosity. "I have come to feel a . . ." Dante paused, searching for an appropriate word. When he couldn't find one, he simply said what he felt. "A certain fondness for your family, Rhea. And although our son is a Leighton first, I want him to feel like a member of the Dominick family as well," Dante admitted. It was not an easy admission.

Rhea gazed down at their son, noting the delicate fringe of eyelash covering his closed eyes. She got to her feet slowly and, walking over to the wooden cradle beside their bed, carefully placed the sleeping babe beneath the down-filled coverlet. When he stirred she gently rocked the cradle for a moment. Soon, yawning, he drifted into that innocent sleep only the newborn know.

Rhea straightened, stretching her tired shoulders, then sighed as she felt Dante's hands massaging her tense muscles. Then the warmth of his lips was caressing the nape of her neck. Leaning back against him, she allowed his hands to slip lower, moving to cup her tender breasts beneath the parted bodice of her gown.

"Shall we stay awhile, m'lady?" he whispered against her ear, his teeth nibbling the soft lobe. Even through her many petticoats, she could feel the hardness of his ardor as he held her pressed against his hips, his hands sliding along the silk covering her thighs. "I think 'tis time we became reacquainted."

"But they will be expecting us in the salon, m'lord," Rhea whispered, her heart beating wildly.

"I never like to disappoint a lady," he murmured, turning her in his arms so he could gaze down into her flushed face before his lips covered hers in a hungry kiss. "You did issue an invitation. Or was it a challenge to prove my manhood, lest you think young Christopher an accident?"

"Dante," Rhea objected in growing embarrassment even as she lifted her lips to his, savoring the hard feel of them against hers. As she stood there in his embrace, she felt once again the trembling sensation that had the power to make her forget everything and everyone but Dante Leighton.

Dante felt her trembling response to his rising passion, and with a satisfied smile curving his lips, he lifted her in his arms and carried her to the four-poster.

"Dante, what if someone comes looking for us? What—"

But Dante silenced her with his lips. When he finally lifted his mouth from hers, she was breathless.

"Forget about everybody, for there is nothing that can come between us now," he promised, and proceeded to prove the truth of his words.

> *My pride fell with my fortunes.*
> Shakespeare

Chapter 12

SEAWYCK MANOR squatted on a rise overlooking the sea.
It could not be considered a pretty house, yet there was a
certain charm about its gray walls and stone-tiled roof. When
the sun shone, the armorial glass in the mullioned windows
was highlighted and the garden stretching along the east front
blossomed. But they were the only touches of color against
overwhelming grayness. Toward the southwest, beyond the
outbuildings and stableyard, beyond the formal gardens and
the parkland grazed by deer, beyond the gently rolling hills,
lay the village of Merleigh.

And directly west, beyond the woodland of beech and chestnut, planted to shield Seawyck from the cold winds blowing
in from the sea, the dark towers of Merdraco rose against the

horizon whenever there was no mist enshrouding the curve of coastline.

But those towers, visible or not, were never forgotten by Lady Bess Seacombe, mistress of Seawyck Manor. And even when the towers were hidden by swirling fog, she knew they were there, a continual reminder that Merdraco was still there, even if its master had fled.

Lady Bess eyed the setting sun with little appreciation of its golden splendor, for it meant that darkness would soon fall and remain until dawn; for this was to be a night of no moon.

"Damn!" she muttered beneath her breath. Turning away from the window, her eye was caught by the threadbare condition of the velvet hangings. With another curse, she pulled the heavy burgundy draperies together, closing off the dramatic view of sea, and the glorious reflection of the sun sinking in a fiery ball of copper.

Recklessly, Lady Bess poured herself another sherry, carelessly banging the crystal decanter on the polished tabletop. She quickly emptied the fluted glass, thinking she had need to bolster her courage for what she had planned for this moonless eve.

"Dear Lord, how can I do it?" she whispered, her bejeweled hands shaking as she set the glass down.

"I cannot do it," she told herself, tapping her fingertips against the mantelpiece in nervous agitation. "'Twould be madness." Then looking up, she cast an ill-favored glance at the man in the portrait above the fireplace.

"'Tis a pity you were such a fool," she said, eyeing him with renewed dislike. Although he'd been dead for over two years, he still had the power to irritate her. "More the fool I was in ever marrying you, Sir Harry Seacombe," she complained. "But who knew at the time that you were in debt and had no head for business? And then, later, to invest in that Indies plantation! What rot that turned out to be, eh, Harry?" she asked the silent man whose pale blue eyes continued to stare beyond her expressionlessly, as if uncomprehending. Indeed, they had often looked that way when Harry Seacombe was alive.

"Hounds and horses, Harry, that was all you ever knew or cared about," Lady Bess accused him. "You had your nerve marrying me under false pretenses. Not that I blame you, for I was a beauty, eh, Harry?" she demanded of him. As she caught sight of her reflection in one of the wall mirrors, she had to admit that she still cut quite a fine figure, even if she was past thirty and had given birth to two children. But the bloom was gone from her cheeks, and she had gotten too thin, she thought with critical assessment of her décolletage and the firm, perfumed flesh so temptingly revealed above the lacy edge of her corset.

"You cheated me, Harry. Not only were you in financial trouble, but you weren't even a good lover, not like . . ." Lady Bess' words trailed away and, with a sigh, she turned away from her mirrored reflection and the portrait. They both brought back too many unpleasant memories of a time when she was fifteen years younger and had made the biggest mistake of her life.

"Mama?" a young voice sounded. "Mama? Where are you?" the girl's voice grew shrill, rising to a note of fear. "Mama?"

"In the salon, Anne," Lady Bess answered reluctantly, unwilling for the moment to relinquish her dreams. The present was a discouraging place to be without some manner of escape.

"What are you doing sitting in here in the dark?" the girl demanded. Although only fourteen, Anne Seacombe was already developing into a beautiful young woman. She bore, in fact, a remarkable resemblance to her mother at that same age. "Shall I light the candles?"

"No, 'tisn't worth the expense. I shall not linger long, my dear," Lady Bess told her.

"Then shall I have Janey light a fire? 'Tis still too chilly not to once the sun has set," she offered, inadvertently reminding her mother of approaching eventide and all that would follow the darkness.

"No, she has enough to do in helping her mother in the kitchens. Besides, I do not want the house to look as if we were awake," Lady Bess said, more to herself than to her daughter. Anne's puzzled expression gave way to an unhappy one as she realized what her mother meant.

"I forgot. There is no moon tonight, is there, Mama?"

"Whatever do you mean, child?" Lady Bess demanded.

"Oh, Mama, you needn't pretend you do not know. And

I am no longer a child. Why, Lucy Widdons was wed by the time she was my age, and had a babe suckling at her—"

"She was fortunate she made it down the aisle at all, so rounded with child was she. Besides, she is a common village girl, not a Seacombe," Lady Bess reminded her restless daughter.

"I don't see how being a Seacombe makes any difference these days, for we seem to have as much trouble putting food on the table as the poorest villager," Anne said. "I know that is why you let those smugglers use our horses. 'Twould just about kill Father if he knew how they were being abused, having to haul kegs through the countryside. He wouldn't have allowed it."

Lady Bess opened her mouth to speak, to deny the charge, but just as suddenly she shut it. There really wasn't much point in lying, especially now that she had made up her mind to change things. "Your father, my dear, would have sold his soul for a keg of untaxed French brandy, but he will rest easy tonight, for I am not going to let the smugglers have our horses. In fact, I am going to sell several of them at the fair in Westlea Abbot on Saturday." Lady Bess spoke confidently, though her insides were quivering.

"But, Mama, you can't. Don't you remember what happened last year to the Webbers' farmhouse? Charles said 'twas because they wouldn't give the smugglers their horses," Anne told her mother in a breathless voice.

"How many times have I told both you and Charles not to listen to gossip?" Lady Bess said harshly, for of course he did not need to be reminded. "Charles does not know what he is talking about. Besides, no one would dare trespass here at Seawyck. Who do they think we are? Common folk? Easily terrified?" Lady Bess demanded scornfully, swallowing her fear. "And if there was one thing your father was accomplished at and had the good sense to teach me, 'twas shooting. I can load and shoot a pistol as well as any man. Let them dare raise a torch at Seawyck," Lady Bess promised.

"I hope you are right, Mama," Anne said, her eyes drifting toward the drawn window hangings, wondering if that could truly keep a determined intruder at bay.

"Of course I am," Lady Bess reassured her, forcing a smile.

"Now go and tell Mrs. Bickham to start dinner, for we shall be dining earlier than usual tonight," Lady Bess informed her daughter, determined that they would all be safely tucked away in their beds when midnight visitors arrived.

"Mama?"

"What now, Anne?" Lady Bess demanded sharply, for her nerves were bad despite the two glasses of sherry.

"I think I heard the bell."

"Nonsense. Who would be calling at this hour?" Lady Bess asked. A moment later, Bickham, their butler, coachman, gardener, and gameskeeper, announced quite grandly, "Two gentlemen to see you, m'lady."

"Their names, Bickham?"

"Captain Sir Morgan Lloyd and Lieutenant Handley, m'lady. Shall I tell them you will see them?" the butler asked, noting the unlit candles with disapproval.

"Oh, very well, but give me a moment," Lady Bess ordered, and as the door closed on the ancient retainer—he'd been at Seawyck Manor half a century when Lady Bess had arrived as a young bride fifteen years before—she hurried to the secretaire against the wall. After fumbling inside one of the drawers, she held out her hand to her daughter. "Here, light some candles."

"But I didn't think you wanted to light any—"

"Oh, Anne, do not question me now. Just light the candles," Lady Bess told her. "Damn! What the devil do they want? Who is this Sir Morgan Lloyd? The name sounds familiar. Do we know him? I know Handley."

"No, Mama," she replied as she moved around the room, an illuminating glow following in her footsteps.

"Damn. Of all nights. If they are seen coming here, there will be the devil to pay, let me tell you," she fretted, thinking of what had happened to others unfortunate enough to have been suspected by the smugglers of being informers. "Lud, just what I need, two officers of the Crown sitting here taking tea!"

Carefully she spread out her skirts on the settee, successfully hiding the darned spot in the silk cushion. "Now run along, dear, and have Bickham show our guests in," she told her daughter.

"Mama? They haven't come to arrest you, have they?" she asked tremulously.

Lady Bess choked. The thought had not entered her mind until her daughter kindly mentioned it. "Of course not," she hissed, but she eyed the imported lace adorning her gown with less pleasure for it had come from smuggled cargo. "Now do as you were told. Our guests have been kept waiting too long, and I'll not have it said that Lady Bess Seacombe is ill-mannered."

"Very well, Mama," said Anne. She hurried through the entrance hall, her breathlessly spoken words to the butler barely heard by the old gent. She risked a quick glance at their two visitors, but when she caught sight of them, she wished she hadn't. Never had she seen so stern-visaged a man as was the taller and older of the two officers. She was suddenly thankful that she had been sent from the room, and she pitied her mother having to face that man and tell lies.

Lady Bess Seacombe was thinking much the same thing as the two men entered, and she met the steely-eyed gaze of the older officer. "Gentlemen? Please sit down. To what do I owe the pleasure of this visit?" she asked politely, managing a welcoming smile while noting that there was something tantalizingly familiar about the tall naval officer. Undeniably, he was a handsome man, but his blue eyes were cold and assessing, and his well-shaped lips were drawn together in a grim line. This officer, unlike his subordinate, was no weak-willed fool.

"'Tis not on pleasure that I have come to call, madam," Sir Morgan Lloyd responded, his directness confirming her speculations.

"Indeed, sir?" Lady Bess said, her tones becoming frigid. "Why, 'pon hearing that two officers had come to call, I suspected that some of my cows must have gotten loose again and strayed off our property. But since my cows cannot swim, and you, sir, are a naval officer, I must have been mistaken." She met Sir Morgan's gaze with haughty arrogance. "Or, has the navy taken to milking cows?"

There was no flicker of humor in those icy blue eyes. Neither Dante Leighton nor Rhea Claire would have recognized the man who, only months before, had drunk to their good health.

He was a changed man. "I have come merely to introduce myself to you."

"Oh?" she asked in a tone which implied that he would have gone beneath her notice otherwise.

"Madam, I am now the highest-ranking officer in this area, and as such have been invested with special and full authority to deal with any crimes against the Crown which result from the illegal smuggling of goods—by order of the Admiralty, the Board of Customs, and His Majesty King George himself. And I am giving you, as well as other members of the community, fair warning that I shall rid this coastline of its infestation of smugglers."

Even though Lieutenant Handley had been privy to this dialogue before, he seemed just as startled as Lady Bess was while listening to it. "I am indeed impressed," Lady Bess murmured, thinking the man must be extraordinary to have been given such powers. "And, you, Lieutenant? You answer to the good captain, too?" she asked innocently enough, never having cared for Lieutenant Handley. He was too humble, too fawning and subservient. She never had been able to stand sniveling, servile people. Too often a toadying attitude hid a mean streak.

"Naturally, m'lady, I have assured Sir Morgan that he will have my complete cooperation. I can only hope that I will be able to be of some small service to him." Lady Bess did not miss the look of disgust which passed across Sir Morgan Lloyd's austere face. He must have suffered much of the lieutenant's lickspittle humility.

Lady Bess asked, "But, Captain, what does your assignment have to do with me? I am but a grieving widow, with two young children to raise. I am hardly likely to cross, ah, what is that charming saying?" she paused, looking thoughtful. "Ah, yes, to cross bows with you."

"Whether that possibility is likely or not, madam, I have yet to discover, but I am also thinking of those people who have been living in fear because of this smuggling gang," Sir Morgan explained.

"In other words, sir, you would look kindly upon an informant?"

"I beg to differ on the appellation, for I think that any man or woman would be doing a great service by giving me information. It could also save his life."

"And *I* beg to differ there, for I am certain 'twould ensure his death. However, as I know nothing of this gang's affairs, I cannot see how the matter concerns me," Lady Bess said.

"Forgive me then, madam, for taking up your valuable time," Sir Morgan murmured. The contempt in his voice flicked Lady Bess like a whiplash.

"Not at all, Captain. May I offer you gentlemen a brandy? Or perhaps you would care to share a pot of tea with me? I have longed for a cup for quite some time," Lady Bess asked courteously. Her face reddened with embarrassment when the captain's narrowed blue eyes lingered on the sherry bottle and then returned to her.

"No thank you, madam, I have other calls to make yet," Sir Morgan declined. For some strange reason, Lady Bess felt his response as a rebuke.

"I shouldn't wish to keep you, Captain Lloyd," she said, rising in dismissal.

Sir Morgan Lloyd got slowly to his feet. Lady Bess realized then that those sharp eyes had not missed the darned spot on the settee, or the threadbare carpets and draperies. His eyes were taking note, no doubt, of the peeling paint, and the one lighter wall where a painting had hung before being sold to pay the butcher's bill.

"You have far to ride?" she asked, trying to draw the captain's attention away from the beggarly condition of her salon.

This time Lieutenant Handley couldn't quite control his feelings. He sighed in exasperation. "Yes, m'lady, I am afraid so, for although I told Sir Morgan that Merdraco stands empty, he insists on seeing the castle. And from there we must travel back to Westlea Abbot, where I hope I can persuade Sir Morgan to stop and enjoy a warming rum before continuing on to Wolfingwold Abbey."

"Indeed?" Lady Bess seemed startled.

"Yes. I thought I saw a light in one of the towers of Merdraco a few nights past," Sir Morgan commented casually.

"Merdraco is not likely to be inhabited ever again," Lady Bess said, smiling as she remembered the shining lights and the strains of music which used to fill the night air. She sighed with regret.

"You think not? And why is that, Lady Bess?" Sir Morgan inquired.

"Since you are a stranger hereabouts, you wouldn't know. The marquis, Lord Jacqobi, left Merdraco when he was but a young man, and no one has seen or heard of him since," the lieutenant replied, eager to repeat the gossip he had overheard.

"I see," was all Captain Sir Morgan Lloyd said.

"Of course, were he here," Lieutenant Handley continued conversationally, despite the awkward silence that, for different reasons, existed between Sir Morgan and Lady Bess, "'twould make your job all that much easier."

"Oh?"

"Yes. He was quite the wild one, or so I've been told. He was even accused of murdering a young girl out on the moors."

"And what does that have to do with making my job easier, Lieutenant?" Sir Morgan wanted to know. His dislike of the young man was becoming even more intense for he could guess what the lieutenant's next words were going to be.

"Why, he would be, of course, the most likely suspect to be the leader of the smuggling gang. He lost his inheritance through gambling, and what better way to regain a fortune?"

"One must have proof, Lieutenant. We cannot hang a man merely because he possesses a bad reputation," Sir Morgan responded.

"My pardon, sir. Of course, you are right," the lieutenant quickly changed his tune. "But I still do not see any reason for going to Merdraco. My horse always acts crazy when I'm there," he said without thinking.

"You have had cause to go there often, Lieutenant?" Sir Morgan asked quietly, and Lady Bess told herself never to make a slip of the tongue around the man. He missed nothing.

Lieutenant Handley coughed, clearing his throat nervously. "My troop and I have had to patrol all along the coastline, sir. And in the course of that duty, we have ridden to Merdraco. But we've never even stumbled across a mouse," the lieutenant reported with a sickly grin, knowing he was going to look a fool with his next words. "I really believe, though, that the place is haunted. Yes, really. There are always people claiming to see lights flashing. Nobody goes up there anymore.''

"Then what better place for the smugglers to land their goods than Merdraco?''

"Can't do that very well, Sir Morgan. Dragon's Cove is the devil to sail in and out of. Most don't make it. Why, just a few months ago—'' the loquacious lieutenant began, only to swallow the last of his words. "Sir Morgan, please forgive me, I meant no offense. I forgot about the relationship,'' he pleaded, genuinely sorry this time.

Lady Bess stared hard at Sir Morgan Lloyd. "Lloyd? I thought the name sounded familiar. Where have I heard it before?''

"Perhaps, madam, you knew my brother, Captain Benjamin Lloyd, late of H.M.S. *Hindrance*, which was wrecked in Dragon's Cove not half a year ago?''

"Good lord, of course,'' Lady Bess exclaimed, and as she continued to stare up into Sir Morgan Lloyd's hardened face, she realized the reason behind his assuming command of his brother's former station. No wonder he had managed to get additional powers. "I was very sorry to hear of his ship's sinking. I met your brother on several occasions and always thought him a most polite young gentleman.''

"Thank you,'' Sir Morgan said abruptly, distinctly not inviting her condolences.

"I am surprised, however, that on the strength of that relationship alone, you were given so important a command,'' Lady Bess asked.

"Sir Morgan Lloyd, Lady Bess, has had command of his own ship for many years, and was considered one of His Majesty's most illustrious captains on duty in the colonies,'' the lieutenant supplied. "If anyone can catch those smugglers, then 'twill be Sir Morgan.''

For the first time since he had entered Seawyck Manor, Sir Morgan Lloyd smiled. Lady Bess gasped at the startling change it made in the man, and she found herself wondering what he must have been like before his brother's death.

"Let us hope you are correct, Lieutenant Handley,'' Sir Morgan said, eyeing the young officer with interest. "Naturally, I shall not expect to achieve that end without your help,'' he added, his smile widening as Lieutenant Handley grinned, unable to contain his pleasure.

"A pleasure, Lady Bess," Sir Morgan said, nodding with the minimum of acknowledgment for her presence. "We still have a long way to ride, Lieutenant."

"Oh, did I hear you say you were planning to pay a call on Wolfingwold Abbey?" Lady Bess asked. At the impatient look which crossed the insufferable Sir Morgan's face, she smiled, keeping her information to herself. "Then please give Sir Miles my best." She did not inform them that she had passed him on the road the day before, bound for London.

As the door shut on the two figures, one in blue, the other in scarlet, Lady Bess smiled. They were destined for a long, frustrating ride, and it even looked like rain.

Lady Bess drew the brush through her daughter's long, black hair with slow, even strokes. Grasping the soft strands, Lady Bess parted them into three lengths and began to braid them.

"Mama?"

"Ummmm?"

"There really was a light in one of the towers of Merdraco the other night. I saw it."

"Nonsense, child," she said absently. Then her voice sharpened. "Were you listening outside the door? Haven't I warned both you and Charles time and time again against so rude an activity?"

"I was coming to see if you wanted tea," Anne explained. "'Tis haunted, though."

"Of course not."

"But didn't the Lady Elayne jump to her death from the cliffs near there? They say 'tis she who wanders the halls."

Lady Bess sighed. She wasn't in the mood for ghost tales that evening, what with worrying about the padlock she'd had Bickham put on the stable doors. "She fell."

"Couldn't the smugglers have pushed her?"

"There weren't any smugglers at Merdraco fifteen years ago," she murmured, thinking that everything good in her life had happened fifteen years ago.

Anne Seacombe caught the unconscious sigh. Glancing up,

she stared at her mother curiously. "That was about the time the Marquis of Jacqobi left, wasn't it?"

"Yes, it was the same time."

"Was he truly as wild as they say he was? And as handsome?"

"And who has been speaking of him? Janey? That girl talks too much."

"Well?"

"Well, what?"

"Well, was he?"

"Yes, I s'pose he was."

"Did he really murder that girl?"

"You certainly are full of questions this eve, Madame Nosey," Lady Bess said.

"Did he, Mama?"

"No, he didn't," was the emphatic reply.

"You sound very certain. How do you know?"

"I just do. I would never believe such a monstrous thing of Dante. When you love someone, child, you can believe no wrong of them."

"But you broke off your engagement to him. If you loved him, why did you forsake him?" Anne's dark brown eyes searched her mother's flushed face. "Ouch! You pulled my hair too tight!" she cried.

"Because he had gambled away his inheritance," Lady Bess said tersely while she tied a red velvet ribbon in her daughter's hair. "Unfortunately, one must have means of putting bread on the table, and Dante was more concerned about the cards he was laying down on the table. How could I marry a man who couldn't support me?" Lady Bess demanded. Even to her, she sounded hollow. "At least, I thought so at the time. I was so young. And so very foolish."

"I am sorry, Mama. I did not think you still cared for him," Anne said softly.

"What? This is ridiculous. 'Twould have been a most unfortunate match! He was wild and arrogant and damned everyone's eyes, and I was too used to getting my own way, and not sympathetic to other people's needs. We most likely would have killed one another before the month was out," Lady Bess said wryly.

"You are still in love with him, aren't you, Mama?"

But Lady Bess Seacombe remained silent. That was an admission she dared not make even to herself, for how much more empty could her life be than it was already? And there was no future in dreaming.

"I know you were not happy with Father."

There was a startled silence, and then Bess asked frankly, "Was it so obvious?"

"How could you be happy with him when he was forever drunk? And when he did speak, 'twas always of his hounds," Anne said, surprising her mother by her keen memory. "I can see that you might long for a former love, especially now that you are widowed."

"Thank you, my dear," Lady Bess said, and for the first time she saw Anne as the thoughtful young woman she was becoming, and not as just her little girl.

"Do you ever think of him?"

Lady Bess smiled, tugging gently this time on the long black braid. "Yes. More than I should. And who knows if he is even still alive?"

"Maybe one day he will come riding up to the house on a big black charger and carry you off to his castle," said Anne, who was still young enough to believe in romantic dreams.

"If he were to return, he would probably shun me, and with good reason. I betrayed him. He will never forgive me," Lady Bess said sadly, knowing she would not forgive herself.

"Oh, Mama, no. He must still love you. He will if he ever sees you again, for you are so beautiful," Anne's dark eyes mirrored admiration.

"Fanciful child," said Lady Bess affectionately, pleased by the compliment.

"Besides, Mama, your grandfather would never have allowed you to have wed him once his reputation was ruined, especially once he became penniless. You were underage, and you would have needed permission."

"You are right, my dear. Grandfather refused permission when he discovered Dante's gambling had led him to lose his inheritance. And, of course, when Dante was accused of murder, he forbade me even to see Dante again." Lady Bess' expression became sadder. "He later came across information which proved Dante's innocence—while convicting me in his eyes."

"What was that?"

Bess hesitated, then explained. "Something I said. I was ill with fever, and I rambled on and on about something which, until then, had remained a secret between Dante and me. I do not think that Grandfather has ever forgiven me for it, or for what I did to Dante Leighton by lying. I know I have never forgiven myself."

"I always wondered why Grandfather visited us so rarely."

"He bears you and Charles no grudge. He is a good man and an honest one, but very rigid. I disgraced him by breaking his code of ethics. And oddly enough, disreputable though Dante may have seemed, in Grandfather's eyes he acted the gentleman. Now," Lady Bess ordered, pressing a kiss against her daughter's forehead, "off to bed with you."

"Good night, Mama," Anne said, and kissed Lady Bess' cheek. Spinning around and around, her nightdress billowing out, Anne danced to the door, then paused, listening. "Did you hear something, Mama?" she asked, suddenly frightened.

Lady Bess swallowed hard. "No." She managed to sound firm.

"Go to bed, child."

As the door closed on the small figure, Lady Bess sighed tiredly, but her eyes strayed to the shuttered window rather than to her bed. Her rooms overlooked the stables. She conquered the temptation to glance out, in case someone standing out there in the darkness was looking up. Clad only in the thin lawn nightgown, Lady Bess shivered, but with cold, not nerves, she reassured herself as she glanced at the darkened hearth.

Pulling a wool shawl around her shoulders, she crossed her arms over her breasts, hugging herself protectively, and then began to pace. She would wait for the clock in the entrance hall to strike once, and then . . .

Lady Bess awoke with a start, her heart pounding. It was too quiet. What had awakened her? Tired of pacing, she had curled up in the winged-back chair near the fireplace, but that had been hours ago, she realized as she heard the clock strike the hour. It was well past one, the hour she had been dreading, yet nothing had happened.

Lady Bess sighed. She uncurled her legs and glanced around the floor for her slippers. She froze as her bare foot struck something cold and hard. In the half light she just barely managed to make out the broken padlock she had locked on the stable doors earlier that evening.

"Did ye really think 'twould keep me out, Lady Bess?" a harsh voice demanded.

Lady Bess' scream died in her throat. She stared up at the man leaning negligently against her bed, a glass of brandy in his large hands. Tall, he was broad of shoulder and lean of hip. Clad in leather breeches and frock coat, he looked like any villager, but his heavy jackboots were caked with mud. The man was accustomed to much more walking than was normal.

"You!" she whispered hoarsely.

"Ah, *Lady* Bess, I thought ye smarter than that. 'Tis a pity."

"Get out! How dare you set foot in my house!" She sounded sure of herself, though her body was shaking.

"Ah, Bessie, ye're a cruel woman, ye are, to be turnin' out a man who has been workin' hard all night long, and who's been makin' ye some money. Ye've disappointed me, ye have."

Jack Shelby was standing in her bedchamber, drinking her brandy. Lady Bess Seacombe shook her head. That couldn't be happening to her! Oh, what a fool she had been to think she could double-cross Jack Shelby and get away with it. He and his cutthroats ruled the farms and villages lying along the whole nearby coastline. Nobody told Shelby what to do. He had defied the authorities for too long to know fear of the law.

Lady Bess eyed the man who had broken into her home and who stood so boldly before her, gazing down at her with that sadistic smile. And as his narrow, catlike eyes moved slowly over her, she suddenly knew another kind of fear. Many women sought his favors, for there was a certain sensual attractiveness in his coarse-featured face and firmly muscled body, but he preferred taking women by force.

With a suddenness that caught him off guard, Lady Bess jumped to her feet and flew to the door. She even managed to turn the knob and open the door before she felt herself being lifted off the floor. The door was kicked shut. He held her struggling body against him with one arm, the warm, brandy-scented breath of his laughter striking her on the face.

Quickly, Jack Shelby pressed his lips against the slender column of her throat.

"By God, but ye're still a beauty, Bess Seacombe," he whispered against her mouth before his mouth covered hers, the hard pressure forcing her lips apart.

As if she were standing aside, watching, Bess felt his big hands moving across her hips to fondle her buttocks, the thin lawn nightdress giving little protection. His large fingers moved up her back, tracing her backbone in a way that told her he could as easily snap it in two as caress it.

An indistinct roar filled her ears and she felt faint when, his mouth moving away, she heard the ripping of material as he tore her nightdress from her.

His mouth was on her breasts, licking and biting at them like a wild animal gorging on its kill. Bess whimpered as she felt him pressing against her.

"I've often thought of takin' ye, Bess. I've watched as ye and that pretty little daughter of yours rode on the moors, and I've wanted to feel ye naked flesh against mine. Annie, that be your daughter's name, eh?" Jack Shelby said thickly, his yellowish eyes staring hypnotically into her dark eyes. "She reminds me of ye at that age, when ye were goin' to marry the young lord of Merdraco. Did he ever get the chance to fondle ye like this, Bessie?" Jack demanded as his hands moved sensuously along her bare thigh.

"Please let me go," Bess cried, tears on her pale face.

"No, I don't reckon he did, 'cause he was too busy seducin' my Lettie. Meetin' her out on the moors, tellin' her lies. Strangled her, didn't he, Bessie?" Jack Shelby demanded, his eyes glowing madly while the long fingers of one hand curved around Bess' neck, pressing against her throat.

"N-no, please. You're wrong. H-he didn't kill her. He was with—"

"Aaaah, shut up, woman!" Jack Shelby spat. "Still in love with him, eh? After all these years, ye still defend him? Well, not to me, Bessie. I know who murdered my sweet Lettie, and now I think I'll enjoy what the young master of Merdraco was too busy for. Ah, Bessie, ye smell good," he murmured, burying his hot face between her breasts.

He dropped her on her bed and feasted his eyes on her pale

flesh while he unbuttoned his breeches. Bess closed her eyes against the sight, her scalding tears trickling beneath her dark lashes. She heard him mutter something, then felt the bed sag as he fell on top of her.

His heavy body covered hers, but he stopped moving. Opening a wary eye, Bess stared in amazement at the sight of her daughter standing over the unconscious form of Jack Shelby, a raised poker held in her shaking hands.

"Oh, my God, Anne!" she cried out.

"I killed him, didn't I?" Anne's voice sounded as if it was coming from a long way off.

"No, damn it. He is still alive. I can feel him breathing." Here, lift him and I'll slide out the other side of the bed. Hurry, we don't want to him to wake up."

Anne braced herself. She didn't want to touch the man. Dropping the poker with a thud, she grasped one of Jack Shelby's arms and pulled with all her strength. And although she couldn't move him much, it was enough to allow her mother to climb out of bed.

Anne glanced away while her mother searched frantically for a dressing gown. "Now, what the devil are we going to do with him?" Lady Bess asked as she eyed the big man with distaste, and had she a sword in her hand, she most likely would have run him through.

Suddenly Anne started to weep, her shoulders shaking as her hysteria grew. "I'm so scared. He's an awful, horrible man."

Lady Bess put her arms around her daughter, holding her tight. "My child, 'tis all right now. You saved me," she told her, the truth of it just sinking in. "How did you know he was here?"

Anne sniffed, wiping away her tears with the back of her hand. "I couldn't sleep very well, and when I heard the hall door squeak, I wondered who was awake. I thought, if it was you, I would come and talk with you. B-but then I saw *him* climbing the stairs. I don't think I have ever been so frightened."

"Thank God Bickham never got around to oiling those hinges," Lady Bess breathed. "And you could have stayed in your room. You should have, too, you know. Jack Shelby is a dangerous man. He could have done you great harm, my dear."

"I couldn't leave you alone with him. I found the poker and when I cracked open the door and saw him, I—I just ran in and hit him."

"Wonderful child," Lady Bess said, then cast a speculative glance at the unconscious form of the most feared criminal in Devonshire. "I would be doing everybody a favor if I finished him off now, but..." She continued to stare down at him, wondering what they could possibly do with him. She didn't want him anywhere nearby when he awoke.

"I wish we could just throw him out the window," Anne said, eyeing the man from a safe distance behind her mother.

Lady Bess remained thoughtfully quiet, but her eyes strayed to the window more than once. "A splendid idea, child. We could never get him down the stairs, or even to the door. He's too heavy. But we can get him to the window, and then send him on his way," Lady Bess mused.

"But Mother, won't the fall kill him?" Anne exclaimed nervously, glancing again at the man. She thought she heard a groan.

"More's the pity it won't, but he'll live. The roof of the kitchen wing is just beneath my window. When he rolls off that, he'll most likely land in the rhododendron bushes. Come along, Anne. You've shown more courage than I would have. "Don't let me down now. I intend to have this swine out of my house and in the barnyard by the time he comes to," Lady Bess said breathlessly, for she had managed to hook one of his arms across her shoulders, and it had cost her no little effort.

Anne took a deep breath and grabbed hold of his other arm. Between them they managed to drag him backward a few steps, where, with a mighty push, they sent Jack Shelby sprawling backward through the window.

A heavy thud sounded, and then a scraping noise as he rolled off the steeply sloping roof. Then there was a final thump. Lady Bess and Anne exchanged a glance, then looked out the window.

All was dark below, and quiet. For a heart-stopping moment, Lady Bess thought he might not have survived the fall.

But as she strained to see into the darkness, she heard a rustling movement followed by mumbled cursing.

Drawing Anne back from the window, Lady Bess quickly pulled it shut. Then without a word she hurried from her bed-chamber and down the darkened stairs. She reached the hall door and rushed through it, not stopping to think that Jack Shelby might already have reached the kitchen door. Breathing raggedly, she bolted it firmly from within, then ran back through the kitchen to the hall, bolting that door as well. Leaning against it, Lady Bess stared up to the landing where Anne was standing.

"We're safe—for now," Bess Seacombe whispered. The clock was chiming the hour, and soon the sun would be rising.

Anne came hurrying down the stairs, throwing herself into her mother's arms. "Mama, what if he comes back? What will we do? Who is there to protect us? What if he brings those other smugglers with him?" Anne cried.

Lady Bess rested her chin on top of her daughter's head. "I don't know what we are going to do, child," she admitted slowly, her voice shaking with pent-up emotion. The past hour had seemed the longest of her life. "He's a vengeful, vicious man, and he will try to get even with me. Not you, Anne, for he doesn't know you were there. And he must never know that. Promise me?" she asked.

Anne nodded, her tears dampening the silk of Lady Bess' dressing gown. "Can't we ask that officer who was here earlier to protect us, Mama?"

"No! That would be the worst thing possible. Although Captain Sir Morgan Lloyd would certainly like to see Jack Shelby hanging from the gibbets, for 'twas Jack who murdered the captain's brother. Everyone knows that. But I'm afraid Jack Shelby and his Sons of Belial are too strong. Sir Morgan Lloyd will surely end up dead long before Jack Shelby does. No, I am afraid no one can help us. We must try to survive this on our own. We can only pray that someone comes along to distract Jack Shelby's attention from us. Pray, child, that the person who does has the devil's own luck."

As the ancients
Say wisely, have a care o' th'
      main chance,
And look before you ere you leap
For as you sow, ye are like to reap.
                                          Samuel Butler

Chapter 13

"**B**ETCHA can't stay on his back this time, either," Robin Dominick challenged Conny Brady. Conny had just picked himself up off the ground for the second time since climbing on the back of the gentle little mare.

"Ye be all right, then, Master Brady?" Butterick demanded, for he was responsible for the lad's safety. The task of teaching him to ride horseback had been placed in his hands, and he wanted no harm to befall the young ward of the Marquis of Jacqobi. That was not what certain other individuals were wishing, Butterick thought as he eyed young Lord Robin's grinning face. "Don't be despairin', Master Brady," Butterick said bracingly. The lad was looking quite dejected as he tried to wipe some of the mud off his breeches.

"Why, I even managed to teach young Lord Robin how to ride," Butterick said, grinning as Robin's mouth dropped open.

"Is it true that Robin landed on his head so many times it was nearly flattened?" Stuart Fletcher asked, and grinned. His smirk became a grimace as Robin's elbow connected with his ribs.

Butterick's appreciative laughter did little to ease the tension.

"Aye, we'll have the young gentleman riding with the best of them soon enough," Butterick predicted as he gave the lad a hand up into the saddle again.

"Haven't you always said, Butterick, that you could tell a gentleman by the way he kept his seat?" Robin asked. "Does that mean, then, that if one isn't a good rider, that he is no gentleman?"

Conny Brady's lips trembled. Holding the reins firmly, he gripped his courage. He was trying desperately not to slide off the horse's back and provide further entertainment for Lord Robin Dominick. He walked the horse around and around the stable yard, ignoring the remarks he couldn't help but overhear from the unsympathetic gallery of cousins watching him from the stone steps beside one of the stable buildings.

"Now ye be doin' better, lad, but don't be holdin' so tightly to the reins. Relax," Butterick told the petrified lad. "There ye go, that's better, now," he said, his booming voice reassuring Conny. The boy actually began to enjoy the feel of the horse beneath him. "Now give her a little nudge in the side and let's see ye trot some," Butterick called.

"Aye, or you'll be until midnight tomorrow getting back into the stables," Robin called, pleased by the loud guffaws that followed his joke.

Butterick sent the lad a disapproving glare. Young Lord Robin had become a bit of a troublemaker of late. He'd always been a high-spirited lad, indeed, a real little mischief-maker, but there had never been any harm done. Since Conny Brady had showed up, however, the childish horesplay had turned rough, and the good-natured banter had turned into ridicule. It had him worried, Butterick admitted. He liked young Lord

Robin, and until just last year, when Lady Rhea Claire was kidnaped, he had been such a nice young gentleman. He wondered if the Duchess realized how much her son had changed.

"Ye're doin' nicely, lad. Keep it up," Butterick called to Conny, who was trotting the mare around the yard with more assurance now.

"I bet he'll be down before he comes around again," Robin whispered, and with a quick glance around, he stretched out his leg and knocked out a pail which had been left on a step just beneath where the boys were sitting.

The sudden clattering of the pail against the stone as it rolled down the steps had the desired effect. The little mare was startled, and she unseated an unsuspecting Conny Brady for the third time that day.

"Are ye all right, Master Brady?" Butterick cried again as he ran to help the young boy to his feet.

"Aye, and 'twill take more than a chicken-hearted shonky who wouldn't know the difference 'tween a jack pin and a shackle crow to get the best of me. Well, that spouter's wet as a scrubber if he thinks he's tubbed Constantine Magnus Tyrone Brady," the lad said, rubbing his aching elbow. "I may be shippin' it green right now, but I'll scupper that milksop yet, even if he is Lady Rhea Claire's brother," Conny Brady promised between gritted teeth.

Butterick, who'd never been aboard ship, much less to sea, shook his head in amazement, wishing the lad would speak proper English. If what he suspected was true, then young Lord Robin had better keep an eye out, for this young buck was out to even the score, and between the two, he thought Conny Brady might well be the toughest, and where this young lad learned to fight, there was no such thing as a gentleman.

"I reckon that be enough for today, Master Brady," Butterick decided, thinking he'd better not set the lad up for any more of Lord Robin's pranks. He was about to say as much and he sent a warning glance toward the snickering group of cousins when several outriders in unfamiliar livery rode into the yard. Their arrival preceded that of their master's coach. The Grand Ball would be held that evening, and lords and ladies and fancy gentlemen and their wives had been arriving since the day before.

"Off with the lot of ye!" Butterick roared. The stableyard would be too busy and he couldn't have mischievous children underfoot.

"Don't s'pose we'd be seeing any more riding today anyway," Robin Dominick commented, alluding to the fact that Conny Brady had spent more time on the ground than on horseback.

Conny Brady sniffed, unconsciously imitating Houston Kirby when the little steward was getting ready to fire one of the salvos which could be shattering. Conny Brady walked past his nemesis and, casting him a sly glance, said, "Hey, dab toes, ye think ye're sittin' pretty tall when ye're on the back of that pony of yours, eh? Well, ye ain't seen anythin' until ye've ridden the riggin' or climbed to the topgallant mast. Reckon, though, ye landlubbers ain't got the guts. Aye, we'd probably have to stonnicky ye to get ye movin' up the mast," Conny Brady said, his expression insultingly disgusted. He sized up the violet-eyed, dark-curled son of the Duke of Camareigh with great disdain. "'Course, the cap'n, he did it all the time. And I bet His Grace could do it easily. *He's* a man, all right. I bet even your baby brother could do it. Lord Andy would be up there in no time," Conny added as a final insult. Then with a challenging grin, he sauntered away.

"Better lift a leg, mates," Conny advised over his shoulder, "or Mr. Butterick might have ye helpin' his boys clean out the stables."

"I don't think he likes you, Robin," Anna commented, her soft gray eyes full of admiration as she watched Conny Brady's swaggering figure disappear around the side of the stables. "He certainly knows a lot. But then, none of us has traveled around the world like he has."

"He hasn't traveled around the world. Just to the colonies and down to the Indies," Robin corrected her, unable to hide his envy.

"Do you really think Andy could climb to the top of one of those tall masts?" Maggie wanted to know, her eyes looking her cousin Robin up and down as if now questioning his abilities.

Robin Dominick could stand no more. Jumping to his feet, he hurried after the braggart Conny Brady. Oddly, the boy hadn't gotten too far ahead, and Robin caught up with him near one of the tall, stately chestnuts lining the drive.

"You think you know everything, don't you?" Robin Dominick demanded as he reached out and spun Conny Brady round to face him.

"I don't know everything, but I figure I know a lot more than you," Conny Brady baited.

"Like what?"

"Like this," Conny said quickly, now that the bait had been taken.

Robin Dominick, surrounded by his cousins, watched in amazement as Conny Brady pulled off his boots and scrambled beneath the overhanging branches of the big chestnut. He disappeared for a few minutes, then suddenly appeared overhead, his grinning face staring down at them from high above.

"Ooooh, how did you get up there so quickly?" Maggie demanded, her eyes round with disbelief.

"'Twas easy, if ye know how. Why, this isn't anythin' at all compared to climbin' the riggin' aboard the *Sea Dragon*," Conny boasted. He disappeared again, only to reappear even higher up.

"I bet if I was to look hard, I could see all the way to the sea," the onetime cabin boy stated, little realizing how much longing there was in his voice.

"If you were as smart as you think you are, then you'd know you couldn't. We're too far inland," Robin Dominick called.

"Ye think not, eh? Well, at least I can see beyond Camareigh. Maybe, if I climb higher, I might even be able to see beyond those hills in the distance," he speculated. And Conny Brady climbed higher into the tree.

"Why don't you try to touch the sun while you're up there, Master Brady?" Robin called scathingly.

"Why don't you, Lord Robin? Or are ye afraid of heights? Ye may be quite the gentleman on horseback, but I don't reckon ye'd make much of a sailor, at least not on board the *Sea Dragon*. The cap'n would have ye scrubbin' the decks," Conny Brady called down to him.

Robin Dominick glared at his cousins. He didn't enjoy finding himself the laughingstock, especially because of a scrubby little guttersnipe who had connived his way into Rhea Claire's affections.

"Well?" Stuart asked.

"Well what?" Robin said, not meeting the challenging glance.

"Are you going to let him get away with calling you a coward?" Stuart demanded, quite put out about the matter, but then he could afford to be in high dudgeon, for he wasn't the one who was going to have to climb the tree.

"Hey, down there!" a faraway voice called. "Ye sure look little and insignificant to me from way up here on top o' the world," Conny Brady's triumphant voice drifted down.

"I'll take that puffed-up jack-pudding down a peg or two before I'm finished," Robin Dominick promised as he disappeared into the tree.

His cousins backed away from the overhanging branches. Craning their necks, they stared up at the two boys climbing higher and higher into the tree. They were unaware of being observed by a rider who, having seen the little group, had halted his horse along the drive, curious.

Robin Dominick continued to climb higher, but he was definitely not enjoying the experience. His face flushed, his breathing coming quickly with anxiety, Robin Dominick glanced around, wondering what had happened to Conny Brady. He had been above him not a moment before. Thinking that he might have fallen and feeling a certain guilty concern, Robin Dominick quickly glanced down. He wished he hadn't, for the world swirled and spun, and the branches looked as if they were reaching out for him.

Robin closed his eyes, pressing his hot cheek against the rough bark of the tree trunk and gaining some comfort from the sturdy feel of it. With a sigh, Robin felt the sky and earth right themselves, steadying enough for him to regain his balance. He managed to keep his luncheon inside his churning stomach, but just barely.

"You all right, Robin?" a voice called from somewhere far below, reminding Robin of exactly how far aboveground he was. He stared out toward the hills in the distance, then closer, at the roof of his home. It was a view never seen before, and as he thought about it, he realized he really did not care to see Camareigh from this perspective again.

"Robin! Can you hear me?" Stuart called up. His cousin certainly had more courage than he did, climbing up into the top of that tree!

"Cat got your tongue?" Conny Brady called, startling Stuart Fletcher, for the voice came from right beside him.

"How did you get down? I thought you were even higher up than Robin," he exclaimed.

Conny Brady gave him an incredulous look. "Ye think I'm crazy enough to go that high?" he demanded, chuckling as he saw his enemy stuck at the top of the tree. Robin was apparently holding on for dear life. "Reckon some folk be dumber than they look."

"And some people should know better, Master Brady," said a deep voice from behind the children.

Conny Brady spun around, blinking nervously. "Mr. Marlowe, sir!"

Alastair Marlowe eyed the *Sea Dragon*'s former cabin boy. "Now, Master Brady, who is the unfortunate lad you've made game of? And who," he added with a worried glance upward, "now seems to be stuck?"

"That's my cousin Lord Robin Dominick," Anna declared, her eyes full of tears as she imagined the funeral they most likely would be having to honor the recently deceased Robin Dominick.

"Lady Rhea Claire's little brother?" Alastair Marlowe demanded incredulously. Conny Brady must have lost his mind. He was, after all, a guest at Camareigh, and as such he shouldn't be putting one of the family in danger.

Conny Brady hunched his shoulders, a defiant glint in his eye, and stood his ground. "Reckon he knows what he's doin'. Leastwise, so he's been braggin' to everyone. 'Course, he don't seem to be laughin' so hard now," Conny Brady couldn't help but add, and Alastair Marlowe, dismounting, caught the satisfied smile.

"You going to leave him up there, Master Brady?" Alastair asked quietly.

Conny Brady eyed his former shipmate carefully. Mr. Marlowe didn't seem overly concerned about Lord Robin's predicament. "He climbed up there without any help from me."

"Aye, but then he probably wasn't thinking clearly, was he? You made him mad with your insults," Alastair Marlowe guessed.

Conny Brady glanced at him, startled. How had he known? "Reckon Lord Robin can get down well enough," Conny said confidently, but when he risked a glance to the top of the tree, Lord Robin Dominick was still clinging to the same place. "Reckon if he was in need of help, he'd call out."

Alastair Marlowe smiled. "You know he won't, Conny. You wouldn't, would you? You wouldn't lose face before your enemy," he commented, correctly guessing the situation.

"Robin sure can be stubborn sometimes," Stuart confided, confirming Alastair's thoughts. "Robin likes his own way. He always manages to get us in trouble, but he's not a bad fellow, really he isn't. I know if I needed help, he'd be right there," Stuart continued, thinking of the time he'd gotten his hand stuck down the neck of a valuable vase and Robin had helped him get it loose. Of course, it *had* been Robin who'd hidden the shoe buckle in there in the first place. "Maybe I ought to go get Uncle Lucien?"

Alastair Marlowe frowned, then shook his head emphatically. "I do not think it will be necessary to inform His Grace. Let us wait a few minutes more," he suggested, hoping that either the Duke's son would find the courage to climb down, or . . .

But he didn't have to wait for long, because Conny Brady was suddenly climbing back up the tree, this time to help his bitter rival. Alastair Marlowe smiled. He hadn't misjudged the lad. Or perhaps it was the thought of the Duke of Camareigh standing here looking up at his son that had stirred Conny.

Several silent minutes passed before they caught sight of Conny Brady's small figure nearing the place where Robin Dominick roosted.

"Aren't you worried that Conny'll get stuck up there, too?" Stuart asked.

Alastair glanced down at the red-headed lad, then at the other two red-headed children, their expressions mirroring genuine concern for the two boys. "No, Conny has climbed to comparable heights since he was breeched. He's like a monkey. You'll notice that he took off his shoes. 'Twill give him better footing. Besides, Conny has no fear of heights. He'll bring down young Lord Robin," Alastair said reassuringly, but if they had glanced behind his back, they would have seen his fingers crossed.

"Lord Robin?" Conny Brady said, standing on a thick bough just below Robin Dominick's booted feet.

There was no response. "I was thinking that I was wrong. Ye certainly might make a sailor. Not many of the mates like to climb up so high. In fact, they have to be ordered to by the cap'n. Well, reckon I'm headin' down now. Figure Mrs. Peacham might have some more of them hot tarts comin' out of the oven," Conny said. "If ye be comin', then I'll wait for ye. Here, sit down on that limb, and I'll give ye a hand down to this one. Could use a hand, myself," Conny Brady lied, thinking that Robin Dominick wasn't going to budge, and then they'd both be in trouble with His Grace.

Conny was about to give up when Robin moved his foot, and then his legs were dangling down. With his hand in Conny's, Robin slid down beside Conny Brady on the lower branch.

Robin Dominick pulled his gaze away from the tilting sky and met Conny Brady's dark blue eyes. He stared at him for a moment. Finding no derision or gloating in Conny Brady's expression, he said, "Thank you. You didn't have to come back up, but you did. So I figure you win, Conny Brady."

Conny Brady was startled. He had not expected so generous a remark, and certainly not a capitulation from someone he'd thought to be little more than a spoiled brat.

Conny smiled self-consciously. "Reckon ye did real well considerin' ye'd never climbed the riggin' before. Wish I could say I'd done as well on horseback."

The two boys made their way back down the tree, moving slowly this time. Gradually faces below became more than just blurs. And as the two climbed down to the lowest branches, Robin paused to catch his breath.

"Reckon those tarts might still be warm?" he asked.

"Aye, reckon so," Conny replied.

"Actually, you've been doing quite well, considering you've never ridden horseback before."

"Ye think so, Lord Robin?" Conny Brady asked, surprised and pleased by the compliment.

"Aye, I reckon so," Robin grinned, and it was the first time he had looked upon Conny Brady with anything but dislike. "Butterick is the best. He'll have you riding so well that by next week you'll be able to jump the yew hedge in the south gardens," Robin predicted.

"Ye really think so?" Conny Brady asked doubtfully, thinking he'd be satisfied just to stay on the horse's back.

"Well, I see you both made it back down without incident," Alastair Marlowe commented, eyeing the two boys as they dropped to the ground from the lowest branch.

"Oh, aye, Mr. Marlowe, 'twas nothin' to it, eh, Lord Robin?" Conny asked with a wink.

"Nothin' to it," Robin replied stoutly, much to his cousins' amazement and admiration.

"Weren't you scared, Robin? You sure looked green in the face from where we were standing," Stuart wanted to know. "I thought you were going to get sick."

"I thought you were going to fall," Anne said, thinking Robin was very brave indeed.

"And I thought you were going to land on top of us," Maggie chimed in.

But Robin maintained his calm demeanor while he explained the intricacies of his climb in detail. Now that he was safely back on the ground, he described most glowingly the wonderful view he had seen from on high.

Leading his horse, Alastair Marlowe walked alongside the little group as they made their way back to the big house. He didn't mind the company, for he had been apprehensive of approaching the home of the Duke of Camareigh, even though he had a proper invitation tucked safely away in his coat pocket.

"This is Mr. Marlowe, Lord Robin," Conny Brady made the introduction. "He was the supercargo aboard the *Sea Dragon*, and is probably the cap'n's best friend. And a finer gentleman ye'll not be findin' anywhere, says Mr. Kirby," Conny Brady boasted, thinking Mr. Marlowe looked quite the gentleman in his fine gray frock coat and breeches, his boots as shiny as new guineas and three times as expensive, Conny guessed.

Alastair Marlowe looked embarrassed when seven pairs of curious eyes were suddenly trained on him. "Well, that is very kind of you, Conny, but I certainly make no claim to being the captain's best friend. I just did my duty while serving aboard the *Sea Dragon*," Alastair Marlowe said modestly.

"Mr. Kirby says Mr. Marlowe never takes full credit for anythin', unless 'tis some mistake, then he's ownin' up to it like a decent man oughta," Conny stated. He proceeded to regale the awestruck Fletcher children with some of his former shipmate's more daring exploits.

"Did you really find a sunken galleon, Mr. Marlowe?"

"Did you really swim in the sea?"

"Did you see any sea monsters?"

Alastair Marlowe was still trying to satisfy their curiosity when he first set foot inside the hallowed halls of Camareigh, passing beneath the noble coat of arms of the Dominick family. The arms were emblazoned with the motto, "Yield Not Truth, Valor, or Purpose."

Alastair Marlowe, who had faced many a bloodthirsty foe while serving aboard the *Sea Dragon*, was almost sorry to see the children leave once they had entered the hall. It was crowded with liveried footmen, who were standing under the critical eye of a very haughty-seeming old man called Mason, who had probably been the butler at Camareigh for close to a century, or so Alastair surmised. Escorted into the Chinese Room, Conny Brady having scurried off to tell the captain that Alastair had arrived, Alastair Marlowe anxiously awaited the arrival of his host and hostess. Never before had he been in such exalted surroundings, and he expected that already half of London was here for the Grand Ball held in honor of the Duke and Duchess' daughter and son-in-law.

"Alastair! You've come!" Turning around, Alastair Marlowe smiled into that violet-eyed gaze.

"Lady Rhea Claire," he murmured, thinking that his memory had played him false, for dressed in a gown of rose brocade trimmed with lace, she was more beautiful than he had remembered, and he found himself staring dumbly at her.

"'Tis wonderful to see you again," Rhea said, holding out

her hands in welcome. "Alastair?" she spoke again, her smile fading. "Is something amiss? You're not ill?"

"Forgive me, Lady Rhea Claire," Alastair apologized as he took her outstretched hands in his, "but the sight of you brought back so many memories."

"I know. I often find myself thinking of those days," Rhea confided.

"The crew would be pleased to see that you are wearing their gift and that they have not been forgotten," he said as he spied the jeweled brooch gracing the white satin of her stomacher.

"Never," she promised. "Have you seen any of them since we parted in London?" she asked. But before Alastair could respond, the door opened and a tall figure strode toward the two people standing so close together, their hands still clasped.

"Alastair. I thought you had forgotten us," Dante Leighton said. Holding out his hand, he watched the quick unclasping of their hands and the slightly guilty look on his former supercargo's face. But then, he had always known that Alastair Marlowe was in love with Rhea.

"Captain, 'tis good to see you looking so well, and I—"

"Not 'Captain.' Have you forgotten that I am now respectable?" Dante asked, sliding his arms around Rhea's waist.

"You were always quite respectable in our eyes, m'lord," Alastair said quite seriously.

"I am not 'm'lord' to my friends. Please remember that," Dante ordered, his voice sounding like an echo from the days aboard the *Sea Dragon*. "And I seem to remember a time when you thought me not respectable enough to pursue Rhea. Since you are slightly more respectable than I am, did you harbor thoughts of engaging the lady's affections yourself?" Dante asked with a smile.

"Dante, really," Rhea laughed, wondering what had gotten into Dante.

Alastair Marlowe eyed his former captain nervously. He had seen that glint in the narrowed eyes too often not to heed its warning. "How can any man not be half in love with so beautiful a lady? However, since the lady is spoken for, there can be nothing for me but to compose lovesick poems and adopt an attitude of abject despair," Alastair jested.

"I do seem to have the devil's own luck, do I not?" Dante said, and smiled.

"Aye, Cap'n, that ye do," Alastair said, breathing easier. "And may I extend my deepest and sincerest felicitations on the birth of your son? I heard the news when I was in London. I am afraid that gossip is still rampant where the captain of the *Sea Dragon* is concerned," the sensitive Alastair admitted, his face flushing with anger when he remembered some of the more outrageous remarks he had overheard.

"Thank you," Dante spoke softly, his eyes meeting Rhea's and mirroring that extraordinary pride he had felt upon seeing his son for the first time.

"I must admit I was surprised. I had no idea," Alastair said, glancing between Rhea and Dante.

"I should hope not, since I only heard the glad tidings on the day Rhea left London."

"Had the crew known, I am afraid Lady Rhea Claire's departure would have been delayed so there could be many more toasts," Alastair said, and laughed.

"You have been in London recently, then?" Alastair nodded, and Dante, who still felt a deep sadness about the disbanding of the crew, asked, "Have they all left, then?"

"Aye, I think so, although I did meet up with Cobbs. He was newly arrived from Norfolk, where he had bought that manor house. He was in the process of buying out all of London. Nothing but the best for Squire Nabobs, he said, and proceeded to buy half the tavern several rounds of drinks," Alastair said.

"Speaking of which, you must be thirsty and tired. We have kept you talking here for far too long," Rhea spoke quickly, for she hadn't missed that faraway look in Dante's eyes when he had asked about his crew. She wondered if perhaps, deep down inside, he would prefer to be standing on the deck of his ship.

"Yes, as a matter of fact I am rather fatigued. And I shouldn't wish to appear in polite company without changing out of these dusty clothes," Alastair Marlowe said, embarrassed as he became aware of the dried mud spotting his boots. "I only hope the coach I hired is not too far behind me. I rode on ahead. I'm afraid that sailing for so many years has made me dislike closed-in places, so you'll not catch me inside a coach. Nor could I have put up with the incessant chatter of my valet. I hired the fellow in London, or I should say that Barton condescended to become my valet. A more disapproving and snobbish man I've yet to meet. He'll have a paroxysm when he sees these boots," Alastair said, and sighed.

"You came straight from London?" Rhea asked. "I thought you might have come from the South, where your family lives."

Alastair Marlowe became most uncomfortable. "Shortly after you left London, Captain, I did, too. I went home. Only, it wasn't really home anymore. My brother is master there, and he has a wife and seven children. I felt like a stranger. And I am afraid that my brother's opinion of me hasn't changed over the years. My parents are long dead. They died before I left to sail with you. So, except for my memories, there was nothing to hold me there," Alastair said slowly. Rhea's heart went out to him, for he had spoken with such longing of returning home. But time had not stood still while he sailed the seas.

"I am sorry, Alastair," Rhea said, touching his arm lightly.

"'Twas my own fault for thinking that, perhaps, since I returned a wealthy man, they would welcome me. But they have their own lives, and I am no longer a part of that world."

Rhea glanced at Dante. He was standing so tall and proud, but she couldn't help but wonder what reception he would receive when he at long last returned to Merdraco.

The prince of darkness is a gentleman.
                                              Shakespeare

Chapter 14

BEDAZZLED and bewitched by the resplendence shimmering like a thousand captured suns, the eye blinked, only to find a brilliant reflection of the scintillating light within the carved and gilded frames of the mirrors adorning the gold and white walls of the Great Ballroom of Camareigh. The muraled ceiling, with its clouds swirling around mythological scenes, soared fifty feet above the floor, while the sparkling crystal chandeliers seemed like stars, with Hesperus and Aldebaran burning brightest of the heavenly lights. Melodious strains of chamber music drifted from the Minstrels Gallery at the far end of the great hall, mingling with the sound of voices. Even Bacchus would have envied the feast prepared for that evening's revelry. Against the far wall, several long banqueting

255

tables had been set up and were surely groaning under their burdens.

Alastair Marlowe was as awed as the other guests were. Never had he seen so many people enjoying themselves with such abandon. Taking a sip from his goblet of wine, which was never allowed to go empty, he glanced around the crowded ballroom. Guests had been arriving continuously for the past hour, and Alastair knew he would be fortunate to remember even his own name by the end of the evening and certainly not the countless names and titles which had been so impressively announced by the stentorian-voiced majordomo standing guard at the double-doored entrance.

Alastair Marlowe's bemused gaze rested on the small group standing just within the entrance. He was thinking what an attractive couple the Duke and Duchess of Camareigh were. The Duchess was dressed in scarlet velvet, and her black hair, left unpowdered, as the Queen herself had been doing recently, was arranged in soft curls and threaded with pearls. Around her neck hung an exquisite pearl necklace with a pearl and ruby pendant. It sparkled with a warmth that was a mere reflection of the welcoming smile on the Duchess' delicately featured face.

As Alastair observed the Duke of Camareigh, he told himself that his memory of that stern-visaged gentleman had served him well. The man seemed as much the imperious patrician as he had the first time Alastair met him, perhaps even more so. Dressed in gold Italian silk embroidered in a delicate floral pattern, he was indeed a gentleman of distinction and lord of a noble household.

The former supercargo of the *Sea Dragon* smiled slightly as his gaze rested on the elegant, eminently respectable figure of his former captain. The gentleman was presenting himself with so dignified and gentlemanly a demeanor that Alastair suspected he was a great disappointment to those guests who had expected a bloodthirsty, snarling pirate.

Alastair Marlowe wasn't even aware of the obliging footman who replaced his empty goblet with a brimming one, for his eyes were held captive by the stunning vision in gold standing beside Dante Leighton. Suddenly he found himself remembering his captain's words of earlier that day, and he had to agree that Dante Leighton had the devil's own luck. Lady Rhea Claire was the most spellbindingly beautiful woman in the room.

Dressed in a gown of gold tissue and lace, her golden hair sparkling with diamonds, she was more beautiful than Alastair thought any woman could be. And she belonged to Dante Leighton.

Alastair sighed. Would he ever have Dante's luck? His eyes lingered almost sadly on that golden figure, and then they drifted down the receiving line to where Lord Francis Dominick stood, looking very much his father's son. He was a handsome young man, and already he possessed that air of quiet dignity and even arrogance which only the born aristocrat exuded.

Beyond Lord Francis stood General Sir Terence Fletcher and his wife, Lady Mary. She seemed almost insignificant in her sky-blue silk, until one gazed into those remarkable gray eyes. Alastair had had the strangest sensation from Lady Mary, as if she knew all about him. Standing next to Sir Terence and Lady Mary were three handsome young men, introduced to him as the Fletcher brothers.

Alastair Marlowe's gaze traveled the room, pausing with interest on one person and then another, but when he saw a buxom young woman approaching, dressed in pale pink, an enormous rose-tinted feather bobbing in her powdered hair, he ducked behind a crowd and hoped he had not been spied.

With a sigh of relief he watched Caroline Winters sweep past, a determined glint in her eye. For once he was thankful he had no title to fire that glint further. Too late, he had been warned about Caroline Winters. The unfortunate experience still vivid in his mind, Dante Leighton had shared with his friend the details of suffering through several days of Caroline Winters' company. Unable to get around because of his broken ankle, he had found himself being waylaid far too many times by that insufferable young woman.

Alastair Marlowe, after having found himself with yet another brimming goblet of wine, was beginning to enjoy himself. A feeling of well-being spread through him. He nodded politely to a bejeweled lady eyeing him seductively from behind an undulating feather fan, and was about to address her when, as if in a nightmare, he heard the majordomo announce, "Sir Miles Sandbourne!"

Alastair Marlowe spun around, his sudden action leaving the bejeweled woman smiling at his broad back. But he had forgotten her. His attention was centered on Dante Leighton, who looked as if he had been turned to stone. Dante stood there staring at the man he hated for the past fifteen years and had once vowed to kill when he returned to England.

"Excuse me, but is that *the* Sir Miles Sandbourne of Wolfingwold Abbey, Devonshire?" Alastair Marlowe demanded abruptly of the tall, pompous gentleman standing before him.

The gentleman glanced down with imperious disdain at the vulgar upstart who had dared engage him in conversation. But upon eyeing him closer and ascertaining that the fellow's tailor was reputable and his breeches without wrinkle, he deigned to reply. "Quite. Though I confess I am surprised to see him here. There used to be bad blood between Sir Miles and Lord Jacqobi. But I s'pose they've buried the hatchet," he drawled with a bored sigh.

"Most likely in each other's backs," Alastair Marlowe murmured, and without begging leave, walked away. But as he did he caught sight of that plump figure swathed in pink and heard the shrill cry, "Wesley! There you are!"

With a feeling of apprehension he'd not experienced since his first battle at sea, Alastair Marlowe moved closer to his captain's side.

Rhea Claire was unaware of the turmoil. Sir Miles Sandbourne was just another guest as far as she was concerned. But the name must have struck a chord in Lucien Dominick's mind, for he glanced quickly at his son-in-law's paling face, then back again at the smiling face of the gentleman standing before him.

"Your Grace," Sir Miles Sandbourne spoke in that beautifully cultivated voice. It was the second thing a person noticed about him. The first was his extraordinarily handsome face. Although the man was at least fifty, he did not look his age. And he exuded a great sensuality.

"Sir Miles," the Duke responded stiffly, trying to sort his confused thoughts.

Dressed in black velvet, with lace ruffles and frills a startling contrast to the overall darkness of his figure, Sir Miles Sandbourne was the epitome of elegance and grace. He lifted a delicately scented handkerchief to his lips in almost an effeminate gesture. But it would have been a mistake for anyone to dismiss his masculinity, and the look in his dark eyes was lustfully appreciative as he gazed at Sabrina Dominick.

"Your Grace," he said softly, his eyes caressing her, lingering on the soft curve of décolletage. "As always, your unparalleled beauty leaves me quite speechless." He bowed low, his breath warm against her gloved hand.

"Not quite speechless, Sir Miles," the Duchess responded with a slight smile. She had never really cared for Sir Miles Sandbourne and had long suspected that there was a hollowness and insincerity beneath that façade. But his charm entranced people, and her opinion of Sir Miles placed her in a minority.

Although there had once been rumors of corruption and depravity where Sir Miles' conduct was concerned, nothing had ever been proven. Even had it been, people would have been hesitant to close their doors against Sir Miles Sandbourne. It was never wise to make an enemy of such a powerful gentleman.

"Witty as well as beautiful," Sir Miles murmured with that twisted smile. "I suffer perpetual envy of His Grace's good fortune in having carried you away from London before I had a chance to woo you. I can guarantee that he would not have had so easy a time of it had I been on the scene," Sir Miles pronounced.

"You underestimate me, Sir Miles," the Duke remarked coldly. He was never patient when it came to watching another man lust after his wife.

Lucien Dominick caught a look of anticipation, almost of excitement, in Sir Miles' eyes when he moved past Sabrina and stood before the pale-eyed Dante Leighton.

The two men, of a similar height, gazed into each other's eyes. Whatever thoughts were passing behind those expressionless faces remained unreadable. Neither man moved, nor blinked, nor even seemed to be breathing.

Rhea glanced worriedly between the two men. What was the matter? She had seen that cruel, pitiless look in Dante's eyes only a few times, but those had been the times he talked about the man who had betrayed him. Rhea's eyes widened as she stared at Sir Miles Sandbourne. This must be the man!

"Well, well, what have we here?" murmured Sir Miles Sandbourne, oozing honeyed sarcasm while he eyed the younger man from head to toe with contemptuous thoroughness. "I wonder if 'tis indeed true, as Shakespeare said, that the smallest worm will turn being trodden upon?" Sir Miles asked. His smile included not only his long-ago victim, but also others.

Dante Leighton smiled. It was a hard, cold smile. "Only time can tell, Sir Miles. But then, time is something I have plenty of. Do you?" Dante inquired with just enough doubt in his voice as to leave a listener wondering if Sir Miles were already on his deathbed.

Sir Miles' smile seemed a great effort for him, and Lucien Dominick reflected that when Sir Miles had first seen Dante Leighton, the older man seemed startled. Had he been unprepared to meet so dignified a gentleman, one who possessed such a cold, calculating gaze? For in Dante, Miles saw a man who could not be easily baited, as a younger man might have been.

"My, my, some things don't change, do they?" Sir Miles asked conversationally. "When I arrived in London, all I heard were stories about Dante Leighton, the Marquis of Jacqobi— or, as he was more often called, the captain of the *Sea Dragon*. I was not surprised to learn of your rather disreputable profession. You always did enjoy taking risks, whether you were gambling or attempting seduction. I fear you will always be notorious," Sir Miles predicted with an understanding sigh. He had aimed his remarks at the Duke and Duchess, as though commiserating with them about their son-in-law. "I suppose," Sir Miles asked kindly, "you *have* told them *everything* in your shadowy past?"

"If you are referring to that slanderous murder accusation, then, yes, we know everything about Dante's past." Rhea spoke quietly, but her voice was shaking with fury, and she wondered how Dante could control himself.

"Ah, Lady Rhea Claire, how lovely you look," Sir Miles responded easily, the dark eyes missing nothing. "It was most distressing to learn of your kidnaping. How extraordinary that you should meet up with Dante." He laughed softly as he eyed the two. "Going from bad to worse, eh? You have my sympathies, my dear."

"Please keep them to yourself, Sir Miles," Rhea told him. "I am very much in love with my husband."

"How noble of you. But then, one must keep up appearances," Sir Miles said with a pitying look. "Of course, I doubt you had any choice in the matter, knowing Dante as I do. Ah . . . I did hear, did I not, that you recently became a mother? As I said before, some things never change, do they?"

But Dante Leighton appeared untouched by Sir Miles' snide innuendoes. "Some things change, Sir Miles. You would be wise to remember that," Dante spoke softly, and the calm, self-assured tones irritated Sir Miles. The dark eyes narrowed as he dabbed at his lips with his scented handkerchief.

"Do they?"

"Yes. You will discover that soon enough," Dante added enigmatically, and he eyed the older man pityingly.

"You seem very sure of yourself, Dante. I have heard of your great fortune, but you should remember that even though you possess considerable wealth, some things may still remain out of your reach," Sir Miles reminded him.

"Perhaps," Dante said evenly. "Of course, I may already possess everything I desire. I planned carefully for fifteen years. You may not be as cognizant of certain facts as you think, Sir Miles." Dante was baiting him.

Sir Miles became silent, evidently trying to fathom Dante's meaning. Something was bothering him, and he suddenly seemed to realize that Dante Leighton knew what that something was.

A muscle beside his mouth twitched as he continued to stare at Dante with those narrowed dark eyes. "I suppose you will be returning to Merdraco?"

"Naturally. I am still master there," Dante pronounced the words he knew had the power to infuriate Sir Miles Sandbourne, "as all Leightons have been masters there for centuries."

But Sir Miles did not react quite the way Dante expected. A guarded look entered Sir Miles' eyes, and a twisted smile curved the thin mouth. Dante began to feel a growing uneasiness.

"It has been a long time since you were last at Merdraco. And as I warned you before, many, many things may have changed since you ran away. Had you remained, instead of being a coward, we might have been able to work something out. But as it is"—he threw a mocking glance at Dante—"I am afraid I have had to sell the lands that once belonged to the great estate of Merdraco. I fear 'tis not the magnificent estate the great Leighton family has always believed it to be. Of course, you have only yourself to blame, for you are the Leighton who lost it all by gambling. And there is no way you can get your hands on that land anymore. Even if I still held deed to it, do you think I would sell it back to you? I can truly pity you, for you may be master of Merdraco the castle, but you will never achieve the greatness of your forebears, for you will have no land around that castle. It is now merely a castle high on a hill. A place for dreamers, eh, Dante?" Sir Miles charged.

But Sir Miles Sandbourne had misjudged his enemy, for he was no longer dealing with the same reckless man who had left England. He was facing the man who had been captain of the *Sea Dragon,* a man who had stood and faced far worse than anything Sir Miles Sandbourne could attack him with.

Dante Leighton smiled, and his crew would have known to beware, for what was to follow boded ill.

"I shall not kill you tonight, Miles," Dante said bluntly, insulting the older man by the informal use of his name, "because I want you to suffer some of the agony of uncertainty and then defeat that I suffered at your hands. I shall enjoy watching you see your world crumble. And then, if you beg me, I shall put an end to your suffering."

Whether Sir Miles or Rhea and her parents were more startled it would have been hard to say. But Sir Miles well knew the extent of Dante Leighton's hatred and the magnitude of his sins against the younger man, and he felt the greatest disquiet upon hearing those calmly uttered words.

The arrival of a guest brought to an end the confrontation. With a slight nod to the Duke and Duchess of Camareigh, Sir Miles continued down the receiving line until his black-clad figure disappeared into the crowded room.

"What a horrible man," Rhea breathed before she smiled at the couple approaching her, sighing in relief when they moved along the line after greeting her. "That is the man who was your guardian?" she asked, incredulous.

"Yes," Dante replied, his pale eyes searching for that black figure in the crowd.

"How is it that *he* was entrusted with your inheritance?" she demanded.

Dante smiled. "Why shouldn't he have been? After all, he is my stepfather."

The first pale mauve shadings were highlighting the eastern sky when Dante Leighton entered the private drawing room of the Duchess of Camareigh. He crossed the room and stood broodingly before the tall mullioned windows. Rhea, sitting with her parents in front of the warming glow of the fire, did not need to see his face to know what was uppermost in his mind. She realized that they had stayed too long. There could be no further delay.

"When do you wish to leave for Merdraco?" she asked.

Dante turned around, startled by her perception. "I—"

"Please, Dante, I understand," Rhea told him. She knew he had longed to return to his home for many months, but had stayed at Camareigh out of deference to her and her family. Not that he would have gotten far on his broken ankle, Rhea realized, but she believed that even had that not happened, they would have remained at Camareigh for the birth of their child; but now, it was time to go.

She knew that her parents understood.

"He has already left for Devonshire," Dante spoke, and there was no need for him to explain himself.

"I am sorry for this evening, Dante," the Duchess said, genuinely concerned lest Dante think they had purposely arranged the embarrassing incident. "I had no idea of the bitterness between you and Sir Miles."

The Duke of Camareigh rubbed his scar thoughtfully and then startled everyone by echoing the apology. "I had forgotten the relationship. And even had I remembered, our guest lists were drawn up by my secretary, not by us. And besides, the same people are invited to every party. Sir Miles may well have come as the guest of one of our guests."

"I haven't checked the list in years, except for adding a name or two," the Duchess admitted. "You do believe us?"

"I do not blame you, and the meeting between Miles and myself was bound to happen sooner or later. I suspect that Miles was rather looking forward to this. He wanted to bait me, to let me know that he would be waiting for me when I returned to Merdraco."

"I do not think it went as well as he thought it would," the Duchess remarked. "I think he was unprepared for you, Dante Leighton. You must have changed much since last he ridiculed you."

"Yes, I have, and he'll not drive me away from Merdraco this time," Dante swore, his eyes narrowed, as if he were already savoring the defeat of his enemy.

Lady Mary Fletcher awoke screaming. Her heart pounding, she fought her way out of the blackness enshrouding her. But even when she opened her terrified eyes, she saw only darkness, and still felt the cold dampness of the cave. In the distance was the bellowing of the sea in tempest as it challenged the howling winds.

Lady Mary began to weep softly. Pulling the rumpled bed-clothes around her shaking shoulders, she buried her ravaged face in the tangle of red hair spread out on her pillow.

"Oh, dear Lord," she prayed. "Please protect them." It would all come about as she had seen it, and there was nothing on this earth she could do to stop it. She did not have to be in Sabrina's private drawing room to know that Dante Leighton and Rhea Claire were soon to leave Camareigh. Nor did Lady Mary need to travel to Merdraco to see again those dark, solitary towers standing sentinel against the dawn sky.

*It was now the hour that turns back the longing
of seafarers and melts their hearts, the day they
have bidden dear friends farewell, and pierces the
new traveler with love if he hears in the distance
the bell that seems to mourn the dying day.*

Dante

Chapter 15

FIVE days later a caravan of coaches was sending up a cloud
of dust as it moved along the narrow road winding out of
the valley. Through the small, sleepy hamlet of Camare it
traveled. Its passage did not go unnoticed, for most of the
villagers who had gathered beside the road had known many
of the travelers since they were small. They were gathered to
bid a fond farewell to one of them. Rhea Claire was bound for
a new life.

She leaned out of the coach window time and time again,
partly to wave to familiar faces and throw tuppence to the
young children running alongside the coach, but mostly to catch

last glimpses of Camareigh. But the golden walls blurred before Rhea's eyes, and then the coach rounded a turn and the great house, her home, disappeared from view.

Rhea leaned back against the cushioned seat, feeling a deep sense of loss. But then she looked down at the sleeping baby snuggled warmly beside her on the seat and she knew that a wonderful future must surely await her.

"Aren't you excited, Rhea?" Robin Dominick demanded, his violet eyes sparkling. Except for an occasional visit to London, he'd never traveled far from Camareigh, yet here he was traveling into the wilds of the West Country. "You aren't crying, are you?" he asked with curious impatience, for this was the start of a great adventure and Rhea should be happy.

Conny Brady, sitting next to Robin Dominick on the seat opposite Rhea, eyed her uneasily. Ladies reacted in the strangest ways sometimes. For no good reason they would start to cry, and he didn't want the cap'n to think either he or Lord Robin had done anything to upset her.

But Rhea surprised them. Composing herself, she smiled. "Are you excited about the journey?" she asked them, banishing the melancholy vision of her mother and father standing on the steps of Camareigh, waving good-bye.

"Been hearin' about this Merdraco since I first signed aboard the *Sea Dragon,* so I reckon I'm lookin' forward to seein' it now. Glad I don't have to be ridin' horseback all the way there, though," Conny Brady said with a wide grin. He hadn't quite mastered the art yet, and his seat still smarted from being saddlesore.

"You're doing quite nicely, Conny," Robin told him, wanting just what Conny didn't want. He'd like to be riding alongside Dante Leighton, Francis, and Alastair Marlowe, all of whom were riding a short distance ahead of the first coach.

"I was afraid Papa and Mama weren't going to let me accompany you, Rhea," Robin admitted, still concerned that they might change their minds at the last minute and send someone to fetch him back. "But I guess since Francis was coming, they didn't think it fair not to let me."

"They probably thought Francis wouldn't know what to do unless he had you around to keep out of trouble," Rhea said. She would not tell her brother of her parents' deep concern about him. They hoped Robin would regain the disposition he had had before the kidnaping if allowed to go to Merdraco. They had always been close, and perhaps his staying with her for a while would reassure him that his world had not really fallen to pieces.

Rhea sighed contentedly. With Robin and Francis along she really did not feel that she was abandoning her home. She remembered now how Francis, looking rather ill-at-ease, had come to her and Dante, and had asked if he might accompany them to Merdraco. He had declared that he had always desired to see the Devonshire coastline, but Rhea suspected that he was exercising a bit of brotherly concern, and wished to keep an eye on his sister and young nephew for a while longer, and although on good terms with Dante Leighton, he most likely wanted to make certain he had not been hoodwinked by the man. Dante was not displeased. Indeed, he had genuinely welcomed his brother-in-law to join their party, perhaps with the intention of setting to rest once and for all any fears the Dominicks might still possess concerning his suitability as a member of the family. The group had already grown in size with the announcement that Alastair Marlowe, who claimed he had nothing better to do, would be traveling with them. Perhaps he would even purchase an estate near Merdraco, he had joked, and then they would be cursed with his presence forever. But Rhea suspected that Alastair Marlowe still felt a deep loyalty to his former captain and wished to be at his side should events turn against Dante Leighton.

Houston Kirby, who would always remain at his captain's side, had insisted on riding in the second coach with several other new members of the Leighton household. He had promised, with a glint in his eye, to acquaint them with the rules to be set down at Merdraco. There was Nora, the granddaughter of Mason, butler at Camareigh, the old man proudly watching his granddaughter become personal maid to Her Grace's daughter; and Thompson, Nora's cousin, who was personal valet to Francis. Although excited about the adventure, he was looking forward to returning to Camareigh and resuming his courtship of Alys Meredith. There was Betsie, one of the upstairs maid from Camareigh. She had hoped to succeed O'Casey as nanny for the youngest Dominicks, having helped to raise her own

young brothers and sisters, but with the arrival of Alys, she
had been displaced. She was happy to have been invited to
become young Lord Kit's nursemaid. Finally, there was Barton, Alastair Marlowe's valet, who most certainly had not
imagined himself traveling into the wilds.

In a third and fourth coach, respectively, were several other
maids and footmen, all of whom sought to better their positions
in a new establishment. Among them was a kitchen maid who
had tutored under Mrs. Peacham and had many of the acclaimed
cook's recipes safely tucked away in her trunk, which was
wedged in with countless other trunks in the heavily laden
wagons that trundled along at the end of the procession.

Rhea glanced down lovingly at her son's sleeping face. With
a smile curving her lips, she reached out and lightly touched
a soft, rosy cheek. Such a sweet little mouth and chin, she
thought admiringly, wondering once more if he would grow
up to look like Dante. He already had his father's chestnut
curls. Rhea continued to gaze down on her son almost disbe-
lievingly, for she was still incredulous at having created a life.
He was so tiny, Christopher Dominick Leighton, and yet he
would inherit Merdraco one day.

Feeling a cool draft across her knees, Rhea rearranged the
fur rug more carefully around the peacefully sleeping child,
but even the sudden jolting of the carriage as the wheels rolled
into a pothole hadn't the power to awaken so innocent a rest,
or to disturb such a lazy feline as Jamaica, who remained
contentedly curled against the corner of the seat.

Rhea rested her head against the cushioned seat, wishing
she could put everything out of her mind as easily as Robin
and Conny had. They had spread Robin's wooden soldiers out
on the seat between them and were absorbed in lining up their
armies. But she kept remembering her Aunt Mary's face.

Lady Mary had taken her niece aside and, cupping Rhea's
face in her hands, had stared deeply into those unshadowed,
violet eyes. She looked confused, and Rhea had felt for a
moment that her aunt didn't recognize her. Then Lady Mary
smiled that sad smile of hers. Pressing her cool cheek against
Rhea's, Lady Mary whispered, "My dear child, if only I could
spare you the oncoming darkness! But I cannot, for what must
happen will happen. But please, you must not despair or believe

the worst, for your doubts will rob you of great happiness if you allow them to. I am very confused and unhappy, my dear, for I have had many visions lately, but I cannot seem to sort them out. If only I could discover the key, but I cannot, and what information I do have might confuse you, bring you harm. No, 'tis best you go to Merdraco with a clear mind, for you must discover the answers yourself. However, there is one thing I must tell you," Lady Mary said, an underlying urgency in her words. "It is vitally important, my child, that you remember this: *The answer lies in the grave.* 'Tis madness, I know, but humor a half-mad woman, will you?" she had begged, her gray eyes dark with whatever fearful visions she had experienced.

"I promise, Aunt Mary," Rhea told her, though of course she didn't understand.

Lady Mary kissed her lightly, her smile understanding. "I know you do not understand," she answered Rhea's question before it was voiced.

Rhea sighed in frustration, beginning to understand a little better some of the anxiety that her aunt had lived with all her life. "The answer lies in the grave," Rhea murmured to herself just then, but Robin glanced up curiously from his soldiers.

"What was that, Rhea?" he demanded.

"Nothing important, Robin," Rhea answered as she glanced out at the sun-filled day beyond the coach windows and hoped that, for once, her Aunt Mary had had a plain, ordinary nightmare and not one of her visions.

The sun had climbed high into the cloudless blue sky by the time the weary travelers broke their journey, pausing for their own luncheon and to rest the horses. Before a stream with wild woodland and meadow, bright with spring's first buddings, wicker hampers were unloaded and blankets were unfolded and spread across the soft grass.

The sun was an opiate. Sitting slightly apart from the others, Rhea was feeling drowsy as she glanced down at the small chestnut head resting against her breast. Pressing a kiss against his soft curls, Rhea lifted her face and glanced up at the sun, her eyes closed. She dozed for a moment, a languorous feeling enveloping her. Suddenly everything seemed so peaceful, set apart from the rest of the world.

Rhea opened her eyes. She had been enjoying a false security. They could not remain in this tranquil setting forever. Soon they must resume their journey and face whatever awaited them.

The realization took away some of the magic of her surroundings. No longer did she smell the sweet woodruff carried by the gentle breeze, or see the pale-hued buttercups swaying in the meadow, or hear the spotted woodpecker's busy tapping. There came a sudden rustling in the hawthorn scrub, then the flash of a shyly curious deer fleeing back to the safety of the deep woods.

Rhea's gaze came to rest on the familiar figure of her husband as he stood in conversation with Alastair Marlowe and Francis. Her loving gaze remained on that tall figure and she murmured softly, "Dante Leighton. Captain of the *Sea Dragon*. Marquis of Jacqobi. Master of Merdraco. So many titles. So many different men. Yet sometimes all I can see is that brokenhearted young man who had no family, no friend to stand by him. My poor Dante," Rhea whispered as she thought of the pain and sorrow he must have suffered over all of his stepfather's treachery.

Miles Sandbourne had pretended to befriend a fatherless young boy, while all the time planning to revenge himself against the heir to the family he hated.

Rhea smoothed her sleeping son's curls, then glanced up toward her husband, feeling a sudden fierce protectiveness toward both of them. She had felt the same way when Dante told the tragic tale of his youth to her and her parents. He talked softly yet coldly, refusing to allow the remembrance of his pain and humiliation to surface. He first talked about his mother, Lady Elayne. Orphaned at a young age, Elayne Shambry came to live at Merdraco. As great-niece of the old Marquis, she was accepted as a member of the Leighton family. Raised at Merdraco with her cousin, it was not surprising when she became engaged to the old Marquis' son. Only one person was surprised, and that man knew that he, not John Leighton, possessed the lovely young Elayne's heart. That man had been Miles Sandbourne. But it was Miles' misfortune to be second in line to inherit the family estate, Wolfingwold Abbey. His prospects were bleak. But even if he had possessed a great title and fortune it would not have mattered. The old Marquis wished to see Elayne married to his son. And because she felt indebted to him for his kindness, Elayne agreed. But her heart belonged to Miles.

So the beautiful, flaxen-haired, gray-eyed Elayne wed the handsome heir to Merdraco, much to everyone's delight. But there was no fairy-tale ending. Lord John Jacqobi died within seven years of his nuptial day. He had done his duty, however, by leaving to Merdraco an heir.

By that time, Miles Sandbourne had, through the untimely death of his elder brother, inherited Wolfingwold Abbey. He had been knighted as well. Quite naturally, he had sought out his newly widowed former love. They were married shortly thereafter. And all should have been blessed, as true love sometimes is.

But Sir Miles had not forgiven his lady for marrying another. He nurtured that hatred over many years, waiting for the time when he could make her suffer, as he had suffered when he watched her walking arm in arm down the aisle with another man.

Miles' revenge was subtly played. Too late Lady Elayne realized that his love had turned to hatred. By then he had destroyed her life and her son's life as well. Dante Leighton, who had been an ever-present reminder of Elayne's first husband, was an important part of Miles' plans for vengeance.

With the death of the old Marquis, Sir Miles moved his family from Wolfingwold Abbey into Merdraco, where he could savor more completely his revenge while he destroyed the great family. Under Sir Miles' influence, the heir to Merdraco became a rakish young man for whom honor and decency held little importance. Fulfilling his base appetites was all Dante cared about. All the while he never understood that he was a pawn in an evil game.

Lady Elayne suffered in silence for many years and spoke of her fears too late. She was humiliated and debased as Sir Miles, a man she had once loved so deeply, took her to bed without love or tenderness. He flaunted his many mistresses before her, even daring to bring them to Merdraco, where he would fondle them before her eyes, holding her up to ridicule before his friends.

Then, much too late, she realized that Sir Miles' revenge had not centered on her alone. He had been cunningly turning her son against her, leading Dante into a world of debauchery. Soon his presence would be tolerated by no decent person. And because Sir Miles was the heir's guardian, he had had full control of the estate. He had nearly bankrupted the Marquis of Jacqobi.

Because he was the dissipated young gentleman's stepfather as well as his guardian, he had been generous enough to buy up all the Merdraco lands, thousands of acres, on condition that he would sell them back to Dante when that young man realized another inheritance upon his twentieth birthday. Sir Miles had also been pitying enough to buy many of the family heirlooms, saving them being lost forever. In the opinion of society, Sir Miles Sandbourne had done more than enough for the dissolute young Lord Jacqobi.

Known only to Miles and Elayne was the truth, that Dante Leighton had been betrayed by Sir Miles. Dante Leighton himself would not learn of the treachery until his twentieth birthday. On that day, he discovered that his inheritance had been borrowed upon by his guardian. There was but a quarter of the inheritance remaining, barely enough to pay off Dante's debts, much less to buy back the family lands.

In the second week of that terrible autumn, when fog enshrouded the coastline, and the countryside had seemed so unnaturally quiet, as if it were waiting with bated breath for the tragedy that was to follow, Dante Leighton had been accused of murder. Swiftly, his fiancée had spurned him. And after an argument with his mother, who had finally spoken out against Sir Miles, Dante stormed off to London, refusing to hear the truth about the man he thought of as a father.

But the news of his mother's tragic death had sent him back to Merdraco. He arrived too late for the funeral services. Feeling it her duty to speak up, his mother's personal maid had told Dante that his mother might not have slipped while walking the narrow path along the cliff. Perhaps she had taken her own life. The brokenhearted maid—she had loved her beautiful mistress dearly—sobbed her story. Lady Elayne's disappointment in her son was not what had killed her. The night of her death, she had been horribly beaten by Sir Miles. The master had hurt her terribly. Her face swollen beyond recognition, the Lady Elayne had run from the house seeking death. The maid, having told her story, packed her belongings and left, bidding no fond farewell to the single remaining Leighton.

Confused but beginning to feel a dreadful certainty, Dante Leighton confronted his stepfather. At last he came face to face with the bitter truth. Sir Miles' hatred of him and all the Leighton name stood for had poured forth, shattering what little self-respect and self-control Dante Leighton still possessed. Never before had he faced such malevolence. His blood hot, he and Sir Miles fought.

But Dante, although younger, was fighting in the heat of passion, while Sir Miles had full, cold-blooded control. He might easily have killed Dante, but Sir Miles preferred to further humiliate the Marquis of Jacqobi. After disarming him, having wounded him in the arm, Sir Miles took his whip and beat his stepson on the steps of Merdraco. Then, his laughter ringing in Dante Leighton's ears, Sir Miles closed the great doors against him, leaving him trembling in disgrace on his own doorstep.

Time and the whims of fortune had changed many things since that infamous day. In allowing Dante Leighton to live, Sir Miles might have signed his own death warrant; for the Marquis of Jacqobi had become a determined, cold-blooded man, and that was due, in part, to Sir Miles' treatment of Dante and the example he had set.

During the past few years, Dante bought back much of the land stolen from him by Sir Miles. He had always used a surrogate. Each transaction, over the years, had been carried out by a person who would not arouse Sir Miles' suspicions.

Rhea shuddered, wondering what Sir Miles' reaction would be when he discovered that Dante Leighton once again held the lands of his heritage.

"What are you daydreaming about?" the object of her fears demanded with a smile as he lowered himself to a place beside her on the blanket. His hands balanced two plates piled high with food.

Rhea opened her eyes, startled. She flushed as she tried to

straighten her bodice. Kit, having appeased his appetite, was now sleeping peacefully.

"Here, let me take him so you can eat," Dante said as he held out his arms for his son. Holding him for a moment while he stared down into the tiny face, he felt that sense of amazement at being a father sweep over him.

"I'll never be able to eat all this," Rhea complained as she took a forkful of ham and egg pie while eyeing the cold chicken, buttered buns, thick wedge of cheese, salmon mousse, and chilled lemon pudding.

"You have to stay strong, my dear. After all, we can't have the next Marquis of Jacqobi growing up to be a runt, can we?" Dante said as he helped himself to a large bite of apricot-stuffed ham. "Delicious. I hope this girl Her Grace sent along with us raided the pantry and the recipes without conscience," Dante said appreciatively.

"If she raided the pantry then she'd better not return to Camareigh, for I cannot see my father dining on suet roll," Rhea advised. For just an instant she felt a deep homesickness as she thought of Camareigh and the people left behind.

"Not sorry, are you, to be going to my home?" Dante read her mood.

"Of course not. I am looking forward to seeing Merdraco, though I am sure it cannot compare with Camareigh," she added, looking too innocently demure.

Dante laughed. "You will be speechless when you see Merdraco for the first time."

"I hope not completely so, for I shall wish to make the obvious comparisons between my home and yours," Rhea smiled. She was surprised by his abrupt change of mood.

"*Our* home, Rhea, always remember that. You are a Leighton now. You belong to Merdraco," Dante said, his pale gray eyes suddenly remote, and Rhea knew that he was no longer there beside her, but was traveling the miles to Merdraco.

Dante Leighton had returned home from the sea and, soon, Merdraco would once again know the sound of its master's footsteps along the corridors long unused. With a deep dread, Rhea found herself wondering if Merdraco remained the same. Or had it changed, as its master had changed?

> *The night that hides things from us.*
> Dante

Chapter 16

BISHOP'S GRAVE INN was so named because, a hundred years before, a bishop lost his way in a snowstorm. His frozen body was found three days later just outside the archway leading to the stable yard of the old coaching inn. At that time, the inn was called Ye Goode Knight's Reste. It is still believed that there were no complaints when the name was changed.

Bishop's Grave Inn was approached from the deeply rutted, sunken lanes converging at Merwest Cross. The inn was an unassuming two-story building of gray stone aged by centuries of lichen and moss covering its surface in velvety clusters. The place did not give an impression of offering great welcome until, on a stormy night, one caught sight of the lights shining from its small mullioned windows. Seeking shelter beneath its gabled roof, the thankful traveler would discover a great hearth in the dining room. While warming himself before the fire, he would sip a sillabub, a heady mixture of cream and mulled cider Dora Lascombe had become famous for brewing.

Sam Lascombe, the genial host, would seat his guest at one of the oak tables crowded close to the warmth of the fire, his beaming smile taking in the shining brass candlesticks on every table. His glance would be brightest when it encountered the brass chandelier he'd ordered from Bristol not more than a year past. The much-admired fixture hung from one of the great beams crossing the room, its candles illuminating Dora's prized earthenware in a corner cabinet and capturing the gleam of pewter lining the mantelpiece.

The weary traveler might ease his hunger with pea soup, buttered shrimps, mullet pie, jugged celery served with roast vension or hare, hash of lamb in cider, peas, and scones served with clotted cream and strawberry jam.

Safe and snug inside that stone-walled inn, the traveler would retire for a night's rest after gratefully accepting a mug of warmed, spiced brandy from his affable host. Climbing the stairs to his room, he would find that the quilted coverlet had been turned back and a warming pan placed in that cavernous cold spot lying in wait between the sheets.

As ill chance had it, that night in early April was a night of wrathful storms. By the time the clock on the inn landing struck twelve, it would become a night long remembered, and not just because of the storm venting its wrath over the steeply slanted roof of the Bishop's Grave Inn. It was the night Dante Leighton came back to Merdraco.

It was the kind of night that lent credence to the old legend, especially the one about the Demon Hunt. The villagers, their imaginations fueled by the howling winds and flashing lightning, almost believed they heard the Dark Huntsman's horn and the baying of his yeth hounds as they raced from the moors in search of lost souls.

You'd not catch any sane folk out of doors on a conjuring night, for should anyone have the misfortune to see one of the Dark Huntsman's headless hounds, he would have died within the year. Everyone knew there was truth to the tale, for hadn't two fishermen drowned after seeing the Pale Lady a month before? And there was Dora Lascombe's brother, Ted Samples, who had told everyone who'd listen about seeing that spectral figure while he was prowling the cliffs near Merdraco. He had disappeared soon afterward.

On that stormy April night, Bishop's Grave Inn was locked up tight against the cold wind-blown rains. The roads could be little better than quagmires, and any traveler out on a devil's night like that one would have a difficult time in getting as far as Merwest Cross.

Yet a small caravan of coaches had indeed reached Merwest Cross, and with a rumbling that echoed the thunder overhead, the coaches rolled into the empty stable yard of Bishop's Grave Inn. Following the coaches were the wagons, laboring under the weight of their loads and with mud coating the big spoked wheels. Swinging open the door to the first coach, Dante Leighton peered inside. The coach lamps had long ago expired, and all was darkness within. "Are you all right, Rhea?" Dante demanded of the shadowy shapes inside and was rewarded by the loud wail of his son's voice in angry response.

"'Tis a bit chilly," Rhea said, her teeth chattering.

"I'm freezing," Robin Dominick declared, sneezing.

"Aye, 'tis colder than winter in the Mid-Atlantic in here, Cap'n," Conny Brady contributed.

"Where are we?" Rhea asked as she glanced past Dante into the darkness. The sound of the wind had lessened, but rain still pelted against the coach.

"Is this Merdraco?" Conny demanded, disappointed. He couldn't see much of it in the darkness, and he wanted to see those towers the cap'n was always talking about.

"No, we'll never reach Merdraco in the darkness, or in weather like this. We have arrived at the inn at Merwest Cross. There is no other inn for miles, not until you reach either Merleigh or Westlea Abbot, and we can't travel farther on these roads tonight."

"Everyone accounted for, Cap'n," Alastair Marlowe reported as he came up beside Dante, forgetting for a moment that he was no longer aboard the *Sea Dragon*. "Everyone shipshape here?" he asked. The past few miles had been arduous. "Lady Rhea Claire?"

"We're fine, Alastair, but you must be like ice, and I imagine you are soaked to the skin," Rhea said. The door of the coach was opened and the icy rain was striking her directly in the face.

"Tell them to rest easy while I see if I can rouse the landlord from his bed. I doubt if he was expecting guests this evening," Dante said as he held out his arms to take Kit from Rhea. Holding him with one arm, he reached out and hooked his other arm around Rhea's waist and swung her safely down from the coach. "He's bound to have stable boys who'll see to the horses. I want to check that last team. One of the leaders seems to be limping."

"Aye, Cap'n," Alastair said without thinking.

With his cloak held protectively over both Rhea and Kit, Dante hurried them toward the entrance, prepared to pound against the door until he received an answer. But suddenly a stream of welcoming light shone through the open door.

"Here I was thinkin' there wasn't a soul out on a night like this, when I suddenly thought I heard coach wheels and voices. Dora said 'twas probably just a ringin' in my ears, but I felt certain we had visitors," a gruff voice greeted them. Holding wide the heavy door, Sam Lascombe led his tired guests inside, thinking that the storm he had been cursing earlier was a blessing. It had brought him so much trade. With a look of disbelief he saw that his stable yard was packed full of coaches and wagons. Later, however, he was to wish that he'd listened to Dora and kept his door closed against the night, and what had come out of it; which in his mind had been the devil and his gang of demons.

But for now Sam Lascombe was glad to have the unexpected business and, with a gleam in his eye, he led his guests into the darkened dining room. Without wasting time on conversation, he laid a fire and then went to fetch Dora. His guests were sure to be hungry, and many rooms would have to be prepared. These folk weren't going anywhere else tonight, he thought with a satisfied grin as a deafening clap of thunder rattled the windows.

"If ye'll be excusin' me now, I'll get my wife to fixin' ye somethin' good and hot. I'll bring ye some cider, or wine, or ale, whatever the gentlemen will be wantin'," Sam Lascombe stated, noting with approval the two young gentleman who had just entered the room and were shaking out their wet cloaks.

Though their breeches and boots were splashed with mud, the quality of their apparel was not lost on his critical eye.

A small, cloaked figure bustled past Sam, and with a cursory nod to the fellow, Sam Lascombe continued on down the hall. But then he paused and, glancing back, he looked for the small figure. But the man had disappeared. There was something tantalizingly familiar about the little man, but Sam put the thought out of his mind. He had work to do and hungry guests to see to and Dora still to coax out of her warm bed.

Bleary-eyed, Dora Lascombe trudged downstairs, gray wisps of hair escaping from beneath her hastily arranged mob-cap while she struggled with stiff fingers to tie the ribbons beneath her chin and felt one of her stockings unrolling down her calf.

Soon, however, a cup of steaming coffee laced with brandy had wakened her. She had the two scullery maids set the fire, and within a few minutes the big kettle swinging over the flames was sending a cloud of steam into the room. Pouring the boiling water over the loose tea on the bottom of the pot, she set it aside to steep while she arranged a tray with one of her best sets of cups and saucers. Sam had said there was a fine-looking lady of quality traveling with the group. Dora knew she would welcome a cup of hot tea while the men enjoyed their wine.

Dora picked up the tray and made her way to the dining room. It seemed as if Sam was already seeing to the gentlemen's needs, effectively emptying the hall of its newly-arrived guests.

"Good evening, m'lady," Dora smiled as she entered the room, for Sam had told her he'd caught sight of a crest on the door of one of the coaches. "Thought ye could be usin' a bit of tea, seein' how ye must have been on the road for quite a while now." Dora set the tray down on the table where the young lady was sitting, warming herself before the fire.

"Oh, and aren't ye the pretty one," she blurted out, for Rhea had removed her cloak. In the glow of the firelight her hair looked like burnished gold, and the heat from the fire had brought a rosy tint to her cheeks. "Why, I haven't seen hair as yellow as yours since the Lady El—, well, ye wouldn't be knowin' about her, and may her poor soul rest in peace one of these days, but I guess it won't if people keep seein' her ghost," Dora said. At Rhea's look of horrified fascination, Dora said quickly, "Beggin' your pardon, m'lady. Guess I'm still half asleep," Dora apologized.

"Thank you for the tea. It was very kind of you, and I am sure it will taste quite delicious," Rhea said. "I can already smell something mouth-watering coming from the kitchen. My husband tells me that Devonshire scones are the sweetest in all of England."

"Oh, well, m'lady, right he is about that," Dora Lascombe agreed with a beaming smile, thinking that the lady certainly had nice manners. "Your husband be a Devonshireman, then?" she inquired curiously, wondering if he was from anywhere nearby.

"Yes, but he has been away for fifteen years," Rhea said quietly, wondering what the woman's reaction would be when she discovered the identity of her guest.

"Oh? If ye don't mind my askin'," Dora continued conversationally, forgetting the bubbling pots in the kitchen, "what is your husband's name?"

Rhea hesitated. "I am not certain you would know it."

"Oh, I've lived hereabouts for nigh on fifty years now. Reckon I've known or heard of most folks from around here," Dora told her.

"His name is—" Rhea began, but Kit's timely cry interrupted her and drew the attention of Dora Lascombe. "There, there, Kit, Mama's here," Rhea murmured softly, gently rocking her son in the small wooden cradle Dante had brought in.

"Oh, now isn't he the darlin' boy," Dora said with a wide smile. "Your son, m'lady?"

"Yes," Rhea said, her attention centered on the chuckling baby, whose tears had miraculously vanished.

"Well, who would've guessed, ye look so young and innocent," Dora commented, forgetting herself again. "He's a healthy-lookin' lad. Takes after his papa, I bet, with those chestnut curls."

"Yes, Kit does resemble my husband, much to Dante's delight," Rhea said, but her voice was muffled as she kissed the tip of Kit's tiny nose.

Rhea sat down again and gratefully accepted the cup of steaming tea.

Dora Lascombe glanced around curiously as two small boys came hurrying inside, their cloaks dripping. Shrugging out of them, they left them hanging on the pegs near the door and came forward, rubbing their hands together.

"The cap'n said this was for Lord Kit's cradle," Conny Brady said as he folded the sable rug across the end of the cradle, winking down at the wide-eyed baby staring up at him.

"Is he coming?" Rhea asked, glancing nervously from Conny to the landlady, who was watching the proceedings with avid curiosity.

"In a minute, m'lady. He said he wanted to check the last team of horses," Conny informed her, his glance resting on the steaming teapot while he blew on his cupped hands.

"Here you are, Conny. Robin," Rhea said, holding out brimming cups of tea, both heavy with cream and sugar.

"Thank you, m'lady," Conny said as he squatted down close to the fire, the cup held gingerly between his linked fingers.

Robin accepted his cup gratefully but couldn't help but notice the tray was bare of any food, and his stomach was beginning to growl with embarrassing loudness.

"Aye, young fella, there's an ovenful of scones bein' warmed now," Dora Lascombe told the dark-haired lad, for she had seen that wistful look on her own grandchildren's faces too many times not to guess its meaning. "Well, I'd best be gettin' back to the kitchens or those two girls will set fire to my best pots," Dora Lascombe said with a worried look.

"Would you see that our maids, and Nora and Betsie here, are served some tea?" Rhea told the landlady as she saw the two girls enter, hovering uncertainly near the door. "Come closer to the fire and warm yourselves. You're shivering," Rhea exclaimed. Mason would never forgive her if anything happened to his granddaughter. For the first time, Rhea began to feel the responsibility of having servants of her own.

"We was just makin' sure that the proper trunks were unloaded and put in the right rooms, m'lady," Nora said, wishing she were in her own narrow little bed, the same one she'd slept in all of her life, snuggling beneath her warm quilt back at Camareigh. This didn't seem at all a hospitable country.

"Aye, m'lady, I'll get a couple of more cups," Dora Lascombe said. She had started toward the door when a tall, cloaked figure entered. As he removed his hat and turned down the high collar of his cloak, Dora Lascombe gasped. She remembered only too well those pale gray eyes. And the demoniacal effect wasn't lessened any when a bandy-legged little man carrying a cat in his arms, the feline's slitted green eyes glaring malevolently at her, came scurrying into the room. Dora Lascombe had never forgotten his face either. At one time, when she had been just a rosy-cheeked girl without a gray hair, she had hoped to have him court her.

"Mrs. Lascombe, isn't it?" the cool-toned voice spoke her name. "It has been many, many years, has it not?"

But Dora Lascombe looked as frozen as the unfortunate bishop the inn had been named in honor of.

"Oh, Lord," she murmured, and her uneasiness increased when a smile curved Dante Leighton's lips. God help them all, but he was even more the handsome devil today than he had been at twenty.

"I was afraid this would be the reaction to my return to Merdraco," he said softly. "I was foolish to think anything might have changed."

Dora Lascombe couldn't seem to find her tongue, but Sam Lascombe had. He was yelling her name as he came striding in from the taproom, where a member of the Leighton party had mentioned his employer's name.

"Dora? Dora?" Sam Lascombe demanded as he stomped into the room, halting abruptly as the tall man turned to face him. Sam felt his worst fears being realized, for the fat would be in the fire when Jack Shelby learned that Dante Leighton was back and that Sam had given him food and shelter.

"I had to be seein' it with me own eyes," he said incredulously, his eyes not missing a detail of the man's prosperous appearance. "Lord Jacqobi."

"Yes, and 'tis a pleasure to see you again, too, Sam Lascombe," Dante murmured, for he had often come to the taproom of the Bishop's Grave Inn for a brandy when returning from Westlea Abbot on a cold night.

Sam Lascombe was beginning to become infected with the same ailment Dora was suffering from, for he opened his mouth, but no words came forth until he caught sight of the short figure standing beside Dante Leighton. "I knew it!" he roared, frightening Jamaica out of Houston Kirby's arms. Like a streak of lightning, the tom shot through Sam Lascombe's booted feet and disappeared beneath Rhea's chair.

"I knew I recognized that short, swaggering figure. Houston Kirby, aye, ye've not changed any, ye haven't," Sam Lascombe said, and whether he meant it as a compliment or an insult, only Houston Kirby and Sam Lascombe knew. "Should've known ye'd still be by his side."

"Aye, some of us know what 'tis to be loyal," Kirby said, eyeing the larger man unflinchingly. Although they'd been friends as boys, Sam Lascombe had always been too quick to think the worst of the captain. "Been havin' my doubts about whether or not this particular inn was good enough for the likes of the cap'n and his lady," Kirby said as he glanced around the neatly furnished room as if little impressed by his surroundings.

"Kirby, that's enough. We are guests at Bishop's Grave Inn," Dante said. "Aren't we?" he asked pointedly. "Or would you prefer that I take my family and leave?" Dante asked with such quiet dignity that Sam Lascombe was ashamed.

"I reckon ye oughta know, Lascombe, before ye do somethin' stupid," Kirby said, "that Lord Jacqobi be a very wealthy, respected gentleman nowadays. I don't s'pose his father-in-law would take kindly to seein' his daughter and grandson put out on a night like this. Did I mention that Lady Rhea Claire Jacqobi is the daughter of the Duke and Duchess of Camareigh?" Kirby said, his grin widening as he heard Dora gasp.

"We would not wish to stay where we are not welcome," Rhea said quietly, her voice cold.

"Oh, Sam, come to your senses," Dora said, nudging him none too gently. "Ye can't be thinkin' to deny these people a place to sleep tonight. Why, look at the wee one sleepin' in his cradle before the fire. Would ye be so cruel as to be sendin' the babe back into the storm? And her ladyship, why, 'twould be criminal to ask such a thing of so delicate a lady, and her just havin' given birth. And the lads, why, the one looks as blue as a plum," Dora told her husband. But she knew he didn't really need much persuading. He was no fool, and if times had changed the fortunes of the Marquis of Jacqobi, and he had come back to live at Merdraco, then Sam would not make an enemy of the man and Jack Shelby could go to the devil for all Dora Lascombe cared, she thought defiantly.

"Sam Lascombe has never turned away a guest, so ye be welcome to stay as long as need be," he said. Eyeing the short figure standing so proudly beside Dante Leighton, Sam Lascombe's fingers itched to pull him aside, to sit on Houston Kirby if need be, in order to find out what had happened to Lord Jacqobi during the past years.

Alastair Marlowe and Francis Dominick exchanged relieved glances. Neither had wanted to draw his sword—or to have to climb back on his horse for both were weary and had been looking forward to a warm bed.

Conny Brady and Robin Dominick exchanged smug grins, for the captain knew what he was doing, which was something the former cabin boy was forever telling Dante Leighton's young brother-in-law. Maybe now he would believe it, Conny thought as he returned his attention to something important, like the logs burning in the hearth.

"How is the little fellow doing?" Francis asked, sitting down opposite his sister at the table.

"He's finally fallen to sleep. I don't think he felt the cold, for I kept him bundled up ever since darkness fell," Rhea said, glancing down at the peacefully sleeping child.

Francis shook his head. It was still hard for him to believe that his sister was a mother. He found himself remembering back to a year earlier when she had insisted on saving a litter of half-drowned pups from a ditch beside the road. She would make a good mother, he decided. She had the kindest heart of anyone he knew, and as Francis eyed his grim-faced brother-in-law, he promised himself that Dante Leighton would have him to deal with if he ever hurt Rhea. He was glad now that he had accompanied Rhea, considering the hostility the name Leighton seemed to inspire in the locals.

"Please, make yourselves comfortable, and Dora will get dinner," Sam Lascombe invited his guests as he grabbed Dora, ignoring her outraged expression, and escorted her from the room. Thank heaven for the storm, thought Sam. At least it kept other visitors from arriving. He had in mind a certain person whose arrival just then would be disastrous.

Two hours later Dante Leighton was standing before a small

square of mullioned window in a bedchamber, his eyes searching the darkness beyond. The storm still blew furiously over the countryside.

Curled up like a contented cat on the soft feather bed, Rhea was brushing her unbound hair with long, even strokes. Pulling several thick strands across her shoulder, she glanced up at Dante.

"What are you looking at?" she asked, for she could see only blackness.

"Merdraco."

"It lies in that direction?"

"Yes. And although I cannot see it, somehow I *do* see it. The night may hide it from me, but it is there, waiting for me to return."

He continued to stand there silhouetted against the night. Then he drew the heavy drapes, closing the darkness out. In the shadowy light from the hearth and the flickering candle beside the bed, his expression was unreadable.

Sitting down on the edge of the bed, Dante took the brush from Rhea's hands and began to draw it through the long, silken strands. Then his hand slid around her waist and he pulled her back against his chest, her head resting against his shoulder while his lips caressed her cheek lingeringly.

"Tomorrow, Rhea. Tomorrow I shall take you and our son to Merdraco. We will have come home after so many years of exile," Dante murmured. Then his lips found hers, and he lost himself in her gentle warmth, content to let the darkness reign a little while longer.

Dark with excessive bright.
John Milton

Chapter 17

THE storm which had blown in so furiously from the sea, spawned of the Devil's Hole, the locals said, stayed for another two days, keeping Bishop's Grave Inn isolated from the rest of the world. It also kept an impatient Dante Leighton pacing back and forth before the small mullioned windows while he stared at the torrential rains soaking the countryside. The road to Merdraco would be little better than a stream.

Little did he realize, however, how providential that storm was, for it allowed Sam and Dora Lascombe a chance to learn what sort of man the wild young Lord Jacqobi had become. And it allowed Houston Kirby, never one to miss an opportunity, to tell a few truths about what had really happened fifteen years before. Sir Miles Sandbourne emerged from the stories looking quite different from the way people had always seen him.

In Dora Lascombe's mind, poor young Lord Jacqobi had been done a grave injustice. Now she saw a man very much in love with his beautiful wife, and who was always finding an opportunity to hold his son. Could there possibly be a more loving and gentle husband and father than Dante Leighton? She also saw, though she'd not have admitted it, a handsome and virile man who always had a polite word for her. That was more than she could say of most people in his station.

Sam Lascombe was quite favorably impressed as well, but mostly on account of listening avidly to the exciting tales told by young Conny Brady and the gentlemanly Mr. Marlowe about his life aboard the *Sea Dragon*. In his mind, Sam suddenly saw himself sailing with the crew of the *Sea Dragon* and sharing in that incredible sunken treasure. To Sam Lascombe, the measure of a man was to be taken by the respect other men held him in. It seemed that Dante Leighton had been a fine captain, much admired by his crew. Any man who could do what he had done had Sam Lascombe's respect and admiration—neither come by easily. And so, during those two days of confinement, the Lascombes came to know the man who had captained the *Sea Dragon* and to forget the young lord they once had cursed and had been so quick to judge guilty of murder.

It was due partly to Rhea Claire and her two brothers that the Lascombes suddenly found themselves staunch supporters of the Marquis of Jacqobi. The lady and the young Dominicks seemed such good, decent people and little did any of them realize how important it would be for Dante Leighton to have all the friends he could find; for not everyone would be so generous to forget the past, or their hostility for the master of Merdraco.

The third morning after that stormy night when Dante Leighton had arrived at Bishop's Grave Inn, the dawn broke to reveal clear skies. The sun had hardly dared to show its face when Dante, in buckskin breeches, frock coat, and boots, roused Rhea from her slumber.

"Come on, sleepyhead, out of bed with you," Dante ordered,

sounding like the captain of the *Sea Dragon* sending his men into the rigging.

Rhea rolled onto her stomach, burying her head beneath the pillows. She was tired, having been up with Kit for his feeding in the middle of the night. Hunching her shoulders, she tried to ignore the bothersome tickling sensation at the nape of her neck. She yawned loudly and sighed, preparing to continue her sweet dreaming. But Dante Leighton was not to be denied. Suddenly Rhea felt the covers being thrown back and a rush of cold air on her bare legs.

"Go away," Rhea complained in a husky voice. Opening her eyes, she glanced up at him. Her eyes widened in surprise, for he had already dressed and was staring down at her with a wide grin. "What time is it? Surely 'tis still dark outside?" Rhea asked, deciding she disliked people who managed to be so cheery this early in the morning.

Dante sat down on the edge of the bed and grasped hold of her shoulders, bringing her limp body into a sitting position. "It is no longer dark. The sun has risen, my love, and we have much to do today."

"Merdraco?" she asked, lifting her head from his shoulder.

Dante pressed a kiss against her lips. "Are you up to it?" he asked, a questioning look in his eye as he held her warm, soft body against his chest. For a moment he wished he had remained beside her in bed. "The roads will still be too muddy for the coach, so we shall have to ride. Shall I have Skylark saddled for you?" he asked. Her mare had been brought along as had been several other horses, gifts from Lucien Dominick. He knew Dante Leighton would have to set up stables, and the Dominick stock was some of the best in the country.

"You'll not go without me," Rhea warned, even as her heavy-lidded eyes closed for just another irresistible moment of sleep. But her own thoughts kept her awake this time. "What of Robin and Conny?" she asked. "Will they have to stay behind?"

"No, Francis said he'd take Robin up behind him on El Cid, and Alastair will take Conny. Kit will have to stay behind, but Betsie and Nora and Dora Lascombe will all keep an eye on him. I do not think we need worry on that score."

Rhea nodded. "What of Kirby? I don't think I've ever seen him on horseback. Will he stay here?"

"Kirby? Stay here, while we see Merdraco?" Dante asked incredulously. "Nothing on earth could keep him from going with us today, though horseback riding *is* one of his least favorite pursuits," Dante said, and laughed. Houston Kirby had become as nervous as a bridegroom on his wedding day whenever he chanced a glance toward the dark towers rising out of the mists.

Rhea glanced up at the hard, bold curve of Dante's jaw. Suddenly she felt some of Dante's excitement coursing through her own veins. "Dante?" she said urgently.

"Yes?"

"I want you to be happy," she said in an odd voice.

Dante bent his head, kissing her mouth. "I shall be, Rhea, now that I have returned home," he assured her, apparently feeling none of her anxiety.

Seldom did the expansive view of sea disappear from their sight as the riders drew closer to the towers in the distance. At one point, the narrow lane seemed to fall into the sea as it wound down through a steep canyon. The roar of waves crashing on the rocks below deafened them.

Every so often, Rhea caught one of Robin's excited exclamations before it was carried away on the wind. Never before had he seen such a wild shore, or been so close to the foaming white water surging against the base of the cliff. Francis was more circumspect, but Rhea could tell that he was impressed. Conny, of course, was an old hand when it came to the sea, and he was more interested in reaching Merdraco than in hearing the landlubbers' exclamations. He knew that you really couldn't know the sea until you'd sailed her.

Rhea, too, was awed. This was the land Dante had ridden across as a boy and a young man. She wondered if it seemed much changed to him.

Dressed in a severely tailored riding habit of sky-blue wool with a claret-colored silk waistcoat and ruffled chemise front, dark red feathers and ribbons decorating her hatband, Rhea might have been out for a casual afternoon's gallop through the parklands surrounding Camareigh. But she found herself staring out to where the foaming, wind-driven waves crashed against the rocky headlands before rolling toward shore and the small crescent of sandy beach curving along the base of the cliff. As her eye climbed that precipice to where the dark towers stood at the summit, she knew a sudden desolation. When she looked back down to that sandy shore, she shivered, feeling as if something horrible had taken place on that innocent-looking beach. For the first time in her life, Rhea had a brief sensation of what her Aunt Mary must feel when she had one of her visions. She also knew that Mary Fletcher would have been able to tell her what had happened on the beach that night. Strangely, Rhea didn't even wonder how she knew the horror had occurred at night. But as sure as death, she knew it had.

"You feel it too, don't you?" Francis Dominick demanded, startling Rhea. She hadn't known that he and Robin were so close.

"I saw your face when you were staring down at the sands. It reminded me of Aunt Mary when she is having one of her visions," Francis spoke loudly, for the sound of the sea threatened to drown him out.

Rhea shrugged, feeling more understanding for her aunt than she ever had. "I cannot explain," she said.

"Now you even sound like Aunt Mary," Robin said, and grinned.

"Did you sense something, too?" Rhea demanded of Francis, and he nodded, not needing to say more. The expression in their eyes said it all.

Dante Leighton, leading the way, glanced back in time to see the exchange of glances between the brother and sister who bore such a startling resemblance to one another. Their deep golden curls stamped them as Dominicks. Dante wondered if Rhea would ever come to think of herself as a Leighton.

"Is anything wrong?" he demanded as he slowed his pace and allowed the dainty-legged mare to come abreast of his horse. That caused Francis to fall behind, as there wasn't room on the path for three horses.

"We were wondering what this bay is named," Francis called out, deciding to take the initiative. Once Rhea met that pale-eyed gaze of Dante's, she always seemed to lose track of her thoughts.

"It is known as Dragon's Cove."

"Can ships sail in here?" Francis asked doubtfully as he eyed the waves breaking in the distance. "It looks as if there are reefs at the mouth of the cove."

Dante glanced at the young man in surprise. "You are right, Francis, and 'tis very dangerous to try to sail into Dragon's Cove unless you are familiar with the channel that cuts across it. Even then, if the seas are rough, as they are today, you could very easily run aground."

"Have there been very many wrecks?" Robin asked.

"Yes," Dante said with a bleak look out to sea.

Rhea and Dante both stared up at the sheer cliffs curving along the shore. "Is this where it happened?" Rhea asked softly, too softly for Dante to hear, but he had seen her sadness and he understood the question. He nodded.

"Yes, she fell from there," Dante said. His voice sounded harsh.

Houston Kirby, sitting astride a sturdy little moorland pony hired from the inn, didn't need to overhear the conversation to know what was being discussed. He, too, stared up at the cliffs as though seeing them for the first time. He thought of the beautiful Lady Elayne's battered body lying against the rocks before it was carried out to sea on the tide. It hurt him bad, it did, to think of Lady Elayne's tragic death. And he felt a rekindling of all of his hatred of Sir Miles, the man he and Dante both held responsible for Lady Elayne's death.

The narrow lane wound back on itself, heading inland as it began to rise and, gradually, climbed ever higher toward the summit of the cliff where, from the distance, the towers which had now disappeared had crowned the escarpment.

Rhea held her breath as they neared the top, her smile forced as she glanced back at Francis and Robin, who were in line just behind her, followed by Alastair, Conny holding on tightly to Alastair's waist. Then, his face wizened beyond his years, Houston Kirby brought up the rear.

Skylark seemed to fly those last few yards up the lane, and then they reached the top and were riding along the gentle rise of hilltop. That was when Rhea pulled up, coming to a sudden halt just short of Dante's stilled figure. Both he and his mount looked as if they had been turned to stone.

Rhea no longer heard the pounding of the surf, or the singing of the winds. She was listening to a roaring in her ears as she stared up at the two dark towers of Merdraco.

And at the rest of the castle . . . which lay in ruins.

"Rhea?"

She heard Francis' voice, then felt a supporting arm sliding around her waist. She turned to see Alastair Marlowe's pale face.

"Merdraco, i-it has been destroyed," she whispered to him.

"Coooeee!" Conny Brady's voice pierced the air. " 'Tis a ruin. Looks like someone sent cannon fire through here. What *happened* to it?" he demanded angrily, looking as if someone had slapped him hard. His lips were trembling and his eyes were bright with tears.

Robin Dominick, his mouth hanging open in surprised dismay, peeked from behind his brother's back at the huge gray stones that looked as if the wind had tossed them about as easily as sticks of straw.

Francis Dominick shook his head. He had never seen such a desolate, gloomy place. Suddenly it reminded him of the ruins of Timeredaloch before his Uncle Richard rebuilt the great castle. Francis glanced back to Rhea's stricken face. He didn't know what to say. She was staring at her husband's broad back, and Francis realized that the Marquis of Jacqobi had not moved or spoken since he had come to a halt just within the shadow of the ruined towers of Merdraco.

Francis Dominick bit down hard on his lip, wondering if he should make some move to console his brother-in-law or, perhaps, to restrain him.

But Francis needn't have worried, for Dante Leighton did not react as one might have expected. Indeed, a rage would have been preferable to the sound of his laughter filling the air as Dante held out his arms to embrace the limitless view of the sea and sky now afforded him through the ruins of Merdraco.

"Dante? Dante, please! Stop laughing!" Rhea finally cried. "I don't understand. Why are you laughing?" she sobbed, for all she could see was the destruction of the home he had so long dreamt of returning to, and that was certainly no cause for joy.

Her panicked words got through to Dante. He glanced back at her in surprise, becoming first amazed and then confused.

Dante dismounted and went to her side. Lifting her from her mount, his body shielding her from the wind, he said, "Rhea, my love. I am sorry. I never realized that you did not know. It never entered my mind to explain. Look," he said, pointing to a gentle rise of land in the distance. It was not as high as the rocky crag the dark towers rose from and, sheltered by the curve of the coast which protected it from the full force of the storms blowing in from the Atlantic, was covered in rich woodland. Nestled in that sheltered place was a magnificent house of aged gray stone, the sun a blinding reflection in the countless faceted windows gracing the east front. Great chimneys rose as proudly as had the original towers of the castle. "That is Merdraco, my home, Rhea. Our home. And, for centuries to come, it will be the home of the Leightons," proclaimed Dante Leighton, the former captain of the *Sea Dragon*.

> *O! I am Fortune's fool.*
> Shakespeare

Chapter 18

RHEA CLAIRE LEIGHTON, the new mistress of Merdraco, glanced back at the dark towers which were no
more than hollow shells crumbling down around the spiraling
steps that climbed ever upward toward turrets silhouetted
against the blue sky. The towers were all that remained of the
baronial castle begun in the eleventh century by a Norman
adventurer seeking to hold the conquered lands he had won
from defeated Saxons. As a feudal stronghold, Merdraco had
been inaccessible because of its position atop a rocky mound
dominated by sheer cliffs on three sides.

Originally a wooden tower surrounded by palisading, Merdraco, as the years progressed, had grown into a fortified stone
edifice, with a stone keep with fifteen-foot-thick walls, and a

towering gate house guarding its vulnerable flank, and closing the gap between the encircling, turreted rampart walls.

As the centuries passed and the threat of invasion lessened, and the turbulence of civil disorder had quieted, so had the need for a fortressed castle perched high above the sea where it was under siege by the storm-blown arctic winds which invaded and conquered in a manner no army could have hoped to achieve with catapult and battering ram. It was no longer necessary to stay in so drafty and forbidding an abode. Nor, indeed, had such a place been acceptable once Gilbert Leighton, the sixth Earl of Sandrake, was created the Marquis of Jacqobi.

So the great castle of Merdraco had been torn apart—not by an enemy's hand, but by masons. Under the guidance of an architect and with the assistance of glaziers and plasterers and an army of workmen, the masons reassembled it into a magnificent Tudor mansion of gables and slim chimney stacks, of mullioned windows and stone carvings, of arches and court-yards.

And all that remained of the Norman castle were the two dark towers standing in solitary beauty, a tribute to Raoul de St. Draquet, the Norman who had conquered the wild stretch of coast. The towers also served as a reminder to the locals of their first liege lord and of the allegiance to the Leighton family expected of them.

"Well, what do you think?" Dante demanded as he halted atop a gentle rise and stared down at the somber gray stone of the house he had been born in.

It was certainly not Camareigh, Rhea thought, or anything like her home with its stately, well-balanced wings of honey-hued stone and the classic, porticoed entrance. Merdraco looked as though it had stood empty and neglected for over fifteen years, which it had. But strangely enough, there was a wild beauty about the house. Ivy grew unrestrained along a garden wall, and aged trees were overgrown with climbing roses. The yew hedges had grown tall and bushy, while bram-bles and weeds encroached upon the flowerbeds of the fore-court.

There was also a sadness about the abandoned house. Did it long to hear voices echoing once again down its empty halls while sweet woodsmoke, drifting from the chimneys, scented the cool air? Rhea suddenly felt as if the house were beckoning to her. She wanted to open it up to the light again, to banish the darkness that had enveloped it for so many long, lonely years.

Dante, who had been watching her anxiously, felt all his fears vanishing with the tender look in her eyes. She had accepted the house.

"I could not have wished for a more beautiful home, Dante," Rhea spoke softly, seeing beyond the ravages of time to a home where they would find happiness.

Robin Dominick and Conny Brady, however, were not so wise, and to them the mansion looked as if it had seen better days. They wondered if this was truly Merdraco.

Houston Kirby, seeing the great house for the first time since he had followed its master to sea, was speechless with remembered awe. In his eyes, Merdraco had not changed. He did not see the weeds choking the gardens or the broken panes of glass or the gaping hole in the steep roof. Houston Kirby was seeing the Merdraco of the past, when coaches rolled up the circular, yew-lined drive and when lights sparkled behind every pane of glass, and the gardens held an unending supply of flowers to be arranged in vases in every room.

Alastair Marlowe, on the other hand, was seeing both the past and the present. He had heard stories of Merdraco for years, and so he guessed how great a house it had once been. He could sense some of that glory despite its dilapidated appearance. But he knew that there was quite a lot of work to be done.

Francis Dominick, like Rhea, was accustomed to the classic beauty of Camareigh, with its well-cared-for lawns and gardens. And because he would not have to live at Merdraco, he found it less easy to be generous. He found the house quite depressing, and although he didn't envy Rhea coming to live here, it was certainly better than if the original castle still stood upon that rocky promontory.

The master of Merdraco urged his sorrel-maned chestnut down the incline, following the lane through the woodland, which seemed to be the only link connecting the outside world, the ruins of the castle, and Merdraco.

Suddenly, rising up before them was an imposing, two-storied gatehouse with mullioned oriel windows and turrets. Wrought-iron gates across the gatehouse should have kept out trespassers, but the gates were hanging free of their hinges.

Dante Leighton frowned. They had not become unhinged by themselves, and as he inspected the hinges he saw that they had been purposefully sprung.

"Looks as if there might have been some uninvited visitors," Alastair Marlowe spoke quietly.

"Does this lane lead only here, to Merdraco?" Francis Dominick asked abruptly, for something had been worrying him since they had left the castle ruins.

Dante seemed surprised by the question. "Yes, but it continues a little farther into the woods. This is the only way one can reach Merdraco by way of Merwest Cross. Why?"

Francis Dominick shrugged self-consciously. He did not want to sound fanciful.

"Well, it seemed to me, when we were at the ruins, that there had been a bit of activity thereabouts. The lane we came up on from Bishop's Grave Inn showed signs of much travel. Didn't you notice how deeply rutted its surface was, despite all the recent rains?" Francis asked, his eyes meeting Dante Leighton's.

"I can't say that I did. I was so preoccupied with reaching Merdraco," Dante admitted, then glanced back toward the dark towers looming in the distance. "But now that you mention it, the lane was in rather good condition, considering that no one should have been traveling it for the past fifteen years."

"I saw signs of activity, too," Alastair Marlowe said as he thought back on what he had seen at the ruins. "I remember thinking that one of the stone dragons at the base of the tower had taken quite a bit of abuse, but I figured 'twas only natural considering how old it probably was. It was almost as if someone had been using it for a target," Alastair said, glancing around apologetically. "Of course, it could have been my imagination, but I wonder if—" he started to say, then shook his head.

"What?"

"No, 'tis nothing, really," Alastair remained silent.

"You don't think it was a ghost, do you, Mr. Marlowe?" Conny Brady breathed in growing excitement, little realizing how deeply his words might hurt the captain. "The Pale Lady of the Ruins is what Mrs. Lascombe calls the ghost. Says nobody comes up here anymore 'cause they're frightened of seein' her."

"The maids say we've got a ghost now at Camareigh because of the horrible death that happened there," Robin confided, not helping to relieve the tension.

"Robin!" Francis warned. "That is ridiculous. And if you start repeating it, you'll have half the staff afraid of the dark."

"I do not think that is what Alastair is referring to, is it?" Dante asked slowly, his gray eyes narrowed thoughtfully. "You were thinking that some enterprising smugglers might have been running contraband through Merdraco. What better way to keep the villagers at a distance than to invent a ghost to haunt the ruins? The flashing of a lantern's light, with perhaps a green cloth thrown over it to lend an eerie glow, that would do it."

Rhea found herself remembering something Dante had told her in London. He had spoken of his mother, saying that some of the locals claimed to have seen her windswept figure standing on the cliffs near Merdraco. But how had Dante, who had not returned to Merdraco until now, known of that?

But Rhea forgot her speculations when she heard Dante's amused laughter. Much to her amazement, Alastair joined in, and she glanced at the two men in confusion.

"'Tis ironic, isn't it, that Merdraco should be used by a smuggling gang while I have been trying to make my fortune smuggling between the Indies and the Carolinas in order to return to my home and lead a life of respectability," Dante said, the humor of the situation amusing him terrifically. "When in London, Sir Morgan Lloyd was questioning me about the smugglers hereabouts, for he had heard something of their activities from his brother, who is stationed along this coast. I am afraid Sir Morgan believes that I could never give up my former profession," Dante remarked as he dismounted and then assisted Rhea from her mount's back.

"Really? I had no idea," Alastair said, lowering Conny to the ground.

"'Tis just as well he has returned to the colonies. If he were on duty here, he would most likely suspect me of being the leader of the smuggling gang. After all, I have the best credentials for it."

"I don't see how he could think such a thing," Alastair said. "You've not even been in these parts for years. I should think that fact alone would absolve you of suspicion."

"Have you never seen a puppeteer, Alastair?" Dante asked curiously, his mind on something.

"Yes, of course," his former supercargo replied with a frown, wondering what a childish amusement from a fair had to do with so serious a subject.

"Then you will know that a person does not always have to be seen in order to be in control of something. The puppeteer pulls the strings of his puppet, but he is never seen. What better protection could I have, should I be the leader of this notorious smuggling gang, than not to have been here at all? And, who better than I to be their leader? But now that I am a wealthy man, who would suspect me of smuggling except, perhaps, the very suspicious Sir Morgan Lloyd, who knows that I might still desire the daring of the game rather than the profits?" Dante said. His argument almost had Francis and Robin Dominick and Conny Brady believing that he was indeed the leader.

And even Alastair Marlowe, for just a second's doubt, could almost have believed it true, until he saw the laughter in Dante Leighton's eye, and the shaking of the little steward's head in that manner which left little doubt that he felt he was putting up with an awful lot of spoofing by someone who should know better.

"What does that say, Cap'n?" Robin demanded, having picked up Conny Brady's style of addressing Dante Leighton.

Dante followed Robin's gaze to the family coat of arms supported by dragons, which had been carved into stone above the curving arched entrance to Merdraco. "'Chance not, win not,'" Dante spoke softly the words that had served his family well throughout the centuries. "If my ancestor, St. Draquet, hadn't taken a chance and crossed the Channel with William, then there would be no Merdraco today. And had that not been our family creed, then there would have been no *Sea Dragon* and no sunken treasure to make all of us wealthy. Nor would I be standing here now, master of my fate, my beloved by my side," Dante said, speaking the last words so that only Rhea could hear them.

"'Twould seem as if you have defied them all, Cap'n, and won," Alastair Marlowe said, thinking that Dante Leighton, captain of the *Sea Dragon,* Marquis of Jacqobi, and master of Merdraco, indeed had the devil's own luck.

Alastair breathed easier. It seemed as if all would turn out as the captain had dreamed it would. Still thinking about Dante Leighton's good fortune, which had certainly benefited Alastair, he walked beneath the arched entrance to Merdraco.

"Come, let me show you Merdraco," Dante said, and taking Rhea's small, gloved hand in his, the reins of their horses grasped in his other, he led her beneath the arched gateway, passing freely beneath the dragons' stony gaze.

They entered a large inner yard, where a curving drive surrounded by once-magnificent terraced gardens led to the great house sitting on a gentle slope at the opposite end. The inner yard was overgrown now, and once tamed hedges of yew and box overran the paved road, and rhododendrons and hydrangeas were splashes of color spilling across the green slope of lawn in the center of the drive, where leaves floated in the filthy water of an ornamental fountain. Once through the gatehouse, one could see the high stone wall that ran the distance of the yard until connecting with the gabled stable block. That block closed off the rest of the forecourt on the right side until it reached another arched entranceway near the great house. Directly across from the stable block, on the other side of the yard, was a wing of the house. It also connected to the high stone wall which completed the enclosure on the left side of the gatehouse.

A strange silence engulfed the group as they walked along the curving drive. It was as if they were trespassing in a cemetery. The tall weeds breaking through the cracked paving stones reached out for Rhea's skirt, pulling against it as she passed. The slow clop, clopping of the horses' hooves sounded like thunder to Rhea's sensitive ears. She felt like an intruder in this abandoned place.

If Dante was at all disappointed in the dilapidated appearance of Merdraco, he certainly kept it to himself. As they walked past the long stable block, he said conversationally,

"Thanks to His Grace, we have the beginnings of a fine stable. I only wish that we might be able to persuade that young man in charge of the coach horses to come back here after he returns to Camareigh with the other coaches and wagons. He certainly knows his job."

"He should," Rhea explained. "He trained under Butterick's critical eye. We have lost quite a few of our stable boys to other families just because Butterick teaches them everything he knows. I wouldn't be at all surprised if that isn't why Butterick sent him along. He knows we need a good master of the horse. Butterick could have sent someone else, for even a new hand in the stables could have handled the teams. Perhaps he wanted Clauson to see Merdraco, and find out if he could get along with you."

"If he could get along with me?" Dante asked incredulously.

"Yes. And the fact that Butterick sent one of his best assistants is quite significant," Rhea was saying as she eyed the rundown stables.

"Oh, and how is that?"

"Because if Butterick did not like the way you sat a horse, or treated your horses, he would not recommend you as a future employer. Nor would my father have made a gift of any of the horses from his stable if Butterick had not approved of you," Rhea told a startled Dante who had not realized how much had depended upon the opinion of Butterick.

"I am not certain, then, that I should allow Clauson to see these stables, for I fear Butterick would be scandalized at their condition," Dante said, and although he said it in jest, there was just a tinge of underlying bitterness in his voice.

"I bet Saunders would wring his hands if he could see this garden," Robin said.

"And who is Saunders?" Dante asked, but his eyes were trained on the main block of the house, which, with every step they took, drew closer and closer. Rhea could feel Dante's growing excitement.

"He is the head gardener at Camareigh," Robin explained. "He really gets upset if anyone dares walk through his flowers."

"That isn't quite true, Robin, and you know it," Rhea corrected him. "'Twas Shoopitee he objected to, and with reason, you must admit."

"Who's Shoopitee?" Conny Brady wanted to know.

"He's a pony that Robin used to ride, and rather recklessly," Rhea explained.

"I'll say. Remember when Robin knocked Lord Rendale into the lily pond, just when he was about to propose?" Francis said with a chuckle.

Dante Leighton laughed. That was something he would have enjoyed seeing. He found the man insufferable, and hoped that Caroline Winters managed to become the next Countess of Rendale. The two deserved one another.

A short flight of shallow steps led to the entrance of Merdraco. An arched, covered porch framed the carved oak door. Rhea almost expected the heavy door to resist Dante's weight when he placed his hand on the great brass door handle. To her surprise, it opened, but not without the squeaking protest of rusty hinges.

A stifling mustiness overwhelmed them as they entered the shadowy great hall with its arch-braced roof. The only light was that which slanted down through the stained glass of the oriel window high above the entranceway.

In this hallowed place of spiritual light, a desecration had taken place, and it was a scene never to be forgotten by the horrified witnesses.

> *All hell shall stir for this.*
> Shakespeare

Chapter 19

DANTE LEIGHTON was no longer aware of anything or anyone. He stared transfixed by the destruction surrounding him.

For the trespasser at the gates had not been content merely to steal inside in search of shelter or profit. He had, with calculated viciousness, set about ruining the great house.

With shaking hands, Rhea pulled a scented handkerchief from her pocket. Holding it to her nostrils, she glanced around the great hall in disbelieving horror. Never had she seen such filth and defilement. The odors rising from the hall were an abomination, for the stately hall had been used like a stable by both man and beast.

Piles of rubble and rotting off-scourings were scattered across the filthy floor. Near the great fireplace was a disorderly stack of kindling; it was no ordinary firewood, but the splintered oak of the carved, once-beautiful furniture. The massive trestle table with its bulbous legs that Dante had spoken of as always having a vase of wildflowers gracing its surface, was no more, and the deep chest with the mythological creatures carved across its top, where Dante the small boy had hidden from his nanny, had also disappeared. The great oak settle, the high-backed cane chairs, and the side tables had become powdery drifts of ash in the hearth.

Jagged strips of the carved oak paneling had even been torn from the walls, leaving gaping holes. Part of the carved balustrade of the great staircase at the far end of the hall had been ripped loose, and had most likely come to an end in the fireplace along with all the rest.

"Coooeee!" Conny Brady's voice rang through the hall like the pealing of a bell. "This place smells worse than a privy!" he exclaimed, his face showing his disgust, and disappointment, for the lad had expected the captain's Merdraco to be a magnificent house.

The young cabin boy's contemptuous words hit Dante Leighton like a splash of icy water, waking him from the nightmare holding him spellbound in this macabre scene. Turning round, he saw the other people gathered close behind him, all standing like statues in the oppressive silence.

The change in Dante Leighton's face was more horrifying than the condition of the Great Hall. It was as if the spirit had fled from his body and all that remained was the graven image of a man turned to stone.

"Dante," Rhea said softly, drawing those pale gray eyes to her. They could have been a stranger's eyes, they were so cold and lifeless. Rhea held out her hand to him, wanting to touch him, to comfort him somehow.

Dante stared at her. Seeing the pity in her eyes and in the faces around him, he closed his eyes. He could not face pity. Then, with a suddenness which took them all by surprise, Dante grasped Rhea's outstretched hand and pulled her over to the door. He dragged her through the door into the blinding light outside.

"Dante?" Rhea pleaded, her free hand touching his coat

sleeve fearfully. "I," she began, but there were no words. What words of comfort were there for this?

"I do not want you to enter this house again," Dante said, breathing deeply of the sweet air warmed by sunshine. "Do you understand me, Rhea?" He held her gaze. "I do not want you degraded by that place," he said.

"But Dante, I want to be with you. The rest of the house cannot be in such a state. It will not be easy, but I know there will be something we can save. They cannot have destroyed everything," Rhea said optimistically, not wanting to give in to the despair threatening to overwhelm her, as she feared it had overwhelmed Dante.

"You think not?" Dante asked, his gaze straying to the adjacent wing of the house. "Damn their souls to everlasting hell. They'll pay for this. By all that I hold holy I swear they will," Dante Leighton swore softly.

"Dante, do not go back inside," Rhea beseeched.

"Cap'n," Houston Kirby approached Dante's side, "ye stay out here like Lady Rhea asks. I'll go back inside," he offered, the tears wet on his wrinkled face. "I'll see what needs to be done. There's no need for ye to hurt yourself anymore."

Dante shook his head and turned away, but before he took a step, he placed his hand on the little steward's shoulder. Houston Kirby raised a shaking hand and placed it over that strong hand. For a moment they remained that way, then Dante strode back into that man-made hell, refusing to hear Rhea's pleas. Then came the distinctive sounds of a door being slammed shut and a bolt being shot into place.

"He's been shamed before ye, m'lady," Houston Kirby spoke huskily. "He's got to go back inside. He's got to face the devils that are ridin' him. 'Tis a tragedy," Houston Kirby said, sniffing loudly and wiping the back of his hand across his cheeks. "'Tis a damnation, that's what 'tis. Oh, Lordy, the poor cap'n. Oh, 'tis a shame, such a shame," Kirby muttered, and, pulling out a handkerchief, he blew his nose loudly.

"Dante should feel no shame. If only he would let me share this with him, but he won't let me give him comfort," Rhea said. Feeling Francis' arm sliding around her shoulders comfortingly, she glanced up at his face and saw that he was badly shaken. But they could face the tragedy together. She only wished that Dante would let his pride go long enough to accept the others' sympathy.

"Good Lord," was all Francis could find to say.

"The cap'n is a proud man, he is. I had hoped your love would take some of that stiff-necked pride out of him, but he seems to be worse than ever, maybe because he loves ye too much. He always seems to get hurt when he lets his guard down. He's been betrayed so many times, m'lady." Houston Kirby, who probably knew the captain better than anyone else, tried to explain. "He was so proud to be showin' ye Merdraco. He'd waited so long to return to his home and with his self-respect restored to him. And now, to be findin' this, well, he feels degraded, m'lady. Oh, 'tis blasphemy, 'tis. And if 'tis the last thing I do, I'll help the cap'n get his revenge."

Alastair Marlowe was wiping his face as he listened to the little steward's words, and silently he vowed the same. He took a deep breath of the clean air, trying to banish the remembrance of those fulsome odors.

Robin Dominick was standing beside Conny Brady. The boys' faces expressed only too well the revulsion they felt.

"Who would've done such a thing?" Robin Dominick found his voice first, his violet eyes wide with shock.

"Animals," Francis answered as he guided Rhea toward the low stone wall that edged one of the terraced gardens.

"Animals?" Robin demanded, not understanding how they could have chopped up and stacked the furniture, and he could have sworn he saw a half-eaten drumstick sitting on the mantelpiece.

"The two-legged kind," Alastair explained as he walked alongside them, still disbelieving. The sweet fragrance of honeysuckle and roses filled his senses, and he wondered how that horror could be.

"Aye, reckon a couple might even have familiar names," Houston Kirby added as he sat down on the stone wall before his wobbly legs gave out beneath him.

"Ye think it be the smugglers, then, Mr. Marlowe, sir?" Conny Brady demanded incredulously. He himself had been a smuggler, and no smugglers of his acquaintance had ever acted so badly.

"Aye," Houston Kirby said, staring down at his round-toed boots as if seeing them for the first time.

"But why?" Francis demanded. "The smugglers obviously found Merdraco a perfect hiding place because it stood empty for so long. But why destroy the house? I can find no reasoning behind it. And I am curious about something, Mr. Kirby. Was there no groundskeeper or steward left at Merdraco? I would suggest we speak with the authorities. We ought to get the local magistrate to investigate this immediately," Francis said, thinking that would not be difficult. He was surprised to hear Houston Kirby's chuckle.

"I beg your pardon?" Francis Dominick demanded, sounding just like the Duke of Camareigh.

"Ah, Lord Francis, I am sorry, but ye see, 'twould be for naught. For this smuggling gang don't fear no man, authority or not. I been talkin' to Sam and Dora Lascombe, and, although they'd not admit as much, 'twould seem this gang, these Sons of Belial, as they've taken to callin' themselves, pretty much have a free run of the countryside. Everyone is scared to death of them—and if they aren't scared to death, then they end up dead for not havin' been," Houston Kirby informed them. "Dora reckons they killed her brother for wantin' to quit this smugglin' gang and form his own. You do realize that everyone hereabouts is involved in it somehow or other. Although," he added quickly as he saw Francis Dominick's outraged expression, "most be decent, God-fearin' people, and they aren't the ones goin' about terrorizin' the countryside. And, aye, there was a bailiff once, but he was fired, and the man who had been hired to watch Merdraco died a couple of years ago. Even if he were still alive, there wouldn't have been anything he could do against the smugglers. They probably would have driven him off, or killed him."

"Then these smugglers must be stopped!" Francis said.

"A man can't be doin' it alone. 'Twould take most of the decent smugglers turnin' against their leader, and other folk helpin' 'em."

"Well, from what I know of my brother-in-law, I would say the Sons of Belial have made a dreadful mistake in trespassing at Merdraco. They have made an enemy of Dante Leighton, something *I* would not care to do," Francis said wisely. "I should think the Marquis of Jacqobi had enough power and influence to see that justice is done. If I were Dante, I would get that magistrate out here to see the damage and then go after these swine." Dante Leighton was a member of his own family now, and Francis was deeply offended.

"Ah, m'lord," Houston Kirby said with a tired shake of his grizzled head, "I wish it were as simple as that."

Alastair Marlowe rubbed his chin thoughtfully, wishing the old crew of the *Sea Dragon* were sitting there. The captain could count on them to back him up in whatever he did. "Reckon we're sailing into dangerous waters, Kirby," Alastair speculated.

"Aye, Mr. Marlowe, that we are, only ye don't know the worst of it," Houston Kirby said, and sighed. He wasn't going to keep them in the dark. "Maybe ye might want to be headin' back to London before the goin' gets rough. There's a good chance we'll be founderin'," he advised the younger man.

Alastair Marlowe's face turned dark red with anger. "I'll forgive you that, Mr. Kirby, but never again suggest that I would abandon the captain."

"Aye, I'll remember, lad," Houston Kirby said, pleased by the quick denial. He'd always considered Alastair Marlowe a gentleman.

"You had better be telling us the worst," Alastair said quietly.

"Yes, please do, Kirby," Rhea said, startling the men, for they had almost forgotten she was sitting beside them, and neither one wanted her to know how bad things were.

"Well? I shall be here at Merdraco, too, so do you not think I should know exactly what danger Dante is facing?" Rhea demanded. Her reasoning could not be faulted.

"From what I gathered from Dora and Sam Lascombe, the leader of the Sons of Belial is none other than Jack Shelby," Houston Kirby told them. The name meant nothing to Alastair, Conny, or Robin, but Francis and Rhea understood the significance.

"He is the father of Lettie Shelby, whom Dante was supposed to have murdered," Rhea explained.

The whispering that had been going on between Robin and Conny halted abruptly as they stared at Rhea.

"Coooeee!" Conny Brady said, a long, drawn-out whistle coming from between his pursed lips. "Oh, m'lady, ye've got to be wrong. The cap'n would never do such a thing," Conny argued hotly.

"Of course he didn't murder the girl. But her father thought Dante had," Rhea explained, realizing now why Houston Kirby seemed so worried. "That is why the smugglers tried to destroy Merdraco, isn't it, Kirby? Because Jack Shelby is their leader and he hates Dante."

"Aye. It has me worried plenty, m'lady," the little steward said with a sigh. "If he did this to Merdraco while it stood empty, what is he likely to do when he finds out that its master has returned? And if Jack Shelby *is* the leader of this smugglin' gang and the magistrate has not stopped their activities, then I don't think we can look to him for help. The Sons of Belial are a mighty powerful organization. So, once again, the cap'n will find himself standin' alone."

"That is what you were alluding to at Hawke's Bell Inn when you said that some people might not have forgotten the past." Alastair remembered Kirby's warning.

"Aye, and 'twill be worse when Sir Miles discovers that Dante has managed to buy the lands Sir Miles lost for him," Houston Kirby predicted. Privately he thought he would give half of his own fortune to see Sir Miles' face when he discovered that fact. "Sir Miles, who is a powerful man and who could help rid the area of the smugglers, will just sit back and watch. There's nothing he would like to see more than Jack Shelby and Dante Leighton at each other's throats," the little steward added, looking more woeful than ever as he anticipated that reckoning.

"Rhea?" Robin's voice broke into his sister's thoughts. "Conny and I are going to look around the grounds. Is that all right?"

Reluctantly, Rhea looked away from the house and to Robin's small, heart-shaped face watching her so expectantly. "Yes, but don't go far," Rhea told him worriedly, wondering what other unpleasant surprises they would find.

Dante Leighton carefully righted a tumbled-over, defaced table, his hands lingering over its scarred top. He placed it gently against the wall where it had always been, and in his mind's eye he saw his mother's delicate leather gloves resting against its shiny surface. A velvet upholstered chair, its cushions slashed into strips, was toppled beneath a window, but he could see his mother sitting in it, rocking her young son to sleep. The velvet hangings that had once been pulled against the cold darkness of a winter's eve had been torn from their supports. The windowpanes were broken into a thousand pieces of splintered glass and wood, and these had been ground underfoot into the muddied carpet.

Dante Leighton walked from room to room in silence. Each step kindled his wrath until, savagely, he picked up a table and, with a yell that would have frightened the devil out of hell, threw the table through what was left of the window. The sound of the table crashing to the courtyard below seemed to release his demons, and with the inhuman strength of a madman, he went from room to room, wreaking his own destruction. He cleansed Merdraco of its malignancy, overwhelming the desecration with his fury.

His fury spent, Dante returned to the Long Gallery and buried his face in his arms as he leaned against the mantelpiece. As he stood there, catching his breath, he banked the fires of his rage and they began to smolder, to grow white hot with a virulence sparked of dispassionate thought, and he coolly planned his revenge.

The light streaming in through the gallery windows drew Dante's attention to the bare walls, and a slight smile curved his lips. All was not lost, it seemed, and he had Sir Miles Sandbourne to thank for that.

For the paintings of his mother, of the old Marquis, and all of the other family portraits had long since left Merdraco. They were safely stored in London, along with other priceless family heirlooms. They had been sold by Sir Miles long before to pay off his dissolute ward's debts—though Dante suspected that Sir Miles had profited from the proceeds. Through Sir Miles' intervention, the Leighton family heirlooms had been saved from destruction. Through the years, having hired a private agent for the search, Dante had tracked down most of his family's possessions, bought them back, and had them stored.

Dante walked over to one of the broken windows and

breathed the sweet-scented air drifting in. He stared out over the adjacent wing of the house, toward the chapel at the far end, where the old Marquis had been buried and where his mother and father lay. And then his glance fell on the group of people sitting along the stone parapet in the forecourt. Dante's narrowed gaze lingered on the still figure in pale blue, and he vowed on the memory of those buried in the chapel and on the future he and Rhea would create for their descendants that Merdraco would once again know the greatness of its heritage.

> *Yield not thy neck*
> *To fortune's yoke, but let thy dauntless*
> *mind*
> *Still ride in triumph over all mischance.*
> — Shakespeare

Chapter 20

"IT has been so quiet for so long now," Rhea said worriedly. They had all heard the smashing of wood and glass and could only guess what Dante was doing.

But for the past half hour, there had been silence. It had been so silent, in fact, that Houston Kirby had thought about going in search of the captain.

Rhea must have been of a similiar mind, for she abruptly stopped her nervous pacing and stared at the closed door with a determined glint in her violet eyes. "I should be in there, Kirby. I should be at Dante's side. If only he wouldn't close me out. When I married Dante, I pledged to stand by him for better or for worse, and I intend to keep that vow whether

Dante approves or not," Rhea told them, snapping her riding crop against her skirt with the impatience of fear, not of anger.

Francis and Alastair exchanged glances. Francis shrugged. He knew his sister too well not to take her words seriously, for despite her gentle demeanor, she could be a very stubborn young woman.

"Oh, m'lady, I really don't think ye should be goin' back inside. Why, what would Her Grace be thinkin' of me if I was to allow ye to see such filth?" Houston Kirby fretted, but he was also thinking about the Duke of Camareigh and what His Grace's reaction would be.

"If it were my mother standing here instead of me, then she wouldn't be standing here at all. She would be inside with her husband," Rhea stated.

"Lord Francis," Houston Kirby entreated.

"Kirby, I know I should, and I would if I could, but I can't," Francis Dominick said with a grin, confounding the little steward.

Houston Kirby glanced between the brother and sister as if they were involved in a treacherous plot against him. He turned to Alastair Marlowe, who had been known for clearheaded thinking, but that gentleman was wearing a grin from ear to ear. Houston Kirby could see no humor in the awful situation and thought them all crazed. What he didn't understand was that a bit of humor could make things seem a bit less bleak than they were.

Of course, that first little twitch could lead to hysterical laughter, and that was precisely what happened. Rhea started to giggle and then to laugh until tears were streaming down her face. And soon Francis' shoulders were shaking and the sound of Alastair's deep laugh was blending in.

Houston Kirby's frown deepened as he stared at the three in bewilderment. He glanced up at the blue sky searchingly, for surely they were moonstruck. He shook his grizzled head as he stared at the young lady leaning against Lord Francis for support. But her brother wasn't much better off, for he was holding his side, and Houston Kirby thought if he lived to be a hundred he'd still not have seen it all.

It must indeed have seemed a scene out of Bedlam to the man who approached so quietly and stood watching the merry trio, the fourth member of the group looking as if he were gallows-bound.

"Might I inquire what the jest is?" the cold voice cut through the laughter like the cutting edge of a blade.

"Cap'n!" Houston Kirby cried, spinning around to face Dante Leighton, who apparently had left Merdraco through one of the doors in the adjacent wing. "Lord, but ye gave me a fright," the little steward declared, his hand shaking as he held it to his heart.

"Dante!" Rhea cried, her greeting less restrained as she ran to him and threw herself into his arms. "Oh, I have been so worried!" Her eyes searched his face, but those chiseled features seemed to give so little away.

"So I noticed, and I was most concerned lest you do yourselves an injury with such an excess of good spirits," he commented with a quizzical glance.

Alastair Marlowe and Francis Dominick looked sheepish, for their laughter seemed to hang in the air still, and they wondered what the devil they had found so amusing.

"Forgive me, Cap'n," Alastair mumbled, his face turning bright red with his embarrassment. "There was no disrespect meant. Indeed, I am not even certain why we were laughing," he added.

Francis Dominick swallowed and cleared his throat. "Mr. Marlowe is quite right. There was certainly no reason for it," Francis explained a trifle lamely. "I most sincerely apologize. You must think us insensitive louts," Francis said with little hope that the apology would be accepted.

"I am sorry, Dante," Rhea said. "'Twas my fault. I started it, and I truly do not know why. We really are all deeply distressed by what has happened to Merdraco. I cannot offer you any excuse for our odd behavior," Rhea added, mortified.

But Dante was not insulted. He understood the reason for their laughter better than any of them. He had often seen brave men, who had just fought a victorious battle, suddenly begin to laugh uproariously for no reason.

So Dante Leighton surprised them all by smiling, and with that smile of understanding, some of the grimness left his face. Francis and Alastair relaxed, and Houston Kirby let out a sigh.

Rhea could feel the tense muscles in Dante's arms relaxing

and he held her more easily. "The rest of the house?" she asked him softly.

Dante nodded. "Much the same. Although, 'tis strange, but I do not think the smugglers have been using Merdraco very recently. I'm not surprised, for even animals like a clean stable," Dante said bitterly.

"These swine that call themselves the Sons of Belial aren't even fit to wallow in a pigsty," Houston Kirby said, spitting contemptuously onto the ground, then grinding the heel of his boot over the offending spot.

"Their day will come, never fear, Kirby," Dante told the little steward grimly.

"Aye, that's exactly what worries me," Kirby said. He hadn't missed the moment when the captain's hand moved toward his sword hilt, as if he were already savoring driving its point through Jack Shelby's black heart.

"Well, what's to be our course, Cap'n?" Alastair Marlowe asked. His words were an echo of the past, and when his eyes met Dante Leighton's, it was as if they were still aboard the *Sea Dragon*, preparing for another adventure and possible danger.

Dante Leighton seemed startled. Perhaps he had not expected his former supercargo to remain by his side any longer. The man was wealthy, and he need no longer serve anyone. "It could get rough," Dante said.

"So Mr. Kirby was telling me," Alastair said, disdainfully unimpressed by the fact.

"You are certain you want to sign on again?" Dante questioned him further. "Merdraco, as you saw, is not fit to live in. There will be much to do before the house is habitable. And there are those who will wish to see me fail. Perhaps they will even go so far as to plot an end to the Leighton family forever," he warned the younger man. "The odds are not in our favor, for I have few friends who will help us."

"The crew of the *Sea Dragon* faced worse odds," Alastair Marlowe replied evenly. There was much to be said for action, and he was not accustomed to idle worry.

"Then I shall give you fair warning now," Dante advised, his eyes glittering with purpose, "that I intend to destroy this smuggling gang and see that its leader either rots in gaol or hangs from the gibbet."

Francis Dominick was the only one of them who had never before witnessed that side of Dante Leighton. Having seen it, he believed all of Conny Brady's wild tales. And if Dante Leighton, a gentleman born and bred, could sound so bloodthirsty, then what had the *Sea Dragon* crew been like? Francis shook his head in amazement. That his sister had actually sailed with smugglers! Straightening his carefully tied stock, he decided that he was in no great hurry to make the acquaintance of the cutthroats who had wreaked havoc at Merdraco.

"I think I've seen all I need to for now. Shall we return to the inn for luncheon?" the former smuggling captain suggested, apparently having a stronger stomach than the others.

"Kit will most likely be hungry by now," Rhea said, much relieved. She was beginning to feel very strange, as if eyes were watching her from every gaping window, so that if she looked too quickly, she might catch a shadow moving. She shivered. "Since we cannot stay at Merdraco now, where will we live while the house is being restored?" Rhea asked, concerned now with the housing and feeding of her family.

"I've been quite comfortable at the Bishop. 'Twill be a bit cramped with all of us there, but 'tis convenient to Merdraco," Francis suggested helpfully. "I imagine the Lascombes could use the extra money."

"It would be the ideal place," Dante agreed, "but I would prefer not to involve anybody else in my affairs. Once Jack Shelby learns of my presence here, he will threaten anyone who gives me aid. I have enough to concern me without having to worry about the safety of others."

"Is there no place else?" Rhea demanded.

"There's Sevenoaks House, Cap'n. We could go there," Kirby suggested quietly.

But Dante shook his head emphatically. "No, it is too far away from Merdraco, and I would just as soon keep Sir Jacob out of this. He has already done enough to help me. He owes me no more," Dante said with finality. "We will do this on our own. We need no help from anyone."

"Too damned proud, that's all," the little steward muttered under his breath. Turning away, he said, "I'll fetch the horses."

"Who is Sir Jacob?" Rhea asked, glancing curiously between Dante and Kirby, for it seemed that Dante had been irritated by Kirby's suggestion.

Dante shrugged. "Someone I once knew," was the brief response. Then glancing around, he said, "Conny? Robin? Where are they?"

"They went exploring," Alastair remarked while glancing around the empty forecourt. He hadn't realized they had wandered off so far. "The last time I saw them," he continued, "they were heading in that direction. But I don't see where they could have gotten to."

Dante glanced at the long stretch of stone wall Alastair pointed to and it did indeed seem impenetrable, and certainly too high for either lad to climb over. Dante Leighton began to walk in that direction, Rhea's hand firmly locked within his. The others followed, and even Houston Kirby was mystified until they saw the gate. Set discreetly in the wall, it was covered by the same tenacious ivy growing along the entire length of the wall. How the two boys had spied it, Houston Kirby wasn't even going to try and guess.

Surprisingly, the gate gave easily when Dante pushed against it, as if it had been swung to and fro quite often through the years. And then Houston Kirby remembered that the groundskeeper would have made use of it when making his rounds, for the main gates would have been locked.

"Where are we going?" Rhea asked, glancing around curiously as they followed a narrow, winding path through a copse grown thick with oak and fir. And through the jumble of branches to her left, she caught the glitter of the sun on the sea. The gentle cooing of a woodpigeon marked their passing, while a rustling in the tangle of undergrowth caused Rhea to watch her step.

Bright patches of blue sky appeared and disappeared overhead as Dante led the way along the sunlit path. Magpies and jays fussed at one another, fighting over the ripe holly berries dotting the hedgerows and only pausing long enough to scold the trespassers in the wood.

Suddenly a clearing opened up ahead. Across a grassy plateau bright with the pink and mauve and purple of wildflowers, the sea stretched away to the horizon. And nestled against the curving hillside, beneath a canopy of oak and birch, was a quaint, two-storied stone building.

"The old hunting lodge. I had forgotten about it," Dante said as he eyed the building. It looked like a small, medieval manor house. There was even a belvedere tower, with mock turrets and dragonlike gargoyles. Mullioned windows encircled the tower, allowing a limitless view of the sea and the towers of Merdraco in the distance.

"What a quiet place," Rhea was saying when a shrill battle cry sounded, followed by a shower of small pebbles falling from the heavens.

At the sudden cry, Dante pulled Rhea close to his side. Holding up a protective arm, he glanced upward, spying two grinning faces in the top of the lodge tower.

"Who goes there?" a young voice demanded. There was a glint of metal, then a ringing noise as the long blade held with two hands was banged threateningly against a shield, held high by another pair of straining arms.

"May we have permission to proceed?" Francis Dominick called out, wondering where his brother and Conny had found a sword and shield.

"Lord, but that scared a couple of years out of me," Houston Kirby muttered, promising himself to get a tweak or two of young Master Brady's ear for scaring an old man half to death.

"Come inside, Cap'n," Conny called down. "This place isn't near so bad as Merdraco," he advised them with a youthful lack of tact.

"Aye, mates, come aboard," Robin Dominick agreed.

They entered the hunting lodge through an arched porch where, once again, the Leighton family motto had been carved into the stone above. It was hidden almost entirely beneath a thick ivy vine. There was a short, covered corridor, and then a door opened directly into a large hall with a hammerbeam roof. The timbers were ornately carved and curved, giving stout support to the arched roof.

Even though the parquet flooring was hidden beneath a layer of dirt and cobwebs dangled from the beamed ceiling, the lodge exuded a feeling of warmth. And Rhea suddenly envisioned a fire glowing in the large fireplace with its scrolled plaster overmantel and brass firedogs. The oak long table would be set with china and crystal, which would be reflected in the gilded mirrors adorning the walls. A thick coating of dust covered everything, but with a little oil from sweet marjoram and lavender to polish the floors and tabletops, the hall would soon be fit for a king, Rhea thought.

At the far end of the hall was an oak staircase with an openwork balustrade. Rhea was certain there would be several bedchambers upstairs and perhaps even a small parlor. Yes, she thought, it would do quite nicely. There was quite a bit of housecleaning to do, but at least the smugglers had, for whatever reason, left the lodge undisturbed. It seemed as if the lodge had been lost in peaceful sleep for centuries.

Dante seemed to read her mind. When the others drifted away to explore the hall, he whispered, "This is not quite the home I had intended for us, but 'twill do for now, do you not think so, my sweet?"

"It will be our home, filled with our love, therefore 'tis as grand as anything I could dream of," Rhea replied. She never failed to give replies that warmed his heart.

"My love. My dearest heart. I don't know what I'd do if I ever lost you. This is one of the blackest days in my life, yet I stand here with you in my arms and I cannot feel despair. As long as you are by my side, I know I will always triumph," Dante murmured. Rhea looked up into his face and his lips found hers, and for one enchanted moment everything and everyone were forgotten.

Houston Kirby came bustling into the hall, his voice preceding him. "Cap'n, the rest of the lodge, the kitchen, the servants' rooms, and the bedchambers upstairs are in perfect condition. The smugglers must have forgotten this place was here. We can move in without much trouble. I'll have the footmen over here in no time, and—"

Houston Kirby came to an abrupt halt, coughing in embarrassment when he saw Lady Rhea in the captain's arms. Since they had evidently not heard and were not aware of him, he backed slowly from the room.

There would be time enough later for planning and revenge. For now it was enough that Merdraco's master had, at long last, returned home from the sea.

> *The owl, night's herald.*
> Shakespeare

Chapter 21

"**G**OOD LORD! What the devil's that? Get the poker, Dora! I'll knock it senseless before it can get into the parlor," Sam Lascombe roared, glancing quickly around the kitchen in case there were more creatures lurking in the shadows, for he'd hate to have one catch him by the ankle.

Dora Lascombe placed her hands on her hips and gave her husband a frown. "Sam Lascombe, hush that big mouth of yours," she said. "I don't want ye scarin' our guests." She moved quickly, hiding something by moving in front of it.

"All right, woman, let's see what ye've been up to. Ye've been actin' strange all day long. What have ye got behind your back ye're not wishin' me to see? Can't be as dangerous as I first was thinkin', or ye'd not be standin' there with your back

323

to it. Could nip off your whole rear end, Dora, in one bite," Sam told her with a wide grin.

"Oh, Sam Lascombe, what would the vicar say?" Dora fussed, flushing with embarrassment as she eyed the maid sitting on a stool beside the big fireplace. She was rotating the roast browning on the turnspit. Nodding toward her, Dora said, "Hush, now. Be mindin' your talk."

"Vicar would probably be too drunk to care," Sam commented, sidling behind Dora's back. His mouth dropped open in surprise as he stared down at the reptile in the center of the kitchen table. "Mercy!" he exclaimed, giving it a quick poke on the snout. "Ain't alive, is it? Whatever is it?" he demanded suspiciously, much to the giggling amusement of the young maid.

"Oh, Sam, ye do carry on so," Dora said, but she was, nonetheless, pleased as she stared down proudly at her creation. "'Tis in honor of the Marquis of Jacqobi having returned home to Merdraco," Dora explained. "Reckon someone oughta be welcomin' him, seein' how most other folk won't even be givin' him the time of day. 'Tis such a pity, the sadness he's known. And I'm doin' it for the Marchioness, too. Such a nice young lady she is. Well? What d'ye think, Sam?" she had to ask.

Sam Lascombe stared down hard at the creation occupying the middle of his supper table. "Well, Dora, I can't say I've ever come across one of 'em before," he admitted reluctantly. He was trying to be diplomatic, for Dora was standing very close to her pots and pans and he was wary.

"'Tis a dragon, of course," Dora prompted him.

"Oh, yes. Wouldn't have thought it to be anythin' else," Sam allowed, and, thinking about it, he saw that it truly did resemble that mythical beast.

"Think they'll be likin' it, then?" Dora asked nervously, for it was to be part of Lord Jacqobi's dinner that night.

Sam Lascombe swallowed. "Well, they'll certainly be surprised," he declared, then added generously, "and I can't see how they wouldn't be impressed, Dora. Aye, 'twill certainly be somethin' to be remembered. I won't be forgettin' it soon."

That was an understatement. Dora Lascombe's creation was extraordinary. At first glance it certainly seemed that some reptilian creature had wandered into the kitchen of Bishop's Grave Inn and taken up residence on the large platter in the center of the kitchen table.

The creature had green scales and a pointed snout. His eyes were red and beady-looking, and his tail curled off the plate, while his stubby legs had a hold of the table, and for a moment, Sam was concerned that it might take a swipe at the plate holding the baked mackerel.

Of course, that was nonsense. The scales were made of cucumber, and its eyes were currants. Beneath were several boned chickens tied together and stuffed with sausage meat and mushrooms. Dora carefully arranged sections of lettuce alongside the creature, with sweet red pepper and radishes cut into roses serving as decorations.

"Well, 'tis mighty fine indeed, but why did ye go to so much trouble, Dora?" Sam thought that her usual spring chicken with rice was tasty enough.

"'Twas because of what happened yesterday. I don't like to see such cruelty, Sam. 'Twas Jack Shelby who did that to Merdraco. Tried to destroy it, just like he destroyed my only brother. Reckon I'm just gettin' tired of seein' him goin' around hurtin' people and gettin' away with it. Oh, don't worry, Sam. I'll say nothin' about the man to anyone. I'm not as brave as my Teddie was, God rest his soul."

"Ah, Dora, I know ye be missin' him. 'Twas a real shame," Sam said with a sad shake of his head. He was ashamed that he could not have done anything to protect Dora's brother.

"Ended up stabbed in the back, most likely," Dora said. Wiping her hands on her apron, she continued, "Heard them talkin' about what they found at Merdraco, and because I'm still thinkin' kindly of the Lady Elayne, I got to wonderin' what I could do to welcome her son back to Merdraco. There was no cause for them to be doin' that to his home. No cause for it, Sam, except downright meanness."

"Aye, ye be right, Dora. Although I'm wonderin' if they did it on purpose."

"What d'ye mean, Sam Lascombe?" Dora demanded. "How could such viciousness be done without it bein' on purpose?"

"Them Sons of Belial are used to livin' like dogs. Don't suppose they know better."

"Well, Jack Shelby knows better," Dora said while she quartered a tomato, and Sam couldn't help but wonder if she was thinking of Jack Shelby while she cut and sliced with such precision.

"Well, I'm thankful they still have the huntin' lodge. 'Twill make it easier on us if his lordship and his party aren't stayin' here—not that I would have turned them out," Sam added quickly, "but at least we won't have the Bishop burned down around our heads. 'Tis goin' to be hard enough to explain to Jack Shelby why we let Dante Leighton step through the front door, much less sleep under our roof," Sam worried, thinking of Shelby's black temper.

"Can't say it hasn't helped havin' that extra money comin' in," Dora remarked, thinking of the more than generous amount her ladyship had given her for keeping an eye on Lord Kit. "Was a real pleasure, Sam, bein' able to buy these plump chickens at market and not have to pick through the wilted heads of lettuce. Got it nice and crisp, I did, Sam. And, ye know, I was thinkin' that life hasn't been at all good lately. Livin' like hunted animals, we have, just 'cause we be worryin' about that Jack Shelby, and whether or not he's in a foul mood, or if ye've said somethin' to rile him. Why, yesterday, when I had that sweet Lord Kit on my lap, I felt as if I hadn't a worry in the world. 'Twas like it used to be around here, Sam, when ye didn't have to bite your tongue, or glance over your shoulder," Dora said with a sigh.

"Aye. Wish I could change all that's happened, but—good Lord, I'd forgotten," Sam said suddenly.

"Forgotten what?" Dora demanded, sniffing. "What's that I smell? Imogen, are ye keepin' an eye on them gooseberry tarts? I don't want them brownin' too much, d'ye hear?" Dora warned the girl, who hurried over to the oven and peered inside at the delicately browned tarts.

"D'ye know what night 'tis?" Sam spoke softly.

Dora thought for a moment. "Tuesday night."

Sam snorted rudely. "Think, woman! 'Tis a night of no moon."

Dora's lips compressed into a thin line. "And here we are with the Marquis of Jacqobi sittin' at our table and me fixin' a feast for him and his family. I just hope it ain't goin' to be the last meal he eats," Dora said darkly.

"Aye, there'll be hell to pay if Jack Shelby shows up tonight after runnin' the goods inland," Sam agreed.

"Ye think it likely?"

"Aye, the storm's held them up for over a week now. And this be the first moonless night, Dora. They'll be runnin' the stuff tonight for sure," Sam said, glancing around uneasily as if darkness had already fallen and he could hear the tramping of feet drawing ever closer.

"Ye can't be gettin' word to him not to land the goods in Bishop's Creek?" Dora asked. Shrimps in a spiced wine mixture were coming to a boil over a low fire in one of the fireplaces, and she stirred them slowly.

"Not likely. He's been in France for the past fortnight. He had to find a different source for the goods. The man the Sons had been dealin' with died, or maybe he was cheatin' them and they killed him. Heard they weren't too happy with the Frenchy."

"Well, then, get the word to one of them who'd be down on the beach waitin' for the goods. Tell them it won't be safe to land 'em here," Dora said worriedly, moving to check the crab pie baking in the oven.

Sam Lascombe rubbed the back of his neck. "Don't know if I remember the code anymore. Never had a need to use it, what with the dragoons always bein' down the coast when we're landin' the goods up the coast. Or, seems they're up the coast when we're—"

"Jack Shelby's goin' to learn that his lordship's returned to Merdraco one of these days, Sam Lascombe," Dora interrupted him. "Ye just don't want to be the one to tell him, eh?"

"Would ye?"

"No, can't say I would," Dora agreed, her hand shaking as she stirred the shrimps and wine into a heated egg and butter sauce. "Ye don't have to be givin' particulars, Sam. Just get the word out that 'tisn't safe. We've got guests stayin' here, and 'twould be better if they didn't run the goods through here. 'Tis all they need to know," Dora suggested with a pleading look at her husband.

"Aye, reckon that's the best I can be doin'. Wouldn't want

his lordship stumblin' across the Sons, especially if Shelby is with them," Sam Lascombe muttered, suddenly feeling as if the Bishop had been built on top of a gunpowder keg.

A log burning in the hearth fell in a shower of sparks, drawing an uneasy glance from Sam Lascombe as he watched the flames licking voraciously at the wood. Soon he'd have to add more fuel to the fire. He heard the chiming of the tall case clock on the stair landing, and he glanced toward the darkened windows nervously, for although he'd gotten word to the smugglers not to use Bishop's Creek, he usually expected the worst to happen.

This situation had the makings of an explosion, Sam speculated glumly as he eyed the laughing people sitting around one of his oak tables. They were enjoying their dinner before the warming glow of the fire, and acting as if they hadn't a worry in the world.

Aye, 'twas all a pity, he thought, for they were real fine folk. They were highborn and needn't say a kind word to anybody, but they weren't that way at all, and the Marchioness was a real lady. She always showed gratitude for Dora's efforts, and never once had he heard her raise her voice to her own maids. She had reminded him on more than one occasion of the late Marchioness, for Lady Elayne had been a real fine, gentle lady also. Sam glanced at Rhea and couldn't help but admire her beauty. Dressed in a pale yellow gown embroidered with flowers, her golden hair waved back in soft curls and secured with colorful ribbons, she seemed heaven-born. And when her dimpled smile turned into a low laugh, he found himself envying the clear conscience that allowed her to look so pure. He hoped she would always be able to look at the world so innocently and that her life would never know the deception his had.

Sam Lascombe's gaze rested on the Marquis of Jacqobi. He was amazed that a man could change so drastically. Oh, he was still a handsome devil with those pale gray eyes and classical features, but his gaze was narrowed and hard, as if he were continually searching for an enemy on the horizon, and his face was bronzed from years spent raising it to the sun while he watched the sails of his ship billowing with a fresh-

ening breeze. Dante Leighton had become a man with a sense
of responsibility, a determined man.

Aye, real fine folk they were, Sam Lascombe thought as
he listened to their laughter. He watched the two young boys
sneaking food from each other's plates when each thought the
other wasn't looking. And the Marchioness' brother, Lord
Chardinall, was a handsome lad. What a privilege for the
Bishop to have the heir to a dukedom eating and sleeping under
its roof. Mr. Marlowe was a fine gentleman, quiet, but sharp,
always keeping a wary eye.

"Oh, Mrs. Lascombe, you really shouldn't have," Rhea was
saying as she stared down in amazement at the cucumber dragon
sitting so proudly on that large platter that Sam Lascombe had
to carry in, so heavy it was. The reaction to it had been amazement. Everyone was impressed, though perhaps a little bemused as well.

"This is quite stunning," Rhea said, for it truly was an
amazing feat of culinary expertise.

Dora Lascombe smiled widely. "I'm glad ye like it,
m'lady," Dora beamed, and sending Dante Leighton a sidelong
glance, she straightened her best mobcap. "'Tis in honor of
Lord Jacqobi returning to Merdraco, and in honor of his
family," she said, and there was an almost defiant note in her
voice. She exchanged nervous glances with Sam, something
both Alastair Marlowe and Francis Dominick noticed and wondered about.

The former captain of the *Sea Dragon* shook his head in
disbelief, surprised by the generosity and kindness. Getting to
his feet, the others quickly following, he lifted his goblet and,
catching Dora Lascombe's eye, said, "To Dora Lascombe, a
very special lady. Thank you," Dante toasted the woman. When
she met those pale gray eyes that said so much to a woman,
her cheeks turned as rosy as the radishes garnishing the platter.
And she a grandmother, too!

"Coooeee!" Conny Brady whispered in awe as he stared at
the dragon, itching to touch it. "How'd ye do it, Mrs. Lascombe? Is there a real lizard beneath?"

"I bet Mrs. Peacham couldn't do this," Robin commented,
impressed. "She does make the best cherry tarts, though,"
Robin amended, his loyalty to the Camareigh cook forcing him

to say so, even if it meant Mrs. Lascombe might not give him quite as large a slice of blackberry roll the next time.

Houston Kirby sniffed. "Aye, 'tis a fine job ye've done, Dora Lascombe," the little steward said gruffly, shuffling awkwardly.

Those rather begrudging words of praise seemed to mean more to Dora Lascombe than all the others. "Well, thank ye kindly, Houston," she said, the expression in her eyes warming considerably. Catching her husband's eye, her smile warmed even more, for she had the admiration of the beau from her youth, who had first stirred her passion, and from the man she had wed and come to love.

For a few more minutes, the small group stood around the table admiring their dinner. It was that stillness and the tantalizing odors coming from the tabletop that drew the attention of a green-eyed feline. With purposeful stealth, Jamaica slowly approached the table, sinuously winding his way through the forest of legs blocking his path. He leaped to the table, his quarry one of those buttered shrimps that had been tempting him for the past half hour. What met his startled eyes, however, was hardly the succulent, bite-sized morsel he had been anticipating. Instead, a vicious-looking beast crouched, guarding the table, its beady eyes glowing red.

Jamaica arched his back, his fur standing on end as he faced the miserable-looking creature with the slimy green scales.

"Good Lord, what was that?" Alastair Marlowe demanded as he heard a strange hissing at his elbow, and although he was crazed to even think such a thing, he nonetheless risked a quick glance at the green dragon that was supposed to be his dinner, expecting to see it slithering off the table, its tail swishing angrily.

"Jamaica!" Conny squealed as the tabby took a swing at the dragon's pointed snout.

Dora Lascombe watched in horror as the cat hooked a slice of cucumber to his curved claw, his expression of surprise surpassing Dora's as he stared down at the limp thing clinging to his paw.

Sam Lascombe's rumbling laugh filled the room. Dora looked as if she had sat on a mouse, she was that startled. But she was no more startled than the cat. His tail was puffed up and rigid, spitting a final, insulting hiss at his cowed adversary, Jamaica leaped off the table across Houston Kirby's small shoulders, which seemed to cause Sam Lascombe no end of amusement.

Bishop's Grave Inn was silent and dark when Dante Leighton let himself out the door some five hours later. He had left Rhea sleeping soundly, her face partly hidden by the wild disorder of her hair. Their son slept peacefully in his cradle beside the bed. The fire in the hearth had burned down to glowing coals but still gave off comforting warmth.

Dante Leighton made his way stealthily to the stables, the silvered light shining down from the myriad stars guiding his step across the darkened yard. In the twinkling of an eye, he opened the stable door and disappeared inside. Speaking in low, gentle tones, he made his way to his horse, slipped the bridle over the chestnut's neck, and saddled him.

Leading him by the reins, Dante left the stables, where only the curious neighing of one of the horses indicated a disturbance. Dante glanced back at the dark inn. No light shone in any window. Mounting quietly, he walked the chestnut along the narrow, rutted track winding toward Merdraco.

The only sound was that of the restless sea.

The dark towers rose up before Dante as he sent his horse up the path to the top of the cliff. An owl hooted, followed by the eerie sound of flapping wings. Then all was silent again. Dante dismounted, the leather of his stirrups creaking softly. He looped the reins over the jagged edge of one of the large stones scattered across the courtyard of the castle, then unhooked from his saddle a lantern he had borrowed from the stables. His step light against the paving stones, he walked to the gaping entrance of one of the towers. He paused for a moment, staring up into the surrounding darkness, then entered.

Enshrouded in darkness, Dante stood where he was, listening. Then there was a striking sound, followed by a spark, then a pale, flickering light filled the small area, lighting Dante's way to the first, narrow step of the stairs that spiraled into the tower above.

Slowly, the lantern's yellowish light casting strange shadows that grew and shrank along the walls, Dante climbed upward, his every step placed carefully, for the stones were slippery with dampness and mold. Two of the three floors inside the tower had long before rotted out, so he didn't even pause before the openings leading to those levels. He crept ever higher until reaching the third floor of the tower. He hoped it was intact. For one thing, the old Marquis had insisted on keeping it repaired. But it wasn't that alone which made Dante guess that the floor still could bear the weight of a man; it was the suspicion that the smuggling gang had been using the tower to signal their ships lying offshore.

There was no ghost haunting Merdraco.

Dante Leighton glanced around the third-floor room. A grim smile curved his lips as he stared at the discarded rum bottles thrown across the floor and the rumpled pile of blankets spread across one of the stone seats flanking the deep window embrasure. The nights could be cold when a man was standing watch.

After glancing around again, Dante left the room and walked past the opening to the wall walk, the only remaining section of fortified wall which connected the two towers. He climbed higher until he reached the top of the turret. From there he had an unobstructed view of the whole length of coastline.

Should anyone be signaling to a ship out at sea, he had a very good chance of spotting it, Dante thought as he leaned against one of the low embrasures and stared out into that mysterious blackness. Far below him, the tide crashed against the rocky shore, sending spindrift floating into the cool night air. Dante breathed deeply of the sea he had come to love and once again he could hear the loud flapping of the *Sea Dragon*'s square sails. He longed to feel the salt spray against his face while the deck slanted beneath his feet and the little brig's bowsprit swung toward a new course.

Dante shook his head. That belonged to his past. Now he must channel all his energies into building Merdraco again. Dante glanced away from the sea, staring instead at the dark shadows that were Merdraco. Soon, he promised, the house would light the black skies with a thousand candles, and the sound of voices would drift with the winds.

As Dante Leighton, master of that abandoned house, and of a castle in ruins, stood silhouetted against the night skies, his gaze traveled along the coastline to where a stone house sat silent in the pervading darkness. Seawyck Manor was the home of Lady Bess Seacombe. Despite himself, he couldn't help but wonder how the years had treated his lover. Had they been kind? Or had time ravaged the beauty that once held him spellbound?

It was while Dante stared in that direction that a flash of light caught his eye. Then there was another flash, and that was followed by three more flashes. Dante smiled. He had been expecting as much. He continued to watch, but this time looking out to sea, and he caught the flashing of yet another lantern's light. That signal was a reverse of the other, with three flashes followed by two.

He had seen Sam Lascombe's nervousness as Sam listened with increasing anxiety to the chiming of the clock. And because it was the first moonless night following a storm, Dante had figured on that night being the one when the Sons of Belial would land a cargo of contraband. He suspected that Bishop's Creek, a safe deep-water cove with no hidden shoals or reefs, often saw contraband beached on its shore. But Dante had further figured that Sam Lascombe would somehow manage to get a message to the smugglers not to land their contraband in Bishop's Creek. Sam Lascombe was no fool, and knowing that he had a former smuggler sleeping under his roof, and, that that man hated Jack Shelby, he wouldn't risk a chance encounter between the two men.

The lantern held in front of him, Dante quickly descended the spiraling steps, halting at the bottom to douse the light before he stepped out into the night.

Rhea sighed sleepily and, rolling over, reached out for Dante, but there was only a cold emptiness where his warmth should have been. She sat up and stared into the dark room.

"Dante?" she called out softly, wondering what had awakened her. Fumbling, she managed to light a candle. Glancing down at the cradle beside the bed, she saw that her son was curled up, fast asleep. "Having the sweetest of dreams," Rhea murmured as she reached out and tucked the soft, downy blanket closer about his tiny shoulders.

Throwing back the quilted coverlet, Rhea swung her legs

from the cocoon of warmth beneath the blankets, making a face when her bare feet came in contact with the cold floor. She shivered, trying to remember where she had left her wrapper. As she caught sight of it, she noticed something else.

Dante's dressing gown was still beside hers. Quickly she looked for his boots, for he had left them standing at the foot of the bed. They were gone. Standing on one foot, she rubbed her other one against the back of her calf, trying to warm it while she wondered where he was. He had gotten dressed, but why?

Where could he be? She slipped into her wrapper and absent-mindedly tied the sash around her waist. Reaching behind her neck, she pulled the thick waves of hair free of her collar, allowing the long, golden length to fall over one shoulder, where the ends curled down to her hip.

Taking the candlestick with her, Rhea made her way from the bedchamber. She paused before the door where Conny and Robin were sharing a room, and she carefully opened the door. Holding the candlestick before her, she peered into the room. Both Conny and Robin were asleep.

She walked to the head of the staircase, nearly dropping the brass candlestick when the clock chimed. It was close to dawn. She was debating whether to continue downstairs or return to her room, when she heard muffled voices coming from behind the closed doors of the taproom below.

With a sigh of relief, Rhea walked more quickly down the stairs, her step certain as she followed the sound of voices. She thought she might even get herself a cup of tea, now that she was up. Apparently she wasn't the only one who couldn't sleep, she was thinking as she opened the taproom door.

Hell's broken loose.
Robert Greene

Chapter 22

WIPING the back of his hand across his lips, Jack Shelby lowered the tankard of ale, his eyes widening in wonder at the vision standing in the doorway. Clad in a rose silk dressing gown, her hair cascading over her shoulder like molten gold, she was the most exquisitely beautiful woman he had ever gazed upon.

Rhea stood absolutely still, her eyes mesmerized by the group of rough-looking men gathered close to the warmth of the fire in the hearth, their hands cupped around tall tankards. The flames seemed to be reflected a thousandfold in the gleaming of pewter and brass filling the shelves behind the bar. Several large oaken casks had already been tapped, their contents filling those tankards.

The scene was not at all what she had been expecting. She

335

was further surprised not to see Sam Lascombe serving the group that had obviously just reached the inn. Many were still bundled up in coats, their boots coated in mud. Indeed, they had tracked up Mrs. Lascombe's spotless floor.

"Well, by all that's holy, what have we here?" Jack Shelby demanded as he walked toward the slight figure wrapped in rose silk and standing so still in the opened doorway. "Did ol' Sam get rid of that sour-faced wife? Are ye keepin' him company now, lass? Sam mustn't be the fool I've been thinkin' him. Of course, he's more fool than I thought if he let ye get out of his bed on a cold morn like this," the leader of the Sons of Belial commented, to the appreciation of his men. "Maybe he sent ye down here as a peace offerin' for sendin' me that harebrained message? Hasn't he learned yet that no one in this land can raise a hand against me?" Jack Shelby's hard eyes rested on the slim, ivory throat of Rhea Claire Leighton, Marchioness of Jacqobi and wife of the man he had sworn to kill.

"Come on, lass. Come to Jack. What's ye name, then? Somethin' sweet and pretty, I reckon, eh?" he said with a leering grin. His yellow eyes roved over her with insulting appraisal.

Rhea eyed the big-shouldered man with rapidly increasing distaste. She did not bother to hide her abhorrence, much to Jack Shelby's amusement. He liked a woman with some fight in her, and this little golden-haired lass seemed spirited.

That this man was Jack Shelby, the leader of the Sons of Belial, or that these men were the smugglers who had destroyed Merdraco never occurred to Rhea. Thinking herself safe in Bishop's Grave Inn, her family around her, it never entered her mind that she was in any danger. So, with a complete lack of concern, she spun on her heel and turned to leave the room.

Her second mistake was turning her back on Jack Shelby. Her first mistake had been entering the taproom.

A large hand clamped her shoulder and spun her back around, and she found herself staring up into the coarse-featured, laughing face of a man who knew no kindness. "Uppity, aren't ye?"

"Let go my shoulder," Rhea spoke in a soft yet commanding voice, and her carefully enunciated words told Jack Shelby that she was a lady.

"My *pardon*, m'lady," he said sarcastically. "Ye be a guest here, then? Should've known Sam Lascombe couldn't get somethin' as sweet as ye in his bed," Jack Shelby said with a laugh. But his eyes said that Jack Shelby could.

"Think ye'd have more luck, Jack?" a thin-faced man goaded, his eyes darting between the two people in anticipation.

"Luck?" Jack Shelby roared, his gaze searching out the man who had asked the question. "Jack Shelby takes what he wants. There's no luck to it," he said, his grin widening as he saw the startled look of fear in Rhea's eyes. "Heard of me, have ye?"

Rhea swallowed hard. Even shivering with cold and fear in the hold of the *London Lady*, she had not known such terror as this.

"I think she likes ye, Jack," someone called. "She's not strugglin'."

"Speechless with awe in your presence, Jack."

"More like she's too scared to move," someone else suggested.

"Aye, but she's a beauty. Such bonny eyes," Jack Shelby murmured. "I'll be damned if they ain't as purple as violets. To be sure, I've never seen such a color," he breathed. "Betcha all the lads wanted a tumble with ye, m'lady?" he asked, his fingers tightening painfully on Rhea's shoulder.

"Release me this instant," Rhea said, her voice quivering with anger and humiliation.

"Ah, m'lady. No kind words for Jack Shelby?" he demanded, then before Rhea could stop him, he grabbed her hand and was staring down at her wedding ring. "A married woman. Didn't think ye'd be stayin' a maiden for long, not with that golden hair and soft white skin. Ye smell real sweet, too," he said softly, for her fragrance had intensified with her fear.

"Your husband upstairs? No doubt fast asleep dreamin' about ye, but ye don't think he would be missin' ye, d'ye, if ye stayed down here for an hour or two with Jack Shelby? Reckon I could be teachin' a lady like yourself what 'tis like to be with a real man, a man who knows how to sweat—not a sweet-scented fop who needs help to get out of his breeches. Ye'd not be disappointed, m'lady," he said, his eyes lingering on her delicate-shaped lips. He knew a sudden longing to feel their softness beneath his.

"You will be grievously mistaken should you think my husband a lily-livered milksop. And, if I were you," Rhea spoke bravely, "I would not give him another reason to send you into hell, where you should be suffering eternal damnation right now."

Jack Shelby looked as if he'd been poleaxed. Rhea, herself, was just as surprised by the audacity of her reply. As if she were standing outside herself, she had suddenly heard herself speaking bravely.

Suddenly Jack Shelby's deep laugh filled the room. It helped to relieve some of the tension. His men had been sitting in awed silence, for none of them would have had the nerve to say such a thing to Jack Shelby, though many would have given their right arms to do so.

His head thrown back with laughter, the broad, muscular column of his throat looked like a tree trunk, while his big chest barreled out from his narrow waist and hips. Rhea was suddenly aware of the rampant maleness of him. He was like some rutting stag, and Rhea felt an instinctual awareness of danger that was as old as mankind itself.

She began to struggle, fighting desperately to free herself. Her violet eyes betrayed her as she stared up into that hard face, for Jack Shelby became aware of her fear of his masculinity. It heightened his desire.

"By God, but ye'll be mine before this night is ended, m'lady," he swore, his arms sliding around Rhea's slender waist. With no effort at all, he lifted her clear of the floor and held her high above his head.

Jack Shelby's triumphant laughter filled the room, drowning out Rhea's cry. He was master here. What he wanted, he took. Used to having absolute power over cowed villagers and frightened farmers, he had forgotten that there might be others of power and position of their own, others who would not be cowed.

And so the all-powerful Jack Shelby was indeed surprised to hear a voice ordering him to release the woman, or die.

Rhea knew that voice only too well, and she became even more fearful.

Jack Shelby lowered Rhea to the floor but kept an imprisoning hand clasped to her shoulder. His eyes grew wide with wonder as he stared at the man standing in the doorway. The man was holding a pistol centered on Jack Shelby's big barrel chest.

The smuggler nearly choked. "Good Lord! Is *this* your husband?" he demanded incredulously.

"I shall not tell you again to release her," Francis Dominick spoke softly, his blue-gray eyes narrowed with deadly intent.

"He's but a babe. Ye don't mean to tell me that ye be wed to this bratling? No wonder ye still have such an innocent look about ye," Jack Shelby laughed, and his men joined in, looking forward to a good fight.

"Francis, please, you don't know what you are doing. Go and get Dan—" Rhea began, then stopped, afraid to reveal Dante's presence at the inn.

"*Francis,* is it, now?" Jack Shelby mimicked. "Why, what a sweet name, and for such a sweet nestling. Be a good lad, now, and go back to bed, or ol' Jack will have to put ye there himself," he baited the younger man. "But if ye don't mind, I'll be keepin' the lady with me for a while longer. And I promise ye, lad, she'll be far more woman than she is now when she returns to ye. Ye really should be thankin' me, lad."

Jack Shelby could not be blamed for underestimating the young gentleman standing there facing him. Dressed in a nightshirt hastily stuffed into his breeches, bare feet and legs showing beneath, his golden hair ruffled from sleep, he didn't look at all formidable. But Jack Shelby also didn't know that this was Lucien Dominick's son and that he was accosting the young man's sister.

Francis cocked the pistol, its distinctive sound banishing laughter from the room. "Come here, Rhea."

Rhea tried to draw away from the big hand holding her close against Jack Shelby's chest, but she couldn't move.

"I am Francis Dominick, Marquis of Chardinall," Francis spoke proudly. "I thought to introduce myself to you only because I would not like to send a man to his grave without a proper introduction," Francis stated with a cold detachment that would have made the Duke of Camareigh proud. It certainly made Rhea see her brother in a different light.

Francis Dominick's words had at least the effect of sobering the Sons of Belial. A titled gentleman was not the same as a frightened farmer. And these blue bloods could draw the notice of the authorities, something they would prefer not to have happen.

Jack Shelby, however, continued to eye the young gentleman with insulting disdain. His big hands slid down to Rhea's waist and he pulled her directly in front of him, using her slender body as a shield. "Ye think your aim is good enough not to hit the lady? And even if ye get lucky and shoot me, laddie, there be close to twenty men behind me. They won't take kindly to seein' Jack Shelby shot down in cold blood," he challenged.

Francis' eyes widened slightly as he realized who the brute was. He knew a moment's confusion, for the man had suddenly become more than just a lout accosting his sister.

Jack Shelby, who had lived by instinct all his life, sensed the momentary hesitation, and with a deceptively casual movement, slid his fingers inside the loose sleeve of his frock coat and grabbed the cold hilt of his knife.

Rhea felt the movement and glanced down just in time to see the flash of metal in his hand, and she screamed.

Francis Dominick's index finger jerked on the trigger. The roar of the pistol was deafening as the powder exploded in a bright flash. The air was heavy with the odor of sulfur, and for a moment there was utter silence.

Rhea's scream shattered that when she saw Francis' figure crumpled next to the door, the hilt of the knife protruding from his shoulder. Jack Shelby smothered her cry with his hand as he stared at the young gentleman who had threatened him, a grin of satisfaction spreading across his face as he saw the blood staining the lad's shirtfront.

"Ye all saw it. The lad tried to kill me," Jack Shelby said conversationally. "Pity if he doesn't survive the wound. Might even become delirious and wander off in the darkness. Might even fall to his death from the cliff. His young wife here might run after him and he might drag her with him over the cliff," Jack Shelby speculated sadly.

Jack Shelby glanced back at his men, signaling to them to lend him a hand. But they were staring beyond him to the door. Thinking the wounded whelp was stirring, Jack turned back toward the door, his grin still wide.

He felt a tightening of his muscles, however, as he stared at the shadowy figure in the doorway, for he sensed danger in the stranger standing there so silently.

"If ye're wise, gent, ye'll be on your way. And ye'll be forgettin' what ye've seen in here," Jack advised the cloaked figure.

"And if you are wise, you will release the lady this instant," the cold voice ordered. And just so the gentleman was not underestimated, he cocked his two pistols warningly.

"Either ye be a fool, or ye don't know who ye be talkin' to," Jack Shelby said, still smiling.

"Oh, but I do know exactly who I am talking to, and I would most sincerely advise you to release the lady, for she is *my* wife, and I will not have your filth touching her," the man replied, and taking a step forward, he moved into the light, revealing the features of Dante Leighton, master of Merdraco, for the first time.

To say that Jack Shelby was surprised would be an understatement. The man was stunned speechless. Had he been staring at the devil himself, he could not have been more surprised. And because his mind was reeling under the revelation of the stranger's identity, his grip eased for just a second. It was enough for Rhea to free herself.

So relieved and thankful was she to see Dante's beloved face that Rhea nearly tripped as she rushed to his side, hot tears streaming down her cheeks. Then she slipped behind Dante and dropped to her knees beside her wounded brother.

"You do remember me, do you not?" Dante Leighton asked the silent, grim-visaged Jack Shelby.

Jack Shelby spat on the floor between them, his face suffused with bottled-up rage. "Damn your black soul to hell!"

"You may rest assured that I'll be waiting there for you, Jack Shelby," Dante said softly, his pale gray eyes glowing.

Jack Shelby looked possessed. His eyes were bulging and saliva drooled from his lips as he stared at the man he believed had murdered his daughter and who now stood so arrogantly before him. But even with half his senses, Jack could see that this man was not the dissolute young lord who had turned tail and run.

The man standing before him was a dangerous man. Jack

could see that in the cold deadliness of those pale gray eyes and the way Dante Leighton stood there, waiting, showing no emotion, though he must have felt violent rage. Jack Shelby actually knew a moment's fear, something he had not felt in many years. Suddenly Jack Shelby understood that his adversary wanted him to make a move, wanted to be able to put a hole through his heart. Dante Leighton was hell-bent on revenge, and nothing would satisfy him except the sight of his enemy fallen at his feet.

Jack glanced back at his men, feeling some of his courage returning, for he had nearly an entire army at his back. Dante Leighton was, after all, only one man.

"You will be the first one to die, Jack Shelby," Dante Leighton spoke quietly, reading his thoughts. "And I will die gladly knowing that I have sent you to hell. One of your men will die, too, if he means to kill me. But he will have to wait until the fire cuts through his flesh," Dante added cunningly, knowing just how to plant the seeds of worry in the other men.

Jack heard an uneasy muttering go through his men, and wished he could shoot all those sniveling cowards. "Just in case ye've forgotten, we're all in this together," he shouted. "If I go to the gallows, I'll take the whole lot of ye with me. Don't be forgettin' that ye be the Sons of Belial, and there's many a Redcoat who'd like to make a name for himself by arresting even one of them. And I know your names, ye curs, and where most of ye came from, and what ye was wanted for before ye joined me," he reminded them.

One or two of the group were braver than the others. Or perhaps they had more notorious pasts to protect, for, stepping forward, they gave their support to their leader. After that, the others seemed to think twice about abandoning the man who kept food in their bellies and ale warming their blood, and they began to move forward menacingly.

Rhea, holding the edge of her nightgown pressed firmly against the blood seeping from Francis' shoulder, glanced up nervously at the men steadily approaching. Her heart was pounding as she caught sight of the evil grin widening across Jack Shelby's face. He had won, the grin said.

"Rhea, take Francis and get out," Dante ordered, sure he would not leave that room alive "Get out, Rhea!" he said again. He did not risk a glance at her, but he knew she was still there.

"No," Rhea said weakly. She would not leave him. Francis, although his face was as pale as death, was struggling to his feet. But he was so weak that he could only sink back into her arms.

"Come on, men, we can take him. He's only one. But if ye can do it, take him alive. I'd like to make him suffer for all the lonely years he deprived me of my Lettie," Jack Shelby told his men quietly, allowing them to close the distance at his back.

"You are mistaken," a voice announced from the darkness behind Dante's back, startling the men who, only moments before, had felt so brave.

Out of the shadow of the doorway moved Alastair Marlowe, a pistol in one hand, a sword in the other. Then, slipping in behind him came a short, bandy-legged figure. Houston Kirby was suddenly at his captain's side, two pistols held firmly, while a knife protruded from his waistband.

"Aye, looks like the odds have changed a bit, but then ye never were good at bettin', Jack Shelby," Houston Kirby commented as he eyed the big man with dislike. "And I ain't the gentleman the captain is, so I might not even be waitin' for them pigeonhearted mongrels of yours who ain't fit to dig in a dunghill to turn tail and run before I'm puttin' a hole through your head," the little steward said earnestly.

Jack Shelby returned Houston Kirby's stare with equal hatred. He'd never liked the man. "One of these days I'm goin' to squash ye like a beetle," he spat, his narrowed, yellow eyes glaring at Alastair Marlowe in turn. "Ye be lucky this time, *m'lord*, but next time ye might not have them cullions at your side. Then we'll see how brave a man ye've become," Jack Shelby challenged the man whose pale-eyed stare had never moved from his figure.

"Reckon ye've been back to your home? Heard tell there's been a few changes. Reckon ye was a bit surprised, eh, *m'lord* Jacqobi? Reckon all ye be is the master of some reeky, maggoty jakes. But then, 'tis where the stinkin' likes of ye belongs, *m'lord*," Jack Shelby said, forgetting danger as he baited the man. But his men weren't so blind with rage, and they murmured to him in low voices.

Rhea could sense Dante's rage building, and she knew it wouldn't take much more for him to pull that trigger. "Dante, please," Rhea said. "Francis needs attention. No one can win now," she said, her words the first sane ones spoken.

"Cap'n, Lady Rhea's right," Houston Kirby added. "If ye shoot down that dog, then the others might be on us like a pack of wild hounds. Ye can't be riskin' the lives of Lady Rhea and Lord Francis, and ye know there'll be another time for ye and that bastard to be settlin' your differences," he said.

But it was Sam Lascombe, his big hairy legs sticking out from beneath his nightshirt, who settled the argument—and most diplomatically. He appeared in the doorway with a long-barreled blunderbuss, which he swung around the room with no concern for whom it was aimed at.

"Reckon I'm findin' it difficult to tell friend from foe in this crowd. The Bishop's closed. Ye gents can come back later. Or ye can be meetin' someplace else to continue your argument, but this ain't the time or the place," he suggested, that big-barreled blunderbuss raking the group again, making everyone nervous, for Sam Lascombe still looked half asleep.

"Get Francis," Dante said. Alastair didn't wait for further orders before bending over Rhea's fallen brother. Handing her one of his pistols and tucking the other in his waistband, he slid his arms around Francis and carefully helped him to his feet.

Holding him firmly, Alastair led Francis from the room, Rhea following slowly behind. She kept glancing back to make certain that Dante followed, but she needn't have worried, for Houston Kirby was of the same mind, and he lingered in the doorway until the captain moved backward into the shadows.

Jack Shelby watched that tall figure disappearing, those pale gray eyes never once leaving his face. The message was only too clear: Without question they would meet again, and only one of them would walk away the next time.

We have scotch'd the snake, not kill'd it.
Shakespeare

Chapter 23

FRANCIS DOMINICK made a grimace as the bandage was tightened around his arm. "Ouch, any tighter, Kirby, and my arm will drop off," he said, trying to get a better glance at the little steward's handiwork. As he caught sight of the blood seeping through the white strip of bandage, he swallowed, glad he was sitting down. The sight of one's own blood made him only too aware of mortality, Francis thought, sitting there on the edge of his bed.

"Now, now, Lord Francis, 'tis just a flesh wound and shouldn't be causin' ye any trouble at all. Reckon ye be mighty lucky Jack Shelby's aim isn't as good as it used to be, otherwise we'd be makin' plans to bury ye," Houston Kirby told the young gentleman with such a total lack of concern that Francis actually felt the ache in his arm lessening, which was exactly what the cagey little steward had intended. That, and to set her ladyship's mind at ease, for Lady Rhea was as nervous as a mother hen. She was standing just behind his shoulder, watching with what he thought was an overly critical eye. It only reminded Kirby that his patient was, after all, the Duke of Camareigh's son and heir.

"So that was Jack Shelby?" Francis said with an incredulous look at the people standing around. "If I'd known that when I'd entered, I would have shot him before I'd taken the time to introduce myself. Lord, he's even worse than I thought he'd be," Francis exclaimed. "He meant to kill me, didn't he? Even though he knew I must have friends who would avenge my death? Didn't he even care that those friends might have been nearby?" Francis demanded. How could Jack Shelby have such a total lack of fear? the young man wondered.

"He's crackbrained," Houston Kirby muttered, and he slit the bandage with the knife that had been resting in his waistband only moments before. As he tied the two ends of the bandage together, he wished he were tightening a noose around Shelby's scoundrel's neck.

"No, he isn't crackbrained, Kirby. He believes in his own power," Dante disagreed, his booted feet stretched out before him as he sat in a chair watching, "and that has made him arrogant, perhaps even careless. At least we shall hope it has."

Rhea, satisfied that Kirby knew what he was doing and that her brother wasn't in any immediate danger, left her watch at Kirby's shoulder and walked around the bed to Dante.

"Where were you?" she asked quietly. "I awoke to find you had left, and I was worried. Where did you go?" she questioned him anxiously, for she had not missed the thick coating of mud on the soles of his boots, or the green stains on the side of his breeches. The stains reminded her of that velvety coating of mold covering the stones of Merdraco. "I was frightened, Dante."

Dante quickly got to his feet. Taking her in his arms, he felt her slim body shaking. "Forgive me, but I did not wish to disturb you. I had to go to Merdraco. I had to find out if the smugglers really had been using one of the towers to signal from. I hoped to catch one of them in the act," he admitted, knowing what her reaction would be.

"Oh, Dante, you might have been killed! Why didn't you wait and ask the authorities for help?" she asked, for she still placed her faith in the law. "Or, at least, take Alastair with you?" Rhea said, turning an accusing eye on that young gentleman, who managed to look guilty even though he'd had nothing to do with the captain's stealthy errand, having been fast asleep at the time, a circumstance which still irked him. But as the lady implied, he should have been at his captain's side. "And why tonight?"

"My dearest, have you forgotten that I am a former smuggler? I know how a smuggler plans. This was the first night he could move the contraband. So . . ." he said with a shrug.

"So you decided to face the smugglers by yourself? How could you do such a thing?" Rhea demanded angrily. Why, she might have been sleeping peacefully in her bed while he died.

"Never have I been so surprised or so frightened as I was when I found you with Jack Shelby, the man I'd been out searching for," Dante said, his eyes kindling again with wrath as he remembered coming into the inn, but quietly so as not to awaken anyone, only to hear the roar of a pistol shot, then the sound of a woman's scream. Having rushed to the open taproom doorway, he had halted, his pistol ready, thinking he'd fallen into hell itself, for a sulfuric cloud was hanging over the room and a figure lay crumpled against the floor, blood seeping from a wound. In the hazy light, the dark shapes had seemed figments of his imagination, but the woman straining to release herself from the imprisonment of a man's embrace certainly had not. It was Rhea. Her unbound hair had seemed alive as she'd struggled against the force holding her, the long, curling length of gold undulating with her every thrashing movement.

Dante finally dragged his mind away from the memory, shuddering, as Francis demanded, "Were they using the tower?" Now that he knew he wasn't at death's door, he was burning to know what Dante had found out.

"Yes. I climbed to the top of the tower without having to sweep aside one single cobweb. And on the top floor, I discovered several blankets and empty bottles where the lookout must have spent many an uncomfortable night waiting for that signal from the sea," Dante explained.

"A pity one of them wasn't up there when you arrived," Francis commented, suddenly feeling quite bloodthirsty and hot for revenge.

Rhea sent her brother a hard glance.

"I had hoped so, too," Dante admitted. Then frowning thoughtfully, he added, "But I do not believe there was any chance of that. I got the strange impression that the tower has not been used in a while."

Houston Kirby, who was a man of no nonsense, glanced curiously at the captain while placing several blood-soaked cloths into a bowl of water.

But Alastair Marlowe had a bit more imagination. "Why would they use it, only to stop? You felt it was not being used as a watchtower any longer?"

"It does seem strange, but I couldn't help feeling that way. I've no logical explanation," Dante murmured.

"You sound like Aunt Mary. If she were here, Rhea, we could get her to tell us where the smugglers were meeting and even where they were landing contraband," Francis said warmly, ignoring the disbelieving shake of Houston Kirby's grizzled head.

"Reckon we got enough wild stories of ghosts and Wild Huntsmen to last a lifetime, Lord Francis, without ye addin' more by usin' the Lady Mary's good name," Kirby told him severely, for he had the utmost respect for the kindhearted Lady Mary.

"Maybe one of them standing guard had a bad dream and awoke screaming about seeing ghosts. Most likely they have frightened themselves with their own ghost stories," Alastair said, preferring that explanation of the tower's abandonment to the only other explanation.

The sound of feet shuffling beyond the closed door, followed by a sharp, imperative knock, found Alastair standing against the wall on one side of the door, his hand resting on his sword as Dante pulled Rhea behind his back, his hand moving to the pistol lying on the chest at the foot of the bed.

"Enter," Dante called. Although he had watched the Sons of Belial leaving the Bishop as dawn was breaking, he wouldn't have put it past Jack Shelby to sneak back.

But it was Sam who entered the room, a group of tall

tankards and a china teapot on the tray he was balancing on one large hand. "Dora thought ye might be in need of somethin' bracin'," Sam explained as he set the tray down on the chest by the bed. "She thought her ladyship might like a spot of tea, seein' there's a chill in the air," he added, looking around for Lady Rhea. "I'm sorry, I thought for sure her ladyship was in here."

"Thank you," Rhea said, stepping out from behind Dante's broad back. "I could use something to warm me. I'm still shaking." But she smiled, which relieved Sam Lascombe's mind, for he felt partly responsible for the dangers the lady had seen. After all, it had happened under his roof. He thanked his lucky stars that he had gotten down to the taproom in time to halt further bloodletting. That the Duke of Camareigh's son had come to harm at the Bishop would give Sam Lascombe nightmares for months to come.

"I wish I had some of Mrs. Taylor's Special Treat," Rhea said with a wry smile at Francis, who grimaced.

Sam Lascombe stared blankly at her for a moment, then allowed himself a grin. "Reckon Dora was thinkin' somethin' the same, m'lady, for she added a goodly portion of somethin' special to your cup. 'Tis her Uncle Alf's secret brew. He was always a strange one. Bit of a wanderer, he was, but finally settled down, he did, somewhere around Buckfastleigh, in the South. Don't know what he's up to nowadays, most likely no good, which wouldn't be no surprise considerin' Alf's mother. They say she was part Gypsy," Sam Lascombe explained as he noticed the curious looks, then he shook his head as if including all his wife's relatives in his disapproval.

Silence descended, and Sam Lascombe continued to stand there, looking around him, his eyes never quite meeting anyone's. "I—I don't quite know what to be sayin' to ye, m'lord. I wouldn't have any harm befallin' Lady Rhea for anythin' in the world, and I'm grievously upset by what happened to Lord Francis. I—I hope ye're believin' me?" he asked worriedly, his big hands twisting and untwisting as he faced that pale-eyed stare.

"You warned them off, didn't you, Sam?" Dante stunned the innkeeper by asking. "I am familiar with the ways of smugglers. Surely you have heard about my former exploits from

Master Brady?" he questioned the red-faced Sam Lascombe. To be suspected of smuggling was one thing, but to be admitting to it was something altogether different.

"Well, reckon we get all sorts in here, bein' the only inn between Merleigh and Westlea Abbot," was all Sam Lascombe was willing to admit. "I know, of course, of the bad blood between ye and Jack Shelby, and if I could be keepin' that kind of vermin out of the Bishop, I would, but . . ." Sam Lascombe's voice trailed off uncomfortably. "Lots of things have changed around here since ye left, m'lord," he said with dark meaning. "A person has to look out for himself, or he's likely to end up in the sea like a bloated haddock."

"You don't need to explain, Sam. We do what we must to survive," Dante told him, receiving a grateful nod from the tired innkeeper. "And you needn't worry any longer about any more incidents here, or that your inn will be burned to the ground, for we shall be taking up residence immediately at the hunting lodge. You have already done enough for us by giving us your hospitality," Dante said sincerely, and even Houston Kirby was impressed by the captain's graciousness.

"Well, it has been a privilege, that it has," Sam Lascombe said just as sincerely, but he couldn't hide the relief in his voice. Now that his lordship and his party were leaving the Bishop, he would be sleeping a bit easier.

Dante Leighton went on, "I do not think you need concern yourself with Jack Shelby. He will be too busy trying to find a way to get his revenge against me to be bothering with you. Besides, the Bishop is too important to the smugglers' operations for them to burn it down," Dante told him. The argument didn't relieve Sam Lascombe's mind very much, however. He couldn't help but be concerned for his lordship's safety.

The danger Dante was courting was uppermost in Rhea's mind as she met Dante's hard gaze. She knew he was still savoring the moment when he had faced Jack Shelby and known he could end the man's life.

The thought was indeed occupying Dante Leighton's mind, for he said softly, more to himself than to anyone else, "And you may expect there to be some changes around here. I am once again the largest landowner hereabouts, and I will not be bullied by this rabble. I promise you now, Sam Lascombe, that

I will see the Sons of Belial in hell before they set foot anywhere near Merdraco again. I pledge that vow."

The stunning revelation had startled the innkeeper. Sir Miles Sandbourne owned most of the land around there, including that which had once belonged to the Leighton family, or so Sam thought. He rubbed his chin thoughtfully, and as realization began to grow, so did dread. It seemed Dante Leighton had yet another enemy, for the changes the Marquis of Jacqobi was promising were certain not to sit well with some. Sam Lascombe would have bet his life on that.

And his own life might well be what Dante Leighton would have to forfeit in order to vanquish his enemy, thought Sam with a pitying look at the lovely Lady Rhea. She was gazing up into her husband's grim face with an expression of undying love, and the innkeeper felt as if he were intruding into an intimate moment between lovers. He wondered what the young lady would do if the winds of fortune turned against the man who had fought so valiantly to return to Merdraco.

Chapter 24

COBWEBS and dust. Dirt and grime. Mildew and dryrot. They were all swept away and the lodge was scrubbed and scoured. Soon the dark corners no longer offered refuge for crawling things. Every small, diamond-shaped pane of the mullioned windows allowed the light of day to shine into the lodge. The soaring ceiling beams were no longer draped in gossamer threads. And the parquetry flooring began to reflect a rich patina from the wax being rubbed into the parched wood.

The great fireplace at the end of the hall had been scraped of layers of soot and laid with fresh kindling and logs. A warming fire spread its cheer throughout the hall. The heavy tapestries, having been beaten, were rich again with a jewel-toned vibrancy to their colors.

The velvet and damask bedhangings and draperies were

shaken free of their deep folds and aired, and new, plump feather mattresses were placed on the beds. Lavender-scented linens from Camareigh were laid on them. Swords and shields were removed from their places of honor on the walls and rubbed clean of the discoloration that years of neglect had wrought, and soon gleaming crossed blades were shining brightly against the mellowed oak hall paneling.

Dust mops and scrub cloths. Brooms and brushes. Lye soap and beeswax. All were wielded by tireless maids and footmen, who worked throughout the day to make the hunting lodge habitable for their lord and lady as well as for themselves. This would be everyone's home until the great house of Merdraco was once again fit.

Their spirits grew as the lodge came to life under their ministrations, and throughout the day their voices could be heard in song and laughter, for, except for Alastair Marlowe's valet and the coachmen, none of the young people had ever ventured farther than the somnolent valley where they were born. Many had known no other home than Camareigh. But for most, this was a great adventure, and they were determined to enjoy every minute of it.

> Home came our goodman,
> And home came he,
> And then he saw a saddle horse,
> Where no horse should be.

> "What's this now, goodwife?
> What's this I see?
> How came this horse here,
> Without the leave o' me?"

> "A horse?" quoth she.
> "Aye, a horse," quoth he.

> "Shame for your cuckold face,
> I'll make ye see.
> 'Tis nothing but a broad sow,
> My mother sent to me."

"A broad sow?" quoth he.
"Aye, a sow," quoth she.

"Far have I ridden,
And farther have I gone,
But a saddle on a sow's back
I saw never none."

Home came our goodman,
And home came he,
He spy'd a pair of jackboots
Where no boots should be.

"What's this now, goodwife?
What's this I see?
How came these boots here,
Without the leave o' me?"

"Boots?" quoth she.
"Aye, boots," quoth he.

"Shame for your cuckold face,
And ill may ye see.
'Tis but a pair of waterstoups
My mother sent to me."

"Waterstoups?" quoth he.
"Aye, waterstoups," quoth she.

"Far have I ridden,
And farther have I gone,
But silver spurs on waterstoups
I saw never none."

Alastair Marlowe grinned as he listened to the verses, the
rhythmic movement of his duster keeping time with the old
ballard being sung below. Alastair was precariously balanced
high up on a rickety ladder propped against the wall. His helping to clean raised as many eyebrows as some of the verses of
the song had raised, for a gentleman was not supposed even

to acknowledge menial tasks. A shocked observer would have been further surprised to discover a bandy-legged little man scrubbing the grimy surface of a kitchen table, while two small dark-haired lads were busy polishing the balustrade of the staircase. A young gentleman, his stock askew and his golden curls in disorder, was attempting, none too successfully, to clean the dirt from the armorial glass in one of the bay windows. And a slender maid, her golden curls covered beneath a mobcap, was snipping herbs and flowers from the garden long overgrown with weeds. The only one not working was the baby, dozing peacefully by his mother's side. The sun's golden rays warmed him through the fine netting draped over his cradle.

And clinging like a sailor in the riggings of a ship, a bare-chested man, his fine cambric shirt tossed carelessly over the stone parapet, could be seen high atop the belvedere tower affixing a banner to a pole rising above the turrets. The sun was reflected a thousandfold in the twelve-light windows encircling the tower, the leaded glass having been painstakingly cleaned by the man who was staring proudly at his handiwork. Apparently he could swing a mop as easily as he wielded a sword.

> Home came our goodman,
> And home came he,
> There he spy'd a powdered wig,
> Where no wig should be.
>
> "What's this now, goodwife?
> What's this I see?
> How came this wig here,
> Without the leave o' me?"
>
> "A wig?" quoth she.
> "Aye, a wig," quoth he.
>
> "Shame for your cuckold face,
> And ill may you see.
> 'Tis nothing but a clocken hen
> My mother sent to me."

* * *

"A clocken hen?" quote he.
"Aye, a clocken hen," quoth she.

"Far have I ridden,
And farther have I gone,
But powder on a clocken hen
I saw never none."

In went our goodman,
And in went he,
And there he spy'd a sturdy man
Where no man should be.

"What's this now, goodwife?
What's this I see?
How came this man here,
Without the leave o' me?"

"A man?" quoth she.
"Aye, a man," quoth he.

"Poor blind body,
And blinder may ye be.
'Tis a new milking maid
My mother sent to me."

"A maid?" quoth he.
"Aye, a maid," quoth she.

"Far have I ridden,
And farther have I gone,
But long-bearded maidens
I saw never none."

Alastair Marlowe joined in the song as he climbed down
the ladder, a satisfied gleam in his eye as he glanced around.
The hall was finally beginning to show the efforts of a hard
day's work in the deep shining of polished wood and brass and
the crystalline sparkle of sunshine through the windowpanes.

Flexing his tired shoulders, Alastair made his way out into

the daylight and breathed deeply. The afternoon air was redolent of sweetbriar and honeysuckle, which grew in wild tangles throughout the garden. But dominating all was the scent of the sea. In the distance Alastair could see the glistening, frothy white waves rolling in toward shore, and he suddenly knew that he would never be happy unless he could live within sight of the sea. Subtly, like a woman, it had worked its magic over him. He was captive to its changing beauty and mystery as surely as if it were his mistress. On that seductive thought, Alastair heard a sweet, melodic humming and glanced up to see Rhea Claire's slender figure approaching him. She was holding Lord Kit in her arms, while a wide, shallow basket full of cut flowers and herbs swung from her elbow. Seeing her dressed in a simple linsey-woolsey gown and a plain linen apron with bib, which she had borrowed from one of the maids, no one would suspect that she was the lady of the manor.

"I know you're wondering when luncheon will be, but are too polite to inquire," Rhea said, smiling as she saw Alastair watching her, a hungry look in his eyes. "Shall I go to see how Kirby and Hallie are getting along? Famously, I hope," Rhea added, "or our meals may become quite an experience. If each adds his own seasoning when the other's back is turned, I shudder to think what the stew will taste like," Rhea said with a laugh.

"Here, let me take the basket. It must be heavy," Alastair offered, but Rhea surprised him by handing over the bundled-up Lord Kit instead. Had she placed a beehive buzzing with angry bees in his arms Alastair could not have been more surprised. "Lady Rhea! Please, I—I don't know what to do. Good Lord! What if I drop him?" Alastair said in growing panic as he held the tiny babe in his arms, not daring even to breathe deeply lest he disturb the sleeping infant. "Where are you going?" he demanded as he watched Rhea walking away from him, leaving him at the mercy of the sleeping child.

Rhea smiled back at the stunned Alastair Marlowe, who seemed as helpless as the babe he was holding. "He won't bite you, Alastair," she reassured him. "I saw some daffodils and I'm going to pick them. They are Dante's favorite, as they were his mother's. His mother used to place a vase of flowers on an oak table in the entrance hall at Merdraco, and I thought he might like to see the same thing in his home now," Rhea said as she moved carefully through the garden. "Ah, and here," Rhea murmured thoughtfully as she caught sight of a delicate blossom, "a white violet. 'Tis the sweetest smelling of all flowers."

Alastair Marlowe glanced down at the baby nestled against his chest. As he continued to stare into its funny little face, he felt a sudden longing to know the feel of his own son in his arms. Alastair's gaze drifted to the woman who had given birth to the fellow he was holding, and he knew more longing. With a heartfelt sigh, Alastair shook his head, scolding himself for his foolishness.

"Is something wrong, Alastair? You look sad," the object of his desire spoke solicitously as she came up beside him, her arms full of daffodils and violets.

Alastair actually blushed as he met her gaze, and he glanced away, feeling even more tormented. He had never been good at keeping secrets. "I was worried that I might be holding Lord Kit too tightly," he lied lamely.

"Not at all. In fact," Rhea said with a teasing glint in her eye, "I think you would make a very good father. Once we are settled in here, I shall have to think about finding you a wife. But I shall be very selective, for I expect you to visit here often, and I shouldn't care to take a dislike to your wife. Yes, now that I think of it, we must find a lovely Devonshire lass for you. That way you are sure to stay nearby," she said, little realizing how deeply she was wounding the sensitive Alastair. He had never been in love before meeting Rhea.

"But before you can meet your intended, you must have the cobwebs out of your hair," she said with a laugh. Standing on tiptoe, she brushed the fine webbing from his light brown hair, her laughing face raised to his.

The man staring down from the tower watched his wife and his best friend standing closely together, as if they were exchanging secrets. And because Dante Leighton was so much in love with his wife and was deeply vulnerable, he knew a sudden jealousy as he watched her hands touching Alastair's hair. No man but himself had the right to know that touch.

Dante was still staring down at them when he became aware

of riders approaching along the narrow lane that winded down past the entrance gates to Merdraco.

Startled, Rhea and Alastair turned around in surprise. To the riders, their startled expressions made them seem guilty, as if they were lovers caught in a tryst.

There were three riders, but it was the one in the lead who caught one's eye. She was dressed in scarlet and her prancing black stallion had bells jingling on his bridle. Rhea thought she had never seen such a beautiful woman. Her hair was as black as midnight, and her eyes as dark as thunder. They even seemed to flash with lightning as she pulled up on the reins, bringing her mount to a halt before Rhea and Alastair.

"Where is your master, girl?" the woman demanded. Her arrogance was not affected, but had been with her since childhood. "Well, I haven't all day to wait here while you gawk," she said impatiently, her horse snorting sympathetically. "Well? Haven't found your wits yet, miss? How about that handsome husband of yours? Does he have a tongue? He was obviously glib enough to entice you," she added, for she hadn't missed the blanketed bundle being held so gingerly by the man standing beside the girl.

Alastair Marlowe's mouth fell open at the impertinence of the woman. But when he met Rhea's eyes, he found amusement there instead of anger. Gradually he became aware that they did indeed look like servants.

"May I ask who is calling?" Rhea asked softly, her cultivated voice catching the woman by surprise. That dark gaze narrowed thoughtfully and she eyed Rhea more carefully.

"You certainly may not!" the woman said hotly. "Who the devil are you? Who is your master? Where is he? What is he doing here at Merdraco? If you are trespassing, then I'll see that the authorities arrest the lot of you," the woman warned, a glint in her eye.

"That will not be necessary, Bess," an amused voice called casually from the entrance to the lodge.

Lady Bess Seacombe jerked her head around, prepared to deal a stunning setdown to the impertinent fellow who had dared to address her with such familiarity. When she caught sight of the man walking out of the shadows, she nearly tumbled from her horse. Only once before had she ever seen so handsome a man, and as this one came toward her, his bare chest glinting with sweat, she felt she must surely be dreaming.

"Dante?" she whispered, her dark eyes inky pools as she stared at her onetime lover. "You are alive? You've come back?" she said shakily, her expression disbelieving.

"I can assure you that I am no ghost," Dante Leighton spoke smoothly, his pale gray eyes not missing a thing about Lady Bess' stunning appearance. She was still a very beautiful woman, even more seductive today than she had been as a young girl of fifteen.

"Dante," Bess repeated the name, caressing it, Rhea thought, as she continued to stand there beside Alastair, apparently forgotten. The two former lovers stared into each other's eyes as if it were yesterday and there had been no misunderstanding.

Lady Bess Seacombe was stunned and could hardly catch her breath as she stared in fascination at Dante Leighton, a man she had thought never to see again. She really could not believe it, and she shook her dark head several times, the rakishly tilted straw hat decorated with a profusion of fluttering scarlet feathers looking as if it might take to the skies.

Lady Bess' warm gaze lingered on that bronzed chest, so muscular and broad, tapering down to narrow hips covered by a soft buckskin molded to those hard thighs. She realized that she had been in love with a mere boy all those years ago. Dante Leighton had become devastatingly handsome. He still had the power to make her heart pound.

Suddenly, when her gaze locked with his, she became uncomfortable, for she couldn't help but wonder if he, too, was remembering those long nights they had spent together. And then Bess bit her lip nervously, wondering as well if he were remembering her cowardly betrayal.

But when she looked more deeply into those pale gray eyes, she was surprised to see an amused look there. Was he laughing at her? She was prepared to deal with anger, yes, but amusement?

"How did you know I was back?" Dante asked as he moved closer to Rhea and Alastair.

"I didn't. We were out riding and saw the smoke rising from a house I thought stood empty. Then we saw the wagons moving down the path and followed. I felt it my duty to investigate," Bess explained, her cheeks flushing a deep pink. "I must say I certainly did not expect to see you here," she added, although whether that was true or not, Bess didn't want to admit to herself. Deep down inside, she had indeed possessed a wild hope that she would find Dante Leighton returned to Merdraco.

As soon as she saw the smoke she knew she had to come, even though he might not have welcomed her. He had every right to hate her still, but perhaps he had forgiven her. She silently prayed it was true as she drew close to the house she had once dreamed of living in.

"Why are you here at the lodge?" she asked. "I would have thought you'd move into the big house. Or aren't you planning to stay at Merdraco?"

"I have come home to stay, Bess," Dante said quietly. "But we shall have to live at the lodge for now. While I was away from Merdraco, someone—and I think we both know who— broke into Merdraco and deliberately made it unfit to live in," Dante said harshly. His forbidding expression sent a nervous shiver through Bess Seacombe. Dante Leighton had become a man who could hate.

"We?" Bess asked.

"Yes. I did not return alone," Dante said, his gaze lingering on Rhea's flushed face.

Lady Bess did not miss the softening of his expression as he stared at the young maid. She sighed. He hadn't changed all that much after all. In fact, he was probably more expert at seduction than he had been at twenty. Bess found herself wondering what it would be like to be held in his arms again.

A moment passed and then Bess tapped her riding crop in irritation, for she seemed to have lost Dante's attention to the golden-haired maid. Not quite understanding her sudden jealousy, she said sarcastically, "Your servants are impertinent, Dante. And this maid of yours was hardly accommodating when I demanded to see her master. She even went so far as to demand my name!"

"Her master?" Dante asked, glancing between the two women. He frowned, but then he became aware of the misleading impression of Rhea's costume. He laughed. "I doubt she considers me her master," Dante murmured. "Do you, little daffadilly?" he asked as he saw the golden daffodils she was holding.

Dante didn't wait for Rhea's reply, but went on quickly, "I have been remiss in not introducing these two people—no, three people," Dante corrected himself as he reached out and took his son from Alastair.

Lady Bess Seacombe raised a delicately arched brow. Was he really going to introduce her to servants? Even if one happened to be his mistress, the idea was astonishing. "Do you really think that is necessary, Dante?" Bess asked patronizingly. "I heard rumors that you lived in the colonies, where, I am told, servants are treated as equals to their masters and where tradesmen are the most respected members of society. Indeed, they seem to *be* society, for those colonials respect any man who works, even one who dirties his hands! 'Tis an outrageous practice which can lead only to difficulties. I am surprised that you should adopt such a revolutionary policy, Dante."

He startled Lady Bess by laughing. "I had forgotten how regal you were, Bess," he said. "But I fear that you have been misled. This gentleman here, is Alastair Marlowe, a former member of my crew aboard the *Sea Dragon,* and a very good friend of mine. And this lady is my wife," Dante spoke the words softly.

"And this child is my son," Dante continued, his words ringing in Bess' ears and destroying her dreams. She had hoped...no, she wouldn't even think about what she had hoped, she told herself as she stared down at the woman who was mistress of Merdraco and wife to Dante Leighton.

"Rhea, this is Lady Bess Seacombe, an old friend of mine from many years ago. Almost too many to count," Dante added. He intended no malice, but his words slapped Lady Bess in the face as she stared down at his incredibly beautiful and very young wife. Bess had to admit that Rhea was a beauty.

"Well, what a surprise. And when did the blessed event take place? I shouldn't think your wife is long out of the nursery," Bess remarked.

Dante smiled. "We were wed this past year."

"I am surprised I did not read about it." Bess' questioning voice cast doubt on the fact.

"We were wed in the colonies."

"Ah! Now I understand. I should have guessed by your bride's quaint attire. You really will have to teach her propriety if she is to accompany you in polite society," Bess suggested kindly. "I should be happy to tutor her in the art of being a lady."

"I shouldn't think that would be necessary, Bess, or that you were qualified," Dante said, his voice cutting. "As it so happens, my wife is English. In fact, you may have met her parents."

"Indeed? I shouldn't think that likely," Bess responded coldly. "I doubt whether we move in the same circles."

"Her parents are the Duke and Duchess of Camareigh. Before we wed, my wife was Lady Rhea Claire Dominick."

Lady Bess nearly choked. "Well! 'Tis an honor, for I have indeed met your parents in London on several occasions."

"Lady Bess. It is a pleasure to meet an old friend of Dante's," Rhea said politely, not intending the word "old" as a criticism. But that was how Bess Seacombe took it, for she wanted badly to dislike the chit who had captured Dante Leighton's heart and who wore his ring.

"Yes, well, as a former acquaintance of Dante's, I remember when he left here. He had hardly a farthing to his name, and now he has come home to Merdraco with a very, very wealthy bride. You shouldn't have any trouble at all rebuilding Merdraco," Bess said, leaving no doubt that she believed Dante had wed Rhea for her fortune. "But really, Dante, did you have to snatch a bride from the cradle? Why, she's hardly any older than your son," Lady Bess said scathingly, for her pride was still smarting, and she wanted to strike out and hurt the man she refused to admit she still felt something for, even if he felt nothing for her.

Dante's pale gray eyes narrowed thoughtfully as he eyed the other two riders. "'Twould seem as if Rhea isn't much older than your daughter, Bess?" Dante queried, and his barb struck deep. "I do not believe I have met her or the lad. Your son, Bess?"

Bess Seacombe's nostrils flared with anger. But she steeled herself and, smiling proudly, said, "Yes, this is my daughter,

Anne, and my son, Charles. Children, come and meet Dante Leighton, Marquis of Jacqobi."

As the two approached, their horses moving slowly, Anne Seacombe stared in bemused fascination at the man who very easily could have been her father. This was the man her mother had been so very much in love with. "Hello," she said softly, her dark brown eyes wide with wonder as she stared at that muscular chest. She began to understand her mother a little better.

"You are very beautiful, Anne," Dante said with a smile, charming Anne further. "You remind me of your mother when she was that age. Only she was not as shy. Were you, Bess?" he asked, for he could remember her riding across the moors, her dark curls blowing free, daring him to catch her.

"You should remember, Dante," Bess reminded him with an intimate look. Then she glanced down at Rhea pityingly. "Dante and I were quite close at one time. I doubt whether he told you that we were affianced?" she said. She was sure that Dante had not told his wife about his former lover. And because she wanted to place doubts in Rhea's mind, she brought up a subject that she should have left buried.

"Indeed, Lady Bess," Rhea answered smoothly, her smile understanding this time as she stared at the older woman, "Dante has told me *everything* about his relationship with you."

Bess Seacombe's lips tightened with her anger and then with shame as she met Dante's gaze and knew that Rhea spoke the truth. "I see," Bess mumbled, mortified before Dante and the child he had married. When they discovered that the high and mighty Lady Bess Seacombe was an impoverished widow, they would probably laugh their heads off.

But Bess Seacombe did not know the manner of woman Rhea Claire was. She would never enjoy another's unhappiness. And as Rhea watched the play of emotions crossing Lady Bess' face, she sensed some of her anguish. She didn't know that the woman was nearly destitute, but she knew that Bess had lost Dante through her own foolishness, and she pitied her. With that in mind, Rhea said tentatively, "It must have been a long ride. We would be honored if you and your son and daughter would join us for tea."

Rhea's friendly invitation seemed to startle Dante and Alastair as much as it had Lady Bess, for they all stared at her as if she had lost her mind.

"I am afraid the lodge is in a bit of an uproar. We are in the midst of cleaning it, as you may have noticed from my attire, but I promise the tea will be strong and hot, and in the china cups which will have been unpacked by now. And Hallie's scones will be quite delicious," Rhea said with a smile which included the lad sitting quietly on his mount. At the mention of pastry, Charles Seacombe's homely little face showed its first spark of interest.

Lady Bess Seacombe was flummoxed. She understood that the offer was being made in kindness, and all she wanted was to heartily dislike Rhea, whose existence destroyed her hopes.

Bess Seacombe was a proud woman. Perhaps that was what had caused her downfall, for it was almost impossible for her to admit that she needed help. She'd choke on those scones if she had to sit across from Dante and his wife, pretending that she was pleased about their happiness, for it was only too apparent that theirs was a love match. She was about to refuse, her chin rising with affronted dignity, when the sound of horses' hooves along the lane drew everyone's attention. All eyes turned toward the approaching riders. They moved as though they had a purpose in visiting, and from the expressions on the riders' faces, they were not bringing good tidings.

> *It oft falls out,*
> *To have what we would have, we speak*
> *not what we mean.*
>
> Shakespeare

Chapter 25

LADY BESS SEACOMBE was the only one not surprised by the visitors. Dante, Rhea, and Alastair were stunned, for one of the riders was none other than Sir Morgan Lloyd. They had bid him farewell in London thinking he was returning to the colonies. They did not know the young man accompanying Sir Morgan. But his red coat with its gilt buttons and his black tricorne with its gold lace binding identified him as an officer of the Crown. Dante Leighton saw that this was no casual visit from Sir Morgan Lloyd, his old nemesis with whom he had established a truce.

Alastair frowned and tried to catch his captain's eye, but Dante's attention was on the two riders, his gaze narrowed, which confirmed Alastair's suspicions that something was amiss; for it brought back memories of the captain standing on the deck, his narrowed gaze searching the horizon for that first sighting of the enemy. Rhea saw nothing strange in Sir Morgan's being accompanied by another officer, and she stepped forward, her arms still full of flowers, and a smile of welcome curving her lips.

"Sir Morgan! How wonderful to see you again," Rhea exclaimed, her words of welcome and recognition startling both Lady Bess and Lieutenant Handley, for neither had thought this to be anything but a meeting of strangers. Both remembered a conversation at Seawyck Manor when the good captain had professed little knowledge of Merdraco or its master.

"Lady Rhea Claire," Sir Morgan surprised them by speaking the lady's name with a gentleness that neither Bess nor the lieutenant had ever heard in that stern voice. "I had remembered your uncommon beauty, m'lady, but I confess to being once again startled by it. You are a breath of spring after a very long, bleak winter," Sir Morgan said with so charming a smile that Lady Bess raised a haughty eyebrow. The man had been barely civil to her. Indeed, the impertinent fellow had issued her a warning to watch her step, and here he was fawning over this fair-haired chit and smiling one of his rare smiles.

"You are too kind, Sir Morgan. But what brings you here to Merdraco? I thought you would be in the Carolinas by now. What a coincidence to find you here. I am afraid that we are ill prepared for entertaining, for we have just arrived at Merdraco," Rhea explained apologetically, glancing toward the lodge, "although we would be delighted to have you stay. I hope you accepted my invitation and paid a visit to Camareigh? I know my mother and father were delighted to see you, Sir Morgan. Is that how you discovered where we were?" Rhea was about to inquire about her family when she was interrupted.

"I do not think a social visit was Sir Morgan's intention, Rhea," Dante spoke for the first time. He had been watching Sir Morgan's expression while Rhea conversed with him, and Dante knew that something was bothering Sir Morgan Lloyd, so he was not surprised when that man turned a cold eye on him.

"I am afraid, Lord Jacqobi, that I am here on official business. It is my intention of . . ."

"'. . . of giving you fair warning that I shall rid this coastline of its infestation of smugglers,'" Lady Bess concluded for him. "I give you fair warning now, Dante, that Sir Morgan Lloyd is a man who takes his responsibilities most seriously. Almost to the point of being a bore."

"Lady Bess," Sir Morgan said patiently, but his blue eyes were as cold as the arctic winds. "Forgive me, I hadn't noticed your presence until now," he said, which must have been bending the truth a bit, for he could not have missed that scarlet figure perched arrogantly on her black stallion, which in his opinion, was too much horse for the lady. "And may I compliment you on your remarkable memory. I can only hope that you have the good sense to follow my warning and not simply to mimic me."

"Indeed, sir," Lady Bess smiled provocatively, her dark eyes shimmering with anger. "I have found myself pondering your words of advice often, or at least until I find myself nodding off," she confided to him. "But what is this? You are friends with the lady? Now, this is an extraordinary coincidence. Or did you purposely get yourself transferred here so you could resume an old friendship? I must agree the idea has merit," she said with an arch look at Dante Leighton before glancing at his embarrassed wife. But it was on meeting Sir Morgan's flinty stare that she remembered, too late, the reason for Sir Morgan's presence. She began to feel uncomfortable, for she had not intended to be insensitive to his loss.

"I met Sir Morgan when I was in the colonies. He came to my aid and I consider him a gentleman and a friend," Rhea said stiffly. Lady Bess didn't miss the blush that spread across her rival's cheeks.

"How very interesting. Do you know, I still find it difficult to believe that you have actually been to the colonies? You certainly have traveled rather extensively for one so . . . so young," Bess managed to say the cursed word. "I suppose that is where you met Dante? Or was it in London? Of course, I'm not at all surprised that I didn't hear of your nuptials, since I haven't been to London in over a year. Lud, but it seems an eternity since I left the country. I don't know when was the last time I attended a soiree, or . . . well," Lady Bess stopped herself, for she certainly didn't wish to admit to her lack of funds. "Actually, I must admit that I mistakenly thought *that* young man," she said, indicating a dumbfounded Alastair, "was Lady Rhea's husband. And the father of her child," Bess said with an apologetic laugh which had nothing to do with being sorry. "Isn't that just *too* awful of me? But you have to admit they do make a handsome couple and seem well suited to one another, at least in age. Wouldn't you agree, Dante?"

"Age has nothing to do with maturity. Indeed, I found Lady Rhea Claire to be one of the most courageous and decent young women it has ever been my privilege to meet," Sir Morgan said, surprising everyone again by his unexpected comment, and it certainly set Lady Bess' teeth on edge.

"My, my, it would seem as if the good captain is not only heroic but honey-tongued as well. You will have to keep an eye on this young wife of yours, Dante, what with these two handsome and obviously lovesick gentlemen by her side. I shouldn't turn my back for long, if I were you, Dante. I should hate to have to console you, my dear," Bess said pityingly, but the look in her eyes was telling Dante Leighton something altogether different.

"You were never very good at consoling, Bess," Dante said, and Bess felt her cheeks pinkening with shame. To add to her annoyance, she caught Sir Morgan's hawklike stare on her. She felt a sudden urge to raise her riding crop to him and smash that damned holier-than-thou attitude off his face, for Sir Morgan Lloyd had the strange ability to make her feel small. Lady Bess sent him a smoldering look that should have left him a smoking cinder in the saddle.

"Perhaps you won't need consolation. Perhaps this marriage of yours is one of convenience? At least on your part, my dear?" Bess inquired casually of her former lover before she met Rhea's wide eyes with an understanding look. "I am sure, once he set out to woo you, that you fell head over heels in love with Dante. He can be such a persuasive lov—" Bess let her words trail off discreetly. "Of course, Dante, poor dear, has always been in need of a fortune, and I should imagine that you came with quite a dowry?"

"Mother, please," Anne Seacombe was embarrassed enough to speak up, even though she knew she risked being punished later.

"As a matter of fact, madam," Alastair Marlowe said shortly, unable to hold his tongue any longer either, "Dante Leighton is a very wealthy man. He needed no wealthy wife. And were you more observant, you would see that the captain is very much in love with Lady Rhea Claire."

Lady Bess Seacombe eyed the handsome young man with dislike but decided to ignore him. "Is this true? Are you really rich, Dante?" she demanded incredulously, wishing away the last fifteen years.

"I would not have returned to Merdraco otherwise," Dante answered simply. "And had Rhea been a beggarmaid, I would still have married her," he said, and the look that he and Rhea exchanged hurt Bess in a way that no stinging rejoinder could have done.

"Well, I must say, I am quite speechless with surprise," Bess said, glancing quickly at Sir Morgan and daring him to make the obvious comment.

"If you haven't come on a social visit, then what is your business here, Captain?" Dante drew the conversation back to the naval officer's visit. To see the former captain of the *Sea Dragon* standing there so casually, holding his son, one would have thought the question merely conversational.

For a moment, Sir Morgan's gaze lingered regretfully on that peacefully sleeping babe. Then he seemed to put the feeling aside and said in an authoritative voice, "I am giving you fair warning, Lord Jacqobi," Sir Morgan began, only to be interrupted by Bess' amused voice.

"Oh, lud, here we go again," she complained, ignoring Sir Morgan's irritated glance. There was something about the man that seemed to bring out the worst in her and made her act more outrageous than she thought wise. But sometimes she was helpless to control her tongue.

"As a former smuggler, you are, Lord Jacqobi, the man most likely to be the leader of the local smuggling gang," Sir Morgan stated matter-of-factly. He indicated the lieutenant. "In fact, Lieutenant Handley here thinks you are indeed their leader."

Lieutenant Handley looked most uncomfortable, for he preferred to make his remarks behind a person's back, not to that person's face, especially if that person was a very wealthy marquis who happened to be married to a duke's daughter. "Well," he said with a nervous laugh that sounded more like a gurgle, "I do not believe I actually said that in so many words. And surely you do understand, m'lord, that everyone must be suspect if we are to rid this area of the Sons of Belial," he said with an earnest glance at the man he had been so quick to accuse.

"Indeed. I agree with you that *everyone* must be under suspicion," Dante surprised the lieutenant by admitting, his eyes meeting Sir Morgan's for a moment.

"I can scarcely believe it," Bess said with another shake of the scarlet feathers crowning her head. "You, the Marquis of Jacqobi, a smuggler? That will amuse certain people," she said obliquely. "Is that how you became rich? Well, I s'pose there is hope then for the rest of us," she spoke unthinkingly, not realizing what she had said until she heard Anne's gasp. She glanced up to see a slight smile curving Sir Morgan's lips. "Well? Where the devil do you think my dressmaker got the lace for my chemise? After all, Sir Morgan, even the vicar drinks tea smuggled in from across the Channel," Bess defended herself, trying to make the best of her mistake.

"I was not accusing you of anything, Lady Bess," he said softly. "But I am afraid I must disabuse you of something, should you think of making the trip across the Channel yourself. Lord Jacqobi did not come by his fortune because he was a smuggler. The captain of the *Sea Dragon* found a sunken galleon with a hold full of gold and silver. His methods in achieving his goal are well worth remembering—and I do remember them, Captain, never forget that.

"I warn you now, Captain, if you think you can resume your smuggling activities from Merdraco, or indeed, if you are the leader of this smuggling gang, I shall deal with you as you dealt with Bertie Mackay in the Straits of Florida. You do remember that, don't you?" Sir Morgan asked.

Alastair Marlowe was frowning, for if he remembered the incident correctly, and he should, for he was aboard the *Sea Dragon* at the time, the captain had set one of Bertie Mackay's men adrift in a gig. The man had come aboard the *Sea Dragon* to spy. Accompanying him in the gig was a lantern. Soon the gig was carried away on the swiftly moving currents, and with the lantern's light glowing in the dark of night, the rival smugglers aboard the *Annie Jeanne,* which had been following in the *Sea Dragon*'s wake, found themselves being misled by the very same light which earlier had been used by the spy to signal Bertie Mackay's ship. And as the *Sea Dragon*'s bowsprit swung toward the Carolinas, Bertie Mackay and his crew of cutthroats had been sent on a wild goose chase and had nearly run aground before discovering that they had been tricked.

Alastair shook his head. Why would Sir Morgan wish to put Dante Leighton adrift in a gig? That did not sound like the Sir Morgan he knew. But then, as Alastair eyed the naval officer closely, he realized that the man had changed in the months since they had seen him in London.

"Sir Morgan," Rhea spoke his name doubtfully, her violet eyes searching his face for some sign of the man she remembered so fondly, "I cannot believe you are the same man who came to my rescue in St. John's Harbour when I was in trouble."

"I only wish that I had realized then exactly who you were and had been able to return you to your home in England before you became further involved with Dante Leighton and his crew. I fear that you have married a man who will be unable to settle down and give you a peaceful life. He has become used to a life of adventure, and he will never attach himself to the life of a gentleman of leisure. Wealth changes nothing, Lady Rhea. It was the excitement of privateering that kept Dante Leighton sailing, not desire for wealth."

"You are wrong, Sir Morgan," Rhea told him, her eyes full of hurt as she stared at his hardened face.

Sir Morgan inclined his head slightly. "For your sake, and for that alone, I hope you are right and I am wrong," he said.

"I seem to recall a conversation in which you warned me against continuing my unlawful activities. Like the lieutenant here, you seemed to think that once a smuggler, always a smuggler," Dante reminded him. "Perhaps. But you are correct about one thing, Sir Morgan. I did enjoy adventure and excitement. But I think I am going to find enough excitement in being master of Merdraco to satisfy my adventurer's heart.

"But what has me puzzled is this: Exactly what you are doing here? Last I heard, you were captain of H.M.S. *Portcullis* and stationed in Charles Town. You threatened to warn your brother, who is also a naval officer and stationed along this coast, of my disreputable past. Had you so little faith in his abilities that you came along to help him? Surely I am not as dangerous as that?" Dante inquired of the grim-visaged Sir Morgan Lloyd.

"My brother is dead."

There was a stunned silence, and then Rhea cried, "Oh, no! I am so sorry, Sir Morgan." Her anger evaporated and she began to realize why Sir Morgan seemed so changed. Dante was staring at Sir Morgan, too, but with an expression of enlightenment on his face.

"How did it happen?" he asked.

"He was murdered."

"How?"

"His ship was lured into Dragon's Cove," Sir Morgan said, startling Dante.

"How do you know that?" Dante asked, his words masking Rhea's gasp. At last she knew what had happened upon that sandy shore. "Were there any survivors?"

"No, but my brother did not go down with his ship. He and several others managed to make it to shore. He died of knife wounds. He was unarmed and probably half drowned when he was attacked."

"And you suspect me of his murder?" Dante asked, his raised hand silencing Alastair's and Rhea's protests. "Rather brazen of me, wasn't it, to wreck a ship beneath the towers of Merdraco?"

"This is outrageous!" Rhea exclaimed angrily. "Dante wouldn't do such a thing!"

"If you will excuse me for saying this," Lieutenant Handley broke in, "Lord Jacqobi *was* accused of murder many years ago."

"Suspected but never accused and certainly not convicted," Rhea cried, her violet eyes glaring at a flustered Bess Seacombe, who suddenly couldn't seem to meet the younger woman's contemptuous gaze. "I should think you would be ashamed of yourself for even repeating such a rumor, Lieutenant," Rhea chastised the man. "And you, Sir Morgan, do you believe Dante capable of cold-blooded murder?"

"Anyone is capable of murder, Lady Rhea, if pushed too

far. If they become desperate. If, perhaps, they are cornered," Sir Morgan said quietly.

"When did this occur? Your brother must have been alive when we returned to England with you. And Dante has been at Camareigh since he left London. He couldn't possibly have had anything to do with your brother's death," Rhea said.

"You actually think Dante is the leader of the Sons of Belial?" Lady Bess asked with an incredulous glance at Sir Morgan. "Lud, but that's rich, and, as the lady has said, Dante wasn't even here when your brother's ship sank. Besides, he is the last person who'd be—"

"One can be involved in a murder without actually bloodying one's own hands," Sir Morgan interrupted Lady Bess impatiently. "Since arriving here, I have come to believe that there is some twisted mind behind these Sons of Belial. Although their leader has remained a mystery, I shall discover his identity and find the men responsible for my brother's death and the deaths of his crew," Sir Morgan vowed. "And I shall consider anyone who has information concerning this smuggling gang, and who has not stepped forward with it, to be my enemy. I shall deal harshly with those individuals, whether male or female," Sir Morgan said.

Lady Bess licked her dry lips, thankful that she had been interrupted before saying that Dante Leighton was the last person to be suspected of leading the Sons of Belial, for Jack Shelby hated the Marquis of Jacqobi. Bess couldn't see him taking orders from Dante. Nor indeed would the Sons of Belial have vandalized Merdraco had Dante been their mysterious leader.

Those were two things the good captain had yet to discover, but until then, he would continue to suspect Dante Leighton. And that, Bess thought with a sigh, would no doubt please the Sons of Belial just fine, for they would be free to go about their business while Sir Morgan Lloyd, who wasn't as smart as he thought he was, chased shadows.

"I will take my leave now," Sir Morgan said stiffly. "No doubt you and I shall be meeting soon, Captain," he commented. "I am sorry, Lady Rhea Clare," he added, but glanced away quickly from those violet eyes staring up at him accusingly. Nodding briefly at the others, he turned his horse and rode back along the lane, the lieutenant endeavoring to catch up with him.

"Impertinent man," Lady Bess muttered, but sighed in relief as the two riders disappeared around a curve in the lane.

"It saddens me to see how much Sir Morgan has changed," Rhea said, watching the lane as if she still could not believe that he had said those things.

"We all change, Rhea," Dante said, his eyes meeting hers and holding them for a long moment.

"I hate to interrupt, but I must be going," Lady Bess said tartly. This had turned into a miserable day, and she was beginning to feel a migraine coming on. "Dante, I—" Bess began, but what she might have said, even she was not certain, for Dante merely shook his head.

"Good-bye, Bess," he said tiredly. Taking Rhea by the arm, he turned and walked away.

Bess continued to sit on her horse for a moment longer while staring at Dante and his young wife, their young son held in his arms, as they disappeared inside the lodge. She wasn't even aware of Alastair Marlowe as he drifted away, his farewell acknowledged by her daughter Anne, whose cheeks blushed like a wild rose as she watched his tall figure striding away.

"Welcome back to Merdraco, Dante," Bess Seacombe whispered. Never before had she felt quite so alone.

Men should be what they seem.
Shakespeare

Chapter 26

THE streets of Merleigh cascaded down the hillside toward the sea like a wild moorland stream flowing with cobblestone. Crowding close along the banks were half-timbered, bay-windowed shops and cottages, each with steeply pitched, stone-tiled roofs. A multitude of stone chimneys stood above the picturesque jumble of rooftops, but rising above all was the tower of the parish church. From its lofty perch at the steep end of Merleigh's main thoroughfare, its bells pealed the day of the month with precise strokes after the church clock had struck five and nine of the morning and evening. As darkness fell, it chimed the curfew for any who would have wished to carouse after eight o'clock, as it had in medieval times. Nowadays the curfew law was no longer enforced. The bells also served to remind any forgetful parishioners of the Sabbath.

But it was market day, and the narrow, cobbled streets were filled with people. A heavily laden dray pulled by stout-chested oxen made its slow, creaking way up the lane, passing a team of pack horses loaded down with neatly cut sections of dried peat. The moorland vagabond leading the sturdy ponies did not have far to look for customers, for peat was cheap and made a good fire on chilly nights. Half doors opening onto Merleigh's High Street allowed the passerby a quick glance of the busy shoemaker or tailor or baker within.

At the base of the hill, where the cobbled lane ran into the sea, was a quay stretching out to the small curve of a peaceful bay. The masts of numerous fishing boats swayed to and fro with the tide, their crews mending nets spread out on the sands or standing by their day's catch while the fishmonger and matrons from village and farm surveyed the catch, preparing to haggle.

It was this scene, one that had changed little over the centuries, that met the gazes of the riders approaching the small coastal town.

"This is Merleigh," Dante Leighton said, his hand outstretched to encompass the hamlet, which seemed to have spilled over the edge of the cliff and tumbled down to the sands below.

"'Tis quite a lovely town," Rhea said, urging Skylark along the high road which led into the village about midway in its descent into the sea.

"Hasn't changed much since I last saw it," Houston Kirby commented from the back of his little moorland pony, his narrowed gaze raking the gable-fronted shops. He studied the villagers wandering along the lane as if seeking faces he remembered.

"You were born hereabouts, weren't you, Kirby?" Alastair Marlowe inquired, trying not to notice the curious stares they were receiving.

"I was born at Merdraco, not Merleigh. There's a big difference," Houston Kirby said proudly. He was no simple villager or fisherman. "Merleigh ain't even a very old town. Used to be over by the castle, it did. That's how it got its name.

'Twas on Leighton land, then. In those times, the villagers needed to live close to the castle 'cause, not bein' fightin' men, they needed a place to run and hide when the enemy approached," Houston Kirby commented with a contemptuous glance around. "But when the land became settled, they moved the town here, where they had a better bay for fishin' and shippin'. Dragon's Cove was too much of a challenge for them. Always thinkin' of their purses, these merchants. No respect for the past," he said, forgetting that the Leighton family, with more regard for their comfort than for their heritage, had moved into better quarters and abandoned their ancient castle.

Francis Dominick grinned at Rhea. He had come to like the tart-tongued little steward and enjoyed the grumbling comments Houston Kirby continually made.

"Looks like ol' Tom Morcombe's been busy," Kirby said as he eyed a short, swaggering man being followed by a tall, thin, harassed-looking woman. She held a baby, and another child held tightly to her skirts. Behind them came a line of children from about three to fifteen years old, the varying degrees of height making them look like a moving staircase. "Didn't think he had it in him," Houston Kirby said with a sniff.

"Bet you could show them how to sail those ships," Robin told Conny, who was holding on for dear life as he bounced up and down behind the second son of the Duke of Camareigh on the small moorland pony rented from Bishop's Grave Inn.

"Aye, reckon so, Lord Robin," Conny admitted, wondering why he'd never felt seasick on board ship, but now felt green as a head of cabbage.

"Robin," Robin Dominick reminded his friend. "There's no need for the title between friends."

"Aye, your nibs," Conny said with a wide grin.

"Aye, yourself, spouter," Robin said, chuckling as he sent the little pony even faster down the steep lane, much to Conny Brady's dismay and Rhea's unease. Robin had a penchant for sending ponies into places where they shouldn't be.

Francis was reading her mind, grinning and thinking of the time Robin had sent his pony Shoopitee through the gardens and knocked Lord Rendale into a lily pond. But he kept a wary eye on the lad lest he send his pony through some farmer's penned chickens.

The strangers were beginning to draw a crowd of interested spectators. So many riders, mounted on such fine horses and dressed as only gentry could, were a rare sight in Merleigh Towne.

"I'll leave you here with Kirby, Rhea. He doesn't seem to think Hallie made up a proper list for the greengrocer," Dante remarked. Although Hallie had assumed control of the kitchens, Houston Kirby could be found close by with words of advice, words too often given and never requested.

"I am certain that Kirby's expertise will be most appreciated," Rhea replied diplomatically, and a wide, satisfied grin spread across the little steward's face. Dante shook his head. There'd be no living with him now.

"I will not be long, Rhea," Dante said as they halted their horses at the edge of the marketplace. Dante dismounted and lifted Rhea from the saddle. "I am going to the tavern up on High Street. It is just a short way up the hill. If you need anything, that is where I'll be, and where I hope to find most of the unemployed men of the village. I want to let them know there are jobs for them at Merdraco and that I am paying a day's wages for a day's work," Dante explained abruptly, for he wasn't certain of his reception. The Sons of Belial might have influenced the villagers against working at Merdraco.

"Can you use some company?" Alastair inquired, for he knew little about selecting vegetables and poultry.

Dante nodded. After guiding Rhea through the milling crowd, he turned on his heel and left her standing before several open crates of freshly picked berries, a frowning Houston Kirby and an amused Francis Dominick standing guard on either side of her. Robin Dominick and his grinning cohort Conny Brady had already disappeared into the crowded square, mischief, no doubt, uppermost in their minds.

The tavern Dante Leighton sought was squeezed between a wigmaker's shop, which advertised combing, cutting, and shaving, along with bloodletting for those suffering all manner of physical disorders, and an apothecary's genteel establishment. Situated next to a public house, the apothecary had an appropriate location for a thriving business.

Dante came to a halt before a small, two-storied building with ornately carved gables and long, narrow mullioned windows. Descending beneath a carved wooden sign that creaked with the sea breeze, he took the several steps down to the entrance, but then Dante Leighton paused and went back to stare at the sign, a strange expression on his face as he looked up at it.

Alastair Marlowe nearly bumped into that broad back when Dante stopped so abruptly. Following his gaze, Alastair glanced up and he drew in his breath sharply.

The wooden sign was carved in the shape of a woman. She was dressed in a flowing white gown, and beneath the phantom shape was the name of the tavern: The Pale Lady of the Ruins.

Alastair swallowed nervously. But Dante Leighton said nothing. He just stared at the sign a moment longer, then walked down the steps into the tavern. Alastair followed his captain into the shadowy hall beyond. A small staircase filled the space at the end of the narrow hall and led to the second floor and whatever rooms the tavern had for overnight guests. Following the sound of voices, Dante turned to the right. The coffee room was filled with men sitting and standing as they drank ale and talked of the weather.

Seemingly oblivious to the men and to the strange silence which had fallen over the garrulous group, Dante Leighton walked across the room, coming to a halt at the counter. An aproned man stood behind the counter beside a large keg, from which he filled a tankard.

"Afternoon to ye and welcome to the Pale Lady," the man greeted them. "What's your pleasure?" he asked while eyeing the two well-dressed gentlemen curiously. He didn't know them, but he suspected they'd have plenty of coin. "Ye be strangers to Merleigh?"

"No, not really," Dante replied, ordering two ales.

"Oh? Well, ye might have noticed then that the tavern be under new management. Used to be called the Royal Oak and Ivy, but when I bought the place—I'm from Barnstaple—I changed the name. Changed the serving girls, too. Skin and bones, the others were. Can't be workin' the roses out of their cheeks, eh?" he confided with a chuckle as one of his buxom young maids threaded her way through the crowded room, much to the appreciation of the patrons. They stopped her to place more orders, and the cunning innkeeper grinned.

" 'Tis from local legend, the name," the innkeeper continued conversationally while he filled their tankards and then handed them across to the tall, gray-eyed gentleman and his friend, who was looking on the peaked side. "Seems as if this highborn lady, from a great family she was, even named the town after them, they did, well," he continued, glancing around just in case anyone was eavesdropping, "she jumped off the cliff over by the castle ruins. Merdraco, 'tis called. Well, they say she was so brokenhearted over her blackguard son, and him a marquis, that she took her own life. But what's got everyone scared senseless is that her ghost has been seen wanderin' along that cliff, cryin' and moanin' fer her son. Figure namin' my tavern after her was a wise business move. No one will be forgettin' the name, that's fer sure," he said with a widening grin of satisfaction. But it didn't seem the gentleman found his story amusing, and it was only then that he became aware of the strange silence in his usually noisy coffee room.

Glancing beyond the two figures, he frowned thoughtfully, wondering what was amiss. It seemed all his regular customers were staring at the two strangers, and at the tall, gray-eyed one in particular.

The innkeeper cleared his throat nervously. Something was wrong. "Ah, don't believe I caught the name," he said. "Like to greet my guests proper like, I do," he added, his uneasiness growing when the gray-eyed gent smiled slightly before turning around to face the curious patrons of The Pale Lady of the Ruins.

Taking a sip of his ale, Dante Leighton eyed the men who had been watching him so intently. "Some of you may know who I am. If not, then allow me to introduce myself. I am Dante Leighton, Lord Jacqobi. I have returned to Merdraco. But in my absence, the house and estate have fallen into disrepair."

That was putting it mildly, thought Alastair as he took a hefty swig of ale.

"I will hire anyone interested in working. There's good, honest money to be made," Dante told the group of silent men.

"Reckon I'm one of them who remembers ye, Lord Jacqobi.

Only then ye wasn't one to be payin' your debts," a weathered-looking man commented from a table directly in front of where Dante Leighton was standing. "Dunno as how I have any reason to be believin' otherwise today, although I'll be admittin' ye've got courage in comin' back here. Figure there might be some folk hereabouts who haven't forgotten ye, or what ye was accused of doin'. Ye didn't leave many friends around these parts, milord."

Alastair wiped the back of his hand across his lips and decided to keep a close eye on the surly man who had questioned the captain's honor.

But Dante Leighton surprised Alastair. He merely nodded acquiescence to the impertinent fellow's remarks. Then his hand disappeared into his coat pocket and, a second later, a small leather bag landed dead center on the man's table. "Open it," Dante Leighton said, sounding like he had when barking an order to the helmsman aboard the *Sea Dragon*. The man picked up the bag, albeit gingerly. Untying the cord, he poured the contents of the bag onto the table, the sound signaling only one thing—money.

"Every man who comes to work for me will be paid daily for the work he does. There will be no promise of money. There *will be* money. But do not be lulled into thinking that this will be easy money, for I shall expect any man who works for me to carry his fair share. I worked hard for this money, and so I shall expect you to work hard for yours. Anyone who does not, will no longer work for me," Dante warned them. The man who remembered the dissolute young lord who had squandered away his fortune couldn't believe that this was the same Marquis of Jacqobi.

This was a man who seemed accustomed to speaking his mind without fear or hesitancy, William Brownwell thought as he eyed the tall, muscular man with the bronzed face. He liked to think he judged another man accurately by the look in his eye. As he met Dante Leighton's pale-eyed stare, he saw something he liked. The eyes didn't slide away. They continued to meet his squarely, and William Brownwell read a sense of purpose in Dante Leighton.

"Should anyone doubt my word that I can pay you well for your services, then you have my permission to talk with my bankers. A large sum of money has been deposited in the bank here in Merleigh, as well as the banks in Westlea Abbot and in Bristol and in London, where my solicitor would be pleased to respond to your inquiries."

"I can assure you, gentlemen," Alastair heard himself saying, "that Dante Leighton is indeed a man of his word. I was the supercargo aboard the *Sea Dragon,* a privateer that engaged the enemy on countless occasions, and never turned tail and ran because her captain, Dante Leighton, would never admit defeat. And I can promise you that he had the respect and admiration of all his crew. You may rest assured that if the captain makes a promise, he keeps it," Alastair concluded, the light of battle in his eyes. He was embarrassed at being outspoken, but the time sometimes came when a man had to say what he felt.

"Could be as rich as the King himself, and I still wouldn't dirty me hands workin' fer the likes o' him!" an angry voice called from the back of the room, successfully gaining the attention of the same men who had looked impressed after Alastair Marlowe's outburst.

"Jack Shelby's me friend, and that's somethin' the rest o' ye ought not to be fergettin'," the man warned them. An ugly glint in his eye, he pushed his way forward through the group and came to stand in front of Dante Leighton. "Reckon Jack Shelby is one to be rememberin' who's his friend and who ain't. Reckon I might even be able to remind him," the lout said, looking around the room as if memorizing the individual faces.

"I wouldn't worry too much about Jack Shelby," Dante spoke quietly, unimpressed.

"Oh, and how's that, *milord?*" the man wanted to know as he eyed Dante Leighton up and down contemptuously before spitting at his booted feet.

"Jack Shelby's days are numbered. You can take that message to him," Dante told the red-faced man, whose anger seemed about to get the best of him. Then, before the man knew what had happened, the indolent-looking Marquis of Jacqobi reached out and grabbed both his arms. Pulling them behind the fellow's back, he locked them together at the wrists with one of his own hands. Then his lordship's other hand locked around the back of the malcontent's neck, and the man was escorted to the door. The other men were delighted, for they knew the bully all too well and enjoyed seeing him brought down a peg.

Out the door and up the steps he was hustled, and the man promised himself, as he was propelled into the street, that he'd not forget the laughing voices. He fell to his knees, his hat sailing onto the cobblestones next to him.

"Ye'll be sorry, m'lord," he vowed, picking himself up and glaring at the open doorway. "And I'll not be fergettin' your faces, either! Ye'll be sorry. Ye just wait and see. Just wait until I'm tellin' Jack Shelby of this. Ye'll see!" he hollered as he hurried down the street, glancing back over his shoulder time and again. The sound of laughter fueled his rage.

Dante Leighton turned back to face the men standing there watching him, a different expression in their eyes. They were really seeing him for the first time, and not the rakish young lord he once had been.

"You may also pass the word that I am looking for tenants to farm the lands adjacent to Merdraco. The rents will be low, and as your landlord, I shall see that the farmhouses are in good condition. Anyone who works Leighton lands will find it a good living, and you and your families will be under my protection," the master of Merdraco told them.

"Didn't think them lands belonged to Merdraco anymore. Thought they were Sir Miles Sandbourne's."

Dante smiled. It was not a pleasant smile. "The lands that once belonged to Merdraco belong to my estate again. Sir Miles Sandbourne no longer owns one foot of Leighton land."

William Brownwell held out the bag of coins that Dante had tossed on the table. "Here's your money back," he said. Alastair thought the man was rejecting Dante's offer, but then he added, "At least until I've done a day's work and earned my share of it. Then it'll be mine."

Dante took the leather bag. "I'll look forward to seeing you at Merdraco, then," Dante said.

"Aye, ye can that. Reckon a lot of folk will be pleased to hear that ye be their new landlord. Sir Miles wasn't very popular. Raised the rents every year, he did. Reckon that Houston Kirby returned to Merdraco with ye?" William Brownwell asked casually. "Used to be a friend of mine until he disappeared about the same time ye did, m'lord. Always figured he might have caught up with ye somewhere."

"Aye, that he did, and he's come home now, as I have," Dante Leighton responded, his cold, pale eyes showing the first warmth William Brownwell had seen in them.

"Beggin' your pardon, but does Jack Shelby know ye've returned?" he asked. He wanted to know what lay in front of him, since it seemed he was walking onto a battlefield.

"Yes, as a matter of fact we met face to face the other evening at the Bishop. He left rather abruptly, but he knows what to expect," Dante told the man, figuring he had a right to know what to expect if he was going to work at Merdraco.

"Ye been stayin' at the Bishop?" asked a man who probably knew more than he should, for he knew the smugglers were fond of drinking ale there.

"Yes, Sam and Dora Lascombe have been most hospitable," Dante replied.

"Aye, reckon so," William Brownwell agreed. "Sam Lascombe's no fool. Reckon I'll have to be stoppin' by there one of these days. Pay our respects to Dora, will ye? Lot of us thought it a real shame what happened to her brother. Aye, reckon there be a lot of us who think it's about time for a change," William Brownwell suggested with a meaningful glance around at his friends.

Dante Leighton eyed the men speculatively, then nodded. "I do believe there will be some changes now. It has been a pleasure, gentlemen," he said, and, with a slight smile, he tossed the bag of coins to the startled innkeeper, who wasn't so startled that he missed catching it in his big palm. "See that the gentlemen here have all the ale and food they wish."

"Ye be most generous, m'lord," William Brownwell commented as he noted the men who were looking kindly at their benefactor.

"Not really," Dante Leighton said with a grin. "They will be cursing me soon enough when I have them sweating for every shilling they earn. But perhaps they won't really hate me when they remember that I can be most generous and that I deal fairly with any man who deals fairly with me."

"Aye, m'lord, reckon ye've learned a lot about life in your travels," William Brownwell said slowly. "And I reckon we might deal quite nicely together, now that ye've returned to Merdraco."

"Aye, that we shall," Dante agreed, and with a slight inclination of his head, he walked away from what remained of the group standing outside of The Pale Lady of the Ruins, the others already having disappeared inside for their fill of ale.

"Reckon things are goin' to be changin' around here fast enough now that yon master has returned to stir up trouble," William Brownwell muttered as he watched Dante Leighton striding down High Street as though he hadn't a care in the world.

"Kirby, I do not see whortleberries listed here," Rhea was saying to the little steward, who was selecting several baskets full of the dark blue berries.

"That's because Hallie ain't from Devonshire, m'lady. They're berries picked from the moors, and a sweeter tart covered in clotted cream ye've yet to find anywhere in the realm," Houston Kirby declared.

"And what of this cider, Kirby? Hallie will never be able to use so much. Perhaps we should only order about half this amount," she suggested kindly.

"Ah, m'lady, if ye knew how long 'tis been since I had a good swallow of mulled cider," Houston Kirby said with such a pitiful look on his face that Rhea almost felt sorry for him. "Of course, next year I'll have made my own. Packs quite a wallop, if I do say so myself, m'lady. We used to have the makin's for it at Merdraco, but I'll most likely have to get my own wheel and trough. And of course we can't use the straw from the stables at Merdraco. 'Twould have us all six feet under by nightfall."

"What's wrong with the straw at Merdraco?" Francis asked, eyeing the little steward as if he'd lost his mind.

"It has to be clean straw, Lord Francis," Kirby replied, looking at the young lord and wondering where he'd been all his life. "Ye see, I take the apples—selected by me for their juiciness—and ground them up with a big stone wheel in this specially made, round stone trough. Then I place the pulp between layers of *clean* straw, m'lord, and press it in the cider press. The juice runs out into the kieve, a flat tub. I'll leave it there for about four or five days. That's where it starts to get that kick. I skim off anything that's drifted up to the top, and then get myself some nice oak casks and fill them up with the brew and let them sit. Won't touch them for a good while, of course."

"Of course," Francis agreed.

"Aye. Next year I'll let ye have one of the first sips of the first cider I've brewed in over fifteen years. It oughta be somethin', m'lord," he confided with a chuckle. "Can hardly wait for the wassailin'. Ye be sure and be here at Merdraco for the eve of Twelfth Night."

Francis managed a smile. "I'd be honored," he said, privately vowing he'd not be anywhere nearby come January.

"Well, let's see," Rhea said as she glanced down at the long list of items she had ordered sent to the lodge. "Eggs, chickens, hams, cheese, veal, haddock, potatoes, celery, carrots, peas . . ." she said, her eyes scanning the list. Looking up, she caught sight of Dante and Alastair making their way down the street. She waved, but they didn't see her, for at that moment a small boy ran up to them and yanked on Dante's sleeve. He stopped and glanced down, and as Rhea watched she saw the boy hand him a piece of folded paper. Dante glanced at it quickly before tossing a coin to the lad. When next Rhea looked at Dante's hand, the note had disappeared, and he and Alastair were continuing toward the marketplace.

Rhea waved again, and this time he saw her. His tall figure wove through the crowded square toward her.

"I hope I haven't kept you waiting," he said, noting the crates of vegetables and fruits being loaded into a nearby cart. "Did you have any trouble?" he asked casually, remembering the surreptitious glances cast their way as they rode into Merleigh.

"You should know by now, Dante, that Rhea could charm a smile from the devil himself," Francis remarked jokingly, then thought perhaps his sister had done so just then, for a slight smile curved Dante Leighton's mouth.

"We had no difficulties. How did it go with you?" Rhea asked nervously, for she had dreaded his first encounter with the villagers who had been so quick to turn their backs on him years before.

"It went far better than I thought it would," Dante admitted, his smile widening. "So you had better buy even more cider, Kirby," he told the startled little steward, who actually looked a little guilty.

"Don't look so surprised. That's all you've been talking about since we set foot back in Devonshire. Your cider had better be as good as I remember," Dante warned him. "Where are Robin and Conny? We should be heading back to Merdraco." He glanced around for a glimpse of two small figures and was rewarded by the sight of Conny Brady and Robin Dominick. They were running as fast as their short legs could carry them, trying to outrun several village boys who were tossing rotten fruit at them.

Rhea shook her head as she saw Robin duck behind a rotund woman, waiting his chance to take aim at one of the village boys. The tomato he had been holding so gingerly found its mark, but Robin didn't wait to make certain, and was already hotfooting it after Conny, who had thrown his potato with unerring aim and retreated toward the safety of those familiar figures in the distance. He knew the captain wouldn't let this village riffraff accost him and Robin.

Rhea stood beside Dante, laughing with him as they watched Houston Kirby and Alastair try to stop the horseplay. She caught sight of a scarlet figure hurrying up High Street, scarlet feathers waving with every step, and Rhea wondered if the note Dante had received had been from Bess Seacombe. Rhea couldn't help but find it strange that Dante had said nothing about it. For the first time since they had wed, she wondered what he was hiding.

> *To many a watchful night.*
> Shakespeare

Chapter 27

"I must say you were rather unfriendly the other day," Dante commented, his quiet tones sounding like thunder in the quiet night.

Sir Morgan Lloyd spun round, startled by the amused voice coming out of the shadows. "Do you always arrive early for a rendezvous?" he demanded, put out that the captain of the *Sea Dragon* had managed to catch him off guard.

"Apparently not much earlier than you do," Dante responded while moving into the revealing moonlight, for Sir Morgan was a good quarter of an hour early for their meeting.

"I trust you are here because you received my note?" Sir Morgan inquired.

"Naturally. I do not leave a warm bed at midnight to traipse about the countryside without a reason," Dante responded easily. "I had been expecting to hear from you. I had hoped that your hostility of the other day was feigned."

"Had I truly believed you responsible for my brother's murder, I fear I would have taken the law onto myself and called you out, Captain," Sir Morgan answered quite seriously.

"I was very sorry to hear of his death," Dante said. In the pale moonlight Sir Morgan's face looked like it was chiseled out of marble.

"His murder," Sir Morgan corrected.

"I feel a little responsible because his ship was wrecked in Dragon's Cove. The waters *are* notoriously treacherous," Dante said, "and even the best of captains can run his ship aground," he suggested as an alternative to murder.

"He made it safely to shore, Captain. It was on shore that he met his death," Sir Morgan reminded him sharply.

"Could not the ship's running aground have been simple mischance? There are many wrecks along this shore, and when that happens, the villagers come from miles around to salvage what they can. I've seen a horde of them descend on a ship foundering on the rocks and strip her clean within an hour. I have even seen scavengers strip the dead of their belongings. If anyone survived the wreck and made it to shore, he most likely would have been too weak to put up a struggle if someone wanted his possessions. Perhaps that is what happened to your brother. Or, since he was an officer of the Crown, his attacker panicked and killed him," Dante said. His explanation was quite reasonable and had his listener been anyone but the late captain's brother, he might have been persuaded.

"My brother was betrayed. Indeed, he suspected the traitor. He told me as much in a letter he wrote shortly before his death. But Ben made a mistake somewhere and lost his life as a result," Sir Morgan said bitterly. "He was a good captain, and he knew this coast well. He would not have run aground in Dragon's Cove; he was too good, too cautious. No, something drew him in there, and if my speculations are correct, he was unaware of his position until it was too late. I suspect he was misled by the smugglers' signals. Someone flashed him a signal from shore, knowing he would sail onto the reefs. I think his murder was plotted carefully because he was close to discovering who the traitor was."

Leaning against one of the fallen stone dragons, Dante eyed Sir Morgan through the gloom. "Why did you not suspect me of being involved? As you said, I might be behind all of this, even though I have been absent from Merdraco for many years. And, even if I were not directly involved, my sympathies might very well remain with the smugglers because I used to be a smuggler. Many of them are poor farmers and villagers just trying to make a living, and I might see no harm in their activities. So why are you taking me into your trust, Sir Morgan?" Dante asked flatly.

Sir Morgan ran a tired hand across his forehead, massaging his temples. "Because, as the master of a ship, you would never wreck one. It would go against your blood, Captain," Sir Morgan said simply. "Once you have known a command of your own, you can never shirk responsibility for your ship or your crew, no matter what the circumstances. I cannot believe you would ever put a ship or her crew in jeopardy. I sailed against you long enough to know what manner of man you are, and you are not the sort who would betray another by so cowardly an act. You played a game with Bertie Mackay in the Straits, but you knew he and his crew were never in any real danger. You are simply not a murderer.

"I never thought that the day would dawn when we would be allies, but I think it has, hasn't it, Captain? As the master of Merdraco, you should be especially interested in seeing justice served," Sir Morgan spoke quietly, meaningfully.

"You've heard about Merdraco, then?"

"Yes, word of an atrocity like that spreads quickly. I am sorry it happened, but I would think it gave you good reason for seeing the smugglers put out of business. Especially Jack Shelby," Sir Morgan Lloyd said slowly.

Dante nodded. "You also are aware that Jack Shelby truly believes he has good cause to commit crimes against me?" Dante asked, wondering just how much Sir Morgan had learned.

"He is the father of the woman you were suspected of murdering. I must say, however, that time seems to have dulled some memories and old hatreds. I was in Merleigh earlier this evening, and I happened to be drinking in a popular tavern there and heard some flattering things about you, Captain. You and Mr. Marlowe paid the place a visit earlier in the afternoon and escorted one of Jack Shelby's men off the premises most emphatically. Your actions were well appreciated by the majority. They seem to think Jack Shelby is half mad and has been for fifteen years. They also seem to think that they might have judged you harshly over the death of his daughter. Some remember her as being free with her favors. They say that just about anyone—including a jealous wife or two—might have killed the girl."

"I suspect they are willing to give me the benefit of the doubt now," Dante commented, unimpressed, "only because I have returned a wealthy man."

Sir Morgan smiled sadly. "You are bitter. I suppose that is only natural. You are also quite modest, for you made a considerable impression on these villagers, beyond your wealth. Your laying down of law took them by surprise, as did your authoritative presence, which is, I gather, just the opposite impression of the one they had of you.

"I rather hate to spoil things for you, Captain, but I need to cast suspicion on you if I am to mislead the smugglers. I want them to grow careless, especially one man in particular, and then I'll catch them in the act and have those responsible for wrecking the *Hindrance* brought to justice," Sir Morgan promised.

"You and your brother were very close?"

"Yes, we were. My father died when we were just boys. Ben was younger than I. I suppose, as the elder, I always felt responsible for both my mother and my brother. But now they are both gone, and I am left with a promise I made to my mother a long time ago, and that was to watch out for my brother. I now shall keep that promise in the only way left to me."

"This might seem strange coming from me," Dante said, "but make certain you have the right men and that you have irrefutable evidence. I should hate to see your desire for revenge bring you to ruin."

"Except for the mysterious mastermind behind the Sons of Belial, I know exactly who I am after," Sir Morgan reassured him.

"Jack Shelby."

"Yes," Sir Morgan said.

"And, perhaps, your Lieutenant Handley?" Dante guessed.

"I thought I was so subtle the other day," Sir Morgan said in dismay.

"Threatening to put me adrift in a rowboat is hardly subtle, but your dislike of the man was only too obvious to me, although I doubt the lieutenant realizes it. Do you think he is behind this smuggling gang?"

"He may well be the man who has planned every move the Sons have made. But I don't quite think the lieutenant, unless he is a brilliant actor, has the intelligence to run this operation. I think he is merely following orders . . . like the rest of them," Sir Morgan said thoughtfully.

"What of Jack Shelby?" Dante questioned. "He's a cunning devil."

"It is a possibility, but he seems too hotheaded to have planned the wrecking of the *Hindrance* and to have set up this web of smuggling runs. No, I think he takes his orders from someone else, too."

"And you would like the smugglers to think that you suspect me of running their operation. No doubt that will bring Jack Shelby much amusement," Dante predicted. "If I agree to say nothing of your suspicions, then I want to be a part of whatever trap you are setting," Dante bargained. "Either that, or I'll do some exploring on my own in order to dig up evidence against Jack Shelby."

"Since there are not many people around here to whom I would trust my life, I think I will find your assistance helpful," Sir Morgan commented wisely. It seemed as if two former enemies were indeed becoming allies, but for different reasons.

"I am afraid Rhea will have a hard time forgiving you for the other day," Dante told him.

"I regretted having to upset her so, but I was doing it to impress the lieutenant. Perhaps, when all of this is over, and if we are still here to talk about it, she will allow me a chance to explain. Perhaps she would even invite me to tea," Sir Morgan asked, and Dante was surprised to hear the note of longing in his voice.

"You will find that Rhea is a very understanding person.

Once she understands the facts, she will forgive you, Captain, never fear."

"I shall look forward then to that cup of tea," Sir Morgan said on a lighter note. "But what of Lady Bess Seacombe?" he asked suddenly, startling Dante.

"Bess?"

Sir Morgan caught the hesitancy in Dante's voice, as well as his casual use of her name. "You sound as if you know her well. I ask only because I like to know what to expect from a person."

"Bess and I grew up together. In fact, if you haven't already heard about it, she and I were supposed to marry. She changed her mind. Not that I blame her, for I was debt-ridden at the time and under suspicion of murder," Dante added, thinking the latter explanation gave Bess a legitimate reason for breaking off their engagement.

"No, I hadn't heard that. I suppose you know that she is a widow?" Sir Morgan asked curiously, wondering if there might still be warm feelings between the two.

"Yes, I had heard," Dante remarked, but didn't say how.

"She is also very much in debt," Sir Morgan informed him.

"No, I didn't know that," Dante said slowly, his mind going back to the painful time when she had spurned him because he had little hope of keeping her in the style she believed she deserved. "What happened? Do you know?"

"Bad investments by her late husband. Apparently he was a bit of a fool and invested in some crazy scheme involving a plantation in the Indies. Lost his shirt, too, as did several other people around here. Then the bank he had invested in closed. Seems the largest account was suddenly withdrawn and that caught the investors short. They had mismanaged their capital, made bad loans, and finally became insolvent. A rumor got started that they could not honor their other depositors' accounts, and there was a run on the bank. In order to stay out of gaol, Sir Harry and some other investors, including Sir Miles Sandbourne, who is a very respectable gentleman, had to make the bank solvent out of their own pockets. From what I understand, it nearly bankrupted all of them." Sir Morgan said all of this without any apparent pity for the late Sir Harry Seacombe. If he had a wife and a young daughter and son, he would not have taken any chances with their welfare. "It also seems Sir Harry cared more for the well-being of his hounds and horses than he did his family. Spent lavishly on his stables. I wonder why the woman married him," Sir Morgan said with an exasperated sigh.

Dante was strangely silent. At last he said quietly, "I remember Harry Seacombe. You are right, he was a bit of a fool, but he was harmless enough. I can understand why Bess married him. Fifteen years ago he was very wealthy and handsome and knew how to amuse people," Dante remembered.

"Lady Bess is still a very attractive woman, wouldn't you agree?" Sir Morgan asked casually.

Dante cocked his head slightly. "Yes, I would say she is as beautiful as she was when I left Devonshire," Dante admitted. "Why? Are you interested in the lady?"

Sir Morgan, had Dante been able to see his face clearly, would have appeared uncomfortable. He surprised Dante by stating coldly, "My interest is official, for I think she is involved with the smugglers right up to that slender throat of hers. And I would hate to see any woman's neck stretched," Sir Morgan admitted. Dante got the impression, however, that he would indeed stand by and watch that very thing happen if it meant bringing his brother's murderers to justice. As far as Sir Morgan Lloyd was concerned, no one involved would go unpunished.

"Bess? Involved with the smugglers? That would mean being involved with Jack Shelby, and I do not see Bess giving the likes of Jack Shelby the time of day," Dante scoffed.

"When a person is in need of money, trying to keep food on the table, that person might do just about anything," Sir Morgan replied. "Look at yourself. You changed from an indolent young lord who gambled away his inheritance into a man who fought hard," Sir Morgan reminded him.

Dante remained silent for a moment. "I'll not assist you in sending Bess to the gallows."

"You still care for her that much?" Sir Morgan asked harshly. Whether it was because he was thinking of Rhea or because he was thinking of his brother, perhaps even he didn't know.

"I have my reasons," Dante replied.

"I see," said Sir Morgan.

"No, I don't think you do, but it doesn't matter, for I shall help you catch Jack Shelby and the Sons of Belial," Dante promised. "What exactly is your plan?" he asked. Only the pale moon observed the shadowy figures and heard what was said.

"There, there, Kit," Rhea said reassuringly, pressing her lips against his soft curls. "Mama's here," she spoke softly while gently rocking him in her arms. But her eyes were staring at the empty space in the bed where Dante ought to have been lying.

Opening her nightdress, she guided Kit's little head to her breast and sat back against the pillows while he nursed, his fine fringe of lashes fluttering against his cheeks as his eyes began to close. Rhea continued to sit there rocking him while she hummed softly, and soon his tiny hands stopped their kneading. His head rested heavily against her breast while he slept in her arms, contented.

Carefully Rhea placed him back in his cradle and arranged the fine wool blankets around his shoulders, rocking the cradle for a few minutes when he gurgled and threatened to waken. Then he sighed and slept.

Pulling her gown together, Rhea walked to the window. A bright silver stream of moonlight poured into the room, and it was almost like standing in daylight. She stared out on the wild disorder of the gardens below.

Where was he? With dread she remembered the other night when she had awakened and found the bed beside her empty. Rhea strained to see into the night, but the gardens and trees seemed to darken and crowd closer to the lodge as she watched. In the distance the shimmering sea looked blindingly brighter. The shadows around the lodge seemed to be moving. Rhea rubbed her eyes, staring harder at the line of trees that suddenly seemed to hide secrets.

She gasped as she watched a tall shadow grow taller, then detach itself from the copse and move closer to the lodge. Then she sighed, for she knew that walk. As he drew closer, she could almost make out his familiar features. She smiled in relief. She was acting as foolish as Robin and Conny, and she would never listen again to their stories of ghosts and Wild Huntsmen.

Rhea continued to watch as Dante's figure approached, then disappeared from view as he walked along the path leading to the lodge entrance. She was about to turn away from the window when she saw another shadow sliding away from the trees, and her heart began pounding deafeningly, for the figure was a lady dressed in flowing white robes.

Dread rising inside her, Rhea knew she was seeing the spectral figure of the Pale Lady of the Ruins, an omen that meant certain death.

Guess if you can, choose if you daré.
Pierre Corneille

Chapter 28

IN the cold, revealing light of dawn, Rhea found herself questioning what she had seen the night before. She still believed that she had seen something moving through the trees, but she had said nothing about it to Dante. Her mind was occupied with something more important, for he had denied leaving the lodge. Or, rather, he neglected saying anything about leaving the lodge for a midnight assignation, which she was beginning to believe had been his purpose in stealing away.

She found herself remembering the note he had been handed in Merleigh and had also neglected to tell her about. Had he, perhaps, gone to meet the person who had sent him that secret missive? And could that person possibly have been what she

saw from the window? In the back of her mind she kept remembering that scarlet figure she had seen in Merleigh at about
the time Dante received the note.

Whatever he was involved in, he apparently had no intention
of telling her, for, upon entering their room, he had met her
inquiring gaze and said nothing about leaving the lodge. He
had explained that he couldn't sleep and had gone downstairs
to get some brandy. Indeed, he was holding a dram glass of
the burnished liquid. As he stood there in his bare feet, his
nightshirt tucked into his breeches, one would almost have
believed his story. But Rhea suspected that his muddied boots
and his coat were lying outside the door and that the brandy
was for taking the chill out of his bones. But she doubted that
he'd been out searching for the smuggling gang, for there was
a moon riding high, and he had said that the smugglers preferred
to work in darkness.

Dante asked what had awakened her, and her explanation
that she was feeding their son seemed to relieve his mind. He
smiled at her and seemed to relax. Then he placed the glass
on the bedside table and, sitting down next to her, took her
into his arms as if nothing out of the ordinary had occurred.

Rhea had felt the pressure of his lips against the side of her
neck. His hands moved caressingly across her shoulders before
encircling her waist. His brandy-scented breath was warm
against her face, then his lips found hers for a long moment.
Despite herself, Rhea felt that quivering sensation growing
inside of her, that need to respond to his every desire. But she
would not do so this time, she argued with herself, not with
a lie between them. Especially not with the suspicions she felt,
for that would make a mockery of their love.

So she had freed her lips from his and turned her face away.
It was the first time she had denied him since they had declared
their love to one another. Rhea thought she would remember
forever the stunned expression on his handsome face. Their
eyes had met for a long moment, and then he released her
abruptly.

Getting to his feet, he stood there with an expression of hurt
bewilderment, and Rhea had wanted to reach out to him and
hold him against her. But something prevented it.

"What is wrong?" he demanded, his hand rubbing through
the wiry hairs covering his chest where his shirt had parted.

"Nothing," she lied, unable to meet his eyes.

"You have never been a very good liar, my dear," he'd said softly, and grasping her chin in his cupped hand, he raised her face to his searching gaze. "I shall ask you again, Rhea. What is wrong?"

Rhea could still feel the tenderness where she had bitten her lip while wondering whether she should keep silent, or tell the truth. But she had never been one for subterfuge, and so she stared him straight in the eye and said quite distinctly, "I was standing at the window, Dante. I saw you coming through the gardens from across the lawns. I know you went out. You needn't have lied to me, Dante."

Dante had stood there, a strange expression on his face, an expression of indecision, and his silence convinced her that he did indeed have something to hide.

Finally he spoke. "Yes, I did leave the lodge. I went for a walk," he had told her, which she suspected was only part of the truth.

"Did you not meet anyone?" Rhea asked hesitantly, and Dante laughed.

"Just whom would I be meeting at this hour?" he demanded, almost daring her to accuse him.

Then, at Rhea's stricken look, he knelt down before her and took her hands between his.

"Rhea, little daffadilly," he said, forcing her to meet his ardent gaze, "you need never be jealous of another woman. Is that what you fear? Believe that, and trust me. I once asked you to promise me that you would never turn away from me, no matter what you heard, and even if you had doubts. As surely as the sun will rise tomorrow, you may believe in one thing, and that is that I shall always love you." Meeting those pale gray eyes, Rhea had believed him.

A little later, when he took her in his arms, she did not draw away from him. And in the heat of passion, she forgot to tell him about the pale figure she had seen moving through the woods. Or perhaps she did not forget. Perhaps she did not want to know the truth.

Rhea glanced around her at the sparkling beauty of the lodge that would be her home for most of the coming year, and she knew a deep sense of contentment. She had risen early, before the servants, and in the silence of the first light of day, she enjoyed a rare moment alone. How different the lodge hall looked, she thought as she touched the golden daffodils gracing the oak table, their reflection shining in the brilliant waxed surface. A tall case clock chimed the early hour as Rhea walked over to the hearth. Several tall-backed cane chairs and a pair of velvet upholstered winged chairs were positioned in a semi-circle around the clean hearth.

Rhea stood for a moment staring up at the painting above the mantelpiece. Dante himself had hung it with great care. It was the portrait of a very beautiful woman and a boy, the sea mists swirling around the woman's figure while the boy seemed to stand apart, his small hand clinging to the folds of the woman's silken gown. Her flaxen hair was tousled and blowing free while she stared down with compassionate, soft gray eyes. And the color of her eyes was reflected in the young boy's eyes. Until Rhea gazed at that portrait, she had never seen such an innocent, trusting expression in Dante's eyes. Time had banished that expression and replaced it with one of cynical wariness, and Rhea cried for that loss of innocence.

She sighed, thinking of the tragedy that had befallen those two people so many years after the portrait was painted.

"Aye, 'twas a real shame, what happened," a voice commented sadly from behind her.

Rhea gasped in surprise and spun around. "Kirby! You scared the life out of me," Rhea said, but felt an overwhelming relief as she stared at his familiar face.

"I'm sorry, m'lady. I didn't mean to startle ye," Kirby apologized as he came forward carrying a small silver tray, a china cup and saucer sitting squarely in the center. "I heard someone down here and came to investigate, but ye was so lost in your thoughts that I didn't disturb ye. I thought ye might welcome a cup of tea." He set the tray down on the tea table beside one of the winged chairs, then waited for her to sit down before handing her the brimming cup.

Rhea smiled. "You must be a wizard, Kirby, always anticipating a person's thoughts. This tastes wonderful," Rhea complimented him.

"I took the liberty, m'lady, of preparin' it for ye. I reckon by now I know how ye like your tea," he said with a grin.

"You should have brought a cup for yourself," she told him, wondering if he would ever remember that he was no longer a servant.

"Oh, m'lady, what would the captain think if he was to come down and find us in here sippin' tea?" Kirby asked, grinning widely. He truly did believe it would be improper, especially with her still clad in her nightdress.

"He would think that two friends were sharing tea," Rhea responded, but her smile didn't come quite as easily as it should have. "What was she like, Kirby?" Rhea asked, glancing up at the portrait.

Houston Kirby sighed deeply. "Ah, the Lady Elayne, she was a saint, she was. The kindest, most thoughtful lady I've ever met, exceptin' for yourself, m'lady. And, of course, Her Grace," Kirby added, for the Duchess of Camareigh was a lady he would not soon forget. "The Lady Elayne adored Dante. Lived for him, she did. I imagine 'twas because she wasn't all that happy with Lord John. He was a fine man, but he didn't care for anythin' except books and paintin's and all them things he liked to collect. Loved fine things, he did, and spent more time lookin' over his sculptures and paintin's than he did with his family. Even collected engravin's, medals, gems, all sorts of little gewgaws. And, beggin' your pardon, m'lady, just in case ye happen to run across one, he brought back some statues of half-naked women and naked gents from one of them foreign countries he visited on his Grand Tour. Remember like 'twas yesterday, I do. Nearly sent the old housekeeper, her bein' a maiden lady, into an apoplectic fit when she caught sight of them bare-as-s-ah, forgive me, m'lady," Houston Kirby choked.

"A dilettante," Rhea remarked, unembarrassed.

Houston Kirby looked embarrassed. "M'lady, really, he wasn't like that at all."

Rhea smiled. "I meant no offense. A dilettante is someone who has a love and appreciation of the arts. It sounds as if Lord John wished to surround himself with beauty. I think that is admirable."

"Oh, is that what it means, then?" Houston Kirby said, rubbing his chin thoughtfully. "Aye, reckon ye be right. I sometimes got the feelin' that Lord John looked upon Lady

Elayne as one of his possessions. And he was always pushin' away Lord Dante. He was a high-strung young lad, and I guess Lord John thought the lad would break one of his figurines or somethin'. Can still remember the hurt expression on the captain's face every time he was told to get out by an irate Lord John. All the lad wanted was a wee bit of affection. Lord John was the same with Lady Elayne, and if ye ask me, she was a far sight prettier than one of them marble statues without their proper clothes on," sniffed the little steward. "Reminds me a lot of ye, m'lady," Houston Kirby said unthinkingly, then turned a bright, painful red. "Oh, m'lady, I didn't mean what it sounded like I said," he said, flustered.

"Oh, Kirby, I know what you mean. I am honored that I remind you of Lady Elayne," Rhea told him, her lips twitching.

Houston Kirby stared up at the portrait, feeling the same strange melancholy that Rhea had been feeling. "I wish with all of my heart, m'lady, that ye'll be happier than Lady Elayne was. I'd hate to see ye suffer the way she did. Sometimes I feel it would be worth hangin' for, just to see Sir Miles punished for what he did to her.

"Never liked him, I didn't," Kirby said. "Never trusted the man. Always figured I couldn't go wrong if I believed just the opposite of what he said. Always lyin' and connivin'. Usin' people, he did, then he'd sit back and smile that evil grin. He took real pleasure in sellin' them things of Lord John's.

"Aye, 'twas probably a blessin' Lady Elayne died. Only way she could escape him," Houston Kirby declared. "Always thought it real queer like, 'cause it was almost as if Sir Miles both loved and hated the Lady Elayne." Then, glancing around nervously, he added in a whisper, "Ye don't really think her ghost is hauntin' the cliffs, d'ye, m'lady? I'd hate to be thinkin' she wasn't at peace," Kirby said, his face screwed up with worry. Rhea was about to reassure him, despite the fact that she had seen that pale figure in the darkness, when Kirby suddenly cried out. Jumping up in surprise, he felt something rubbing against his stockinged legs.

"Jamaica!" he growled, picking the big tom up in his arms. "Ye old reprobate. How did ye get in here? Where have ye been? Hasn't been home in three days now. Out courtin' the ladies, eh? Aye, once a tom, always a tom, that's what I say,"

Houston Kirby pronounced. "Say hello to Lady Rhea Claire. Not that she should have been worryin' about ye, but she asked me where ye was time and time again. Ye oughta be ashamed of yourself, causin' the lady such concern."

"Hello, old boy. Where have you been? Have you a lady friend?" Rhea asked, rubbing the purring tom under his chin while Kirby gingerly held him close to her. He thought he'd better check Jamaica for fleas before he let her ladyship hold him.

"Not talkin', eh?" said Kirby with a disapproving shake of his head, for Jamaica was no youngster. "Got your secrets to keep. Well, reckon I might think about cuttin' up some chicken livers for ye if ye behave yourself and don't get greedy. Last time I was doin' that, he took the whole dam—the whole chicken instead," Houston Kirby grumbled, but Rhea knew that the little steward was very pleased to have Jamaica home.

"Can I be gettin' ye any more tea, m'lady?" Kirby asked.

"No, I really should dress before the footmen come down and I embarrass them," Rhea said with a grin that was reminiscent of Robin Dominick's when he was up to mischief.

"Aye, m'lady," Houston Kirby agreed. "'Tis disgraceful that ye should be up before your maid is. Lettin' her sleep in like ye do. I dunno what Her Grace would be sayin', and I know her grandfather wouldn't be approvin', Lady Rhea Claire. I'll see that she gets up before another few minutes have passed. I only hope she has brushed out the wrinkles and dust on your ridin' dress. But don't worry, I'll make sure 'tis ready for ye," Houston Kirby told her with a glint in his eye, for he knew how to crack the whip over sluggards' heads, even if Lady Rhea Claire didn't. Too kind, she was, he thought.

"I don't think I will have need of my riding habit today, Kirby," Rhea informed him. Placing the empty cup back on the tray, she got to her feet, glancing one last time at the portrait of Dante and his mother. She knew that Kit would one day look very much like that boy.

"Oh, but, m'lady," Kirby said, stopping her as she left the room, "the captain said ye was to ride over to Westlea Abbot today."

Rhea halted. "That is strange. Dante did not mention it to me," Rhea said curiously.

Houston Kirby looked uncomfortable. "Reckon he's become a mite forgetful of late, m'lady. Got a lot on his mind. Reckon we all do," the little steward said with a deepening frown. There they were, just settling in, and there were people who wanted them gone as soon as possible.

Westlea Abbot was a larger and busier town than its nearest neighbor, Merleigh. It was located along a gentle slope of sheltered hillside, and its cobbled streets, lined with white-washed stone shops and cottages, followed a gradual descent to the floor of the valley which was covered by forest and meadowland. Westlea Abbot was located along the center of a wide, sweeping bay with a curving sandy shore, but there were no foaming breakers rolling in from a rough sea. This was a safe harbor, one that had a fishing fleet moored along several stone piers.

The small group of riders attracted much less attention than they had in Merleigh. Their horses' ironshod hooves striking noisily against the cobblestones, they passed quickly through the village streets, their destination an estate on the far side of Westlea Abbot.

Sevenoaks House sat at the end of a short drive lined with three oaks on both sides. A noble oak of magnificent proportions stretched its ancient limbs into the sky at the end of the lane, forcing the drive to encircle it and partly hiding the house from view.

It was a dignified brick house with a hipped roof and massive chimney stacks, which perfectly balanced the octagonal cupola perched in the center. Two neat rows of tall, stately mullioned windows marched along the front of the modest house. A short flight of wide steps with a curving stone balustrade led to the entrance.

At the arrival of the riders, several young grooms hurried over from the stable block, which was hidden in a grove of trees off to the right. After the grooms took their horses, Dante took Rhea's arm and escorted her up the steps. Francis and Alastair followed. A footman in plain livery opened the door as they reached it, and allowed them entrance to Sevenoaks House.

"Good afternoon, Lord Jacqobi," the stiff-backed, stern-visaged butler greeted Dante.

"Oliver. It has been a long time. But you haven't changed at all," Dante said with a smile as he handed over his gloves and hat to the footman by the butler's side.

"Thank you, m'lord," Oliver responded, and Rhea could have sworn there was a look of genuine pleasure in the old man's eyes. "And if I may be so bold, m'lord, 'tis good to see that you have returned to your rightful place at Merdraco."

"Thank you, Oliver. That is very kind of you." After a warm silence, Dante asked, "Is your master at home?"

"Yes, m'lord. Shall I tell him you wish to see him?" Oliver asked with a polite look of inquiry at the strangers accompanying the Marquis of Jacqobi.

"My pardon, Oliver. This is my wife, Lady Rhea Claire Jacqobi, her brother Francis Dominick, Lord Chardinall, and Mr. Alastair Marlowe. The gentlemen are our guests at the lodge," Dante made the introductions.

"Your wife, m'lord?" Oliver repeated, and for the first time he seemed disconcerted. But he quickly regained his composure and bowed. "I shall announce you," he said. He had started to turn away when he stopped. Looking back he said sadly, "I heard a rumor about Merdraco, which it would sadden me too much to even repeat. I suppose, if you're living in the lodge, the rumor might be true?" he asked. Seeing Dante's expression, he shook his head, mumbling as he made his way to the double doors opening off the hall.

They had a brief glance beyond of a comfortable-looking salon as footmen opened the doors. The old butler reappeared a moment later and nodded to them to proceed while he announced them in a surprisingly loud, authoritative voice. Alastair and Francis exchanged humorous glances as he roared their names.

Rhea glanced around the colorful room, which was handsomely furnished with several plump, upholstered winged chairs in dark burgundy velvet and sapphire blue. The silk hangings were a rich golden hue. A Turkey rug was a splash of color against the floor, and flowers of every shade and type abounded in delicate vases. The room was resplendent with sunshine.

"Dante! My boy, how very good to see you again!" a frail voice cried out as they entered.

"Sir Jacob!" Dante called just as enthusiastically, and then, to Rhea's further surprise, Dante hurried to the old gentleman's side and clasped his arms around that bent figure. "It has been too long, Sir Jacob," Dante said, staring down into those twinkling but sharp blue eyes. They peered at the world from beneath bristling white eyebrows that looked as if they had taken to flight.

"My boy, you are looking splendid. And I don't care if you disagree with me or not, but the best thing that ever happened to you was in having to leave Merdraco. Going to sea made a man out of you, Dante. I'm proud of you, boy," the old man said with a gleeful chuckle. "Oh, yes, sir, wish I were twenty years younger. I'd be at your side, boy, when you get them hornets all stirred up," he said, laughing, then wheezing, much to the consternation of Oliver, standing in watchful silence by the door.

"Shall I order tea, sir?" he intoned.

"What? Oh, yes, yes, do that, Oliver," Sir Jacob said, waving him away. "Now, who are these people? Don't see as well as I used to, but I know a pretty lady when I see one," he said with an audacious wink.

Dante threw back his head and laughed. "Some things never change, do they, Sir Jacob? Always had a sharp eye for the ladies, you old devil. Well, I give you fair warning now to keep your distance, for this is my wife, Rhea Claire. Rhea, meet Sir Jacob Weare, the best friend a scoundrel like me could have. He has been my eyes and ears in Devonshire for the past, what, fifteen years?" Dante questioned.

"Over fifteen, but not as long as it would have been if I'd been on my toes instead of listening to gossip. I didn't realize you weren't quite the scoundrel I thought you to be until you had already left Merdraco. More the fool me, eh?" he said, slapping his forehead.

"Whatever the amount of time, I could not have succeeded without you, Sir Jacob. You have my undying gratitude," Dante said seriously.

"Ah, boy, forget it. 'Twas the least I could do for going against you like I did. Anyway, let's not talk of dying. I'm too close to it to like the sound of it," Sir Jacob said as he came closer to where Rhea stood. Taking her hand in his, he stared down into her face. Although bent with time and arthritis, he was still a tall man. "So this is the little lady who finally managed to get your ring on her finger, eh?" he chuckled, and Rhea worried that he might start to wheeze again.

"I am afraid that I gave her little choice, Sir Jacob. Once I gazed into those violet eyes, I could not rest until I had made her mine," Dante said, much to Rhea's embarrassment.

"A real beauty, lad. Love him, girl?" Sir Jacob demanded, his beetling brows lowering over those bright blue eyes that seemed to miss nothing.

"With all my heart, Sir Jacob," Rhea answered without being at all coy, much to Sir Jacob's delight.

"Ah, a fine woman you've got, Dante," he said. His bony fingers held Rhea's chin tilted up to the light so he could examine her face. "Too pretty, boy. You'll have to keep her with child if you intend to keep her by your side," he said with a sly glance at Dante.

"I already have," Dante admitted. Rhea would have sworn that even he was slightly embarrassed by the old man's blunt talk, especially when Dante glanced over toward an old woman sitting in one of the winged chairs close to the window, where the light shone on her embroidery.

Sir Jacob caught Dante's meaningful glance and waved his hands dismissingly. "Don't be mindin' Essie, she's half deaf, won't hear a word we say. Don't suppose she even knows we're here. She's always falling asleep this time of the day. Comes in here to do a bit of sewing and ends up snoring," he said with a loud guffaw which seemed to prove his point, for the little lady sitting so demurely in the chair didn't move. Then, her nodding head, its white curls covered by a finely starched mobcap, dropped lower as she dozed.

"Who is Essie?" Dante asked quietly.

"My cousin. Or is she my niece?" Sir Jacob asked himself, a puzzled frown on his finely wrinkled brow. "Gettin' so old I can't remember anymore. Well, whatever, she's a harmless old biddy. Now, who are these young gentlemen here?" he demanded, leveling that hawkish gaze on Francis and Alastair.

"Sir Jacob, this is Alastair Marlowe, my good friend and

a former member of my crew aboard the *Sea Dragon*. And this young gentleman is Francis Dominick, Lord Chardinall, my brother-in-law," Dante made the introductions.

"A pleasure, Sir Jacob," Francis and Alastair said simultaneously.

"And a pleasure it is to be meeting you both," Sir Jacob said, pumping their hands. "Dominick? Know the name. Any relation to Lucien Dominick? Used to see him in London when I went calling on the Duchess. Thought there for a while that me and Merton were going to have to call each other out, both of us courting Her Grace like we were, and both being hot-blooded. Then she called us both fools, and that was the end of it," he laughed. "You've got the look of her, girl. Any kin to you?"

"She was my great-grandmother," Rhea responded quietly. She could hardly wait to write her father about this old reprobate.

"Well, imagine that," he said, shaking his head. "Great?" he added with another shake of his head as he realized just how young Dante's wife was. "Lord, but I'm gettin' old. Ah, here's Oliver with tea. There'd better be a bit of brandy for Lord Jacqobi, Oliver," Sir Jacob questioned, but the butler wasn't fooled.

"Indeed, Sir Jacob, and I brought along your medicine, too," the officious Oliver added with a stern glance. "You know what the doctor said about taking it every day."

"Bah, he's a fool if there ever was one. Why, I was considered old even before he was born. Reckon those extra years have added to my intelligence, and I oughta damn well know by now what's best for me," Sir Jacob snorted, winking at Francis. "A glass of brandy a day, that's what did it. 'Tis good advice, young fella, and if you follow it, why, you might live to be as old and smart as I am," he said with a laugh, which was a horrifying thought for a lad who had yet to reach his twentieth birthday.

"Come, come. Sit down, now. Over here, we'll leave Essie to her napping. Doesn't have much to say anyway. Not so far away from me, girl. My eyesight is one thing that's let me down. But then, it never was very good," he said with a grin, then frowned when he saw the amount of brandy in his glass.

"I'm going to get rid of you one of these days, Oliver," Sir Jacob warned the butler, who looked almost as old as his employer.

"Indeed, sir, whatever you think best," was Oliver's un-ruffled response. Dante could remember hearing that very same threat when he'd come to see Sir Jacob years before. He shook his head. Some things never changed.

Rhea sat down between Francis and Alastair on the sofa, facing the room, while Dante settled into a winged chair po-sitioned at an angle next to the one Sir Jacob was lowering his thin body into, the tray with the brandy close to his elbow.

"Now, I want to hear about everything. I do not want you to leave one single thing out about what has happened to you during all the time you were away. You told me precious little in those brief, businesslike letters of yours through the years," Sir Jacob complained. "Want to hear about pirates and some of your exploits at sea, boy. The bloodier the better, eh?" he said.

"Now, what was I saying?" Sir Jacob questioned, tapping his fingers impatiently on his knee.

"You were complaining about Dante's correspondence with you throughout the years," Rhea reminded him gently, curious to hear more on that subject.

"Oh? Ah, yes. Fine piece of business, that. Eh, Dante? Reckon Miles will be fit to be tied when he discovers you bought back all the Leighton lands he stole from you," Sir Jacob said with a wicked grin. "Enjoyed helping you, boy. Yes, sir, a real pleasure, that," he said, rubbing his hands together just like some smug villain eyeing his stolen booty.

Rhea's questioning glance met Dante's smiling gaze. "Sir Jacob was my surrogate. He made all the arrangements for the purchase of my lands. Did Miles ever become suspicious?" Dante wanted to know.

"No. Too smart for him. Sometimes I dealt with him di-rectly; other times, when I thought he might wonder why I wanted so much land, I got some of my friends to purchase it, then bought it from them. Miles was too busy worrying about trying to keep Wolfingwold to be worrying about any plots I might be hatching right under his nose. Heard that Miles lost quite a bit of money, nearly went bankrupt, he did. Don't suppose he would have sold the land otherwise. Just like him to hold onto it for spite."

"That was certainly a stroke of luck," Francis commented, missing the exchange of glances between Dante and Sir Jacob. Both of them knew that Miles had lost his money in several schemes of Dante's which had been falsely represented to Miles, and which established the need for Miles to sell the Leighton land he had held onto for so long.

Dante coughed, clearing his throat as he said, "I understand that there were several other people who became involved in Sir Miles' business ventures and suffered staggering losses themselves. I want you to know that I feel a responsibility to make good those losses," Dante startled Sir Jacob by declaring.

But Sir Jacob snorted. "No need, boy. No need. Warned them, I did. Quietly, of course, so as not to raise Sir Miles' suspicions. Thought I should, especially seeing how you had warned me against investing in that West Indies plantation, and in the bank, but some of them wouldn't listen. Thought me a foolish old man. Well, by God, I proved them wrong," he said with a satisfied grin. "Was it Harry Seacombe you were thinking about?" Sir Jacob demanded. "Harry was always a fool. Thought he knew best. Reckon he deserved what he got," was the old gentleman's unsympathetic comment. "I warned him personally not to invest, but he went right ahead and gambled his savings. Listened to Sir Miles' advice and not mine. You don't need to be feeling guilty about Harry or his family," Sir Jacob told Dante.

"Harry Seacombe?" Rhea questioned.

"Aye, Bess' late husband. I wrote to you that he had died, didn't I?" Sir Jacob demanded of Dante, then glanced back at Rhea. "Don't reckon it would have mattered at all seeing what you brought home with you, boy. Don't reckon Bess would've had a chance, if that's what she was hoping."

"Bess Seacombe is Sir Jacob's granddaughter," Dante explained, startling Rhea. She understood now how Dante had known so many things about the happenings in Westlea Abbot and Merleigh. Sir Jacob Weare had kept him informed all these years. Rhea wondered how many questions Dante had asked in his letters about his former fiancée. Had he ever entertained the thought of a reconciliation with her?

"How are things between you and Bess?" Dante asked.

Sir Jacob shrugged. "Not much different than they always have been. She never would listen to me. Hardheaded female, if you ask me, and she has gotten what she deserved."

"She is too much like you, Sir Jacob," Dante contradicted him. "You have always adored her, and part of her problem was that you spoiled her."

Sir Jacob stared hard at the younger man. "Aye, perhaps I'm to blame. And maybe she has suffered for her mistakes," he said. Then, glancing at Rhea's golden hair, which seemed aflame with the sun shining on it, he added, "And I imagine she will be beside herself once she catches sight of your wife." Sir Jacob spoke wisely, for he knew his Bess.

"She has already met Rhea," Dante said.

"Oh? Didn't waste any time, eh?" he chuckled. "Hotfooted it over to Merdraco, I'll wager. Had a good excuse on her tongue, too, I'll bet."

"We also met your two great-grandchildren," Dante told him.

"Oh? Don't get to see them as much as I would wish. May have to change that. The girl, what's her name? Pretty little creature, eh? Looks a lot like Bessie when she was that age. Going to be a real beauty one of these days. I'll have to see that she gets a good dowry. Can't have one of mine going around in rags, and she won't make a good match otherwise. What's the lad like?" Sir Jacob wanted to know, and apparently he was indeed interested in Bess' children as well as Bess, for his next question was, "And how did Bess look? Not ill or anything, is she? Looked a bit haggard last time I saw her," he said, a remark which would have annoyed Bess no end.

"The girl's name was Anne, and the boy is Charles," Rhea said, surprising not only Sir Jacob but Dante as well. "Anne is a very lovely girl. The boy seems rather quiet. I don't believe he said a word while he was at the lodge."

"Knew it! That lad needs a man around to teach him proper. That Bess will spoil him. Run his life, she will, unless that girl gets herself another man who's willing to take the boy under his wing," Sir Jacob said unhappily, thinking it was a pity that Dante had wed. Privately, he had thought that there might still be a chance for Bess when Dante returned. And

Dante certainly would have shaped up young Charles. Aye, 'twas a pity, for Bess needed a man, too, and Dante had certainly become one, Sir Jacob decided with a nod of approval. But as he eyed Rhea Claire, he shook his head. Ol' Bessie wouldn't have had a chance at all, no, sir.

"I thought Lady Bess was one of the most beautiful women I've ever seen," Rhea admitted generously, swallowing her resentment of the other woman and the influence she probably had over Dante because of their previous relationship. Even if it had been over fifteen years, Rhea knew the power of a first, all-consuming love. That was the way she felt about Dante, for he had been her first lover. But it must surely be different for Dante because she was not the first woman he ever had loved.

Francis glanced at Rhea, thinking she was too kind for her own good. He hadn't met this Lady Bess, but he hardly thought a former fiancée and the woman she had lost out to usually got along. But then, Rhea was different, and if she decided she liked Bess Seacombe, then nothing bad would be said of the woman in her presence.

"If you like, Dante, we could invite Charles over to play with Conny and Robin. They are of a similar age," Rhea suggested.

"Who?" Sir Jacob demanded. "Never heard those names before. You got sons, boy?" Sir Jacob asked, his gaze narrowing as he looked at Dante sitting there so casually, sipping brandy.

"A son. But Robin is Lord Robin Dominick, Rhea's young brother. And Conny is Constantine Magnus Brady—at least I think that is correct." Dante glanced at Rhea doubtfully.

"Constantine Magnus *Tyrone* Brady," Rhea corrected him.

"Ah, yes, a name almost longer than he is tall," Dante said with a grin. "He is my ward, and the former cabin boy aboard the *Sea Dragon*. He was orphaned at a young age and has been aboard my ship since he was about six. I'm beginning to think that we have done Devonshire a disservice by ever allowing those two to put their heads together."

"Mischievous, eh?" Sir Jacob said with an appreciative chuckle.

"Alastair and Kirby had to rescue them from a pack of

village boys yesterday when we were in Merleigh," Rhea said with a smile of remembrance. Houston Kirby had complained all the way back to Merdraco about the rotten tomato which had splattered his breeches.

Sir Jacob suddenly looked concerned. "Good Lord, you didn't bring them with you, did you?" he demanded.

"No, we left them at the lodge. They wanted to do some exploring, but now that I think of it, I fear we may have made a big mistake. I only hope Kirby can keep them out of trouble," Dante muttered.

"I thought I heard you mention the name of that little bandy-legged salty-tongued valet of yours. Been with you all this time, eh? Don't know why you've put up with him all these years. Always was an irritable little man," Sir Jacob reminisced good-naturedly.

"He's always been by my side. He stood by me when I didn't deserve it, and he's stayed through all the bad times, even when he must have thought he would get blown to pieces. But stay he did. I really don't know what I'd do without Kirby," Dante admitted.

"Aye, reckon you can't buy loyalty like that," Sir Jacob agreed, then slapped his knee, surprising Alastair into nearly spilling his brandy. "A son? What's this? Are you a father?" Sir Jacob demanded, glancing between Rhea and Dante. "Ah, why, you sly devil. No wonder you're sitting there so calmly while that handsome gent sits next to your wife," Sir Jacob pronounced, causing Alastair Marlowe much discomfort as the captain's pale-eyed stare centered on him for a moment.

"Christopher Dominick Leighton was born in March, at Camareigh, and is the most beautiful son a man could have. But then, his mother is the most beautiful wife a husband could wish for," Dante said, bringing a rosy blush to Rhea's cheeks.

Sir Jacob laughed deeply. "Oh, you haven't changed at all. Still a sweet talker with the ladies. Not surprised at all that you've got a son, only surprised that you haven't more of them hanging onto your coattails," he said, laughing heartily at his own quip.

"Only this lady," Dante corrected him. "And only a son by her," Dante said, gazing ardently at Rhea.

"A love match!" Sir Jacob chortled. "Excellent! Excellent!

Does this old heart of mine good," he said. "So you didn't marry the lass for her dowry. Seeing how much money you've spent on getting back your land, I wouldn't have thought you'd be left with much, Dante," Sir Jacob asked, his former jocularity disappearing. "'Twill not be easy, my boy. I've been hearing some shocking things about Merdraco. You know if you need any help at all, I'll be more than willing to assist you. Would've helped Bess, but she's too damned proud to ask, much less accept anything I might offer. Don't be the same, boy. I've got plenty of money, and I don't have all that much time left to be spending it," Sir Jacob offered.

"Thank you, Jacob," Dante replied, touched. "But you may keep your money, and I hope you have many more years to spend it in. I am quite well off. I had the good fortune to discover a sunken treasure, which, after dividing it with my crew, left me a very wealthy man. I have already let it be known that I shall be hiring men to work at Merdraco."

"Oh? And how did that go?" Sir Jacob asked suspiciously.

"Better than I thought, Sir Jacob," Dante told him. "It would seem there are quite a few men around these parts who are willing to put in a day's work. Most of them seem to think working for me might be better than continuing with their . . . former employer."

Sir Jacob scratched his chin, eyeing Dante carefully. "Reckon you be speaking of Jack Shelby?" he asked, and at Dante's nod, he continued gravely, "The man's no good, Dante. And he's gotten meaner and madder as the years have passed. He still blames you, boy, for Lettie's death. He won't rest easy once he finds out you've returned to Merdraco. It has me worried, lad, that it does," he said in a grieved voice. His gaze was troubled when it lingered on Rhea.

"He already knows I have returned. In fact, we have already come face to face, and I am afraid that I did not endear myself to him," Dante admitted. "If it is the last thing I do, I shall make him pay for the destruction he wrought at Merdraco."

Sir Jacob shook his head and sighed. "He's a powerful man, Dante. You know he's the leader of the Sons of Belial? He's got a gang of cutthroats standing behind him, and it causes me no end of concern to hear you talking about going after him."

"It is either that or have Jack Shelby strike a blow against me when I am least expecting it. I have no intention of letting him do that," Dante was saying when the door to the salon opened to admit Oliver with a fresh pot of tea.

At about that time, the old woman started mumbling as she woke from her nap. With a slowness that was painful to watch, she got to her feet. Without even being aware of the group sitting just beyond her, she started to make her shuffling way to the door. About halfway there she dropped her embroidery. Before Oliver could make a move to assist her, for he was filling the teapot with boiling water, Dante had gotten to his feet and was at the woman's side, the embroidery in his hand.

"Here is your embroidery," he said loudly.

"Eh?"

"Your embroidery. You dropped it," Dante repeated patiently, a gentle expression in his eyes as he stared down on the frail little woman.

"Very nice, but I have my own embroidery, thank you,' she said in a quavering voice. "You do good work, young sir,' she complimented him.

Dante glared over at Francis and Alastair, suspecting they would be grinning, which they were.

With a shake of his head, he tucked the embroidery in the woman's basket hanging from her arm. Placing his hand over hers, he guided her toward the door.

Patting his strong, bronzed hand, she continued slowly out the door. Oliver, who had reached her other side, assisted her from the room.

As the door closed on the two figures moving into the hall, Sir Jacob reached out and added more brandy to his glass, winking conspiratorially at Rhea.

"Now I want to hear all about this sunken treasure," Sir Jacob ordered, settling back in his chair as he anticipated exciting tales about pirates.

> Two lads that thought there was no more behind
> But such a day tomorrow as today,
> And to be boy eternal.
>
> Shakespeare

Chapter 29

". . . and his deck bloodied, he forced that Portuguese to eat his own cut-off ears," Conny Brady confided knowingly while Robin Dominick listened raptly, raising a hand to touch his own ears, pleased to find that they were still where they should be.

"Really?" he shuddered, his voice barely a squeak.

"Aye, and that wasn't the worst of that blackguard's crimes, either," Conny informed his friend as they made their way along the narrow path winding toward the two towers standing against the sky in solitary beauty.

"Aye, he was a mean 'un all right," Conny said with obvious relish. "All blackhearted men, they were. D'ye know, Robin, there was this one pirate who actually blew himself up right on the quarterdeck of his ship!"

"He did? What happened? Did he get hit by a cannonball?" Robin asked in amazement.

"No, he put too much gunpowder in his rum," Conny said, stumbling with laughter.

"Ah, come on, 'tisn't so," Robin scoffed.

"'Tis so! Them pirates were famous for spikin' their rum with gunpowder. Why, ol' Longacres, the bos'n aboard the *Sea Dragon*, was a pirate. He was even a cabin boy aboard Bartholomew Roberts' *Royal Fortune*. Sailed off the coast of Africa, he did. Of course, I've sailed off there, too, but not with pirates—though them slavers be just as bad," Conny confided. "Betcha didn't know that one of them pirates, Henry Every, was a Devonshireman? They say that when the time came for him to quit piratin', he sailed from the Bahamas and made port in County Donegal, Ireland. Most of the crew got arrested, but Cap'n Every, his pockets full of pieces of eight, disappeared. They say he was last seen walkin' the streets of Bideford without a care in the world. Ye don't suppose, d'ye, Robin, that any of ol' Cap'n Every's kin could be walkin' the streets of Merleigh?" Conny asked. "Why, maybe even some of them pullets chasin' us yesterday might have been his great-grandchildren, d'ye s'pose, Robin?" Conny asked innocently.

"Aye, they might at that," Robin replied seriously. "Of course, some of them look enough like pirates now, what with having to wear black patches over their eyes where you hit a couple of them with potatoes," he added with a grin.

"Coooeee, Robin, ye be all right for a lad who's never gone to sea," Conny said with a wide grin of his own. It was quite a compliment coming from a lad who had spent most of his life aboard ship.

"Aye, and ye be all right for a lad who's still got to learn the difference between the front and back end of a horse," Robin complimented his friend, ducking just in time to avoid Conny's elbow.

The two boys, dressed in loose-fitting frock coats and well-tailored breeches, their silk stockings of the finest quality and the silver buckles on their shoes glinting their worth, wandered along the path, stopping now and again to examine a pebble or two that caught their interest. The towers in the distance loomed even closer as they walked.

"Think ye'll have to be leavin' soon for Camareigh, Robin?" Conny asked sadly, wondering how he'd keep busy when his friend had gone.

"I don't know. Francis hasn't said anything about it. And we haven't had word from home yet about it. I suppose we'll have to soon, though. Maybe within a month," Robin speculated. Although he'd never admit as much, he was homesick, and not just for Camareigh, but for his parents and even the twins. And by the time he returned home, his cousins would probably have returned to Green Willows.

"Guess ye'll be comin' back for a visit sometime, though. Maybe even the Duke and Duchess might be comin', too."

"Oh, yes, I'm sure they will, especially when Francis and I tell them all about Merdraco. And of course Rhea and Dante and Kit will come to Camareigh for Michaelmas and stay through Christmas, I'm sure. So you'll be coming, too, Conny," Robin said. "And Kirby and Jamaica, too, I bet."

"Ye reckon so?"

"In fact, I heard my mother saying to Rhea that you might want to come and stay for a while and study with me. Mr. Teasdale seems to think he could teach you a lot, Conny," Robin told his startled friend.

"School?" Conny said in dismay. "Don't need any more learnin' than I've already got, Robin," Conny reassured him.

"Can you read and write?"

"Oh, aye. Learned that from Mr. Marlowe. Always tellin' me 'twas important, especially if I was hopin' to become a captain of my own ship someday."

"How about sums? Can you do additions and subtractions?" Robin made a face, for that was one of his least favorite subjects.

"For sure, I can," Conny spoke proudly. "Used to assist Mr. Marlowe some when he was checkin' the cargo, makin' sure we didn't get cheated. And then the cap'n himself taught me how to read the compass and take our bearin's and set course. Know all about points, half points, quarter points, and degrees. Oh, aye, I figure I'm as well learned as any that sails the seas," Conny decided.

"Can you read Latin?" Robin demanded.

"Latin? Coooeee, whatever for?" Conny demanded in return. "Know how to speak some French and Spanish, and even a little Dutch. Had to, bein' in the Indies."

"Reckon you could probably teach Mr. Teasdale a thing or two. However, now that Rhea and Francis are out of the schoolroom, he doesn't have much to do. Figure he might be real happy to see you come swaggering in, Conny," Robin predicted with a grin, thinking that if Conny did come to be tutored by Mr. Teasdale, those long hours of study might not be quite so boring.

"Reckon it be up to the cap'n what I do. And he's a fair one. Knows I'm not in need of any more learnin'," Conny said stoutly, but Robin had put a worrisome thought in his mind.

"You know, Conny," Robin said, reading his friend's mind, "if you did stay at Camareigh after the New Year, then Butterick could really teach you to ride. And I might even be able to beat you to the top of that tree this time."

"Oh, ye think so, landlubber?" Conny said, challenge in his eyes. "Betcha can't even beat me to them stone dragons," he called out, running toward the massive stone statues in the distance. But Robin Dominick was fleet-footed and had caught up with him by the time they reached the castle ruins.

"Well, what d'ye think?" Conny demanded between breaths.

"About what?"

Conny glanced to the top of one of the towers blocking out the sky. "Reckon we'd have quite a view from atop them turrets."

"Race you!" Robin issued the challenge this time, and within the minute stamping feet and childish voices echoed through the ruins.

> Fe fi fo fum!
> I smell the blood of an Englishman;
> Be he alive or be he dead,
> I'll grind his bones to make my bread.

Robin Dominick chanted with each step. Hearing that verse, Conny Brady started to sing an old sea shanty he had heard countless times while watching the crew of the *Sea Dragon* climbing into the rigging.

> Where is the trader o' London Towne?
> His gold is on the capstan,
> His blood is on his gown,
> And 'tis up and away for St. Mary's Bay,
> Where the liquor is good and the lasses are gay.

They were laughing as, breathless, they reached the top of the tower, and they felt as mighty as kings while staring at the rocky shore stretching away for miles in either direction.

"Coooeee, what a sight!" Conny exclaimed.

Robin Dominick swallowed, for the view reminded him a little too much of the one he'd had from the top branches of that tall chestnut at Camareigh. But conquering his trepidations, he sidled up beside Conny at the edge and, leaning over the parapet, stared down at the waves crashing against the rocks far below.

"'Twould be a long fall," Conny said, which eased Robin Dominick's mind not at all. "Probably be flattened like a flounder when ye hit the rocks below," Conny added helpfully.

Robin pulled his gaze away from that surging water below. He was beginning to feel dizzy, watching its rolling movements back and forth, back and forth, back and forth.

"Hey, ye're lookin' kinda green, Robin," Conny said. "Here, have a bun. I snatched them from the kitchens while Hallie's back was turned," Conny offered, holding the lightly sugared, golden crusted pastry under Robin's nose. "Freshly baked, too. She sure knows how to cook, eh?"

Robin took the bun, a strange expression on his face, especially when he saw Conny taking a mouthful of buttery bun. With a feeling of impending doom spreading through him, he took a bite, chewing it carefully. He wasn't certain he could get it to go down without it coming up again. But after a few minutes the nauseous feeling passed, and he was beginning to enjoy the heady sensation of being on top of the world.

There was shimmering water as far as the eye could see, and sky with clouds climbing into the heavens. The sea was silvered, with shafts of gold shining through the clouds on the far distant horizon.

"Guess we oughta be goin' down now," Conny said with a sigh, for being up so high reminded him of being in the rigging aboard the *Sea Dragon*. Although he was still at his captain's side, he kind of missed hearing the flapping of the sails filling with the trades, and the excitement of setting a new course.

"Aye, reckon so," Robin Dominick agreed, less regretfully.

"Want to go all the way down?" Conny asked.

"What other way is there?" Robin demanded.

"I mean, d'ye want to go down below, to the beach?" Conny explained. "'Twill be safe enough. The tide's out. If it were in, well, we could get stranded, I s'pose. But it looks as if there be plenty of beach. Well?" he asked.

Robin licked his dry lips. Conny was certainly the adventurous one, and because he didn't wish to look the coward before his new friend, Robin said, "How are we going to get down there?"

"Look," Conny said, pointing to a narrow footpath that seemed to drop straight down to the beach below.

"That's the way down?" Robin asked incredulously, wishing now he'd acted the coward.

"Aye, unless you can fly," Conny answered with a grin. "Race you down!" he challenged before disappearing down the steep flight of steps that spiraled down to the ground below.

Taking a deep breath, Robin followed Conny, and soon the boys were making their way along the dirt path that led to the beach at the base of the cliff where the dark towers of Merdraco stood sentinel over them. It was a steep path, apparently vertical in some places, but Conny and Robin managed to reach the bottom without serious incident, their feet sinking into the deep sands that covered the small sliver of land that had escaped the hungry grasp of the tide.

With the energy that comes of pure enjoyment, the boys raced along the sands, daring the waves to wet their shoes, their laughter drifting on the winds like the spindrift being blown about their small figures. And all the while they frolicked in the sands, the clouds at sea blackened and climbed higher into darkening skies.

Finally, Robin and Conny sank down onto the damp sand, their breath coming quickly as they lay there with nothing more on their minds than guessing what shapes the clouds would form themselves into next.

"Looks like a dragon," Conny said, pointing to one especially swift-moving cloud.

"Do you believe in dragons?" Robin asked, his eyes full of the innocent wonder of cloud-dreaming.

"Of course! How d'ye think the *Sea Dragon* got her name? D'ye know what Merdraco means?" he demanded, but Robin shook his head. "The Cap'n says it means dragon of the sea. *Mer* is French for sea. *Draco* is Latin and means dragon, but that's the only Latin I'm ever goin' to learn," Conny warned. "There's even a dragon in the night sky. It lies between the Dippers. Dragons have always been ferocious beasts, just like the *Sea Dragon*," Conny said with pride of one who had actually sailed on that almost mythical ship.

Suddenly their reverie was interrupted by the distant rumble of thunder, which drew their attention to the black clouds hanging low over the water.

"Coooeee, what a storm brewin'," Conny breathed, whistling between his teeth as a bolt of lightning flashed through one of the clouds.

"We'd better get back to the lodge before we get soaked," Robin advised.

"Be a while yet, Robin, before the storm hits here," Conny said knowledgeably, for hadn't he sailed long enough to predict when a storm would hit?

They continued to stand there for a few minutes longer, watching the fiery streaks lighting up the stormy skies, and all the while the tide was rising, and the waves were becoming louder and angrier as they were fed by the storm.

"Reckon we oughta be goin' now, Robin," Conny finally said, thinking the storm had built up faster than he had expected. A deafening clap of thunder sounded directly overhead, startling both of them.

During their exploration of the beach, they had made their way to the far end, which curved up higher than the rest. As they glanced back toward the distant end of the beach, where the path to safety lay, they realized that the tide had come in almost without their having been aware of it. Had it been a normal tide, they might have been able to race past it, soaked shoes and stockings the only casualties. But this was a tide rising with the storm, and it had already covered the sandy shore in swirling water that foamed against the rocks.

Robin frowned as he stared at the water racing up the beach. "Come on, Conny. We can beat it," Robin said nervously, listening to its crashing roar.

"No, we can't, Robin," Conny said. "There's too much of an undertow. I've seen those before, and we'd have our feet pulled right out from under us. I don't know about you, but I can't swim," Conny admitted wryly.

"You can't *swim?*" Robin asked incredulously. "But you were a sailor! I thought you'd *have* to know how to swim," he demanded.

"If you've got a good captain at the helm, there ain't no reason to be learnin' how," Conny replied matter-of-factly. His eyes were gauging the distance across the sands, figuring their chance. He shook his head.

"Come on, Conny!" Robin yelled, for the sounds of the storm and the sea were becoming deafening. "Let's climb higher!" he said, for by then the waves were beginning to eat away at their small stretch of sand. They would soon be left without a grain of sand beneath their feet.

Conny glanced up at the sheer cliff rising above their heads and even he felt a moment's fear as he thought of scaling that precipice. One misstep and the shore below would become a watery grave.

Robin was already finding a foothold in the rocks, and after a last look at the rising tide, Conny wasted no more time before following his friend. But Conny couldn't help but wonder where Robin was going. There was only a narrow ledge a few feet above the beach, and he hadn't the heart to tell Robin that the tide would more than cover that in less than an hour.

Somehow Robin Dominick managed to find enough small crevices in the jumble of rocks to carry him above the water surging around the base of the rocks. He glanced back. Conny had just been caught by a wave, which left him soaking wet.

Robin's foot slipped out of the next foothold and he nearly

tumbled back down on top of Conny, who had managed to move beyond the greedy reach of the tide.

"You all right?" Robin asked, ready to reach down a helping hand, but Conny couldn't hear him. They continued to climb higher until, with a sigh of relief, they spied the narrow shelf that stretched along the face of the cliff. It was safely out of reach of the sea.

Sliding onto it after Robin, Conny sat down, his tired legs and feet dangling over the edge.

Looking worried, Conny eyed the precipice rising so sharply above them and knew with a sinking heart that they could climb no higher. Yet they could not stay where they were.

Robin gasped as a wave splashed over them, leaving him drenched. "That was a big one," he said nervously.

"The tide's going to get higher, Robin. We can't stay here," Conny finally found the courage to admit. He felt responsible for their predicament, though Robin had not placed the blame on him.

"Higher?" Robin asked, appalled, wondering how there could possibly be so much water. Everywhere he looked, it surged around him.

"A lot higher," Conny said, pointing to a strange discoloration on the rocks above their heads. "That's the tide mark, and we're sitting below it."

Robin Dominick's violet eyes were wide with fear as Conny Brady's words sunk in, and more so when he glanced along the narrow shelf they were sitting on and saw no place else they could go.

"Come on, maybe we can find some more footholds farther along," Conny said heartily, though he didn't really hold out much hope. "Look, let's go this way; the ledge looks like it curves back some. There's nothing down that way," Conny decided, for even though they had more ledge that way, it led back out over the beach, and there were only sheer cliffs there for as far as the eye could see above that ledge.

Slowly the two boys made their way along the ledge. It was slippery with the waves splashing over it, and in Conny's mind it seemed to get narrower and narrower with every step.

"Isn't this ledge becoming narrower?" Robin voiced Conny's

suspicions. And then to their utter dismay, they rounded the curve and found that the ledge disappeared altogether.

But then they saw that it disappeared into the cliff. It was, in fact, the entrance to a cave. The entrance had, from the beach below, remained hidden. Without pausing any longer than it took to take a step inside, Conny led the way into the darkness, promptly falling to his knees when he lost his balance on the slippery floor of the cave.

Robin leaned against the cold, damp wall, holding onto it for dear life. He found himself breathing easier now that the roar of the waves sounded farther away.

Conny Brady got to his feet quickly and peered into the shadowy darkness. The cave was filled with a strange grayish light filtering in from the entrance.

Watching his friend, Robin said, "Don't tell me we can't stay here either."

Conny grinned a sickly smile. "'Fraid so, mate. How d'ye think this cave got formed in the first place?" he asked. And even as he spoke, Robin discovered how, for the first wave broke across the mouth of the cave, sending a wall of water rushing into its shadowy depths. "Through the centuries the tide eats away at the rock, forming a cavern. I've seen lots of these on islands in the Indies. If we're lucky, there might be another opening topside. Sometimes the ceiling will have caved in, or there even might be several other caverns farther back, which might be above the tide."

Robin began to feel his way along the dripping walls. The angry roar of the sea seemed to grow louder with every second. How long, the boys wondered silently, before the tide caught up to them?

When the stormy winds do blow.
Martin Parker

Chapter 30

SKYLARK shied nervously as the blackening clouds in the distance lit up with the brilliance of crackling lightning.

"There, there, girl," Rhea soothed softly, patting the little mare's sweating neck. Her words were nearly drowned out when thunder rumbled through the darkening heavens.

"I think we're in for a soaking," Francis Dominick commented, his gloved hands keeping a firm rein on his skittish mount.

His gray eyes narrowed, Dante Leighton gazed out to sea, to where the thunderstorm was building. A silvery squall cloud was hanging low over the heavy seas. "I would estimate we have at least three quarters of an hour before the rains hit. What do you say, Alastair?"

"I'm not quite as optimistic, Cap'n, so I'd guess about half an hour. But I hope you are correct, since this is one of my newer suits," Alastair Marlowe said, casting a worried eye at the somber clouds obscuring the horizon. The winds and waves were probably swirling and churning toward the shore.

"I hope Robin and Conny are not out in this. I told them not to stray too far from the lodge," Rhea said, concern growing as another flash of lightning lit the skies. She knew both her brother and Conny too well to assume they had heeded her words.

"You needn't worry," Dante said with all the assurance of a man who was accustomed to having his orders followed, "I warned them against leaving the grounds. They are likely to be curled up before the hearth sipping hot chocolate. That's how we'll find them when we arrive," he predicted.

But Francis and Rhea exchanged knowing glances, for they had lived with Robin's escapades too long to believe that. And with Conny Brady, another adventurous spirit, on hand, Rhea felt it wise to expect the worst. The worst, to Rhea's mind, meant watching them straggle home, soaked to the skin and shivering. She could only hope that Dante was right.

Briefly, Rhea glanced back along the road that led to Sevenoaks House, but that high roof was blocked by the trees which closed in behind them and were bending under the stormy winds. After declining a third cup of tea for herself, while Dante and Alastair stopped Sir Jacob's generosity by covering their brandy glasses with their hands, the party had bid a fond farewell to Sir Jacob Weare. But he would not allow them to leave until he had exacted a promise of another visit very soon.

Reading her thoughts, Dante suddenly asked, "And what did you think of Sir Jacob?"

"I liked him . . . although I am not certain I trust him," Rhea said, startling Dante. "At least, not over the card table. I think he is not as forgetful as he would like people to think," she explained. "For example, I think he knew quite well what his great-granddaughter's name was. I suspect he is a very sly old fox."

Dante laughed. "I shall have to tell him that he failed miserably in deceiving you, my dear."

Francis and Alastair looked mystified. They both had

thought him a harmless old gentleman, rather amusing, in fact, if opinionated.

Dante nodded. "Everyone who knows Sir Jacob thinks him the most amiable of fellows until he wins time and time again at cards or horses, or drinks them under the table. He is no fool, despite what many think, and that is why he was able to get my lands back from Sir Miles. Sir Jacob was the ideal man for that job because no one, especially Sir Miles, would suspect Sir Jacob of having my interests at heart. It was well known at the time that Sir Jacob forbade Bess' marriage to me when he discovered that I was not only penniless but also under suspicion of murder. And there was no reason for anyone to think he had changed his opinion of me over the years."

"What did change his mind about you?" Alastair asked.

"He found out certain information, something I am not at liberty to reveal, that cleared me as far as he was concerned. But I didn't know anything about it, so I was quite surprised when he tracked me down. I had been away at sea for about three years, returning now and again aboard the *Perdita* when she came in for supplies. Finally we needed refitting, and we docked in Portsmouth. You can imagine my surprise when, within the week, I saw Sir Jacob walking along the docks, looking for me. I am not certain, even to this day, exactly what I was expecting when he approached me, but certainly not a hand offered in friendship.

"That was when we formed our secret alliance. I discovered that I hadn't lost an old friend and that there was somebody who would keep an eye on Merdraco. I had, by that time, regained some self-respect, but I still hadn't succeeded in getting my inheritance back. In fact, I assumed that was a hopeless proposition. I had saved a bit of money from my share of the prizes we won in battle, but it was barely enough to purchase my family's heirlooms, the ones sold by Miles, much less the lands he had stolen from me. I didn't even know how to begin.

"And how was I to search for my lost possessions when I might be away at sea for months at a time? How could I get Miles to sell me back the land? Those were the problems. I thought they were insurmountable, but Sir Jacob didn't seem worried. He proclaimed himself my guardian, at least in spirit, and told me to set my mind at ease, that he and his trusted

solicitor would see to everything. He said for me to go back
to sea and make some money, for he wasn't going to be able
to buy back my land on his good looks alone."

Dante smiled. "And do you know, by the time the *Perdita*
was seaworthy again, he had a warehouse full of paintings,
furniture, silver, and crystal that had once filled the rooms of
Merdraco? It was extraordinary, and I suspect that he thor-
oughly enjoyed doing it. When I shipped out again I was full
of hope. I knew that my dream was indeed possible, and after
that day I never lost sight of it again. I owe everything to Sir
Jacob, and to my captain, Sedgewick Christopher, for if it
hadn't been for their faith in me, I don't think I could have
continued fighting and hoping for so many long years, all the
while thinking of my home standing abandoned on a lonely
stretch of shore."

Francis Dominick was deeply moved. Dante Leighton was
quite a man to have taken the chances he had. He thought that
if his father and Dante could just sit down and talk, the way
Dante had been doing, they would find they had quite a lot in
common. He decided to bring the subject up with his mother.
She had a special way of getting his father to do things.

Rhea was thinking that Sir Jacob Weare was an exceptional
man just by virtue of his tracking Dante down to tell him that
he had misjudged him. Then to have helped him regain his
lands was an act of kindness which Rhea would always remember. Part of her happiness came because of that unselfish
loyalty of so many years.

Then another thought struck Rhea, and she asked softly, her
words barely audible above the thunder, "Did Lady Bess know
that Sir Jacob was assisting you?"

"No. It was a secret between Jacob and me. No one else
knew. You should know that the only way to keep a secret is
to keep it between two people. Why?"

"No reason in particular. I was just curious," Rhea replied,
but she wondered what had happened to cause Bess Seacombe
to tell her grandfather the truth about Dante. Had her conscience
forced her to come out with the truth? Bess could not have
been past fifteen or sixteen, and she might have been as much
a victim of those tragic events as Dante was.

The streets of Westlea Abbot looked lonesome when they

rode back through it, the clattering of their horses' hooves against the cobblestones echoing loudly. They drew even less notice than before, for already shutters were closed against the approaching storm. The market square was quickly being emptied, the stalls hastily dismantled, and the produce carefully crated until the next day. Many items would have to be sold cheap then, especially fish that was already a day old and beginning to smell like it.

As they began to make their way across the wide square, they became aware of a coach halted beside a shop at the far side. It wasn't until Rhea caught sight of Dante's grim face that she realized whose coach it was.

Because of the scurrying people seeking shelter, they'd had to slow their horses to a walk as they crossed the square. In fact, they had halted completely while a tradesman pushed his cart in front of them. While they waited, the owner of the coach-and-six stepped out of the shop, where bolts of materials were being handsomely displayed in the bay window. An elegantly dressed woman was on the gentleman's arm.

Sir Miles Sandbourne was assisting the lady into the coach when another woman approached him from behind, a small boy holding onto her hand as she dragged him closer to the shiny coach. From their vantage point across the square, it seemed Sir Miles was startled when the woman addressed him. Even from the distance she looked angry.

She pulled the small lad in front of her, holding his face up to Sir Miles. Then she reached down and picked up a handful of what looked like horse droppings and threw the contents of her hand at Sir Miles' elegantly shod feet.

Rhea gasped when Sir Miles raised a hand and slapped the woman full across the face, sending her stumbling backward. Without another glance, he climbed into his coach, his coachman whipping the team into action while a hurrying footman slammed the door. He barely had time to climb aboard.

"It would seem Sir Miles hasn't changed any. Still the perfect gentleman where the ladies are concerned," Dante said bitterly, remembering the story of his mother's beating at Sir Miles' hands. "Sir Miles seems reluctant to accept his responsibilities toward a former mistress and the bastard he sired. Charity is something Sir Miles is unfamiliar with. Now that he is through with her, he'll let them both rot in the gutter," Dante said, his lips hardening into a straight line as the coach drew abreast of them and, to their surprise, halted.

Rhea could barely stand to meet Sir Miles' sardonic gaze. He put his head out the coach window and stared at his stepson.

"I heard a rumor that you had finally gotten up the courage to return to Merdraco," Sir Miles greeted Dante, and Rhea had her first inkling of what Dante's life must have been like with this creature as his stepfather.

"I am surprised that you found the courage to remain," Dante commented, his gray eyes raking the other man contemptuously. "Especially considering that others seem to hold the same opinion of you that I do," Dante added while drawing a clean, scented handkerchief from his coat pocket and touching it to his nostrils as if offended by some noxious odor.

Mesmerized, Rhea watched Sir Miles tap his cane with its silver wolf's head against the coach door, his anger barely held in check as he parried words with his stepson—apparently none too successfully, which must have been a shock to Sir Miles.

"I dealt quite easily with you once before, Dante," Sir Miles reminded the younger man. "I shall do so again," he threatened quietly.

But Dante Leighton, well used to facing the enemy, merely smiled. That was insulting enough, but the words which followed had Sir Miles' gloved hands tightening on his cane as if he were about to strike.

"Actually, Miles, I have you to thank for my good fortune. If it hadn't been for your betrayal, I would never have left here and been forced to live a life that I can now look back on with pride. Nor would I have been in the Indies to stumble across that treasure map. You might as well admit defeat. Give up, Miles. You've lost, for I have succeeded in returning to Merdraco, and I have no intention of leaving again," Dante promised.

"Ah, but what indeed have you returned *to?*" was the contemptuous rejoinder. "I hear that Merdraco is little better than the laystall I always thought it to be, along with the offal spawned of it and which insists on calling itself a man," Sir Miles sneered, his dark eyes watching for signs of uncontrollable rage or anything to show that he had managed to get under the other man's guard.

But Dante showed no annoyance or anger. Indeed, he seemed amused by Sir Miles' outburst. "Soon Merdraco will be as it once was. You might as well accept that, Miles," Dante said softly.

"As it once was?" Sir Miles Sandbourne asked doubtfully. "I seriously doubt that. There is nothing left of the past but your name, and that has been spat upon. Oh, you may buy yourself new carpets and chairs, and landscapes to decorate the walls, but the portraits will be of strangers because the Leighton portraits are gone. Your home will not be Merdraco, not the Merdraco you were driven out of.

"You have no heritage, nothing to remind you of the almighty Leightons, masters of Merdraco. Have you forgotten so soon that I was forced to sell at auction all the fine possessions of the Leightons? For all your wealth, you have nothing," Sir Miles taunted, enjoying the looks of outrage on the faces of Alastair Marlowe and Francis Dominick.

"Ah, Miles, I do so hate to disappoint you, but since you will not be able to gaze upon the halls of Merdraco, I shall tell you now that I possess all that was stolen from me by you. Through the years I have bought back almost all the furnishings that left Merdraco. I even have the portrait of my mother. It now hangs in a place of honor over the hearth in the lodge. And every time I gaze upon her beautiful face, I thank God that she had the courage to escape you, Miles. You were cheated of your revenge against her for having chosen another when she decided death was preferable to living with you.

"And as I ride across the land that is once again Leighton land, knowing that the enemy has been vanquished, banished from ever setting foot on that which is mine, I can only pity you, Miles. For you are the one with nothing to show for all of the long years of plotting and planning, for savoring a revenge you never truly had. And, ultimately, revenge has become mine, Miles. It is mine now to savor," Dante told an ashen-faced Sir Miles Sandbourne. His gloved hand was so tightly clenched around his cane that Rhea thought it would surely snap in two.

Rhea glanced nervously between the two. Although she

could not blame Dante, she couldn't help but worry about what Sir Miles Sandbourne would do to get even. This was not a man who would ever admit defeat, certainly not at the hands of Dante Leighton.

"Miles? I'm cold. Are we goin' just to sit here all day? My teeth are chatterin' and I'm beginnin' to shiver. If ye'd bought me that fur like I was askin' then I wouldn't be complainin', now would I?" a petulant voice sounded from inside the darkened coach. It seemed to break the spell.

Sir Miles Sandbourne smiled. It wasn't a very nice smile, Francis Dominick thought, especially when those dark eyes of Sir Miles' lingered on Rhea.

"Ah, Lady Rhea Claire, how beautiful you look. What a pity that soon those lovely eyes will be red-rimmed with tears."

"Indeed, Sir Miles."

"Yes. I fear that your husband is not at all well liked in these parts. And I do fear that some harm must surely befall him one of these days. 'Twill be such a pity for one so young and pretty to become a widow. But do not despair, for I am certain that some handsome young gentleman—perhaps one much like that gentleman there"—he pointed to an indignant Alastair Marlowe—"will come along and help you forget your unfortunate first marriage. In fact, since you are a Dominick, and your son is the first grandson of the Duke of Camareigh, your new lover will be more than pleased to raise Dante's son as his own . . . much as I did Dante. And being so young, the child will have no memory of his real father," Sir Miles speculated with a sad, understanding smile. "Please, Lady Rhea, feel free to come to Wolfingwold anytime. You are always welcome in my home."

And with that, he withdrew back into the darkness. With the tapping of his cane on the roof, the coach pulled away.

"What a horrible man," Rhea murmured, her gloved hands shaking slightly as she held the reins. The gentle little mare could feel her mistress' distress and neighed uneasily. "He frightens me."

"The man's contemptible, and certainly no gentleman," Francis expostulated angrily. As a member of a highly respected family and the heir to a dukedom, he had never experienced such rudeness. "Why, he actually threatened you, Dante. It's disgraceful! I shall personally see that he is never invited to Camareigh again," Francis Dominick promised with an angry glint in his eye, and Rhea, glancing at his profile, thought he not only sounded like her father but looked like him as well.

Alastair Marlowe risked a sideways glance at Dante Leighton, for the captain had yet to say anything, and that was when he was at his most dangerous. Dante Leighton's face looked cast in bronze. Not a muscle moved as he continued to stare after the coach, which disappeared along a narrow street leading off the square. His pale gray eyes were as light and clear as crystal, and just as cold.

"Dante?" Rhea reached out her hand to him, and for a moment it remained outstretched between them before Dante became aware of it and reached out to grasp it. For what seemed an eternity, he stared down at that small, gloved hand clasped in his, that hand which always seemed to be there for him, reaching out to comfort. It was as if Rhea knew that Sir Miles had wounded Dante, that he was vulnerable in his possessive love for her and his son. And to hear Miles' vicious words about another man taking his place in the hearts of Rhea and their son must have hurt him terribly.

But even Rhea did not know how deeply scarred Dante had been by his unhappy childhood and by never having known the security of a loving family around him.

Glancing up, Dante met her gentle stare and knew a return of peace. The look that was exchanged between them caused Alastair a brief moment of sadness and envy, for the glance included deep love and mutual respect and understanding, and it excluded the rest of the world. A love such as that which Rhea and Dante shared was wholly unknown to Alastair, and he wondered if he would ever meet someone he could share his life with and know that his love was returned as deeply as it was given.

"Come, let us go home," Dante said softly, and the memory of Sir Miles' hurtful words were put aside as they sent their horses through the empty streets of Westlea Abbot.

The winds blew more fiercely as they rode along the winding road toward Merdraco, racing the storm-driven clouds. With the storm so close, it was something of a surprise to overtake three riders approaching them on the road leading to Merdraco.

Most people had to taken to shelter. As they drew closer, they could see that one of the riders had dismounted and was leading a lame horse.

Lady Bess Seacombe was relieved to see the other riders, but relief turned to dismay when she saw who the riders were. She cursed beneath her breath. Her hair was in tangles, her boots were dusty, and she felt hot and bothered.

"Bess?" the voice Bess both desired and dreaded called to her. "Are you all right? You weren't thrown, were you?" Dante asked, confirming Bess' fears that she must look a poor sight indeed.

"No, this old boy wouldn't throw me, would you?" Bess asked, her voice softening for a moment while she patted the stallion's velvety nose. "We were hurrying back from Westlea Abbot, trying to beat the storm, when he came up lame. I debated waiting at the Bishop until the storm blew over, but then I thought it might last until darkness, and I didn't want to travel with the children after dark. We were going to take one of the paths across that wild bit of moorland between here and Merleigh and save some time, but then Bristol Boy started limping. I'm afraid he's sprained a tendon." She sounded worried.

Dante dismounted. Handing his reins to Francis, he approached the agitated stallion, his sleek coat shiny with sweat. Squatting down beside him while Bess tried to hold her horse steady, Dante took the beautifully tapered foreleg in his hands and gently felt it.

"You're right, Bess," he said, carefully placing the injured leg down. "It's beginning to swell and there's heat. Hurts, doesn't it, boy?" he asked, rubbing the horse behind the ears before patting his strong-muscled neck. "I am afraid you wouldn't have gotten far with him if you'd continued cross-country. But why were you heading back this way? Merdraco is far closer," Dante said, gazing at Bess with those pale eyes she had dreamed about for so long.

Raising a haughty chin, she said shortly, "I did not wish to intrude. In fact, if we are to make the Bishop before it begins to pour, then we should be on our way," Bess said, for already several raindrops had started to fall.

"Bess, you—"

"We cannot allow you to get caught in this storm," Rhea interrupted Dante, her voice nearly drowned out by the thunder overhead. "And think of poor Bristol Boy. If you do not want him lame, then we'd better get some kaolin paste on his leg. I really think we should have Clauson look at it. He worked with Butterick, who has been in charge of the stables at Camareigh for ages, and your horse really could not be in more competent hands, Lady Bess," Rhea suggested kindly, irritating Bess Seacombe all the more. But the wisdom of the younger woman's words was inescapable, as well as the fact that the rain was beginning to fall in earnest.

"Thank you," Bess said between tight lips. "Anne, up behind your brother, now," Bess ordered, for their plan had been for the two lighter children to ride double while she rode Anne's horse.

"I think it might be better if Anne rode with one of us," Dante suggested, for the thunder was already making the horses nervous, and the narrow track running along the edge of the cliff could be dangerous even in fair weather. During a thunderstorm, with a young, inexperienced rider, it was too much of a risk. "And I think it would be wise if one of us took Charles' reins, just in case his horse frightens and bolts."

Dante glanced around, making his decision. "Alastair, you take Anne up behind you and take the lead. Francis, you take the reins of Charles' horse and follow Alastair. Rhea, you can follow me. Bess, you bring up the rear with Bristol Boy." Dante gave his orders, expecting compliance, but Bess wasn't accustomed to taking orders, nor indeed was she used to hearing Dante Leighton barking them out, and it left her stunned.

"Well, really, who the devil gave you leave to decide what—"

"Let's get a move on, Bessie," Dante said impatiently as she continued to stand there staring at him. He was in no mood to humor her. Without further ado, he lifted Anne from her mount's back and placed her up behind Alastair. Then, without so much as a by-your-leave, he placed his hands around Bess' waist and lifted her onto Anne's horse.

Bess swallowed painfully when she felt those strong hands touching her and smelled the familiar scent of him, something else she'd not been able to forget over the long, empty years, not even when she'd lain in her husband's arms. Harry had favored a cloying sweet scent which he'd used without restraint, yet still managed to reek of the snuff he couldn't seem to do without. With Dante you'd hardly been aware of the subtle spicy scent he used so sparingly.

Rhea did not miss the look of anguished longing which Bess could not hide while being held in Dante's arms, and Rhea felt a moment's jealousy. She did not need to be a soothsayer to know that Bess would welcome Dante's embrace.

Dante, however, seemed oblivious to the emotions of Bess Seacombe. He released her almost as soon as he placed her on horseback, making certain she'd hooked her leg over the saddle horn before handing her the reins.

They wasted no time in traveling along the lane winding up to Merdraco, and Dante promised himself that soon he would see that there was a new road leading there. The old Marquis had been drawing up plans for a safer, wider road inland when he died, and then, afterward, Sir Miles had shown no interest in the project. But as Dante stared down at the angry sea, the waves boiling up over the place where the beach had been, he vowed to rebuild Merdraco with a good, new road.

The sweet pungency of woodsmoke drifted down into the mists as they neared the lodge. Welcoming lights shone into the gloom of a stormy afternoon, and Rhea knew that Kirby would most likely have hot chocolate and warm buns waiting for them in front of the fire. She knew a sudden longing to hold Kit's snuggling body against her breast and hear the sounds of Robin and Conny giggling while they played leapfrog or hide-and-seek. Yes, she had come to think of the lodge as her home.

Like the good apprentice he'd been, Clauson was patiently awaiting their arrival, a concerned expression on his young face. Francis wasn't fooled. He suspected that Clauson was more concerned about the condition of the horses than about their riders. And, sure enough, when Clauson caught sight of the limping, sleek-coated black stallion, his face went through several contortions—from amazement to admiration to horrified dismay.

They left him shouting orders to footmen and grooms, sounding just like Butterick.

"Ah, m'lord, m'lady, 'tis good to see ye safely back," Houston Kirby greeted them with genuine relief, for he'd been watching the blackening clouds on the horizon, then glancing down the empty lane, all the while worrying about everything under the sun. Both Conny and Robin had gone out in the storm, too.

"How is Kit?" Rhea asked as she pulled off her hat, shaking it free of raindrops.

"Sleeping like the innocent babe he is, m'lady," Kirby responded with a wide grin, which faded when he caught sight of the dark-haired woman with the scarlet plumed hat entering the lodge beside Dante.

"And Conny and Robin? I hope they didn't wander off and get caught out in this rain," Rhea asked while pulling off her gloves and glancing around, hoping to see them sitting before the fire blazing at the end of the hall.

Much to her relief, she saw them sitting exactly where Dante had predicted they would be, sipping steaming hot chocolate. Their dark heads were close together while they whispered whatever secrets the young boys apparently thought too important to share with adults.

"Well, I must admit I was gettin' kind of worried on that score, m'lady. They were out for a powerful long time, and I could see that the storm was growin' worse by the minute. I'd been up in the tower watchin' for ye and had hoped to spy them two rascals at the same time, but I didn't have any luck. Then in they come, soaked to the skin," Kirby confirmed Rhea's fears, "and not more than a half an hour past. Shiverin' and shakin' and as pale as ghosts. Why, ye'd have thought they'd been to hell and back, they were so jittery," Houston Kirby said with a chuckle, thinking he'd never seen such round eyes as those boys' when they came walking in from the back of the lodge, every step leaving a puddle of water.

"Where had they been?" Rhea asked curiously, but her eyes were watching Bess, who had moved closer to Dante as they stood before the fire. Her dark eyes were laughing up at him while she said something amusing, or at least it seemed to amuse Dante, for he smiled and cocked his head lower to catch the rest of her softly spoken words.

"Said they'd been out explorin' the woods," Kirby said with

a shake of his head. "Sent them right up to get out of them wet clothes, I did."

"And had they been out exploring the woods?" Rhea questioned doubtfully, knowing that Robin's first answers were sometimes in need of closer scrutiny.

Kirby sniffed, apparently annoyed at himself, for he said, "D'ye know, I didn't even see them come into the lodge. Goin' blind as well as deaf, I'm beginnin' to think," Kirby grumbled, for he'd been staring all around the property, right at the woods they'd claimed they'd been exploring, and yet he hadn't caught sight of them. "I'll set out more cups, seein' as how we've got unexpected guests," he said with obvious disapproval as he glanced over at Bess Seacombe.

"Please, Kirby, see that *everyone* is made comfortable," Rhea said with a smile as she started up the stairs. "I want to see Kit. Then I'll be back down."

Rhea's steps carried her along the corridor past the room that Robin and Conny shared. She paused before the half-open door, for on the floor lay a pile of hastily discarded clothing. With a sigh, Rhea went in and started to pick up the wet cambric shirts before they were faded on by the other clothes. Then something Kirby had said struck her.

Half an hour ago Conny and Robin had returned soaking wet from their wanderings, but it had only started to rain about a quarter of an hour ago, and even then not heavily enough to soak them through to the skin. And as Rhea stood there holding the wet shirts, she became aware of a grittiness coating the material. Touching her fingertip to her lips, she tasted salt. Looking closer at the pile of clothes, she saw for the first time the sand around them.

They had been warned against going down to the beach, and yet they had headed there straightaway upon being left alone. She would have to have a word with them about that, and if her warning did not suffice to keep them from exploring where they shouldn't, then she would have to mention it to Dante, Rhea decided, thinking that at least for now it was something that she could keep to herself.

And on that thought she went to see to the needs of her son, wondering if he would be as mischievous as Robin and Conny when he was their age.

Downstairs, Bess was enjoying a sherry while warming herself before the fire, her eyes lingering on Dante's hard face and encountering his gaze too frequently for it not to be purposeful.

"You have done wonders with this lodge," Bess commented, glancing around the cozy hall with a sigh of pleasure.

"You must tell Rhea that, for she has worked hard to make it comfortable," Dante said, taking no credit. "And, of course, Alastair and Francis, who saw to the cobwebs and grime," he added with a laugh, although Anne Seacombe would never have believed that either of these handsome gentlemen could have been found cleaning like scullery maids.

Anne Seacombe glanced shyly between the two men, but her gaze lingered longer on Alastair Marlowe's tanned face, for, although Francis Dominick was the handsomer of the two, there was something about Alastair Marlowe that had Anne watching his every move. He was older than Francis, yet there was a boyish quality in him, almost a shyness, which Francis Dominick, accustomed to wealth, had never known. Every time those hazel eyes of Alastair's met hers, she felt she had known him all her life. It was ridiculous, but it was a pleasurable feeling nonetheless, she thought as she smiled at him, thinking he was very kind even to acknowledge her presence. She must seem a silly young thing.

But Anne Seacombe would have been surprised to read Alastair Marlowe's mind at that moment, for he was fighting the memory of her soft young body pressed against his back while they rode along the road. The mere thought of those small, firm breasts hard against him was having a strange effect on his senses, and he hoped it wouldn't become too embarrassingly apparent.

Having found Kit still asleep, Rhea returned to the hall in time to find Bess accepting another sherry from her host. As soon as Dante heard Rhea's step, he turned away from Bess, a smile touching the hardness of his face as he watched Rhea approaching, the firelight held captive in the gold of her hair.

"And how is Kit?" he asked, knowing where she had been.

"Fast asleep, as indeed Kirby said he would be," Rhea said with a smile while she poured herself a cup of tea. "More tea,

Anne?" Rhea inquired politely, startling the girl from her daydreams.

"Thank you, m'lady," Anne spoke softly, not wishing to draw any more attention to her blushing cheeks.

"I hope you're not coming down with a cold, Anne," Bess commented. "You look feverish," she said, far from realizing the real reason for her daughter's flushed appearance. Nor would Bess have believed it, for she thought Anne was still a little girl.

Rhea glanced around, making certain that no one was in need of anything. For a brief moment her eyes met Robin's, and she frowned thoughtfully when those violet eyes quickly glanced away. She promised herself a word with that young man. Rhea's frown gave way to a smile as she watched Charles Seacombe edging closer to where Robin and Conny were sitting cross-legged on the floor before the hearth. And in a few minutes he was sitting beside them, a look of amazement on his face while he listened to one of Conny Brady's more outrageous tales.

"We saw Sir Jacob today," Dante said, eyeing Bess curiously.

"Oh? How is he?" she asked. Her eyes were locked on the fire, for she could not meet Dante's searching gaze.

"He seems quite well. He's aged some, but Rhea seems to think he is a wily old fox," Dante said with an appreciative grin.

"Indeed? How very astute of Lady Rhea," Bess said. "He always has been one for snooping into other people's affairs. He just cannot seem to leave well enough alone."

"I am surprised that, if you were in Westlea Abbot, you didn't stop in to say hello to him. I think he is lonely, Bess," Dante said, and to the oversensitive woman his words sounded like criticism.

"You may as well know, if he has not already told you, that things have not been good between us for some time. He seldom comes to call at Seawyck. Besides, I had quite a lot of shopping to do. The shops there stock far more fashionable items than do the ones in Merleigh," she explained, forgetting to say that, as the highly respected Sir Jacob's granddaughter, she could get better credit in Westlea Abbot. In fact, she could barely show her face in Merleigh any more without some tradesman cornering her on the street and demanding to be paid.

Bess glanced at Lady Rhea Claire, taking note of the fine quality of the other woman's sapphire blue riding habit. Bess couldn't quite control her envy. "That's a beautiful skirt and jacket. I see the style of cut is more severe than it was last year. I must confess that I rather liked the one you had on yesterday," she heard herself admitting, and then could have cut out her tongue for complimenting the other woman.

"Why, thank you," Rhea said, but her smile did not come as easily, for Bess' casually spoken words confirmed to Rhea that it was indeed Bess she had seen hurrying up the street in Merleigh yesterday. Perhaps she had been the person who gave Dante the note. "You must have been in Merleigh. I am sorry that we did not have the chance to speak."

"Errands, you know," Bess said airily, not saying that she'd been to the bank and tried unsuccessfully to take out a loan. "One is so busy nowadays. What with going to the silversmith to give approval to a special design he is working on for a new tea service I've ordered, and to the jeweler who is resetting my rubies, and then to my mantuamaker and dressmaker, well, there just do not seem to be enough hours in the day," Bess said, ignoring the look of surprise that had spread across Anne's face, for Anne knew they had been selling some of their silver, certainly not buying any. And the rubies, well, they had been sold last winter in order to keep food on the table. "And, of course, Anne seems to grow an inch taller every year," Bess said, thinking to halt anything indiscreet Anne might say. "I am having constantly to buy new shoes for her. But you know how the young seem to shoot up overnight. Why, I swear Charles grew two inches in a month."

"How old are you now, Anne?" Dante asked, thinking Anne bore a startling resemblance to Bess when young.

"Eleven," Bess answered quickly.

Alastair Marlowe choked on his brandy. Whipping out his handkerchief, he wiped his tearing eyes, a look of guilty dismay on his face as he eyed Anne Seacombe.

"Mother!" Anne said in disbelief. "You know I am fifteen. Why, we just celebrated my birthday last month," she reminded her mother, staring at her as if she'd gone mad.

"Really?" Bess said with an embarrassed laugh. "I can scarcely keep up with the years anymore. Fifteen?" Bess said weakly, thinking that Dante's child bride couldn't be much older than that. Glancing at Rhea, she was struck again, unpleasantly so, by her incredible beauty. Damn her, Bess thought, and glancing down into the sherry swirling around in the glass she held so tightly, she could see her own reflection. Suddenly she seemed old and haggard, for the face reflected there was distorted and seemed horribly to point to the future. "Good Lord, Dante, do you realize that your wife was hardly out of swaddling when you and I knew one another?" Bess asked incredulously, turning the ever-increasing years against him now. "It may not seem like so many years between you and your wife now, but wait until you get a little older, my dear. I hope you'll be able to keep up with her, for I should hate to see her having to look elsewhere for"—Bess paused delicately, then continued—"well, for an escort."

Despite Bess' hateful words, Rhea suddenly felt very sorry for Bess Seacombe. She hadn't missed the stricken look on the older woman's face when her daughter said she was fifteen. Rhea knew that Bess must be suffering for losing Dante at all, let alone to a much younger woman. Rhea understood the despair Bess was feeling, for she herself would not be able to go on living if she lost Dante.

The hour that followed seemed an eternity. Finally Bess thought she heard the winds dying down. She wasted no time bidding her host and hostess farewell, for she could stomach only so much, and seeing that possessive, loving expression in Dante's gray eyes when he gazed at his wife was almost too much for Bess.

The worst of the storm had indeed passed when Bess was helped into the saddle by a strong young groom. She was riding a horse borrowed from Dante's stable.

"We'll keep Bristol Boy here as long as you like, Bess," Dante offered, standing beside Rhea as they watched their guests depart.

"Thank you," Bess replied shortly. She had looked in on her horse and couldn't find anything to complain about in the way his injury was being handled. Clauson seemed to know his job. "I'll be back over in a couple of days to see how he is doing. I should be able to take him home then."

"Are you certain you want to take that path across the moors? It'll be muddy after the rains," Dante asked, concerned. "I'm going to send a couple of the grooms along to escort you," he decided suddenly, for he would hate to see Bess and her children stranded on the moors when darkness fell. "There is no hurry about sending the extra horse back, Bess. If you need it to replace Bristol Boy, then keep him awhile."

"That is not necessary, Dante," Bess said, but she was pleased that he should care. It had been a long time since anyone had been concerned about her welfare. "And thank you for the offer, but I have a well-stocked stable. It's one of the few things Harry left me," Bess said with a bitter smile.

"Nevertheless, I intend to see that you reach Seawyck with no further delays." Dante intended no slight, but to Bess it sounded as if he could hardly wait to get her off his hands.

"Thank you," she said in such a subdued voice that both Dante and Rhea glanced at her in surprise, wondering what was wrong.

Rhea and Dante remained standing together in the opened doorway of the lodge, watching the Seacombes and the two grooms ride away.

"She is not a very happy woman, Dante," Rhea spoke sadly. "I feel so sorry for her."

Dante glanced at his wife, smiling. "I can remember quite well when you were of a mind to send her to the gallows," he reminded her.

"She has suffered enough for the mistake she made all those years ago. She lost you. Instead, I have you," Rhea said, looking up at him, little realizing how seductive her look was.

"I would have said that *I* have *you,*" Dante responded, and since they were alone on the small entrance porch, he took Rhea in his arms and held her close, the warmth of her body burning his. Then his lips met hers in a long, tender kiss.

Bess Seacombe glanced back at the lodge just in time to see them locked in that passionate embrace. Her eyes filled with tears. It was not fair, she thought, feeling such a deep bitterness that it almost tasted like poison in her mouth.

"Mother? How could you possibly have thought I was only

eleven years of age?" Anne demanded, which was the wrong question at the wrong time. "You knew very well that I was fifteen. We spoke only recently of how other girls my age were wed and even giving birth," Anne continued, and the unpleasant thought that she could very easily be a grandmother soon hit Bess like a blow to the stomach.

"Well, my dear, you know how *old age* makes a person forgetful," Bess said between gritted teeth, little realizing how very beautiful she was looking with her windblown hair and her cheeks flushed to a rosy hue, her dark eyes sparkling with anger.

"I cannot believe how very beautiful Lady Rhea is. And she is so nice, too. Not at all what you would expect of a duke's daughter," Anne said, salting the wound. "And, Mother, I can see why you were so much in love with Dante Leighton. Why, he is the handsomest man I have ever seen," Anne went on. "He looks just like a Greek god. Don't you think so, Mother? And did you see how very attractive that nice Mr. Marlowe is?" Anne asked hesitantly, blushing.

"No, I didn't, but then my eyesight isn't what it used to be," Bess muttered. "If you are casting your eyes at any one, then I should take a closer look at Lord Chardinall, for he will be a duke one day, and a very, very wealthy young man. He's damned attractive too—for a mere boy, that is," Bess added on a savage note.

"Mr. Marlowe is very wealthy, too, Mother. He had quite a large sum of that sunken treasure they found. I overheard that young Conny Brady talking about it. It was quite an adventure. But anyway, I would think you would be pleased that I care more about my feelings for a man than for his bank account. After all, that was the mistake you made," Anne reminded her mother, which was the last thing Bess wanted to hear.

Anne eyed her mother in growing concern, for her mother could have a terrible temper. Not that she ever hurt them; it just made her more difficult to live with. "What is wrong, Mother? Have I said anything to anger you?"

"Anger me? Of course not, my child," Bess denied in a tight voice. "I am just surprised by some of the things that seem to be on your mind of late. Like men," Bess couldn't resist adding. "There is plenty of time, Anne."

"But, Mother, you were little older than I am when you were engaged to Dante Leighton. Why should it be different with me?" Anne asked.

"Mother? Conny and Lord Robin said I could come over anytime and go exploring with them," Charles' young voice piped in, reminding Bess of yet another responsibility. It didn't help to think that her son was the same age as Dante's wife's brother. "Can I, Mother? Can I?" he pleaded.

"Oh, Charles, not now," Bess said, cutting off his pleas, but when she saw his hurt expression, she relented. "I shall have to think about it. Ask me tomorrow, dear."

"Yes, Mother," Charles said in his usual subdued tone.

"I thought you were very rude to Lady Rhea, Mother," Anne said suddenly, much to Lady Bess' surprise. "She is a very polite person, and I could see that she was trying to be very nice to you."

"Nice? Pity, is what it was," Bess said harshly, her anger spewing forth at last. "You could see it in those big violet eyes. Who ever heard of a person with violet eyes? Lord help me if I don't scratch them out," Bess said, glancing back to make certain the grooms from Merdraco hadn't overheard.

"I don't understand you, Mother," said Anne. Having never been in love, Anne couldn't understand the desperation her mother felt.

"That is because you are so damned young. Well, you just wait, my girl, until you are my age and you see the only man you have ever loved come swaggering home with a wife young enough almost to be your daughter, and I'll wager you'll not be welcoming her with open arms. Talk about rotten luck," Bess raged, her vision blurring with hot tears. "It isn't enough to have made a mistake, but to have to keep on paying for it, well, 'tis just too much. Who would have thought Dante would become the man he has? Or return to Merdraco as rich as Croesus? Lord, the infamy of it all," Bess cried, wondering what more could happen.

"Mother?"

"What?" she sniffed, wiping away her tears with the back of a gloved hand.

"I think that is Jack Shelby coming toward us with some of his men," Anne said in a quivering voice. She still had nightmares about the night Jack Shelby had attacked her mother.

Bess Seacombe could have cried all over again. Jack Shelby was fast becoming one of her more vexing problems. Sniffing back her tears, she raised a haughty chin and prepared to face whatever insults would come of this encounter. She was glad that Dante had insisted on sending the two grooms with them, not that either lad could really have done anything to help should Jack Shelby turn meaner than normal.

"Well, well, what have we here?" his hateful voice called. Bess found herself shuddering at the mere sight of the man, for she could remember only too painfully the feel of his hands on her body. "Been out for a ride, have we?"

"How very observant," Bess said coldly.

"Still the uppity one, eh, Bessie?" he asked, thinking he'd never seen her looking more seductive. "Thought I'd taught you a lesson or two about not showin' me proper respect," Jack Shelby said with a meaningful glance at her bodice. The wild beating of her heart was causing the lacy jabot at her throat to flutter.

"It must have slipped my mind," Bess remarked, as though anything he might have to say was not worth remembering.

"Ah, Bessie, you're quite a woman. Reckon I'll have to be teachin' ye that lesson again real soon. Only this time," he said with a piercing glance at a pale-faced Anne, "I don't think there will be any interruptions. Will there, Annie girl?"

Bess saw the petrified expression in Anne's dark eyes and cursed Jack Shelby to hell for frightening her daughter. "If you don't mind, we are in rather a hurry to reach Seawyck before it rains again," Bess told him.

"Oh, well, by all means, m'lady. I wouldn't want ye catchin' your death of cold because of me," Jack Shelby said in elaborately polite tones, then asked with a suddenness that took Bess by surprise, "What ye been doin' on this path? It leads to Merdraco. Oh-ho, so you couldn't resist payin' a call on your old beau, eh, Bessie?" he said, roaring with laughter at her outraged expression.

"Get out of my way!"

"And how does he look to ye after all this time?" Jack Shelby taunted unmercifully. "Reckon ye paid your respects to that pretty young thing he's brought back with him, eh, Bess old girl? Now, that is one sweet little girl he's got warmin' his bed. Aye, that bastard always had an eye for a slim ankle."

Bess Seacombe glared at Jack Shelby's gloating face, knowing how fast she could wipe away that grin. "We took tea at the lodge, which Lady Rhea has fixed up to look absolutely beautiful. And, of course, now that Dante has returned so wealthy, 'twill be no time at all before he has Merdraco looking just like it did fifteen years ago—perhaps even grander. Now that he has an heir to inherit Merdraco, the Leighton line will continue."

Jack Shelby's face changed with every word Bess uttered, and for a moment Bess was actually afraid. But he had pushed her too far, and the memory of that tender scene between Dante and Rhea still hurt her, and she did not feel charitable toward anyone just then, least of all this swine.

"Reckon his lordship oughta be enjoyin' every single moment he's got, for he's not goin' to be around much longer to enjoy his money or that pretty wife. His son may inherit Merdraco a lot sooner than he thinks. He may have gotten away with it once, but he'll pay for killing my Lettie, you just wait and see," Jack Shelby vowed.

With a curt nod at Bess, he sent his horse down a narrow, twisting path that led off across the moor, his men following close behind. Jack Shelby was one of the few men who knew how to steer clear of the dangerous bogs, and Bess could have sworn that she heard his laughter drifting back to them as the riders became specks in the distance.

"Mother?" Anne asked softly, but Bess pretended not to hear. "Mother, why didn't you say something? You could have told him that Lord Jacqobi didn't murder his daughter. You told me you had proof. Why did you let him go on believing that? Why did you let him threaten Lord Jacqobi like that? Why, Mother? What if he murders Dante Leighton? It will be your fault," Anne said. And for the first time ever, when Bess met her daughter's dark eyes, she saw contempt. It struck deep into Bess, and she knew suddenly she had done wrong. She was horribly ashamed.

But having lived the lie for so long, she wondered what she

could possibly do now. Was it not already too late to do anything about the secret she had kept for so many years?

"'Tis our secret, Robin," Conny Brady whispered between sips of hot chocolate.

"Aye. Just like pirates' buried treasure, eh, Conny?" Robin whispered back excitedly. Besides, he'd be in trouble if Rhea learned they had gone down to the beach in defiance of Dante's warning, and when Robin exchanged glances with Conny, who was keeping a careful eye on the captain, he knew that Conny was worrying about the very same thing.

So neither boy told about how they had nearly drowned. Neither boy talked about their dangerous climb up the slippery rocks, or about the cave. And neither boy revealed the startling discovery of the underground passage they found leading out of the second cavern they fled into when the sea swelled into the cave. That passage, the sides and roof shored up with hand-hewn timbers of great age, led up through the darkness for what seemed like miles, to a flight of stone steps that led directly into the lodge! It was an exciting discovery, and they were sure that nobody else had made it.

That was why Houston Kirby had not seen them return to the lodge. The boys had climbed the stone steps, which stopped before a wooden panel. Peering through a peephole which was disguised on the other side as a plain knothole, they stared in amazement into the empty corridor leading back to the lodge kitchens. They slid back the panel, Robin's expertise with the secret corridors of Camareigh having located it, and emerged into the safety and warmth of their very own home. That was when Houston Kirby spotted them, assuming they had entered through the kitchens.

Thus another secret came into their lives. It was a secret that might very well end in tragedy.

> *After a storm comes a calm.*
> Matthew Henry

Chapter 31

GREAT black curling plumes of smoke rose into the cloud-less blue skies over Merdraco. Seeing from a distance the glowing copper flames tinged with indigo, one would have thought this was some bizarre *danse macabre*. In the courtyard the blackened skeletons of chairs and tables and chests were stacked high into a funeral pyre, purging Merdraco of the defilement perpetrated against it.

Dante Leighton stood close to the heat of the fire, raising his face to both sun and flame as he cleansed himself of the vileness and dishonor which had marked Merdraco. And like the immortal Phoenix rising from the ashes, Dante saw in the burning bright flames a new beginning for Merdraco.

The flames leaped high into the sky, trying to outdo the sun, but Dante continued to stand there in silence, honoring

455

the memories of those Leightons who had gone before him and in whose name he would carry on the traditions of Merdraco.

Blinded by the dazzling light, Dante heard rather than saw the peregrine falcon soaring overhead in search of prey. His cry was the harsh, predatory cry of the hunter, but it lasted for only a second, and in the ensuing silence, Dante heard the soft, melodic cooing of a wood pigeon. It was the gentle song of that ringdove which remained in his thoughts, for at last he had found peace within himself. He had banished all the old, haunting memories, as well as purging Merdraco, so perhaps the dead could at last rest in peace and he could get on with the day-to-day joys and sorrows of living.

With a sigh of satisfaction, Dante turned away from the fire, which was consuming the past. He left to the workmen from Merleigh, who had arrived punctually that morning, the pleasure of completing the task he had started. Some pieces of furniture had escaped the flames. They were the ones that a little sanding and refinishing would restore. But Dante had not wanted them, and had told the workmen to keep whatever they felt they could use.

When they had first come into the courtyard and heard what he had to say, he had caught concerned glances exchanged among the men. But when they entered the great house, he saw that doubt turning to disgust, then to anger, for no decent man would condone what had taken place within the halls of Merdraco. Soon the men entered into the spirit of the purge. They made a giant bonfire, reminiscent of a Guy Fawkes celebration, only without an effigy to burn. But Dante, judging by the grumblings, thought the villagers had a likely candidate in mind. Everyone knew who had been behind the brutality.

Brushing the ash and cinders off his coat sleeve, Dante started to walk away. Then he paused to glance back at the men, laughing and joking while they stood around the bonfire watching the dancing flames. Dante had recognized William Brownwell and several others from the tavern in Merleigh, but what surprised him was the men he did not recognize, and whom he discovered came from Westlea Abbot. He stared thoughtfully at several of those men and reminded himself to thank Sir Jacob, for these were men who might very well be tenants of Sir Miles Sandbourne; yet they had come to Merdraco to work for him. He wondered if perhaps, over the years, Sir Miles' genial mask had slipped askew and others had come to see the corruption which lay beneath. But with Sir Jacob, still a highly respected gentleman, standing by his side, Dante thought he could win against Miles.

His step lighter than it had been for many a day, Dante walked past the stables to the arch, which led to another, smaller courtyard. He stopped for a moment, gathering his courage, then entered the small chapel where his mother and father were entombed. Until that moment, he had not been able to step into the cool darkness. He had been shamed by the past and what had happened to Merdraco because of his weaknesses. Because he had run away from his responsibilities and had failed to protect what was trusted to him, he had lost all that had been held sacred by his forebears.

But now he could face all of that and face the memory of his parents. He could make his peace with them without shame, for he had returned to Merdraco victorious. He had reassembled his father's beloved collection of fine *objets d'art* and regained the Leighton lands. And he had, he hoped, become a man his mother would be proud to call her son.

He had cheated Sir Miles of his revenge. And by doing that, he had avenged the crimes committed by Sir Miles against his parents.

Standing before their sepulcher, Dante, his head bowed, stared at their effigies. He reached out and touched the cold stone of his mother's cheek. "Too late," he whispered. Then he abruptly turned away from the gloomy, damp, airless chamber.

Outside the air was thick with smoke which burned his eyes, and as Dante walked toward the fire, his eyes were luminous with tears. He breathed deeply of the smoky air, reveling in it, for it signaled the end of misfortune. Soon the winds from his beloved sea would catch the smoke and scatter the ashes.

Blinking away the tears, Dante glanced around the courtyard. He was seeing the great house, the stables, and the gardens as they had once been and how they would look one day soon.

Tomorrow the floors and walls would be scraped and scoured. A week later would be heard throughout the great house and across the courtyard the sound of saws and hammers as carpenters set to work replacing the rotten timbers and the shingles in the roof. The gaping holes in the floorboards and walls would be patched, sealing off the drafts that swept through the house. Then the windows would be repaired and new glass fitted into the countless panes. The blacksmith would forge new hinges and a lock so the iron gates would once again bar entry to trespassers. Merdraco would soon know again the sound of its master's voice echoing along the corridors and resounding throughout the Great Hall.

From London would come the finest architect to redesign many of the rooms, his specially trained artisans carving a new balustrade for the great staircase; putting in paneling and mantelpieces; creating elegant plaster ceilings to bring an airy lightness to the rooms of Merdraco; replacing the cracked and scarred marquetry floors. And from the most exclusive shops in the land would be chosen wallpaper and materials for chairs, settees, carpets, and draperies. And then, when all was as it should be, the treasured possessions that had graced the halls of Merdraco long ago would be sent for. And from the windows, with their sparkling panes of leaded glass, would be an expansive view of the gardens and arbors and terraced walks, the emerald green stretches of lawn and parkland, all brought back to life by a veritable army of gardeners who would weed and prune and plant.

As Dante Leighton began to see change taking place in his beloved Merdraco, that first day of beginnings passed. It gave way to another day and then another. The sun retreated against the fall of darkness, which in turn gave way to the moon's rising. The pale, silvery light spread across the black landscape, where shadows took on a life of their own.

And it was on such a night as that, when an ivory crescent of light traveled across the sky, that those shadows first began to threaten the peaceful existence that Rhea and Dante had established at the lodge. The day's activities were examined and discussed over a finely prepared meal served on the great banqueting table. Flickering light from several silver candelabra reflected the gleam of fine china and crystal. Lively conversation was punctuated by laughter while the diners lingered over dessert.

"Tell me more about this Charles Town smuggler called Bertie Mackay. Did he really wear black velvet breeches all the time?" Francis asked.

"Oh, aye, that he did," Houston Kirby confirmed, eyeing his dessert suspiciously because he hadn't been the one to prepare it. "But that wasn't the worst of it. 'Twas mostly the size of them breeches which caused so much concern among the townspeople. Just to make one pair took several yards of material. Seein' how he fancied wearin' a fresh pair every day, there never was so much as a black velvet ribband to be found in all the Carolinas. All the black velvet went into makin' breeches and jackets for Bertie Mackay. In fact, some said that half of what he smuggled into the Carolinas was black velvet cloth just to keep himself in breeches."

Francis laughed. "I am not certain I believe you, Kirby."

"Kirby is prejudiced, for he never cared much for our smuggling rival," said Alastair.

"Aye, right ye are, Mr. Marlowe, for Bertie Mackay would have slit your throat from ear to ear as soon as smile at ye," Houston Kirby reminded his former mate. "Doesn't ever pay to let your guard down. There be folks out there just waitin' to catch ye dozin', mark my words," Houston Kirby pronounced with a worried glance at the captain, who, with a fine show of indolence, was slowly swirling brandy in a glass. Receiving no acknowledgment, Kirby sent a disgusted glance at Jamaica, who lay curled up before the hearth. "Reckon some folks and critters might be gettin' a bit soft nowadays. Reckon ol' Jamaica couldn't catch himself a fat old mouse even if it were sittin' before him on a platter."

"Coooeee, that'd sure look funny," Conny said with a wide grin. One of the maids grimaced with dismay, and Conny exchanged knowing glances with Robin, but before ideas could take root in their minds, Rhea coughed, drawing their attention.

"I think it is well past your bedtime, boys," Rhea suggested, much to their displeasure despite the fact that both had been yawning widely.

But Rhea was adamant. She was beginning to remind Robin more and more of their mother. With a shrug of defeat, snatching a tart to be split between them later, Conny and Robin said good night. Their steps, interrupted by an occasional scuffling noise, faded up the stairs.

"I wonder what the big secret is that they've been keeping?" Francis asked as soon as they were out of earshot.

"You think they've been up to something?" Dante asked while he toyed with the dessert in front of him, most of which he had left uneaten.

"I know my brother too well not to be suspicious when things go too smoothly. I have been expecting to find something slimy and crawling in my bed each night, but as yet I have managed to escape their pranks," Francis said.

"I think Conny must be a very good influence on Robin," Rhea commented, much to the amusement of the captain and two of the crew.

"How did the stallion do when you took him back to Seawyck?" Dante startled Alastair by asking. Under those penetrating gray eyes Alastair found himself growing uncomfortable.

"Didn't limp at all. In fact, I had a devil of a time keeping him from racing most of the way there. I don't know how that woman controls him. I hate to admit it, but he was almost too much horse for me," Alastair said with a shake of his light brown curls. He hoped that would end the subject, but the captain's eyes were too sharp, and Alastair heard him ask the question he dreaded hearing.

"Did you happen to see the lady of the manor? And, perhaps, her lovely daughter?" Dante's quiet tones always held a wealth of meaning.

Alastair Marlowe actually blushed while stuttering out what he thought sounded like a reasonably intelligent reply. "Uh, yes."

"And how were they?" Dante asked, enjoying teasing him. Alastair had been rather too eager in his offer to return Bristol Boy to Seawyck Manor, and had Dante not caught a certain look in Alastair's eyes when he gazed at Anne Seacombe the other day, he would have suspected his former supercargo of having a penchant for Bess.

But it was her daughter Alastair Marlowe was interested in, and that fact would be enough to set Bess off on another tirade, Dante thought. It was too obvious that she was becoming concerned about her age. As Dante thought of the possibility of Bess Seacombe becoming Alastair Marlowe's mother-in-law, he stared at Alastair with both amusement and pity. What that man might have to face in the future! Still, Dante was pleased to see Alastair show an interest in courting. He was becoming annoyed by Alastair's constant attentions to Rhea.

"Quite well. Invited me in for tea," Alastair finally admitted, much to Dante and Francis' amusement. But Rhea was frowning slightly, for it sounded to her as if Dante were trying to elicit information about Bess from Alastair. In his next breath, Alastair confirmed the fact that Bess was trying to learn more about Dante's recent life.

"I felt as if I were being questioned by the Inquisition, so curious was Lady Bess about everything you've done, Captain," Alastair said with a grin, getting even with his friend for putting him on the spot. Too late, he realized how that sounded to Rhea, and he glanced at her apologetically, but she was smiling politely.

"I am sure that Anne was impressed to hear of our privateering days. You did tell her, did you not, about finding that sunken Dutch merchantman?" Dante asked thoughtfully.

Alastair Marlowe looked embarrassed. "Well, as a matter of fact, the subject did come up."

"Don't suppose, though, that you told her about how we met the cap'n?" Kirby asked with a sly grin.

But Alastair Marlowe surprised Kirby and his captain by his answer. "Why, yes, I did, much to the amusement of Lady Bess. She enjoyed hearing about your caped figure coming out of the gloom, the torches smoking and flickering in the rain," Alastair said. It was a situation few men trying to impress a woman would have admitted to, since he had been drunk at the time and was being chased by a press gang.

"I am sure the ladies were quite concerned to hear about the danger you were in," Francis remarked with an understanding smile that should have warned Alastair.

"Yes, do you know, I believe they were, especially Anne. I really wasn't certain if I should continue with any more stories about our bloody battles," Alastair Marlowe said. If it had been anyone besides Alastair, they would have found his concern for the ladies' sensibilities quite suspect.

"But you did?" Dante asked.

"Well, yes, but only at Lady Bess' insistence. Rather blood-thirsty woman," Alastair muttered, remembering how those dark eyes had shone with excitement.

"It struck me that Anne Seacombe seemed a very sensible girl. Rather subdued, yet I suspect there is a bit of Bess lying beneath that gentle exterior," Dante said, for Anne possessed the same dark sensuality that her mother did.

"Yes, I thought much the same myself," Alastair agreed readily, pleased that Dante should think so highly of Anne Seacombe. "She also seems very mature for her age. But of course fifteen isn't all that young," Alastair said quickly.

Rhea stared at her friend in amazement, realizing for the first time that Alastair Marlowe was interested in Anne Seacombe.

"Hmmmm, Anne Seacombe. Yes, she is quite a beauty, isn't she?" Francis said, a speculative look in his blue-gray eyes. "Next time you call on the Seacombes, perhaps I shall accompany you," Francis said, much to Alastair Marlowe's dismay. Francis Dominick was a handsome young man, and Alastair knew he could never compete against a duke's son for a woman's hand.

Seeing Alastair's uneasy look, Francis took pity on him and added, "But, of course, I shall probably be returning to Cama-reigh before I have a chance to pursue that friendship."

Francis nearly laughed aloud, for Alastair Marlowe quite visibly relaxed. "I shall be sorry to leave here, for I have enjoyed your company, Alastair," Francis said, and Rhea could have hit him. Poor Alastair was no match for Francis' jesting.

Alastair looked ashamed. He truly liked Francis Dominick, who seemed at times far older than his years. "I shall miss our conversations, too. But, of course, you will be returning often."

"Yes, but will you be here when I do?" Francis asked.

Alastair Marlowe remained silent, as if that thought had never occurred to him. Suddenly it caused him concern, for he had come to think of this as his home, and the thought that he might have overstayed his welcome caused him great con-sternation.

Reading his mind, Rhea said, "I hope you are not planning to leave while we are in the midst of rebuilding. You have been so much help to us. I really don't know what we should do without you. Why, Dante was telling me just the other day how much easier he is, knowing that if he isn't at Merdraco supervising the work, then you are. He trusts you to see that his wishes are carried out. Of course, we cannot be selfish and expect you to stay here forever. I do know you are interested in finding an estate, and we shouldn't wish to keep you from doing that. But since you haven't found anything suitable yet, why not stay here with us? Unless, of course, you *must* leave us," Rhea concluded sadly, not meeting either Francis' or Dante's eyes.

"Oh, no, I wouldn't abandon you! Especially if I can be of service to you," Alastair Marlowe reassured Rhea, suddenly feeling much lighter of heart. It seemed he'd just been given an open invitation to stay at the lodge until he wished to leave, as if he were a member of the family. The captain apparently agreed, and he was even smiling.

Dante Leighton was eyeing his wife in wonder. He had always known how very charming she could be, but he hadn't realized exactly how conniving she could be until he listened to her adroit maneuvering of Alastair. The gentlemanly Alastair Marlowe had never had a chance against Rhea.

"Oh, I'd almost forgotten," Alastair said suddenly, looking sheepish. "When I was returning from Seawyck, someone came up to me and gave me this note for you. I am sorry I forgot about it until now," Alastair apologized.

With apparent lack of concern, Dante took the note from Alastair and pocketed it without a glance, and also without satisfying the curiosity of the others.

Alastair Marlowe's future was still in Rhea's mind later in the evening while she sat before her mirror and brushed out the tangles from her unbound hair. Crowded across the surface of the small rosewood and gilt dressing table which had survived the journey from Camareigh were crystal and porcelain bottles of delicate scents, a silver patch box inlaid with precious stones, the silver comb which matched the brush in Rhea's hands, a pastille burner filling the room with a fragrant blend of honeysuckle and roses, and other things necessary for a lady's proper toilette.

While she brushed the long, golden strands of hair, Rhea

hummed the melody coming from the tinkling music box which occupied some of that precious space on her dressing table. Humming, she smiled at Dante's reflection in the mirror. He was taking off his shirt and stretching his tired muscles.

"We shall have to make certain that Alastair and Anne Seacombe come to regard one another as more than friends. 'Twould be a good way of making certain that Alastair stays here in Devonshire. I would miss him terribly if he were to leave and go to live in York, or some other out of the way place."

"Many consider Devonshire a wild, unsettled place," Dante reminded her.

"That is because they are not here with us. Why, if we were in York with Alastair, then I shouldn't think it an inhospitable place at all, because I would be there," Rhea stated with a last long brush.

"To my dismay, I am actually beginning to understand you at times," Dante complained. Sitting down on the edge of the bed, he began to remove his shoes while watching Rhea, who left the dressing table and began tucking in the blankets round their son. The baby's hands were reaching out to her and he chuckled, gazing up at her with big wondering eyes.

"I cannot believe how fast he is growing. Every day he seems an inch or two taller," Rhea said, pressing a kiss into each tiny hand.

As she moved away from his cradle, she passed in front of the fire and paused a moment to warm herself. In the glowing light, Dante could see the contours of her body outlined through her thin lawn nightdress. His gaze traveled along the slender line of calf and thigh to the womanly curving of hips, to the small waist. Once again he could encircle it with his hands. The uptilted outline of her small breasts caught his eye, and he felt that tightening in his loins that would find relief only in a slow, sensual exploration of every scented inch of that body, the body he had come to know better than his own.

His expression must have given him away, for when Rhea met his gaze, she blushed. But she didn't look away. She came toward him, pausing just before she reached him to drop her nightdress from her shoulders, leaving it rumpled at her feet.

Dante stared at Rhea, thinking she had never seemed quite

so stunningly beautiful as she did just then, standing before him, revealing all her womanly secrets, giving of herself so naturally and so completely.

"You are so lovely," he whispered, his hands reaching out to pull her close, his lips caressing hers with lingering sweetness as he sought to taste of what she offered so temptingly.

Rhea wound her arms around his neck, moving against him, the heat of his bare chest burning her breasts as they pressed against him. When his hands moved along her spine, she felt a melting pleasure inside her. He caressed her soft buttocks while he held her closer against his hips, and soon the physical needs of his love for her could no longer be controlled.

Picking her up in his arms, he gently put her down on the bed. She seemed to disappear into the soft folds of the silken comforter. Within minutes he had joined her, his body covering hers while he buried his face in her golden tresses and breathed deeply of her scented flesh.

"Little daffadilly," he spoke against the softness of her mouth, "I love you so."

Rhea cradled his head against her breasts, feeling his tongue against the hardening nipples, and then his mouth was against hers, robbing her of her breath, and then the hardness of him was against her, driving deep inside her, and she gave herself to him without restraint of heart or soul. Dante was a part of her, and she knew that she could never exist without him.

The fires of their consuming passion left Rhea weak but contented, and she dozed off. But she awakened with a start, feeling the bed moving beneath Dante's weight. She opened her eyes to see him sitting beside her, fully dressed.

"Dante?" she asked in sleepy confusion. "What is amiss? Kit?" she demanded instinctively.

"No, nothing is wrong. I have to go out, Rhea," Dante said quietly. "But since you are such a light sleeper, I thought you might awaken while I was gone and I did not wish you to concern yourself. I shall not be long," he told her, pressing a kiss against her troubled brow.

"But why? Where are you going?" Rhea demanded. Despite his wishes, she was most concerned. "It has to do with that note Alastair gave you, doesn't it?"

"I cannot tell you, but will you trust me?" he asked, his fingers caressing her sleep-warmed shoulder.

Rhea remained silent. In the darkness he could not see the indecision crossing her face. He must have sensed it nonetheless, for he found her lips in the darkness and kissed her deeply.

"Trust me, Rhea. You can, you know. I would never do anything to hurt you," Dante said, his breath hot against her face.

Rhea put her arms around his neck, as if she were seeking desperately to hold him to her. Her lips clung to his. "I do trust you, Dante. I do, but that does not keep me from worrying. This has to do with those smugglers, doesn't it? Must you go? Can't you leave everything as it *is?*" she pleaded, but he shook his head and, moving her arms from his neck, kissed the palm of each hand, as she had kissed Kit's hands earlier.

"Go back to sleep now and dream of me, little daffadilly," he told her. Then she heard the sound of his boot heels against the floorboards, and then there was silence.

Rhea hugged her arms around her shoulders. "Dream of you? That is the problem. I can do nothing but dream of you— even during my waking hours," Rhea whispered. Throwing back the coverlet, she climbed from bed. Finding a shawl from the big chest at the foot of the bed, she wrapped it around her shoulders and curled up in the big winged chair beside the fireplace and prepared to wait until Dante had returned safely.

> *Bait the hook well: This fish will bite.*
> Shakespeare

Chapter 32

"**Y**OUR informer keeps late hours," Dante Leighton commented, shifting his weight from his left leg, which had gone to sleep.

"He can afford to," Sir Morgan Lloyd responded, his voice not much above a whisper. He carefully parted the prickly holly leaves and peered through the hedge they were hiding behind. He was looking at the lone man standing impatiently by his horse underneath the overhanging branches of an ancient oak.

"What makes you so certain there will be a meeting tonight?"

"I made certain that there would be by baiting the hook well. I often tried to do that with you, but you were never hungry enough to bite," Sir Morgan said wryly.

467

"Or, perhaps, greedy enough?" Dante retorted.

"Perhaps. I let it be known that I would be in Bristol day after tomorrow, and—"

"—that happens to be the first night of no moon. And who will be in charge of your command while you are away, Sir Morgan?" Dante inquired.

"Why, Lieutenant Handley, of course," Sir Morgan commented casually. "In fact, I have left him in command quite often over the past few weeks. He has done an exemplary job. He has not apprehended any smugglers, but he's managed to confiscate a hidden cache of several casks of brandy and bolts of velvet. He and his men discovered the caches hidden in an abandoned farm cottage on what is, I believe, Leighton land. It does look bad for you, Captain," Sir Morgan murmured, but he sounded unconcerned.

"It was not black velvet by any chance, was it?" Dante asked, smiling in the darkness.

"Thank God we don't have Bertie Mackay to worry about," Sir Morgan responded after a moment of silence. He had finally remembered the story about that jovial smuggler's fondness for velvet.

Dante rested his head against the rough bark of the tree trunk he was leaning against and stared up at the pale sliver of moon. "'Tis rather ironic, wouldn't you say, that we should be standing here together waiting to catch a traitor working with smugglers. After all, I am a former smuggler and was once an enemy of yours."

"The irony of it had crossed my mind," Sir Morgan said smoothly.

"I have, in the past, paid well for such information, Captain," Dante admitted.

"I know, but you never plotted the murder of an officer of the Crown, no matter how close he might have come to catching you. You couldn't have or I would probably be long dead."

Dante was silent for a long moment. "You have taken rather a risk in trusting me. I gather that precious few people are aware of your plans. Should you be mistaken about me, you could very easily end this night with a knife in your back."

"A minute ago you spoke of irony. 'Tis strange, Lord

Jacqobi, but you are the only person I truly do trust. In part that's because I know what happened to Merdraco at the hands of the smugglers, and I imagine that you are as anxious to catch them as I am. But as I told you before, I came to know you as an opponent, and sometimes a man comes to admire and respect an enemy more than he would a friend. I would turn my back on you without hesitation, and there are few other men I would trust that far. Why do you think I walked so calmly out of White Horses Tavern in Charles Town the night we drank rum together? I knew that, if you had seen anything dangerous in that scurvy bunch of smugglers, you would have warned me."

His admission startled Dante Leighton as few others things had ever done. "I am honored," he said quietly.

"Then you do not mind if I call you by your given name? Titles become rather cumbersome after a while," Sir Morgan suggested.

"Indeed, if you had not suggested it, I certainly would have, Morgan." Dante's smile matched the smile curving Sir Morgan Lloyd's mouth at that very instant.

But their smiles faded quickly at the sound of approaching hoofbeats. They stared through the hedge and, in a few minutes, saw two men engaged in earnest conversation.

The two were Jack Shelby, whom Sir Morgan Lloyd and Dante Leighton had followed from Merleigh, and Lieutenant Handley, whom Sir Morgan had been expecting. Indeed, Sir Morgan would have been surprised if the lieutenant had not shown up. The two were arguing, so their voices carried clearly.

". . . and not a farthing more!"

". . . or you'll not be receiving any more information."

"Don't be threatening me, you—"

". . . a cold day in hell before I deal with you again, *Mister* Shelby," the lieutenant spoke up bravely, surprising both Dante and Sir Morgan. Neither had thought the baby-faced blackguard had it in him.

"One of these days, laddie . . . just ye wait . . ." came the threat, and then there was the jingling of coins as Jack Shelby tossed a small leather pouch at Lieutenant Handley's outstretched hand. "He won't be likin' this."

"... your problem ... Bristol ... Thursday night ... and where shouldn't I patrol?" was all the spies heard of that exchange.

Dante felt the hairs on the back of his neck rise as he heard Jack Shelby's low laughter and saw the lieutenant take a step backward. Just then Dante heard the words that chilled him. "Dragon's Cove."

He heard Sir Morgan's gasp, and Dante knew that Sir Morgan was thinking of savoring his revenge against Jack Shelby and the smugglers who had wrecked H.M.S. *Hindrance* and killed his brother.

"You must be crazed. Why there? ... too dangerous."

"D'ye care now that ye've got your blood money? Watch it! I've got me knife handy, and I've got me reasons for wantin' to land in Dragon's Cove," Jack Shelby growled.

There was silence except for the jangle of that money pouch, and then there was a harsh laugh.

"Countin' it? Aye, reckon ye shouldn't be trustin' anybody if ye expects to live very long."

Suddenly the lieutenant turned on his heel and stalked away into the trees. There were the sounds of hoofbeats and then silence.

"Fool!" Jack Shelby spat. "Wouldn't live long if I was in charge. Reckon that highborn whore might want some company tonight, seein' how her lover has such a pretty little wife. 'Twill be a long, lonely trip," he went on, raving aloud. "Teach her a lesson. Let him know I've had her, too, just in case he cares." Jack Shelby was muttering as he disappeared into the trees, unaware that his display of bad temper had been a great boon to two men hiding nearby.

"Well. I've got my traitor. And soon I shall have my smugglers," Sir Morgan said softly after a long silence. "And then I shall have their leader, for this rabble won't keep silent when their necks are so close to being stretched."

"Have you any ideas?" Dante asked absently, his thoughts elsewhere.

"Some, but I haven't any proof," Sir Morgan admitted. "What do you know of Sir Jacob Weare?"

Dante nearly laughed. "Jacob? You can't seriously believe he is the leader of the smugglers. I think you've got your man, and that's Jack Shelby."

"You know Sir Jacob well?" Sir Morgan asked.

"Quite well. Besides, he is too old to go gallivanting around the countryside hiding contraband."

"The leader of these Sons of Belial needn't dirty his hands with the actual smuggling. I have discovered that Sir Jacob is quite well off, whereas many of his neighbors have suffered losses. He seems to have enough income that he warrants close investigation. I also understand that he is the grandfather of Lady Bess Seacombe and that your engagement to her was broken off because of him. You must have had bitter words. Perhaps he bears a grudge against you and ordered the smugglers to ransack Merdraco?" Sir Morgan was saying until he heard Dante's low laughter and stopped, surprised.

"Although it has been a secret, Sir Jacob Weare has been my confidant for the past fifteen years. If it hadn't been for his tireless help and his belief in me, I would not be in possession of my family's lands and heirlooms. Sir Jacob Weare, contrary to what people have been led to believe, has been my eyes and ears here in Devonshire for years. Believe me, he is not the man you are looking for," Dante assured Sir Morgan.

"Thank you. That helps considerably. And I shall keep your secret," promised Sir Morgan. Then he said, "I shall see you day after tomorrow?" They made their way back through the woods to their horses.

"Naturally," Dante replied.

"I thought as much."

"How will you clip the lieutenant's wings so he doesn't fly the coop?" Dante asked.

"I shall put him aboard ship. I believe he cannot swim. And with a troop of marines, all of whom I can trust, I shall be waiting for our smugglers when they land. I shall have a ship stationed just outside the cove so that when the smugglers flee, they will be apprehended."

"Just make certain that the captain of your revenue cutter doesn't come into the cove," Dante reminded him.

"He will have orders to stay at sea no matter what happens," Sir Morgan said. A bit later, becoming aware of the other man's silence, he asked, "What is wrong? Is someone coming?" he demanded then. They had ridden back to the road and were about to part when Dante suddenly halted.

"I was thinking of something I heard Jack Shelby say just before he left, about visiting a certain woman. I think the woman is Bess Seacombe, and I doubt she is expecting him," Dante shocked Sir Morgan by saying.

"Bess Seacombe and Jack Shelby?" he asked incredulously.

"I do not think it an association she desires. What if she has had no choice but to lend her horses to this gang, or let them store their contraband at Seawyck?" Dante asked. Already he was guiding his horse across the lane and toward the path he knew cut across the moors to Seawyck Manor. He had spied a lone rider on that path minutes before but had said nothing.

"I warned her that I expected cooperation from anyone who knew anything about the smuggling gang," Sir Morgan said, following Dante along the winding path.

"Bess will do as Bess sees fit. She's hardheaded. She has fallen on hard times, too, although she would not admit that to anyone, not even to her grandfather, who would help her if only she would ask." They moved more swiftly across the moors, their horses becoming accustomed to the path.

"I noticed the threadbare appearance of Seawyck Manor," confided Sir Morgan.

"If I know Bess," Dante worried, "she will not have spared Jack Shelby's feelings if he made any overtures to her. And Jack Shelby is a man who enjoys carrying a grudge." They were close enough to see the solitary stone house squatting on the distant rise.

When they entered the yard, everything was quiet. "I think you ought to wait here," said Dante. "If Jack Shelby is in there, we don't want him to see us together. He might cancel the smuggling run if he becomes suspicious of you. Most likely he thinks you a fool, like most of the King's men, so let's just let him keep on believing that," Dante suggested as they dismounted behind the shelter of the stables, out of sight of the house.

"Very well," Sir Morgan agreed. "But if you're not back within fifteen minutes, or if I hear anything strange, I shall not hesitate to come in." Sir Morgan would not hide while Dante faced danger.

Dante moved slowly along the side of the stables, keeping an eye on the main part of the house as he slid from shadow to shadow. As he approached one of the outbuildings, he spied a horse. Coming up alongside, he patted the big bay's rump. It was covered with sweat.

Dante moved closer to the windows of the house which overlooked the entrance. But they were dark.

He moved onto the steps leading to the front door, but the door was firmly locked. Moving around the side of the house, he made his way toward the kitchens, passing through the garden full of spicy herbs and ripening vegetables. There he discovered how Jack Shelby had gotten into Seawyck Manor. The door leading into the kitchen wing of the house had been splintered at the lock and it stood ajar.

Dante had made his way through the dark rooms into the hall when he heard Bess' scream, followed by a man's laughter. He bolted up the stairs just in time to see Anne Seacombe come running out of another room farther down the hall, a poker raised high above her head. She sank against the wall, shivering, when Dante silently waved her back.

The door to Bess' bedchamber stood open, and as Dante approached it, he heard Jack Shelby muttering with pain. Dante reached the door in time to see Bess' teeth biting down hard on Shelby's thumb.

With little effort, he jerked his hand free and, with the other hand, ripped her nightdress away. Bess, dazed, couldn't believe the horrible nightmare was actually happening all over again. She might have remembered her recent wish that someone would come along whom Jack Shelby wanted revenge against and who had the devil's own luck. Had she opened her eyes to glance behind the broad-shouldered form leaning over her, she would have seen her wish enter the room.

Dante Leighton's cold voice nearly caused both Jack Shelby and Bess Seacombe's hearts to stop. Shelby spun around, looking as though he had just been shot. And that would have been his fate had he taken a step closer to the pistol barrel leveled at his chest. "You!" he spat, yellow eyes glowing like the eyes of a trapped wild animal.

"I think you had better take your leave now before I thrash you to within an inch of your life," Dante said so calmly that it took Jack Shelby a moment to realize what had been said. He was about to snarl a retort when the expression in those pale gray eyes made him think better of both the remark as well as the sudden move he was planning. Death was written in those eyes, his death. He knew, as he had known that night in Bishop's Grave Inn, that it wouldn't take much to persuade his enemy to pull the trigger.

"Reckon ye got the pistol *and* the woman tonight, *m'lord*. But there will be other nights, and other meetin's between us, and soon I'll be takin' a great deal of pleasure in makin' ye beg me to put an end to your life. Ye'll be pleadin' with me, beggin' for mercy, and I'll laugh in your face," Jack Shelby promised. "Ye won't be lucky next time. And then I reckon I might have to pay a visit to that sweet little wife of yours. Reckon she'll be mighty lonely with ye lyin' cold in yer grave.

"Reckon she might even be lonely *now*, seein' ye've got yourself a mistress. Wonder what she'd be thinkin' if she knew where ye was tonight?" He turned back to Bess. "I'll be back to teach ye another lesson, Bessie. Ye and I ain't finished yet," Jack Shelby told her with a leering grin as he stared at her naked body.

"No, not that way," Dante said when Jack Shelby started for the door.

"What?"

"'Tis rather stuffy in here. Why don't you open the window?" Dante said, much to Jack Shelby's dismay. "Don't bother closing it on your way out," Dante finished softly.

Jack Shelby's eyes narrowed with hatred. With an obscenity thrown over his shoulder, he went to the window. Opening it wide, he climbed onto the sill. It was farther than he had hoped for, but the pistol gave him little choice. He jumped.

There was a thud, then a scraping sound, and then another thud. Jack Shelby hit the ground in about the same spot he had landed before.

Dante hurried to the window and stood watching until he saw a horse and rider galloping away from the house. With a grim smile, Dante closed the window, drawing the draperies securely shut. Suddenly he became aware that Bess was laughing.

Her midnight black hair tumbling across one shoulder and swinging around her hips, Bess was shaking with laughter.

"Thump, thump, thump. Poor Jack, 'tis the only way he knows how to leave Seawyck," Bess gasped.

"Everything is all right now, Bess. You are safe," Dante told her gently. That gentleness broke Bess' control, and she started to weep, cupping her face in her hands.

Dante hurried to her side and took her in his arms, rocking her, his hands smoothing her hair as she sobbed, her tears soaking into his coat.

It was this scene that Sir Morgan Lloyd walked in on, his eyes widening as he saw Dante holding the naked Lady Bess Seacombe, her pale skin so startlingly white against the blackness of her long hair.

"I beg your pardon," he said harshly, the image of Lady Rhea Claire crowding his mind.

Dante glanced up and when Sir Morgan met those pale gray eyes, he saw no lust in them, only pity and concern, and he realized he had come to the wrong conclusion. His eye was caught by the ripped nightdress and he cursed under his breath.

"He didn't—" he began, leaving the rest of the sentence unfinished.

"She became hysterical. She's shaking with fear now, but in a moment, unless you get that coverlet around her, she'll be shaking with cold," Dante suggested to the suddenly flustered Sir Morgan, watching as he carefully placed the coverlet around Bess.

"H-he has been threatening me ever since I wouldn't let him have my h-horses. H-Harry would be turning over in his grave if h-he could see h-how the smugglers have abused them," Bess was saying between gulps of air. "I-I didn't want to help, but I needed the money. I h-have a family to raise. What was I to do? I couldn't let my children starve, could I?" She asked, gazing up into Sir Morgan's compassionate blue eyes, her fingers locked on the lapels of his naval uniform.

Dante walked back to the window and pulled the heavy draperies aside. He stared out on the lightening skies. Dawn was breaking, and the shadows which had seemed so ominous were fading, but he felt no lightening of spirit. He wondered where Jack Shelby was and what would happen if they failed to catch him when he next tried to run his goods ashore; for Shelby was hellbent on revenge.

> *Sits the wind in that corner?*
> Shakespeare

Chapter 33

ESMA SAMPLES hadn't been a coward. She put up a valiant struggle before she died. Her body was discovered the next morning by some workmen from Merleigh as they followed the narrow path across the moors to Merdraco.

It was ironic that one of the men who came across her battered body had, as a boy of fifteen, discovered the body of Lettie Shelby over fifteen years earlier, and in exactly the same place. That might even have been why he looked in that direction, for he had never been able to pass the spot without thinking about the grisly find he had made that day while hunting rabbit.

He had known Lettie Shelby, and he had also known the

widow of Ted Samples, who had disappeared while crossing the moors and was never seen again.

It was only human nature that the frightened villager from Merleigh would remember who had been suspected of the murder of Lettie Shelby. The Marquis of Jacqobi had just returned to Merdraco after a fifteen-year absence. There hadn't been a murder like this one in fifteen years, he realized.

Dressed in the rose brocade with the white silk stomacher embroidered in a pale green leaf pattern with small satin rose-buds which Dante had purchased for her in London, the jeweled replica of the *Sea Dragon* adorning it, Rhea looked as lovely as the flowers she was arranging in a crystal vase on the hall table.

"Oh, that is pretty, m'lady," Betsie said, eyeing the golden daffodils with pleasure. "Why, even Saunders would approve of these," she said, the head gardener at Camareigh springing to her mind. "What d'ye think of that, Lord Kit?" she cooed, cradling the baby. Lord Kit's mother smiled as she went about arranging the colorful spring blooms throughout the lodge.

"There, that should do for now," Rhea finally said, satisfied. "Take the rest of these flowers and put them in a vase for your room, Betsie. I'll take Kit," Rhea said.

"Oh, m'lady, thank you. 'Twill be like sleepin' in the garden for sure," Betsie giggled as she handed the chuckling baby over to his mother. She gathered up the bundle of flowers. "M'lady?"

"Yes?" Rhea glanced up, smiling. Kit's tiny hand was wrapped round her thumb with surprising strength.

"I just wanted to tell ye that we, well, the others and me, we're real pleased to be here at Merdraco with ye. 'Tis kind of nice livin' by the sea. And although the lodge isn't Camareigh, it's very nice. And one day soon we'll be movin' into the great house, and that'll be like a palace, I'm sure," Betsie rushed on. "Well, we just wanted to thank ye for bringin' us with ye to Merdraco. We are all real proud to be servin' ye and his lordship," Betsie said. "And we're real glad ye married him and not the Earl of Rendale."

"Why, thank you, Betsie," a deep voice commented, surprising the women. They turned around to see Dante Leighton standing at the head of the stairs. Betsie's young heart fluttered, so handsome he was with his dark chestnut curls brushed back from that bronzed face, and his pale gray eyes smiling down. And dressed in a stylish blue frock coat and fawn-colored breeches, his waistcoat cinnamon, his stock elegantly folded, he was every girl's desire.

"Oh, m'lord!" Betsie squeaked nervously, worrying that she had been indiscreet. Curtsying hastily, she hurried off with her armful of flowers.

"I do believe that is one of the nicest compliments I have ever received, being considered preferable to the good Earl of Rendale," Dante said with a grin. "You and our son are up early."

"'Tis getting well into the summer now, and we have many things to do before winter," Rhea told him. She did not look forward to the howling storms she knew would blow in off the sea and isolate Merdraco. But as she glanced around the cozy lodge, she realized that she wouldn't mind too much. She had come to think of it as home. And with her family around her, Rhea decided she could outlast the storms.

In that special way of lovers, Dante guessed her thoughts and said softly, "So you wouldn't mind being stranded here with me during the long, cold months of winter?"

"Not if every night could be spent like last night," she said without any pretense of coyness. "Well, *most* of the night," she amended, for she had spent a few uncomfortable hours curled up in a chair, waiting for Dante. It wasn't until nearly dawn that she had finally heard him on the stairs.

Dante reached out and captured one of the golden curls dangling over her shoulder, pressing a kiss to her temple.

"It won't be much longer, Rhea. It will be all over soon, and then we can begin to live here at Merdraco as I have long dreamed of doing. After tomorrow night, there will no longer be any shadows. We and our family will be able to live out our lives in happiness at Merdraco, our home. I swear to you that our children will have a life different from mine. I ask no more than for our children to know the happiness that was your life at Camareigh," he said quietly, his fingers caressing the nape of her neck.

Their son cradled between them, they stared at one another's eyes, and each felt a new kind of belonging which strengthened their love.

The spell was broken by the sound of running feet as Conny and Robin charged down the stairs, excitement shining in their eyes. Each day presented new adventures for them.

"I'm hungry," Conny called as he landed on the bottom step with a thud. He was nearly knocked off his feet by Robin, who slid off the waxed balustrade.

"And a good morning to you, too," Rhea said firmly, thinking that her mother would wonder what she had let Robin get up to recently.

"Top o' the mornin' to ye," Conny mimicked the former quartermaster of the *Sea Dragon*. "I wonder what Mr. Fitzsimmons is up to," he asked Dante.

"Probably no good," Houston Kirby replied as he came out of the kitchens carrying a silver teapot. He placed it alongside several other silver pots of varying sizes and shapes, the aromatic steam rising from them drawing Conny and Robin to the table. There were dishes of freshly baked bread; scones and buns still warm from the ovens; muffins and crumpets; jams, jellies, and preserves; and thick cream for the coffee and sweet chocolate.

Cooking odors have a way of sneaking through a house, and soon Francis Dominick was making his way down the stairs, politely shielding a yawn. It was apparent that he had dressed in a hurry.

"I am beginning to see why sailors seem so hearty. I swear I haven't had an appetite like this since I was Robin's age. It must be the sea air," Francis commented as he reached the last step. He nodded a good morning to everyone, then paused to grin down at his young nephew and tickle his tiny pink foot. Kit giggled, delighted.

"Good morning!" Alastair Marlowe called from the top of the stairs, a wide grin of pleasure on his handsome face. He started down the steps. "Looks like a fine day. I think I might take a ride over the countryside. Might even pay a call on Sir Jacob. Perhaps he can advise me about some land around here." Alastair had decided to let his intentions be known.

Dante Leighton met Alastair Marlowe's rather hesitant gaze, then smiled. "I am very pleased to hear that. I was hoping you would decide to settle near here," he said. "I may be able to help, since I have been buying up most of the land around here for the past few years," Dante said with an apologetic look at the younger man.

"Are you quite certain you wish to remain in this wild countryside?" Francis asked with a serious look. Rhea was experienced enough not to trust that look, but poor Alastair fell for it every time. "I happen to know of some rather good land over toward Buckinghamshire way. Maybe we should have a look at it before you decide on Devonshire. I should be more than pleased to show you around that area."

"Well, that is generous of you, but I wouldn't wish to waste your time, Francis," Alastair began.

"Not at all. We can even stay at Winterhall while we are looking around. I am sure that Sir Jeremy and Caroline would be pleased to see us," Francis added matter-of-factly, but he had put the broad width of the table between them by the time he said it.

Alastair Marlowe looked like he had been broadsided, then his laughter blended in with the Francis' and they sat down at the table, still laughing. But before anyone else could sit down, an imperious knock sounded.

"Now who on earth could be calling at this hour?" Francis demanded, not pleased at the prospect of his coffee growing cold.

But Francis, and even Conny and Robin stopped thinking about their stomachs when the footman escorted three grim-faced gentlemen into the lodge.

Sir Morgan Lloyd was about to speak when the elegantly clad man in plum-colored silk who was at his side stepped forward and demanded arrogantly, "I demand that you arrest this murderer at once." His gaze fastened on Dante.

To say that Sir Miles Sandbourne's statement had caused a deathly silence to fall over the room might have been ex-aggerating a bit, but it certainly caught everyone by surprise, especially the man he had pointed to and demanded the arrest of, and that was Dante Leighton.

"Did you hear me, Captain?" Sir Miles repeated, his eyes not missing one detail of the spotless and comfortable appear-ance of the lodge, the table set for breakfast, or the friendly atmosphere which his entrance had disturbed.

"Yes, I heard you, but I shall use my own judgment in this

matter," Sir Morgan said quietly. His tanned face was pale as
he faced the residents of the lodge. It was especially hard for
him to meet the violet eyes that had smiled at him so warmly
once, long ago.

"What is the meaning of this, Captain? This is my home,
and I will not stand here being accused. This man has dared
to trespass onto Leighton land despite the fact that he was
warned against doing so," Dante spoke coldly, his contemptuous glance flicking Sir Miles like a whip. "Please tell me
what this is about."

"There has been a murder," Sir Morgan began, signaling
to the third man in his party. "Esma Samples, Mr. Lascombe's
sister-in-law, was found strangled out on the moors this morning. She was last seen in Merleigh sometime last night. Apparently she was hurrying to some assignation, and it ended
in her death."

Dante Leighton, his pale gray eyes narrowed, looked more
like the captain of the *Sea Dragon* than the master of Merdraco.
"And why should I be under suspicion? No! Let me guess,"
he said, holding up his hand. "This woman's body was found
in about the same place Lettie was found. Perhaps there were
other similarities between the two murders. And since I was
suspected of the first murder, I am now suspected of this one.
Is that correct?"

"You are the *only* suspect, my lord," Sir Miles Sandbourne
corrected.

"This is absolutely outrageous. How dare you come into my
home and accuse my husband of killing?" Rhea cried, her eyes
sparkling with anger as she moved between Dante and Sir
Miles.

Sir Morgan looked away, unable to meet her eyes. "I am
sorry, Lady Rhea Claire, but I have to carry out my duty
regardless of the circumstances."

"Even if outright lies are involved?" she demanded incredulously. "Oh, Sir Morgan, I was so mistaken in you. You are
not a friend to us. You never have been," Rhea charged. A
single tear fell down her cheek.

"Rhea, please don't," Dante said, but he could not say
anything further without revealing the secret of his partnership
with Sir Morgan. And as Dante thought of their night together,

it suddenly came to him what a dilemma Sir Morgan found himself in. He was Dante's only alibi, but he could not say anything without jeopardizing their plans.

"I can understand why you are here, Sir Morgan," Dante said. "I respect you for doing your duty. But what I fail to understand is why you are here, Sir Miles. Is it to satisfy your curiosity about the lodge?" Dante inquired softly.

Sir Morgan looked most uncomfortable as Sir Miles declared grandiloquently, "I happen to have every right to be here. In fact, I have a greater right than Sir Morgan, except for his having been granted certain powers over civilian authorities," he complained. "I am the local magistrate. As such, I have the authority to apprehend anyone I suspect of wrongdoing."

"What proof have you that I murdered this woman?" Dante asked.

"It does indeed seem strange, and perhaps 'twill be convincing enough to a judge, that there was a murder fifteen years ago. You were suspected then. Indeed, your watch was found clutched in the young woman's hand. Now you return after fifteen years and there is another murder, identical to the first one!" Sir Miles sounded as if he were already the prosecutor.

"That is ridiculous!" Alastair Marlowe exploded, but Sir Miles was unruffled. "I am sure any judge would find it hard to believe that a murderer other than you would be so patient as to wait over fifteen years to commit murder simply to implicate you," he sneered. Sir Miles' arguments, as presented by a smooth-talking prosecutor, would be believed by judge and jury, for Dante Leighton would be a stranger to the court.

Sam Lascombe was shuffling his feet back and forth. "I just dunno if that's the truth," he finally said, much to Sir Miles' irritation. "Reckon it looks bad for his lordship, true, and reckon 'tis strange that another murder should take place just when his lordship returns. But..." he paused, not knowing how to continue.

"But?" Sir Miles urged, making a great show of containing his impatience. He pulled out his watch and sighed.

"Well, she was my sister-in-law. Married to my wife's late brother, she was, and, well, Dora and me think the smugglers killed them both. Yes, we do."

"That is ridiculous!" Sir Miles snorted derisively. "Why

should smugglers harm a village woman? What is Lord Jacqobi paying you to buy your silence? If you're perjuring yourself, I'll see that you're hanged for standing in the way of justice," Sir Miles threatened, and Sam Lascombe, deeply frightened, kept silent.

"Please, let the man finish," Sir Morgan said, and Sam began again, though reluctantly. "We figure, Dora and me, that the same ones who killed her brother Ted also killed Esma. She probably knew too much about the smugglers. See, Ted threatened to leave the group, and then he disappeared. Well, reckon they thought Esma could cause them trouble, too. Ted would have told her whatever he suspected. She was mad enough to do some talkin' 'cause they murdered him and left her with them fatherless children. We'll be takin' the children into the Bishop, I guess," Sam Lascombe finished, looking down at his big gnarled hands. "Never thought when she and her boy stopped t'other day at the Bishop, on their way to Westlea Abbot, that it'd be the last time we'd see her alive."

"And I suppose Lettie Shelby knew too much about the smugglers, too?" Sir Miles scoffed, dismissing the entire theory. "Your story is absurd. We know who killed Esma Samples. Dante Leighton did. He killed fifteen years ago and now he's killed again. I'll see that he is hanged this time," Sir Miles swore, his eyes glowing.

"But you see, Sir Miles, he did not murder Lettie Shelby fifteen years ago," a voice called from the opened door. "He was with me that night. In my bed. And he did not leave me until well into the morning. So you see, he did not murder that night." Bess Seacombe had made her admission at last.

Sir Miles Sandbourne looked ready to strangle her. "It seems strange that you did not say as much fifteen years ago," he murmured. "Even if this were true, which I doubt, that does not explain last night. Before we entered the lodge, we checked the stables and found a horse with mud splattered on his legs and flanks. It appeared that someone did leave here last night. I should imagine it was Dante Leighton, and I am wondering where he went," Sir Miles said silkily. Finding that horse had been a fine stroke of luck.

"You are right, it was Dante who rode last night," Bess said. "He was with me last night, and did not leave until well past dawn." Her eyes met Rhea's startled gaze just briefly. Then she looked at Dante's for his reaction. Relief and regret, both, were reflected in his eyes. He was cleared of the murder of Esma Samples, but he was damned in the eyes of his wife.

Dante glanced over at Rhea. She was staring at him as if seeing a stranger. He wanted to reach out and touch her, but she looked away as if she couldn't bear the sight of him.

"I think we had best leave now," Sir Morgan sighed, deeply unhappy over what had happened. Still, if all went as planned, then they would be able to reveal the truth to Rhea tomorrow night. "I think we have more than overstayed our welcome," he said.

"What? Are you going to *believe* this woman's tale? She is obviously his whore, and she will say anything he wishes her to. You cannot take her seriously?" Sir Miles' voice was shrill. He had been cheated out of an easy case against Dante and he was furious.

His anger turned to amazement when Rhea spoke up. "You, of all people, Sir Miles, should know that what Lady Bess says is the truth. Dante confided in you fifteen years ago that he was with Bess that evening, yet you chose to keep silent about it all this time. It suited you to see Dante's name blackened. Lady Bess has come forward this time and cleared Dante's name of both crimes. You had better look elsewhere for your murderer and for a chance to hurt Dante," she finished in a clear, steady voice. Her listeners were stunned by the declaration. She had been faced with his infidelity only moments before, yet she gave no indication of that fact.

"You're a fool, Lady Rhea," Sir Miles spat, taking a step backward as Dante moved toward him. "He got Bess to lie for him then and she's lied again now. I did not believe his story. That was why I kept silent." Sir Miles made a futile effort to defend his actions, but the fact that he hated Dante and would do anything to destroy him was apparent to all the others. "I insist that you investigate this matter, Sir Morgan. I have friends in London who will see that you are court-martialed if you don't do your job properly," Sir Miles warned.

"I said, Sir Miles, that I would decide this as I saw best. Now I suggest we leave." Then Sir Morgan added a bit of his own malice. "I will not be held responsible for what happens to you after I leave, Sir Miles." With a slight bow, he turned on his heel and left, Sam Lascombe following quickly after him.

Sir Miles stood where he was, fuming. Then he turned and stalked to the door, throwing one last barb to Rhea. "Remember this, Lady Rhea. Dante Leighton cannot be trusted. He's made a fool out of you and a whore out of Bess, and may you all three be damned."

After the three men had left, a terrible silence descended. There must have been a hundred different expressions crossing those stunned faces. At last Rhea could not bear the strained silence any longer. With a mumbled apology she hurried to the stairs, climbing as quickly as she could while holding Kit and managing her skirts.

Rhea stared around her at the sudden emptiness of her room. Kit was in his cradle, waving his hands and feet, his baby sounds comforting her a little as she stood there, numbed.

"Rhea?"

She turned away from the voice.

"Rhea? God, don't turn away from me," Dante cried as he came into the room: "Rhea, please, don't turn away from me," he pleaded. He tried to take her into his arms, but she was stiff and unyielding.

Dante turned, pacing back and forth as he tried to find the right words. He couldn't possibly tell her the truth. What if they failed to catch the smugglers tomorrow night and Jack Shelby went free? How could he endanger Sir Morgan's plans and even his life? And what danger might too much knowledge mean to Rhea? No. He could not endanger her.

Dante stopped his pacing and glanced down, surprised to find her staring up at him curiously. Looking her straight in the eye, he did the best he could.

"Rhea, I asked you before to trust me. I also asked you not to believe what might seem the truth, stories which make me out to be a liar and a cheat. You must believe me that it is truly not as it seems. I was with Bess this morning, but nothing happened. Nothing. I swear to you, Rhea," Dante spoke softly, his pale gray eyes never leaving her eyes.

"Dante," Rhea said, but he held up his hand to silence her.

"I love you with all my heart. There is nothing dearer to

me than you, Rhea. You are the most precious thing in my life. You are my love, my wife, and my friend. I trust you as I would no one else, and I think you have trusted me, too. I would never do anything to destroy that trust. Believe in me, Rhea. I know it is asking a lot of you, but please do, Rhea. I don't think I can survive unless I know I have your love," Dante said, bowing his head in pain.

"You will always have my love," Rhea said simply. "And if you tell me that nothing happened between you and Bess, then I believe you. I have to. If I could not trust you, Dante, then I could not go on loving you. And if I could not go on loving you, then I could not go on living. It is as simple as that." And taking his face in her hands, she pressed her mouth against his.

After a moment she said, "Whatever it is you must do, then know that I shall always be here waiting for you," she promised. With her gentle kiss sealing their love, with her unselfish, unquestioning loyalty, Dante knew that he would triumph.

> *There sighs, lamentations, and loud wailings*
> *resounded through the starless air, so that at first*
> *it made me weep; strange tongues, horrible lan-*
> *guage, words of pain, tones of anger, voices loud*
> *and hoarse, and with these the sound of hands*
> *made a tumult which is whirling through that air*
> *forever dark, as sand eddies in a whirlwind.*
>
> Dante

Chapter 34

UNDER cover of darkness, the smuggling sloop was once again running contraband ashore. Two flashes of light followed by three had signaled the all-clear and, boldly, the sloop had come within three miles of shore, delivering her cargo into the small waiting boats.

On shore, a group of silent men stood waiting, ready to sling the brandy, tea, and tobacco from the boats and make the long, hard climb back up the cliff. From there, they would tramp along the narrow, rutted lanes to a nearby farmhouse or inn and unload their casks and crates onto the backs of horses. That was the plan.

But at sea, things were going wrong. The smuggling sloop found herself under chase by a revenue cutter that had sailed out of nowhere. The cutter tried to eat her out of the wind by sailing so close to the wind that the sloop dropped to leeward. All her canvas set, the cutter gave chase. After firing shots across the sloop's bow, she caused the lesser armed ship to heave to, and the cutter's troop of armed marines took the smuggler's crew into custody without so much as a stubbed toe among them.

On shore, the waiting smugglers found the beach invaded by troops of marines and dragoons. Many of them carrying torches, the troops swarmed onto the beach from hiding places among the rocks, their muskets firing warning shots into the air and sand.

But the smugglers on shore were better armed than their counterparts at sea. Their muskets firing back at the King's men, they stood their ground. They had nothing to lose. Soon clubs were brandished, and torchlight glinted on sharp-edged knives. Cutlasses swished through the air with deadly accuracy.

Dante Leighton knew he was dreaming, for he could see Rhea's pale face drifting in and out of focus before him. That long, golden hair was floating around her bare shoulders like seaweed on the tide, a phantom, sometimes there and sometimes not. But the violet eyes never disappeared. He could feel them staring at him, drawing him away from the darkness threatening to overtake him.

Gulping for breath, he felt cool water lapping against his face and choked on the salt water. Suddenly he felt a hand gripping his shoulder and, with a desperate strength, he knocked the arm away and rolled over. His knife flashed in a murderous arc, but he stopped in time to recognize Sir Morgan Lloyd above him.

"Don't forget, we are on the same side," Sir Morgan yelled over the roar of voices, some raised in pain, others in rage, but most unintelligible, ringing out around them.

Dante shook his head to clear it, realizing that Sir Morgan had been standing guard over him until he regained consciousness. He had probably saved Dante from being clubbed to death or drowned. Beside him, however, one of the smugglers hadn't been so lucky. He was floating facedown in the water, arms outstretched while his blood seeped into the sea. Dante wondered if it had entered Sir Morgan's mind that this particular smuggler might have been the one who had murdered his brother.

"Are you all right?" Sir Morgan demanded, his gaze probing.

"Yes. *Thank you*," Dante said, and coughed, struggling to rise, his feet slipping out from under him as the tide rushed out. When he glanced up again, Sir Morgan was engaged in a wrestling match with some unfortunate smuggler. Sir Morgan would be invincible that night, Dante thought, for he had his chance to avenge his brother's death.

Dante staggered through the tide, moving his leaden legs out of the water until it was just swirling around his ankles. He stumbled up the beach, his step steadying as he searched for one particular face. So far, the man he wanted more than anybody else had managed to elude him.

Jack Shelby stared through the peephole in the paneled door that opened into the dark hallway of the lodge where Dante Leighton and his family had been living. He was breathing heavily, for it had been a long climb up to the cave, then a tiring walk through the dark, narrow tunnel that winded away from the beach, from that hellish scene of betrayal and death.

Jack Shelby's yellow eyes were glowing with madness that precisely reflected the scene he had fled. Torches had glowed eerily, and the tide roared like thunder, drowning out the sound of pistol shots. And through it all he had seen one figure, a man who strode toward him, the pale gray eyes searching only for him.

Dante Leighton was like the devil after his soul, Jack Shelby thought. In his mind Jack suddenly saw his beautiful Lettie, so full of life. She had been only fifteen when all that vitality had been stilled forever.

But Dante Leighton was still alive. Dante Leighton still walked the earth. Dante Leighton still laughed and took his pleasures. Dante Leighton still breathed, while his Lettie rotted in the ground.

Dante Leighton had returned a wealthy man, and once again he was lording it over all the land, destroying others. His own men had thrown down their weapons and had fallen to their knees begging for mercy. Aye, they'd been that cowardly lot from Merleigh and Westlea Abbot. They had either stood there watching, putting up no fight, or joined the King's men and turned their clubs on his best men from Bristol and London. Well, he'd get even with them all, Jack Shelby vowed, just like he'd get even with Dante Leighton.

A slow smile crossed his face as Jack Shelby quietly opened the panel and stepped into the hall.

Time's glory is to calm contending
kings,
To unmask falsehood, and bring truth to
light.

Shakespeare

Chapter 35

SITTING at her dressing table, Bess Seacombe stared at her reflection in the gilt-edged mirror. She didn't like what she saw, and that shocked her. She had always rather liked herself, but now she stared hard at herself, and the more she saw, the more she disliked herself.

"Damned if I'm going to play the harlot or the bitch any longer," she muttered, dragging the comb through her long dark hair. Until she had gazed on hair the color of molten gold, she had always been pleased with her black-as-night tresses.

Tilting her head sideways, she eyed the firm line of her chin, patting it just in case, noting the softness of her skin. Try as she might, she couldn't find any wrinkles or even laugh lines—but then, there hadn't been much to laugh about lately.

Bess avoided the dark eyes staring back at her. She couldn't forget the stricken look on Rhea Claire Leighton's face when she heard Bess' declaration. Damn it all, the woman was her rival. Why should Bess care how Rhea felt?

Bess turned her back on the mirror, staring at her big, empty bed, the one she had slept in alone for two years. She took a deep breath. It would probably be easy to cause trouble between Dante and his young bride. But she remembered Dante's face when he saw Rhea's hurt expression. With a woman's true instinct, Bess knew she had lost him. Never had she seen such a tender, caring look on Dante Leighton's face. Or on any man's face, for that matter.

And try as she did, Bess couldn't dislike the child bride Dante had brought back to Merdraco. Bess knew that the girl was head over heels in love with Dante. Too, there was a sincere, honest quality about the chit that even Bess had to admire.

Taking her hair in her hands, she twisted it into a chignon, pinning it firmly, then got to her feet. She risked one last glance in the mirror. This time, however, she didn't have to look away when she met her own eyes. She knew what she was about to do, and though some might call her a fool, Bess Seacombe had found respect for herself at long last. She was going to make certain that Lady Rhea Claire Jacqobi knew that nothing had happened the other night between Dante and his *former* love. Bess glanced at the clock. It was late, but she'd be damned if she was going to lose another night's sleep fighting her conscience. Late, and uninvited, she was going to Merdraco.

Jack Shelby waited in the shadows of the hall, a terrible look in his eyes as he watched the people sitting before the hearth in companionable silence. He smiled. They were completely unaware of danger. It was a shame, he thought, eyeing the beautiful golden-haired Lady Rhea with regret. But the best way of hurting his enemy would be to deprive him of the thing he loved the most, and that was his beautiful, golden-haired wife.

She was sitting there so innocently, gazing into the flames, waiting for her loving husband to return. And all the while, Dante assumed that she was safe.

Jack Shelby stared at the fire burning so brightly in the hearth. He could almost feel its warmth from where he stood, out of sight in the hall. He glanced around at the beams rising high above his head and at the fine wood paneling and then at the wood floors and the heavy oak·furniture. It would all burn so brightly.

With a smile which would have made the devil himself uneasy, Jack Shelby crept back along the corridor.

"I really don't understand you sometimes, Rhea," Francis Dominick said softly, wishing not to disturb Alastair Marlowe, who was sitting nearby, reading.

"Why?" Rhea asked, glancing up from the embroidery she was trying to keep her attention on.

"Why?" Francis repeated, raising his voice without meaning to. "Because you are so damned trusting. That's why!" Exasperated, he ran his fingers through the curls that were the same shade of gold as his sister's.

"You mean Dante?" she asked.

"Of course I mean Dante. Here you sit while he runs off again, and I suppose Bess Seacombe will show up soon to claim he has been with her all night," Francis said hotly, then shook his head in regret. "I'm sorry. I didn't mean to bring that up, Rhea."

"I understand. But I'm afraid that you don't understand, Francis," Rhea said calmly. "You have never been in love. One day you will be, Francis, and when you are, you will understand that unless you trust fully, you cannot love fully. The one cannot exist without the other," Rhea explained as if talking to a child. "Dante asked me to trust him, to have faith in him. If I claim to love him as much as I do, then how can I not believe in him? How can I be true to myself if I cannot be true to him?"

Francis was mystified.

"One day you will understand, Francis," Rhea said. "Although Dante has not told me as much, I fear that he is involved in trying to track down these Sons of Belial, and that causes me far more worry than a possible rendezvous with Bess Sea-

combe. At any rate, Dante denied that anything happened between him and Bess, and I believe him," she said. Also, she
had the memory of his lovemaking on that evening, and she
knew he could not go from her to another woman like that.

"Why he was with Bess Seacombe, I do not know. But
when he can, Dante will tell me," Rhea said serenely. Francis
stood up and kissed her on the cheek.

"You are too good, my dear. I only hope that you are right
about Dante. I really hope you are, for I have come to like
him quite a lot," Francis admitted, grinning as he settled himself
back into the chair across from her. Glancing over at Alastair
Marlowe, he was surprised to see that gentleman staring
thoughtfully into space, as if pondering what he had overheard.

Francis' smile widened. Resting his head against the back
of the chair, he closed his eyes for a moment. But then he
opened them, thinking that the fire was smoking a great deal.
Francis sniffed, growing very concerned. There was little
smoke from the fire, yet it seemed the whole room was filling
with a smoky haze. Then he saw flames licking at the windows
all along the front of the lodge.

"Rhea! Oh, my God!" he screamed hoarsely, jumping to
his feet just as the fire, with a shattering of glass, spread into
the lodge.

Alastair Marlowe jumped to his feet, incredulous. How
could any fire spread as fast as this fire was spreading? The
flames were already eating away at the west side of the lodge.
In a minute, unless they got out through the kitchens, they
would be completely surrounded by the red-hot flames.

Rhea had already started for the stairs, for Kit and Conny
and Robin were all in their beds.

"I'll warn Kirby and the servants," Alastair cried as he ran
toward the kitchens, where a small corridor led to the several
rooms tucked away in back.

Francis had hold of Rhea's arm as they stumbled up the
stairs together, choking for breath. The upstairs was already
filling with smoke.

"I don't understand how the fire could become so hot so
quickly!" Francis yelled. "I just spotted it less than a minute
ago. How could it already be here?" he asked. They could see
flames climbing up the second-story windows.

"Oh, Francis, I'm scared," Rhea cried as she hurried along the smoky corridor. She could see smoke seeping out from under her door, where Kit was.

Francis stopped at Conny and Robin's room. "I'll be right there, Rhea!" he called out to her as her figure disappeared down the hall. He threw open the door and shook the boys, one after the other.

"W-what's wrong?" Robin mumbled groggily.

"Too early," said Conny.

"Get up!" Francis hollered, shaking him until he thought he heard Conny's teeth rattling. He reached across and pulled Robin from beneath the blankets.

"Francis, leave me be!" Robin yelled at him, thinking his brother had lost his mind.

"The lodge is on fire! We've got to get out of here!" Francis cried, grabbing each and pulling them from the room after him. "Wait here. Don't move! I've got to get Rhea," Francis was saying when she appeared farther down the hall, a bundle wrapped up tightly in her arms as she hurried toward them.

"The only way out is through the kitchens. Alastair must have gotten the maids and footmen out by now," Francis cried as he led the way down the hall, trying not to jump backward when he saw how close the fire had traveled in only minutes.

"Coooeee!" Conny Brady coughed his favorite saying, his eyes horrified. The flames stood taller than he, and they raced along the floor of the hall where the family had dined that evening.

Robin Dominick was blinking his tear-filled eyes, his hand tightening painfully on Francis'. As they neared the base of the staircase, they could feel the heat of the fire like a blast from an oven door. "Francis!" Robin screamed when his hand slipped from his brother's grasp. "I can't see! Where *are* you?" he cried.

"Here I am. Don't worry," Francis said, and choked. He wondered where his next breath would come from. The smoke had become so thick. "Rhea? Are you all right?" he demanded, for he had lost sight of her.

"I'm here," she said, and suddenly she was right next to him, Conny close against her side as he hung onto her waist. "Francis, where is the hall? I can't see!" she cried out.

Francis stared at the wall of flame approaching them, then turned around to stare at the flames licking up behind them, closing off the stairs. He was sure he was going to pass out.

They were trapped.

Bess Seacombe saw the flames as she approached along the lane to Merdraco, Bristol Boy snorting and shying nervously when he smelled the smoke. But Bess became iron-willed as she saw the fire. Even from there, she could see that it was an inferno.

As she drew close to the gatehouse, a figure in black jumped out and grabbed hold of her reins. Big hands grabbed her and pulled her to the ground.

She tumbled, lying there stunned for a moment. But when she glanced up and saw Jack Shelby pulling the sidesaddle from Bistol Boy's back, she struggled to her feet. "You!" she spat, hatred and terror of this man consuming her.

"Goin' to see your lover, Bessie?" he snarled. "Ye'll be findin' him down on the beach. Maybe he survived without gettin' a hole through that black heart. If he did, he's goin' to wish he were dead when he finds his wife and brat have been burned to cinders." His harsh laughter rang. It was demoniacal.

"You trapped them in there? In that lodge?" she cried, her heart pounding deafeningly. "My God, why?" she cried. "What have they done to you?"

"He loves them, that's why. Just like I love my Lettie, who was murdered by him," Jack Shelby said. "Let him know the hell I have known all these years. Let him cry for his dead, as I have cried for mine. He'll never see that pretty wife or son again," Jack Shelby bellowed as he climbed onto Bristol Boy's back.

"You fool! Your blind fool!" Bess Seacombe screamed, and he paused for just a second. "Dante Leighton didn't kill Lettie. He was with me that night fifteen years ago. He was with me!" she yelled again just to make certain he understood.

"Ye're lyin', tryin' to save his neck. One of these days, I'll get him. I'll come back for him," Jack Shelby said.

"I'm not lying. For once in my life I am facing up to the truth. But it's too late. I am responsible for this," she cried, and something of her despair seemed to reach Jack Shelby, for he remained where he was, staring down at her strangely.

"The truth, woman," he growled suddenly, and Bess looked up to see the pistol pointed directly at her head.

"The truth, Jack Shelby? All right. But you won't like it, because when I tell you, you won't have anything to hate anymore. Certainly not Dante Leighton," Bess told him, staring up unblinkingly into that pistol barrel.

"Dante Leighton was with me the night Lettie was murdered. He stayed with me the whole night, and did not leave until morning. But the next day, when we learned of her death and learned that he had been implicated, I said nothing. I said nothing because I was selfish, because I had learned from my grandfather that Sir Miles had been to see him and had told him that Dante was in debt. When Dante fell under suspicion, I wasn't about to risk my reputation by saying that I was his mistress. I was young. I wanted a good match. I couldn't risk the scandal. And Dante said nothing about us. He allowed me to keep my spotless reputation while he lost his own. He was run out of Devonshire."

"You could still be lying," Jack Shelby thought wildly, trying to put everything together and make it look the way it always had.

"Yes, I could be, but the woman found murdered on the moors yesterday was killed in exactly the same fashion Lettie was killed. This time I gave Dante his alibi, for suspicion was cast upon him again, but I—" Jack Shelby interrupted her.

"What woman?"

"Don't you know?"

"No. What murder?" he asked again.

"Esma Samples. And I find it strange that you didn't know about her, for if her family is to be believed, then she was murdered because she knew too much about your smuggling gang," Bess told him. "But don't you understand? If Dante didn't kill Lettie fifteen years ago, and if another murder was committed in exactly the same way yesterday and he didn't do it, then someone else killed both Lettie and Esma Samples. You saw Dante at Seawyck last night. You know he didn't kill Esma Samples."

"He could have done it after he left you. Or before he got there," Jack Shelby stated.

"No. You see, Sir Morgan Lloyd was there as well, and Dante and Sir Morgan were together the whole evening. Dante is not the man who killed either Lettie or the other woman. Why would he make it look like Lettie's murder?" she continued, ever aware of the pistol pointing at her unwaveringly. She had his full attention, and she rushed on. "I was talking to the man from Merleigh who found the body. It's unbelievable, but that man also found Lettie's body. What he remembered was the strange shape he saw on Esma's body, a bruise. It reminded him of another bruise. He's going to take the information to the authorities tomorrow."

Jack Shelby was deadly quiet. "What kind of a bruise?" he finally asked.

"He said it looked like a dog's head, something like that. He swears he saw it on Lettie's body, too."

As Jack Shelby sat there on the back of Bristol Boy, Bess sensed a horrible change taking place in the man. The horse felt it too, for he whinnied nervously. The pieces of a puzzle were falling into place for Jack, and as Bess watched fearfully, the pistol began to shake. At last he spoke. It was just one word: "Miles."

Then Jack Shelby turned Bristol Boy around and laid the whip to his backside as he galloped down the road, leaving Bess standing there afraid to believe that she was still alive.

"Damn, I don't see how he could have gotten away," Dante swore softly.

"I don't think he did. A lot of bodies were carried out into the cove," Sir Morgan reminded him. "Eventually, he will wash ashore." That Jack Shelby could be walking around was unthinkable.

Dante Leighton and Sir Morgan Lloyd had reached the top of the cliff and were walking through the ruins when they both caught sight of the flames reaching high into the sky, lighting up the heavens with a sullen, orange glare. Both froze, then raced ahead.

Dante reached his horse first and was already galloping down the road when Sir Morgan sent his mount in pursuit.

By the time Dante reached the lodge, it was totally engulfed in flames. The heat was unbearable, and the small group huddled close together were standing back against the trees, cringing as if they were watching the end of the world.

Dante jumped down, letting his horse gallop away from the flames as he ran toward them. It was only when he drew close that he heard the weeping and moaning. But what stopped him in his tracks was the sight of Alastair Marlowe sitting on the ground, his head in his hands, sobbing.

Alastair felt a hand touch his shoulder, and he knew without looking whose hand it was. He just shook his head, his sobs coming harder.

"Cap'n," Houston Kirby whispered hoarsely, his face streaked with tears and smoke, "it happened so fast. One minute everything was fine, the next the place was all in flames." His gnarled hand shook as he kept rubbing Jamaica's ruffled fur. The cat's eyes glowed with reflected fire.

"Mr. Marlowe came running in and woke us, said it was spreading. He said Francis and—and—" but Kirby's voice broke. He started to cry. Then, sniffing, he gasped, "Lord Francis and Lady Rhea had gone upstairs to get Conny and Robin and young Lord Kit. They were coming back down. W-we saw them. Then suddenly there was this sheet of flame. It cut them off. That was the last we saw of them. Oh, Lordie, I-I—" Houston Kirby sobbed, his body shaking as he buried his face in Jamaica's fur, holding onto the tomcat as if he were the dearest thing in the world.

Sir Morgan Lloyd shielded his eyes against the flames. He had heard Houston Kirby's story, but even though he was staring at the raging fire, he still could not believe that Lady Rhea and her brothers, and her son, and young Conny Brady had all died that fiery death.

Glancing at Dante Leighton, he thought he'd never seen a man look so stunned, or so lifeless. It was as if he had somehow died himself in that moment when he had learned that his wife and child had died.

Sir Morgan Lloyd jumped a foot as someone touched his arm. He looked down to see Bess Seacombe staring up at him, her dark eyes haunted.

"It was Jack Shelby. I-I was coming here to explain to Lady

Rhea Claire about the other night when he jumped me on the road and stole my horse. He boasted about setting fire to the lodge. He's mad. He did it because of Lettie, because he thought Dante killed her. But I told him he hadn't. I think he finally believed me. Then he said the strangest thing." Bess' breath was coming raggedly.

"What?" Sir Morgan questioned, his arm around her waist all that kept her legs from giving out.

"He said, 'Miles.' I don't think I've ever seen such a murderous look on somebody's face."

"What did you say to him?" Sir Morgan asked, trying to go slowly to coax the answers from her.

"I was trying to convince him that Dante didn't kill Lettie, or Esma Samples. I told him that Dante was with me that night fifteen years ago, and he already knew that Dante was at Seawyck the other night. Then I told him that you had been with him all night. He knew then that Dante could not have killed Esma Samples. I told him about the bruises on the bodies," Bess said tiredly.

"What bruises?" Sir Morgan said in a hard voice.

"Bruises that looked like a dog's head. The man who found the body said he remembered seeing one just like it on Lettie's body. And that was when Jack Shelby said 'Miles.'"

"Dante! Don't! Come back! No matter what, you can't do it!" Sir Morgan called suddenly. But it was useless, for Dante had overheard all of it, and Sir Morgan Lloyd knew where he was going.

Dante had reached his horse and flung himself into the saddle when, suddenly, he slid back to the ground and stood staring straight ahead.

"What the devil?" Sir Morgan whispered as Dante ran wildly across the stretch of cliff that led to the towers of Merdraco. For a horrible moment, Sir Morgan thought that Dante had lost his mind from grief and was going to throw himself off the cliff.

But then they all caught sight of figures making their way across that stretch of cliff. There were four of them. One of them was a woman cradling something close to her breast.

"Oh, my God!" Houston Kirby blubbered, his sobbing loud and unrestrained as he understood. He recognized those two short figures running ahead of the other two now, and awkwardly he ran out to meet them, Jamaica eyeing him as if he'd gone completely mad.

Francis Dominick's face was nearly black from the smoke, and his teeth seemed startlingly white as he grinned, stumbling into waiting arms. He glanced back over his shoulder to see Rhea disappear entirely as Dante Leighton wrapped her and their son in his arms, holding them as if he would never let them go, as indeed he never would.

> *Truth is truth*
> *To the end of reckoning.*
> Shakespeare

Chapter 36

THERE was no darkness before the rising sun on that day, for the skies had been aflame all night long. When dawn broke, the first streakings turned to scarlet, reflected by the smoky skies above Merdraco.

The daylight revealed a lodge reduced to little more than ashes, soon to be blown away on the winds.

It revealed, too, all that remained of the smuggling gang, footprints in the sand, soon to be washed away on the tide.

News of the fire spread quickly, and soon the homeless were on their way to Sevenoaks House, having received an invitation from Sir Jacob Weare to be his guests until Merdraco could be made habitable.

But before the master of Merdraco could rest, he would

have to face his enemy. So Dante Leighton left Rhea and his
son with Sir Jacob and rode from Sevenoaks House to Wolfingwold Abbey, the home of Sir Miles Sandbourne and the
place where Jack Shelby would surely be found. With him rode
Sir Morgan, Alastair, Francis, and Houston Kirby.

What that group of bedraggled, grim-faced riders had expected was not what they saw.

Sir Miles' servants were standing in the Great Hall of the
onetime monastic property, their faces clearly showing fright.
Jack Shelby had indeed come to Wolfingwold Abbey demanding to see Sir Miles. Apparently he had found him in the salon.
None of the servants had dared to open those closed double
doors since they had heard the pistol shot ring out.

Dante and Sir Morgan put their shoulders to the locked
doors and broke through. The sight which met their eyes was
enough to sicken even a man accustomed to death.

Jack Shelby had discovered that he had been duped by Sir
Miles all these years. It had been that fine gentleman, in fact,
and not his stepson, Dante Leighton, who murdered Lettie.
When Jack Shelby started to choke the life out of Sir Miles,
the older man managed to reach inside his coat pocket and
grasp his pistol. Pulling the trigger, he shot the larger man in
the chest. But Jack Shelby, his big hands still clasped around
Sir Miles' throat, continued to crush Sir Miles' windpipe before
he succumbed to his own wound. Finally, both lay dead at
each other's feet.

They had not lingered long in that place. Back at Sevenoaks
House, Dante found Rhea freshly bathed, smoke washed from
her hair, and clad in a gown borrowed from Sir Jacob's niece,
the hard-of-hearing Essie.

Kit was snuggled on her lap, his eyes drooping heavily as
he nodded off. Rhea sipped a sherry and tried to put the horrible
memory from her for at least a while.

Sir Jacob Weare, still wearing his dressing gown, was waiting for Dante. He knew there would be more to this day. Essie
was in her chair by the fire, and Dante wondered idly if anything
ever budged her.

Alastair, Francis, Houston Kirby, and the boys had found
seats around the room. They had scrubbed their hands and faces
clean of the black smoke, but their clothing still reeked of it.

Dante ran a tired hand through his own disorderly hair and, finding a footstool, drew it up close to Rhea and Kit, a large snifter of brandy in his hand.

Jamaica, understanding that they were guests in the strange house, made certain of his next meal by attaching himself to Essie. He began to weave in and out around her legs, much to Houston Kirby's annoyance. When it came to his stomach, that cat had no loyalties.

"They killed each other," Dante startled everyone by suddenly announcing into the expectant silence.

"Sir Miles is dead?" Sir Jacob asked. Perhaps repeating it would make it absolutely true.

"Yes, but he managed to shoot Jack Shelby before he died," Dante said.

"Good Lord, the madness that comes of hatred!" Sir Jacob shook his head. "Well, at least neither one of them will be able to hurt anyone anymore. Is it all over now, do you suppose? So many years, so many long, wasted years all because of one man's corruption. After a silence, he said, "May I ask why Jack Shelby went after Sir Miles all of a sudden? If what I have heard is correct, then Sir Miles was the leader of the Sons of Belial, and the two of them have been working together for years. Why did he turn on Miles now?" Sir Jacob asked, thinking about rabid dogs turning on their masters.

All eyes moved from Jacob to Dante, who explained, "Sir Miles was indeed the leader of the Sons of Belial, but, as was his way, he stayed in the background for all these years, letting Jack Shelby be visible, and letting him enjoy the small tastes of power Miles allowed him. If anything had gone wrong, then the rope burns around the neck would also have been Jack Shelby's. I suppose I am partly to blame for Miles' involvement with the smugglers, for I caused him to become almost bankrupt. He had to have some revenue coming in," Dante speculated, staring into his brandy as if seeing everything clearly in the glass.

"Nonsense, boy. Miles was rotten the day he was born. Never did like him, even when he was a boy Francis' age. Would've turned bad no matter what," Sir Jacob expostulated. "Don't be silly. Now continue."

"Well, apparently Esma Samples knew Miles' identity. Her

husband must have known, and that was why he was killed. He told his wife, and so she was killed."

"Ah, I am beginning to see," Sir Jacob said, rubbing his chin. "I had heard about this murder and its similarity to the Lettie Shelby killing. No doubt Miles planned it to look as if you had done it. Since you had been suspected of the Shelby girl's murder, what better way to discredit you all over again and stir up Jack Shelby as well."

"Yes, but Sir Miles did more than just *plan* this murder. He dirtied his hands this one time, and that was when he became careless. He was so desperate to silence the woman and protect his identity that he killed her himself, but he also couldn't resist the opportunity to cast suspicion on me. He was greedy. He let his desire to destroy me blind him to good sense."

"How did it come about that Jack and the authorities suddenly suspected Miles of Lettie Shelby's murder?" Sir Jacob wanted to kow.

"Apparently there was a bruise on Esma Samples' body which matched one seen on Lettie's. It was the bruised impression of a dog's head. Something that might have been made by a blow from the head of a cane."

"A wolf's head, not a dog's! Sir Miles and his vanity," Sir Jacob said, smiling strangely. "He always carried that damned wolf's head cane. He signed his own death warrant with it. Jack Shelby, slow as he might have been, would have remembered seeing a wolf's head."

"Actually, we have Bess to thank for that," Dante surprised Bess' grandfather by saying. There was a soft note in his voice.

"Bess?"

"Yes, she met Jack Shelby on the road right after he set fire to the lodge," Dante said, his hand touching Rhea's, "and she told him that I had been with her the night of Lettie's death and that Sir Morgan had been with me that other evening in question. As he already knew I had been at Bess' the night of Esma Samples' death, he knew I could not have done either killing. Then Bess told him about the bruise, and she said he looked as if he'd seen the devil."

"But what was Bess doing on the road near Merdraco at what must have been a rather late hour?" Sir Jacob demanded.

"She was coming to tell me that nothing had happened

between her and Dante," Rhea spoke for the first time. "She wanted me to know the truth, that he and Sir Morgan concluded that Jack Shelby would go to Seawyck Manor and they found him there. But because Dante and Sir Morgan were working together to trap the smugglers and this Lieutenant Handley who had betrayed Sir Morgan's brother, they couldn't let it be known that Sir Morgan had been there that evening, and since Jack Shelby hadn't seen him, they were still safe. Sir Morgan prevailed upon Bess not to say anything, and Bess, being grateful for their assistance and very willing to see the end of Jack Shelby and his smugglers, was more than agreeable," Rhea explained, glad, as Bess had been, to bring everything out into the open.

"Sir Morgan told me that he would have explained to Rhea if Bess hadn't," Dante said, knowing what Rhea had gone through.

"If I were not so pleased to find out that Sir Morgan had never really turned against you, then I should be very displeased with him for not taking me into his confidence," Rhea said calmly. "I shall look forward to having a few words with him. Where is he?" Rhea asked.

"He stayed at Wolfingwold to make arrangements, and no doubt to collect whatever evidence there is. He will be quite busy making certain that the lieutenant stands trial without delay."

Sir Jacob Weare leaned back in his chair and sighed. "I can scarcely believe that Miles Sandbourne is actually gone. I have worried for so long about that man and the threat he presented," Sir Jacob mumbled.

"Ye've been worried?" Houston Kirby said. "Think how I've felt all of these years, knowin' the cap'n was determined to come back here and wreak his vengeance against that hell hound. I don't s'pose I've had a night's rest since I've returned," the little steward sniffed.

"You do look as if you've aged a lifetime, Kirby," Sir Jacob commiserated with the little man, who raised a bushy eyebrow at that.

"Aye, thought 'twas the end there for a while, and I don't s'pose hell could be any worse than the sight of that lodge on fire," he said with a shake of his head. He raised the brandy glass to his lips gratefully.

Sir Jacob stared at Rhea and her son, sitting there so close by Dante, and then at Francis Dominick who seemed truly to be enjoying a brandy for the first time, and at the two boys, who were sitting close together on the settee, their eyes still wide with the terrors they had seen.

"How the devil did you get out of the lodge?" Sir Jacob suddenly demanded.

Francis shuddered. He had come too close to death to think about it even now without feeling the heat of that fire singeing his eyebrows. He glanced over at the two boys, a loving look in his eyes, and said, "We have those two intrepid but secretive explorers to thank for our being alive."

Conny Brady and Robin Dominick looked shamefaced even as they straightened their shoulders proudly. They knew that by keeping the underground passage from the beach to the lodge a secret, they had been partially responsible for Jack Shelby being able to escape Sir Morgan's and Dante's trap.

"I thought we were done for," Francis admitted. "The flames had cut us off, and we were huddled there in the hall, when Conny and Robin suddenly started hollering about some secret underground passage that led from the lodge to the beach below. They started to fumble against the panel in the corridor. Finally, clearing some of the smoke from my brain, I started to help them. We found the latch and got into the tunnel just in time. A minute later and . . ." Francis struggled for the words that did not need saying.

Dante eyed the boys thoughtfully. "I had forgotten about that underground passage. It was boarded up long ago. It served its purpose during the Civil War, when my ancestors needed to escape Cromwell's men. I didn't think it had been used in over a century. In fact, I assumed the roof had fallen in by now. Apparently Jack Shelby hadn't forgotten about it. That must have been how he escaped us on the beach and how he got into the lodge to set the fire. He probably found the tunnel when he was bailiff at Merdraco and then remembered it when he started smuggling. I wonder whether Sir Miles ever knew about it, or whether it was Jack Shelby's private escape route. I shall have to explore this tunnel with you later," Dante promised. He also promised himself to keep a closer eye on the two fearless young fellows.

"I still wonder how all of this would have ended if Sir Miles hadn't killed Esma Samples and if Bess hadn't told Jack Shelby about that bruise," Alastair Marlowe mused, thinking that their lives had depended rather too much on a few chances of fortune and the caprice of fate.

Sir Jacob Weare shifted most uncomfortably, but Rhea could have sworn his eyes gleamed with excitement as he said, "It would have ended as it has, although Sir Miles might not have met his death at the hands of Jack Shelby."

"How can you know that for certain?" Dante asked, thinking that Sir Jacob had a lot of faith.

"I think it is time to reveal everything," said the old man. He glanced at the little woman sitting so quietly by the fire, Jamaica curled in her lap. "Essie? Don't you think so?" Sir Jacob inquired gently. Everyone was surprised to find that she had no trouble hearing Sir Jacob. And when the old woman got up, she moved quickly and easily.

Dante Leighton and the others stared as the woman turned and faced them, allowing the bright light of day, streaming in from the broad row of windows, to hit her full in the face. After a moment she removed the deeply ruffled mobcap which had concealed so much of her face. Then her hands, no longer shaking with age, slid into her silver curls and, with a quick movement that caught them all by surprise, she pulled the wig from her head, revealing her own golden hair, pinned tightly in a topknot.

Using a lace-edged handkerchief, she carefully removed the caked powder which had made her seem old. At last, removing her spectacles, she held her face up to them. It was the woman of the portrait.

"Mother!" Dante cried hoarsely, rising to face the woman he had thought dead for fifteen years. "Mother!"

"Dante. My son. My beloved son," she said softly, holding out her arms to the lost son who had finally come home to Merdraco.

Two weeks passed while they remained at Sevenoaks House, and in that time Dante and his mother came to know one another again. Rhea smiled joyfully watching Lady Elayne, looking almost as young as her portrait, sitting in the shade of the big oak tree, her grandson cradled in her lap. She sang softly to him, as she had once sung to her Dante.

Rhea remembered every moment of that stunning discovery of two weeks before, when Dante learned that his mother was alive and had been living at Sevenoaks for the past ten years.

Sir Jacob had been under oath to keep the secret, he told Dante apologetically. Elayne pleaded with him, and although he had not wished to, he had gone along. As the years had passed, he came to see the wisdom of Elayne's decision. The others in the salon listened to her story and came to see why she had made that decision.

The night she fled from Merdraco and the beating Miles had given her, she stumbled on the cliff edge. She had thought of ending it, for she knew she could no longer face Miles' brutality, or the revelation that he had murdered Lettie Shelby. Miles had been involved with her and was the one she had boasted would set her up in a house in London. He admitted as much when beating Elayne, for she could not be a threat to him. It was her word against his, if she ever did say anything, and he warned her that her son would suffer the consequences of her betrayal. At that time Dante was still blind to Miles' treachery.

Stumbling on the cliff path gave her the idea. Elayne knew that if she were thought dead, then, when Dante eventually learned the truth about Miles, her son would be free to make a new life. If she were still tied to Miles, then Dante would feel responsible for her. He would never leave Merdraco.

She made it down to the beach and left her shawl spread out on a rock, as if it had drifted there after she fell. Then she had made her way back up the path. She walked through the night, trying to get as far away from Merdraco and from Miles as she could. Now that she knew who had killed Lettie Shelby, it might be only a matter of time before Miles killed her, too.

And that was when Sir Jacob Weare found her. Returning home from a meeting, he saw her staggering along the road. Recognition had come hard because her features were so swollen. He lifted her into his coach and took her to the safety of

Sevenoaks House. There she had poured out her whole story to Sir Jacob.

He arranged her funeral, then helped her travel to France, where she stayed in a convent for the next five years. But when Sir Jacob sent her news of Dante, she was unable to stay away any longer and had returned to Devonshire, content to live at Sevenoaks House as Sir Jacob Weare's hard-of-hearing niece, Essie.

When the loneliness became unbearable she went out during the dark of night and visited Merdraco, to walk the halls and remember the times she had been happy there. That was how the legend of the Pale Lady of the Ruins got started and how she had inadvertently scared off the smugglers from using Merdraco. She admitted, too, that she hadn't been able to resist a look at her son. It was she whom Rhea had seen that night, wandering through the trees near the lodge, her cloaked figure looking like the ghost of legend—the Pale Lady of the Ruins.

When Dante returned with a wife and child, she and Sir Jacob realized the terrible danger they were in. They spoke with Sir Jacob's solicitors in London, and had been prepared to come forward with their story. Although there was no proof, their claims would at least have alerted the authorities to watch Sir Miles Sandbourne.

Rhea stood at the window, a smile of contentment curving her lips as she stared at Lady Elayne holding Kit up high in her arms, then hugging him close. While she watched, Dante came up behind her and his arms slid around her waist. He pulled her pack against his chest, resting his chin on her head. They stood there in companionable silence.

"I have been thinking that perhaps 'tis time we paid a visit to Camareigh. I know the Duke and Duchess must be anxious about us, and they did not get to spend much time with their grandson. I know my mother would enjoy the visit. I also was thinking that we might travel on to London afterward. Then, with a new crew, we will sail the *Sea Dragon* home to Merdraco."

Rhea reached up a hand and touched his tanned cheek, remembering the first time she had seen him. That had been aboard the *Sea Dragon*, and it seemed right that they should sail again. Without her being aware of it, Rhea's other hand touched the jeweled brooch pinned to her stomacher and she smiled. Luckily, she had been wearing it the night of the fire, and she truly believed that the jeweled replica of the *Sea Dragon* had kept fortune with her that night. She vowed always to wear it.

"Shall we go out into the sunshine and join them?" he asked, his eyes meeting Rhea's for a long moment before his lips touched hers. Together they left the room, which suddenly seemed full of shadows. Dante wanted nothing to remind him of the past. As he heard his mother's laughter and his son's squeal of delight, he knew that he wanted only to look ahead into the future, and there would be no backward glances into the past.

The brightness of the sun was almost blinding as, hand in hand, Dante and Rhea stepped out of the shadows and strolled through the garden toward his mother and their son. A future of bright tomorrows awaited.

> *Long is the way*
> *And hard, that out of hell leads*
> *up to light.*
>
> John Milton

Epilogue

THE sea gull spread his wings, soaring then gliding, as his shadow drifted across gentle slopes of green. It was early in the season of wild thyme and blackthorn. The small plum hung heavy on the bough, its pale clusters yet to feel the ripening sweetness of a midsummer sun.

The gilded petals of the primrose bespoke of mildness that had not yet warmed the earth, for the winds roaming the wild north coast of Devon were spawned by angry, maelstrom-fed gales far out at sea. Raw with lingering winter bleakness, heedless of the first tender buds of spring, the northern winds drove the foaming waves against the storm-swept headlands and the jagged reefs.

But the solitary stone tower stretching against the black

horizon had withstood far greater onslaughts than the squall now threatening the dawn where eastern skies were rich with clouds edged in sungold. The isolated tower was all that remained of a castle in ruins. Merdraco.

The massive stones, chiseled and fitted with such care by masons long gone, were strewn about like so much kindling. The lichen-covered walls, which had seemed insurmountable for centuries, were fallen, defeated in the end by the steady advance of ivy, the tenacious vine entwining itself year after year in the rotting mortar.

Sky was visible through the crumbling arches, where once a vaulted ceiling had risen high above walls adorned in the splendor of heroic shields and shining swords, where noble flags of silk had proclaimed a never-to-be-forgotten glory.

In the desolate courtyard dandelions pushed their way up between the cracked paving stones. No beat of horses' hooves or rattling of wagon wheels had disturbed the peace for many moonless nights.

A stone dragon, fallen from its lofty perch, still guarded the entrance, its sightless eyes gazing upon its domain in a never-ending search for trespassers. But there was no reason to fear intruders. No enemy waited for the fall of darkness. And even the subtle movement of shadows was merely the reflection of the sun's course across the heavens.

There were only memories left to haunt the deserted battlements and the abandoned tower, those enduring testimonials to an age long past.

Bewitched by sun and moon, the ebbing tide crashed against the rocks far below the ruins of Merdraco. And the tower stood alone, perhaps forgotten. . . .

But the fates had not decreed so unworthy an end. Adrift on the wind came the sound of children's voices raised in laughter, echoed by the frenetic barking of hounds. Had there been anyone atop the tower, he would have seen a small group approaching the ruins.

A man dressed in the finest of silks, and a woman clad in blue velvet and whitest lace walked arm in arm toward the ruins from a stone house where sweet-scented woodsmoke rose from a score of great chimneys. The sun, reflected in the mullioned windows, burned like a thousand candles.

The man's gray eyes were narrowed against the glare from the sea as he watched the thunderclouds darken the horizon. For a brief time he forgot that he was no longer captain of a brigantine and that he need never again worry about keeping his ship under press of canvas, the wind filling her sails as she ran free before storm and man. For only an instant his thoughts lingered with what had once been.

His gaze was caught and held, as it had always been, by the pure gold of his wife's hair as the wind tousled it about her flushed cheeks. He thought, not for the first time, that she grew more enchantingly beautiful with each day.

She looked at him and knew intuitively, when his eyes turned away from the sea and the faraway look faded, that she had lost him to old memories for a spellbinding moment. But as her eyes met his and, together, they walked the land that was his heritage and would be their children's, she knew that the past did not beckon him. The future was theirs.

A smile of contentment curved his mouth as he watched his eldest son, a boy tall for ten years, scolding his younger brother and sister as they sat astride the fat, shaggy pony Kit was leading. Its bridle jingled with bells. A young man, not more than twenty, walked a little ahead of them, his long strides shortened to accommodate the wobbly steps of the child holding tightly to his hand. With an indulgent laugh, he hoisted the little girl onto his shoulders, her golden curls swinging while he bounced her.

The young man's blue eyes were filled with the bright dreams of manhood, dreams encouraged by the man and woman who had welcomed him into their home so many years before and whose love was more precious to him than a sea chest filled with Spanish treasure.

Conny Brady glanced back at the man and woman whose daughter he held securely in his arms. He called out something to them, but his words were carried away on the winds. So he waited, knowing, as he leaned against the sun-warmed stone dragons, that he had all the time in the world. The lively chanty he was whistling drifted upward toward the unfaded emerald, scarlet, and indigo banner flying high atop the solitary stone tower, the tower that continued to stand sentinel against time

The moon had become a pale shadow without the dark

before the rising sun. The sea continued to bind its spell upon the wild shore beneath Merdraco.

There was the sun and moon, the sea and Merdraco. Ever changing, yet forever constant.

BESTSELLING ROMANCE
by Johanna Lindsey

GLORIOUS ANGEL   79202 $3.50

This powerful novel of a nation and a family divided by Civil War follows the passionate romance between a sharecropper's daughter and a plantation owner's son, that leads from Alabama to Boston, to the wilds of Texas.

PARADISE WILD   77651 $2.95

From high-bred Boston society to the wilder shores of Hawaii, Corinne Barrows and Jared Burkett find a love so violent that it must either destroy them—or give them completely to the wild abandon of tropical nights in paradise!

FIRES OF WINTER   79574 $2.95

Abducted from Ireland across an icy sea, the lovely and dauntless Lady Brenna vows vengeance on her captors. But the Viking leader Garrick claims her, and between them is forged a bond of desire.

A PIRATE'S LOVE   75960 $2.50

Caribbean breezes sweep a ship westward, carrying Bettina Verlaine to fulfill a promise her heart never made—marriage to a Count she has never seen. Then the pirate Tristan captures Bettina's ship and casts his spell over her heart.

CAPTIVE BRIDE   79566 $2.95

Recklessly following her brother from London to Cairo, beautiful Christina Wakefield is abducted by a stranger who carries her off to his hidden encampment, where she is made his prisoner. Soon she learns to want the desert sheik as he wants her—and to submit to a stormy and passionate love.